RAISED BY WOLVES

THE COMPLETE SERIES

CASEY MORALES

Edited by
CARLEY SLATTERY

WWW.AUTHORCASEYMORALES.COM

READER ADVISORY

The following story is best categorized as an MM Romantic Comedy in which the main plot depicts gay men and their entanglements. There are scenes describing sexual acts, some of which are explicit and may be inappropriate for those below a certain age.

Casey Morales

My Accidental First Date

Raised by Wolves Book 1

PREFACE

You're going to find this hard to believe, especially when you learn how Gomer-Pyle-gullible I was at twenty-two, but what you're about to read is a true story. What can I say, I was *that* preacher's kid. You know, the one who never knew he was supposed to be secretly rebellious and get away with a hidden wild side? Yeah, I missed that memo. I was the PK who was actually into being righteous and good, whatever that means these days.

I grew up in a kind, loving household, with three older sisters—stop snickering already.

Now, years later, I know that was a perfect setup for a coming out later in life. But at the time, I had no clue. I was convinced that I would one day have a beautiful wedding in a massive church with flowers and candles everywhere— you're snickering again.

Anyway, you get the picture. Good boy. Innocent. Completely clueless. And definitely straight. Did I mention that? I was *straight*, doggonit.

I made it through high school and college without ever meeting a single gay person. I was convinced, as was taught fervently from the pulpit on Sundays, that all gays lived in California or New York, and as long as we stayed away from those evil places, everything would be fine. Little did I know my best friend from fourth grade through high school was a screaming queen. How was I supposed to know? Just because he was the drum major in the marching band—and your snickering continues.

I see now that we are not going to have a serious, adult conversation, so I may as well get on with the story. Yes, yes, I changed the names and places to protect the guilty, but the story itself is a real account of my very first date. Although, looking back, I don't think you could actually call it a date. That kind of insults the idea of dates. Alas, it's in the title, so it was a date.

Just roll with me here.

1

BORING SATURDAY

It's a terrible idea to leave a twenty-two-year-old guy alone at home on a Saturday. There are entirely too many parts of a young male's overactive, yet still developing brain that can wander and find trouble. A girl would read a book, watch a movie, or find some other semi-productive way to use her free weekend. But not a boy.

At least, not this boy.

So, we've established I'm home, alone, and bored on a Saturday. There's bad football replays and bowling on tv. I tried the other channels, but Lifetime didn't call to me. It rarely did. There were reruns of Star Trek, but I'd long ago reached my tribble-tolerance, so I tossed the remote aside and wandered aimlessly around our poorly appointed apartment, briefly considering attacking the pile of dirty laundry in the corner. Unfortunately, it was much larger than the sacred pile of laundry quarters on the counter. My roommate, Peter, would be frustrated that I'd violated the immutable law of laundry quarter hoarding, but I'd found a vintage Ms. Pacman machine at a Pizza Hut around the block from our place earlier in the week. What can I say? Ms. Pacman and I have a thing. So much for the stockpile.

Quarter issues aside, the thought of lugging a basket of laundry down the stairs to the complex's common room, then babysitting my poor collection of hole-ridden undies wasn't appealing. I'd had a massive load of my best fairly-new sweatshirts stolen from that laundry room, so babysitting was a requirement. But, the clothes had sat on the floor for a few days without stinking, and I figured they'd be okay a little longer. Just to confirm this decision, I did the only thing a self-respecting young man can do in this situation. I sniffed my t-shirt. It didn't kill me, so I assumed I was stronger for the effort and moved on.

Frustrated at my fruitless apartment tour, I tossed myself back onto the couch, grabbed the remote off the cardboard box we used for an end table, and resumed Olympic-level channel flipping. Some guy was babbling about the strategy behind championship bowling. Strategy? Hit the pins, right? I flipped on Mr. Strategy as fast as possible.

The phone rang.

No one ever called. This was exciting, and something new to shake me out of my boredom.

Yes, this was an old-fashioned land-line. There was no Caller ID—or any other fancy features we take for granted these days. The ring sounded like the rapid whirring of a teacher's bell in school, kind of annoying, but something you couldn't ignore. My roommate, Peter, and I shared the number. He was a struggling model/trainer, and I hadn't found my place in life. We shared pretty much everything that involved spending money on a monthly basis. He was a good roommate that way.

I answered, "Hello."

"Hey. Peter?" The voice was friendly, masculine, and held a note of anticipation. That last part was a little odd, but whatever. He wasn't calling for me anyway.

"No. This is Michael. Peter's not here," I said, disappointed this welcome interruption would likely end as quickly as it began.

"Oh, ok," the voice said. "Thanks."

"No problem." I reached behind the couch to hang up while keeping my eyes on the awful Lifetime special the remote decided was worthy of my Saturday. The receiver slipped out of my hand and clunked against the linoleum, then rebounded by its Slinky-esque cord to bob and wiggle off the back of the couch. Annoyed, I made my way around the couch to hang the dangling phone up.

The voice crackled. "Michael? You still there?"

Butterfingers finally got the receiver to his ear. "Yeah, I'm here. Sorry. I dropped you. Did you want to leave a message for Peter? Should've asked before."

"No. That's ok. I'm Joseph, a friend of Peter's." He paused. I remember the sound of that pause. It was thunderous. "I was just bored at home on a Saturday and called to see if he wanted to catch a movie."

"Oh, ok. Well, I don't know when he'll be back. He left early this morning." I said.

"So," He paused again, the silence louder this time. "What are *you* doing?"

Okay, that wasn't what I thought he'd say next. Not even close. "Umm. Nothing really. Just flipping channels, staring at laundry, kinda bored."

"Wanna go see a movie?" Joseph asked without hesitation.

Now it was my turn to hesitate. This was more than a little odd, right?

I didn't know this guy, and Peter hadn't ever mentioned him. At least, I don't think he had. I didn't always pay great attention to the list of people who followed Mr. Photogenic. As a model, he had a flock. But sitting here, staring at bowling or tribbles wasn't making me less bored. At least this would get me out of the apartment. And if Joseph was a friend of Peter's, he had to be okay. That makes sense, right?

"Umm. Yeah, I guess," I said.

"Great, I live a couple blocks from the theater on Pine. You know it?"

There was no silence this time. The movie angels were signing. You know, that one note that always accompanies the bright white light and announces something *really* cool?

I totally knew that theater. It was the newest, nicest, *coolest* theater in town, the one with the puffy leather stadium seats. I hadn't actually been to a movie there yet, but everybody was talking about it. And when I say everybody, I mean all the cool kids I wanted to hang out with but never really had the chance to because of the stick-up-the-ass PK thing.

"Yeah, great place," I said, trying to sound like I knew what I was talking about.

"Great. Why don't you come here and park at my place? We can just walk to the theater and save the five bucks."

I was all about saving five bucks.

"On my way."

2

THREESOME

I drove my maroon Saturn lazily to the other side of town where Peter's mysterious movie-loving friend lived.

I loved that car, by the way. I got it when I was in college a few years ago, and was among the first to ever own the new breed of horseless carriage known as Saturn. People would stare as I drove up to the gas pump, point, and ask their friends, "what is that?" The occasional brave soul would wander up and ask, "That's a cool car. What kind is it? I've never seen one before."

Add to the mystique of mounting a horse whose breed no man had seen before, that car saved my life—literally. I'd spent the day in class, then went to work for a few hours, and was driving home around eleven o'clock. I was beat. You know, exhausted to the point I was seeing two of everything? No alcohol, just plain pooped-ness. I'm usually a careful driver, but didn't see the flashing red light at the intersection a few blocks from home. I slammed into a poor old man driving a gunmetal gray battleship of a Lincoln. Tboned him. His car barely budged, but mine struck, spun in two complete circles, then slammed directly into a large oak tree. It struck precisely where the artistic *S* of Saturn's logo rested on the hood and the entire front of the car crumped in on itself. The only thing that saved me was a safety feature pioneered by the intrepid engineers at Saturn, sharp guard thingies that cut the engine free in the even of a collision. The heavy car-part-thing that would've slammed into my soon-to-be-lifeless body was sliced free of the chassis and fell harmlessly to the ground.

When I came to and noticed the blinding blue lights of cop cars and ambulances, I heard an officer turn to his partner with wonder in his voice, "Hey, the kid's *alive*."

Thankfully, the old man driving the USS Eisenhower was also unharmed. Hell, the Eisenhower barely had a dent.

With a little help from the cop and a paramedic, I stumbled away from the car without even a scratch. Unfortunately, Betty (that's what I named the Saturn), didn't fare so well. It took some pretty skilled car medics a month to get her back into fighting shape.

None of this is terribly relevant to the date, but it was still amazing.

I was a Saturn-driving stud. What can I say?

Back to Joseph…

True to his word, Joseph's condo was right around the corner from the amazing new theater. The four-unit red-brick building wasn't anything fancy, but it was in a nice part of town and looked well-maintained, each unit featuring a neat row of shrubbery and shadowboxes filled with brightly colored flowers. I didn't want my black thumb to suck the life out of anything, so I admired the landscaping from a respectable distance. The parking lot was above the level of the condo, forcing a descent of several steps to reach the door. I hopped over all four steps to land at his dark green door and knocked, suddenly nervous at the prospect of going to a movie with an unknown dude, even if he was a friend of my roommate's.

The door opened to reveal a guy about my height, in his late twenties, maybe thirty. He made eye contact, and a hand went from the doorknob to his wavy brown, almost black, hair, moving a few stray curls that tried to obscure his view. He smiled broadly.

"Hey. I'm Joseph." There was a split-second pause, then he stuck a tentative hand out to shake. Were we supposed to shake hands? Was that the right thing to do in this situation? I gripped his hand with my best business-man's grip and shook.

His smile turned into a grin.

"Give me a minute. I need to throw on some shoes. There's a bunch of new movies playing. Any idea what you want to see?"

He disappeared through a short hallway, leaving me alone in his cozy den that wasn't much bigger than the apartment laundry room I'd so artfully avoided earlier.

Before we dive too deeply into movie selection, it's important to note that I'd spent the summer working for a city councilman on his reelection campaign. He and his wife didn't have kids, and they'd pretty much adopted me for the months I'd hauled yard signs and called old ladies for envelope stuffing. Apparently, one of the perks of being a good councilman is a movie pass for you and your family. That's right. Unlimited *free* movies at the local theater, even the fancy new one around the corner. There's probably some ethics law in place now, preventing our good coun-cilpersons from receiving such generous support-on-the-side, but there wasn't one back then. And you'd better believe I wore that sucker out. I was just a campaign bee. Ethics be damned! By the time the Joseph-called-Peter-but-got-me Saturday arrived, I'd seen pretty much everything released over a very busy summer for Hollywood. Answering Joseph's simple question was a challenge.

An odd, nerdy pride filled my chest out as I explained my stud-level movie ticket connection loudly through the opening toward the back of the condo. And, true to my nerdiness, I laughed awkwardly. "Guess I should've thought about that when you asked about seeing a movie."

"It's okay. Have you seen *Threesome*? The one with Stephen Baldwin?" he called from somewhere shoes apparently go to die.

Imagine that. He asked about one I hadn't seen. It might've been *the* one I hadn't seen. I couldn't even remember seeing it advertised. What were the odds?

"No. Don't think I've heard of that one."

"Perfect. Threesome it is." I heard a chuckle, but didn't think much about it.

Note to self. People don't chuckle for no reason. There's *always* a reason. Pay attention, kid.

His minute of putting on shoes stretched to five, so I decided to snoop. I've always been an inquisitive lad, some might say nosy, but I prefer inquisitive. The light in the den came from two ancient-looking lamps crowned with those grandma shades with little dangly things around the bottom rim. I guess they were pretty. At least they tried to be. The bulbs in them cast a soft yellow glow more than light, so I had to really get close for my snooping to be effective. I immediately turned to scan the photos staring back at me from the bookshelf. Joseph, arm around a girl our age. Joseph and two other guys. Three guys in swim trunks on a beach—well, not trunks. Those little Speedo things that pretty much showed what religion a guy was. Banana hammock, I think was the correct term. But the guys were really fit, and I guess I'd want to wear something like that if I had abs on my toes. They sure did.

The pictures seemed normal enough, so I turned again and took in the room.

At the far end was a large television resting in an antique case that spanned wall to wall. Vines crawled across the caramel-colored wood and thumb-sized lion faces growled back where you'd normally find pulls. Wait, *those* were the pulls. Cool. Under the tv, on a shelf built into the case, were rows of video tapes. For you youngsters, before there were CDs or DVDs, we used tapes. Just think of them as movies and stop thinking I'm old.

A love-seat-sized couch took up most of the far wall. It was cream or beige or off-white. I really don't know decorating or colors. But it looked comfy. More bookshelves covered the wall above the couch, and from floor to ceiling on either side, and were filled with hardback and leather-bound volumes. The kind you have to buy *on purpose* at expensive specialty bookstores. This guy really liked his books, and knickknacks, and photos.

I couldn't match black and white, much less make a room look nice like this. Shoot, after a year of hard living, our apartment was decorated in Early Cardboard. But just because I was a neanderthal didn't mean I couldn't appreciate when someone else did well at—design? Is that the term? I don't know. It looked nice.

Opposite the couch sat the tallest, grandest high-back chair I'd ever seen. It looked like one of those ancient thrones you'd seen a movie about Queen Elizabeth. Muted gold fabric, embroidered with green and blue patterns, covered the cushioned back and halfway up each arm. Rich cherry wood framed the top, feet, and uncovered parts of the arms. No, I don't know what any of that's called either. But when Joseph's head appeared in the doorway, I was firmly enthroned and trying to figure out how to fit the chair in my Saturn sedan. It was one ridiculously amazing chair.

"See anything you like?" Joseph's voice startled me.

"What? Uhh…" I was articulate as ever.

He laughed and moved to the door, brown eyes glittering with amusement. For some strange reason, I thought he'd actually worked on his hair while he was finding his shoes. It looked freshly fluffed, or whatever you call it. And he'd exchanged his faded t-shirt for a trendy crisp blue number that clung to his chest and arms.

"Ready when you are," he said.

I stood, turned, and gracefully banged my knee on the edge of the chair. Joseph barked a laugh. I shot him an annoyed glance, but his smile never wavered. He was *enjoying* this. My knee ached a little, but I recovered my lost dignity and followed the chuckling roomie-friend out the door.

It was a pleasant late-summer afternoon, but in our little berg humidity was the order of most days. By the time we made the short walk to the theater, my forehead was dripping and Joseph's newly quaffed hair had dipped into a waterfall of waves and curls about his ears. Mine had always been cropped short, so there was no risk of anything. Hell, I ran a towel over it in the morning and *bam*, I was ready to go. But his black locks were full and wavy, and totally vulnerable to a hot summer day. How can someone's hair fall flat from moisture and still look perfect?

Something about the humidity kicked his cologne into

high gear and the scent of some manly spray, tinged with a hint of sweetness, drifted by. His slinky blue shirt was now a darker shade of navy and sported very happy nipples. I don't remember noticing them, but guess I did. Headlights are hard to miss in the dark.

3

OPIE

Before we get to the theater…

Context matters. Isn't that what they always say? So, in order for you to fully appreciate what happens next, I need to give you a quick primer on my humble upbringing.

A few years ago, my dad retired from his lifelong work as a minister in a very conservative church. I know what you're thinking. All churches are conservative. But that's not true. On one end of the spectrum are religious groups who believe loving your fellow man and woman pretty much punches your ticket into heaven. No rules or heavy lifting required. In fact, if you don't want to darken the door to their building, that's fine. Just think about them now and then—and be a good person—maybe drop a coin or two in the basket now and then. On the extreme other end of the spectrum are religions who dictate what you can wear, how long your hair grows, what you eat or drink or— you get the idea. Now *that's* conservative.

For the record, my view today is this: if you are sincere in your beliefs and live your truth, go team. I don't question their sincerity or faith. I've watched my parents live theirs my whole life. They're positive examples of how their beliefs guide their actions, both inside their home and with others.

I grew up in a loving, Beaver Cleaver family, and still respect both my parents' beliefs and their commitment to living lives by them. They're not folks who simply say they're religious or spiritual or whatever. They walked the walk, letting their beliefs guide their actions and generosity toward their fellow man. But, *accepting* and *tolerant* were not words I would use to describe my folks or their church.

Was that enough of a disclaimer to get me out of a deep philosophical debate on various religious beliefs, movements, cults, and other systems? Good. I don't have the ink —electronic or otherwise—to go there.

The church my dad led, which I attended from my earliest recollection, fell somewhere to the right of the Baptists. Yes, we viewed *them* as liberal. How dare they have potlucks and instruments in their buildings! No, we weren't into snakes or self-flagellation, but we thought about it occasionally. We attended services every Sunday morning, evening, and Wednesday night—religiously (excuse the pun).

And while my dad was the preacher, my mom was the real conservative force in the family. Curse words, such as "fart" or "darn" were strictly forbidden. How dare we bring such filth into her house. Dancing was bad because it's too much like sex standing up. Sex was bad because it caused dancing. And so on. Pick a topic and she planted her flag— and consequently our little flags—on the extremely conservative side of the conversation.

In my younger years, my youngest sister would practice her lifelong dream of being a teacher by forcing me to sit through "class" every day. We had one of those old school-desk-chair-combo-things and she made me sit there while she lectured on whatever her teachers had covered earlier in the day. The bright side of this was that I started elementary school ahead of my peers, by several classes. The downside was the utter boredom that comes to a child who has to wait three years for something new to be taught in class. I was four, maybe five, and already hated the idea of school. Thanks, sis.

Our family ate dinner together most nights, many times enjoying fresh veggies from the garden my dad tended out back. We lived in the heart of a good-sized city, but he insisted on having a garden in the back yard. We were definitely *those* neighbors. But hey, the veggies were really good.

We crowded around the tv and watched "our shows" together. It never occurred to me that kids my age did sleepovers or went to the mall or hung out. Other than in school, I wasn't really exposed to what other kids did. And for some unknown reason, I never thought to ask. Weren't they all at home on Friday nights watching tv with their parents? What were they thinking?

I attended a local private church-affiliated school, the same one from first grade through high school. And while I'm thankful for the quality education I received, the school was basically an extension of our church. We attended chapel and bible class every day. That's right, every day. Girls were required to wear skirts or dresses that stretched at least a few inches below the knee. It was common to see teachers walking about with well-worn wooden rulers enforcing this modesty principle. I never understood what it was about a girl's knees that drove boys crazy, but apparently they did.

Sports have always been a passion. I played Little

League baseball and YMCA basketball, but wasn't blessed with speed, size, or skill. A couple of tryouts for our school teams taught me to love the game from the sidelines, because that's as close to the action as I'd ever get. Especially at my high school, where we bled for state championships every year. So, off to band and chorus I went.

In other non-school hours, I poured myself into the Boy Scouts. Yes, I know, that illustrious organization has had their issues over the years, but the leadership training and camaraderie I gained through Scouting made those lonely, formative years tolerable. I didn't come from a rich family, and I wasn't ever going to be a popular jock in school, so Scouting gave me an outlet to make something of myself without all those high school prejudices or expectations. I *totally* rocked knee-length green socks and a merit badge sash.

OK, so I was a little nerdy. Give me a break. It was a good childhood, even if I wasn't exposed to many people who looked or lived differently from me. Again, raised by wolves.

Now, back to Joseph…

4

STEPHEN BALDWIN

S tadium seating was a glorious invention that deserves much more notoriety in the history books than it's received. How long had us short folk suffered behind the heads of our height-blessed friends? Or had to sit crouched to one side, peering desperately around Aunt Millie's giant beehive hair-do? Stadium seating solved all that, and with it came world peace.

Ok, it wasn't that dramatic. But it was really cool.

We walked to the acne-riddled kid behind the glass and I presented my Golden Freebie. Joseph's eyes widened appreciatively as zit-face gave me a sharp, awe-filled glare. Yes, I was a free-movie-going-stud. He punched a few buttons and gave me a respectful head nod as he handed us two tickets stamped, "VIP" in giant red letters. I couldn't help flashing them to Joseph and grinning like a three-year-old with county fair cotton candy.

He *winked* at me.

Huh.

Tickets in hand, I headed for the theater, but Joseph pulled at the back of my shirt, asking if I wanted popcorn. I was perplexed. Buying concessions violated the whole theory behind the Golden Freebie. Besides, Ms. Pacman had devoured my savings. There was no room for popcorn.

Joseph grinned at my befuddled expression and turned to buy popcorn and a Sprite whose size should've read "gargantuan" on the board. That was nice of him.

We entered the theater and it felt hot, crowded. People stood gawking at the amazing leather chairs that rose straight up toward the ceiling, rather than flat toward the back wall. A few ran their hand along the smooth, tan leather, before flopping down and being absorbed in its softness. Kids laughed and adults chatted. This was a movie theater as God intended.

Looking back, there were probably twenty people in a room that could seat two hundred. I guess I was more nervous than I thought.

We crawled across our row to take middle seats. I wasn't sure whether to leave the traditional "I'm not *with* that guy" middle seat empty, but Joseph made that decision for me by plopping down in the chair next to me and offering to share his popcorn. That was nice, again. Who doesn't love buttery, salty movie popcorn? When he took a giant sip of Sprite, then offered it to me, straw extended, I thought it a tad odd. I pried the lid and took a sip of sugary goodness from the rim of the cup. I handed it back to him, and his eyes twinkled in amusement. I didn't understand what was funny. I sure wasn't putting my lips where some dude just sucked.

We were comfortably munching our Heaven-sent, butter-slathered corn when an extremely large woman who should've been cited for illegal use of Spandex wedged herself into the seat next to Joseph. Don't get all offended here. I'm just describing what happened. The woman was large enough to need that seatbelt extension on a plane, and would likely have been required to buy an extra seat. No judgement, but she was gargantuan, like our Sprite, only bigger.

She'd also clearly missed the memo regarding personal space, resting both of her fleshy, naked arms on the rests to either side, intruding beyond the center line and well into Joseph's seat. Didn't she know Movie Law allowed her to claim *one* rest, but *never* both? Barbarian!

Ms. Barbarian had one of those enormous buckets of popcorn and a jug of Coke. I was jealous of her bucket of salty, buttery goodness.

The smell of woman-straining-against-Spandex mingled with popcorn and drifted into my own personal space. Oddly, it wasn't unpleasant. Joseph scooted closer to me and crammed our pitifully small popcorn container into the crack between our seats. Our shoulders pressed firmly against each other. For a second, I thought he pressed a little harder than was necessary, but thanks to our malodorous neighbor, I didn't give it too much thought.

The lights dimmed and previews started.

Previews.

My favorite part of the movie-going experience.

This is the point where any self-respecting movie-goer pretends to be Ebert—or the other one—and gives each preview a solid thumbs-up or thumbs-down. There are no middle votes or abstentions. Don't be a wuss. This is a sacred ritual, and you will lose your hard-earned council-man's movie pass if you skip it or can't commit to a vote.

Most people, heretics really, were unaware of this hallowed tradition. Miraculously, Joseph was not. In fact, Mr. Perma-Smile beat me to the first vote, giving some poor film Caligula's best "kill that gladiator" gesture. My eyes must've widened because he grinned. For the first time that day, I grinned back and immediately concurred with his condemnation, offering my own thumbs-down to underscore the point. We moved to the next contestant. And the next. And the ten other previews that followed.

Some hallowed traditions should have maximums to their hallowed-ness so the darn movie can start.

Ancient ritual complete, the movie intro finally began, and I settled comfortably into my puffy leather seat, barely noticing the warmth from Joseph's shoulder, which had somehow pressed even closer. I had claimed the armrest between us, and he respected that claim, but his hand brushed my arm each time he reached for more popcorn. For some reason I failed to comprehend, that sent a thrill up my arm.

And then the movie started. *Threesome.* Joseph's idea.

Do you remember those old air raid sirens that would sound every time the Germans bombed London? I know you weren't *actually* there, but surely you've seen movies about those days. They'd wail loudly, starting low and growing in volume until the pitch reached an opera tenor's girth, then gradually descend back to the depths of a low roar. There was no mistaking what they meant. The enemy was coming, and they weren't dropping cupcakes.

Fifteen minutes into the movie, I heard the air raid siren —in my head.

When Joseph suggested we see *Threesome*, I'd had no idea what it was about. I hadn't even given the obviously suggestive title much consideration. I was busy rifling through his pictures and VHS collection and barely heard the name he'd suggested. Even if I'd heard it clearly, the implication didn't sink in. What raised-by-wolves preacher's kid thinks about threesomes? Ever?

By thirty minutes into the movie, I understood what the title meant. Quite clearly.

Here's the gist. A girl named Alex was accidentally assigned to live in a dorm suite with two guys, Stephen Baldwin's character and a gay dude named Eddy. After some initial drama, they became friends. More than friends, actually. As it turned out, Stephen Baldwin had the hots for the Alex. Alex wanted in Eddy's pants, but he was gay. Eddy wanted dear Mr. Baldwin.

See what we did there? Mr. Isosceles would be proud. It was a love triangle with a gay guy sandwiched in the middle. Or would Stephen prefer to be in the middle? Never mind. That wasn't important.

What *was* important was the righteous indignation bubbling up through my PK soul as I watched the wanton display of vulgarity panning across the sacred screen. It was *Three's Company* on steroids. By the way, I wasn't allowed to watch *Three's Company* as a kid because a woman lived with two men—and them men pretended to be gay to make everything okay. How could being gay make anything okay? That didn't make sense. The whole show was sinful and therefore banned from my childhood watch list.

But the whole family crowded around the TV every Friday nights to watch *Wonder Woman* despite her bare knees. Wolves, I tell you.

Stop distracting me. Back to the movie…

Stephen didn't want to take the girl to a nice dinner, or win her with his charming wit or perfectly-white-toothed-smile, or offer to walk her home and respectfully kiss her cheek as she disappeared inside. Oh, no. He wanted to do nasty things to her, over and over, and he wasn't shy about it. And the things she wanted to do to the poor gay guy—

don't get me started. She was not a well-behaved, church-going, knee-covering girl. Oh, and while I'm talking about the gay guy—there was a *gay guy* in my movie! What was with that? Weren't there supposed to be decency standards in Hollywood? I was horrified on pretty much every level.

Joseph loved every minute.

He never turned to me, or said anything, but I got the feeling he was watching out the corner of his eye, amused at my discomfort. What was wrong with him? Why wasn't he asking if I wanted to leave? How could he tolerate such filth? I was confused, offended, and a few other things I couldn't put into words. And it was a theater. It would've been *rude* to put anything into words. And I was raised in the South. There might've been sins in the church—but being rude was a sin against *your people*. Simply unthinkable.

Somehow we made it to the end. Not to spoil the movie's intricate plot, but the triangle ends up, well, becoming connected—and not just in a geometrically correct way. Somehow, all sides of this triangle met and each of the characters got some of what they wanted. Did that make it a star or a parallelogram? I never was good at geometry.

Anyway…

Joseph was clearly more patient with restraining his disgust than I was. He was still smiling. We left the theater and began the five-minute walk back to his condo and the safety of my beloved Saturn. He asked what I thought of the movie, and I didn't hesitate. All the pent-up PK guilt transformed into volcanic lava, and I erupted all over Hollywood's vile, corrupting influence. I attacked the idea of men living with women, of poor Stephen's loathsome desires to do naughty things to not-so-innocent Alex, and of some director's nerve to put a g— guy on the screen. I whispered the g— word so no one would hear, or the g— fairy wouldn't get me, or some other nonsense.

Yes, I actually said "g— guy." I couldn't bring myself to use the word.

Joseph took it all in stride, never speaking, smile never faltering.

When Mount St. Michael's righteous eruption ended, Joseph turned to me and asked the strangest question. If I live to be a hundred, I'll never forget his words.

He asked, "I get all that, but don't you think Stephen Baldwin is just the cutest thing?"

5

———

DIE HARD 2

I thought it was odd in the moment, but was so fired up, and had been so sheltered and world-blind my whole life, that I didn't connect the obvious dots. I didn't even know there *were* dots. I get it now.

I shook off the odd question that somehow continued to echo in my head as we reached my car. Joseph, a step ahead, turned and leaned against my door, blocking me from getting in. His hands went casually into his pockets, and his big brown saucers met my own timid blue eyes.

"Where are you going now?" Joseph asked, shaking me out of my internal struggle with his Stephen Baldwin question.

"Umm, home, I guess."

We'd seen a matinee, so it was early afternoon, and we were both about to resume our home-alone-on-a-Saturday-boredom. I didn't welcome another round of bowling strategy and channel flipping, but hadn't planned very far ahead. Apparently, Joseph was in planning mode.

"Why don't you come inside and check out my movies? See if there's something your magic pass missed? If you go home now, we'll both just be home on a Saturday, bored again."

Was he in my head now? And by the twinkle in his eyes, he *knew* he was in my head.

That damned twinkle.

But he had a point, and I knew it.

"Okay. Sure." I used my world-class vocabulary.

We tromped back into the cozy den, and I immediately claimed the throne, running my fingers along the deeply carved kudzu—or whatever vine they carve on fancy throne-like chairs. I really did love that chair.

He pointed to the shelves to the right of the couch, the ones I hadn't had time to inspect earlier. It was his own personal Blockbuster. Somewhere, angels were making that holy, "Ahhh" sound again. He turned the accent light on and I swear it lit up the movies in time to that ancient siren's music.

"I have over a hundred tapes, pick one. I'm gonna get something to drink. You want anything?"

"Sure. You have tea? Or Coke?" I asked.

I didn't understand why, but he chuckled and shook his head like I was some eight-year-old who'd just broken his window with a baseball. I actually did that when I was eight.

"Sure. Be right back."

I heard ice rattling against glass in the kitchen, so I stood and focused on the mighty wall of movies. He wasn't lying. It was impressive. And he didn't just have the old stuff, or the tapes he'd failed to return to Blockbuster (not that I knew *anyone* who did that sort of thing), he had some new stuff I hadn't seen. Very cool.

I immediately pulled the most recent Die Hard movie. It had been in the theater a while, but I'd made the mistake of telling my sister I wanted to see it. This would be my sister Lisa, the most conservative wolf among the pack of religiously-rabid wolves who'd raised your dear story teller. At the *suggestion* I wanted to see an R-rated movie, she laid a guilt trip on so thick I thought I'd never see another movie not made by Disney, and even those were suspect. She went on for thirty minutes about how the executives in Hollywood were all good Christians and put ratings on movies to protect us—and we should respect their work. Never mind the not-so-Christian religious adherence of our Jewish brothers and sisters who ran much of Hollywood the whole concept was flawed. It sounds ridiculous now, I know. But, I was Opie and didn't know better.

Once again, wolves.

I was still gawking in awe at the movie wall when Joseph returned from the kitchen and deposited two squatty, fancy crystal-looking glasses on the coffee table. One contained some golden looking liquid I didn't think was appropriate for a good Christian. The other was my Coke, fizzing loudly and happy to see me.

"Be right back. I'm gonna change out of these jeans." He disappeared into the hallway before I could respond. Why did he need to change out of his jeans to watch a movie? Whatever. His condo. He should be comfortable. I moved on.

I took a sip of Coke, set Bruce on the coffee table, and settled back onto the throne. I was leaning forward slightly, squinting across the room at the people in Joseph's pictures, when the warmth of a smooth hand pressed gently against my neck. A jolt of electricity shot down my spine, somehow making my heart beat faster, while paralyzing everything else at the same time. The hand was joined by its partner, and they began flowing down the line of muscles on my neck to the base of my head, then down to my shoulder. And again. And again.

I did the only think my body permitted in that moment of indecision—I scrunched up my neck, trapping a few fingers, and asked in a squeaky, trembling voice, "What are you doing?"

Joseph's tone carried amusement again. "You just seem so tense. I wanted to help you relax before the movie."

Yes, there were more red flags in that den than in all of China, but don't forget my wolfy-upbringing. Add to that wonderful childhood, a college buddy recently talked me into taking a massage therapy course with him. I did it, more for moral support than anything. As a result, I was always the one giving the massage. It never occurred to me to ask for one. And here Joseph was offering without me even asking. How cool. I relaxed my neck-grip on his fingers and bowed my head to give him easier access to the muscles he so accurately diagnosed as tense.

There was a part of me that started piecing things together. Home alone. Antiques. Three guys in banana hammocks. Threesome. Stephen Baldwin.

Yeah, I'm slow.

I gripped the arms of the beloved throne so tightly that my knuckles turned white. A tiny voice in the back of my head whispered, "I think he's the G-word." No, I couldn't bring myself to say the word, even in a mental conversation with myself. I wanted to jump out of the chair, to run. My heart was racing and a bead of sweat tickled my forehead. The voice began screaming, "Get out!" After all, my virtue was at stake. I couldn't stay in the home of a *G—*. I certainly couldn't allow one to massage my neck. But man, he had good hands. And my neck was really sore. Maybe it would be okay.

Ten, maybe fifteen minutes later, I'd lost track, the hands stopped rubbing and Joseph materialized on the couch opposite my throne, sipping from his un-Christian drink. He was now sporting a loosely fitting light blue t-shirt and even looser navy shorts. Did I mention the shorts were the silky athletic kind? The ones that need tube-undies, or whatever they're called, to keep the boys from roaming? Yeah, those shorts. And his boys roamed freely.

I rolled my now loose neck and reached forward to take a sip of Coke. My hand shook slightly.

Joseph gave me a sideways glance as he picked Bruce up from the table and unceremoniously shoved him into the VCR. Sorry Bruce. Dramatic movie music blasted from speakers I couldn't find, and I nuzzled myself in to the most comfortable position possible, fixing my eyes on the TV in a death-stare so I couldn't possibly make eye-contact with the g— guy sitting across from me.

Joseph settled into the couch, and I heard the rattle of ice and a satisfied sip.

Then he asked something curious. "Why don't you come over here?"

Opie didn't understand. "Why?"

He smiled. "I just thought you might be more comfort-able on the couch." He patted the cushion next to him.

I didn't think it was possible, but my heart raced faster. "I really like this chair. I'm—um—really comfortable." I took another shaky sip of Coke.

He grinned wolfishly. No, not like the ones who raised me. The other ones.

He *knew* I was scared to death, and clueless, and confused—and a hundred other things. He knew all those things and grinned anyway.

"Just come sit over here, okay?"

Opie stared, stunned, mute. PKs are nothing if not obedient. "Umm. Okay."

I shuffled around the coffee table and snuggled as close to the opposite end of the couch as possible. The "I'm not a gay dude" empty seat was firmly established in the middle, even if it was just a sliver of cushion on the tiny loveseat sized couch. I was safe.

But I'd forgotten my Coke. Damn.

Joseph reached across the table, plucked my Coke and the cork coaster, and set them both in front of me. He artfully repositioned himself into the sacred "I'm not a gay dude" space. Didn't he know the rules?

I tried to turn my attention back to the TV, but familiar hands gripped my shoulders and pulled me back. Before I had time to think or react, I was leaning against his chest and his lips were tickling my ear.

6

BRUCE WHO?

I remember the feeling of being frozen, unable to move. My racing heart and rapid breath were the only things still working. Even my eyes had bugged open and wouldn't close. All the while, Joseph kept nibbling, first at the top of my ear, then gently down the outer edge, until he reached my Irish pot of gold, the lobe. His teeth tagged out, and his obviously experienced tongue took over, barely brushing the tender skin. His breath was hot and smelled buttery, with a hint of popcorn. His hands dropped to his side, as if afraid to intrude across some invisible barrier, but his tongue held no such notion of propriety. When it finally found its way inside my ear, the magical spell was shattered and bodily control returned, however shaky it might've been.

I sat forward and turned halfway to face him, unsure of the exact gymnastic feat required to actually sit facing him from our pretzel-like position.

"What are you doing?" My now tiny, childlike voice asked.

He must've seen the terror in my eyes because he

leaned back, granting blessed distance from his sensuous Orville Redenbacher breath. His eyes twinkled more than before, their deep pools swirling as if to hypnotize. I'd never been this close to another guy. Do all men's eyes do that?

He gave me a lopsided grin. "Nothing serious. Just having a little fun."

Fun? I didn't get it. "We're gonna watch a movie. That's fun, right?" I pulled back as if to resume my seat at the edge of the world—I mean couch.

Smooth hands reached out and gently gripped my shoulders. He didn't pull me back this time. He just squeezed, one of those "it's going to be okay, trust me" gestures. Then his hands turned into fingers caressing my arms. He let each finger hover far enough from my skin so they barely touched the hairs on my arms. The sensation that streaked through me, the fire, I'd never felt before.

My inner voice screamed to jump from that couch. It cursed me for betraying everything I'd ever been taught, everything I'd ever believed. Being here with Joseph was wrong, a sin, and I should run out the door as fast as I could. Let Betty carry me to righteous freedom on the other side of town, as far from this g— man as I could get.

But his fingers tickling the fuzzy hairs on my arms felt *so* good. No one had ever done that to me. Hell, I'd only ever been on one date before, with a girl who was part of my nerd pack, not really anyone I was interested in. Besides, my good Christian morals wouldn't let me touch someone that made them feel this way. It could only lead to…

His hands finally reached my wrists, which now pressed against my legs, petrified, unmoving flesh against jeans. He maintained his finger-touch and gradually dragged them across the back of my resistant hands. I dared not move. The effort brought his body forward and his chest again pressed against my back. The warmth of his steady breathing made my neck pimple. When his fingers finally stopped tracing and interlaced with my own, I was so startled that I squeezed reflexively. That was apparently the universal gesture for "bring it on," because his lips pressed against my neck and fire bloomed throughout my chest, spreading through every artery and vein and whatever else spread through a body. Holy cow, that fire. I'd never imagined feeling like that. I'd never dreamed it. I couldn't even be sure I knew what it was, but I knew I didn't want it to stop.

All thoughts of religion or beliefs or fears or popcorn (yes, I did occasionally think of popcorn throughout the evening) vanished. I let my roommate's friend grip our interlaced fingers tightly and raise them to my chest so he held me with all his strength. He stopped kissing my neck and nuzzled his chin over my shoulder so our cheeks pressed together. I'd never been held like that. I'd never been held by someone who wanted to hold me *that way*.

The fire grew hotter, but in ways I couldn't identify. It wasn't just some twenty-something guy hormone thing. It was the awakening of feelings I never knew existed. I drew the deepest breath possible and held it, held his strength and breath and scent inside my lungs, savored the safety and warmth of his embrace.

He must've sensed something because we sat there for an eternal moment. When his voice finally broke the stillness, it was quiet, compassionate.

"Are you okay? he asked.

"Yeah." I released the breath I'd been holding. "I'm good."

"You sure? Have you ever done this before?"

This? I didn't even know what *this* was. But something inside me screamed for the comfort and security of his touch. I didn't want it to end, regardless of what that meant. I'd deal with that later.

"No. I've never—I mean, I… "

"You've never been with a guy before, have you?" he whispered.

Damn that buttery whisper. It was silky and made me want to press closer into his embrace. I tightened my grip on his fingers and pulled his arms more snugly around me, then leaned my head back onto his shoulder.

"Is it that obvious? Am I doing something wrong?"

A warm chuckle tickled my ear and he kissed it. "No. You're doing fine. Just know we can stop. We don't have to do anything you're not comfortable with."

Bruce Willis blew something up in the background and gave me a moment to think while the sounds echoed through the room. I untangled our fingers, which he released without protest, then stood and sat again, facing toward him. I took both his hands in mine and held them while staring into his eyes. My fear vanished. My guilt vanished. Everything, except Joseph's twinkling brown eyes vanished.

Without thinking, I leaned forward and brushed my lips against his in the gentlest, faintest touch. I drew in his breath, closed my mouth to hold it and leaned back again, locking eyes once more. His breath was inside me. The idea battered my senses and a goofy grin burst from my face as his breath escaped my now parted lips.

He smiled broadly.

It was that same warm smile he'd given me when I first arrived at his door. It was so unsettling then. It wasn't wanton or lecherous or anything like that. It was generous and kind and open—and desirous. That anyone—especially a man—desired *me?* That idea had never crossed my mind before.

He watched patiently as my emotions warred, then reached one hand to cup my cheek. His fingers traced the line of my jaw, then my lips. There wasn't anything sexual in his touch. Just an explorer discovering new, uncharted territory, curious what he might find when he searched further.

So I let him search.

7

———————

THE OLYMPICS

B ruce blew stuff up for two hours and four minutes, and I remember when the credits started rolling. We were still on the couch. Not a single article of clothing was out missing, but we'd remained tangled throughout the on-screen action, only separating to reach for a glass of Coke or whatever Satan-inspired liquid he was drinking.

Kissing. Talking. Laughing. Kissing more. Giggling.

I know. Giggling wasn't manly. But I couldn't help it. I had somehow missed the little dimples that formed when he smiled. The first time we unlocked our lips long enough to breathe, he grinned and I saw them. Those little puddins. They made me giggle.

By the end of the movie, I knew Joseph was originally from Iowa where his parents still ran a farm. He had two older brothers who were both married with kids. None of his family cared that he was g— and he returned to potato-land several times each year to see them. He'd attended college in Nashville before landing a job working with numbers or books, or numbers with books, that moved him a few hours away, to a city with a shiny new stadium-seat theater. He'd lived here for a year, was slowly making friends, but liked to keep his circle small. He loved his antiques, not just for the beauty of the pieces, but for the history behind them. A good story made his heart flutter. Hence the Blockbuster-wanna-be wall. He wasn't terribly tall, but he liked to play volleyball on Friday nights in a social league for g— guys. Who knew there were such things?

He offered to take me to volleyball one Friday night and I cocked my head, confused.

"Isn't that for g— guys? You know I'm not g—, right?"

He barked a laugh and his puddins glared accusingly. "Yeah, I know," was all he said.

Even then, he was kind and respectful, and understood that while I was clearly ready to suck his face off, there were certain truths I wasn't brave enough to examine. Not yet. Joseph really was a good dude.

When the credits stopped, he looked at me with one eyebrow raised. "So, if we go to my room I can help you relax some more. Just give you a massage."

Okay, stop laughing.

I didn't know this was the most well-used line in the gay lexicon. I had no idea what "massage" might be code for or what it might lead to. I barely knew there *was* a code. There's a code, right?

Anyway, Opie grinned and followed his new puppy, Dimples, into the bedroom.

I heard the click-click of an old-timey lamp switch and dim light bloomed from across the room, revealing another antique wonderland that must've been stolen from Queen Victoria herself. The wood of the four post bed and oversized end tables was dark and rich. The bed's headboard stretched nearly halfway up toward the ceiling, and was heavily carved. The side table didn't really lend itself to close inspection, so I don't know whether there was more kudzu or some other carving. But it was fancy. The lamp now lighting our way looked like one of those old Tiffany's pieces you'd see on *Antiques Roadshow*. You know them—the ones with the church window glass that made the appraiser squeal before they ever start talking. He had *that* lamp.

On the wall opposite the bed stood a massive armoire that must've taken four burly dudes to carry down the stairs when Joseph moved into the place. It was elegant and rich and old—and monstrously large. While every-thing else in the room screamed Queen Vicky, the armoire had a distinctively Asian flair. Something from the early Quin Dynasty, perhaps? What do I know? It was amazing.

Joseph smirked as he watched me ogle his furniture, but his patience ran out when I started tracing the armoire's doors with my fingers.

"Why don't you lay down on your stomach? I'll go get some oil."

"Umm. Oil?" I asked nervously.

He chuckled. "Massage oil."

"Oh, right. Great. Perfect."

When he returned from the mysterious oil stash, I was on the bed as instructed. I felt his presence in the doorway, but only heard his chuckles.

"Do you want me to oil up your shirt?" he asked through grunts of laughter.

"Oh, right," I said, flipping around and sitting up to remove my shirt. I tried not to look terrified, but must've failed. He padded to the bed and sat on the edge, placing a hand on my fully-clothed leg.

"We can stop. I've had a great night." I can still hear the sincerity in his offer.

I tossed my shirt and it landed bunched against yet another antique I hadn't inspected, a waist-high table with a glass top to display things I couldn't see from the bed.

"I'm okay. Besides, I'm never on this end of a massage." I gave him my best "I'm not about to pee my pants," grin.

He stared a moment, considering, then smiled. "Good. I was hoping you'd say that. But remember, we can stop anytime."

"Thanks, I'm really good." My bravado ground dissonantly against the quaver in my voice. He motioned for me to resume the belly-flop position, and I happily complied. A hidden band struck up wordless, cool jazz.

I heard the pop of the oil cap and squirt of liquid on flesh as he greased up his palms. Then, for the longest moment, I heard his hands rubbing together like he was trying to start a fire with two sticks. When the skin of his palm came to rest on my now-chilled shoulder, I understood. He'd warmed his hands for me. Another point to Joseph.

The smell of tea leaves drifted from rubbing flesh. It tickled my nose, but warmed my back. Another sensation I'd never felt before.

For thirty minutes, the sax and trombone and trumpet played, while Joseph expertly—platonically—massaged muscles I hadn't realized needed it. He started with the upper part of my back, then worked his way carefully, methodically down to my lower back. Satisfied, he moved back up to my neck and shoulders where the real tension waited. I heard a soft, "wow" as his fingers tried to dig into clenched muscles.

I found myself drifting in and out of the music, my mind seeing Stephen Baldwin, then Bruce Willis, then Joseph. It lingered every time Joseph appeared. My heart shifted from a relaxed first gear to a racing third just seeing his smile with my closed eyes.

Somewhere between dreaming and awake, he asked, "Want me to do your legs?"

I grunted something unintelligible he assumed was assent.

His hands rested on the small of my back before traveling toward the button holding my jeans together, guarding my virtue. I arched my butt slightly to give him access, to give him permission. A moment later, jeans lay near my crumpled shirt and Joseph was rubbing re-oiled hands together.

When the last pinky toe had received a proper caress, he hesitated. I could sense it. Odd. He hadn't hesitated all night.

A hand found my shoulder, wedged itself underneath, and lifted to turn me onto my back. I got the gist and turned the rest of the way on my own. His eyes found mine, then wandered slowly down to my chest. He did that gentle-finger-thing again, this time starting with my neck, across my chest and down to below my belly button. My body screamed at his touch. In a good way. My soul was on fire, and my skin couldn't decide whether to tingle or burn. It was the most electrifying, intense, passionate thing I'd ever experienced—until he hit my belly button and I giggled like a Catholic school girl in trouble. His eyes popped wide, and recognition flashed before he took his other nine evil, sadistic, oily fingers and tickled the shit out of me.

The tickling made me need to pee. Talk about mood killer. I shuffled into the bathroom, eyeing the armoire on the way, giving it one little stroke as I passed. He was still laughing from his sneak-attack as I disappeared into the bathroom.

A moment and a flush later, I returned to find him standing by the bed, oil bottle in hand.

"Back on your back. I didn't get to finish. And close your eyes this time. No peeking."

"Yes, sir." I smiled, forgetting I stood in some man's bedroom in nothing but tighty-whiteys. With holes. I would never be a good g—.

For the next twenty minutes, Dimples used his magic hands along every part of my body's front, at least that parts not covered by ratty fabric. He started with my shoulders, pressing firmly, tracing muscle lines and tendons—or whatever you trace when running your hands over a man's shoulders, down his chest and stomach, toward no-man's-land, excuse the pun. This time, he avoided the ticklish spots, skipped the Underoos, and focused of my legs and feet.

I reached up a couple of times to touch his arm, but he pushed my hands back down onto the bed. "Lie still. Just enjoy this."

Yes, sir, I thought, happy to comply.

I don't think Joseph was a professional masseuse. And maybe it was the whole day or night or something, but that was the best massage of my life. Even to this day, nothing has topped it.

I know. I said, "topped it." Stop laughing.

But what he did next took my breath. He'd saved the finger-tingle thing to the end. Starting with my feet, he traced the tips of his fingers up my legs, over the fabric of my undies, up my stomach, and across my chest. He lingered there a moment, tracing little circles across my nipples as if studying them intently. Then, as a blind man searches a face for the first time, his fingertips found my chin, then cheeks, then temples and forehead. My whole body tingled and spasmed. I couldn't stop it. Was this what it was *supposed* to feel like?

I still hadn't opened my eyes or moved my hands, so when his breath brushed near my mouth, my heart nearly jumped through my chest. I tasted him before ever feeling his lips brush gently against mine. I shivered. He drew closer and ran his tongue above them, only letting it hint of a touch. The shiver grew.

The air warmed as he hovered above my body. When he finally lowered himself to press against me, my skin thrilled at the surprise of his now naked flesh against mine for the first time. His lips pressed again, no longer gentle, now urgent. I ran my hands along his sides, then around his back, holding him closer. I found his bare buttocks and gripped it with both hands, pressing him closer. He caressed my face as we kissed, then ran a hand across my short hair, pulling my head back. His tongue attacked my neck, teeth scoring gentle lines where it traced, and my body writhed as his tongue found its way to my chest again, then tickled my stomach in a far different way than before.

I'd never felt so—*alive.*

His mouth reached the top of my underwear, and he carefully gripped the elastic band in his teeth. His hands gripped my arms and held them flat against my sides. I thought my heart would explode. Ever so carefully, he lifted the underwear over my granite-like erection and pulled them down my legs. I'll never know how he managed that without using his hands, but I remember feeling the last of my clothing slip over my feet.

I still hadn't opened my eyes. He'd told me not to.

He moved up from my feet, his breath tickling the hair on my legs, then across my groin and stomach, to my chest and back to my mouth. He kissed me gently this time. Passionately. He wasn't holding back, and I could feel how much he wanted me.

He wanted *me*.

I'd never been wanted before. Not like this. By anyone.

When he finally pressed his body to mine again, our nakedness joined for the first time, my world spun. His manhood pressed against my own, and he was *enormous*, not just because he was excited. That thing was huge! I was a little startled, but didn't want to break the mood, so I kept quiet. Besides, his lips wouldn't let me speak. Good lips.

I wrapped my arms around Joseph and lost myself in the feeling of his touch, losing all sense of time or thought. He was the only thing I knew, and I couldn't get him close enough. My hands explored, eager to learn what awaited around every curve. His lean, muscular frame excited my senses, and fireworks of adrenaline and emotion exploded through me.

An hour into this make-out session, Joseph pulled back and stared down at me. I reached a hand up and ran it through his hair, cupping his head as he stared into my eyes. I couldn't move. I didn't want to move.

"Are you okay?" he asked.

I smiled uncontrollably. "Yeah. I'm great."

"Are you *sure* you've never done this before?"

I cocked my head, confused, a little embarrassed. "Can you tell? Am I still doing ok?"

He laughed and ran a hand along my face. "Okay? No,

you're not doing okay. You're amazing. We've been going for over three hours when you count the movie we barely watched. This is Olympic level making out."

I blushed, making him laugh again.

"Maybe we should stop," he said, concern creeping into his voice.

Shock flooded my face. "No. Please."

I hesitated, my eyes never leaving his. "I want to feel you inside me."

His eyes widened. "Really? You've never done *any* of this and you know *that's* what you want? How do you know that?"

I shrugged as much as I could under his weight. "I don't know. It's all I could think about a minute ago. All I can think about now."

He stared a moment, thinking, unsure. Something clicked in his eyes, a decision made. He leaned forward and gave me a gentle kiss before rolling over to his nightstand. I traced my hand along his back as he opened the drawer and pulled out a bottle of some clear liquid I'd never seen.

"What's that?" I asked.

He chuckled. "Just trust me."

Ever considerate Joseph squirted some of the clear goo into his palms and did the fire-starting thing again, ensuring I would never receive the rude shock of cold against my skin. When his hand gently gripped me, an earthquake started in my toes and raced up my spine. My hair bolted upright and I started to shiver. He stopped immediately and smiled.

"Oh, no. Not yet you don't."

I didn't understand, but trusted him.

He oiled himself and then took a healthy handful of the liquid and used a finger to tease between my cheeks.

Wholly different shock waves shook my body. What was this guy doing to me? Then he heated more and pressed his hands across my chest. Before I knew it, my whole upper body was glistening in the candlelight.

Hey, when did he light candles? The random thought popped into my head.

When he pressed against my body, and my slick, oily skin slid against his, he moaned for the first time. We ground against each other, kissing and rubbing. I felt him harden further and my hand strayed, curious what it would feel like in my palm. I'd never held another man's penis, and the idea thrilled me as much as the act. I didn't understand why. I didn't care.

He pressed his palms against the bed beside my head and sat himself upright, then lifted my legs to rest atop his broad shoulders. He added more clear liquid and guided himself gently with one hand, seeking entry.

And here's where things went sideways.

Have you ever driven down a highway or road and approached a tunnel with one of those signs reading, "Seven Foot Clearance" in big, bold lettering? They're everywhere. So, what happens if your truck is eight feet tall, or nine, or more. Would your girth—er, height—be able to squeeze into the tunnel? Would any amount of—um —truck grease (just roll with me, I'm making a point) help that truck traverse the tunnel's tight, confined opening? And to make things more challenging, what if it was a brand new tunnel, one that hadn't ever had a truck enter its dark confines? A *virgin* tunnel, so to speak?

Nope. Of course not. Not gonna happen.

And we darn sure tried to get that truck home. Over and over.

Joseph smiled and sat up on the fourth or fifth, maybe it was the twentieth attempt.

"I don't think this is going to work. Want to finish together?" he asked.

I was disappointed and it must've shown on my face. He ran a hand across my cheek, kissed me tenderly, and said, "Please don't be upset. You've been incredible. You just need a little practice."

Unsure how to respond, I nodded.

His gentle hands found my still-firm shaft and began to rub in odd, circular motions, up and down. When his palm brushed the tip, I quivered. I pulled him on top of me and searched his eyes as he continued his rhythmic stroking. He kissed my lips passionately, then moved to my neck. I couldn't focus, couldn't think. My body was all sensation and feeling. My heart raced.

And then all my excitement and anticipation burst forth. He sensed my body tense and release, returning his kisses to my lips, no longer gentle, again urgent. His grip tightened and released in time with his body pressing then pulling back. I lost all control and our bodies were soon covered in more than just warm lube. His hand surrendered its grip, but he continued grinding against me with his penis, mimicking the motion of the sex I'd hoped we'd have in a very different way. My oily body, now slick with all manner of life, gave him pleasure. I saw it in his eyes. The ones that never left mine.

His hands never left my body and he finally reached climax by the blessed friction of our sweaty, oily torsos. He ground against me long after he'd left his mark. I wish he'd never stopped.

After a moment of lingering kisses, he moved to rise. I

pulled him back and pressed his flesh against mind, holding him as close as I could.

I wanted him close. I needed him closer.

I buried my nose in his neck, then in his hair, savoring his scent and taste and touch.

We fell asleep like that.

I've never slept so well.

8

———

SHE'S A WITCH! BURN HER!

Sunlight intruded through the open window around seven o'clock and roused me from my peaceful slumber. My bleary eyes found the Joseph's lustrous black curls spread across the pillow next to me and my first reaction was to smile and bury my nose in those curls, breathing deeply his scent and the feel of his locks against my skin. But as I pulled back from that ecstatic moment, a second, less expected flood of emotions flooded into my mind.

Overwhelming guilt.

watched the man next to me sleep, fascinated by the rise and fall of his chest, and it struck me that I was in bed with another man. Yes, that's obvious now—but in the moment, the idea struck me like a mallet whacks a gong. And that darned gong rang loudly in my head.

From my earliest recollection in Sunday School or Bible class, I'd been taught that men laying with men was sin, an abomination, something for which stoning outside the city walls was appropriate. At least that was the punishment back in the days of walls and stones.

In one night, I'd betrayed everything I'd ever known to be true and right.

And here the sun rose on His day, and light streamed through the window to find me naked in bed. It lightly warmed my face with accusatory heat. My heart—the same one that had thrilled at Joseph's lingering touch hours before—now fell into a dark despair.

It ached.

I ached.

I dug my legs out of the tangled covers and stood as quietly as possible. I stared down at Joseph while the war of emotions raged in my head. A few moments later, I was dressed and sneaking toward the door.

He sat up. I don't know how long he'd been awake and watching, but there was no surprise in his eyes when I turned at his first words.

"You ok?" he asked simply.

Given the adult game of Twister from the night before, that wasn't what I expected. I'm not really sure what I had expected.

"Uh, yeah. I'm good." I tried not to sound like a dying animal. "I need to go."

He threw the covers back and stood. Damn. He didn't mean to make me look, but how could I not? My eyes grazed like a hungry beast until my conscience kicked my inner gut, reminding me why my head was still cowed. And it had nothing to do with grazing—and *everything* to do with it.

I didn't let naked Joseph come any closer. Maybe I was afraid he'd pull me back, tempt me to stay, or ravage me like a bagel smeared with strawberry cream cheese.

Hey, I was hungry. It was breakfast time.

Whatever the reason, and I may never understand, I

gave him a quick nod and turned as quickly as possible, and practically ran through his front door and up the stairs to my car.

I sat in my beloved Betty and stared out the windshield at Joseph's door for a long time. I don't know if I was hoping it would open and he'd come comfort me, or if I was torturing myself over my horrific betrayal of my PK past. Either way, I couldn't move. After an eternity of self-loathsome glaring at Joseph's door, I found the courage to start the car and drive home.

When I walked through the apartment door, I expected Peter to greet me with his perpetually chipper morning-person banter. The thought of answering, "So, where were you last night?" made my stomach churn even faster. Thankfully, he'd already left for work, and my conscience was the only thing asking questions.

So, I KNOW YOU DON'T WANT TO DO THIS IN A STORY primarily about a hot and crazy date, but we need to talk about the conscience. You know, that tiny angel on your shoulder who whispers in your ear when you're doing right or wrong? The one who spars with the leather-clad minx on your other shoulder?

According to legend, there was a Native American medicine man who lived somewhere along the Mississippi River. His tribe honored him, as was befitting his role among his people. It was common for him to sit in a chair of tightly bound limbs while his tribe packed shoulder to shoulder on logs and the ground around a billowing fire. He'd don his untanned, beaded leather jerkin and colorfully feathered crown, adding import and weight to whatever words he might choose that night.

No one knew his age. He wasn't even sure of it. But he was ancient.

One cloudless night, as the people crowded around a fire and the moon dominated the inky sky, a young boy braved a question for the mystic.

"Why does it hurt to do wrong?" his squeaky voice asked over the crackle of burning logs.

Dozens of eyes snapped to the child who'd asked for the shaman's wisdom. The old man cocked his head and motioned the boy toward him. His gap-toothed grin offered more fear than comfort to the lad, but the boy complied. As the quaking boy stood, his shoulders gripped by leathery hands, his eyes met eternity in the shaman's glare.

"Little one, inside you, right here," the man stabbed a bony, arthritic finger in the middle of the boy's chest. "Inside here, there is a stone shaped with three sides. When you were born, the stone was smooth and perfect, its corners sharp as daggers. Throughout your life, this stone weighs your actions and judges them according to our laws and beliefs. When you act against the tribe, or against our beliefs, the stone turns, and its corners prick your heart, causing pain."

The boy's eyes filled with wonder, and a tiny hand escaped the man's grip and pressed to his chest, as if searching for the stone.

But the man wasn't finished. He peered around the fire at the adults assembled and listening to his lecture with the child. When he spoke again, his eyes wandered to each man and woman in turn, his gaze finally landing on a proud warrior across the flames.

"Tell me, why do you sharpen your blade between hunts?"

The warrior was surprised to be called out, but puffed out his chest and answered. "It dulls when used. I must sharpen it before the next hunt or it will fail when I need it most."

"Just so." The medicine man nodded, then returned his eyes to the boy. "Your stone is like that brave man's blade. Each time you do wrong, it turns and its points dull. Eventually, its edges round and you'll no longer feel pain for your wrongdoing."

The boy stumbled through another question. "But— isn't that good? To no longer feel pain?"

"Oh, no, my son. Not so." The old man intoned. "For one who cannot feel the pain of his conscience is lost to evil."

I BATHED UNDER THE HOTTEST WATER OUR APARTMENT could offer. No matter how hard I tried, how much soap I lathered onto my body, Joseph's scent wouldn't fade. I saw him when I closed my eyes, his taught chest, his wavy hair, his sparkling eyes. I shoved bubbles up my nose and was rewarded with a burning sensation, but his scent lingered.

When my skin was wrinkly and raw, I toweled off and threw on some ragged shorts and a t-shirt, then tossed myself onto the couch. Baseball, old football *again*, Lifetime, more Star Trek reruns. TV sucked.

I decided to take a nap. It had been a long night.

When I pulled the sheet to my neck and rolled into my side-sleeper position, the Bible I kept on my nightstand glared back at me. I tried closing my eyes, but could feel the Holy Book scolding me. What had I done?

I couldn't sleep.

Days passed. I was miserable. Joseph never called, but my stone triangle spun faster than I thought possible. Its unworn corners pricked with reckless abandon. Their sharpness didn't fade like the shaman said they would. They just hurt over and over.

But through all the self-doubt and inner turmoil, I couldn't shake one realization that confused everything I thought I'd known for so long. The night with Joseph, not the sex part, but being with him, sharing time and space and experience—it all felt good. No, it felt *right*. In all my uptight years of preaching about rightness to others, I had never felt that rightness myself, until that night.

It's hard to explain.

I'd dated girls before. Well, I'd been on *a* date with *a* girl before. I was nervous the whole time, but that's probably to be expected of a teenage boy on his first proper date. I'd practically lost my shit when she leaned over and kissed me in the car. Her lips were that special soft that only comes from years of wearing lipstick or gloss. Nothing like the crackled, un-cared for lips I offered her. It was nice. Pleasant even. But at no point in that interlude did I think about her naked or want to keep kissing her. It just seemed like what I was supposed to do at the end of a date with a girl.

And I'd been taught that you don't have sex until you're married. It was a sin. It led to pregnancy and disease and, I don't know, more sin? My lack of libido with women was actually a point of pride. I had it all under control. I was very right and holy when it came to the opposite sex.

What I hadn't realized before Joseph—that hit me like

the proverbial light on the road to Damascus—was that I might've been aiming my pointy thing at the wrong target.

All those feelings, both physical and emotional, that our parents and teachers warned us about ad nauseam, avoided me completely when I thought about girls. But when I thought about Joseph, holy cow. They were overpowering.

I wanted him to hold me again, to feel the safety and comfort in his arms.

I wanted to hear him laugh. See his eyes sparkle. Watch him flick that annoying curl out of his eye.

I wanted to see those dimples form when he grinned.

I wanted to rip his shirt off and let my tongue be Magellan to his tight, fleshy ocean.

Was that too much?

Of course not, you prude!

I wanted to feel him next to me, against me, *finally* inside me. I ached for it. I craved it. Thoughts of him filled my mind, waking or otherwise, in ways that no girl ever had. Ever could, I now knew.

It was like the experience with Joseph had pried a door open that I never even knew existed. Sure, it was likely always there. I don't believe that crap about nurture over nature. You either have the penis-loving-gene or you don't. Get over it, Mary.

But that door was open and no amount of pent-up PK guilt was going to close it again.

Hallelujah, a *gay* was born!

9

PARKS ARE FOR BALLS

Two weeks has passed since the *Threesome* encounter. Joseph had called once, spoken briefly with Peter, then disappeared. I don't think he ever mentioned me or told Peter what happened. Part of me was relieved, but another part was a little hurt. We'd had an existential, life-altering movie date and he didn't seem to be singing with the angels like I had been.

My guilt stone wasn't smooth at this point, that would take years, but I'd learned to brace myself when it spun.

I think it was a Sunday. Peter was home, strutting around in his ridiculously tight shorts that were basically underwear with pockets. He was shirtless. There was no question why he was a model, and I noticed for the first time. Sure, I'd known he was a good looking dude before, but I'd never thought about it much. Remember, *that* door had been closed, probably padlocked with one of those religious locks that bites or burns when you touch it.

But today, for the first time, I realized my roommate was stunning. Not just handsome or cute—*f'ing stunning.* Holy cow. How do I shut that damned door?

Anyway.

He said something about volleyball in the park. I wasn't paying attention to his words. Models and words and all. But volleyball stuck. It was a pretty day outside, no humidity, light breeze. So I told Peter I'd meet him at the park and teach him who's boss.

Or I'd set for him since I was short. Yeah, that's what I said.

An hour later, I drove around the sprawling park searching for the promised volleyball game. The road wound a lazy circle around the huge green space. Thick patches of trees interrupted the landscape, and it was impossible to see from one end to the other. So Betty and I drove, windows down, Bruce Springsteen blasting. Guess I had a thing for Bruces, too.

A few minutes later, I spotted shirtless guys sitting at the base of a net erected over a bed of neatly hemmed sand. I parked and trotted up the hill.

As I drew closer, a few things became apparent.

First, Peter wasn't there. I probably beat him. He was on model time.

Second, the guys were really fit. I mean cover-of-GQ fit. My scrawny butt felt out of place.

Third, and most importantly, I could hear snippets of their conversation between smacks of the ball. One guy was telling another about a date he'd had last night.

"… and then he put his tongue up my ass," was all I heard as my legs suddenly stopped working, and I froze halfway up the hill.

"What? That's amazing! Keep going!" another dude urged.

"He stayed back there forever. I thought my head was gonna explode. It was so hot. But when he fucked me…"

And my legs gave out. I flopped to the ground, out of sight of the speakers. Terror filled me.

But curiosity did, too.

Why would one guy put his tongue up another guy's butt? Didn't poop come out of there? I was perplexed. This was a sport I'd never seen before. So I did what any self-respecting guy headed to play volleyball would do, I crouched on the ground out of sight and eavesdropped my never-been-licked ass off.

I had no idea there were so many different things two guys could do. Joseph had seemed impressed with my PG-13 rated kissing and fondling, but this was what an Olympic-level performance was *really* all about. I was so Junior College compared to these guys.

Then Peter walked up and scared the shit out of me.

"Hey. What are you doing? Not gonna play?"

"Uh, yeah, sure." I stammered, "Was just waiting for you."

It sounded good at the time.

Peter helped me to my feet and a lightning bolt struck. *"What if Peter's gay?"* raced through my head. Was I living with an honest-to-Cosmo hotter-than-hell *model* gay? What if… I didn't let myself finish the thought because we were approaching the butt muncher. Or is that munch-ee since he was on the receiving end? That might need research.

When the volleyball guys looked up and saw Peter, all talk of butt munching and dates ceased. Immediately. I was stunned. They greeted him with hearty hugs that ended as quickly as they began, similar to what you'd see from chest bumping football players on the replays I avoided almost as much as Lifetime. Fascinating. What did *that* mean? Why wasn't any of this simple?

Peter introduced me and fist bumps abounded. No one seemed to take special note of either of us, and volleyball resumed. It was fun. They were *really* good. Some had even played in college.

I was disappointed there was nothing to overhear during the three hours we played, but I was sure of two things. I'd just met a bunch of gay men, and they really liked playing with balls.

10

CLOSE ENCOUNTER OF THE SECOND KIND

Four weeks after the magic, door-opening date with Joseph, I still dithered between guilt and curiosity. But more than either of those things, I wanted to see him again.

I'm generally a bright guy. Smart, plenty of common sense, level-headed. But when confronted with my first antique-loving, rippling bodied naked man, I'd lost all ability to reason.

You guessed it. I never got Joseph's phone number.

And since we've already discussed the ancient era in which this epic takes place, you know caller-ID wasn't a thing. So, I put on spy music and crept into Peter's room. Actually, he was at work, so I just walked in. But the spy thing sounded fun.

I dug through the clutter on his nightstand until I found the leather-bound book where he kept all his numbers. Yes, kids, we had to use things like paper and little black books before the dawn of iPhone civilization. Get over it.

Joseph's number was there!

My heart fluttered.

His last name was kind of unique, so I knew immediately it was the right coat-of-many-colors-wearing-Joseph (that's a Biblical reference for you heathens).

I carefully placed the leather book back on the nightstand and ran like a girl who'd just been asked to prom to the den where our antique phone sat. I believe this was my very first proper "queen out." Experts, please rule on this.

My hand shook as I cradled the receiver. I had absolutely no idea what I wanted to say, but I was calling him right then and there. *Buzz buzz*. The familiar sounds of someone else's phone ringing met my ear.

"Hello?"

It was him!

"Oh, hey. Joseph. Is that you?" I was articulate as ever.

"Yeah. Who's this?"

My chest fell. How could he not know my voice after what we shared? The intimacy. The romance. The popcorn!

"Hey. It's Michael."

Silence.

"Uh, from the other week. You know, *Threesome*?"

"Oh, Michael, duh. I'm sorry. I was in the middle of reading and didn't recognize your voice. How are you? You doing ok since…" his voice trailed off.

"Yeah. I'm great." I lied. "Sorry I didn't call. I didn't think to ask for your number."

A chuckle flowed through the phone. "You did bolt out pretty fast."

"Sorry about that," I half said, half sighed.

This wasn't going like I imagined. He was supposed to be fawning all over me, over my prowess, over my passion. At least over my movie pass.

"So, what's up?" he asked casually.

"Well, I was thinking, maybe we could get together again. We kinda bailed on Bruce Willis. I feel bad for him."

He laughed and I beamed that my joke landed. "Sure. That's be great. Maybe I can cook for you sometime?"

And he cooks? What the hell?

"I like to eat." Goober said. Dumbass.

He chuckled again. "You free tonight? It's Saturday, and you sound bored again."

I grinned. "It's a date. Uh—I mean—sure, that works. I mean—it's *not* a date or anything, but yes. Dinner's good. Sure."

I could hear his dimples through the receiver. I'm such an idiot.

"See you at six."

I hung up the phone and did a happy dance right there in front of James Tiberius Kirk on the tv. He didn't seem to notice.

———

THAT NIGHT, JOSEPH MADE CHICKEN ALA-SOMETHING-OR-other with broccoli and couscous. I'd never had couscous before. It's fun to say. It tasted even better. Damn, this boy could cook.

He opened a bottle of wine and started pouring me a glass. I waived him off and asked for a glass of water. At this point in my PK recovery program, I'd still never had alcohol. Yes, I was twenty-two, I know. Just keep remembering the wolves. They're real.

He popped popcorn and added extra butter, just like in the theater. I sat in the throne across from the couch and dutifully waited for his playful smirk and hand wave before practically leaping over the coffee table to snuggle under his arm. We watched Bruce blow things up for two hours. This time, we actually watched. You're welcome, Bruce.

The Disney-like grin didn't leave my face once. It was cute.

When the credits began to roll, Joseph kissed the top of my head and leaned me forward. Well, wasn't that *fatherly*? Not the hot and steamy I was hoping for.

He turned me around and gripped my shoulders, studying me with his piercing gaze. "You ok?" he asked with sincerity.

I nodded nervously. Why was I nervous again?

"I didn't know that was your first—experience. I mean, I knew you hadn't had sex before, but didn't realize you'd never even been on a date. I wouldn't have pushed so hard. I'm sorry."

My jaw must've dropped, because he grinned.

"I'm not sorry you pushed. I just wish you could've pushed something else—into something else."

Oh, words, why did you fail me?

He barked a deep, rumbling laugh. The one that started deep in his core and clawed its way out his throat. I couldn't help it and joined in.

Before I knew it, we weren't laughing anymore because my lips were otherwise occupied.

11

THREESOME CHANGES LIVES

The second encounter with Joseph didn't rise to the Olympic standard set the month before. How can you ever compete with your first Olympics? Sorry Michael Phelps. I know you just kept getting better.

Anyway.

It was still nice. We made out a bunch, and our hands explored again. He was kind and gentle, though not as gentle as the first time. And he didn't once ask, "Are you okay?" or "Do you want to stop?" We just plowed forward. Sorry, bad turn of phrase. There was still no plowing. The fields were just packed too tight and the plow was too fat.

Are plows fat? What do I know? I'm a city boy.

Regardless, there was no plowing, so that experience will have to wait for another story.

Perhaps the most interesting thing that happened that night was my unconstrained blurting of, "I think I love you," about an hour into the action. Joseph bolted upright. Then his brows knitted, and I think surprise morphed in to something akin to pity. Man, that was *not* the reaction I was going for.

He gave me a wan smile and said, "No, you don't. You don't even know me. I'm just your first."

We got dressed after that emotional ice bath, and I headed home.

My PK guilt battled with hurt feelings at his rejection of my undying love. I'd never uttered those words to anyone, much less a naked man. Wasn't it part of The Code that he say them back? How could he reject my sincere pledge of fealty and faith?

Okay, he was right. I didn't even know him.

But he was hot, passionate, sweet—and he was my first. Even to this day, twenty or so (don't ask) years later, I can close my eyes and picture a dark curl escaping and dangling frustratingly across his forehead. I can see his eyes and their sparkle. His smile, the little quirk on the right side that didn't quite match the left.

Joseph will always be special, always my first.

THERE'S A LOT MORE TO THIS STORY, ABOUT THE GRANITE triangle of my conscience and its war inside my chest. That battle lasted years. In some ways, I suppose, it will never end. But it would take volumes to do that struggle justice. It deserves more than a chapter and a few witty quips.

But what I can say is that, while the battle took many years, I won the war.

Regardless of your view of religion, or your religious views, one common thread flows through nearly all of them: the idea of finding inner peace. Sure, spiritual folks want you to find peace through their particular belief system, and that's fine. I respect beliefs, and believers.

But it wasn't how I found my own peaceful calm.

That came after years of making mistakes. Of falling and getting back up. Of questioning *everything* and coming away with more questions than answers. Of learning that there will *always* be more questions than answers. Of learning that those who claim to have all the answers are secretly struggling with their own questions, and need my compassion and support, whether or not they admit it.

Just like I need theirs.

And that's okay.

It'll all be okay.

THANK YOU, JOSEPH.

IF YOU ENJOYED MY ACCIDENTAL FIRST DATE, PLEASE leave a star-filled review. Your feedback helps independent authors thrive!

CONTINUE THE JOURNEY WITH MICHAEL IN THE NEXT DATE, the first novel-length volume in the Raised by Wolves series. **I've included the first three chapters in the following pages** *as a free sample.*

My
Next
Date
Casey Morales
Rescued by Wolves Book 2

Casey Morales

My Next Date

Raised by Wolves Book 2

1

———

I was completely intimidated the first time my roommate, Peter, bugged me about joining the gym where he worked out. He was a Greek god, an actual model who looked like one of those unreal men on the cover of the magazines I *definitely* never looked at every time I passed them in the grocery store. Peter worked out twice a day and coached other people in their workouts for another three or four hours. I hadn't ever met anyone with a body like his, and it was such a waste, especially since we lived together, because he was straight.

Never mind that I thought I was straight too. Yes, I know. I'd had hot man-sex twice and couldn't get the images of Joseph out of my mind, especially as I lay awake at night wishing his warmth was beside me, but I *wanted* to be straight.

So I was. For the moment. I thought.

Sigh.

The third or fourth—or tenth—time Peter asked me to go to the gym and start working out, I gave in. I was *that* skinny kid. You know, the one who could never gain weight. My mom cooked buttery fried goodness most nights, and we drank sweet tea so thick it could give you a cavity just looking at it. It didn't matter. I could eat anything and never gain a pound.

As strange as that might seem to those who struggle with losing weight, I was insecure about my bean-pole-ness and intimidated by all the perfect people I imagined seeing lifting small houses at the gym. Peter said I should be thankful. He said I had "the perfect body type" for adding muscle, and he was sure he could turn me into something hot if I just put in the work.

It sounded like a *lot* of work to me.

I tossed my fear and childhood insecurities aside and followed muscle-god roomie like a lost puppy to the gym. It was pretty much what I expected—men with necks bigger than their heads lifting small houses. They tended to congregate in the section with warnings about not lifting too much without a partner. They weren't just big. They were huge.

Oddly, they were very nice. Every single Popeye acknowledged me with a smile or nod, as if greeting a new brother into their fraternity. I hadn't expected that.

By the third or fourth week, when it became obvious I wasn't going to be one of those guys who paid for the membership and never returned, the muscle gods learned my name and greeted me warmly. They offered to spot me and gave me a high-five when I did something particularly painful. It was nice, in a really masochistic way.

One afternoon, I was straining with all my spindly might and noticed a guy I hadn't seen before. He was running on a treadmill. I blinked through sweat and focused. Blondish-brown hair bounced as he ran, though a few locks stuck to his forehead. He wore a thirsty white tank top that drank every drop of sweat it touched and clung to a ridiculous set of abs. His shoulders glistened as they bobbed. Every time he smiled at a different person who called out his name, his brilliant white teeth lit up that corner of the gym.

Okay, maybe it wasn't that dramatic, but you get the picture.

Despite his obvious sweat-soaked hotness, Mr. Sweaty Runner caught my eye because every few minutes, a different club member would wander up to him and shake his hand or wave or call out in greeting. Nashville was a town where half the people you met were either students or aspiring musicians. I'd become numb to that scene, and barely kept up with who was famous and who wasn't. I had no clue who this very popular hottie was.

Peter smacked the back of my head playfully, pulling me back to our side of the gym.

"Enough rest. You've been sitting there for at least five minutes. Let's go."

I wanted to toss the weights at him, but that would've required lifting them and he would've won, so I asked about hottie instead. "Is that guy up there famous or something? Everybody seems to know him."

Peter grunted. "Yeah, he's a singer, or wants to be. Nice enough guy. Welcome to Nashville."

With that, Peter grabbed my wrists and hoisted them to the bar dangling over my head, giving me no choice but to resume the lat-straining-torture-thing.

Don't hurt yourself on all my technical terms. I try to be precise.

A WEEK PASSED, AND I SAW SINGER BOY AT THE GYM nearly every day, his flock of women—and men—trailing him from treadmill to bicep curl, trying to look like they weren't following his every move. It was pretty funny to watch. When one of his loyal geese would catch me watching, their head would whip in the other direction, and they'd magically find the need to work a random body part not on that day's rotation.

Singer Boy never seemed to notice. He just kept working out and flashing his pearly whites.

Peter and I got to the gym late Friday afternoon. Singer Boy had already showered and changed into tight, faded jeans and a clingy black T-shirt. The black made his green eyes leap out. Holy cow, they were *really* green.

Anyway.

I had just finished a set on the leg-press-device-of-death when someone walked up to Peter. I was facing the wall and couldn't see who it was.

"Hey, Peter. I've got a gig tonight at Rowdie's. A big producer promised he'd be there, so I really need a good crowd. Can I count you in?"

There was a crinkling of paper, probably a flyer.

"I'll try," Peter said in a tone I knew meant he wouldn't go anywhere near Rowdie's.

"Thanks. This could be my big break if it works out. It's been a long time coming."

"Good luck," Peter said, followed by the distinct sound of paper being stuffed into a pocket. He turned back to me. "Again. Two more sets."

I hated Peter sometimes.

An hour later, I staggered into our apartment, thighs ablaze with leg-day pain, and threw myself onto the couch. Peter trotted in without the slightest hint of soreness.

Again with the hating Peter thing.

He tossed his keys on the counter, then emptied his pockets. I looked up.

"What's that?" I asked, indicating the wadded-up paper he'd dropped by his keys.

He hurled the wad into my head. "That wannabe-famous guy at the gym is playing some bar tonight. He says there's a producer going, and it might be his big break. Same story, different night."

That got my attention. "Are you going?"

He laughed. "Nope. I hate bars. Go if you want to. I don't think he cares who's there, just that there's a crowd."

I stared blankly. I'd never been to a bar. Weren't they the den of evil and the birthplace of sin? People drank alcohol there. I'd never had alcohol either.

Did you forget already? I was raised by wolves.

"That's OK. Bars aren't my thing either," I said weakly, wanting desperately to see Singer Boy in his element and find out if bars were really as vile as I had been taught.

"Whatever. I'm meeting Jen for a late bite. We might grab a movie after. See you later."

Jen was Peter's on-and-off girlfriend. At the moment, she was on.

As soon as the door slammed shut and Peter's footfalls faded into the night, I smoothed the flyer against my leg and held it up. Singer Boy's set started in an hour.

I had to move.

I WALKED INTO ROWDIE'S AND BLINKED A FEW TIMES SO MY eyes could adjust to the dim light. The aroma of cigarettes tickled my nose. There were ten, maybe fifteen round high-top tables scattered about, with a brightly lit, makeshift stage holding court from one end of the room. From the flyer and Singer Boy's perma-smile at the gym, I had expected the place to be packed. I was the fifth person to enter. Only seven total would show up. So much for a roaring crowd.

I looked nervously around and picked a table near the back, as far from the stage and other people as I could get. A perky waitress wandered by and giggled when I ordered a Coke. Was that not OK in a bar?

A moment later, Coke in hand, my eyes darted from stage to bar, taking in every detail. This den of ill repute seemed awfully tame. People weren't humping or fighting. They were just sitting and drinking, some eating, enjoying themselves. Interesting.

"Mind if I sit with you?" A voice startled me.

I looked up to find a man with short dark hair and kind eyes blinking at me. His short crop revealed a faint dusting of gray that intruded around his temples.

"I'm Dwayne," he said, extending a hand. Were we supposed to shake hands in a bar? Was this a business thing? I shook it, and he sat without waiting for permission. "Thanks. I hate sitting up front at these things. How do you know Jason?"

For the second time, I was startled. "Jason?"

"The singer. He's supposed to start any minute, but he's always late." He chuckled.

Singer Boy's name was Jason. Check.

"Oh, I don't really know him. We work out at the same gym. He was making the rounds today, handing out these flyers, and I thought I'd check it out." I tried to sound disinterested and casual.

Dwayne looked down at the flyer I had tossed on the

table and smiled. "I helped him make those. He's definitely *not* shy."

Before I could answer, Jason raced up to our table and wrapped Dwayne in a big hug. "Thank you for coming. I'm so nervous." His head swiveled as he scanned the room. "Mr. Best isn't here yet, but he promised he'd come. Dwayne, this could be the night."

He sounded giddy. I guess that was to be expected. Back then, there was no *American Idol* or *The Voice*, or any other competition show that vaulted unknown artists into stardom. To be discovered, you had to actually *be discovered*. It was nearly impossible. If I had been a singer with a shot at a producer, I would've been giddy too.

Dwayne finally turned and introduced me. I reminded Jason about the gym, and he nodded as if he actually remembered seeing me among his throng. He clearly didn't. Then he vanished to prepare for his time on stage.

I caught Dwane watching the interaction with more than passing interest. I guess my stare lingered on Jason's jeans a little too long as he walked away, because he said, "You *like* him?"

Startle number three.

"Uh, I guess. I mean, um, I don't know him or anything. He seems like a nice guy." I was articulate.

Dwayne chuckled and peered over his glass of Jack and Coke. A second glass filled with limes sat next to it. He would squeeze a lime into his drink after every sip; there had to be as much lime in there as there was Coke. Was this normal bar behavior? No one else seemed to be doing it. Weird.

Thankfully, the stage lights flashed as Jason stepped up to the mic, saving me from further examination. I got the feeling Dwayne didn't miss much.

Jason sounded good. I mean, really good.

He played guitar and sang songs he'd written himself. When Dwayne told me he would perform his own work, I'd groaned inwardly, expecting a long evening of bad music. But this guy had talent. He sang about love and loss, and lost love, and love he wished he hadn't lost, and love he was glad he lost—then a song about a lake in a town where he met someone he loved and lost.

My keen sense of observation picked up a theme, but it still sounded good.

The more I watched and listened, the better he looked.

What was it about performers, especially singers, that made them so much more alluring the minute they stepped behind a microphone? Jason didn't get all dressed up or wear makeup or anything, but on that stage, under the annoyingly bright lights zip-tied to the bar's ceiling, he looked even better than he had in the gym that first day. Now that his hair wasn't a sweaty, matted mess, I could see how it curled slightly at the ends and waved in the air from the vent above the stage. It wasn't quite Marilyn and her white dress, but it was nice.

He was dreamy, and he was singing.

A couple times he actually looked over at our table and flashed that broad, incredibly warm smile I'd seen him give others a hundred times at the gym. I tried not to swoon, then realized he was smiling at Dwayne, acknowledging his friend and some secret meaning hidden within the tune.

For his part, Dwayne barely spoke throughout the evening, but I caught him watching me a few times, a catlike grin playing across his weathered face.

When Jason wrapped and the stage finally fell quiet, the lights in the bar gradually brightened. Dwayne stifled a yawn into his elbow and looked up. "What did you think?"

"He's great. I'm surprised he hasn't got a record deal yet," I said.

Dwayne laughed sardonically. "That's *the dream*, but he's been doing this for years. I think if it was going to happen, it would've by now."

"What about the producer tonight?"

He shook his head. "Never showed. Again, that happens all the time. They promise, get the performer all excited, then stand them up. It's sad, really."

"Huh." I'd never known anyone trying to make it in music. This was news to me.

Dwayne yawned again. "There's a group of us going out after this. You should join us."

It was already eleven o'clock. Where could anyone possibly go at that hour on a Friday night? I was baffled.

It must've shown on my face because Dwayne chuckled. His eyes held that amused, knowing gaze of one who'd discovered a baby learning to walk—or at least realizing that walking was a thing. I hadn't even tried to stand yet, much less walk.

"It's just a few of us going to celebrate with Jason on his big performance. We were going to celebrate the producer, but he's still AWOL. Come have a drink."

"Alright. I guess." I didn't even think to ask where we were going. If it was to have a drink, I assumed another bar. My first night was turning into a two-fer. Look at me, becoming a Coke-drinking barfly stud.

Jason stopped by and gave Dwayne another hug. He sure hugged a lot. He acknowledged me with a quick smile and thanked me for coming. I don't think he remembered my name or how we knew each other—again. So much for validation.

I climbed into Betty, my cooler-than-cool Saturn sedan,

and followed Dwayne's eight-hundred-year-old Toyota something-or-other. It was small, zippy, and thoroughly covered in rust—but who was I to judge? It was easy to follow because nothing else looked like it.

We drove for twenty minutes before I realized I was thoroughly lost. I'd never been in this part of town before. It was one of those industrial parks with long, low, sprawling buildings. From an airplane's view, they almost looked like bugs, with all the trailers pulled up to the loading docks serving as legs. Were we going to a warehouse? Who'd put a bar all the way out here?

We finally pulled into a massive parking lot. There were hundreds of cars already cooling. I looked for signage or anything that might tell me where we were, but there was nothing. The building before us was as nondescript as every other factory or warehouse around, save for the line of a dozen people waiting to enter.

I parked and found Dwayne waiting for me near the entrance.

"Ready? The others already went inside. We'll meet up in the country bar."

"Country bar?" I asked.

He nodded. "This is more of a complex than a bar. You'll see."

We waited our turn. I tried not to wince as the doorman held out a palm and said, "Welcome to the Connection. Five bucks."

Ever-observant Dwayne noticed and waved me off, paying my fee. "My invite, my treat."

That was nice.

As we entered, my head spun. We walked through giant double doors into a wide hallway that could squeeze a dozen people shoulder to shoulder without touching the sides. It was packed. We could barely move, and the mass of quickly heating bodies was inching forward. A thunderous rhythm pulsed from somewhere ahead, and I could make out flashes of light through an opening thirty or so yards away.

We got about halfway down the hallway when Dwayne grabbed my arm and pulled me through an opening on the left side. The booming bass was replaced by a happy, twangy tune better played in a Western movie than a bar in the industrial heart of Nashville. The crowd thinned, and tight-fitting T-shirts and tank tops were replaced by gaudy buckles and fringy tops with silver buttons. Walking through that opening, we literally set foot onto a different planet, one filled with country music and very country patrons.

"What do you want to drink?" Dwayne's voice snapped me back to him.

"Coke, thanks."

He shook his head and chuckled. "Come help me. I'll need an extra hand."

I followed and waited with him in the queue that was only a few men deep. As we stood there, something struck, and I turned to Dwayne. "Where are all the women?"

He looked up at me with a furrowed brow. "What?"

"The women. I don't see any in here. Looks like some of the guys had to dance with each other because there aren't any girls here yet."

In that moment, Dwayne gave me a look I'll never forget. His eyes flew wide, and his mouth twitched between a smile and a frozen 'O' shape, as if he couldn't decide—or believe—what was standing in front of him. Maybe it was what I asked, or maybe I had something in my teeth. I'd never seen anyone look so utterly baffled.

Then he doubled over and gripped his sides.

When he righted himself, tears were streaming down his cheeks. He saw me gaping, and his laughter grew into near hyperventilation. Some of the guys standing around us turned to see what was so funny. I shrugged, dumbfounded.

By the time he managed to suck in enough air to breathe again, we stood before a bemused bartender wearing a foot-tall cowboy hat and leather vest. He'd forgotten his shirt; a furry, muscular chest poked through.

Dwayne turned to me and wiped his eyes. "You're going to need a real drink tonight. Trust me, Coke isn't going to cut it."

2

____

I helped Dwayne carry the two glasses filled with limes and three brimming with Jack and Coke to a table on the outside patio. The night was cool and comfortable, and the patio was much quieter than anywhere we'd been in the Connection so far. It was a relief to sit and have a little personal space again.

Dwayne hadn't stopped chuckling to himself. He'd said something to the bartender, whom he obviously knew well, and Cowboy Rick nearly peed himself before pouring our drinks.

I wasn't sure I was ready to know the joke, but curiosity got the best of me. "Care to share what's so funny?"

He looked up, eyes twinkling. "Why don't you take a good sip of that drink first?"

I'd only ever tasted wine once. It had been five years ago in Australia. I was there at the National Scout Jamboree representing the United States, along with two thousand other Boy Scouts.

Don't laugh. It was a really cool trip.

Anyway, the French scouts, Fleur-de-something, had

homemade wine and were passing out samples. I hadn't even noticed when my best friend handed me a cup and I took a sip. I gagged so hard I thought I'd spew all over France. It was awful and tasted like a soured version of whatever drink it used to be.

Yes, I know, that was the point. At the time, I didn't even know I was drinking wine, much less what to expect. It was vile.

And here I sat, with a man twice my age in a bar without women—with men dancing together to country music—about to drink hard liquor. The two-fer just became a hat trick.

Yes, hockey reference. Just roll with it.

I lifted the glass and looked at it with deep suspicion, as if a snake might leap out from behind the ice cubes and snap at my nose. I didn't mean to give Dwayne puppy-dog eyes, but when I looked up, there was a mix of amusement and pity in his gaze.

"Michael, this is a gay bar."

I downed half my drink in one swallow.

"Whoa. Easy. They make them strong here," he said with genuine concern.

I finished the drink and looked up. "*Gay* bar?"

Before tonight, I'd never been to a bar of any kind. I didn't know the gays had their own bars.

He nodded silently and watched as the color drained from my face.

A moment later, he asked, "You didn't know we were coming to a gay bar?"

I didn't trust my voice, so I just shook my head and tried not to make eye contact with the guy at the next table who kept staring at me.

"I need another drink." I stood before Dwayne could

say anything. Thankfully, there was only one person ahead of me at the bar. I had time to gather my wits, but not long enough to be alone in a gay bar without my life raft, if that's what Dwayne was.

"You came. Dwayne said you might."

I turned and was shocked to see Jason leaning against the bar. He'd changed from the outfit he'd worn on stage into a tight white T-shirt with the name of some band I didn't recognize scrawled in script across his chest. I could see the definition of his pecs through the lettering.

"Uh. Yeah. I'm here," I spluttered. "Um. You sounded good tonight."

"Thanks. Stupid producer stood me up, but I'm used to that now." He waved at the bartender, who leaned over and kissed him. He *kissed* him—on the mouth, in front of me; in front of everyone.

My jaw must've still been on the floor when Jason turned around because he started chuckling. "You OK?"

I nodded fervently. I wasn't OK.

I could see his wheels turning, then click into place. He leaned over and half-whispered a question I'd never forget. No one had ever asked me that before. "You like boys, don't you?"

The music faded away. All the men and lights and drinks and smoke—it all vanished. Jason was the only person in the world, and I felt like I was falling. Not falling for him, *actually* falling. My head spun, and I lost track of where I was.

When the warmth of his hand on my arm brought me back to the present, I managed a weak smile. "Sure. I like boys fine."

He cocked his head again, smiled, then vanished into the sea of men.

I blinked a few times as Cowboy Rick plopped another Jack and Coke in front of me. He batted his eyes and gave me a flirty smile as I handed him the last of the paper money in my pocket. I didn't know whether he was actually flirting or angling for a better tip, but he laughed as he walked away. I'm guessing the bar lighting hadn't hidden my blush.

I escaped back to the quiet of the patio to find Dwayne deep in conversation with two other men now seated around the table. They were older—and by that, I mean in their thirties, not *nearly* as old as Dwayne's ancient forties —and both leaning forward on conspiratorial elbows. All three had that same catlike smile that lingered a moment too long when they noticed I'd returned.

"You made it back," Dwayne said. The other kitties grinned. One of them, the prettier one with hair a bit too tall for his face, looked me up and down like he was sizing me for a tuxedo. What was that all about?

Felines One and Two excused themselves, but Pretty Cat made a point of squeezing my shoulder as he walked by. Dwayne's eyes twinkled as he watched the exchange. Had there been an exchange? I didn't even know where we were, much less what was going on with the shoulder-squeezing, puffy-haired puddy tat.

"I ran into Jason at the bar," I said.

Dwayne brightened. "Oh? Is he coming out here?"

"No. He disappeared into the crowd. I think he's headed toward all the music." I paused and stared at my drink.

That moment has lingered in my memory for years. It's one of those still-frame moments when you later realize you'd been standing before the proverbial fork in life's road, but at the time, you had no idea what that tingly feeling in your neck was. My neck was definitely tingling its ass off. Wait, necks don't have asses, do they?

Anyway.

"He asked me the weirdest question," I said, then took a sip.

"Oh?" Dwayne arched a wiry, unkempt brow. He was very un-gay in that regard.

"Yeah. I guess he thought I looked uncomfortable or something. He asked if I liked boys."

Dwayne nearly spat out his drink, but stifled whatever laughter had tried to escape. A second and a swallow later, he looked up. "What did you say?"

"I told him I liked them fine. It just seemed like such a strange thing to ask."

Something clicked. I saw it in Dwayne's eyes.

He realized I was still clueless—that lone wolf cub lost in the woods with bears and otters and every other kind of animal wandering around me. His expression changed from amused observer to something akin to Yoda when he gave Luke Skywalker his first lesson. "Gay you are, asking he was."

OK, he didn't say it like that, but that's the gist. Yoda would've said it better.

I was shocked. *Gay? Me?* I could barely bring myself to *say* the G word. I sucked down my second Jack and Coke and never felt a thing.

"Are you OK?" Dwayne asked.

"Yeah, I am. I mean, I'm not. Yes, I'm fine, but no, I'm *not* gay." Articulate as ever though.

He nodded sagely. "OK. You seem to be handling this place alright. Did you not realize we were coming to a gay bar?"

I shook my head. "I'd never been to *any* bar before tonight, much less a gay one."

His eyes widened as if seeing some exotic animal at the zoo for the first time.

The lights flashed twice and I looked up, unsure if there was a fire or air raid or what.

"The show's starting. That's the two-minute warning," he said as he rose. "Come on. This should be fun."

There was that twinkle again, the one I now understood hid Dwayne's utter glee at exposing me to something else I'd never experienced.

This was going to be a long night.

3

T he herd was definitely moving with purpose. We made it out of the country bar with little trouble, but had to inch our way from there. I'd never seen so many people packed into one place—and the place was huge.

The hallway was crammed with new arrivals who'd skipped line dancing and were headed directly into the main part of the warehouse. It was around midnight, which was apparently when all gays instinctively knew they should arrive. I managed a look back and could see that the line out the glass double doors now wound through the parking lot, so far that I couldn't see its end. Dwayne had said they crammed two to three thousand people into this place every Friday and Saturday night, but seeing the throng of men in their painted-on T-shirts and jeans that nearly revealed which religion they followed—well, I was overwhelmed.

Shoulders bumped and brushed from all sides. The crowd crawled. The doormen didn't seem to care and kept letting more join the flow. They pressed tighter together as we shuffled forward.

I couldn't breathe. I started to sweat.

My eyes darted around, taking in the sea of men. Some locked eyes and smiled in a way that I was sure meant something, I just couldn't imagine what. I looked away as fast as my head would swivel.

And then it happened. My life raft floated away.

I'd lost Dwayne.

The hallway opened into a vast open space half a football field long. Lights flashed. Fast-paced music, heavily anchored with bass, throbbed through my body. Despite the strobing lights, the massive room was dark, and I couldn't make out faces well, only writhing shapes.

A different song began to play, this one with words everyone in the bar seemed to recognize, and a cheer rose with every arm as the dance floor hopped as a single beast.

Long bars on every wall served a constant stream of men. At the center of the room, a towering pillar rose to support the ceiling. Around the base of the pillar was a circular stage, on which shirtless men swayed and wiggled and strutted—*and rutted*—to the beat.

I panicked and found the darkest, emptiest corner I could find. There was no escaping the crowd, but it did thin out a bit around the edges. Leaning my back against the wall gave me some sense of security. At least a gay couldn't sneak up on me from behind.

Yes, I now know that's one of the main goals of the place. I didn't back then.

The lights rotated and flashed, and I looked up. I hadn't noticed the upper level before. This place went on forever.

A balcony encircled the entire dance floor area, but it wasn't just a *look-over-the-edge* kind of balcony. It was wide enough to fit hundreds, and there were three bars on three of the walls. There was even a seating area with couches and puffy chairs at one end. Men were lined along the silver railing, drinks in hand, watching those below.

There was barely an inch of empty space in the whole place—and more men poured in with each passing moment.

Where did all these gay men come from? Had I died and gone to California?

My mind raced as a handsome guy with floppy hair passed by. Our eyes locked for only a second, but that was enough to make the temperature in the room skyrocket. I knew I should just make my way back to the exit, run to Betty, and flee to the safety of my apartment, but I couldn't move.

Couldn't? Wouldn't? I didn't know. I still don't.

Instinctively, I pressed my back to the wall. Good, it was actually a corner. No gay-sneak could get my side *or* my back. Secure in my hiding place, I did the only thing I could do. I watched.

I liked watching people. People were interesting. And this place was a petri dish of interesting.

When my nerves calmed enough for my semi-rational mind to take over, I was again stunned by what I saw. As the child of a very conservative preacher, I'd been taught that all gays were either child molesters or drag queens. It seemed strange. How could a man wanting to get into another man's pants automatically make him one of those two things? But who was I to challenge the wisdom of my father's religious teaching?

As I scanned the crowd, I didn't see anyone who looked like a child molester. In fact, most of the men dancing and drinking looked to be in their twenties or thirties. Weren't most child molesters older than that? All I knew was, I didn't see any obvious ice-cream-truck drivers.

And I didn't see a single man in drag. I'd actually never seen one before, but was sure I'd know one when I saw it.

Everyone looked so normal. They looked happy and relaxed.

They looked like *me*.

Wait. How was that possible? These were *gays*! They weren't supposed to be normal or, I don't know, *anything* like me, but that's what hit me harder than a Jack and Coke with a whole glass's worth of lime.

Here I was, surrounded by more gay men than I knew existed outside their protective borders, and they looked like any other guys you might see in the real world. I mean, this *was* the real world, but it wasn't. This was a giant gay bubble. Right?

A gaggle of gays passed by, clearly headed somewhere in a hurry. They were all laughing hysterically. One of them came up for air and I overheard him say, "Come on, we're missing the show."

Right. Dwayne was headed to a show. Curiosity overcame fear and I followed the giggling gaggle.

They weaved through the crowd with practiced ease, carefully pressing palms against shoulders to move the men blocking their progress. I was the guy with the ball following his blockers. I just wished they'd told me what the goal line looked like before we crossed it.

As we entered another short hallway, the throbbing of lights and music faded and was replaced by the sounds of something decidedly *showier*. The song had more words, was easier to recognize, and there was a performance quality to it that was very different from the mindless rhythm of the dance floor.

Ten yards later, my blockers skipped merrily into another massive room. Like the chamber of dance, there was a balcony on one end that held a bar and room for fifty or so. The main floor was a field of four-top tables crammed with laughing, drinking men. At the end, opposite the balcony, rose a stage roughly four feet above the floor spanning nearly the entire thirty-yard stretch of wall. A catwalk (is that what it's called?) stretched from the center of the stage halfway through the room.

I stopped walking and gaped as the performer I'd barely noticed marched down the catwalk like she owned the whole club. She was the only woman I'd seen in the bar so far, and was by far the tallest woman I'd ever seen in real life. Her dusty blue wig towered higher than Marge Simpson on a bad hair day. I knew performers wore crazy outfits, but I couldn't understand why this one had chosen a bedazzled version of Mr. Hefner's bunny costume, complete with floppy ears that protruded out the top of the mile-high hairdo.

And then I saw her boobs. Man, they were big. No, enormous. And they jiggled like Jell-O that needed more stiffener, or whatever that powder was called. I couldn't stop staring. How were those things real? Did the poor gal have back problems? My mind raced with questions.

Then someone in the crowd behind me said something about "him" lip-synching well. *Him*? What him? I looked around the stage and couldn't find anyone other than Amanda Rabbit.

Then the clouds parted, the sun shone, and two of my repressed, raised-by-wolves brain cells smashed together. This was one of those fabled drag queens, live and in person. I gawked, this time really studying the tall bunny. Her jaw was a little too square, her shoulders too round, and the hair on her chest—WAIT. She had *hair on her chest*, just above the two presidents of her Mount Rushmore.

No one else seemed bothered, but this was one oddity too many for my already whiskey-addled brain. I turned and fled the field as fast as I could. Before I knew it, I was sinking into the safety of Betty's driver's seat and listening to the blessed sound of my door lock clicking into place. My head fell back against the seat rest, and my breathing deepened and slowed.

As I drove home, a slideshow of images scrolled through my head. I couldn't turn it off. A man in fringe dancing with another man in more fringe. Shirtless boys with abs on their toes grinding against each other. A giant bunny looking at me like I was a carrot ... never mind. Bad analogy.

What was really odd were the thoughts that followed.

I was terrified of that place. The idea of spending the whole night there without the safety of anyone I knew nearly sent me into a panic attack—and yet, as I thought about it, I hadn't had that much adrenaline-induced fun in a long time. The music was great, and I loved the idea of going from one area to another when my tolerance for country was exceeded.

Oh, and there were men *everywhere*. They came in every age, shape, size, color, and flavor (yes, flavors are a thing, apparently). Many of the men were shirtless and sweaty and rubbing their hands over chests and arms and—

Sorry. Did it just get warm? Why was I sweating? Thinking about all of them made my skin tingle in a way I'd only remembered once before.

Well, twice.

I'd seen Joseph twice.

4

I woke the next day in a pool of sweat. My dreams had been filled with shirtless men grinding against each other, then all turning and looking directly at me while they continued to rub and thrust. Arms reached out, beckoning me to join them on the dance floor. Every guy in the place had that *come-hither* look in their eyes. So I came … I hithered … I henced. I went out there, and a thousand hands tore off my shirt and—

My alarm clock blared.

I rubbed my head and peeled myself off the disgusting sheets and padded into the bathroom. I could smell cigarette smoke on my jeans and shirt from across the room. That was disgusting too. How could fabric absorb that much smoke when I'd never picked up a cigarette in my life?

I showered, tossed last night's smoky laundry into the closet, and threw on some shorts and a T-shirt. The noonday sun was approaching much faster than I'd expected. Some guys from a volleyball game I'd once joined in at the park had talked about sleeping in after a night at the bar. Was this what they meant? I barely felt rested, but the day was almost halfway over.

Midway through my incredibly healthy breakfast of Frosted Flakes, the whirring sound of our old rotary phone broke through my crunching.

I figured it was someone calling for Peter. It usually was. He had a harem, or pack, or posse—I wasn't sure what the right term was for people who hopelessly followed a model around. Men, women, dogs, non-mammals, it didn't matter. He was hot, and they all wanted him; or at least, to be near him so they seemed hotter. I didn't think it really worked that way.

After a couple rings without Peter bounding into the room, I set my spoon down and grabbed the receiver. "Hello?"

"Michael?"

"Yeah. Who's this?"

"It's Dwayne, from the bar—well, from both bars, I guess."

Huh. The old guy was calling the day after he'd abandoned me in a sea of sweaty sensuality.

"Oh hey. Thanks for keeping me company last night. That was … something."

He chuckled. "I bet it was. Are you OK?"

"Yeah, sure, fine." I had no idea why he'd asked that. Why wouldn't I be OK?

He paused a little longer than usual. "You want to grab lunch? I'd love to hear how your evening went. I lost you on the way to the drag show."

I barked a laugh. "Yeah, you did. I tried to find you, but—"

"Sorry. It's impossible to find anyone in that place when it's packed. So, lunch?"

He seemed awfully intent, but I *was* hungry. Tony the Tiger hadn't done my stomach right. "Sure. Why not?"

He suggested we meet at a little diner close to my apartment so we could get breakfast food. Apparently, that's the requisite post-going-out meal. I threw on my holey socks and tennis shoes and headed out.

———

DWAYNE WAS ALREADY SEATED AND SIPPING COFFEE WHEN I strolled into the diner.

"Hey," I said as I scooted into the seat across from him. It was one of those long booths made for three people on each side. "Planning for the whole bar to join us?"

He grinned. "I took what they gave me. Feel free to stretch out."

The waitress breezed by and gave me the universal *I'll be right back* finger. When I looked back, Dwayne was studying me. I couldn't hold his gaze.

"So, how was last night?" he asked. "Stay long?"

I shrugged and told him about my hiding place by the dance floor. He grinned as I described watching the disco antics. When we got to Miss Bunny, he nearly spat out his coffee.

"You didn't know that was a man dressed up like a woman?" The utter disbelief in his tone matched the upward curl around his eyes. He was loving this.

"I didn't even know there was a theater back there, much less who was singing." I wanted to be positive, even though the drag had scared the crap out of me. "He—she—I don't really know what to call the singer. They were pretty good. Sounded like the original."

Then he did spit coffee.

He set his mug down and dabbed his shirt in his water glass, then went to work on the spots blooming across his sleeve. His shoulders bobbed with laughter the whole time.

"What's so funny?" I asked.

He looked up and cocked his head, like he was trying to decide something. "You really don't know, do you?" His laughter stilled and he resumed that paternal tone he'd used the night before. "That was a man dressed as a woman, and he was lip-synching, not actually singing. You *were* listening to the original singer."

I opened my mouth to say something, then closed it as the *you're an idiot* feeling crept up my neck.

He smiled. "You really hadn't ever been to a gay bar, had you?"

I shook my head again. "Told you, both were my first bars, gay or otherwise."

"You're what, twenty-two?" he asked.

I stiffened. Not sure why. "I'm twenty-four."

He hid a grin behind a sip of coffee, but I saw it in his eyes.

"Why did you want to have lunch?" I asked, teetering between nervousness and annoyance.

He set his mug down again and leaned back. I could see the wheels turning as he debated how to answer. I don't know what I expected. Maybe he'd flirt. He was gay, right? That's what gay guys did when they were around other dudes—but he was so much older, had to be twenty years older than me. Did old men in their forties still flirt? How did they even still walk around?

"Because you looked like you could use a friend, and I'm a good friend."

Huh. I started to say something witty, but my mouth wouldn't work. His eyes were sincere. There was no leering or lust, just genuine concern and empathy. I might not have understood the whole gay world, but I was good at reading people. Dwayne was being a nice guy.

"Oh. OK. Sure. That's great, I guess." Mouth, please start working.

He chuckled at my fumbling. "Look, you said you're straight, and I'm not looking to win a toaster. I'm being honest. You seem like a decent guy who's a little lost and could use a friend. I like helping younger guys figure things out. That's all."

Figure things out? What did that mean? I was more confused than ever—if that was even possible.

What came out of my mouth next surprised us both. "You don't have a toaster?"

He cocked his head, then the lightbulb turned on and he laughed again. "Sorry, I forget you don't know gay slang. It's a joke. When a gay man converts a straight man, or gets him to have sex, he wins a toaster. Think old days when you got a toaster for opening a bank account."

I felt like I was in a foreign land. "You got a toaster at the bank?"

His mouth opened, but the clatter of waffle-laden plates slapping the table made us both turn. I'm not sure which of us was more relieved by the waitress's sudden appearance, but it broke the tension. She looked back and forth, obviously sensing something and trying to decipher it. Her brow quirked.

Finally, someone was more confused than me.

The conversation turned to lighter topics. I learned that Dwayne had spent years working as a corporate executive for a company that did something with blood collection or blood banks, I'm wasn't sure, before turning to the simpler life of a waiter in one of Nashville's most exclusive restaurants. I struggled to wrap my head around that transition.

"Why would you leave a cushy corporate job?" I asked.

"I was working ten or twelve-hour days, six days a week. The money was great, but I had no time to spend it. Work *was* life, and that's no way to live." Again, sincerity poured out of his thin frame. I didn't think this guy knew how to be dishonest or insincere.

"But you gave up so much," I said, still puzzling.

He nodded. "It was tough at first, but I've been at the Atrium for years now. They pay well, and the tips are great most nights—but it's the freedom I like more than anything. Yeah, I live in a one-bedroom apartment, but now I can do things I couldn't before—like have lunch with you in the middle of the day."

I nodded like I got it. I didn't.

He asked what I did for work, and I realized I was just as lost and clueless in that part of my life as I'd felt the night before in the bars.

"I work with my dad," I said. "He owns a company that sells private-label products to pharmacies."

It sounded pretty impressive out loud. The truth was far less sexy. We drove more than a thousand miles each week, visiting pharmacies and selling a pain rub my dad had dreamed up from who-knows-where. I love my dad, but he was never the brilliant business guy he thought he was. His little company barely made anything, and my butt and legs ached every night thanks to the endless hours in the car.

"How do you like working with your father?" Dwayne asked.

I shrugged. "It's alright. The best part is I get to spend time with him. I'm the baby in the family, and my parents are older. I probably won't ever get to spend this much time with him again."

I got lost in the implications of that for a moment. Dwayne waited patiently.

"He asked me to work with him while I was still in my senior year at college. It was easier than doing the job search thing and gave me time to figure out what I really wanted to do."

"What *do* you want to do? Wasn't that what college was for? Figuring that out?"

"I guess, but it didn't work. I went in *knowing* I wanted to go to law school. I was really good at debate in college, and the idea of standing in a courtroom with judges and juries was exciting. I dreamed of being the next Perry Mason. Then I met some lawyers and learned they spent more time in the library than the courtroom. I couldn't think of a more painful way to spend my days."

Dwayne cocked his head. "You know who Perry Mason is?"

I laughed. "I'm an old soul, I guess."

"And I'm just old?" He smirked.

I gave him another shrug and the most innocent puppy-dog eyes I could muster.

He laughed harder.

And just like that, Dwayne became my new best friend.

5

____

My dad and I spent the next week roaming all over
Alabama.

It's funny. Every small town thinks they're unique and
special. I suppose they are in some ways, but I discovered
during our gazillion miles on the road that most of them are
remarkably similar.

There's a town square—and yes, it usually is either
square, with an intersection on each corner, or circular, with
roundabout rules that make every driver uneasy. On one
side is a law office; on the other, a pharmacy. There are
always at least two barber shops or beauty salons. The
more towns we visited, the more I realized salons and
barbershops were more about dissemination of information
than styling of hair. Where else could good rumors spread
so quickly?

Oh, and don't forget the town's bank, which has been
around since before money was invented. The face of the
bank is either brick or stone, usually gray, always with the
name etched into the face to make it look stable and
permanent.

Back then, I was still new to the snake-oil sale, so I'd haul boxes and take notes as my dad marched proudly into each pharmacy and presented his pain rub.

There are salesmen in the world, and then there's my dad. He truly is a category of one.

We would walk into a pharmacy and there would be a pharmacist in a lab coat (always a lab coat). Most of the pharmacists we dealt with were friendly once you got to know them, but had flat personalities. Let's face it, they spent most of their days trying to keep up with the flow of customers and pills without mixing the two up. That would suck the personality out of anyone.

I remember one visit in particular. We walked into a tiny pharmacy barely wide enough for a row of shelves down the middle. The pharmacist was on his knees near the back stocking a shelf. Yes, in a lab coat.

My dad didn't hesitate. He walked up to the pharmacist and introduced himself.

No response. The man kept putting bottles on the shelf.

So my dad launched into his pitch. He told one corny story after another, trying to get the man to laugh or engage —or just turn around.

Nada.

I was starting to wonder why we were still there when my dad turned to me and said, "Put a case on the counter."

I was dumbfounded. The pharmacist had never even acknowledged our presence. But within a minute, an assistant appeared and handed my dad a check.

To this day, I will never know how he did it. If I hadn't believed in magic before, I did in that moment.

That scene repeated itself four or five times each day. That was our life.

FRIDAY FINALLY ROLLED AROUND AND THE TITANIC PULLED back into town. That's what I called my dad's powder-blue Pontiac Bonneville. It was a ship on wheels.

We didn't have cell phones or email back then, so the first thing I always did after a week on the road was check the answering machine. Yes, kids, there was a machine for this. It had a little blinky light that was our version of the endorphin-inducing sound of a text arriving. It rarely blinked for me, but today was my lucky day.

I pressed the button and listened to the whirring of the tape rewinding as I tossed aside my shoes.

"Hey, Michael." It was Dwayne. "Jason's singing down at the Orchid Saturday night. Want to go? I'll protect you from the gays again." I laughed at the same time as he did on the recording, then the click-beep indicating the end of the message sounded. My heart raced as I wondered if Peter was home and had heard Dwayne use the G word. Thankfully, the apartment was empty.

I stripped off my road-wrinkled suit, took a shower, then scavenged for whatever our desert-wasteland-of-a-kitchen might harbor.

Ramen it was.

A few hours and an episode of *MacGyver* later, my mind was divided between utter boredom and the desire to make a nuclear device out of chewing gum and swizzle sticks. I wandered into the bedroom with no clear mission, and found a crumpled wad of paper on the nightstand. Curious, I smoothed it out and held it under my Eiffel Tower bedside lamp. It was Dwayne's name and number. I'd forgotten he'd even given it to me while we were sitting on the patio bar last week. The Connection's name and address was stamped across the top.

For some reason, my heart sped up as I stared at those red letters and numbers.

Images of men line dancing, slow dancing, dancing shirtless, just being shirtless … ugh. Images of men wouldn't get out of my head.

I tossed Dwayne's number aside and tried to walk away, but the magnetic pull of the Connection dragged me back. Before I could think or talk myself out of it, I was pulling on jeans and a ratty white T-shirt. I hadn't really been taking notes last week and missed the memo about the gay-bar uniform. I looked like a poor, straight college student, possibly a homeless one, but I was going to the bar.

STANDING IN LINE AT A GAY BAR WAS A LITTLE INTIMIDATING. Most of the guys were normal- looking dudes just hoping to have fun on a Friday night, but some of them looked like they should've been in front of a camera, not a bar queue. I'd never really noticed how hot a guy was before, but now I couldn't stop looking—and staring. My head was spinning faster than a propellor on a prop plane. The guy behind me had to nudge me with his elbow when it was my turn to pay the doorman.

I wandered into the hallway to find it nearly empty, so I ducked into the entrance I knew led to the country bar and outdoor patio. One guy was practicing his line dancing to some twangy song I didn't recognize. The clomp-clomp of his boots echoed through the nearly empty space. Two older, snow-topped men huddled at the bar, reminding me of the old guys in the balcony from the Muppets.

Hey, don't laugh. Miss Piggy was cool. I had her lunchbox in third grade. *Pigs in Space* rocked.

I turned to the bar to find Cowboy Rick smiling knowingly. I tried to look confident as I ambled up to him, but every eye in the place turned in my direction, even Mr. Clompity's. I was suddenly very uncomfortable.

"Pretty boy, you came back."

My head must've snapped up a little too fast, or my eyes were too wide or something, because the Muppets and Cowboy Rick broke into a fit of laughter.

The fourteen shades of red I turned probably didn't help. Rick at least attempted to stifle his laughter, but the Muppets were unrestrained. I wanted to slink away, but there was nowhere to hide.

Rick leaned over, doing the *look at my muscular arms flex* thing I'd seen last week. His biceps were like softballs tearing at the fabric of his fringe-covered shirt. Damn.

"Eyes up here," he said, with too much mirth in his voice. Then he lowered his volume to a whisper only I could hear. "Honey, you're new, aren't you?"

Somehow my eyes widened further as I nodded nervously.

He put a hand on my arm. I shivered.

"It's alright. We were all new once, even those old goats." He motioned with a nod to the Muppets. "If you get nervous or uncomfortable, you come back to my bar. I'll make sure none of the big bad bears get you, OK?"

He had that same kind paternal look I'd seen on Dwayne's face, despite being only a year or two older than me. He wasn't flirting. He was being nice.

I let out a breath. "Thanks. Is it that obvious?"

He chuckled. "Well, you didn't pee the dance floor, so

I'd say you're doing just fine. Doesn't hurt you look like *that*." He eyed me up and down.

I looked down at my shirt, specifically the holes in it. "Uh, it was clean." I gave him a sheepish look.

He laughed again. "I wasn't talking about your shirt, silly. Nobody cares about that here. Half the shirts come off at midnight anyway. I was just saying you're handsome, and that helps in a place like this."

The fifteenth shade of red found its way to my face. He thought *I* was handsome? I couldn't believe it. I was always that skinny kid, the one with the pasty skin who couldn't tan. I'd never thought of myself as handsome. I still couldn't see myself that way.

But a gay bartender with bulging biceps in tan fringe said I was, so it *must* be true, right?

Rick suddenly turned away and started making a drink. I looked around, but there wasn't anyone new. When I turned back, two shot glasses stared up at me with some kind of pinkish liquid inside.

"Sex on the Beach. Do it with me?"

I nearly fell off the stool. "What? You want … what?"

Rick nearly peed the dance floor. One of the Muppets knocked his drink over as he gasped for breath between snorts.

"It's the name of the drink," Rick said through tears. "I was asking if you'd drink one with me."

"Oh." I looked down at the drink, desperate to avoid eye contact with anyone within earshot. "Uh, sure, I guess."

"You're new to drinking too, aren't you?" Rick asked as I took a ladylike sip. "Down the hatch." He threw his head back and his drink vanished.

I followed his lead.

"I can't let your first shot be a misfire. One more?" He didn't wait for an answer.

The second shot didn't burn like the first one had. I don't remember feeling it at all.

As Rick reached for my empty glass, I asked, "Where is everybody? It was packed last week."

"Give it an hour. You're early."

I looked up at the neon Busch beer clock behind the bar. It read ten-thirty.

One of the Muppets surprised me by gripping my forearm. "Honey, nobody but us old farts comes here before eleven. You'll figure it all out." He patted my arm and the pair headed out, leaving me alone with Rick and Mr. Clompity.

RICK KEPT ME COMPANY UNTIL THE TRICKLE OF NEW arrivals turned into a steady stream. A little before midnight, the stream became an uncontrollable flood of man-flesh. I stepped away from the bar and took a seat just outside on the patio, where I could watch. I'd never seen so many people hug each other. Was that a gay thing? Were they all related somehow, or did they just like hugging?

The Busch clock actually poured a golden shower of neon when midnight struck. Pretty cool. I took the cue from the gay-bar gods and wandered into the main dance floor area. It was just as packed as the week before. I threaded my way through the crowd to my secret corner and felt the security of the wall behind me as I leaned back.

Time to watch the animals at the zoo.

The lights were pretty much off, with swirling strobes and spotlights that gave the warehouse a feeling of dizzying motion. It was a little hard to focus on faces with all the lights flashing, but after a few eye blinks, things cleared up. The thrum of the bass reverberated in my chest. It danced with the anxious nerves bouncing around in there, keeping them company and out of my head. I'd never get used to the overpowering stench of cigarettes, but my nose did stop twitching after about ten minutes. My clothes were really going to stink again.

I got bored watching the same guys dance and decided to wander. The show bar was still fairly empty. A few older men huddled around the bar, a pattern I was beginning to understand. There were a handful of small groups congregated around tables, laughing, chatting and drinking. Everyone looked so happy.

I stared up at the nearly empty balcony and curiosity drove my feet up the stairs. A bored bartender slumped against the glossy surface of his counter. Two guys huddled at a table in the corner, kissing between childlike giggles. If I looked young, they looked twelve.

Noises from below called to me, so I peered over the railing to find the best view in the house. I could see the stage and catwalk, and even the bar below, although some of the guys were merely tops of heads from this vantage point. Guys wandered in and out of the room, seemingly as curious or bored as I had been, but few remained still for long. Looking down gave the place a feeling of energy. It crawled with it—or maybe the people were doing the crawling, I wasn't sure.

I'd lost myself in a voyeuristic trance when an arm bumped against mine, and a voice with more treble than bass spoke. "Hey."

I turned to find an absolutely beautiful blond bombshell of a man standing next to me. My eyes involuntarily dropped to the fishnet-looking shirt he was wearing. I think there was actually more skin than net. While I didn't exactly share his fashion sense, the bulging chest and rippling abs made my already tight jeans pinch a bit more. It must've been cold because his nipples were poking through the net and staring at me.

"Hey," I said artfully. My eyes took their time rising to meet his.

He smiled. Damn. He had *perfect* teeth that practically glowed in the black light of the bar, but I couldn't see what color his eyes were. "You look bored. Want to get out of here?"

I nearly jumped off the balcony. "Uh, what? Leave? Now? I mean … I just got here." I gulped in air. "But, just curious, where were you thinking of going?"

He didn't hesitate. "My condo. It's way more fun than this place."

It wasn't even midnight and this guy wanted to leave. I mean, he was crazy-hot, but did guys just meet up like this and leave together? At least Joseph and I saw a movie first, got to know each other. I was a little baffled, but couldn't stop looking at the abs he'd caught in his net. For once, the little angel on my shoulder had laryngitis, while the devil was dancing an Irish jig.

"OK. I'm kinda bad with directions though. Can I just follow you?"

His teeth flashed again. "Sure."

He grabbed my hand and pulled me along like a little red wagon until we entered the parking lot. I'd never held a guy's hand before, certainly not in public, but no one seemed to notice—except for Cowboy Rick, who was taking a ciggie break by the door as we walked out. He gave me the strangest chuckle and shook his head, then waved with four fingers like he was tickling the air.

The cool, nicotine-free air outside filled my lungs. It was a full moon—naturally—and I now had my first well-lit view of the guy dragging me to my doom.

Holy Mother of Hotness and Sin, Batman.

He was flawless. Whoever chiseled his jaw needed a prize or trophy or whatever they gave chiselers of stuff. In the light, there was even less fishnet and more flesh, if that was possible—and how were his jeans tighter than mine? How was *that* possible? He could crack walnuts with his butt cheeks; they were poking out in their perfect rounded glory through his denim. One back pocket was ripped and flapping, and there was no fabric covering his pale, hairless skin. God bless his wardrobe malfunction.

He walked me to where Betty waited, gave me the appropriate reaction for one who'd never seen a Saturn, then vanished across the sea of cars to retrieve his own. A moment later, he pulled up in a sporty green BMW convertible, top down, golden hair flowing, teeth flashing. My heart raced as he pulled up beside me.

He didn't speak, just grinned and motioned with his hand for me to follow.

6

———————

Halfway to Blondie's house, the little angel decided to wake up and start peeping in my ear. What a nag. For a split second, my preacher's kid guilt kicked in, and I thought about turning Betty around and heading home. Then the little devil licked my lobe and the hard-on that had started as we left Connection threatened to rip my zipper open. I thumped that angel so hard she slammed against the back windshield. I was sure I'd pay for that at some point in life, but not that night.

We pulled up to a blocky brick warehouse with faded lettering across the top that read Nashville Steel. I didn't even know we made steel. Does one even *make* steel? Or shape it? Or melt it? I have no idea. I had even less idea why we were parking at a steel factory. Plant. Warehouse. Steel place.

Anyway.

Blondie flicked his hair back and grinned lecherously, then gave me the *come-hither* finger. Like a dumbass, I nodded and waved from across the parking lot like some kid who'd just spotted his mom picking him up from school. He chuckled.

We walked inside and I couldn't stop gawking at the girders and beams that rose and crisscrossed everywhere. The place was seriously cool. Blondie noticed and explained. "This used to be a factory where they made steel parts for ships and river boats, but was abandoned years ago when the company went under. Some developer bought it and turned it into open-concept condos. I think I was actually the first person to get one."

He seemed very proud of being the first. I resisted the urge to ask what an open-concept condo was.

We were halfway down the eternal hallway when he stopped at the third door. As we entered, I was again in gawker heaven. The same girders latticed the ceiling, making the place feel old, incredibly tall, and somehow new at the same time. There were no walls, just one massive room with a few of those folding divider-screen things I remembered seeing in Asian movies. On one side was a modern-looking kitchen with shiny silver appliances and countertops that looked like medical examination tables. The middle held a long L-shaped leather sectional and flat screen that covered most of the wall. Outside of a movie theater, I had never seen a screen that wide. It was powered on when we entered. The screen saver flipped between landscapes and ocean views—a really nice touch.

Against the wall opposite the kitchen was a sprawling king-sized bed with a mattress that barely rose to my waist. An antique-looking wrought-iron frame swooped in artistic waves above layers of pillows. The contrast between the frame and the brick of the wall was very cool.

I couldn't get over how open the open concept really was. Even the toilet and shower were exposed. The shower head poked out of a concrete slab that reminded me of some bad high school football TV show where half the scenes were of guys showering after practice. I was fascinated and started walking over to see how he kept water from flooding everywhere without a shower curtain.

Before I made it three steps, strong hands gripped my arms, spun me around, and shoved me against a steel beam. Warm lips attacked mine, and a tongue darted between my now open mouth. Blondie was all passion and fire, an urgency driving him to action, and I knew there wouldn't be any small talk—probably no talk at all.

I thought my heart was going to beat out of my chest.

While his tongue explored, his fingers found the end of my T-shirt. Before I could think, white fabric ripped over my head and flew across the room, smacking against the oh-so-dry shower. I fumbled with his shirt, desperate to feel his skin against mine, but the fishnet was awkward and my fingers got stuck. He looked down, then back up at the embarrassment in my eyes, and barked a laugh.

I thought the mood might've been broken, but his laugh fell away, and he pressed his lips into my neck. A shiver ran from my neck to my toes, and I let out a soft moan. I felt him grind against me.

He unwound the stringy netting from my digits and loosened his shirt, dropping it unceremoniously where we stood.

Sweet baby Jesus.

He was even more perfect than I'd thought. His abs were harder than the beam pressing into my back. I couldn't remember ever seeing anyone with such a perfect physique. I reached up and pressed my hand to his chest. It didn't budge. It was like pressing that concrete shower wall, but with tiny pink nipples that begged to be nibbled. I ran my fingers across his arms and could feel the separation of each muscle. He wasn't ogreish like some bodybuilders; he was lean and thick and hard.

In a flash, so was I. Hard, that is.

He reached up and closed my mouth, his eyes glittering, then hooked one finger into the top of my jeans above the button and pulled. Like a pup on a leash, I let him tug me toward the bed. I could barely think. Was this really happening?

When we reached the edge of the bed, he dropped to his knees and took the button of my jeans in his mouth. His face brushed against my stomach and I couldn't stop a shiver. Through some otherworldly gay sorcery, he unbuttoned and unzipped my Wranglers with his teeth. I rarely wore underwear, and his tongue found more than he likely expected as the denim parted. Wide eyes looked up, smiling once again.

I reached down to help remove my jeans, but he gripped my hands, his hold firm. "Tonight, you *only* do what I tell you, alright?"

I wasn't sure what that meant, so I nodded and didn't say anything. He released my hands and gripped my jeans, pulling them down as slowly as he could. He turned his head and rubbed his cheek against where my erection was sprouting.

I can still remember the smooth softness of his skin against mine. I wanted him so badly in that moment.

When my jeans finally found my ankles, his mouth had consumed every inch of me. His head rose and fell as he ran lips and tongue up and down my shaft. I spasmed every time the tip pressed against the back of his throat. He pressed further, willing me deeper inside him. I ran my fingers through his hair while he licked and sucked. He reached up and gripped my chest, then trailed his fingers firmly down my stomach and abs.

Finally, he leaned back and pushed me onto the bed. I flopped onto my back and tried to lean forward, but he pushed me back. "No moving unless I tell you to, remember?"

I nodded frantically.

He finished removing my jeans, then straightened my body so I was laying with my head on a pillow. He was still wearing his jeans, but I could see his excitement throbbing down one leg. He hung to the right. I wanted to reach up and feel it, but he'd told me not to move, and I was a good boy.

"Stay there. I'll be right back," he said with a quick kiss to my nipple.

A moment later, he was back with one hand held secretively behind him. "Close your eyes."

I did as he commanded.

There was a pause and the sound of shuffling. I felt warmth above me as his naked flesh hovered. He crawled up the bed, and his dick dangled and brushed against my own. I could feel the skin of his uncut cock as it pulled back slightly with my touch. Something wet moistened my head.

Then silky cloth covered my eyes, and I flinched.

"Shh. Don't move."

His mouth was over mine, breathing into me, as he tied the silk behind my head. He kissed me deeply, then the heat of his body vanished as I felt his weight leave the mattress.

"Put your arms out like you're reaching for the corners of the bed."

What the f—?

My breath caught, then quickened. Sweat bloomed across my chest and forehead, and my heart thumped faster.

I did as he commanded.

Before I could ask what he was doing, both wrists felt the same tight pull of silk my face had a moment earlier. I tried to lower them, but found they'd been tied to the iron headboard and wouldn't budge. Fear jolted down my spine. What had I done coming here with this guy? How could I have been so stupid? I started to panic and tried pulling against the silk, but was shocked into stillness by the sensation of warm liquid dribbling across my chest and stomach.

"Relax. *Trust me.* I won't hurt you."

I *wanted* to believe him. He was so freakin' hot, and I had twenty-four years of pent-up repression begging for wild, crazy sex—but this man had me blindfolded and tied to a bed. My rational mind was screaming to grab my clothes and run as fast as I could.

Then he pressed his slick body against mine and all rational thought vanished.

He'd apparently rubbed himself down with the same oil he'd dripped on me, and our bodies slid with frictionless ease. His hands ran up my sides, spreading oil everywhere, tickling and teasing as his tongue and teeth reached my neck. I could feel his erection pressing just under my balls, and my back arched.

My whole body trembled. The fear of being bound and blinded by a stranger somehow heightened my other senses, and ripples of pleasure bloomed everywhere his skin touched. He kissed me. No, he *devoured* me, his tongue exploring mine again and again. When our dicks slid against each other, I thought I might explode. My body shook and my breathing heaved.

He pulled back, and the heat of his touch cooled. I could hear him at the foot of the bed.

The mattress dipped as I felt him crawl across the bed on his knees. Oily fingertips traced across my skin, starting at my ankle, up my calf to the inside of my thigh. Then he did it again up both legs at the same time. It tickled and tingled. I could picture his chest and arms, see his fingers touching me, feel his lips, though they were far away.

I clenched, caught off guard, when his finger teased my butt, barely grazing the tiny hairs outside my hole, then pressed inside. I heard a *pop* as his finger came out, then a chuckle. When his finger didn't return for more exploration, I began to wonder if I'd done something wrong. I lifted my head to listen for him. Then I felt the heat of his breath, and my hole quivered. His tongue was hot and wet, and the oil let it slide in without protest. He pressed into me, testing, then thrusted it harder and deeper.

I moaned again, louder. I sucked in a breath as my world spun.

"God, you're tight," he said, as he pulled his tongue out, teased around the edges, then plunged it even deeper and more insistent. His hands went from gentle to gripping, squeezing and releasing my hips, pulsing in time with the rhythm his tongue.

I groaned when he finally pulled back. How could he ever stop that? I wanted him to keep licking and pressing and squeezing. I couldn't imagine anything feeling better than his tongue—

Until, without warning, he slid inside me.

No one had ever been inside me.

With all the oil and sweat, he slipped inside me like he'd been there all his life. I cried out and he stopped, a hand pressed against my chest.

"Don't stop."

"Ask me nicely." His voice carried amusement and desire, an alluring cocktail.

"Please, get back inside me and don't ever pull out. I need you inside me," I pleaded.

"That's my boy."

He eased back slowly, then slammed into me again, this time deeper, driving the breath out of me. I gripped the silk holding my hands, and fear mingled with pleasure as I remembered being tied—but I didn't care anymore. I'd given myself to him, to his pleasure, and he could have whatever he wanted.

My back arched. My toes clenched. He retreated then plunged into me as he pulled my cheeks apart with his hands. The hardness of his pelvis pressed urgently against my hips. He wanted to be as deep as possible in me, and I wanted it too. He *couldn't* get deep enough.

His tip pressed against some fleshy barrier. It resisted him, held him back. He pressed deeper. I felt him lean over and grip my shoulders for leverage, then press again. Something relaxed inside me, and he entered a place I never knew existed. I groaned, and waves of ecstasy rolled where shivers had trailed moments before.

A deep growl rumbled with his groan, driving my senses further into madness. He held himself deep inside me, unmoving, and his hands rubbed my legs, then pressed against my chest. I could feel him hardening even more inside me.

That excited me.

His lips brushed against mine, and I reached up to kiss him. He pulled back to keep us a breath apart, then I felt the silk pull away from my eyes and I could see his face inches from mine.

God, he was beautiful and fierce and *intense*. His eyes were infinite pools of blue brimming with passion and fire, hunger and need. His gaze bore into my soul. No one had ever looked into me like that.

My heart leapt into my throat.

He saw the shift and pressed his lips hard against my mouth, then began grinding himself into me. Wrapping his arms around me, his body melded with my own. The oil heated with our skin, and his thrusting sped up. He raised himself to his knees and held my legs in the air. His chest was slick, and light flickered off his abs.

His eyes never left mine.

He quickened. His thrusts were deep and desperate. I moaned and threw my head back as I felt his body tensing. He was close. I wanted him, all of him. He didn't slow. His hand gripped me and began stroking, his fingers squeezing and caressing from base to tip. He was gentle and firm, the oil giving him permission. He was inside me, raging. He pressed deeper and faster, until finally his head flew back and he released a primal cry. I felt the thrill as he flowed into me. His whole body pulsed as wave after wave left him.

He kept himself inside me and wrapped his hand around my shaft once more. This time, it didn't take long. My body tensed and I felt myself explode across his abs. Through overwhelmed senses, I heard him cry out again, and felt him release a second time, somehow in perfect unison with my own cry.

He smiled, ran a hand across my chest again, then laid his body on top of mine.

7

———

"We fell asleep like that, me tied up, his body spread across mine. I could still feel him pulsing inside me as I fell asleep."

Dwayne and I sat in the corner of the diner. It was a rustic eatery whose tables were level-ish, thanks to stacks of sugar packets shoved under their legs. It didn't look like much, but the food was good and cheap.

"So, what was the guy's name? When are you going to see him again? Tell me more." Dwayne leaned forward on his elbows.

Shit.

He saw the panicked look on my face and started laughing. "You don't remember his name, do you?"

"It's worse than that."

"Oh Lord. What?"

"I never got his name. All I know is—well, I'm *assuming*—he's a flight attendant. There were a bunch of uniform coats with wings in his closet."

Dwayne struggled to come up for air as his laughter

drew looks from other tables. "You let a hot flight attendant whose name you never got fuck your brains out and cum inside you?" He doubled over.

I couldn't help but laugh with him. Before I knew it, we were both giggling through tears as the waitress appeared.

"Care to share?" she asked with a smile.

Dwayne started to say something, but I cut him off with a horrified stare. "No! Sorry, it's an inside joke."

"*Inside* joke. That's priceless!" Dwayne nearly choked on the laughter following that faux pas.

The waitress refilled our tea and scurried away. I think we scared the poor girl.

"So, did you and Fly Boy talk at all?" Dwayne asked through gasps.

"Does grunting and moaning count?"

He couldn't get his tea glass to his mouth fast enough and had to set it down before it spilled. "You didn't even talk at all? Seriously?"

"Well, I tried. When we got to his place, I started to ask about the building, but he threw me against the wall and any thought of steel or smelting went out the window."

"Oh, I'm pretty sure your mind was on steel." He was riding this harder than Fly Boy had. "What about in the morning, before you left?"

I shook my head. "I woke up in the middle of the night, got dressed, and left. He was out of it, so we didn't talk then either."

"Did you at least get to keep one of his ties as a souvenir?"

I couldn't help but chuckle. "No. All I got was to be his baby mama."

He scowled.

Now I was confused. That had been a pretty witty comeback.

"Michael, we need to talk about that." He crossed his arms and leaned back.

Uh-oh. No good conversation ever begins with *we need to talk*. Anyone who's ever watched a movie knows the greatest breakups in history have followed that phrase. This little brunch was about to take a serious turn.

I shifted uncomfortably in the squeaky booth.

"You let him cum inside you. You know you can't let guys do that. *Ever*."

Here I'd just told Dwayne about a rock-my-world experience with a guy, basically admitting I was gay, and he was *scolding* me? I barely knew how to react. Plus, I didn't really understand what I'd done wrong. Sure, it was random sex with a guy whose name I never asked—and he never offered. The whole night went against pretty much everything I was raised to believe, but damn, it was hot. I thought the Gay Handbook encouraged random hook-ups, like it was part of the culture, or a man's rite of passage.

Gay rules were confusing.

His face morphed from concerned to annoyed when I didn't immediately turn contrite. "HIV, Michael."

"Huh? What about HIV?"

He cocked his head as if examining a baby bird. "You don't know *anything*, do you?"

I gave him my best puppy-dog eyes, the ones that usually got me out of trouble with him. They didn't work.

I really *didn't* know anything.

"Unprotected sex is one of the chief ways HIV spreads. I used to work in a blood bank. I know all about this stuff. Hell, I watched too many friends get sick and die. The press doesn't talk about AIDS like they used to, but it's still raging out there, taking great people before their time. Even if it doesn't kill you, you'd have to take meds for the rest of your life, and who knows how other guys would react to you? People are still ignorant and scared. I don't want to watch any of that happen to you."

I lowered my gaze. "Sorry. I didn't know."

"You don't owe *me* an apology, silly, but you *need* to know these things before you go out into the big gay world and stick your butt in the air like a horny hyena."

I couldn't help the mental image that popped into my head. Tea flew out my mouth. "A horny hyena?"

He smirked and shrugged. "I'm just worried about you. This whole life is new to you, and I don't want to see you pay for an innocent mistake. It could cost you your life."

I looked up and saw the most heartfelt concern in his eyes. He wasn't exactly a father figure, despite being old enough to actually *be* my father. I thought of Dwayne more like an older brother. There was zero attraction on my part, but I felt compelled to be around him, to be close and share with him. It's hard to explain. From the day we met, he'd felt special, like family.

He reached across the table and put his hand on my arm. "I don't mean to lecture, and I know we've only known each other a few weeks, but you're important to me."

"Thanks. Really." I put my hand on his and gulped back the emotion threatening to emerge. "I never would've dealt with any of these feelings if you hadn't shown up at that bar to see Jason. You've been so patient and listened, even when I talked out my ass about being straight."

Shit. Did I just say that?

He studied me a moment, then said in his most serious tone, "You're still straight, right?"

I laughed, suddenly nervous. Did he want me to say it out loud, to admit I really did like boys, like Jason had asked that first night? I wasn't sure I could get the word out. I wasn't ready to be that honest with him—*or myself.*

I just rolled with it. "Yep, still straight as an arrow."

"That's what I thought." He raised his glass in salute.

8

I drove back to my apartment, climbed the steps, and stared at the door. Peter was probably inside.

My gut churned. I was excited from the night before. Talking about it over lunch was almost the same as getting to live it all over again. Well, not really, but it was fun seeing the shock on Dwayne's face as I told him about the silk ties. *I* was still in shock from the first kiss of them on my wrists.

As giddy as I might've been from getting laid—I mean, *seriously* laid—there was a part of me that felt a stab of guilt. I couldn't help it. The preacher's kid would always live inside me, and sometimes he decided to stand up and shout. I wished he would just stay quiet and let me have fun. I'd never had fun like this before. Guilt made it, I don't know … less.

Then I felt silly standing outside my own apartment. Peter wouldn't know anything, other than I hadn't come home until after lunch the next day, if he was even awake himself. Why was I so worried what he thought anyway? Sure, I had a bit of a crush on him. Everyone did. Women,

men, even straight guys crushed on him. He was *that* hot and that likable.

So why did my gut clench thinking about facing him?

Would he ask where I'd been? I couldn't tell him I'd gone to a gay bar and hooked up with some random dude, could I? He didn't know I was gay. Hell, I couldn't even admit it myself when Dwayne had asked me earlier. Why did everything have to be so confusing?

I ran my hands through my hair and shouldered through the door.

"Hey. Where've you been?" Peter looked up from his perch at the kitchen bar. He was stuffing half a pound cake in his mouth. I know, weird. He was convinced he could eat as much pound cake as he wanted—as a meal substitute— and his abs would never disappear. And yes, *he* was coaching others on being healthy. That's my Peter.

"Had brunch with a friend. You?"

He snorted through bites. "I meant last night. You never came home."

I tried not to fidget, but I was sure my ears were turning red. "Oh, well, I went out, you know, to a bar."

He set the cake down. Crap. His eyes had acquired missile lock, and I could tell by his smirk he was about to fire. "Huh."

That's it? That was all he was going to say? I scooted past him, desperate to reach my room before he could get off a good shot.

I heard a loud sniffing sound, then he spoke again. "Cigarette smoke mixed with … something. Perfume? Cologne? I recognize that one."

Of course he did. He was the gayest straight guy ever to sashay up to the men's fragrance counter.

I ignored him and tried to stay casual as I darted into my room and slammed the door.

OK, that wasn't exactly casual. I panicked.

Once inside the safety of my personal space, I smelled something awful and realized I needed a shower. My jeans were stuck to my leg from Fly Boy's, um, *cologne*.

Crap.

Crap. Crap. Crap.

Neither of our rooms connected to the bathroom. It was down the short hall, but would force me to pass near him as he sat on his throne of judgment in the kitchen.

I almost made it.

"What was her name?" an amused sounding, cake-muffled voice asked.

I froze. He thought I'd hooked up with *a girl*. Perfect.

"Uh, well, she was really hot."

Nice. *Smooth.* Idiot.

He laughed and I could see bits of cake fly across the bar. "You don't know her name? Seriously? My preacher's kid?" His laughter grew into a full-blown giggle fit.

I hated him.

Not really. I secretly wanted to get in his pants.

Wait, did he just use the possessive *my* when referring to me? My heart fluttered. "Hey, I'm a rock star. What can I say?"

He guffawed as I disappeared into the safety of the bathroom and locked the door. We never locked doors, but I needed it bolted, chained and sealed in that moment. I leaned back and closed my eyes, trying to remember to breathe. I'd *never* lied to Peter before. Now I felt guilty about that too. Perfect.

A few minutes later, as I was finally peeling off my vile

jeans, Peter's voice boomed through the door, nearly startling me into the tub.

"I'm headed to work. In all the excitement of your midnight romp, I forgot to tell you some guy called right before you got home. Dwayne? Number's on the pad by the phone."

"OK, thanks," I yelled back.

Peter's footsteps faded, then the door slammed as he exited our apartment. I could finally soak in a comforting waterfall. The water was hotter than usual. Maybe I was trying to scorch the guilt off my body, along with Fly Boy's children. I don't know. I didn't feel the heat, but my skin was angry when I toweled off and glanced in the mirror. I dropped the towel and studied myself, something I never did.

Like I told you before, I'd always been the scrawny toothpick who couldn't tan. Really attractive, right? Self-conscious didn't come close to describing how I felt about myself, especially about my body—but standing there, sans towel, after a night of silk-bound sex that had been hotter than my shower water, I gazed at myself and, for the first time in my life, thought *I* looked kind of hot. Peter's incessant whip-crack at the gym had helped round my shoulders and chest, and my arms were no longer rail-thin reeds. My stomach had always been flat, but I'd never eaten well enough to reveal abs—and I'd certainly never inflicted crunch-style pain on myself to form them—but there they were, poking through, smiling up at me.

I flexed, impressed, then laughed at my ridiculous Arnold pose. I actually looked pretty good naked. I'd *never* thought that about myself before.

A strange warmth bloomed in my chest, and my hand reflexively rose to touch it. I traced my fingers across the compact muscle that hadn't existed a few months earlier. I squeezed my bicep as my hand moved across it and grinned at the firm ball that formed.

Then the rusty tint in my hair caught my eye in the mirror and the moment burst like an overinflated balloon. I might only be half-ginger, but that's enough to be skittish as hell. What can I say? All gingers see their hair as hottie kryptonite, sealing us away from ever being among the truly beautiful.

Genetics aside, I'll never forget that moment, that glimpse of who I was becoming, what my body was becoming. Pride I'd never known—that I'd never known could even exist—about myself sparked to life.

It took a while to wipe the goofy grin from my face.

Freshly showered and changed, I wandered into the den and flipped on the TV. Bowling. *Star Trek*. A documentary about coral reefs. Awesome.

I remembered Peter's shout about Dwayne calling and decided whatever he had to talk about was better than tenpin, so I grabbed the phone and spun the numbers. Yes, kids, it was an old-school rotary phone. If you don't know what I'm talking about, I'm embarrassed for you.

"Hello?"

"Hey, Dwayne. It's Michael."

"Oh hey. Thanks for brunch today. I realized after we left that you paid the bill. You didn't have to do that."

I really couldn't afford it either, but he'd paid for the last couple. My guilt was now a hat trick. "No problem. Happy to."

There was an awkward pause.

"So, Jason is playing another gig tonight at the Orchid. Please don't make me sit through another three hours of the same songs by myself." He and Jason had been friends for years, and I knew he'd go to any performance our illustrious singer invited him to attend, but he sounded a little desperate for company.

"Sure. I don't have anything going on tonight, and you know how dangerous it is to leave me alone on a Saturday."

He chuckled. That was an inside joke between us now. "That's an understatement," he said. "Meet you there at seven?"

"Sure. I'll eat before we get there though. Peter's got me watching my food, and I'm finally noticing a difference. Don't want to blow it."

I had to pull the receiver away from my ear as his laughter barked through. "Oh, I'm starting to think you want to *blow* everything."

My ears turned red again, I was sure of it. "Ha ha. Very funny. Although, if they all look like Fly Boy …"

"Oh stop! They don't count if you don't get their name. New rule."

"He didn't *need* to count. He just needed to use his tongue—"

"Enough! I'm done with you. See you tonight." Click.

I chuckled. I might not have admitted I was gay yet, but I didn't seem to have any trouble talking about having a man's tongue shoved up my ass, and getting mild-mannered Dwayne to hang up on me had been quite the accomplishment.

Seven o'clock rolled around quickly. Dwayne met me on the sidewalk outside the Wild Orchid, a local bar that packed in the crowds for their live music. The place was famous for discovering any number of successful singers, and everyone working their way up the chain in Nashville wanted to perform on that stage. Dwayne told me it was fairly common for producers and talent scouts to show up unannounced on weekends. Whether they liked the food or were actually looking for singers was unclear. I was a little surprised Jason had landed such a prime gig on a Saturday night, but I really didn't know much about the music scene other than what Dwayne had explained in our time together.

We'd only made it a couple steps inside when Hurricane Jason blew up to us and wrapped Dwayne in an embrace. "Dwayne! Thanks for coming. You're my *only* fan here tonight."

Dwayne looked sideways at me, and Jason followed his eyes.

"Oh hey." He had that look on his face like he recognized me from somewhere, but couldn't remember where. "Were you—"

I saved him. "We work out at the same gym, and Dwayne invited me to hear you sing a couple weeks ago. You're really good."

He beamed at the compliment and the memory-scowl vanished. "Why, thank you." It sounded like his practiced reply to a compliment regarding a performance. He was always on stage, I guessed.

"Gotta go get ready for my set. The table up front with the *reserved* card is for you." He hugged Dwayne one more time, then snaked his way through the tables to the side door by the stage. Dwane shrugged, and I followed him to our promised table. Jason wasn't kidding; we were in the front row, practically bumping against the stage.

Dwayne leaned over. "I hate it when he sticks me under his nose. Let's get a different table. I'll tell him the house needed the prime spot for someone important."

He motioned a waitress and a moment later we were comfortable, midway back and against a wall. Dwayne had been right. We had been pretty much up the performer's nose.

Dwayne ordered a pork chop that made my stomach growl. I got an iced tea and munched on the bowl of bar snacks we'd sweet-talked out of the waitress. Being friends with the artist had its advantages, sometimes in tasty, garlicky nuts.

Stop snickering and get your mind out of the gutter. I'd never tasted Jason's nuts.

We chatted and laughed. Dwayne told me about some new boy who'd started waiting tables at his fancy restaurant. Jeff was twenty-two, had wavy blond hair and emerald eyes. Dwayne got a faraway look when he described how he'd sauntered into the restaurant in his 'Ducks in a Row' T-shirt from the Peabody Hotel in Memphis. Apparently, the shirt was cute and a little too tight, two things Dwayne loved in a man half his age.

In the short time we'd known each other, he'd only mentioned two guys, and both were under the age of twenty-five. Dwayne was forty-one.

I listened patiently, then launched a barrage of playful attacks at my friend's need for an ankle bracelet near schools.

He snorted unapologetically and waved me off. "I can't help it if I like younger guys," he countered.

"Grass on the field, play ball?"

He gave me a sharp look.

"Old enough to pee, old enough for me?"

This earned me a smack on the arm as the waitress appeared.

"Help! This old coot's attacking me. Call Child Protective Services, quick!"

She glanced between us with raised brows as she refilled my tea. Dwayne smacked me again. "Somebody has to keep these youngsters in line," he quipped without missing a beat.

We both laughed, and the poor waitress shook her head, a tiny curl threatening the corner of her mouth. She was in for a long night. At least we'd be entertaining.

Someone tapped the microphone, saving Dwayne from more teasing and my arm from his punches. We turned to watch and listen.

There was a mic stand, a bar stool, and Jason on a raised, round stage barely wide enough for two performers. He stepped up to the microphone with a wide leather guitar strap crossing his shoulder, the instrument cradled in his hands. He strummed a few chords, smiled, then looked out toward the crowd. Light applause returned his greeting as diners divided their attention between the stage and their meals.

I'd seen Jason several times at the gym, usually in a tank top and skimpy shorts. From what I saw, he was in great shape, and was a generally handsome guy—but it was his smile and the magnetic way he drew people toward him that I noticed more than anything. He had this mystical pull. People *wanted* to be near him, to interact with him, to be seen by him. I'd been fascinated by the phenomena a few times while doing leg presses or arm curls. I hadn't been smitten so much as fascinated. I figured that was a required gift for a performer, at least one with any shot at making it in the business.

Charisma is a funny thing.

As Jason started singing, I looked at him. No, not like any old fan in the audience. I *really* looked at him. In some ways, it felt like the first time. His voice smiled with each note, the lyrics recalling happy memories in Austin around Lake Travis, giving the audience a virtual hug filled with warmth. His face, to those who knew him, carried a hint of longing and pain. I leaned forward. Yes, that *was* pain, or, more accurately, heartache. Someone he'd cared for and spent time with on Lake Travis wasn't in his life anymore.

How did I know this? Was I channeling Celine Dion? Or the other Celine? Or Dionne? I get them confused.

I *felt* every word, every note. His pain drifted into my heart and pulled at my soul. I wanted to leap out of my chair, knock Dwayne's pork chop to the floor, and race into Jason's waiting arms to comfort him. He needed me, I knew it.

Damn you, Lake Travis! How dare you hurt my Jason!

The screechy sound of a vinyl record being scratched sounded in my head. You know, that cringe-worthy sound that literally stops life? *My Jason?* Where the hell had that come from?

I looked back up to the stage as he finished his song and gave a shallow bow to the crowd's polite applause. He flicked his hair. His bicep flexed. My heart fluttered.

What was happening to me? Without thinking, I got to my feet.

"Are you OK?" Dwayne leaned over and gripped my arm before I could run out of the bar.

"Uh, yeah. Fine. I just, um, need to go to the bathroom." I shrugged his arm off and wove my way through the tables to find the restroom full with one man waiting outside.

What in the holy gay fuckety fuck was happening?

I gave the waiting man the obligatory *'sup?* chin salute, then leaned against the wall and stared at my shoes, praying I wouldn't break out in a cold sweat.

"Oh hey. Michael, right?" I looked up to find Jason standing in front of me.

Fuckety fucking fuckery!

I tried to smile. "Hey. Uh, yeah. Michael. That's me." Why was English suddenly my second language?

He grinned. "What did you think? I did the Lake Travis song a little different tonight."

"Yeah, I noticed." Had I noticed? I mean, I was practically daydreaming about offering him therapy throughout the song, but had I noticed it differed from the last time I'd heard it? "I really liked tonight better. I could feel it more."

He cocked his head, paused, then smiled. "Awesome. Thanks."

Before I knew what had happened, the dude in the bathroom exited and Jason snuck in, leaving the *'sup* guy and me staring at the locked bathroom door.

9

Dwayne called Sunday morning and badgered me into brunch. I was sleeping in like a champ, but he sounded like a Catholic schoolgirl in trouble, so I knew I had to go.

Around eleven o'clock, I pulled up to our diner to find Dwayne pacing just outside the door. Was he muttering to himself while he paced? Oh, this was going to be juicy.

He saw me walking up and turned toward the door. Without a word, he opened it, went inside and plopped down at a table he'd already secured from Katie, our regular waitress. She gave me a look, something between sympathy and curiosity. A strange tingle tickled the back of my neck as I scooched into the booth and grabbed the creamer to doctor the mug of coffee Dwayne had thoughtfully ordered.

The cream had barely struck the surface when Dwayne's words tumbled out. "So, I met this guy last night. You know, I told you about him. Jim, the cute one from work. We talked after Jason's show, and he asked me to meet him at a bar."

He paused to gauge my reaction. I simply moved from creamer to sugar and raised an eyebrow.

"We met at the Chute."

My brow quirked in confusion at this new place I didn't recognize. Was this supposed to mean something?

"It's a small bar. We haven't been there. Well, you haven't been there. I've been there a million times. It's nice, mostly smoke-free, and has a small drag bar attached to a sporty bar. I like it. Anyway. You're getting me side-tracked."

Wow. Dwayne was babbling. I'd never seen this before. I sipped my coffee and grinned over the rim, enjoying the show. We might get a full-on meltdown today. Maybe Katie could bring me popcorn. Hell, she'd probably throw herself down and munch with me if the show had enough fireworks.

"Are you listening to me?"

I nodded my bleary head and took another sip. "Sorry. Go on. Cute Jim. The Chute. I'm with you."

"Anyway." He was *so* edgy. "We met at the Chute. I said that, didn't I? He had on these tight jeans and a stringy tank top. I'd never seen him wear anything but his uniform at work. Michael, he took my breath away. He was beauti-ful. I mean, *seriously* beautiful." He took a breath and gulped from his water glass. The ice rattled as his hand shook slightly.

"He's twenty-two, right?" I asked, more to confirm in his mind than mine. Dwayne was old enough to be the kid's father. This couldn't end well, and I was starting to get worried my friend was smitten.

"Michael, I'm totally smitten."

Oh shit.

"We got there around midnight and talked until they

kicked us out at two. Then we went back to my place and talked for another three hours. I don't think I've ever talked to anyone that long, definitely not in our first real conversation. It flowed so easily."

The diner gods must've been watching, because Katie showed up in that moment, forcing Dwayne to stop rattling and breathe. She looked at him, then gave me a questioning look. I shrugged and chuckled, then mouthed "popcorn." She nearly dropped her order pad as a cackle burst out.

Dwayne looked up, and she covered her mouth with her pad. "Whatcha gonna have today, sweetie?" she asked Dwayne.

He gave me a snarky look, then turned back and ordered. I got my usual, wholegrain pancakes with a side of bacon and two over-medium eggs. She actually just told me that was my order, and I nodded. We're regulars, what can I say?

"Dwayne might need a side of chicken today. Seems he's been in the mood for it lately."

He wadded up a napkin and threw it at me as I spat coffee back into my cup. Katie cackled again and shuffled away, her head shaking the whole time.

"He sucked me off."

I nearly dropped my mug. Coffee splashed across the table and all over my white shirt. Katie was there in a flash with a bottle of soda water. Bless you, Katie.

"Did I hear you right? The staff diddled your staff?"

He gave me a sheepish grin and nodded. This forty-one-year-old man was *embarrassed*. I had to admit, it was kind of cute to see.

I grinned. "And? You know you can't just cum and run. I want details."

He huffed as if I was putting him out, then smiled.

"Oh … my … God. It was incredible, and I didn't see it coming."

I giggled like a schoolboy who'd heard a fart joke. He tossed another wadded napkin.

"Oh stop. We'd talked for so long that I'd lost track of time. I guess it was around three or four in the morning when he turned to me and, totally out of the blue, asked, 'Can I see your cock?' I was half-asleep until he asked that. I might never sleep again."

Our food arrived and Dwayne awkwardly changed the subject to football, of all topics. Katie nudged me with her arm and giggled. You can't fool a diner waitress.

Dwayne talked for another twenty minutes about the intricacies of a blow job from a twentysomething. He was usually even-keeled and focused on everyone else. It was fun to see him so excited and happy. He deserved it.

Katie brought the check and joked around with us a little, then we shuffled toward the door. Dwayne's nervous energy was spent—apparently for the *second* time in only a few hours. He turned the tables as I started toward my car. "So, what did you think of Jason last night?"

"Jason?" The sudden change in topic surprised me. "He's a good singer. Crowd seemed to like him."

He eyed me. There was a twist to his grin. "Mm-hmm."

"What?"

"I saw you two talking by the bathroom. He was leaning awfully close, and you seemed a little nervous and flushed when you got back to the table."

He didn't miss a damn thing.

I tried to laugh it off. "He just wanted to skip me and the other guy in line for the bathroom. You know Jason, he's a shameless flirt when he wants something."

He nodded and grunted in agreement. "Alright. I won't

press, but you two are my closest friends. If there's something going on, I want to know about it."

"Yes, Dad."

He smacked my arm and shoved me into my car.

———

AS I DROVE HOME, I THOUGHT BACK TO HOW BOYISHLY
happy Dwayne had been describing his close encounter of
the chicken kind. For the uninitiated, in gay vernacular, a
chicken is a young guy. That would make my dear Dwane a
chicken hawk—and if reports from last night were correct,
he was a lecherous one.

I was proud.

Then, for no apparent reason, Jason's face popped into
my head. I could see every strand of murky brown hair as it
fell across his forehead. He'd push it back, feigning annoyance, but knowing that simple act drove the rest of us crazy.
I wondered what it would be like to reach up and push
those locks out of the way. A shiver worked its way into my
chest.

What was I thinking? Jason was Dwayne's oldest friend
—and he was an aspiring singer in Nashville. 'Rudderless
ship' barely did him justice. I couldn't be interest in *him*
—could I?

I tried to shake him out of my mind, but his stupid,
perfect, pearly-white smile kept flashing back to the fore. It
was the same smile that distracted pretty much everybody
at the gym. How could anyone have such flawless teeth?
And how did he get them to do that twinkle thing I was
sure had to be animated, like in toothpaste commercials?

My car somehow found itself parking in the gym's lot.
I'd packed a bag, swearing to make good use of my free

Sunday afternoon. The gym was usually pretty empty on weekends, and I'd planned to get a great workout in. Then I looked up and realized Jason's car was parked opposite mine, its grille mimicking its owner's annoyingly angelic smile.

Focus, Michael. You're here to work out. Jason never pays attention to you anyway. Just go in, endure the pain, and go home. There's no need to even think about him and his hair-flicking madness.

So I told myself.

Five minutes into my workout, I looked up from the bench press to see Mr. Pearly Whites looming.

"Don't stop. I've got you." His hands gripped the pole … I mean, bar. The whole thing slammed loudly into the rack.

"Aw, you had more in you. Take a break and I'll push you all the way when I come back." Jason bounded across the gym floor to work his triceps.

Was every word out of his mouth sexual, or had Dwayne planted a seed that refused to be ignored? It sure was trying to take root and grow, or whatever seeds do when they're all about rolling in the hay with a hot guy. I watched Jason as he pulled the rope down and his triceps flexed to their limit. Despite the blasting air conditioner, he was dripping with sweat; it was soaking through his yellow tank top. I watched a bead fall from somewhere and trail into the crevice of his straining triceps. That might've been the hottest non-sexual thing I'd ever seen. I had to leave the bench for fear my own bar might distract others. It was standing at attention.

I got a drink from the water fountain near the locker rooms, as far from Jason as possible. The walk did me good and allowed Little Michael to droop back into place. It probably would've helped if I'd worn underwear and he wasn't tickled by silky fabric every time I moved, but I hated underwear—always had.

"You can't get away that easy. Back to the bench."

Shit. He was standing behind me. I could smell him, he was *that* close. Little Michael was intrigued and decided to look up again. This was going to be awkward.

"On my way, coach. One more drink," I said, buying time to get my shit back together.

He pressed against me and flames burst across my skin. He whispered in my ear, "I'm waiting. Come lift for me." I couldn't tell if his voice was sensual or playful, but it didn't matter. I was swooning.

I had the presence of mind to take another sip and free my personal space from his—though it was the last thing I *actually* wanted in that moment.

By some miracle of the gods, I managed to get through my final two sets of flat bench without busting a nut all over the gym. Little Michael behaved—sort of—and I don't think Jason ever saw how much he'd affected either of us. I stood and toweled the sweat off my arms, then turned toward the locker room. A familiar voice stopped me cold. "Oh no you don't. You have incline, decline and abs to do. Don't make me follow you around."

I couldn't decide whether to be annoyed he was making me work out more, thrilled he might follow me around—or *terrified* he might follow me around. The whole nut-busting thing was a real possibility if I had a Jason shadow all afternoon. Then again, there were worse ways to work out than looking up into dreamy eyes and a firm, muscular chest.

Stop it! There went Little Michael again, a dutiful soldier standing at attention. Ugh!

Thanks to Coach Jason barking "you got this" every

two seconds, I pushed myself harder than I ever had at the gym. It felt good. No, it felt *amazing*. I had that pump-high that only comes after an intense workout. Add the Jason-high that came from being close to him for nearly an hour, and I was just plain high.

Now, stop that—not *that* kind of high. At that point in my pious, preacher's kid life, I'd never done any of that.

This was a wholesome, muscle-burn, boy-crush giddiness that coursed through my sore muscles. As I wobbled out the door, Jason chuckled and flashed every molar, canine, and whatever those other teeth are. I was too sore to swoon, but my insides did backflips.

Can your insides *do* backflips? Anyway.

He really was stunning. And the boy could sing. Damn.

I caught myself drumming my steering wheel and singing along with *Macarena* in the car as Betty drove me home. It had been a really good day.

10

The next day I worked on reports for my dad. I still worked for him in his wholesale drug business, but was less inclined to spend eternity on the road each week. My job had shifted into the back-office management of the business. Sounds pretty sexy, doesn't it? Don't be fooled. I created paperwork, entered the data that people wrote on that paperwork, then followed whatever instructions were left on the paperwork. It was mind-numbing, but I had no idea what I wanted to do with my life, and it was a job.

That afternoon, I left, packed bag in hand, to drive across town to referee a pair of high school preseason basketball games. That's right, yours truly was a basketball referee. Once the season heated up, I'd don stripes five or six nights each week. I'd even been accepted into a couple NAIA and JUCO conferences, which meant I got to drive a little farther and work college games.

When I was younger, I played YMCA basketball, but was never dedicated enough to get good. The high school I attended competed for state championship hardware every year, so making that team was a pipe dream. When I got into college, I still wanted to be on the court, and the guys and gals in stripes won me over. I got to be close to the action and get some great exercise. It was love at first whistle. Tweet? Blow?

Never mind.

Yes, it was a weird hobby where people constantly yelled at you and called you names that didn't make sense half the time—but any ref worth their stripes learned to tune all that out. There was always one mom hidden midway up the stands whose voice carried over all the others. You couldn't tune *her* out, but she usually yelled funny things we'd laugh about back in the locker room. I lost track of the times my partners or I would start a conversation at halftime with, "Did you hear what mom called you?" We'd all laugh at her creativity. Sometimes her name-calling stuck and a ref would earn a nickname that carried throughout his career, like Mav in *Top Gun*, but without the fighter jets or half-naked volleyball.

Mostly, I loved the game and being part of it. Working college games was a rush and a totally different level of professionalism and pressure. Coaches' jobs and kids' scholarships were on the line. The higher the level, the more money and prestige was at stake for the college or university too, but the rush was worth it. The play was a lot better, and there was an intensity to the game that lower levels just couldn't recreate.

I loved every minute on court.

And the exercise was amazing. They put a pedometer on a referee once and found he ran, on average, four to six miles per high school game and eight miles per college game. Multiply that by five to six nights of reffing, and Holy Roadrunner, Batman, that's a lot of miles!

I could eat *anything* and never gain weight. I know,

most people would kill for that problem, but it drove me nuts because it made adding muscle painfully slow. Somehow, I still managed to grow. Between Peter and Jason punishing me daily at the gym, I started filling out my stripes, and even got called "pretty boy" a few times by wayward spectators. I knew it was meant to be insulting, but it made me smile the rest of the night.

Someone thought *I* was pretty. That blew my mind.

Monday night I worked a college preseason scrimmage, then a pair of high school games Tuesday evening. Wednesday was blessedly free of basketball, so I wrapped work early, determined to get a good workout in and relax in front of the TV. I stopped by the grocery store for a pre-workout snack.

The register ringer-upper cocked her head at the lonely apple that wobbled down the conveyor belt toward the scanner thingy. "That's it?" she asked.

I smiled and nodded, then counted out the change I knew would be exactly right. I did this routine almost every day. The apple gave me a quick boost of good sugars before my workout, just enough to help me push through the pain and get a good pump. It made for a tasty, healthy snack, but also created a funny scene in the store. Great on so many levels.

When I pulled into the gym's parking lot, I was pleasantly surprised to spot a space by the front door. I gave Betty a jolt, determined to not lose my Princess Parking. As I pulled in, I got my second surprise. Jason's car was in the neighboring space.

Maybe Wednesdays were good days after all.

I couldn't suppress my grin as I pictured Jason rushing to the door to greet me. He'd throw his arms wide and wrap me in the same tight hug he gave Dwayne, but with the added thrill of a passionate kiss and open declaration of his undying affection.

It was a nice daydream.

I woke from it a second later and made my way through the door. The only person to greet me was the desk dude who scanned my badge. Jason was nowhere to be seen.

Oh well.

I took the long way through the machines, just to see if I could spot Jason working out somewhere. When that failed, I headed into the locker room and changed into my workout clothes. I'd been working out now for about six months and had finally become proud enough to switch from T-shirts to tank tops. That was a huge adjustment for the skinny kid, a little like jumping out of a perfectly good airplane that first time.

Nope, I've never done that, but this is a story. Use your imagination, for Pete's sake.

As I glanced in the mirror on the way back to the floor, I still couldn't believe *my* body was growing and changing. I looked athletic; I felt stronger. It was exhilarating. For the first time in my life, I wasn't a toothpick.

I was feeling pretty darn good about Wednesday when my shoes struck the familiar rubber mat of the weight room, and then I remembered it was leg day, and all the positive vibes drained away. Nobody in their right mind liked leg day. We worked legs because turning into 'tits on sticks' wasn't attractive, but I knew I'd be walking funny and burning painfully before it was all over.

While that might also describe the hours after Fly Boy did his thing with his giant … silk ties, I can assure you, it's *not* the same pain.

Halfway through my fourth set of leg presses, Jason's upside-down face appeared as he hovered above and behind me. I must've been four shades of red and straining because he stifled a laugh that made me lose my concentration. The weights slammed back into place, sending my knees into my chest. Smooth, Michael. Real smooth.

"Nice set," he teased.

I tried to smile, but was still deciding whether life was worth it on leg day. "Thanks. I think."

"So, I have another performance tonight. It's at the Wildhorse, kind of a big deal. Can I count you in? I think Dwayne's going, so you'll know someone there."

Did Jason just ask me out? Did he want me there to support him—or did he *just want me there*? My heart skipped a beat. "Uh, sure. Sounds great. What time?"

"I don't go on until ten. Hope that's not too late. I know you work a regular job."

"Nah. That's fine. Looking forward to it." I started to stand, but my legs protested. Before I could brace myself, Jason said "thanks" and moved on. He bounced from one person to the next, no doubt drumming up a crowd. He had to do that. The more people who attended, the more times he'd be invited back to perform, and the more tips he'd make. Those other people were all part of the business of a starving artist.

His invitation to me was different. He'd singled me out. He wanted *me* there. Right there in the middle of the gym, surrounded by massive bodybuilders, I giggled. That earned a few odd glances, but I didn't care.

Wednesdays were suddenly awesome.

I'D NEVER BEEN TO THE WILDHORSE.

It was a massive, multi-story country bar owned by

Gaylord, the folks who also owned the Grand Ole Opry and built the sprawling Opryland Hotel. They didn't know how to *do* small. The bottom floor was centered on a fenced-in wooden dance floor and was rarely without a few men and women struggling to grasp the basics of line dancing. The upstairs bars were largely focused on banister viewing of the downstairs, but there were quiet couches and other seating for those wishing an escape from country's finest. Fast-paced, twangy songs blasted throughout, causing even the most stoic barfly to bop his head or wiggle her shoulders.

The place felt alive from the moment I walked in.

I scanned the bars that wound around the edge of the place, looking for Dwayne, finally locating him in the corner, cradling a Jack and Coke with a gazillion limes. Another glass full of limes rested behind him on the bar. Backups, I assumed.

We settled onto our stools and I ordered a Coke, eliciting an eye roll from my gay godfather. "Where's Jason? And where will he sing? I don't see a stage or mic stand anywhere."

Dwayne pointed to the dance floor. "They'll set up a mic for him in the center of the floor. All the lights will drop and he'll be out there alone in a spotlight."

I shivered. "Sounds terrifying."

He laughed. "Jason will eat it up. He's never met a spotlight he didn't crave."

"He does look good in bright lights."

Dwayne shot me a look I couldn't interpret, then held it for a long moment. My skin crawled under his gaze. Had I said something wrong?

The lights flickered and staff worked to clear the dance floor so they could set up for the night's headliner.

A buzz ran through the crowd. That was the first time I thought Jason might be kind of famous. He really wasn't. They did that for anyone who sang. Most of the people in the Wildhorse were tourists who didn't know a lounge singer from an Opry member—not that I was much better.

The lights dimmed and the spotlight flared, forming a stage out of a small circle of well-lit dance floor. One heartbeat, then two. Then Jason appeared and filled that stage of illumination. He was wearing tight jeans and a black cowboy-style shirt with white fringe. He flashed his trademark smile, and I swear his teeth glittered.

My heart fluttered.

I *felt* Dwayne staring at me from the side and turned to give him the universal 'What are you staring at?' shrug and brow raise. He shook his head and leaned toward me as Jason started singing. "He's not on the market," Dwayne whispered. "You know that, right?"

Now my racing heart tripped over its little arterial feet. How had Dwayne known I was crushing on him? I'd been *so* careful. My shock must've shown because he chuckled and shook his head again. "You've been mooning over him for weeks. How many times are you going to tell me what he wore to the gym? I think I know his wardrobe better than he does now."

My ears turned red. "I guess I have kinda talked about him. A little."

He snorted. "A little?" His eyes turned serious. "If I thought you had a shot with Jason, I'd be the first one telling you to go for it. The problem is that *nobody* has a shot with him. He's totally wrapped up in trying to make it in music and doesn't want anything that might be a distraction. There's been a line of men following him for years, but I can't remember the last time he actually went on a date."

My eyes fell. I loved having a friend who would be brutally honest, but hated his brutal honesty in that moment. "But he flirts with me at the gym. Like, *really* flirts."

"Michael, he would flirt with a rock if it could buy a ticket to one of his shows. I'm not trying to be cruel, but there's no hope there. Zero. It's better you realize that now than spend months—or longer—hoping for something that won't ever happen."

My eyes drifted back to the angel in his beam of light. His voice made me warm, and that smile … I didn't want to believe Dwayne, but replaying Jason's *flirting* at the gym made me question my confidence. He had left my side and continued his rounds to every person in the gym. He'd leaned over their machines—just as he had mine. He'd flashed the same smile, given the same intense gaze. He was a performer. It was *his job* to make people feel like they were the only person in the room when he spoke to them.

I wanted to be the only person in the room.

My heart finally settled into a slow, melancholy rhythm. Jason's songs were still amazing, but I struggled to keep my eyes on him as he delivered them. When I closed my eyes to escape, he was still there, smiling and making me feel things I didn't fully understand.

I couldn't escape him. I didn't want to.

Dwayne and I didn't talk much throughout the set. Jason finished, received raucous applause, then exited the stage to a waiting drink the bartender had made especially for the guest star of the evening. He didn't stop by or even glance in our direction.

I left the Wildhorse dejected.

Jason liked me. I *knew* it. He'd breathed on my neck while I did shoulder shrugs. Who did that? At least, who did that without liking the shoulder they're huffing on?

He *had* to like me.

Betty wandered aimlessly around downtown, partly because I didn't know where I wanted to go, and partly because I had the most atrocious sense of direction of any person alive. I could get lost pulling out of my own driveway. I definitely got lost that night.

When I finally found my bearings, it was around two in the morning. I was tired and sad. I wanted Jason to magically appear and tell me everything would be alright as he cradled me against his firm, muscular bosom.

Shit, I had it bad.

Without thinking, Betty found a familiar road. I recognized buildings and street signs. I pulled off to the side, into one of those parallel parking spaces that still confounded my driving skills, and rested my forehead against the steering wheel.

Footsteps jarred me out of my sad slumber. When I looked up, Jason had returned home and was walking from his car to his condo door.

Yes, I'd stalked my man-crush and was sitting outside his condo.

Give me *some* credit. I was parked discreetly across a little park that straddled his parking lot, not actually *in* the lot. The distinction might not sound like much to you, but to me it was the difference between a star-crossed lover and some psycho stalker. I was desperate to stay on the good side of that line, even though I knew I was dangerously close to crossing it.

Jason disappeared inside.

I needed air, so I did the smartest thing I could think of. I got out of my car and walked around the grassy park.

No, that *wasn't* very smart. It was precisely what a stalker would do as he bought time before sneaking inside to dismember his prey. I wanted Jason's member to remain intact. I had uses for his member. Dreams about it, actually. Dreams with condiments, or not.

Too much?

Anyway. Betty glared accusingly from her space by the park, and I finally drove my sorry, sad ass home.

Wednesdays sucked.

<h1 style="text-align:center">11</h1>

"You ended up where?" Dwayne bristled as he spoke. I'd never seen him upset or angry, but the color rising across his neck told me I was about to learn what his wrath was like. I shrank in my seat.

"I didn't go to his condo, just the park across from it."

"Michael, seriously?" He set his lime-laden drink down a little too hard, and poor Jack spilled all over the bar. "This isn't good. Not good at all. You can't turn into *that* kind of person. Do you hear me? What were you thinking?"

The preacher's kid in me knew exactly what I *should* be thinking, what I *should* be feeling. Guilt. That was the go-to. When all else failed, feel guilty. I was good at that.

So, I did.

"I'm sorry," my small voice answered. "I just wanted to see him again."

"That's no excuse. Promise me you'll never do anything like that again."

I looked up and found the most peaceful man I'd ever met glaring at me as though I'd run his mother down with my car. I wanted to crawl under the bar. "I promise," I squeaked.

Dwayne stood there and stared like a disappointed parent whose child had stolen a candy bar from their favorite local store—hands on his hips, brows furrowed, scowling mouth. He had the look perfectly set.

I couldn't meet his eyes.

Cowboy Rick wandered over and stepped in between us —well, as best he could from across the bar. He was like a boxing referee trying to break up two fighters from outside the ring. He leaned over.

"You guys alright? Dwayne, you need another?" He wiped up the spilled drink and swept the glass away.

Dwayne nodded but didn't speak, then the air whistled out of his balloon and he sat beside me. I felt his hand press against my shoulder.

"Michael, you're important to me. I really care about you. I want you to be happy." He sucked in a breath, seemingly buying himself time to measure his words. "I know last night wasn't who you are, and I also know you've got a big crush on a very unattainable boy. You have to let that go. Just trust me here, OK?"

I was so ashamed. Worse, I felt like I'd disappointed Dwayne.

I didn't trust myself to speak, so I just nodded.

12

A couple weeks passed. Most days were spent in utter boredom doing random tasks for my dad's business. Basketball season was entering the busy period, so I donned stripes most nights. On the few when I didn't have to referee, I followed my routine as if it were a religion: leave work at four-thirty, stop at the store for my pre-workout apple, work out, go home. Rinse and repeat.

Dwayne and I met up for lunch a couple times, but never talked about anything more substantial than the latest boy making his ankle bracelet buzz. I joked about getting a button I could use to make the imaginary device vibrate just to watch him twitch. That usually earned a halfhearted slap on the arm, but it was funny. Dwayne could always bring a smile to my face.

I tried not to think about Jason. That was easier said than done.

I'd never been in love before—and I didn't even know if this qualified for that lofty category, but I was definitely in *something*—in over my head, most likely.

Dwayne prodded a few times, ensuring my psycho-stalking proclivity hadn't returned. It hadn't. I was a smitten puppy, but one that took well to training. Daddy Dwayne said don't go there, so I didn't. Although, I *really* wanted to, even just to see Jason walk from his car to his door. His butt puckered as he walked. It was hot.

Ugh. I had to get a life.

I went straight from work to my high school basketball assignment. Officiating always made me feel better. Between the exercise and the intense focus it required, being on court was an escape from everyday problems, such as pining after some unattainable singer with wavy hair and sparkling teeth.

I got home around ten thirty, ate a snack, and tossed myself on the couch. Once again, the television programming gods had taken the lazy route and every channel was showing reruns of some show I didn't care about. I tried watching the news, but that was depressing.

Peter bounced into the room with his perpetually annoying well of bubbling energy. "I'm going out with the gang. Want to come?"

That meant he was going to a straight bar, probably a sports bar, with four girls who would preen and fawn over him all night. Yes, it was *exactly* as exciting as it sounded, especially to the guy who wouldn't be the object of any of the aforementioned fawning.

"Nah. I'm beat, might even turn in early," I said.

He finished lacing up his shoes. "Suit yourself, old man. It's Friday night and you're young. You need to get out more. Who knows? One of the girls tonight might actually like nerdy old men." He jabbed me good-naturedly with his elbow.

Yes, I knew I needed to tell him about the whole *liking boys* thing. A pang of guilt shot through me as I heard the door slam behind him. Peter was such a good guy, and an even better roommate. He deserved the truth—but I hadn't admitted *that* truth to myself yet. How was I supposed to say it out loud to someone else?

I flung my head into the fluffy comfort of our couch and stared at the ceiling, barely hearing the weatherman babbling about rain coming this weekend.

Maybe Peter was right. Maybe I should get out of the house and pull my mind out of my Jason-induced funk. I turned the TV off, wandered into my room, threw on some jeans and the cleanest shirt I could find, then headed out. The Connection was calling. This time, I swore I would stay long enough to actually experience the place—unless Fly Boy happened to be there again. I'd definitely leave early for another round of tie-your-partner.

Thirty minutes and three wrong turns later, I pulled into the parking lot. It was packed; cars were lined up halfway down the street. It had been full that first night Dwayne tricked me into going to a gay bar, but nothing like this. For some reason, butterflies were banging around inside my chest. I watched the guys laughing and hugging as they met each other in the line or ran into friends in the parking lot. The mood was festive.

Why was I suddenly nervous? Hadn't my two past visits been positive experiences, ending in happy … never mind.

A group of five incredibly fit guys in tight T-shirts strutted by. One of them craned his neck to get a look at me after they'd passed. He gave me a sexy grin and a wink.

This was *exactly* what I needed.

It took ten minutes to find a parking space, wait in line, and wade through the sardine can of an entrance. I turned into the country bar out of habit, as if a third visit could produce a habit. Cowboy Rick and two other bartenders were slinging drinks faster than Julia Childs chopping potatoes. For the heathens among us who don't get that reference, that means *really* fast. Think Ginsu knife fast.

I think I'm hungry. Anyway.

I got halfway through the throng before Rick looked up and saw me. I was surprised when he smiled broadly and waved me up to the bar, never missing a beat in his order-taking and drink-mixing. He was a true pro.

He craned across the bar and gave me a warm hug when I got close enough. I hadn't experienced the universal gay version of two kisses on either cheek, so my return squeeze was a little awkward. An old guy standing by, quietly sipping something fruity, grinned at my discomfort.

"You missed the past few weeks. Michael, right?" Rick really didn't miss a beat.

"Yeah, Dwayne dragged me to other places."

He looked around me. "Where is the old coot? I haven't seen him tonight."

I laughed. Anyone who made fun of Dwayne the same way I did had to be alright. "He's working late. I doubt he'll be out tonight. You know, being old and all."

Rick laughed as he shook a margarita. The old guy next to me scowled. Guess Grandpa didn't appreciate the jokes of young folk.

I turned to start scanning the crowd when a thunk drew me back to the bar. "On me. It's good to see you again." Rick winked and blew me an air kiss. "Can't chat. Busy, busy." He darted away to take another order.

I looked down to find a Coke with three limes stuffed on the rim, his little homage to our missing Dwayne. Cautiously, I sipped, wondering if he'd actually given me Dwayne's Drink-o-Death. Nope. Plain ol' Coke.

Damn, he was good.

Drink in hand, I wedged my way through the pack to get some air on the normally quiet outdoor patio. It, too, was packed, but the cooler air felt almost as good as the lack of cigarette smoke smelled. I hated that stuff.

The price we pay for a night of gay. Hey, I made a funny.

I laughed at my own silliness and took another sip, then wandered back inside and watched the line dancers do their thing. The floor was filled, as four full lines of dancers wiggled and kicked to fast-paced music. I was mesmerized. They danced through six full songs before I realized how long I'd been standing there. Each song had its own foot-work, and the pack of men knew every move. How was that possible? The DJ wasn't playing a rehearsed set, yet they could *name that tune* in three notes—mostly with their feet. It was impressive.

My country music tolerance was exceeded by the sixth song, so I decided to visit the main floor.

Holy Mary and Joseph ... and their dogs ... and cats ... and pet fish.

There was music and flashing lights, but absolutely no dancing. It wasn't possible. Overheated bodies were packed in so tight there was no hope of even a bad white-man dance, much less the more exotic kind I'd witnessed on the boxes a month ago. The mass of men just swayed, like one large organism under a microscope wobbling back and forth to the rhythm.

What surprised me the most was that no one seemed to

care about their arms being pinned to their sides by the wall of half-naked, sweaty bodies. Come to think of it, that might've been the whole point of being there.

Little Michael found room to dance as the pack of muscular men who'd passed while I was parking moved in around me. The Winker handed his drink to a buddy then turned to face me. There was no avoiding his chest pressing into mine as the amoeba swayed toward my side of the floor. That sent a thrill up my spine. I looked up and he was smiling, his eyes locking on mine. One of his hands teased my arm, starting with my wrist and slowly tracing a path up to my shoulder. His fingertips barely touched the hairs on my arms, lighting my skin on fire as they passed. When I shivered, his grin broadened.

I was frozen. Little Michael wasn't. Winker's other hand pressed into him and his eyes widened in a smile that matched the one parting his mouth. There was more than amusement in his gaze. There was hunger.

Damn, I was hungry too.

He leaned forward and pressed a soft kiss on my lips, then leaned his mouth to my ear. "Find me later. I'm Thomas."

I tried to breathe. His warm breath clung to the skin of my neck, and I watched as he and his friends vanished into the crowd. He looked back once and winked again.

The sound of applause shook me out of my stare. I turned toward the noise to find two young guys giggling and clapping. One of them called out, "Honey, you tease those boys." Another round of giggles ensued and they drifted away.

When did *I* do any teasing? I was the unsuspecting, innocent teasee in this situation—not that I was complaining.

I'd never had much confidence, and here I was being approached by darn hot men. Not approached—kissed and rubbed and teased. They wanted to tease *me*. The butterflies had to move aside because a wave of newfound pride swelled my recently worked-out pecs. I threw my head up, chest out, and strutted my way through the crowd. My butt was squeezed three separate times during that strut. Anywhere else, we might be calling the police. In that bar, my puffiness grew with every grab. They were grabbing *my* butt! I was a butt-grabbable gay—

Guy. I meant, butt-grabbable *guy*.

I still wasn't G.

I couldn't be *that*.

13

———————

The next night, I couldn't wait for midnight and another visit to the Connection. According to Cowboy Rick, Saturdays were busier than Fridays. I had a hard time believing they could fit in any more people than I'd seen the night before, but Oracle Rick proved himself omniscient.

Holy gays on a stick, it was even more crowded than before. The line to get in was nearly to the street—not the cars, the people queuing out front.

I was giddy.

Committed to my ritual, I visited Rick, got my *on me* Coke, watched some line dancing, then headed to the main floor. Michael must follow routine.

After my third lap around the dance floor—and two glorious butt squeezes—I decided to head to my original hiding space in the corner. I needed a break, and it would be nice to just watch and breathe without so many bodies pressing against me. When I got to that side of the bar, I was annoyed to find someone standing in my spot. How dare he? Didn't he know that was where I lurked in the darkness?

Then I looked a little closer. Oh, this one was hot. Maybe he *could* stand in my spot, after all.

He was tall, maybe six three, with short brown hair. The disco lights flashing in the darkness made it impossible to tell much more than that, but his white T-shirt glowed luminescent. I *could* see a massive chest poking through strained fabric. Little Michael loved some big chesticles. He let me know it too.

I stood three guys over from White Shirt for two songs, sneaking peeks when I thought he wasn't looking.

Holy Massive Man Boobs.

Halfway through the fourth song, I was actually watching someone else as they climbed atop a box when a voice startled me. "You've been watching me."

I jumped as I turned and found myself eye-level with delicious, hard, erect nipples—I mean White Shirt.

His nipples *were* erect.

But fear not, I was smooth. "I, uh, what? No. I wasn't. I mean, kind of. But not really. I wouldn't—"

He laughed and cocked his head, studying me quietly. His eyes twinkled in the flashes of light. "You're cute," he said with a smile.

I was completely befuzzled now. "Thanks. Um, you have big boobs. Ugh, I mean chest. You have a nice chest. It's big and hard. *Your chest*, I mean. Oh, never mind."

The brilliance of my reddened face had surely lit up the darkness, and I turned to seek the fastest exit.

His hand cupped my cheek before I could. He guided my face, urging my eyes back to his. "Thank you."

I had just verbally thrown up on my shoes and all he said was, 'Thank you?' What the actual fuck?

"I'm Carter."

Finally, something I couldn't screw up. "I'm Jason—I mean, Michael. I'm Michael."

"Who's Jason?"

"Not me. I'm not him. He's not me. I mean … I'm Michael."

Had someone struck my head rather than squeezed my ass? What was happening? I swear I'm a smart, well-spoken guy, but in that moment, English was *definitely* my second language.

He chuckled. "Would you like to go into the show bar? They won't start for another thirty minutes, and it'll be easier to talk without all this." He waved his hand at the amoeba.

I nodded, afraid to open my mouth and let stupid fall out again, then followed as he shoved his way into the open space of the show bar.

The lights were still bright—well, as bright as bar lights got before closing—and I could see Carter more clearly. His eyes were a light hazel, made even lighter by the black-light effect of his white shirt. He had a strong jaw and chiseled features that matched the impressive chest my eyes couldn't stay away from.

As he started to speak, his lips commanded my attention—and not for the reason you're thinking, you dirty possum. They formed an incredibly thin line, almost as if no lips existed, only an opening through which he spoke. When his mouth was closed, a tiny speed bump surfaced, giving the impression he was smirking even when he wasn't. It was odd and unlike any lips I'd seen before, but kind of cute in a malformed-Ken-doll's-missing-penis sort of way.

They were different, but definitely didn't make him less hot.

"This is much better. I can actually hear you in here."
He held up an empty plastic cup. "I need a refill. What are
you having?"

I raised my empty cocktail glass. "Just Coke."

His lips quirked. Twerked. Pursed. I really didn't know
what to call it. "*Just* Coke? You're not drinking?"

I shook my head. "Alcohol makes me sleepy. Coke is
good."

He chuckled and shrugged. When he returned, he
handed me a plastic cup filled with fizzy goodness. There
were three limes on the rim. "The bartender said you
needed those. I've learned not to question the staff here."

I looked up and was shocked to find a bartender I didn't
know. He grinned and waved. Apparently, the Gay Force
was strong with this one.

"You come here a lot?" he asked, staring at the limes.

I shook my head mid-sip. "This is just my third time."

He gave the lime a last glare, then looked out toward
the stage. "Yeah. I don't mind the bars, I guess, but they're
not my favorite. All the smoke drives my sinuses crazy, and
half the guys are just looking to get laid."

The little voice in my head spoke. *Guilty as charged,
Your Honor.* I licked his chest with my eyes again. *Seriously guilty, sir.*

My normal voice said, "Yeah, I know what you mean. I
hate how my jeans smell like smoke even after I wash
them."

He quirked his head and smiled, studying me again. It
wasn't the *come fuck me* look I'd gotten from Winker the
night before, though I wasn't complaining about that. No,
his gaze was earnest, curious, intrigued. I think he wanted
to learn about me, not just get me naked.

This was different.

Over the next thirty minutes, I learned that Carter was an executive for a shoe company. He did numbers or stats or something. He spoke in precise, clipped phrases when talking about work, and I got the impression he was a muckety-muck of some sort. My eyes glazed as he described inventory and the inner workings of the footwear business. He'd been with the same company for more than fifteen years and was very proud to have built a 401(k) in the high five figures. I'd have to remember to find out what a 401(k) was later.

He'd been married for a few years and had two small children.

Huh. How did that work for a gay man?

He explained that he'd met his ex-wife in college, and they'd done what was expected. He'd known he was attracted to men, but didn't know any gays and thought *it* would just go away when he got married. He'd joined a church with his wife and had two kids trying to make *it* go away.

It never went away.

Now he was divorced with shared custody. His wife was as good with him being gay as a woman could be. She'd been hurt, wanted to know what she'd done *to turn him*, but in the end loved him enough to want Carter to live a happy life without hiding his true self.

I'd lost track of time when men started filling up the seating. It was getting harder to hear each other.

"Looks like the show is about to start," he said.

I looked around and nodded.

"Do you like drag?" he asked.

I'd never really thought about it. I shrugged. "I guess it's OK. Wearing women's clothes isn't my thing, but if someone else wants to do it, why not?"

He rolled his eyes and chuckled. "I need another drink before this starts. Want one? Still Coke?"

"Sure. Thanks."

He reached out, gripped my shoulder gently and held it a second, then turned to walk to the bar.

This was the strangest bar meeting ever. He was such a nice guy, and genuinely wanted to know about me, who I was, what I liked, what made me happy. In my vast experience of three visits to the bar, no one had wanted to get to know *me*, only Little Michael.

Again, not judging. Little Michael enjoyed the attention; *craved* it, actually. My sheltered youth among the wolf pack cried out for him to get more action.

But there was something about Carter, about this conversation, how he looked at me … I don't know. It was new and somehow *more*. It didn't make me want to strip down and hump like Winker had, but it brought a smile to my face. A strange warmth I didn't recognize flowed in my chest.

A moment later, Carter returned with the promised refill. Our fingers touched as he handed me my Coke, and I let them linger a second before securing the plastic cup. There it was again, that warmth.

We watched three songs' worth of drag before reaching a mutual point of boredom. Don't get me wrong, the drag queens in Nashville were world class, with their massive wigs and even bigger boobs. They probably spent hours squeezing into their heavily sequined gowns. I didn't want to know how much makeup they puttied on before entering the stage—it was Tammy Faye thick. Beyond their appearance, the queens were incredible performers, as comfortable on stage as anyone you might see in Vegas. Sure, most of them lip-synched to the music, but they were on point with it. There were even a few who sang, and their voices were Nashville-starving-artist impressive.

So when I say we reached our tipping point, it wasn't out of disrespect for the quality of the entertainment. Drag just wasn't a passion for either of us, as it appeared to be for the enthusiastic fans currently screaming and waving dollar bills from the front row. They *really* loved men in dresses.

We walked back toward the dance bar and Carter paused, then he committed one of the most grievous gay-bar sins imaginable. He yawned. And not one of those tiny covered-by-the-back-of-one's-hand yawns. This was a full-throated, lay-your-head-back-and-belt-it-out yawn. He didn't even bother trying to cover his mouth, and I could hear the satisfied groan-like sound over the competing disco and drag music. He turned to me with an unapologetic look.

"I think it's time for me to go. My battery's getting low." He gave me a pursed smile, then leaned over and kissed my cheek. "I'd like to see you again, if you're up for it."

I guessed being shocked out of my mind was going to become a regular occurrence at the Connection. While my emotions throughout the night were generally less about forking than spooning, I still thought we'd end up hooking up. Wasn't that what all gays did when they went to a bar? It's practically a rule or something, right? Wasn't that why we paid a cover—to *guarantee* a lucky night? No one had given me a copy of the Gay Handbook yet, and I was sure it would be murky on this point.

I looked up at his sincere face and smushy, thin lips. He had kind eyes. With a quick nod, I said, "I'd really like that."

He grabbed my hand and led me to the long bar by the disco floor, then waved one of the five bartenders down. Five. Seriously. And they were never standing still or without a glass to fill. It was remarkable.

The hottie behind the bar gave Carter two business cards with the Connection's logo and phone number stamped on them. On the reverse side was a series of prompts for patrons to complete, like a questionnaire you fill out when starting a new job.

My name and number:

His name and number:

How I can remember him:

I actually laughed out loud as I read that last one. It made sense. In an ocean filled with pecs, lats, and triceps—and every other kind of exposed muscle—you might need a note to remember which guy had given which card.

Were we all *total* sluts?

Carter handed me his card without completing question three. I did the same, not wanting to presume his memory aid for him, though I got the impression he didn't give his number out often.

He leaned over, kissed my cheek tenderly one last time, then turned and made his way to the parking lot. I watched him until he disappeared. He towered over most of the guys. More than a few of them turned to admire his chest as he passed, and a spike of red-hot something seared through me. Was I jealous? I'd just met him. That was ridiculous. Then a guy reached up and touched his chest, and that spike turned into a Lorena Bobbitt stab—or was she more a cutter? Ew. Never mind.

When he was out of sight, I turned back to the bar and looked at the card he'd handed me, its neat cursive script like a warm smile. I grabbed the pen and wrote my memory aid in spot number three: *Big chest. Tiny lips. Shoe guy.*

14

———

Morning came annoyingly early the next day. Peter was his usually chipper self, blending some kind of terrible concoction that I supposed helped him extend the life of his ever-present abs.

I really hated his perfection, especially since he spent most of his in-apartment time without a shirt. He was just being comfortable and had no idea how *un*comfortable it made me.

God, he was beautiful.

Anyway. Stop distracting me.

I shuffled my bleary-headed butt to the counter and nearly fell asleep watching the blender spin.

"Late night?" he asked with a smirk.

I shrugged. "I guess. Got in around one thirty or so."

"Oh, so didn't get any ass?"

Ass? Oh shit. He'd never asked that before. What did he mean? Was he being literal? Did he suspect something?

Panic rushed through me and I broke into a cold sweat. We couldn't have *that* conversation now. Maybe never.

He grinned as I squirmed. "So you didn't meet any girls worth mentioning? Thought so. Don't worry, we all strike out some nights."

Whew. I breathed again. Girls have asses too, right? "Yeah, totally struck out. That's why I came home early."

Thank you, baby Jesus.

He downed his Titanic-sized glass of protein madness, then padded into his room to *finally* put on a shirt and head to the gym. Sundays were busy with his personal training clients, and I knew I wouldn't see him again before seven or so. On his way out, he gave me a good bro-tap on the shoulder. I tried not to wish it was more, but the little devil was getting louder every day. The angel must've been bound and gagged somewhere in the recesses of my subconscious, probably with silk ties—I hadn't heard her voice in months.

Following Peter's example, I mindlessly prepared a healthy breakfast, of a cherry Pop Tart with icing and sprinkles. Hey, stop laughing. Those things are a gift from the gods. All of them. The whole Mount Olympus gang granted humans a glorious inheritance when Pop Tarts were bequeathed upon us.

OK. Maybe they weren't *all* that, but they were tasty. Especially with a little melted butter.

As I stuffed the last crusty bite into my mouth, our ancient phone whirred and halted my chewing. Who would call at this hour? It was eleven o'clock in the morning on a Sunday. How rude!

"Hello?"

"Hi. Is this Michael?" I immediately recognized the voice. Images of hard, rounded pecs materialized in my mind, and I couldn't stop a reflexive smile.

"Hey, Carter."

There was a second of silence, then he said, "You recognized my voice?" I thought he sounded pleased and was teasing me a bit.

"We did talk for over an hour last night." I decided to tease back. "It's eleven o'clock the day after we met. Miss me already?"

He chuckled, and I could see his itty-bitty lips curling upward. "I wouldn't go *that* far, but I guess I was thinking about you this morning. Does that count?"

That warmth rushed to greet me again. I reveled in its touch. He *had* missed me. Holy cow … and chicken … and pig. Please, English, stay my primary language. "Oh sure. That counts. You *definitely* missed me." My heart thrilled at the adorable giggle I heard through the receiver. "So, what do you do when you miss a boy you just met?" I was getting a little brave, maybe even cocky. This was fun.

He cleared his throat. "Well, in my world, I invite him to dinner. I like to cook, and from the looks of his shoulders and arms poking through his shirt last night, he has to eat to keep growing."

I nearly passed out. He'd noticed *my* arms? A guy with pecs the size of Kansas had noticed *my* chicken wings? English abandoned me. "Yeah, well, uh, I do eat. I mean, I like to eat. And have to, you know, for working out. 'Cause I do. Work out, I mean. And eat."

What had been a giggle turned in to a deep, full-throated laugh. There wasn't a mirror in our living room, but I was surely as red as the sprinkles I'd just devoured. I sounded like a complete and utter babbling idiot.

But the gentleman on the other end of the phone didn't pounce. He didn't take advantage of my obvious discomfort. He simply calmed himself and said, "Good. If you're

OK coming to my place, I'd like to cook you dinner tonight. Say, six o'clock?"

"Six?" I said, as if I'd need to confirm with my social secretary or some silliness. "Sure, I think that'll work."

What a moron.

He gave me a second to grab a pen. The only paper I could find was the Connection card from last night, which was actually perfect. I'd have all his info in one place. I jotted down his address, then hung up the phone.

The second the receiver hit the cradle, I was up in front of the television doing the goofiest white-man happy dance you've ever seen, chicken wings flapping wildly in the breeze. I couldn't contain my excitement. It just came out.

The growing pile of laundry in the corner practically flagged me back down to earth. Shit. I had work to do if I was going to be halfway presentable in a room brighter than the Connection's black-lit dance floor.

Then it hit me. I was actually going on a date—a real, sit-and-eat-dinner date—*with a guy*. For some reason, that made me more nervous than any other interaction I'd had with a man. Fly Boy had tried to shove himself all the way up to my lungs, but the thought of having dinner with a nice guy made me want to run and vomit at the same time. What evil magic was this?

I needed serious help before facing Carter again, so I grabbed the phone and called the one person who would know what to do.

"Hey, Michael. What's up?" Dwayne's warm voice sounded through the receiver.

"Code Red! Or DEFCON One. Or whatever term you gays use when there's an emergency. I need a Dwayne lunch, stat!"

He laughed at my excitement and appalling use of

terms I clearly didn't understand. "Sure. I'm not doing anything. See you at the diner in an hour?"

"Great. Thanks. Oh, and this is a good emergency. Great, actually. The best."

He was laughing as I hung up the phone.

I'm such a goofball.

15

For the first time since we'd met, I beat Dwayne to the diner and was sitting at our usual table, iced tea half-empty, when he arrived. The startled expression on his face was quickly replaced by a broad smile. He was always happy to see me. What an amazing friend.

"Alright. I'm here. What's the emergency?" he asked as he slid into the booth.

"I met a guy last night."

He rolled his eyes. "Yeah, it was Saturday. What's new these days?"

"Dwayne, this one was different. We actually *talked*."

He barked a laugh. "You know that's actually allowed? In fact, I highly encourage it. Did you get his name before he banged you into last week?"

"Ha ha. His name is Carter. He's a shoe guy."

His brows quirked like two caterpillars humping above his nose. He needed to take a weed whacker to them soon or someone might revoke his gay card. "Shoe guy?" he asked.

"Yeah, exec for a shoe company. I think he's their CFO

or comptroller or something. I didn't totally understand, but he sounded like a big deal."

Katie appeared and plopped down beside me, playfully shoving me out of the way with her ample hips. "Scoot it, precious. How are my boys?"

She was perky today.

Dwayne chuckled at my discomfort. "We're great. We're celebrating. Michael actually *talked* to a boy last night."

She feigned being impressed with bulging eyes and her mouth shaped like a giant O. "Good for you, little one. Just be careful. Most men only want one thing."

Dwayne nearly fell out of the booth laughing. When he came up for air, his eyes were moist. "Oh, that's usually what the little one beside you is hunting for. We're celebrating him actually getting the guy's name and having a conversation that *didn't* involve exchanging fluids."

"Dwayne!" I was shocked and embarrassed. Was I really *that* slutty?

"Look, Slutisha."

"Slutisha?" Now it was Katie's turn to cry. She wrapped her arm around my shoulders and gave me a squeeze. "You have your fun. You're only young once. Just be careful, OK?"

Her transition from hilarity to motherly advice jarred me a bit. There was genuine concern in her eyes. "I will. Thanks."

She took our orders and extracted herself from the booth, then shook her head and giggled as she walked away. I could hear her mutter "Slutisha" between chuckles.

Over lunch, I babbled, giving Dwayne every detail from last night with Carter. He listened with his usual attentiveness, asking questions and chuckling when I told him about the bartender loading me up with limes.

"You've only been there three times and the staff are already taking care of you. That's Rick's doing."

I was dumbfounded. "Why? There are thousands of guys there on the weekend. Why would they do that for me?"

He shrugged. "Hanging out with Jason over the years, I've learned a little about the bar community. The staff, at least the ones who've been there for a few years, are like family. They see everything you can imagine—and probably stuff neither of us can imagine. They look out for each other and for those they like or care about."

I still didn't get it. "OK, but why me? I've only talked to Rick a few times, and I'd never even met the bartender in the show bar."

He smiled. "I'm part of the family, and they know you're important to me."

He didn't elaborate. I wanted to ask a dozen more questions because that didn't make any sense to my wolfy brain, but he threw cash on the table and stood. "I need to run some errands, and you have laundry to do." He paused, then gave me a conspiratorial grin. "Please, pick a shirt without holes. I know you haven't earned your gay card yet, but you have to do better than that on a date."

I looked down at the small tear just above my right pec. "Good call."

I ONLY MADE ONE WRONG TURN DRIVING TO CARTER'S house. It added five minutes to the trek, but I'd left much earlier than was necessary, determined to be on time for my first official date with a dude. I found his house, then drove past, stopping in front of a neighbor's home a few houses down. My palms were wet and the lone random napkin in the car was now soaked. Terror struck as I looked at my hair in the mirror. I tried to make it lay down, but more than one cow had licked it to death earlier in the day —and they hadn't even thanked me for the action. How rude.

Realizing nothing would help the hair situation, I took a few deep breaths to try to slow my pulse. Why couldn't I breathe? This was ridiculous. We'd already met and talked for an hour. Now we were having dinner. It was just dinner. I ate all the time. I knew how to do dinner without throwing up on my shoes. There was *nothing* to be jittery about.

The pep talk didn't work. I was about to pee myself right there on Betty's faux-leather seats.

Baby Jesus, please don't let me pee myself. I'm begging.

I parked in Carter's driveway and stared up at the modest, one-story ranch home. His yard sprawled for a good half-acre and was full of lush, well-tended grass. The iconic red and yellow of a Cozy Coupe peeking around the corner caught my eye, and I remembered he had two toddlers. For some reason, that made me even more nervous.

Lord, I was a mess.

The door opened and Carter appeared wearing a long blue apron. On it, a salt shaker was dueling with a pepper shaker, each combatant wielding a steak knife like a sword. It was cute and somehow fit what I knew of him perfectly.

He watched through the screen door, then stepped out and tilted his head to the side as he walked up to Betty's driver's-side door. I rolled down the window.

"You want to eat out here?" he asked, a smirk playing on his lips.

My head swiveled around Betty, as if taking him seriously. I was such an idiot. "Uh, no, sorry. I was just … never mind."

He chuckled as I finally got out of the car. He pulled the oven mitt I hadn't seen off one hand and gave me a hug and peck on the cheek. Holy shit, I piddled. Right there in his driveway, I felt myself piddle my jeans a little bit.

Baby Jesus, why do you hate me? I even begged.

Thankfully, he didn't seem to notice and I followed him inside.

Carter's house was tasteful and simple, as modest and functional as the outside. I couldn't believe how clean it was; I had flashbacks of the mounds of laundry and other unknown objects strewn about my apartment. He was like an adult or something.

I asked to use his restroom, and he pointed down a narrow hallway. I didn't really have to go anymore, but the piddle spot needed work. On the way, I passed a bedroom. A mound of toys rose out of a bin in the corner, and brightly colored sheets and comforters covered the beds. I wasn't up on kids' cartoons and didn't recognize the characters frolicking across the covers. The room was small, but cozy and bright. It felt happy.

The smell of dripping chicken fat made my stomach gurgle. Satisfied the error of my ways had been corrected, I washed my hands and hurried down the hall toward the kitchen. There was no formal dining room, but the breakfast nook held a round wooden table laden with platters and dishes. Either Carter ate way more food than I thought possible, or he had serious portion control problems. I really didn't care which was true. It smelled amazing.

He looked up from stirring and smiled. As I leaned in the doorway to watch him in action, he handed me a tall glass filled with fizzing liquid. The rim was so covered in limes I didn't have room to take a sip. He chuckled as he handed it to me, evidently proud of his little joke, then gave me another peck on the cheek.

Damn if I didn't piddle again. What was this boy doing to me?

I evacuated the doorway and sat quickly at the table to cover my new wet spot. It wasn't like I'd unloaded my bladder, but the tiny bloom was growing and I wanted to protect my dignity.

A moment later, he set the last of the steaming dishes on the table and joined me, a glass of white wine in hand.

"I hope you like baked chicken with Cajun spices. I tend to cook simple and healthy. It's more a lifestyle than a diet these days. When you get to my age, you have to watch it more."

"Your age?" I blurted out, immediately regretting it.

He didn't flinch. "Yep. I'm thirty-six."

Holy cow. He was *old*. I was on a date with an old guy. How was he so hot at that age?

He must've seen the questions spinning in my head. "You're what, twenty-two, three?"

I puffed my chest out. "Twenty-four. Turn twenty-five in March."

He grinned as his brows rose. "Happy early birthday. You're moving up a box."

I cocked my head, confused, and he grinned. "On forms and insurance. You know, the check boxes usually go in five-year increments. You're moving to a new bracket on paperwork. It's sort of a milestone."

He sounded so smart when he talked.

I'd never thought about any of that. I didn't own any insurance and didn't have a 401(k). Hell, I worked for my dad. I suddenly felt tiny and unaccomplished.

He placed a hand on my arm and squeezed. "Enjoy being young. Before long, you'll round down with birthdays rather than up."

We grinned at each other like fools and he gestured for me to tuck in. He didn't need to tell me twice; the spread looked incredible. I just hoped my brain remembered how to use cutlery and, you know, chew without spilling down my front. The last thing I wanted was to have him hand me one of his children's bibs. He asked about working with my dad, and I asked about his work, though it sounded terribly boring. When he talked about his kids, the whole room lit up. Cade was three and Christian was five. Cade was finally learning more words, making it easier to know what he wanted. Carter beamed as he told me Cade called him "Ba Ba," the three-year-old version of Christian's "Daddy."

Carter's cheeks formed little dimples when he smiled. I wanted to reach up and run my thumb over one, but resisted. They were adorable.

He was adorable. No, he was hot, despite his advanced age.

Things grew quiet after that, save for the clanging and scraping of knives and forks. The silence became awkward.

"You OK?" I asked. He met my eyes. I could tell he wanted to ask something, but was afraid to. "Ask me anything. I'm an open book."

He sucked in a breath, and a suddenly tiny voice asked, "Do you like kids?"

I watched him. He was so sincere, so open and honest. I could feel his heart seize as he asked that question. Tension hung in the air. As nervous as I had been earlier, it never crossed my mind that *he* might hold some secret angst too. Yet here it was. Laid on the table as plainly as the Cajun chicken.

I kept my eyes steady and firm. "I do. Like them more than adults most of the time."

The relief on his face was perhaps the most beautiful thing I'd ever seen. I knew in that moment that he loved Cade and Christian more than life itself, and finding someone to share that joy with was core to his own happiness.

I also understood that as warm and loving as Carter was, as much as his children filled his life with laughter, he was *lonely*. He didn't just want companionship, he craved it, but was terrified it would elude him.

How I saw all that in one glance, I couldn't explain, but it was there. It was written across his face, and I could feel it slamming into my every sense.

He finally spoke again. "I don't date a lot, but so many guys run the second they learn about Cade and Christian." His eyes fell to his plate as his head drooped.

My heart ached for him. I reached across and gripped his hand. "I'm not running, Carter. I'm right here."

WE SEEMED TO HAVE BROKEN THROUGH SOME ICY WALL I hadn't realized was there, because Carter relaxed and conversation flowed freely. We finally set our forks down, and I scanned the empty platters. We'd done serious damage, and it was delicious. Sure, it was meat with some spices, but Carter really knew his way around a chicken.

Stop snickering. Not *that* kind of chicken. Although, on behalf of chickens everywhere, I hoped he knew his way around *that* kind too. It would come in handy should we ever get naked. Glancing at his chest again, I really wanted that to happen soon.

Anyway.

His eyes widened when I insisted on helping him wash and put away the dishes. He washed, and I dried. Our elbows bumped more often than the rag hitting the wet plates. We laughed and cut up like little boys. It was odd how such a simple domestic task could turn into something so endearing, but I caught him smiling at me several times when he thought I wasn't looking. I suspect he caught me doing the same a time or two.

The whole night felt good. No, it felt *comfortable*, like putting on an old pair of slippers you found in the back of the closet. They fit just right, and warmed you in ways no new pair ever could.

Was it bad I just compared Shoe Guy to slippers?

Carter suggested we watch a movie. Lord, was that the story of my life or what? Did all gay men use the 'let's watch a movie' thing to get into each other's pants? Flashes of my first date with Joseph played in my head. The more I thought about it, the more I liked the idea, and wondered if Carter would make a move once we hit the couch.

I don't remember what movie we picked, but there were no moves. Carter got a couple pillows from the kids' room and stretched out on his extra-wide sofa. He patted the cushion in front of him, and I took my seat. He chuckled, reached up and gripped my shoulders, then repositioned me so I was prone in front of him. He pulled me tight against his chest with one arm. I nearly piddled again as I felt his pecs pressing against my back and the corded muscles of his arms envelop me.

Once the movie started, and I realized we really were

going to watch it, I settled in and let myself enjoy the comfort and safety of his strength. He was tall enough that I wedged perfectly under his chin. A few times, I felt him squeeze a little tighter and nuzzle his chin against my head.

We just fit.

As the credits began to roll, I stirred and began to sit up.

"Want a snack?" he asked from behind.

I turned to face him, my dirty little mind wondering if he meant what I was thinking by *snack*. "Sure," I said, leaving our options open.

He untangled himself and padded into the kitchen.

Damn it. He meant an actual snack. Oh well.

I followed and watched as he pulled out a tub of cottage cheese and two cans of fruit—you know, the mixed fruit in a can with the little cherries. He scooped out a healthy bowl of cottage cheese, then topped it with the fruit, dropped in a spoon, and handed it to me. He made himself a bowl and lifted his spoon in salute. "I eat this every night before bed," he said, bringing his first bite to his mouth.

I couldn't remember the last time I'd eaten cottage cheese. Mixed with the fruit, it was actually tasty.

Wait, he'd said 'before bed,' hadn't he? My heart skipped a beat between spoonfuls. I looked up to find him watching me intently. My heart leapt into high gear, and I had a little trouble swallowing my bite.

He reached up with a napkin and wiped my lip.

Holy shit. *He just wiped my lip.*

It was the sweetest thing anyone had ever done to me— I mean, *for* me. Stop snickering.

I swooned, but tried to cover it by taking another bite.

"I have to work tomorrow, but you're welcome to stay —if you want to." That last part sounded like it came more from Cade than Carter. Was he as nervous as I was? Was that possible?

I met his eyes and hesitated. He struggled to hold my gaze this time. No way! He *was* nervous.

I asked the first thing that popped into my head. "Will you hold me like you did on the couch?"

His eyes snapped to mine, all hesitation gone, and he smiled. "All night long."

16

———————

"He held me *all night*, Dwayne. We slept in our underwear, and he never tried to do anything other than kiss me goodnight. I don't think I've ever felt so safe and at peace in my life." I took a bite of eggs. "You need to meet Carter. I want to know what you think. He seems too good to be true—and did I mention he has a *massive* chest?"

Dwayne laughed and dribbled a little coffee onto the table. "Yes, thank you very much, you have mentioned his chest at least a dozen times—and yes, I *always* have to approve. Don't you ever forget that. You'd be completely lost without me."

I gave him a childish scowl. "Totally lost, no doubt."

Over the next twenty minutes, Dwayne sipped in silence as I recounted every tiny detail of my first full night with Carter.

I grew up in the South, and, like any self-respecting southerner, can make any one-syllable word stretch into at least three, sometimes four, without much effort. People sometimes get annoyed at how slowly my mouth moves.

Again, not *that* way, you naughty possum.

Despite my drawl, sitting at that table recounting the most magical night of my life—and yes, I actually said that—Dwayne could barely keep up. I bounded from dinner to the couch to the cuddling to the kids, then back to when he greeted me at the door in an apron. Just when he thought I was coming up for air, I went back to something Carter had said at the bar that made me laugh.

I was a babbling, bubbling, blithering, *besotted* boy.

About halfway through my endless monologue, Dwayne began grinning. He sat back against the hard, shiny cushion of the booth and cradled his coffee. Once or twice, I caught him glance up and wink. I assumed Katie was hovering nearby. I'd later learn she was eavesdropping nearly the whole time, and the two conspirators were communicating through some diner-inspired telepathic link as I talked. How rude!

Dwayne took a long sip and slowly set his mug down. I could tell by the gleam in his eyes *something* was up. He was about to spring a trap. Oh boy.

"So." He dragged the word out to a respectable four syllables. "I assume you're seeing him again?"

Not what I expected. I nodded. "He asked me for dinner Friday night, at his place again."

His brows rose slightly. "So that would be a second date, right?"

I shrugged, not sure where Inspector Gadget was headed. "I know. Hard to believe, isn't it? A week ago I was bed-hopping, now I can't wait for Friday to get here so I can see the guy I *didn't* sleep with again. Well, technically, I guess we did *sleep* together, but you know what I mean."

He rolled his eyes, then quirked his mouth into a lopsided grin and cocked his head. I think he was trying to look innocent, like he was about to ask something out of sheer curiosity with no hidden meaning or agenda.

Now I *knew* a trap was coming.

"So, help me understand something. How can a *straight guy* go on a second date with a gay man?"

I froze, the buttery English muffin stopping just before it hit my mouth. I think I dropped it. I don't remember.

His grin smoothed, and he continued. "I think it's time you looked inward and figured some things out. If Carter really is a good guy, he deserves to date someone who has his head together, not someone scared to face who he really is."

Damn. That cut deeper than I expected.

I didn't know how to respond. My face had surely turned pale because I felt a nauseous chill all over my body. When I got the courage to look into his eyes again, he didn't flinch or move or waver. He was a rock.

I looked away.

Part of me was ashamed he even had to say that to me, but another part of me was terrified of the implications of facing his words. Deep down, I knew he was right, but I wasn't ready for that. I *couldn't* be ready. Everything I'd ever been taught—and everything I knew with certainty, everything that was good and right—told me I could never be ready to face—or admit—*that*.

If I ever admitted …

If I said it out loud …

What would my parents …

It would break their hearts.

The diner began to spin and I couldn't suck in air. I

squirmed in the booth, desperate to get comfortable, to stop the clawing heat spreading across my skin.

Then my mind flashed to Carter.

What was I doing? Was Dwayne right, was I leading him on? Was I taking a good man—*and his sons*—down a path I couldn't see to the end, whatever end that might be? Was I letting my desire to be accepted, appreciated, admired, or whatever it was I really wanted but didn't yet understand, cloud my judgment and moral compass? That stupid compass had been spinning out of control for a while. I wished it would just point in one direction so I could know what was right again. It was so much easier before, never questioning, never doubting, simply following the path laid out for me. I was beginning to wonder if my compass was faulty or actually broken.

I wanted to run from the diner, to get as far from Dwayne and his questions as I could, but my legs wouldn't move. I was stuck to the seat—and not in the fun way you're thinking of.

Dwayne's voice brought my eyes back up to his. "I need to use the restroom. Why don't you breathe a little while I'm gone? Holding it in that long can't be good for your health."

There was an undertone to his voice, but I didn't get it. There were often layers to his words, and I wasn't adept enough to see all of them, much less know what they represented. His footsteps faded, but I didn't look up. My eyes were fixed on some indistinct point on the table.

A moment later, someone scooted into the booth beside me. I assumed it was Dwayne, but Katie's slender arm wrapped around my shoulders and pulled me into her. An odd mix of bacon, eggs, bleach, and cheap perfume flooded my senses. Her voice was calm as she whispered in my ear.

"Sweetie, everything will be alright. *You* will be alright. You are beautiful and perfect just the way you are." She kissed the top of my head and squeezed me tighter.

My throat caught.

A jumble of emotions I couldn't name, much less understand, tumbled out of me all at once, and my shoulders heaved. I fell into her embrace, giving up any semblance of control. I couldn't stop the tears. I hadn't known they were there, but they raced forward like a horse released from its paddock, wild and uncontained, desperate to run freely. I felt them streak down my face, but also churn in my gut—and even more in my heart.

I don't remember how long we sat there, how long she held me and stroked my hair with the gentleness only mothers possess. In that moment, I needed her embrace more than I needed oxygen.

Somehow Dwayne had known that and had sent her to me. She knew it too.

Looking back, I'm sure she missed working some tables and had to get another waitress to cover, but she never looked up or fidgeted. No one ever came to interrupt the scene playing out in our booth. What an act of incredible kindness.

How had I been so lucky to have those two in my life?

Dwayne sat quietly at the counter drinking coffee and watching from a respectful distance. When my sobs subsided, Katie lifted my chin with her hand and wiped my cheeks with smooth, soft fingers. She kissed my forehead, rubbed the lipstick off with her thumb, then stood and walked back to resume her work.

I stared after her, a hollow shell, unsure if I could move, unsure if I should.

Then Dwayne appeared beside me, his hand resting on

my shoulder. "Come on. Let's get out of here. I took care of breakfast."

17

───────

Carter called me the next day. He said he was thinking about me and wanted to talk. Was that allowed? The Gay Handbook was silent on the point. That simple call turned me into a giddy, mindless puddle of mush. It felt amazing.

The next day, he called *again*. "Did you get my email?"

Hmm. Email? What was this mystical item of which he spoke? "Um, no. I don't think so."

"Check your AOL. I found you on there and sent you a little note." There was a proud grin in his voice.

Now, kids, some of you may be shocked to learn that the internet was not always as free and easy as the men at Connection. Sometimes, you had to work for it—again, like the men at Connection.

America Online was *the* internet service provider to the gays. Everything was still dial-up through your landline— yes, that's a phone line with wires. When you clicked the *Get Online* button, the whirring of a phone ringing would be followed by an odd series of bing-bong sounds as your computer did a virtual handshake with the AOL supercomputers somewhere in outer space. Or maybe Kansas, I wasn't sure.

There were three features to AOL that made it ripe for the gay picking.

First, a user could create a profile in which he told others basic information about himself. For most people, that included work, hobbies, hometown, and other fun facts. For gays, it *always* included height, weight, waist size, arm size, and, well, the size of other important organs. Hence, the term *AOL inches* was born, indicating someone who exaggerated the size of their, um, feet, in their profile.

The second exciting innovation brought to us by the AOL geeks was the Chat Room, a virtual place to meet like-minded people. These rooms were generally themed. One might talk gardening in a room titled *Keeping Them Green* or tennis in *Holding Court*. More adventurous men might join a group called *M4M Now!!!* Yes, the exclamation points added urgency to their, um, need. Those folks were generally impatient. I'm not sure why.

The third, and possibly most functional feature enjoyed in the AOL's magical land was email. Yes, today we take this tool for granted. It's on our phone, PC, iPad, watch—practically everywhere we turn. Back then, it was only in one place—AOL.

But there was a catch to this groundbreaking new service. They charged *by the hour*.

Stop gasping.

Yes, internet usage was *expensive*. In today's currency, you would be bankrupt, you internet-using trollop. Be thankful you live in the era of basically free interconnectivity, youngsters. We suffered for your right to unlimited online porn. Or shopping—you might like shopping. Whatever, weirdo.

Because of that last little fly in the interweb ointment, a poor twentysomething like me didn't go online very often. Yes, AOL sent CDs with hundreds, sometimes thousands, of free usage hours if you downloaded their program, but I'd long ago burned through those freebies. At that point, if I couldn't pay for it with the holy stack of laundry quarters, it probably didn't happen.

Bottom line, I hadn't checked my email in weeks, and I couldn't check it while on the phone with Carter. I needed the phone line to connect to AOL, remember?

"I need to get back to work anyway. Check your email. Can't wait to see you Friday."

My heart fluttered. He wanted to see me again. *Me!*

God, I was a dribbling mess.

As soon as the receiver hit the cradle, I ran into my bedroom, where the washing-machine-sized computer monitor blinked to life. Holy crap, Windows startup took *forever* back then. I paced for a good two minutes before the hard drive stopped spinning and I saw the happy blinky of 'you may proceed' on the screen.

I logged into AOL and the sexy voice announced, "You've got mail."

Yes, kids, that was a thing before it was a movie. Keep up here.

I clicked as fast as I could, scrolling through the spam and other emails from Nigerian princes who thought I should be their successor. About a third of the way through the stack, I found an email from Carter. It wasn't from an AOL account. It was from his *work* email.

Did people at his job know he was gay? The thought flashed through my mind, then vanished as I opened the message.

Subject: Sunday Night

Michael,

I had the best time Sunday night. I can't remember the last time I held someone all night. You didn't even squirm or turn over. It was perfect.

Bring an overnight bag Friday—but only if you want to. You don't have to. Really, it's up to you.

Work is boring today. I can't stop thinking about seeing you again.

Anyway. I sound sappy. You make me smile. Thanks for that.

See you soon.

Carter.

I lost track of time as I sat and stared at the screen in disbelief. I think I read that email twenty times. My heart was doing backflips. No one—and I really mean no one—had ever made me feel like this before. And from the bit of babble in his email, it seemed his heart was doing some gymnastics of its own.

Could this be real? Was it possible that a put-together, hot guy like Carter could actually be interested in me? I was such a mess, still figuring out life, still having no clue about most of it, and he wanted to spend time with *me*?

A sudden burst of energy sent my body hurtling toward the phone in the den. I couldn't spin the dial fast enough.

"DWAYNE! Oh my God, you're not going to believe this. He sent me an *email*. Like, a real email in my inbox to my AOL—*from his work*!"

I expected at least some enthusiasm, maybe even a show of being impressed. After all, how many people got emails?

Crickets. "Dwayne?"

"OK, I'll bite. What did it say?"

I tried to race back to the bedroom, but the scrunchy

cord on the phone wouldn't stretch that far. "Crap, I can't get the phone back there. He said he's looking forward to Friday and to *bring an overnight bag*."

There was a moment's pause. Dwayne was probably waiting for me to tell him something more earth-shattering since I'd practically declared a national emergency with my initial enthusiasm. "Alright. Is that all?"

I was stunned. How could he not see the immensity of this moment? He'd sent me *an email*. He would probably declare his undying love next. Wasn't that the progression? "Yeah, that's about it."

"Well, that's great. He's thinking about you. It's a good start."

A start? What in the actual holy gay fuck was Dwayne thinking? This was *so* much more than just a start. This was real, tangible, digitally traceable progress.

"Have you thought any more about our conversation at the diner?"

You know the sound when Ms. Pacman gets caught and dies? Yeah, I heard that, loud and clear. "Some, but Dwayne—"

"I'm glad you're excited, but you need to think about what we discussed. Trust me on this. It's important in ways you won't understand for a while, but it will make sense one day. I promise."

My heart returned from the Olympic Gymnastics Training Center and settled back into place. It continued beating, but didn't really have its heart in it. Sorry, that was terrible.

"Can I just be happy for once, without having to think about life-shattering changes? I've never felt anything like this before, and I don't want to mess it up by being all serious."

He was quiet for a few heartbeats too long before speaking again. "Just be careful, OK. And remember—I'll be here, no matter what happens."

As we hung up the phone, those words echoed in my head. What did he mean by that? Carter and I were having dinner, possibly forking and spooning—*hopefully* forking then spooning. We liked each other. What was so dangerous about that? Why did I need an ominous warning?

What could possibly go wrong?

18

I t took forever, but Friday finally arrived.

The week had passed uneventfully. I worked each day, then either worked out or refereed, depending on the schedule assigned by the officiating gods. I saw Jason at the gym a few times, and I didn't trip over myself or issue so much as a single stammer when he greeted me, so I considered that flame suitably extinguished. Carter emailed every day. They weren't long, sappy love notes, just short 'I'm thinking about you' messages. Each one made my heart flutter a little more than the last.

When I opened Friday's email and saw there was an attachment, it felt like Christmas had arrived early. I was sure it was some scantily clad version of Carter with full pec exposure. I couldn't click the little paperclip fast enough, and nearly screamed as the hourglass flipped over … and over … and over. Dial-up sucked.

When the image finally finished downloading, my heart leapt into my throat.

It was a tiny, fuzzy tiger cub standing beside Batman.

Not literally. It was Cade and Christian.

The picture was dated last year, which would've made the boys two and four. They were dressed up for Halloween and ready to hunt for some cavities. Christian, the older of the two, had his arms crossed in his best 'Batman will kick your butt' stare. Cade was smiling, his grin nearly as wide as his face. It looked like Carter had caught him mid-giggle. There's nothing like a little kid's giggle. How can you not smile listening to them?

I stared at that picture for several long moments. The boys were *perfect*. Then I thought to read the actual message in the email, and my heart stopped.

M—

I forgot something. It's my weekend. Guess you'll meet them tonight.

I understand if you're not ready for this. They can be a lot.

C

When my heart started beating again, I was still frozen in my chair. I'd spent an untold amount of money remaining logged in to AOL, so I quickly logged off.

Holy fuzzy tiger, Batman.

My first thought was pure, unrepentant excitement. I was going to meet the boys. This was going to be an awesome, fun, play-filled night. We'd wrestle and race with Matchbox cars and whatever else the boys wanted to do. I loved kids. This was going to be *awesome*.

Then the angel appeared. She'd apparently taken a road trip across the country for the last month only to return hours before my moment of triumph. Her tiny arms were crossed, her tiny foot tapping feverishly—and she looked *pissed*. There was judgment in her eyes.

What do you think you're doing? she asked. *First, you keep lying to yourself about being straight. By the way, you* should *be straight. Being gay is wrong. It's a sin. That's clear in the book. Remember the stoning? How could you not understand stoning?*

I'm not sure which is worse, the lying or the being not-straight. We'll discuss that later.

Next, you're leading a good man down a dark path with no clear future. Now you're going to meet his beautiful, innocent children. You'll play with them and they'll become attached, hoping you'll stay in their lives. That's something you can't *promise. They'll fall in love with you, with the innocence of children, and you'll crush their little hearts. You know better. You were* raised *better.*

Man, she *was* pissed.

Then my bro appeared. He wasn't the devil in the red suit with the pitchfork. Nope. He was Fabio from *I Can't Believe It's Not Butter* fame, wearing tight black leather pants and *never* a shirt, just bulging, rippling muscles that poked through his lustrous blond hair as it shimmered and flowed across his chest.

OK, maybe I projected a little with my devil. It's *my* conscience, and I can make him look however I like. Give me a break.

You love kids, the devil's silky voice said. *They deserve a night of fun. You deserve it too. Don't listen to the old prude over there. Carter likes you—a lot. Trust me. I'm an angel, or I was before ... never mind. That's not important. The important thing is that you should go. Have fun. Stay the night. Get laid.*

Yeah, Fabio was right. I *did* deserve this.

The kids would know me as one of their dad's friends;

the fun one, actually. They were too young to know anything else—and I was just meeting them. It's not like Carter and I were getting married or anything serious.

Yeah, thanks, Fabio. You rock with your not-butter-but-oh-so-tasty self.

Then I shook the image of Fabio rubbing butter all over himself out of my head. That was weird, even for my devil.

Decision made, I turned to pack my backpack for the night and decide which of the remaining three clean shirts I'd wear. I know what you're thinking, but it makes life simple to only have a few options. Closets full of choices are overrated.

I PULLED INTO CARTER'S DRIVEWAY WITHOUT DOING THE stalker-in-recovery circling of the block like I had on my first visit. The front door opened before I could get out of the car, and I saw Carter's tasty frame filling the screen door. He was wearing the same apron as before, this time without a shirt. Pecs poured out where the apron straps failed to contain. Damn.

He gave me a cute wave. If I hadn't known better, I would've thought he was nervous. In point of fact, I was just hoping to make it into his house without another piddle incident, especially now that I'd seen his Michelin stars peeking out from behind his apron.

As I made it halfway to the door, a tiny head poked through Carter's legs, lifting the bottom of the apron. A flash of blond hair, then a poked-out tongue, and the rascal vanished. I guessed it was a parent thing because Carter didn't seem to notice. He never even looked down.

"Are you sure you're ready for this?" he asked when I was a couple paces from the door.

I flashed him my most confident smile. "I've been looking forward to it all day."

He grinned. "So have they. That's what worries me. I get scared when they have time to plot."

I made it past the screen door and enjoyed a warm hug and cheek peck from Carter before the attack began. The same little towhead leapt from my left and attached himself to my leg. A second later, a larger version of the blond disaster darted into the room and grabbed my hand, pulling me further into the house. "Come see my room!" Cade squeaked as he tugged.

Christian just squeezed, determined not to lose his grip as I walked. I did that monster walk, stomping my foot down, just to make him giggle and squeal. That was the best sound ever.

I looked up to find Carter grinning. He started to say something, to call off the assailants, but I shook my head. "I'll go see their room. They won't rest until I do."

He nodded, his eyes brimming with *something*, then headed to the kitchen. "Yell if you start feeling outnumbered. I'll send in reinforcements," he called over his shoulder.

Thirty minutes and twenty toys later, Carter's head appeared in the doorway to the boys' room. "Anybody in here hungry?"

"No way!" Cade yelled. Christian stuck his tongue out at Carter.

"Christian, that's not nice." Carter was laughing as he said it, more amused than annoyed. He surveyed the damage. Toys once neatly housed in their crates littered the floor. There was barely room to walk. Even the bed was now basically a toy shelf.

He shook his head, smiled, and turned to me. "Hungry?"

"Yes, sir. All this playing gives a boy an appetite." I tickled Christian as I answered and was rewarded with that angelic giggle. He squirmed out of my hands and ran for the safety of his father, then looked back, annoyed I wasn't following, and flashed his tongue again.

Carter extended a hand and helped me up. "Looks like you're a hit."

"Told ya before, I do better with kids than adults most of the time."

He cocked his head, then cupped my cheek and kissed me softly on the lips. I nearly fell backward. Where had that come from? There were kids in the room!

As we walked toward the kitchen, he leaned toward me and whispered conspiratorially, "This will be a lot easier if we feed them first, *especially* Christian. We can set them up with a cartoon in the den while we eat."

And that's what we did.

It went about as smoothly as you might expect. Cade was old enough to behave, but Christian decided to put on a show for the new guy. When I sensed Carter getting frustrated—and more than a little embarrassed—I leaned over and made faces until Christian giggled again. "You'd better eat that bite or I'm gonna tickle you." I reached my fingers out and wiggled them.

He squealed and pulled his bare feet back. Carter snuck in a spoonful, then gave me an appreciative wink.

Ten minutes later, Carter and I sat around a much quieter table eating baked chicken dusted with all-purpose seasoning. I was beginning to sense a pattern. Was this what it took to get abs? Or did Carter just really like baked chicken? Either way, it was tasty, and his abs were hot.

After dinner, the four dudes piled onto the couch. Carter sat at one end with Cade cradled next to him under his arm. I had a cushion to myself, until Christian climbed on. I watched his head swivel from Carter to me as he tried to process the scene. I would've given anything to plug into his head to hear what he was thinking. Something clicked, and he scrambled into my lap and pulled my arm around him. He wanted me to hold him tight while we watched TV.

I thought I might die right there on that couch. It would've been a *very* happy death.

I looked down at Cade, his mussed hair scattered across my shirt and bony fingers gripping and releasing my arm, as if testing if I would let go. He never looked up, but I felt the point when he relaxed and nuzzled deeper against my chest.

Carter was watching the whole time, though I hadn't looked up to notice. He reached across the couch and wiped moisture from my cheek—something else I hadn't noticed. Another simple, tender gesture to be added to the list of this evening.

My heart was full.

———

THE CARTOON ENDED AROUND NINE O'CLOCK AND CARTER declared it the boys' bedtime. Cade protested, but Christian didn't peep; he was already asleep in my lap.

I carefully adjusted my arms and picked him up, cradling him tightly under my chin. I almost made it to the boys' room when he shifted. Fingers brushed my chin, then traced my cheek.

I looked down to find him studying me. He smiled and said, "Mika," then closed his eyes again.

This time, when I looked at Carter, his eye was the one with moisture.

***

CARTER AND I WATCHED A RERUN OF *CHEERS* WHILE EATING our cottage cheese and fruit concoction. He wasn't kidding when he said he ate it every night before bedtime. Guess I had a new favorite snack now too.

As the credits began to roll, I turned to him and asked, "Are you sure it's OK if I stay here? I mean, what will the kids think when they wake up and find me sleeping in your room?"

He didn't hesitate. "I've never hidden anything from them, and I won't start now. They don't need to know the gory details. They wouldn't understand them at this age anyway, but they know Daddy has friends who are boys instead of girls. They'll see you as one of my friends."

I was struck by how firmly, how confidently, he answered what I thought was an awkward question. Doubt clawed at my gut, but I saw none in his eyes. He must've sensed my disquiet because he reached up and cupped my cheek, then pulled me into his arms for a tender kiss. I melted into his embrace. It's what I'd wanted all night. It was the perfect cherry on top of this cottage cheese of a day.

God, did I just say that? Shoot me now.

We kissed on the couch until the *Cheers* theme song ended and an equally familiar toilet paper jingle began.

"I can't take that tune. It'll be stuck in my head all night," Carter said, reaching for the remote. "Let's go to bed."

I hummed the toilet paper theme all the way to the bedroom. Carter finished the last two notes, then smacked my arm playfully. "I'm going to make you pay for that."

As his door clicked shut, I growled, "I was hoping you'd say that."

19

———

I don't know what I expected, but it wasn't for the lights to go out before I'd made it two steps into Carter's bedroom. The sudden darkness startled me. Then Carter's hands crawled across the ticklish sides of my abdomen as he pulled me back against him. His warm breath caressed my neck before a sharp bite sent jolts of adrenaline down my body. As his tongue teased and teeth nibbled, his hands explored up my abs to my chest. Without warning, the gentleness of his probing ceased, and he gripped my pecs, squeezing, as he kissed my neck with vigor.

I moaned and couldn't suppress a shiver.

"I'm going to take my time with you tonight. I hope you weren't planning to sleep." His half-whisper, half-growl in my ear was followed by teeth to the nearby lobe. I'd experienced wild, passionate sex before—my two nights with Joseph and the necktie debauchery with Fly Boy could definitely be described that way—but what Carter was doing took things to a completely different level. I thought I might pass out—and we were still fully clothed.

His hand found its way to my neck. Strong fingers with well-trimmed nails crept hungrily upward. When they reached my head, they pressed firmly and kneaded, massaging muscles I hadn't known were tight. The hand worked its way up to my crown, never ceasing its caress, while lips and teeth continued taunting my ear and the tender skin below it.

I reached back with one hand and gripped his neck, pressing him into me, giving him permission to do whatever he wanted for as long as he wanted. He growled and ground his body against mine. The pulsing granite pressed against my lower back told me he understood and wanted the same.

Firm hands gripped my shoulders and he turned me to face him. He held me there, looking down, his eyes searching. Then he smiled and pressed a soft kiss to my lips, barely brushing the skin, letting me taste his tongue as it passed.

I couldn't stop the giggle that completely shattered the sensual scene.

He pulled back and quirked a brow. "What?"

"You taste like cottage cheese," I said, my giggle turning into a fit of laughter. I didn't know why that was funny, but I couldn't stop. Before I knew it, Carter had shoved me onto the bed and was tickling my sides, making me laugh even harder, this time with that bladder-squeezing, piddle-inducing glee. He was too big and strong to escape from, so I did the only thing I could think of—I tickled him back.

Nothing. Not even a flinch.

He grinned like he'd just won some undeclared contest. "Not ticklish. Nice try."

Bastard.

He tickled me harder; tears blurred my vision. Just when I thought I actually would wet his bed, his hands went from attack to entangle. He pressed the weight of his substantial frame against me, and I sank happily into the mattress as he kissed me. His tongue searched mine, as tenderness was replaced by ravenous desire. His hands gripped and squeezed, then moved and repeated. I pawed at his back, feeling the tautness of his muscles, reveling in the flare of his broad lats. Nothing got me more excited than a well-formed physique. I thought I might explode right there, before we'd even taken off our shirts—and then he corrected that error.

My T-shirt flew over my head as he ripped it off, then he bowed his head and gripped my nipple in his teeth. No one had ever done that. Stars exploded at the backs of my eyes, and my back arched completely on its own.

I moaned loudly and he stopped, chuckling. "Shh. The boys."

I turned eight shades of red. "Oops. Sorry."

He winked; then, without warning, attacked the other nipple.

Holy Mother of Batman, the Joker, and the Penguin. What was this man doing to me? How could something feel so good?

I gathered my wits enough to reach up and feel the front of his shirt, determined to do the same smooth ripping-off move he'd demonstrated a moment ago.

Crap. Buttons. Who wears shirts with buttons? Fuck me.

My fingers wouldn't work. They fumbled with the first button while his tongue wound round and round my nipple. I could barely see because every time his teeth brushed against it, my eyes involuntarily shut and my back arched again. When had I lost bodily control?

He finally realized I was never going to get a single button undone, much less remove the darn shirt, so he sat up and began unfastening them himself. That 'I won again' grin pursed his impudent little lips as he moved from the top button to the next—as slowly and deliberately as he could. With each button, I saw a little more of his hairless, rounded, hardened, perfectly massive chest.

Oh … my … sweet … Jesus.

I reached up to touch him, but he gripped my wrist and pushed it down against the bed. What was it with men and restraining my wrists?

"Oh no you don't. Not yet." His grin was infuriatingly sexy and playful.

The third button popped free, then the fourth, and fifth. Damn it. How many buttons could a shirt have? Was this thing made in Fort Knox?

He hovered over the last button, teasing me, then lifted his body and smothered my hardness with his butt cheeks, grinding back and forth with his hips as he gradually opened the last of his shirt, revealing a riverbed of stone-hard abs that made my mouth water. He was beautiful. No, he was sexy. OK, he was both.

And he was grinding. Oh Jesus.

Then he pulled his arms free of his shirt and the moon-light from the thin window above the bed painted his skin in soft light.

My breath caught. Even the audacious little angel let out a sustained "Ahhhhhh" in middle C.

Then he ground again.

He leaned down and pressed his whole body against mine, our naked chests and stomachs rubbing firmly against each other, lighting an even brighter fire in my nethers. He ground his groin against mine and I moaned again. When he kissed me, I forgot my orders to stay still and gripped his head in both hands, digging my fingers into his hair, gripping it, pulling him harder against me.

His hand reached between us and unfastened my jeans. I didn't think it was possible, but my heart raced even faster. He sat up again and trailed his tongue from the middle of my chest to my belly button, then down my happy trail. When he reached my stubborn jeans, he raised up to allow his hands to do their work. Snap; zip. He pulled the zipper flaps back and my erection flew out like some caged beast finally offered its freedom. He looked up, surprised by the lack of underwear, and gave me the most sinful grin I'd ever seen. I loved it.

He licked up my shaft slowly, reaching the rim, then stopped. I looked down to find his hands now gripping the waistband of my jeans, pulling them down past my hips. He crawled toward my feet and slowly tugged everything free.

Every move he made was deliberate and measured, his eyes rarely leaving mine, returning quickly if they did. I'd wanted him before, but now I craved his touch. I needed his warmth against my skin, his lips and tongue tangled with my own.

I watched him toss my jeans across the room with a gleam in his eyes, then stand at the foot of the bed, chest out, shoulders back. He teased the button of his slacks as he'd done with his shirt, then flicked it loose. I'd never heard a zipper's hum take *that* long, but somehow, I didn't want it to stop—until I saw what rose beneath. I definitely wanted that damn zipper to reach its end.

He shimmied out of his pants, and I saw him fully naked for the first time.

Holy Frodo, Bilbo, Sam, *and* Pip …

He was the Dark Lord's mighty tower, complete with a massive roaming eye atop its, um, head. (Yes, that was a *Lord of the Rings* reference. I'm a nerd. Get over it.) He was *huge*—and I'm not talking AOL inches either. There was no exaggerating the scale of his beast. It was monstrous and thick and … *dripping*.

My eyes must've been golf balls, because his grin turned into a full-on 'I'm going to fuck the shit out of you' stare.

My palms started to sweat as he climbed back onto the bed. His hands gripped my thighs and he did a push-up, letting his tongue tease the head of my penis. It flinched and quivered at his touch. He grinned up at me, bared his teeth, then enveloped my head between them, teasing the sensitive skin with cottage cheesy goodness. I never would've thought having another man's *teeth* on my dick would be a good thing—it sounds so painful when you say it out loud—but, as he ran the smooth tips of his incisors across the skin just below the lip of my head, and his tongue swirled around the hole, I suddenly had a new appreciation for man-teeth.

He closed his mouth over me, consuming my most precious member, then pulled back with a startled expression. He smacked his lips as if finishing a snack, then licked them. "Your pre-cum is delicious," the naughty rabbit said.

I'd never had pre-cum. Never. Ever.

My eyes flew downward and there it was, lava dribbling from the mouth of Mount Michael.

He licked it away and my whole body spasmed at the unexpected pleasure.

We spent the next eternity kissing and touching and

rubbing, learning each other's bodies and what made each of us squirm (and what tickled—darn rabbit).

I caressed his chest, licked it, nibbled it. I was obsessed. It was perfection in the flesh and I couldn't get enough of it.

He turned away and my heart skipped a beat, then he lay on his back, his erection casting a shadow in the window's moonlight. He gripped my shoulders and pulled me on top of him, then reached his arm off the side of the bed and I heard the side table drawer slide open. I knew what *that* sound meant. That's the universal gay sound of, 'Loosen that hole up, here I come.' I was suddenly a kid about to enter Disneyland for the first time. Well, I wasn't doing the entering, but you get what I mean.

Give it to me, Mickey. Come, you raunchy rodent.

Never mind. Different genre.

He squirted lube onto himself, then offered to do the same for me. I put my hand on his to keep him from doing it. "I want this for as long as you can last. The second you put that on me, it won't just be pre-cum you're licking off."

He barked a laugh, then quickly set the lube on the table. "Definitely not giving that to you for—"

He lost his voice as I raised my body and slid him inside me. He hadn't seen that coming; his eyes looked as big as the moon that was shining across my body. For once that night, the 'I won' grin was on my face.

"Michael, we shouldn't—"

I rose and fell atop him, teasing his head with the rim of my hole before taking his whole length inside me. His body rocked and his head fell backward. He didn't protest again.

I took him slowly, savoring every inch as he slid in and out, knowing we truly were one person in that moment. My hands pressed against his chest, and my dick twitched in excitement as his fingers traced my abs. Every time I pushed him deeper, he grunted or moaned. He couldn't be close or deep enough.

When I bent down and our lips met, the world fell away. All thoughts vanished. There was only the feeling of Carter and his body mingled with mine, his soul entering me, filling my essence, his warmth and passion and desire. I rode him faster, and his body responded, pushing upward with each thrust. I reached back, pulled my cheeks apart, and willed him past all limits. He struck something inside me and my eyes clouded with pleasure.

He was shaking. I was shaking.

He held that spot for a long moment, prolonging our union, then grabbed me roughly and flipped me on my back, never pulling himself free. The air flew out of my lungs as I struck the pillows, and he drove deep again, slamming past that inner barrier guarding ultimate pleasure and pain.

He gave me one last, slow, passionate kiss, then all tender sweetness fell away.

He was no longer the rational, nerdy shoe guy, he was an animal whose craving *had* to be satiated. He gripped my shoulders and pushed, using my body to brace his effort, harder, then faster. I reached behind my head and gripped the pillows as the rhythm of my ecstasy mirrored the cadence of his thrusts.

His grunts grew louder, his breathing heavy. Sweat poured from his skin, making his chest glisten in the moonlight.

I hadn't noticed him reach for the lube until his hand grabbed my shaft and rubbed slickness across it. When his slippery palm grazed my head, my chest shook, and I bit back a cry. He stroked me in time with his thrust, both becoming rougher and faster. I reached up and felt his abs as they clenched. My own responded, and my body grasped his shaft firmer with each deep dive.

He couldn't hold back. He pushed harder, and all the passion and desire he'd held exploded inside me. I could feel his cum, the warmth of his liquid, as it entered my body. I felt *him* enter me. That thought, more than any physical act, pushed me beyond all control, and I shot across his chest and abs, again and again.

I felt his cock pulsing. We shivered in unison. We didn't speak.

Still inside me, he lay atop me, smearing my cum across our sweaty bodies. Neither of us cared.

He kissed me and ran his hands through my hair. I wrapped my arms around him and held him tight.

We melted into each other, and fell asleep as one person.

20

Sunshine streamed through the window. I lay wrapped in Carter's arms, my head nuzzled in the space between his chin and collarbone. It was *the* perfect place.

Then I felt a sharp pain as a knobby knee found my gut. "Mika!" a tiny voice squawked.

My eyes creaked open to find Christian sitting atop me, his tiny hands clapping.

A heartbeat later, a second jab knocked the air out of my lungs as Cade playfully shoved his brother onto Carter and stole the spot on my stomach. He held his arms in the air, declaring victory in this battle for the top.

Carter grunted a laugh. "I don't think you need to worry about them seeing you here anymore. Looks like you've been accepted into the pack."

Lord, *another* pack. He didn't know about the wolves yet.

Cade bounced atop me and I worried Carter's other children might squirt out.

Too much? Get over it.

"Come on. We're hungry, and you have to play with us. You promised!" Cade knocked the air out of me again.

I glanced sideways at Carter, as if to say, 'Help me.'

He laughed as he tickled Christian. "You got yourself into this mess, Mr. Michael. Don't look to me for salvation."

Cade bobbed a couple more painful times and shouted, "Yay!" before leaping off the bed and racing into the kitchen. Christian, never to be left behind, threw himself down and scurried after his older brother. I watched them vanish and couldn't wipe the grin off my face.

Carter grabbed my shoulders and pulled me into him for a passionate kiss. I savored it, then pulled back.

"What?" he asked, brow raised.

"Next day cottage cheese isn't nearly as sexy." I wrinkled my nose.

He laughed and shoved me off him. "Fine. I see how you are. Can't take a little stink in the name of love."

He threw back the covers and strode into the bathroom, unfazed by his firm, perky butt smiling sideways at me the whole time.

My overactive mind was racing in a different direction though. *Love?* Where had *that* word come from?

I lay frozen in bed. Stuck was probably more accurate. The sheets were attached to my cum-dried chest. I had to peel them off, in that moment thankful for whatever act of genetic kindness had given me a mostly smooth body—the hair pull would've stung.

Carter, apparently an incorrigible morning person, raced from the bathroom and leapt on top of me, planting his lips firmly on mine. The minty taste of mouthwash seeped toward the back of my throat. "Happy now?"

"Much better, Captain Cottage Cheese."

He guffawed. "That's the *worst* nickname ever. I think you pulled it out of somewhere I discovered last night."

His finger suddenly found my hole and poked at it. If he hadn't been on top of me, I would've hit the ceiling.

I gulped back the twinge of pain and wiggled my brows. "It's the best I can do before coffee. Are you going to let me up, or do I need to pee all over your sheets?"

He kissed me again and hopped off. "I'll go feed the beasts while you wash up," he called over his shoulder as he donned a robe, then vanished down the hall.

I stared at the open doorway for a good two or three minutes. Could he get any better? Carter was hot, built, kind, smart, successful, funny, and, from everything I'd seen so far, a great dad. Did I mention *fucking amazing* in bed? Seriously. Holy crap. My butt puckered at the thought, and I realized I was sore back there. He had fucked me into soreness. Was that a thing? God, I hoped so. If not, I planned to make it one. I could deal with *that* soreness every day.

I walked back into my apartment around seven Sunday night.

Oh, don't give me *that* look.

Yes, Carter and I had dinner *Friday* night. Yes, I stayed with him overnight, then another night … then the next day. What of it? You're *so* judgey.

Speaking of judgey, Peter was eating cereal at the kitchen counter, and imagine that, wasn't wearing a shirt. My first thought was, *Huh. Carter has a better chest.*

Shit. I was smitten.

"Somebody's doing the walk of shame today," he said between crunchy bites of Froot Loops. I couldn't wait to hear how *that* healthy gem was supposed to keep his abs in check.

"Oh hey." Yeah, that's all I got out. My brain was muddled. Give me a break.

"Oh boy. He's tired. He didn't sleep much." He stood, grinning from ear to ear. "Out with it. I want details now. Start with her name."

God. "Can I shower and change first? I really need to get out of these clothes."

He hooted. "I think getting out of those clothes is what made you tired in the first place, but whatever. Wash behind your ears. There's no telling what your little tramp did back there with her tongue."

I reddened, remembering the tingle of Carter's tongue in exactly that spot, then earned an Olympic medal for speed dashing from the door to my room. The slam earned a perfect ten from the Russian judge. What can I say? Nobody loves a good bit of door slamming like a Russian.

No, I don't know what that means either. Drop it, OK?

Thirty minutes—and the longest, hottest shower ever— later, I emerged to find Shirtless Wonder still perched on a stool in the kitchen. His arms were crossed, which made his perfect pecs poke out. Why did I have to like pecs so much?

Anyway.

"Time's up. What's her name? I claim roommate prerogative. You have to answer and can't lie. It's the law."

I thought as quickly as I could and lied. "Pat."

"Pat?" He scrunched up his face.

Holy crap. Did I just pull a *Saturday Night Live* skit out of my ass? This wasn't going well.

Then again, the name was androgenous, could've been male or female. It wasn't *totally* a lie, was it? I shrugged off his challenge but didn't say anything, just poured a bowl of colorful sugar and topped it with milk.

I said *topped it*. Shit. Images of Carter beneath me as I straddled him flashed before me and Froot Loops scattered across the floor.

Peter's brow furrowed. "You alright?"

I knelt to gather the errant rings and hide my face from

his scrutiny. "I'm fine, just tired. She didn't let me get much sleep, like you said."

He laughed. "That's my boy. Bang 'em into tomorrow."

"Oh, he did," I muttered to myself.

"What?"

Shit. "Nothing. Right. Bang 'em. I totally did. *She's* walking bowlegged today." I rubbed my sore thigh at the thought.

"'Atta boy." He laughed again. "Speaking of which, I need to get changed. It's my turn to get laid tonight while you rest your tired butt."

"*Sore* butt, more like it," I grunted, grinning.

"What?"

Crap. "Nothing."

THE NEXT MORNING, I DROVE ACROSS TOWN TO MY DAD'S tiny office. It was attached to a gas station. Sexy, right? It was cheap, and we were a struggling family concern.

I powered on my PC and went to make coffee. Windows wouldn't be ready before I got back, so I took my time and stared at the cars as they filled up and drove away. I felt lighter today somehow. Had the sky always been that blue? It seemed deeper, richer—*bluer*—somehow. The coffee stopped perking and I inhaled deeply, savoring the scent. It was the Peruvian mountains in a mug. Wonderful.

Armed with java, I strode across the vastness that was our twenty-by-ten office and plopped down before my still-loading screen. Bill Gates really needed to make Windows faster. I was aging while the darn program powered up.

The familiar welcome tones sounded and I set my mug down, ready to tackle the day. Out of habit—yes, a habit born after meeting Carter, Oh Judgey One—I double-clicked the AOL icon. Another eternity and a dozen beep-pops later, my second favorite voice in the world said, "You've got mail."

It was nine o'clock in the morning. Was it possible Carter had already sent me an email? He'd barely made it to work himself. My pulse quickened.

There were *three* emails waiting, all from the address of the most fastidious shoe manufacturer on the planet. I grinned at the screen.

7:52 A.M.

> *M*
>
> *I woke up smiling this morning. You did that. Thanks for a great weekend.*
>
> *C*

I GIGGLED AND DID A HAPPY DANCE IN MY CHAIR, completing a full revolution, which the now-stingy Russian judge only awarded a nine-point-five. Screw her and her frozen tundra.

I clicked the next one.

8:12 A.M.

> *I forgot to tell you, Christian asked about you this morning. He was upset he didn't get to say goodbye. When I dropped him off at his mom's place, he whispered, "Bye, Mika," in my ear.*
>
> *Have a great day at work.*
>
> *Tell Dad hi (chuckle).*

C

Smart ass. *Tell Dad hi.* Funny, funny man.

Then cuddly Christian flooded my mind and tears threatened. That might've been the cutest, sweetest thing I'd ever heard. I wanted to grab that little guy and squeeze him, hear him giggle, feel his hand on my cheek.

How could anyone feel this way? My chest swelled as I remembered to breathe. Two full revolutions. Stuck the landing. *Perfect ten.*

Then I clicked the last email.

8:42 A.M.

Come over for dinner tonight. I know you have to referee, but I'll wait up, cottage cheese with fruit in hand.

Please don't make me wait until this weekend to see you again.

C

I don't remember what bad white-man dance moves I made after I read that message. All I recall was bawling like a baby from atop the podium as the sobbing Russian judge hung the gold around my neck, and they played our national anthem.

22

The weeks rolled by quickly. Basketball season was about to kick into high gear now we were in the middle of November, and most of my nights were spent officiating preseason games or attending meetings with other stripes.

A new habit formed—I packed two bags every day. The first was my officiating roller-bag filled with uniforms, whistles, and other on-court necessities. The other was my overnight bag in case Carter asked me to stay over again.

He did. Every day.

Did you know your body could learn to crave cottage cheese? I had no idea.

I slept snugly in Carter's corded arms and woke to gentle kisses on my neck.

I didn't think I'd ever been so perpetually happy. My cheeks ached from smiling. Dwayne and I had lunch several times a week, and I grinned throughout each as he endured me recounting every detail of the prior evening's sleepover. Based on how sore my jaw was in the morning, I had slept with a broad grin too.

I needed therapy. Seriously. To all who lived through this period of syrupy sweet, perpetual bliss, I sincerely apologize.

What am I saying? I *don't* apologize. I'd never been so happy, and everyone else had to just deal with it, grin and all. So there.

By our fifth week, the L word slipped out. No, not lesbian, the *other* L word.

This time, it wasn't in the context of teasing or passionate sex. We'd just eaten breakfast, and I was leaving to drive to work. Carter raced from the bedroom, nearly slamming into a wall in his graceless socks-on-hardwood slide, just to give me a kiss goodbye. My hand was turning the knob when he said, "Have a great day. Love you."

I wasn't sure he *meant* to say it. When I turned around, his face had lost all color. Mine was suddenly covered in sweat.

I bridged the two strides between us, cupped his cheek as he so often did to mine, and said, "I love you, Carter."

He didn't hesitate. In a flash, he was squeezing me into him with all his strength, his lips glued to mine, his eyes open and blazing with complex emotion and longing.

Neither of us made it to work that day.

OUR SIXTH WEEK WAS THANKSGIVING WEEK.

Carter had promised his ex he'd take the kids to the annual family gathering in Minnesota. All of his grandparents had passed when he was young, and he was determined his boys would have that special bond with theirs. As much as I hated to see him leave without me, I couldn't argue with the logic. It was part of why I loved him.

On Wednesday afternoon, I tossed my trusty overnight bag into Betty's trunk and drove to my parents' house. My three sisters, their husbands, and about a hundred nephews and nieces would descend sometime that evening. I wanted to beat the crowd.

Don't get all excited thinking I had taken an epic road trip. They live fifteen minutes away. It takes me longer to get to the grocery store.

My mom did the mom thing, hugging me until neither of us could breathe, then chided me for not visiting more often, since we lived so close. My dad did his traditional half-hug and asked about refereeing. We worked together every day, and neither of them knew about Carter—or the G word—so there wasn't much else for him to ask about.

Pleasantries said, I went with Dad to the den, where he would, predictably, fall asleep in his ratty old La-Z-Boy while I suffered through whatever TV show he had on. No, I couldn't change the channel, that was a sure way to wake him up and deal with the 'Why'd you change the channel?' conversation. Life was too short for all that.

Besides, I was too nervous to care what was on TV.

Denise, my oldest sister, would arrive shortly with her side of the pack. Nise, as we called her, was as close to a living saint as there ever would be, at least in my book. She believed she was put on earth to be a mom, and she was determined to be that mom to as many children as possible. She had two birth children, my oldest nephews, and served as a foster mom for a local faith-based adoption agency. Over the past ten years, she'd fostered more than thirty kids in her home, four of whom she'd adopted. My folks weren't thrilled with her life choices, arguing she was stealing time from her *real children* to give to the others. Nise never flinched. She simply crossed her arms, raised a fire-kissed brow, and told my parents it was none of their business, but if they ever expected to see their *real grand-children* again, they'd better want to see *all* of them.

God, I loved her.

Add to all that, she and her college sweetheart eloped when she was in her second year of college. I remember my parents tossing us in the over-packed Bonneville and driving hours to try to beat the 'I do' part of the ceremony so they could object when the officiant asked for feedback. We got there in time for a slice of cake.

Man, they were pissed.

Nise was a badass whose heart was bigger than all the planets and stars combined. There would be a special place in heaven for her one day, probably near the back of the dining hall by a door so she could hear another adopted baby cry. Were there baby monitors in heaven?

Anyway.

Midway through an episode of some poorly acted cop show came the roar of Nise's minivan in the driveway. I couldn't get out of the den fast enough. My dad's groggy voice trailed behind. "Hey. Where ya going? What's happening?"

I laughed. He'd be asleep again before I hit the door.

I got to the van just as the side door slid open. They had one of those fancy new minivans with doors that opened automatically. There was drama in waiting for the space-age panel to creep until it clicked.

The raucous sound of a half-dozen kids who'd been cramped in a minivan for three hours nearly knocked me off my feet. When they emerged, I actually did land on my butt. Uncle Michael was their *favorite*. That should go without saying, but I'm happy to remind you.

Nise tumbled out the passenger-side door, all four-foot-eleven of her. For a woman who stood so tall in my eyes, she was an itty-bitty thing. It made her more adorable to me. I wrapped her in a tight hug and we stood there in the driveway until long after the kids had vanished into the house.

Of the wolf pack, Nise and I were the closest. It had been that way for as long as I could remember. Was it weird for the oldest and youngest, separated by more than seventeen years, to be the closest? I didn't know either, but we were.

"You and I need to talk," I whispered.

She squeezed me and grinned. "Let me go kiss the ring and we'll slip out before dinner."

We both refused to release our hug and waddled together into the house, giggling all the way. It warmed my soul to see her again.

An hour later, we'd freed ourselves from the burgeoning pack and escaped through the back door. It was chilly outside, so I suggested we fire up Betty and chat in the heated privacy of my *fancy Saturn*, as the family had come to call her.

After a few minutes of mindless chatter, she grabbed my hand and gave me that older sister glare that carried more meaning than any look should. "Why do I get the feeling you're nervous about something?"

My eyes fell to my lap. Suddenly my fidgeting fingers were the most interesting thing I'd ever seen.

"You know you can tell me anything."

"I know. Just give me a minute."

Out of the tops of my eyes, I saw her scrunch up her face. She did that when she was thinking hard about something—or when she was worried about one of her kids. I suspected both was at play.

"So, you know how Mom told you I was dating someone, and it was getting serious?"

Her face lit up like a freshly plugged-in Christmas tree. "Uh-huh. Her name is Pat, right?" She leaned forward and her grip became iron around my fingers.

Stop snickering. I know it was a *terrible* fake name to give people, but I had to think fast. Then I had to stick with my bad story so people didn't compare notes and figure it out. How else would I end up dating that ambiguous *Saturday Night Live* character?

"So, I have a confession, and it's kind of a big deal."

She was getting excited. Then it hit me. The sister who'd eloped was getting excited about a girl named Pat I'd gotten serious with.

Shit, this wasn't going according to plan.

Come on, dumbass. Just tell her. "So, Nise, I lied. Her name isn't Pat."

Her face scrunched again. "It's not?"

"No. It's Carter."

Silence.

She somehow scrunched her face even harder. That must've hurt. Then her eyes opened wide as recognition settled in. She covered her mouth with a hand and stared at me.

I felt that stare, physically, in my chest. It ached. The pack's religion was clear on gays. They were good as piñatas—if you threw stones outside the city walls instead of smacking them with sticks for their candy—but not much else. I wasn't worried about physical safety, but the time-honored medieval tradition of ex-communication was a very real possibility that terrified me.

The moment dragged on without her speaking—or me breathing. I closed my eyes, unable to take her glare any longer.

That's when I felt her other hand, the one that had flown to her mouth, gently rest on top of mine. I dared a peek. She wasn't scowling—that was good, right?

"Alright, Michael, I want you to listen to me. I don't want to repeat this, alright?" Her voice was steel.

Oh shit. Here it comes. Goodbye, pack. I'll miss you.

"You are my baby brother." Her voice caught. "I have loved you since the day I held you in my arms that first time. There is nothing, *and I mean nothing*, that could make me love you less. I *am* a little shocked by what you've shared, and it will take some getting used to—but it doesn't change anything. You remember our rule?"

I nodded, having no idea what rule she meant.

"Before you make any serious commitments, *I* still have to approve."

In that moment—that glorious, weight-lifting moment —I ugly-cried worse than Tammy Faye on Sunday morning. Nise wasn't much better. Within minutes, Betty's windows were fogged and we were both trying to keep our noses from running all over each other's shirts. Yeah, that part was gross.

Sweet Buttery Popcorn and Oversized Coke, I'd just told her about Carter! By extension, I guess I'd just *come out* to my big sister.

I hadn't used the G word. It would take years for my brain to command my mouth to make *that* sound. But the most important wolf in my pack now knew my biggest secret—and she hadn't turned her back on me. Or bared her teeth. Or bitten anything.

Maybe everything would be alright.

An hour later, we strolled back inside. Neither of us had noticed our mom watching from the kitchen window.

23

———

The following weekend, Carter had the kids again. It was unseasonably warm for the last weekend in November, and Mr. Hot Boobs decided to mow the lawn one last time before winter set in. We raked leaves for an hour, creating a massive pile as tall as Carter's six-foot-four frame, then he went to the garage to ready his super-sexy dad mobile.

OK, it was a riding lawn mower. Just go with me here.

Cade wedged himself in front of Carter so he could grip the steering wheel and pretend to drive, while Carter kept his arms safely around him in case of trouble. They began making precise rounds, creating near-artistic lines in the grass. The yard would look like Yankee Stadium by the time he finished.

Christian was left to me. We tried playing with a ball in the house, but his wild kicks nearly toppled a family heirloom, so I decided outside play might be better. After several minutes of wresting a very squirmy three-year-old, I had managed to tie his shoes and zip up his jacket, and we headed outside.

The moment I saw the leaf mountain, I knew what had to happen.

Christian was tottering a step or two ahead of me and never saw me coming. I grabbed that giggle bunny and hoisted him into the air, then raced headlong into the pile. We both vanished in a sea of orange and yellow. His squeals and giggles only swelled as I went on the attack, tickling his sides while lifting his flailing body above the leaves.

He screamed out for Carter, but the mower was too loud for his backup to hear.

I dumped him back into the mound and hopped out.

Leaves flew everywhere as scrawny arms flapped to the surface and leaf-ridden blond hair shook with glee. I scooped up leaves between my hands and dumped them onto his head.

He shrieked louder. His laugh was now uncontrollable. I felt my own howling deep in my gut.

Without thinking, I dove into the pile next to him and let him dump armful after armful on top of me. He jumped on my stomach and tried to tickle my sides like I'd done to him earlier. Tears were streaming down both our faces.

The roar of the lawnmower made me look up.

The moment froze. It was as if someone had taken a photo, snapped that moment in time, and nothing could move.

Carter held Cade tight against him, as both boys grinned from ear to ear. Cade's eyes were bugged wide as his hands gripped the steering wheel like an indie racer. My heart soared at the sight. Then I glimpsed Christian's face as he emerged from the pile, leaves sticking out of his thoroughly disheveled hair. His face held a pure, innocent joy.

Our eyes met, and his smile widened, his giggles grew louder.

Click.

Each of us may have three or four perfect moments in our lives, a few more if we're truly lucky. I'll never forget that moment, that frozen instant when everything I loved and cherished—*everyone*—was smiling and laughing with reckless abandon. I can still squeeze my eyes and see Carter glancing at me out the corner of his eye, hear the laughter of a precious little boy as he tossed leaves on my head, feel the bite of the breeze, smell the mix of leaves and cut grass.

That moment will never fade.

THAT NIGHT, WE PUT THE BOYS TO BED AROUND NINE. Carter carried Cade; I, Christian. As I laid my charge into his bed and pulled the covers snugly to his chin, he wiggled his arm out and pressed his palm to my cheek. His giant brown eyes blinked up at me, and he smiled. When I thought my heart couldn't take any more, he whispered a new word I'd never heard him speak: "Love Mika."

I gulped and managed to say, "I love you too, little man." I fled the room before my chest began to heave. I'd never shed so many happy tears. The door clicked shut and Carter wrapped me in his strong arms.

"They get me every time too." He kissed my temple. "Let's get our snack."

I couldn't help but laugh at the absurdity—and pleasure—of our nightly ritual. Cottage cheese and canned fruit. Who knew?

An hour later, we climbed into bed. Carter spooned me

tight against his body. His warmth comforted me; his strength gave me peace. I felt his breathing slow and deepen as sleep overtook him. I wriggled free of his arm and turned to face him, to watch his chest rise and fall, to see his eyes zip back and forth beneath his eyelids as he dreamed. He even pursed his lips. It was cute.

It was Saturday night and my mind found its way to the Connection where we'd met. There were probably thousands of men there right now, dancing and drinking. I'd been so excited to go there each weekend. Now, I couldn't imagine going back. What was I doing there in the first place?

Then I chuckled. It was called *the Connection*. That's exactly what people were doing there; what I'd been doing there. We were looking to *connect*. Maybe some wanted to connect purely on a physical level, but I think most wanted more, whether or not they were ready to admit it.

I nuzzled my head beneath Carter's chin, just above his collarbone, and rested my hand on his chest. It was my special place, the safest place in the world. In that moment, I knew there would be no more searching.

As far as connections went, I'd found mine.

Casey Morales

My Wildest Date

Raised by Wolves Book 3

1

PANCAKE BLISS

"Just breathe between sentences, okay?" Dwayne motioned for me to slow the word vomit spewing out of my mouth. His amused grin belied his annoyed tone and motherly palm.

"Sorry," I said, not sorry at all. "I guess you had to be there. It was the most incredible day I could ever imagine."

Thanksgiving was a couple weeks ago, and perky festive tunes rang throughout the diner. I'd just talked through Dwayne's coffee, pancakes and eggs without touching my own plate. He had practically licked his clean as Katie, our regular waitress, pried it from his bony fingers. They exchanged a wry glance before she shuffled off to her next table.

None of that mattered.

I walked Dwayne through the weekend with Carter and the kids, ending with a Picasso-like portrait of Saturday's lawn-mowing, leaf-pile-tossing, picture-perfect day. Carter had had his older son, Cade, on his lap as they made meticulous lines in the grass with the riding mower. Carter was determined to get one last cut in before winter grabbed us by the, um, throat.

Meanwhile, I was responsible for watching three-year-old Christian. Not to be outdone by Carter's heroic, ride-on-my-lap dad trick, I had taken my little monster to the man-sized pile of leaves and tossed him in. The pile shook with his giggles. Before I knew it, we were both rolling around, tossing leaves at each other and crying with happy laughter.

That's when it happened.

I looked up from the flurry of tiny hands and fluttering leaves and time froze. It was as if someone had pressed a button on a magical camera and everything paused.

In that moment, I had *everything* I'd ever wanted.

I had a partner who loved me, two beautiful boys whose smiles filled my soul in ways I'd never experienced, and hope for an incredible future.

Despite his palm-waving, Dwayne couldn't quell my excitement.

I could see in the tiny, upturned lines around his eyes that mirrored his smile that he didn't want to either. He was happy for me. He was nearly twice my age, but he was my best friend, the one person in the world I could tell everything and know I would never be judged.

Um, okay, that's not exactly true. I knew I *would* be judged. It's what we gays do, isn't it? Our DNA requires it. It's science.

Anyway.

Dwayne's judgment wasn't snarky or self-interested. It was borne of genuine empathy and concern, like a brother or father—or true friend.

"You've been dating how long now?" he asked as he eyed me over the rim of his chipped coffee mug.

"Three months."

My alarms were starting to sound. Where was he going? Was there a lesson coming from the sensei that would sober my giddy mood?

He nodded sagely. "That's a good amount of time. Just guard yourself."

"What do you mean?" I hadn't intended to sound defensive, but there it was.

"I don't want to see you hurt. That's all."

"Hurt? Why would Carter hurt me?" I *really* didn't like this conversation anymore. Maybe his judgment was judgy, after all.

Dwayne set his mug down and leaned forward. "Michael, you've barely slept a night at your own place since you met him. Things have moved so fast I can barely keep up. I know it feels wonderful right now, but Carter's life has complications. That can change things over time."

"Complications?" Now I was totally defensive.

His palms flew up in a *don't shoot the messenger* motion.

"I'm happy for you, really. Just try to take things one day at a time, alright?"

I had no idea what he meant, but nodded as if Confucius himself had just granted his wisdom.

In my moment of Zen-like confusion, Katie's hand found my shoulder. She leaned over and whispered into my ear, "Sweetie, don't listen to him. It's wonderful seeing you so happy."

I reached up and gave her hand a squeeze and smiled up in thanks. Dwayne downed the last of his coffee, tossed his usually healthy tip on the table, and began scooting out of the booth. "Gotta run," he said. "I'll talk to you soon. Have fun with lover boy."

Now *that* I could do.

Maybe Dwayne's sensei abilities were spot-on after all.

2

———

WHERE DID SANTA GO?

The Christmas countdown clock was ticking loudly now. Eight days 'til Santa.

Christian and Cade couldn't talk about anything else. I'd helped Christian make his list, which consisted of more Matchbox cars, stuffed animals, and a Batman costume. Batman and Robin were his big brother's favorite cartoon characters on Saturday morning, so they were now his too. It was cute.

Cade was two years older than my charge, which made his list twice as long. I didn't even recognize some of the toys and games on his crumpled paper. He carried it everywhere he went, as if showing more adults what he wanted would make them more likely to appear. Carter tried prying it out of his hands once, but the fit that ensued convinced us both to leave list management to the little one.

The four of us piled into Carter's SUV and searched for the perfect tree, then hauled it home and spent another hour decorating it. I'd never been into the whole Christmas cheer thing, but the boys had won me over to Santa's side.

There's an inexplicable joy hanging tinsel with a three-year-old—and they get *so* excited as each ornament appears. His deep brown eyes widened when I handed him a plastic Rudolf, then he giggled when I flipped the hidden switch and the reindeer's nose blinked.

I looked up to find Carter lifting Cade so he could place decorations near the tree's top, smiles plastered on both their faces.

My heart felt like it would burst.

THAT NIGHT, DURING OUR THURSDAY NIGHT RITUAL OF snuggling on the couch watching an episode of *LA Law* (hey, it was the '90s, that show was amazing), our little men fell asleep an hour before their normal bedtime, exhausted from another day preparing for Santa. Carter paused the TIVO, and we carried them into their room and tucked them snugly under their covers. I leaned down to kiss Christian's forehead and felt a tiny finger trace my jaw. His eyes never opened, but a thin smile curled his lips.

I heard Carter clanking dishes in the kitchen and knew he was making our bedtime snack of cottage cheese and canned fruit. This was a delicacy I'd never experienced before meeting him, but now I couldn't go to sleep without it. I curled up on the couch to await my gourmet goblet of goodness.

The kitchen quieted.

I let a few minutes pass, then curiosity got the best of me, so I headed into the kitchen. Carter was sitting at the table, staring into his untouched fruit. A second bowl was made for me, sitting in front of the chair opposite his.

This was odd. We always sat beside each other, not

opposite—and our nighttime snack was eaten in the den while watching TV.

As I sat and waited, my Spidey sense began to tingle—and not in the good way. Something significant was about to happen.

"Everything okay?" I ventured.

When he looked up, I knew my world was about to change. His eyes were rimmed red and a trickle flowed down one cheek.

"Carter, what's wrong?"

"I'm so sorry," was all he could get out before he choked on a sob.

I was kneeling by his chair in a flash, one hand on his arm, the other gently rubbing his back. "Hey. I'm right here. Whatever it is, we'll face it together."

That made his sobs grow.

"Her lawyer called," he muttered.

Now I was confused—and deeply concerned. "Lawyer? Whose lawyer?"

"Jen's." Jen was his ex-wife; the boys' mother.

My heart seized.

"Christian was so excited the other day." He sucked in a breath and locked eyes. "When I took them back to her place after their visit, he talked about it all week. Jen hadn't realized you were staying here on my weekends with the boys."

Another wave hit him, and he couldn't talk for a few minutes. I waited, having no idea what to say.

"You can't stay here anymore."

The room tilted.

My head swam.

"Oh. Well, um, that's okay, I guess. I'll just stay at my place when the boys are here. That's not a big deal."

It *was* a big deal, but they weren't my kids, I had no skin in this game. That's what I told myself, grasping for anything that would numb the pain blooming in the center of my chest, but it refused to be dulled.

He shook his head. "No, it's bigger than that. She's threatening to take me to court, to challenge our joint custody, if you sleep here one more night. Her lawyer said something about Tennessee judges not looking favorably on *gay influence* in situations like this."

Gay influence? What the hell was that? I understood the conservative approach to parenting—my own wolves had made sure of that—but I'd never been anything but supportive of Carter's decisions and was a positive influence on the boys. Carter and I never kissed in front of them, just to make sure stories couldn't get back to their mom.

"The lawyer said Cade told them about jumping on you while you were in the bed with me. He said you were naked."

"That's ridiculous." Now I *was* pissed. "I never got out from under the covers. The boys have never seen me less than fully clothed."

"I know, but the truth doesn't matter, only what they can make a judge believe." His head drooped. "I can't lose them, Michael. I can't lose my boys."

His hand was shaking as he took mine and kissed it. My last defense shattered with that simple act, and I began to cry with him. He dropped from his chair, pulled me down, and held me on the floor as we wept.

3

SHOCK AND AWE

"I don't know how long we sat there on his kitchen floor, holding each other and crying. It felt like all night. I kissed each of the kids on the forehead as they slept and haven't seen them since."

Katie's arms were a vise around my shoulders as they shuddered. She pressed my head into her shoulder, tears staining her white apron.

"Have you talked to Carter since?" Dwayne's voice was soft and soothing.

I wiped my face with a scratchy paper napkin and shook my head. "We talked on the phone last week. He said he didn't think he could do this anymore." I spat more than spoke that last part.

"Just like that?" Katie was indignant in my defense. Bless her.

I nodded. "Yeah, just like that. I can't blame him though. If I had to choose—" A new round of sobs slammed into me at the thought of Christian and Cade, realizing I wouldn't see them at Christmas—and might never see them again.

ON CHRISTMAS EVE, THE PACK GATHERED AT MY PARENTS'
house.

A month earlier, as we'd gathered for Thanksgiving, I'd
come out to my oldest sister, Nise, and told her about
Carter. She'd been amazing, telling me she only cared that I
was happy and with someone who loved me. I hadn't
mentioned the boys. That would've been more than even
the most understanding wolf could take.

Apparently, my mom, the unchallenged alpha in this
pack, had seen us fogging the glass in my beloved Saturn
and had grilled Nise about the conversation after I'd left. I
never knew my mom had lived a secret life as a Soviet
interrogator, but her skills at making people talk were
unmatched. Combine that with her Pisces sixth sense and
no secret was safe. Nise was no match for Comrade Nell.
My most closely held secret was dragged out in the open
for the whole family to see.

But here's the best part—I didn't know *any* of that
when I showed up for Christmas. The KGB hadn't sent a
note.

Apparently, they liked surprises.

I strolled into the house, a pack of clothes slung over
my shoulder, pillowcase filled with wrapped presents
weighing down my other hand. The greeting I received was
not filled with the festive cheer I'd expected

My mom and dad sat on one side of their round oak
dining table. Nise glanced up from her seat opposite the
inquisitors. There was something in her gaze I didn't recognize. I now know it was pity.

"Why don't you set your things down in the den and
join us? We'd like to talk before the others get here." My

father's voice was calm and welcoming, as if he was inviting me to eat dinner or grab a coffee. That unnerved me more than if he'd yelled.

As soon as my butt hit the wicker chair, Comrade Mama lobbed her first grenade. "Is there anything interesting you'd like to tell us?"

Oh, this was bad. She was opening with the *I'm not giving you any information* approach. I was well and truly screwed. Nise looked like she wanted to crawl under the table.

"Um, well, can you narrow it down a bit? Give me a topic?"

Mom's gaze was steel. "How about we start with Pat— or should I call *him* Carter now?" She crossed her arms in triumph.

Shit.

As a great philosopher once said, "Resistance is futile." I decided to just go with the conversation, as if there was nothing unusual in talking about a boyfriend with my preacher dad and zealot mom—the ones I didn't know had learned I was gay while my back was turned.

"Sure. Okay. Carter is someone I was dating."

Mom spat her overly sweetened tea across the table. I looked up, brow quirked.

"Dating?" she hissed. "You call it dating now?"

Ah, I understood. She'd switched to the religious *gays don't belong in our world* card. I should've seen it coming.

Honestly, at the time, *I* was uncomfortable calling it dating. Everything still felt new and strange, but there really wasn't a better word, at least not that I could think of. She certainly didn't need to know about the canoodling that went on behind closed doors. That would've destroyed Christmas.

Rather than offer a sharp retort, I nodded and quietly said, "Yes, we dated. We went to dinner and movies. We watched TV and cooked. We did all the normal things you'd expect from two people getting to know each other."

Her gaze was hardening, so I decided to make a peace offering. "But you don't need to worry about Carter anymore. Things...ended."

I heard Nise suck in a breath. When I dared a look in her direction, she mouthed, "I'm sorry."

"Denise!" the all-seeing eye snapped, and Nise's head fell.

My dad finally leaned in.

In all my daydreams—and nightmares—about coming out to my parents, he was the one I feared would slam the door. He was the man who stood in the pulpit and talked about how being gay was an abomination, citing one example after another, where city walls and stones were the only solution to the *gay* problem. He didn't disappoint in his reticence on the issue, but he did surprise me with his calm, empathetic tone.

"Michael, we love you, no matter what," he said.

My throat caught. Was he—

"But, since Carter's no longer in your life, do you think it might be a good time to, I don't know, get some help?"

Help? What in the ever-loving gay hell was that supposed to mean?

My pulse raced, and I began to sweat. Without a word, Nise, my only ally, my lifeline, stood and scurried out of the room.

Whiskey Tango Foxtrot!

I looked up at my dad and thought his heart might be beating as loudly as mine. He looked even more uncomfortable than I felt. "Help? What do you mean?"

He glanced at my mom, but her icy glare remained fixed on me.

He sipped his tea, then carefully set his glass down, the gentle thud of Walmart's finest crystal hitting wood the only sound in the room.

"I found a place that…they help people…boys like you," he stammered, eyes dropping to his weathered hands, unwilling to meet my eyes.

I couldn't believe what I was hearing. My dad was suggesting I consider going to a reform school for gays? I'd heard stories on the news about them. Some used shock or drug therapy to help *fix* a gay person's brain, as if there was some faulty wiring that simply needed an adjustment. Most of the tales about such places were horrific, and the only successes I'd heard of came from the guys who'd managed to hook up while there, sometimes with their instructors (or whatever you call them).

Let's go with Daddies.

"I know someone who went through a program like this. He's married now." My dad's voice was more plea than statement. He was miserable suggesting this, but he also sounded helpless. As confident as my mom's gaze appeared, I knew she was scared of losing me, whether to gayness or my own obstinance. Now my dad looked lost and alone.

Was he just as confused dealing with my feelings as I had been?

Then a realization struck. I'd had time to think through my feelings. It had been a few years since my first experience. While I was nowhere near confident in my new self, I wasn't looking in that mirror for the first time either.

My parents, on the other hand, had just learned everything. There were layers of complexity in their feelings in that moment.

First, in their eyes, the son they thought they knew—the one they raised to follow my dad into the pulpit—no longer existed. Sure, I was sitting right there. But in that moment, their eyes told me they were seeing *a stranger* sitting across that table. They had no idea who I was. Everything they thought they knew had turned upside down when Nise let the truth of Carter slip.

They weren't just afraid for my soul; they were mourning the death of a child they knew and loved.

They were also mourning the loss of a future they'd dreamed about since holding me as their newborn son— their *only* son. They'd dreamed of a wedding, followed by grandchildren. They'd dreamed of a life like they'd enjoyed, except this time with the freedom to spoil that comes with the title grand-whatever. None of that would happen now. I would never father children, grand or other- wise. While I had nieces and nephews, in my dad's pater- nalistic view, *his line* would end with me.

As angry as I was at the suggestion I needed help, I couldn't stop myself from feeling a deep empathy for their struggle. Their religious beliefs weren't an act. They weren't some suits they donned on Sundays to impress the neighbors. Their beliefs were the core of their beings. While our views definitely differed, I still respected theirs. They were sincere, good people, and I loved them both. Seeing their pain added to my own.

Until my mother spoke again. "You know you can never bring a *man* into our home. We could never allow that."

So much for the goodwill gesture.

I stood, nearly knocking my chair over as it slid back.

"Keep telling me I need help and you'll be lucky if I bring *myself* back into this house, much less anyone else." I was proud of that line.

Then I turned to my dad, venom in my voice. "And how dare you. I just lost someone I loved. I came here, *hurting*, feeling more alone than at any time in my life, and the first thing you suggest is I enjoy the warm embrace of electroshock therapy? Nice one, Dad."

His head fell and any pride I might've had in that snappy retort dropped like a stone in my gut.

I grabbed the pack with my clothes and stormed out of the kitchen to the solitude of my old bedroom, leaving a pair of stunned and hurt parents staring at the chair that once held their son.

4

HO, HO, HO

The rest of the pack arrived within hours.

Tension flashed between the adults like light-ning, but we kept everything in check for the kids, deter-mined to let them be children and enjoy their holiday, regardless of whatever Grinch-like havoc I might've wrought.

Family tradition dictated the opening of exchanged presents on Christmas Eve, followed by the opening of Santa's deliveries at some ungodly hour on Christmas morning. The festivities were capped with a glutenous meal around two o'clock on Christmas Day. My dad usually found his La-Z-Boy and passed out within thirty minutes of his fork's final clank, but not this year. I felt his hand on my shoulder and knew there would be another *talk*.

I sighed. Nise, who was sitting beside me, grabbed my hand under the table and gave me a supportive squeeze. Then I rose to face the executioner.

It was freezing outside, so my dad suggested we take a drive down to our gas-station-adjacent office. If you missed that part, yes, we rented space attached to a gas station for our family wholesale drug business my dad ran when he wasn't doing the part-time preacher thing. It wasn't big, nor was it glamorous, but it was close to their house and was all we needed. I sat in my spinny office chair. He grabbed a folding chair and sat with his knees almost touching mine.

This can't be good.

He'd called this meeting, so I kept quiet as a long moment passed and he gathered his thoughts. He was clearly struggling, which was not normal for the always-ready-to-speak preacher man.

"Michael, I want to say…I mean, after yesterday in the kitchen…well, that wasn't…"

Wow, he's really flummoxed.

"I just want to say I'm sorry."

Shit. That wasn't the sermon listed on the program.

"I didn't realize how much he…I mean, Carter…meant to you. If I'd known, I never would've suggested any of those things. I know I shouldn't have anyway, but I really wouldn't have if I'd known." He put his head in his hands, and I thought he might actually cry. I'd only ever seen him cry twice: at his mother's funeral, and as he held my mother at her father's funeral. He'd actually shed more tears comforting her than he had allowed himself for his own loss. He was such a good man in that way.

He looked up. A tear had escaped. His voice shook when he continued. "You're more important to me than *anything* in this world. You know that, don't you? I'm *so* sorry you're hurting. We don't have to talk about anything else. Just tell me how you're doing. Please. Let me help you."

Dammit. I lost my shit right there in our office.

My dad was so sincere, so heartfelt. I fell into his arms and became a five-year-old boy seeking shelter and safety in his father's embrace. All the grief from losing Carter, even more from losing my connection to the boys, poured out of me. Between sobs, I told him how hurt I was, how much I'd thought Carter was *the one*. I know it hurt him to hear me refer to another man that way, but he held me tighter, and his tears fell with my own.

Now, don't get crazy, he wasn't accepting me being gay or giving up hope I might return to the fold one day, but he was putting our relationship as father and son above everything else. This man I'd expected to cast me out of the pack —to stone me outside our city walls—chose to hold me closer when the darkness came.

However long I live, I may never experience a more beautiful moment.

5

AOL INCHES DON'T COUNT

The holiday encounter with the pack had taken place over the weekend, so I got back to my apartment Sunday night, the day after Christmas Day.

For those of us trapped within the borders of our own land, the day after Christmas is known as Boxing Day to the rest of the world. Modern thought suggests it's the day to *box up* everything from Christmas, though the origin of the day was more likely related to servants or workers on estates being given gifts (in boxes) the day following the land-owning family's celebration. Either way, like many traditions that began with the best intentions, it turned into a giant commercial opportunity for retailers to offer crazy sales and handle lame gift returns.

Why am I giving you a history lesson on Boxing Day? I have no clue. I just remember that's the day I escaped the pack.

Stop distracting me.

My roommate Peter had traveled to spend Christmas with his family, so I had the apartment to myself until New Year's Day when he returned. I was glad. A week to myself would let me process everything that had happened over Christmas.

The morning after his return, I walked my bleary-eyed self into the kitchen and was greeted by Peter, who was sitting shirtless on a bar stool eating Frosty Pebbles.

Yes, Peter was a personal trainer with abs on his toes, but he loved his sugary goodness. He could've eaten every Frosty Pebble ever made and still look like a Greek statue. It was infuriating—but not the worst sight to see first thing in the morning.

"You don't look mopey today. That's an improvement."

He'd been trying to shake me out of my funk for months, but, because I was a total wuss and hadn't come out to him yet, he still believed the Pat story and thought I'd been dumped by a Hooters waitress.

Hey! Stop giggling. If I'm going to date a fictitious woman, she's going to have *huge* tatas and tiny shorts. That's just how I roll.

"Guess time does heal."

He eyed me, but kept munching. "Anything you want to share?"

I nearly dropped my coffee mug. What did he mean by that? Had he heard something? Had my mother secretly conspired with him to grill me for information? He didn't know my family. How could he know Pat wasn't real? That's what he was saying, right?

I tried not to freak out. "Uh, I don't know. Like what?"

He finished his overstuffed mouthful and set his bowl down. It took forever for him to stop chewing. I flinched as he tossed his spoon against the empty ceramic with a *clank*. Why was I suddenly so nervous?

"So, two things. You should probably sit down."

I sat, feeling like the kid waiting outside the principal's office.

Peter stood and leaned over the counter. I couldn't help admiring how his arms flexed, despite the tsunami I sensed coming.

"First, I've known Pat wasn't real for months. I get why you never told me, but you should know you can tell me anything. I don't care that you're gay, only that you're my brother."

I swallowed hard.

"Second, and this is the part you may not like, I'm moving out."

My head snapped up. "What? You're—"

"Actually, it's more than that. I'm joining the navy. The recruiter said he could get me into the SEAL program—at least, get me into the tryouts for it. I have to earn my way in from there."

My mouth closed, but my eyebrows shot to the ceiling. "SEALs? Really? But you're...*a model.*"

I didn't mean for that last part to sound so judgy, but there it was.

He laughed. "Crazy, isn't it? My dad was a SEAL. My uncle was a SEAL. It's something I've always wanted to do, but never thought I could. The program's intense and most guys fail out."

My head was spinning. "Wow. SEALs. I don't even know what to say. That's awesome...and totally sucks. I don't want to lose you."

He cocked his head like a confused German shepherd.

"I mean, you're a good roommate and all. I'll hate to see you go."

He reached across and mussed my hair. Was I twelve? What was that? "I'll miss you too." He turned to walk toward his bedroom. "I leave tomorrow. If you want to tell me about Carter before I go, now's the time."

Holy shit. He even knew Carter's name.

I watched him vanish down the hallway, speechless for the third time before my first full cup of coffee. This was going to be a really weird day. I'd have to start getting used to the idea of living alone. I wasn't glad about that.

Peter and I had been roommates for a couple of years. His straight hotness might've been frustrating—and an utter waste of a smokin' hot guy with gay rockstar potential—but he was a great roomie. We lived separate lives, but enjoyed each other's company when our paths converged at home. We respected each other's space, shared the bills, and he was a great coach at the gym. I hated him for that last part some days, but he was largely responsible for my burgeoning physique, and that felt amazing.

Peter had taken a scrawny, scared guy and dragged him into the deep end where the muscle heads swam, somewhere he never would've ventured on his own. He showed that guy it was okay to be new and to struggle, that others had been there and would help. He helped him gain confidence he'd never known.

He helped *me* gain that confidence. I was going to miss him.

I flopped on the couch, more miserable than before. The goal had been to get home and cheer up by the time Peter returned. Nice work.

Something shiny caught my eye on the kitchen counter, so I hopped up to investigate. It was one of those magical discs that granted one thousand free hours of internet access—and it didn't come with a *for new subscribers only* label, which meant I could add a thousand freebies to my account. My mood suddenly shifted as I raced into my room, disc in hand.

A couple minutes and a dozen beep-bops later, a warm voice welcomed me to the World Wide Web. I checked my inbox. Nothing but coupons from Crate and Barrel and several emails bequeathing me an estate in Nigeria and Slovakia. How could there be so many princes out there I'd never heard of—and how did they all know my email address?

Annoyed by my lack of popularity, and still smarting from Christmas and Peter's pending departure, I turned to the only therapist I'd ever known, America Online Chat Rooms.

For those born after the glory that was the '80s, let me explain. Chat rooms were the very first online meeting places. They came in every variety and flavor, much like the people who entered them. For example, one might be interested in gardening. There were probably a thousand different rooms, with titles like *Green Thumbs in Indiana* or *Horticulture Rocks!* Yes, some of the names were lame, but you get the idea.

Now, forget plants.

If there were a thousand rooms for finding gardening tips, there were ten thousand for finding gardeners, and I'm not talking about the spade-wielding kind. These were rooms for meeting and talking with other men or women looking to date.

Yes, *date*—that's what they were looking for. Do you know what a euphemism is?

Anyway.

For our purposes, let's narrow the conversation to any room with a title containing the designation *M4M*, the universal label for men looking for other men. These were the gay rooms where good Christian boys sought other good Christian boys—

Wait, you *believed* that?

Most of the men chatting their lives away in *M4M* rooms were looking to meet other men. I'll be generous and say *some* of them wanted to get to know other guys, maybe have coffee or see a movie. You know, go on a date?

Bah! Most of the men online wanted one thing—and it wasn't the Crate and Barrel coupon.

The rooms with more aggressive appellations, such as *M4MNow!*, suggested those seeking dates would be better served elsewhere. The guys in this club had their own members primed and ready—*now!*

I'm not sure which bucket I fell into in that moment. I'd never been one for casual sex. Then again, I'd thought I was straight most of my life. Not having sex with women was easy. Now that Little Michael was pointed in the right direction, resisting the urge was getting much harder.

Yes, I said harder. Stop that.

I knew my ultimate goal was to find someone special, to get to know him and build a life together. My time with Carter, however brief it might've been, had crystalized that dream in my mind. When it worked, it was beautiful. That's what I wanted.

But at the moment, I didn't have a Carter. I was a free agent.

I entered the benignly named *NashvilleM4M* room. There were twenty-two guys on the menu…I mean, in the directory. I clicked on the first screen name, Chad824. His profile was sparse, but said he liked reading, cooking, and gardening.

What was it with gardening online?

Anyway, Chad824 had committed the ultimate AOL-profile party foul. He'd left any description of his physical attributes out. To any self-respecting, judgy gay, that ruled him right out.

Next.

I clicked on MuscleBrad. He sounded tasty—I mean, educated.

There was only one line in his profile. It read: *GWM, 34, 6'1, 31w, Brown/Blue, 16a, 8cThick—if online, looking —must have pix.*

Yes, kids, this was how a profile was *supposed* to work. Brad was a gay white male, kinda tall with a sexy waistline. He had brown hair and blue eyes, bulging arms, and an even nicer bulge down below. Apparently, he thought so much of his bulge that he specified its impressive girth.

Here's another fun fact for the class: the term *AOL inches* was born from these stats. What if Brad, musclebound though he may be, was only packing six inches of, um, bulge? Surely, someone wouldn't lie about such a vital value, would they? Come to think of it, who even measures their member? Isn't that weird in itself? Anyway, AOL inches was the inside gay joke referring to a guy's real length versus his AOL profile's stated length.

The little *c* next to the eight was confusing to me at first. I had guessed it was a religious abbreviation, maybe Catholic? Alas, dear friends, that's *not* what that stood for, though some might infer which religion a boy belonged to (or didn't belong to) by the letter's presence.

Think scissors. Got it?

Brad was hunting a hookup, and was experienced enough online to only meet guys who could swap pictures. No, there was nowhere to upload a photo onto a profile back then. You had to actually talk to someone and agree to exchange pictures via email. AOL was great in some ways. That wasn't one of them.

I wasn't really looking for sex, but Brad sounded like a good Christian boy. I sent him an instant message (IM for you heathens): *Hey*.

Yeah, I was a literary genius.

While I waited for Brad to reply, I clicked on the next few profiles. Most had the obligatory line with stats, some contained lengthy paragraphs describing that person's ideal match. Others spent more time describing what they *weren't* looking for. Either way, it was fun to meet more people, safe in the anonymity of my own apartment, without having to go to a smoky bar.

After two hours of my magical thousand-hour freebie, I had eleven IM windows open and blinking rapidly.

Holy Mavis Beacon, Batman. I needed typing lessons. IMs moved fast—*really* fast. Just when you started one conversation, three more windows would pop up with prospective candidates seeking an interview—I mean, guys saying hello. If you got stuck chatting with one dude too long, others would start getting annoyed at your delayed response and either exit the IM or send a snarky message. Either way, if that happened, your odds with that particular applicant would decrease.

My fingers had never flown so fast.

And then I committed an AOL mortal sin: I sent a reply to the wrong guy.

The guy I was chatting with about his golden retrievers had a similar screen name to another dude who wanted me to lick his Weimaraner. I was really starting to like talking with Retriever29, but he didn't appreciate me asking whether his weeny dog was cut or not. He logged off in a huff.

In that moment, I had a gay epiphany.

I needed a system, some method of taking notes and cataloging the guys I chatted with. I opened a profile and hit Control-P. What spat out of my printer was a jumbled mess of a dude's profile, but it was workable, and there was enough white space for taking notes.

When my wall clock chimed eleven, I blinked the monitor haze from my eyes and stretched my back. I had somehow spent an entire day in chat rooms, and I wasn't even sorry—it had been exactly what I needed. I looked at my stack of printed profiles. Midway through the evening's adventure, I'd figured out how to copy and paste a photo onto the profile before hitting the print button, thus creating a more complete dossier. Dozens of guys smiled up at me, most shirtless, some showing their *very* happy Catholic wiener dogs.

Profiles of hot guys got a star or two. If the conversation was good, they got another star. If they were hot *and* could hold down a chat, their stars were circled.

I was an organized, AOL-loving…never mind. You get the idea.

As I hit the power button and listened to the whirring of the hard drive cease for the night, I laughed at myself. I knew it was silly and probably crazy, but I felt good again. There were so many guys out there, even in sleepy Nashville, surely one of them would be cool and want me.

For the first time since Carter had kicked me to the curb, I felt a twinge of hope.

Thank you, America Online. You're an *amazing* therapist.

6

THE BIG GAY DIAMOND

Did you know there are groups for virtually any activity or interest in the gay world? And not just on AOL, in real life?

Last night, while trolling the chat rooms like a good Christian boy, I'd found a room titled *GayMen4Chess*. My initial reaction was curiosity at how they'd misspelled the word *chest*, then I realized they meant the board game. Holy cow. It was a group of gay nerds who'd get together just to play chess.

Who knew?

My scrolling intensified and, besides the Kasparov Rainbow Club, there were groups for gay gardening (had to mention that one), gay travel, former military gays, service industry gays, and gays into drag. I suspect that last one was redundant.

There was even a group for gay couples looking for other couples *FOR FRIENDS ONLY.* I thought it was funny how they put that last bit in all caps to ensure everyone knew they weren't there to hook up. Just for fun, I stuck my nose in and chatted with a few lovely gents. Two of the couples talked about their dogs and how they wanted to decorate their homes, but the third asked for my stats and pics right out of the gate.

Yeah, they wanted a threesome. I'd learned all about those in a movie a while back.

I clicked out of that room pretty quickly (although I did print the profile of one couple who seemed nice). No, it wasn't the throuple-seekers. Give me *some* credit.

Among the groups, I discovered Nashville had a gay softball league. I was blown away. Not too long ago, I didn't know another gay man existed near me. Now AOL was telling me there was a whole league packed full of softball-loving queens?

I jumped all over that shit. My email zipped out faster than a fart at Taco Bell.

Sorry, I know you love a sloppy Nacho Bell Grande. Who doesn't?

Five minutes flew by and my PC cried out, "You've got mail." I clicked the envelope of joy to find an email from the commissioner of the softball league. Indeed, they were accepting new players—and there was a tryout this weekend.

The gay gods were smiling on me again. And the congregation said, "Let there be rainbows and unicorns. Amen."

This was exciting. I loved playing most sports, and softball sounded like a fun way to get to know more guys, make some friends, and who knows what else? Add that to a Friday night social volleyball group I read about, and I might actually have a social life before it was all over.

Again, AOL's therapeutic skills were unparalleled. I was now in my first achy-cheek-smiling good mood since Christmas.

<hr>

Saturday arrived, and anticipation bubbled inside me as I strode from my car to the dusty field. There were a few guys warming up, tossing balls back and forth, but most of the gaggle was gathered around the chorus-riser stands behind the home team's dugout.

I slowed my approach to appraise the competition.

The warmer-uppers looked decent, except for one poor dude who couldn't throw for shit. He made it look like an Olympic javelin toss as the ball either sailed miles over the receiver's head or flopped to the ground a foot in front of him. The guy playing catch with him closed the gap between them, grabbed the ball from the ground, and gave some sage coaching advice I wasn't sure would make any difference. I guessed some guys were here more for the social than competitive aspect.

Shifting my attention, I saw that most of the gaggle was unremarkable, dressed in T-shirts and shorts, some limbering up their gloves or swinging bats.

One guy wore a pink tutu. He was about six feet tall, barrel-chested, with a belly that stuck out like Santa and a bushy beard to match. From a distance, I could see wiry black hair clawing its way out of his shirt—the front *and* the back.

Holy Wookiee, Luke. We have ourselves a hairy fairy.

I later learned there was a *whole team* of guys who looked and dressed exactly like our dear Mr. Tutu. From my extensive academic research on the well-known hub of knowledge, AOL, I'd also learned that gays used animal names as descriptors. Guys with big bellies and pelts sprouting out of their pores were called *bears*. I did not, however, learn what one called a bear in a tutu. I made a mental note to research that one later.

"Michael?" a voice called out from the trees beyond the gaggle.

I craned my neck to find a blond guy in his midtwenties waving his hand above his head. He was practically hopping up and down to get my attention. I squinted, but couldn't place him. The social pressure of being called by name in front of a bunch of new guys pulled me to him like a magnet. When I got within reach, his arms flew outward and pulled me into a tight hug.

Whoever he was, he felt good—hard chest, strong arms, good hugger.

"You have no idea who I am, do you?" he said, grinning as he pulled back from the embrace. "It's okay. I'm better with matching profiles to real-life faces than most. I'm Scott, of *Scott and Jay*. We chatted last night."

"Oh!" I said, rapidly sifting through the printed pages in my mind. One with three stars in a bold circle flashed to the fore. "I remember now. You're the couple that lives downtown near Second Avenue, right?"

Scott beamed at being remembered, then took a step back and looked me up and down like I was a slab of beef in a butcher shop. "You need new pictures. Damn."

"Uh, is that a good thing?"

"Sure is. Jay's going to lose his mind when he sees you. He's out there trying to help that poor kid with throwing dyslexia." He pointed to the pair I'd noticed earlier.

"Throwing dyslexia?"

"That's what we call it when the ball goes opposite to where the thrower intends—*every time*." He laughed. "This must be your first time with the league. What level are you playing?"

Huh. They had levels. "I don't know. I played Little League baseball, but never softball on a team."

He examined me again and squeezed my bicep. I wasn't sure that was a necessary part of tryouts, but it *was* a gay league. What did I know? "Well, you look athletic. Come warm up with me, and we'll see how you do."

It took a minute to remember to keep my glove on the ground when fielding, but the mechanics came back quickly. Scott and I warmed up for ten minutes before a tall guy in a bright-orange cap walked out and blew a whistle. Those of us warming up gathered round and waited as the others took their time wrapping up conversations. They moved as one, a group giggle flowing in the wake of the gaggle.

Scott strode up to stand beside Jay. Like Scott, Jay was fit. He wore a white tank top, showing off taut arms and rounded shoulders. Scott motioned toward me with his eyes, and Jay scanned me like a copier, then looked back at his partner. He whispered something I couldn't hear, and they both grinned and nodded.

What had I gotten myself into?

We were divided into three groups: new players with throwing dyslexia, guys who had some basic hand–eye coordination, and skilled players who either played high school or college baseball. I stood with the middle group, a little annoyed that my prowess had been underrated. After another hour of fielding drills and batting practice, I discovered I had been accurately pigeonholed, because those higher-level players were the real deal. Their throws zipped across the field without a hint of an arc, and their batters hit more balls over the fence than inside the park.

Jay and Scott were placed with the experienced players. Scott was good, but Jay was ridiculous. I'd later learn he played baseball at Vanderbilt, which explained why every ball he struck landed in the parking lot well beyond the fence. He was a softball-slamming beast.

At the end of practice, Whistle Dude walked around and thanked each new player for trying out, and asked if they wanted to continue playing with a team. Those who answered affirmatively would be matched up with a team later in the week, and a follow-up email would be sent informing each player of their new assignment.

When Whistle got to me, he said, "Scott tells me you're pretty good. The Shooters need a pitcher. Think you could learn that position?"

He said that with a straight face, so I left the double entendre on the field. Man, that was a hard one to pass up. "Sure. That gets me in every play. I like it."

"Good." He scribbled something on his clipboard, nodded once, then moved on to his next victim.

I turned to leave, but was stopped by a hand on my shoulder. "I hear you just got signed up to pitch. Ever done that before?" The gleam in Scott's eye told me he had left no entendre on the field, double or otherwise.

I tried playing it straight. "No, never have. Should be fun."

Jay strolled up then and asked, "What should be fun? Are you coming over?"

"What—"

Scott chuckled at my wide eyes, then turned to Jay. "I haven't asked him yet. We were talking pitching…I mean, softball."

"I bet you were," Jay said with an eye roll before turning back to me. "Come have dinner at our place. You seem like a nice guy, and we're trying to add to our friend list."

I cocked my head. "You guys need more friends? I find that hard to believe."

"You might be surprised. The minute you get a boyfriend, half the gay world thinks you're dead. The other half just wants to get in your partner's pants." Scott grinned at Jay. "I can't really blame them for that though, can I? Look at him. Who wouldn't want that?"

Jay snorted and tried to play it off, but I could see a blush forming in his cheeks. They were adorable together. There was an intimacy to their banter, a familiarity.

"So, dinner?" Jay dodged his blushing issue.

"Sure, sounds good."

We exchanged phone numbers, and Jay scribbled their address on the back of a softball flier. I waved as I drove out of the parking lot, completely missing the mischievous grins on both their faces.

7

BARBECUE AND FLUFF BALLS

I only got lost once on the way to Scott and Jay's house. The streets of downtown Nashville made my brain hurt; add in my terrible sense of direction, and one wrong turn was actually a victory.

Nashville's downtown was an odd jumble of short red-brick buildings dating back a hundred years or more, and shiny new skyscrapers. You might walk past the Ryman Auditorium where the Grand Ole Opry recorded its show for decades, then enter the lobby of the city's tallest tower, like the Bat Building, only a block or two away. The Bat Building was BellSouth's new headquarters. It wasn't actually named the Bat Building, but that's what everyone called in thanks to the odd glass and girder protrusions on its top that looked like Batman's ears.

There was an odd beauty in the tightly packed juxtaposition of old and new.

The guys lived just across the Cumberland River, almost within sight of historic Second Avenue. Yes, that's the same Second Avenue where the Wildhorse Saloon hosted a performance by my one-time obsession, Jason. I thought about that night briefly as I passed the multi-story bar. Why had I been so taken with him back then?

Jason had joined Dwayne and me for lunch a few times over the past few months. He was still hot, but now that I knew him, I was glad he wasn't looking for anything.

Let's call that a healthy miss.

I crossed the brackish waters of the Cumberland, and the quality of the real estate took a quick nosedive. Tattered public housing rose to my right, while houses barely holding themselves together sprawled to my left. I tried to keep the sinking feeling now churning in my gut at bay, but it was determined to make this an uncomfortable drive.

Three left turns, two gas stations, and one liquor store with a shattered window later, I reached the sign for Pierce Avenue, the dead-end street where the boys lived. The first house I passed had an old refrigerator on the front porch. The fridge matched the rusty white car in the driveway, though the cinder blocks holding the car up didn't quite fit the rusted metal motif.

My family was never wealthy, and I had nothing against folks who struggled financially, but this was starting to make me nervous. Where the hell was I going?

The third house on Pierce towered over the others, a new two-story construction that looked like something off the cover of a real estate magazine. To either side of this majestic home were more houses with appliances as yard art. The yards themselves had less grass than the dusty infield at softball practice.

I finally reached the end of the street and looked up to find another two-story newbie. It was stunning. Most of the exterior was red brick, and each floor had its own deck that wrapped around the entire structure. Even the driveway looked freshly laid, its pearly white concrete barely showing signs of recent rain, much less wear. I double-checked the softball flier and confirmed the 243 on the door was my destination.

The knot in my gut relaxed as I walked up the driveway and Scott appeared in the open doorway. He wore a tall, puffy chef's hat and a broad smile. As I drew closer, he waved a wooden spoon and called out, "Come on in. I need to take the beans off the heat."

The sound of barking dogs grew louder, then abruptly stopped as the guardians of the castle peered out the open door, daring me to enter. I'm not sure what breed they were, something small, puffy, and white. The moment I leaned down, all three attacked my hand with warm, slob-bery tongues.

"Wow. They don't like *anybody*." I looked up as Jay descended the wooden stairs.

I grinned and tried to reply, but words eluded me. The last time I saw Jay, he was wearing baggy baseball pants covered in dirt. Now, slightly above my eye level, sheer, tight-fitting light-blue shorts clung to every curve—and his curve was *huge*. I was pretty sure he wasn't wearing under-wear by the swing on his porch. I really loved swings.

I swallowed the lump that sprung out of nowhere and threw my eyes back down toward the dogs, desperate not to look at the *taken* dude's package.

He chuckled, then turned. "Come on in. Scott's just about got dinner ready. Hope you like barbecue chicken and baked beans."

"Sounds great."

The fluff balls had apparently decided I was part of their pack and surrounded me as I followed the sound of clanking pots and utensils. The house was an interesting mix of log cabin and postmodern minimalist.

What am I saying? I don't know anything about architecture.

The walls were like a log cabin, where the wood had been flattened and polished to a sheen. The gooey stuff that held the logs together was visible, but sealed within the wood's clear coating. It was beautiful; I'd never seen anything like it. As I passed the den, I took a good look at the ceiling; white, with an intricate pattern of massive beams made of the same rich wood as the walls, giving the open floor plan a sense of height and rustic elegance. Long, puffy leather couches created a seating area around a large-screen television. It was warm outside, but the guys had lit a fire in the fireplace anyway.

There were photos everywhere—standing on tables, propped up against books in tall niches, and hung on every wall. Images of varying sizes told the story of Jay and Scott on a cruise ship, riding horses on a mountain path—and a *whole* lot more. In a number of the pictures, the boys were posing on various beaches wearing only speedos. I leaned in close to one photo and…

Sweet Chicken of the Sea, Jay's free-flopping curve looked even *bigger* in a banana hammock.

I turned and led the pack from their den of iniquity, finally reaching the kitchen. Scott was standing at the stove ladling beans into a serving dish. Jay was nuzzled up behind him, sneaking kisses on his neck. I paused, taking them in.

Set aside how beautiful each of them was in their own right—they were fit, muscular, sexy guys in the prime of life—but that wasn't what made me stare. It was the tenderness of the moment, the gentle kiss Jay pressed against Scott's neck, and the way Scott leaned back into his lover's touch. There was something so simple, so honest, in that gesture.

Scott must've felt me staring, because he looked up, winked, then shooed Jay away with his wooden spoon. "Go on now, the table isn't going to set itself." Scott turned to me and issued more orders. "You, come here. Help me put these dishes out."

And just like that, I realized Scott was the mother of the pack.

<hr>

BEFORE WE DOVE INTO THE MEAL, SCOTT DOVE INTO conversation, asking everything he could about my past, present, and future. It felt a little like a job interview, but I secretly enjoyed the attention. I wasn't used to guys wanting to know all that stuff.

Jay finally rescued me. "I'm going to starve if you keep asking Michael questions. Let's eat."

Jay was dad. Got it.

Dinner was delicious. How can you not love barbecue? Scott used canned baked beans, but added so many spices and herbs they were barely recognizable from the original —and they were outstanding. Scott drank white wine, while Jay had beer. They gave each other a look I didn't quite follow when I asked for a Coke.

What is it about me asking for Coke that makes men grin?

The guys were as free with their own information as they had been with questions. Jay spoke like an online profile. "I grew up in Knoxville with my parents and three brothers, am a diehard Tennessee Vols fan, and work for a landscaping company. Scott and I met in college. He's the only man I've ever dated. We've been together for eight years, ten if you count freshman and sophomore years when we fucked but claimed we were straight and it was just a college phase."

They shared a grin and laughed in unison. Jesus, they were like the same person sometimes.

I eyed Jay's golden tan. As an Irishman, I'd always envied those with more than pasty pigments. I'd tried tanning oils, creams, even tanning beds, but nothing worked. The best I could do was make a few patches of freckles merge and pretend it was a tan. Melanin was repelled by my near-translucence.

Snapping out of my skin-tone envy, I turned to Scott. "What about you? Was Jay your first and only?"

"Oh hell no. He was a slut," Jay barked.

Scott grabbed a fork and pretended to toss it at him from across the table, grinning the whole time.

"I was *very* friendly in college, thank you very much," he said dramatically. "I studied nursing, and work at Baptist Hospital now."

"What kind of nurse are you? I mean, where do you work in the hospital?" I asked.

"I work in the NICU, taking care of babies."

I tried not to swoon at the idea of sexy Scott holding a newborn, but it was the *perfect* profession for him. In the short time I'd known him, he'd impressed me with how he took care of everyone around him. He did it at the softball field, and he clearly took care of the pack here in his home.

It didn't hurt that he was a hardy Midwestern boy from Iowa.

He saw my awed expression and joked, "I was raised with good morals, muscles, and mothers."

I quirked my brow at that last statement, completely

lost. Jay laughed and leaned over like he was telling me a secret. "He was raised by a pair of *lesbians*." He slithered out the last word as if he was a snake.

Oh. I think my mouth actually made that O shape.

I'd never heard of such a thing. My brain immediately tried to process the biology of his birth and came up empty.

Scott and Jay each barked a laugh, then Scott saved my impending aneurysm. "I was adopted when I was six months old. My birth mom was a drug addict who died in childbirth. If it weren't for two loving women coming to my rescue, I don't know where I'd be now."

I wanted to smile to show I understood, but the heartbreak of his birth held my pained expression in place—to lose his mother before he could know her.

Scott smiled. "It's all good. My moms are the best. They taught me everything I know about being a man and taking care of my own family."

I'd need to consult the Oracle of AOL for answers later. Women teaching a boy how to be a man puzzled my preacher's kid's mind.

Jay stood and started grabbing dirty plates. "Why don't we clean up, then we can watch a movie or something."

A movie. Or something? This sounded vaguely familiar.

We all moved to the kitchen, and I chided myself for making a naughty assumption. These guys were a couple. From what I could see, they were just about the happiest, most loving pair of dudes you'd ever meet.

What was I thinking?

And then Jay spoke. "I think we should get in the hot tub instead of watching a movie."

I almost dropped the glass I was washing. Hot tub?

"That's a *great* idea, babe. I'm still sore from softball,

and it's so nice out tonight," Scott said enthusiastically. "Is that okay with you, Michael?"

"Sure, I guess. I mean, I, uh, didn't bring any swim trunks or anything."

Jay laughed. "That's perfect. We don't allow *clothing* in our hot tub anyway."

Scott somehow found the wooden spoon in the soapy water and swatted Jay's arm playfully. "You be good."

"Yes, Mom," Jay said without a hint of remorse. Then leaned over my shoulder and whispered, his hot breath brushing my ear, "It's settled. Naked tub in ten. I'm gonna go get it hot for you."

The glass slipped from my grasp, and soapy water splattered everywhere.

Jay's laughter could be heard echoing off the walls until the thud of the sliding door blocked him out.

"Don't let his mouth scare you. He's harmless. Besides, he's got a *great* mouth," Scott said affectionately.

I ignored the burning blush of my ears and focused on fishing the glass out of the bubbles.

***

WAS IT WEIRD TO GO *UPSTAIRS* FOR AN OUTDOOR HOT TUB?

I wasn't sure, but, like a lost puppy, I followed Scott anyway.

We wove our way through a hallway and entered a large bedroom that spanned half the upstairs floor space. Their king-sized bed held court against the far wall, and was cloaked in a fluffy comforter embroidered with a bright floral pattern. Another huge television hung on the wall opposite the bed. Dressers consumed one side, while the other side contained a small sitting area, complete with two chairs and a love seat. Double French doors between the dressers led to their bathroom. I couldn't see much, but a sea of marble gleamed as I strained to check it out.

We exited through a sliding door next to the love seat. The smell of freshly cut grass slapped my nose as we walked out onto the upper deck, where the hot tub gurgled happily. Scott disappeared back into the house to grab towels.

I really didn't connect the dots of the hot tub sitting only a few feet from the entrance to their bedroom. Bookmark that for later. You'll want to reference this moment of gullible idiocy.

As I stared into the frothy water, I couldn't stop thinking about Jay's steamy breath on my neck. The tiny hairs prickled as my fingers tried to scratch the sensation away. I sucked in a deep breath, but an odd mix of terror, anticipation, and something I couldn't identify kept my heart racing—horniness, yeah, that was the other thing. Little Michael made *that* clear. The mixture of those emotions was a cocktail made for, well, a cock—and mine was ready to leap out of my shorts and be seen by the world. I was afraid it might break out into song like in a Disney movie.

Hmm. I wonder what Uncle Walt would name *that* character?

Never mind.

Scott and Jay were inside doing whatever they did before getting naked in a hot tub. They'd left me out to wait, or get ready, or, I don't know, play with the dogs. Three luminous fluff balls had tailed us and now swirled in constant motion around my feet.

I peered over the railing and took in the perfectly manicured yard. Bursts of pink, purple, and blue bordered the green expanse. At the far end, a small wooden pergola sheltered two benches and a bubbling fountain. There wasn't a bloom or blade out of place, and the towering fence encircling the garden ensured total privacy. Even the upper deck had light-brown wicker screens to shield the hot tub from the neighbors' view. Somewhere, on another plane of existence, a Japanese Zen master was pleased by Jay's effort.

"Am I throwing you in fully clothed?"

I nearly jumped over the railing as Jay stepped up behind me.

When I turned, my eyes widened at his naked body only inches away—and we're not talking AOL inches either. I staggered back a step, and the banister pressed into my back. He grinned at my discomfort.

My eyes ignored the command to stay at eye level, wandering down his perfectly tanned and toned physique. His shoulders were even rounder than I remembered, and he had those tiny nipples you just wanted to tickle and call *my little buddy.*

That's not weird. That's what you call them, right? Anyway.

Before I could vomit—I mean, say anything—he stepped forward and gripped the bottom of my T-shirt with both hands.

"Arms up, mister," he commanded.

My arms *flew* skyward as if a dozen policemen had guns trained on me.

His grin widened as he slowly pulled my shirt upward, revealing my abs. He teased my skin, dragging my shirt so the fabric barely tickled it on the way up. I couldn't stop a shiver.

"Stop that!" Scott's voice shattered the moment. I

wanted to thank him for saving me, but couldn't find my voice. "At least wait to strip him until I can watch."

Thanks a lot, Scott. Nice save, dude.

Off went my shirt. Jay looked down at my chest, shot me a devious grin, then tossed my shirt over the banister into the yard. I was so stunned that I forgot the guys and turned my head to watch the shirt flutter to the ground. The sensation of fingers around my happy trail, fumbling with my jeans button, spun my head back around. Jay was on his knees with my button between his fingers. Scott knelt behind him, his eyes glued to the show Uncle Walt never intended.

I didn't know what to do. *Shit*. These guys were a couple. Were they actually coming on to me? Could I get naked with *married* guys?

Technically, guys couldn't get married back then, but you know what I mean. Wait, maybe that technicality actually allowed me to do this? Maybe I was legally bound to get naked. Gay rights or equal marriage rights or something super important might depend on my nakedness. This was a patriotic duty!

In that moment, I decided to give myself to the cause.

I spread my arms out wide, placed my hands on the banister, and arched my back so my head was hovering over open yard. Jay had full access to do whatever he pleased to that little button.

No, the *actual* button. My other thing wasn't little. Really.

Stop laughing.

I heard Scott whisper, "Oh my god. Look at him."

They hadn't unbuttoned my jeans yet. Confused, I looked down to find Jay staring up at my eyes and Scott reaching a hand out to touch my abs. A second later, his fingertips brushed my skin and my whole body convulsed.

All three of us grinned.

Then Jay ripped my jeans off and tossed them over the railing into the yard.

8

SANDWICHES SATISFY

I was first to climb into the hot tub, anxious to get my
pasty-white nakedness out of the open air. According to
the temperature gauge I stubbed my toe on, the water was a
steamy one hundred and four degrees. I sank below the
froth and edged toward the safety of the far wall of the tub.
When I looked up, Scott's balls were swinging at eye level
as he descended the two steps and submerged himself. I
was too startled to be embarrassed. They were low hangers
and happy to see me.

Jay entered immediately after Scott. He was fully erect,
so his balls were huddled tightly together. I swear one of
them winked at me as I snuck a peek.

Can balls wink?

Anyway.

We each claimed a separate side of the watery square.
The boys remained pressed against their respective edges,
their bodies simmering below the surface of the water, only
their heads exposed to the evening air. I dipped down and
doused my hair, then smeared it back with my hands as I
re-emerged. The heat felt amazing.

"So, no boyfriend?" Jay asked as he wiped water from his face.

"I had one." My eyes dropped. "Guess it didn't work out."

Scott's voice was flush with empathy. "What happened? It's okay if you don't want to talk about it."

I gave him a weak smile that barely curled my lips. "His ex-wife threatened to cut him off from his kids. It was them or me. I can't really blame him. No father could walk away from his boys." My voice broke.

Scott waded to my wall. The hairs of his legs tickled mine as he sat beside me. "I'm sorry. That must've been hard. How old were the kids?"

"Five and three. Cade and Christian." My smile was genuine as I recalled their names.

Scott mirrored my expression. "When did all this happen? I mean, when did things end?"

"December, right before Christmas. That's, what, three, four months ago?"

Jay finally entered the conversation. "How long were you together?"

I snorted. "I knew you'd ask that. Just three months—but he was my first, and we were together pretty much every day of those three months. On the weekends he had the kids, I did everything with them. I think I fell in love with the kids as much as I did him."

"Three months may not seem like much, but it matters, especially if he was your first," Scott said, ever the care-taker. His arm rose out of the water and wrapped around my shoulders. I let myself melt in his embrace, needing to borrow from his strength. "If you ever want to talk about it, we're here. Okay?"

I looked up and met his eyes.

Given the earlier aggressive undressing and Jay's very happy penis, this wasn't how I expected our aquatic adventure to go, but it felt *right* somehow. I could see in Scott's eyes the care and concern of one who understood and wished he could relieve my pain. We'd known each other for, what, eight hours? Yet I felt his sincerity, his empathy.

Scott was one of the good ones.

Suddenly, Jay's leg pressed against my other side, and his arm wrapped around my shoulders on top of Scott's. Startled, I turned to see the same empathy in his eyes I'd seen from Scott. For some reason, that startled me. I had no reason to think Jay was any less of a good man, but the fact he demonstrated the same concern as his partner…I hadn't expected that either.

"There are a million bastards out there who just want something, mostly to get into your pants. You're a handsome guy, Michael. They'll be all over you. Whatever you do, don't lose the man who's still hurting because he misses those boys. He's the most amazing man I've met in a long time."

Scott and Jay looked across at each other and shared a smile. On cue, they both wrapped their other arms around me and formed a group hug. There was nothing sexual about it, only the warmth of two men responding to a third who didn't even know he needed the support.

God, I needed that hug.

Right there, in the middle of the hot tub, wrapped in the arms of two incredibly hot, naked dudes, the pent-up emotion from the loss of Carter and the boys poured out of me. The harder my shoulders heaved, the tighter they held me.

No one spoke.

Ten, maybe twenty minutes passed—long enough for

the hot tub's auto-timer to shut off, forcing Jay to leave the circle to reset it.

Scott reached up and wiped the tears from my cheeks. His fingers were gentle—and pruny. We'd been in the hot tub a while.

I took his hand and ran my finger over the elderly ridges and smiled. "I think we've stayed in past the manufacturer's recommended guideline."

He snorted, clearly surprised by my quick return to humor.

Before he could reply, Jay appeared and splashed more water on us than was required by the two-foot journey. "Don't even think about getting out of this water, gentlemen."

I tried to make some smart-ass response, but Jay snatched my breath by plonking onto my lap, straddling my legs, and planting a deep kiss on my lips. When he pulled back, his eyes smoldered, while mine were Puss in Boots wide. He laughed and floated out of my lap.

"Well, that wasn't very fair, Jay. Why'd you get him first?" Scott asked.

My whole head snapped toward him, terrified, as his mouth closed in and locked over my own. Where Jay had been passionate and aggressive, Scott's lips were soft and tender, his tongue teasing mine, tempting it, but going no further. When he pulled back, my whole body surged forward to follow, begging to stay connected.

He grinned as we parted, then turned to Jay and winked. "Come over here, babe. You know I hate it when you're so far away."

So far away? He was in the same hot tub. What the hell?

Before Bambi could run for the woods, *two* sets of lips,

two tongues, dove forward in a mingling of barbecue and heat that sent my head spinning. I tried to resist, to pull back, but I was squished against the tub's wall. There was nowhere to go. Somewhere in the back of my mind, the tiny angel who so often seared me with her acidic guilt was screaming, but everything in me wanted them, wanted *both* of them. I felt myself sink into the steaming water and surrender to their desire.

Scott pulled back, and Jay resumed his straddle position. His lips, no longer tentative, attacked, and I responded in kind. Our mouths were a blur, and I moaned as shivers shot across my skin.

Then Scott took over. My eyes were closed, but I knew the difference in their touch and taste now, the intimate subtlety of Scott's lips grazing my neck, his fingers tracing my chest under the water. He gripped around my waist and lifted me up, his lips never slowing. Fire bloomed as Jay pressed firmly against me, the evidence of his desire grinding, parting my cheeks with strong hands. My head fell back and both men's mouths descended, teeth teasing my skin, tongues tasting my sweat.

And then the timer sounded and the hot tub shut off again.

Jay reached for the dial to reset our time, but Scott stayed his hand. "Let's move inside."

Scott grabbed my hand and led me out of the tub. I reached for a towel and he playfully slapped my hand away. He took the cloth and, with deliberate slowness, found every drop of water on my body and dabbed it dry. Jay kept ruining his effort as he slid his dripping torso against me from behind, nibbling my neck and ears.

Amused, Scott handed him a towel. "Since you keep getting him wet, you do his back."

Jay smirked. "Oh, I plan to."

I leaned into his touch.

Then it was Jay's turn to take my hand. He led me back inside and closed the sliding door, then guided me to the bed where Scott lay waiting with the covers turned back.

I looked from Scott to Jay, checking for signs that either might be uncomfortable inviting a third man into their bed, but all I saw was acceptance and desire. Scott quieted the last of my worry as his hand reached out and pulled me down next to him on the pillow-like comforter. We scooted to the head of the bed where the pillows lay. Jay joined us, stretching his six-foot frame beside me.

We stared in silence for a long moment, then each of them bent their heads to attack a nipple. I nearly peed the bed right there. Scott and Jay broke into a fit of laughter at the horror written across my face.

"I might need to pee."

Jay snorted. Scott came up for air and pointed. "Go on. It's through that door."

Now a tad self-conscious, I padded into the Taj Mahal of bathrooms. Seriously. This thing was insane, and probably spanned the whole length of my apartment. There were three sinks spread along a long vanity wall, each with its own mirror held in modern black frames. The sinks themselves were clear glass bowls that sat atop the counter.

Who needs three sinks? I thought, since there were only two of them.

Three marble steps led up to a tub that looked like it could seat six people. It had jets like those in the hot tub outside. I definitely had tub envy.

Then I saw the shower. Holy sprinklers, Batman.

It was basically a glass box with shower heads sticking out of *everywhere*. It looked more like a car wash than a shower, and I wondered if giant roller things with rags attached would descend from the ceiling if I turned it on. There was a weird silver wand-like attachment hanging on the wall I didn't recognize. I guessed it was used for giving the dogs a bath, but made a mental note to ask later.

Satisfied with my tour of the palatial potty, I used the actual potty, thankful for the moment to process everything that had happened—was *about* to happen. I was pretty sure there were two men outside the door expecting a second half to this ballgame. Hell, I might've wanted it more than they did, and I wasn't even sure what game we were playing. I took a few deep breaths, shook the tinkle off my dinkle, then dabbed it with toilet paper for good measure. I didn't want them to think I was a drippy barbarian.

As I passed the sinks, I spotted a decanter filled with mouthwash and rinsed the barbecue away. I chuckled, thinking how they'd make me taste it again soon.

The image staring back in the mirror grabbed my eye as I set the decanter down. I stood straight and stuck my chest out. *Huh.* I looked *good.* The skinny kid who would never take his shirt off at the beach actually had muscles and definition. I had *abs.* I grinned, almost giddy. Was this what it felt like to be proud of how you looked? I'd never known that before.

"Can we get in on some of that? Or are you going to hoard all the goods?" Jay's voice snapped me out of my Miss America crowning moment.

It was my turn to make them jump.

I turned and ran back into the bedroom and leapt on top of them. Scott tried to roll out of the way, but I grabbed his shoulders and pulled him into the pile. In a blink, three grown men were wrestling and tickling and laughing like kids at a slumber party.

Okay, naked kids who had just made out and were about to do worse—not any slumber party I remembered, but it was definitely going to be fun.

Scott freed himself and trotted into the bathroom. "Now look what you've done. *I* have to pee!" He stuck his tongue out and laughed.

"I'm gonna make you use that tongue, mister," I called without thinking, then clamped my hands over my mouth as I realized how forward I'd sounded.

Jay was sitting up on his knees, his sculpted chest and impressive manhood facing me. He saw my innocence, the way I struggled with sexuality. His head cocked, and I swear something in his eyes clicked. He leaned his long body over mind, then slowly pressed his weight against me, while holding his head up. His eyes never wavered. When our mouths were inches apart, he whispered, "You know you're safe with us, right?"

My throat caught. Safe? In the laundry list of emotions and fears, *safety* hadn't ever come to mind. What was he implying? Would other men physically hurt me? Or did he mean they were a safe place to talk and share? He hadn't been the nurturing one of the pair, and I didn't know quite how to take his declaration.

It must've shown because he rolled over onto one elbow and spoke softly. "We've been together a long time, and we rarely do this sort of thing. Actually, I think you're the third guy we've ever done this with—in eight years. I love Scott more than life itself, and I know he loves me the same way, but we both have this need…" He stopped and his eyes drifted as he thought. "It's hard to explain. We want—no, we *need*—to share our love with someone. We are enough, the two of us, but we know we want more. Am I making any sense?"

I really didn't know what he meant—any of it—except for the part about how they loved each other. Ray Charles could've seen that. The rest? Not so much.

Scott returned and blanketed my other side with his body. "Don't let him get all sappy." Scott gave Jay a smart-ass grin. "That's *my* job in this house and no one gets to take it from me."

My heart pulled at his words. I couldn't explain it, but I really liked these guys, each of them, both of them, together and separately. How was that even possible?

I chuckled. "Yes, sir. You're the sappy one. Got it."

He gave me a gentle peck on the cheek. "What Jay means is that you have nothing to fear in this house. We'd love you to stay, to get to know you more, but we also get this is new to you and is probably overwhelming. Don't feel you have to keep going if you're not comfortable."

"How did you—"

"Oh, Michael, we could spot a newborn gay a mile away." Scott grinned.

"Enough mush." Jay shoved him off me with a laugh and pressed himself down, chest to chest once again. This time he didn't hold himself up. His mouth pressed back into mine as his hands roamed freely, kneading my arms and sides until they reached my butt. He moaned, and I felt his erection return, growing against my own. The friction of our dicks pumping and stretching sent lightning up my spine.

We passed each other back and forth, me to Scott, then to Jay, then the two of them together. I watched as they kissed with the familiarity of time and experience, the depth of love that only comes to those who've lived a lifetime together. It warmed my heart to see their passion for each other, and made me long for the same.

They turned their attention back to me. Scott leaned over, kissing me, stroking my now-throbbing penis, and whispered, "I want you inside me."

Then Jay whispered from behind, "And I want to be deep inside you."

My head spun back and forth. I didn't know where to look or who to listen to. What was I supposed to do?

Waves of exhilaration battered my senses at the idea of having *both* of them—*at the same time*. I'd never thought of such a thing.

Scott rolled over onto his side, urging me to spoon him from behind. I heard the pop of a bottle cap and squirt of liquid, then felt Jay's slick hand wrap around my shaft, teasing the skin with moisture and soaking my head with slippery pleasure. His hand turned toward Scott and he fingered his hole, earning a squirm and moan. Jay leaned back and squirted more lube on his palm, but I was captivated by Scott's hand reaching behind and gripping me. He pulled me into him, pressing back, nudging himself closer and me in deeper. I spasmed with ecstasy as the last of my length entered his body and his head craned back to kiss me.

Then Jay's freshly saturated hand found my hole and I grunted in Scott's ear, pushing hard at the surprise of Jay's touch. I felt him clinch around me and stars flashed. Then Jay pressed inside me and I thought my heart would burst out of my chest. He pushed, I pressed back, Scott arched to drive me deeper. We were clumsy at first, but quickly learned to time our thrusts. Again and again, the three of us became one.

Jay kissed my neck while Scott's tongue drove into my mouth. I reached around Scott and grabbed his throbbing uncut cock and began stroking, teasing his head, toying with the fold of skin now stretched taut. Then I slid my palm down, squeezing tighter. His mouth released mine, and Jay leaned in, stealing my mouth away, kissing me deeply.

The pressing became pumping, then grinding and thrusting. I could feel Scott quicken in his shortened breaths and the pulsing of his cock, so I stroked it faster, alternating between firm and teasingly loose. His hole responded, caressing my cock with a throbbing constriction, a sudden clutch that made me cry out. Scott's body shivered and convulsed as his cum exploded across my hand and his body. Surge after surge coated him, and I could smell the salty sex smeared across his skin. He reached back and held me, telling me not to stop, to drive onward, begging for more.

Jay growled in my ear and his gentleness vanished. He slammed himself inside me as hard and deep as he could, before pulling back and ramming into me again. Something snapped at his renewed vigor and I drove myself further into Scott. He cried out, "God, yes, don't stop!"

I didn't.

I couldn't.

Jay clutched my chest with both hands and he pumped me so fast I could barely keep up—Jay into me…me into Scott…Jay…Scott…

Sweat poured down my forehead. My mind and vision were blurred. I couldn't think, only felt the wild, unhindered passion flowing through the three of us.

Jay's body tensed, his cock throbbed, and I knew he was close. The thought of him inside me pushed my already addled mind over the edge, and I lost control, spilling myself into Scott again and again. I whispered "I'm sorry" in his ear, but his grip on my hips tightened, drawing me into him, refusing my pleas.

Then Jay shouted, "Oh god, I'm coming!"

He slammed again and again until I felt him empty inside me. All three of us shivered, and Jay's arms reached beyond my shoulders to pull Scott close, sandwiching me in between. I kissed Scott's neck as Jay, tenderly, did the same to mine.

We dared not move.

Our breathing slowed.

Our pulses eased.

<hr>

SOMETIME IN THE MIDDLE OF THE NIGHT, I WOKE UP. MY sleep had been peaceful, dreamless, something I hadn't enjoyed in a while. Nature had removed me from Scott and ejected Jay from me, but our arms were still tangled and our bodies mingled tightly.

I lifted Jay's arm and laid it against his side, careful to not wake either of them, then looked down at Scott. I reached out and moved a stray strand of hair from his forehead as I watched the rise and fall of his chest. Then I turned and studied Jay. They were so different, yet so similar. Jay's dark features made my blood boil, while Scott's tender heart made my own skip a beat. They were each beautiful and passionate in their own ways.

I honestly couldn't decide which I liked better.

Is that weird? Isn't one supposed to captivate more than the other? Aren't we made to be with *one* other person who blinds us to all others?

That's what I'd been taught, at least about straight relationships. I'd just assumed gay ones worked the same.

Scott and Jay made me challenge those lessons, challenge what might—

Scott's fingers grazed my chest, and I turned to face his opened eyes. He smiled. With his disheveled hair and genuine grin, my heart melted. I leaned down and kissed him. Before I knew what was happening, he'd gripped me back into stiffness and slid me inside him again. This time he begged me to take him slowly, to press and pull and savor every motion. My skin pimpled with excitement as I slid in and out. I could feel his body react to each thrust.

For a fleeting moment, I worried Jay might wake and be jealous, but that idea shattered when I felt his lips against my neck again. Then his hands gripped my abs. He kissed me like that for a while, letting Scott and me have our moment, then slid himself back into my still-moist hole.

When we fell asleep after our second time, nature didn't remove either of us from the other.

We woke as one.

9

COFFEE TALK

"Wait, you slept with a *couple*?" Jason leaned across the table, eager and incredulous.

I nodded. "Yeah. We kind of did it twice. I mean, after dinner and the hot tub."

"You actually had a *date* with a couple? Are you serious?" Dwayne perked up.

"I don't know that I'd call it a date. We met online, then ran into each other randomly at softball. They invited me over for dinner. I was dessert."

Dwayne and Jason shared a look as Katie ambled over. "I've never seen the two of you looks so out of sorts. This must be good. Spill it."

She refilled our coffee mugs as Jason blurted, "Boy Scout over there banged a couple last night."

"What?" She spilled Dwayne's pour all over the table.

"Technically, I only banged one of them. The other one—"

"Enough!" She held up the palm not laden with coffee. "I don't need details. I get the squishy picture."

As she walked away, I grinned and winked at Jason. "It was pretty squishy."

Dwayne threw the napkin he'd been using to clean up the coffee at me, then pointed a finger at Jason. "*You*, stop encouraging him. I'm trying to raise a respectable gay here."

"Don't look at me, grandpa. I'm actually impressed. The boy scored more last night than I have all year."

"*Not helping!*" Dwayne tossed another soaked napkin on his plate and got to his feet. "I'm getting more napkins. You two behave."

Jason and I laughed as he headed to the counter. During my post-Carter period, Jason and I had become friends. I'd always liked him, but more as one of his lovesick followers than as a real person. Now that those emotions were thankfully out of my system, I'd come to enjoy his sarcastic wit, especially when he aimed it at Dwayne. They'd been friends since the dawn of time, and I could see that closeness through their interactions. Regardless of who was speaking, there was usually an undertone of caring and love, overlaid with sass and fire. They were a perfect odd couple, and now Jason joined most of our lunch dates.

"Are you going to see them again?" He was like a little kid. I'd never seen him so excited.

"I guess so. They both play softball in the league, so I'll definitely see them there."

"No, dummy, *see* them again—as in *get naked* again?"

"Uh, I don't know. We didn't talk about it." I was suddenly uncomfortably aware of Dwayne's shadow darkening the table.

"I think you should. Sounds like they might be open to a throuple."

Dwayne plopped down dramatically beside Jason and

elbowed him to scoot over. "Don't listen to his nonsense. Come to think of it, *never* listen to Jason again unless he's singing—and then, don't pay attention to his words, just the music."

Jason laughed. "Let the boy be happy, old man. Times have changed since you invented the wheel. Throuples are hot."

"You can't even get a *couple* to work. What would you know?"

"You wound me, good sir." Jason mimicked a bow from his seat.

"You two are better than television," I said. "I don't know if they're looking for a third or a throuple or whatever. They said they don't even do three-ways that often, that I was the first in a few years. We may never see each other naked again."

"Why do I hear disappointment in your voice when you say that?" Jason needled.

I hesitated. *Was* there disappointment in my voice? *Did* I want to get naked with them again? If so, was all this purely physical? I'd never heard of a throuple, much less considered one. The very idea went against monogamy and every other principle my preacher dad ever taught me. Hell, getting naked with them had shattered most of those principles. "I…I don't know."

Dwayne leaned over and put his hand on my arm. "You had fun. That's good. Don't read more into it than it was—just sex."

I looked up, unsure I agreed.

"I know losing Carter and the kids was hard, but jumping into something like this is…well, it's not the right thing for you. Just trust me. Your heart is exposed and raw right now."

"Sounds like his ass is raw too." Jason barked a laugh, and Dwayne involuntarily spit coffee on me.

"Hey!"

"Sorry, kiddo," Dwayne said through gasps. "Jason won that round."

10

SOFTBALLS AND YOUNG BALLS

Three uneventful weeks passed.

Jason played a couple more gigs and Dwayne met a new kid—I mean, guy. This one was a twenty-three-year-old who'd just moved from Florida, or Atlanta, I wasn't paying much attention. He babbled about the child's smile and eyes for an hour, only allowing Jason to interrupt a few times. It was good to see him beaming, even if the object of his affection was out of reach.

We'd talked a few times about his attraction to guys half his age, and about the odds anything would actually work out with them, but Dwayne played it off as though he didn't want anything serious. He reasoned, if nothing came of it other than some flirtation or sex, he was fine with that.

I never bought that. Despite his perpetually positive attitude and smile, I could feel the loneliness in him. I could see it in his eyes when he'd talk about someone from his past, or when one of his younglings wouldn't work out.

At least, for now, he was happy and hopeful.

I left the diner and headed to softball practice. My new

team had practiced once each week since the tryouts. We were terrible, but it was fun to learn a new sport.

Our coach met me in the parking lot before my first practice. She was a short, stocky woman in her midthirties and looked like she could drop me to the ground before I could cry for help. I liked—and feared—her the moment we met. Before we walked away from my car, she looked at my closed trunk and asked if I needed help with my equipment. I held up a glove and shook my head, laughing. She seemed perturbed. I later learned that serious players owned their own bats and carried them in fancy bags with their jersey number embroidered on the side. The lack of such accoutrement told her all she needed to know about my experience level.

Sergeant Coachie took her softball seriously.

I was introduced as the new superstar pitcher. Clearly, no one had told Coachie I'd never played the position before, and I didn't bother to correct her. She and I spent much of the practice getting me used to hitting a tiny spot behind the plate. It was a repetitive motion that came naturally, and I quickly learned to control the ball's movement with various spins.

Who knew? Maybe I was a slow-pitch stud.

I didn't see Scott and Jay. They were both B-level players and their team didn't practice on the same day as mine. I thought we'd see more of each other when the season started, but I later learned that B-level games were usually scheduled at different times from C. That sucked, but I figured we could find other ways to meet up. Sure, I was hungry for more hot-tub time, but something inside me was also intrigued—and terrified—by the idea of dating a couple. What would that be like? Could it even work? I had so many questions.

There was part of me still wary of natural jealousies and the perception of others, along with a hundred other fears plaguing my PK mind. A throuple wasn't something sanctioned in the Good Book, and it certainly wouldn't be approved of by the wolf pack. That might even send my dad over the edge, and I didn't want to endanger the tenuous truce we'd established.

It all sucked. I really liked the guys, both of them. I'd talked to a number of guys online about the idea, and every one of them said jealousy usually killed throuples. The third would fall for one or the other, or one of the original couple would fall out with the third. There were far more reasons for a throuple not to work than for it to live happily ever after.

On top of everything, I still struggled with the basics of making a relationship work. The only one I'd ever known went from zero to sixty in one night, then crashed and burned worse than the Death Star. If I couldn't handle dating one man, what made me think I could succeed with two egos and personalities, and everything else that came with dating an already established pair?

In the end, I never pursued another dinner or date or *whatever* that was. I ran into the guys a few times, when our games were scheduled close together, and they were always friendly, but I never chased that dream.

I guess the little angel had found her voice again—or a strong pair of handcuffs.

Wait, that should be the little devil with the handcuffs, shouldn't it?

11

ZOO GUY

The next couple of months passed in a blur.

Basketball season kicked into high gear, and I officiated either high school or small college games five or six nights a week. Between work during the day, squeezing in gym time to avoid my roommate's evil eye, and refereeing, there wasn't much time left for anything else.

That worked out just fine. It kept my mind off how much I missed Carter and the boys.

Midway through February, high schools entered playoffs season. They'd start with Districts, then Regionals, and eventually, the big kahuna—the State Championship. Every high school player in the state wanted to make it to their version of The Dance. What might surprise most folks is how much every referee in the state also wanted to make it to the elite end of the playoffs. There were only three officials in the finals of the State Championship, and we all wanted to be one of those highly talented officials.

Unfortunately, there were politics in the world of officiating, and, while I was a skilled referee, I wasn't great at *that* game. The result was an earlier end to my season than

I'd hoped, just like those high schoolers whose teams missed a shot at the buzzer.

Oh well.

Send in Dwayne, coach. He'll save the day!

THE FIRST FRIDAY IN MARCH MARKED THE BEGINNING OF the State Championship. You know, the one I wasn't invited to be part of? I wasn't bitter. Really.

Dwayne proposed we go to the Chute. He was a regular there, but I'd never been. Were gay bars all different? Were the gays who went to one bar different from those at another? I had so many questions. Dwayne rolled his eyes and laughed. His only answer was, "Come with me and see for yourself."

So I did.

The Chute sat at the end of a short strip mall. It didn't look like much from the street, but it sprawled almost the whole length and depth of the mall building. While the other businesses won street-facing space, the Chute won the battle for actual floor space.

We got there around ten, well before the gay witching hour when most of the boys would show up. What was it with gay men and their nocturnal internal clocks? Were they born with it? Was it somehow instilled in them at a certain age?

Did I just make the *nature versus nurture* argument over time and bar attendance? Wow. I needed a drink.

But it was like magic. At eleven thirty, the bars would be empty. At midnight—on the dot—they'd bulge at the seams.

The bars, not the boys. Although, now that I think about

it, you're right—some of the boys bulged nicely too.

Stop distracting me.

We walked past the doorman, who nodded to me, then stood and hugged Dwayne and called him "Sugar" in greeting. That would *definitely* come back to haunt him. I loved nicknames.

The bar was exactly as he'd described. The front opened onto a large dance floor surrounded by carpeted boxes for sitting and watching. One lonely guy swayed to pounding bass beneath the swirling lights of lasers and strobes. At one end of the dance floor were stairs leading to the DJ booth, and at the other end was the bar, which was actually pretty cool. A tall case holding liquor of every color and variety towered in the center. Around it, the bar top formed a rectangle wide and long enough to house three or four bartenders at any one time. At that moment, Dwayne and I had the place to ourselves—except for the dancer and one bartender, who waved as we approached.

"Back so soon?" he asked as he leaned over the bar to hug Dwayne.

"Is it Friday?" Dwayne grinned. "Donny, meet Michael, the Luke to my Yoda."

I quirked a brow at Dwayne, then turned and offered Donny my hand to shake. He looked at me funny, then snuck a glance at Dwayne.

Dwayne smirked. Donny shrugged. I didn't get it.

He shook my hand, a firm, manly shake that held on a little longer than was necessary. His gray eyes were warm and locked onto mine without flinching.

Dwayne got his usual bucket of limes with a splash of liquid, and I sipped my Coke, earning another odd grin from Donny.

He sure grinned a lot.

A few sips later, Dwayne dragged me away from the bar to inspect the back, which opened into a show bar similar to the one I'd experienced at the Connection. It could hold a couple hundred patrons facing a wide stage with giant curtains and glaring spotlights. Small tables for three or four filled the middle of the room, allowing open space around the stage and in the back, where the bars held court. Another lonely bartender was setting up his station. He looked up, waved, and yelled Dwayne's name, like he was Norm in *Cheers*, then resumed his work.

We wandered back to the main bar and grabbed stools directly in front of Donny. He was busy hauling bottles, filling ice bins, and placing clean glasses on their easy-to-reach shelves below the bar. As we sat, I caught him glance up, then look down quickly. Sandy blond curls flopped as his head darted below the bar.

He was tall, six two or three I guessed, so being sneaky with his peeky wasn't easy.

Now I was curious about Mr. Sneaky Peeky.

Dwayne and I talked about our uneventful weeks while Donny worked. I watched him out the corner of my eye, trying to be casual. I clearly wasn't.

Dwayne looked up as Donny passed, a heavy crate of wine bottles making his bare arms bulge. "Michael thinks you're cute. You two should talk."

Donny stopped in front of us and looked from Dwayne to me.

"What? Wait. I didn't say anything. Where'd that—" I stammered. Dwayne and Donny giggled like schoolgirls.

Dwayne said he had to pee and disappeared.

Donny resumed his box-hauling, so for the first time that night I got a good look. His hair curled slightly at the ends and was cut short except for some floppy coils that bounced around his forehead. It was neat but messy at the same time. I wanted to reach up and push them back every time he talked. As he passed one of the other bartenders, I realized he was taller than I'd thought before, probably six four. Most guys that tall had trouble gaining muscle. Donny clearly didn't. His arms were ripped, and the white Fruit of the Loom tank top he wore was straining across his chest. He was sweating from his work, and the fabric revealed more than it covered. I watched with admiration as his headlights panned the room on high beam. He wasn't weightlifter huge—you know, that neck-bigger-than-his-head look—but he was nicely muscled.

I'd say he was handsome, but not strikingly so. He wouldn't turn every head in the bar when he walked in, but his personality and infectious smile pushed him from a seven to a solid eight.

I've always been a sucker for a nice smile. Color me romantic.

I was so wrapped up in cataloging his looks that I missed the part where he stopped working and turned.

Oh shit.

"Need something?" he asked with that frustratingly cute grin, then threw his head back to toss a curl out of his eyes.

I woke up. "Uh, no. I'm good. Thanks."

His grin broadened. He extended his hand across the bar. "My name's Donny McLeren."

We'd already shaken hands, but it would be rude to leave him hanging, so I took his palm again, careful to mirror his firm grip from before. "I'm Michael Reed. Nice to meet you."

His grip was solid again, warm. He felt good. An involuntary shiver ran up my arm.

He released my hand and gave me a shallow head dip

like you'd see in old movies about medieval England. "It's my pleasure, Mr. Reed."

"So, you work here all the time?"

What a stupid question. I mentally slapped my forehead.

He nodded. "Most weekends. I work at the zoo during the week though."

"The zoo?" My eyes widened. "What do you do there? I've never been to the Nashville Zoo."

He ran a hand through his hair, a gesture that made his bicep flex and my heart beat a little quicker.

"I'm the cat guy."

Huh. My head tilted. "The cat guy?"

"I know what you're thinking. Not *those* cats. Think tigers and lions. They're cats too, and I'm their keeper."

"That's *so* cool," slipped out before I got my Coke to my lips. What was I, eight? Gah!

"You should come by sometime. I'll show you around. Nashville actually has a great zoo."

Dwayne walked up. "Zoo? What did I miss? Are you threatening to throw him to the lions?" He laughed at his own joke, not realizing that's *exactly* what we'd been talking about.

"You should come too, old man. You'd like it," Donny teased.

Dwayne shook his head and downed the last of his drink. "Nope. No zoo for me. You two young bucks enjoy that."

The trickle of guys whose internal clocks needed adjusting streamed in, so we said our goodbyes and headed to the door. Dwayne wanted to get home before it got too late, and I was tired from reffing all week.

As I pushed the glass door open, I felt a groping in my

back pocket and practically leapt out of my jeans. I spun to find the doorman pulling his fingers out. He winked at me and wiggled the offending fingers in a tiny gay wave. I was so stunned that I'd walked all the way to Betty before checking inside the pocket he'd violated.

There, scrawled on a bar napkin, was Donny's name and number. I guess he thought I needed a reference point, because he left two words below his number:

Zoo Guy.

HORSES ARE FOR HEALING

Katie gave me a peck on the head as she set my pancakes down with a flourish. "You look good today, baby." She winked at Dwayne and skipped merrily back to the kitchen.

Maybe the *Cheers* folks were on to something. It *is* pretty cool to go where everybody knows your name.

"You and Donny seemed to hit it off last night."

"I guess. He seems nice." I shrugged. "The zoo thing is pretty cool."

Dwayne pointed his fork at me. "Listen here, mister, you need to pull your head out of your ass and get back on the horse—or under it, if that's your thing." He grinned, proud of his gay dad joke.

I rolled my eyes. "Yeah, I know. I've just been really busy with basketball lately."

"Oh no you don't. You were pissy all last week because you didn't get past Regionals. Your season is over. There's nothing taking up your precious time now. Call Donny. Go see lions or tigers or whatever he keeps. At least, see *his* tiger. Lord knows, Katie and I would love for you to get laid. I love ya, but you've been a lousy lunch partner lately."

"Aren't you the same gay sherpa who was scolding me for sleeping with a couple not that long ago?"

"That was different. You were being a mindless slut for your own empty pleasure." He snorted. "This is about *my* happiness and welfare. I'm perfectly happy to whore you out if it'll put you in a better mood. It'll certainly make these lunches more enjoyable."

"Sorry," I mumbled.

His voice softened. "I'm not complaining. Carter was your first, and I know how much you fell in love with his boys. I just want you to be happy again."

"Here, here," Katie chirped from behind me. The silky scent of brewed Kona beans wafted by as she leaned across the table. "Honey, you call that cat man. He sounds like just what you need right now."

"Cat man? Is he a superhero now?" I quipped.

"Only if he wears a tight leather outfit." She smirked, then put one hand on her hip in that *I'm a teapot* pose. "If he can make you smile again, he'll be a superhero in my book."

As she drifted to her next table, I looked up to find Dwayne chuckling. "She's not wrong, ya know?"

"Alright. Fine. I'll call him later. The napkin with his number is on my nightstand."

"Already keeping him near your bed. I love it."

I couldn't help but laugh. Dwayne could always get me.

AROUND TWO O'CLOCK, I WALKED INTO MY APARTMENT TO find Peter's things strewn about in neat piles. He'd arranged his clothes first by type, then by color. I grinned at his new sense of organization. He'd never cared before. Maybe the SEALs would be good for him.

I tiptoed my way through the minefield of tank tops and T-shirts until reaching my room, where the neat laundered stacks transformed into my unkempt piles of dirty clothes. The SEALs would never help me. It might take the whole navy to change my cluttered ways.

Donny's wadded napkin rested between a stack of quarters and a roll of toilet paper on my nightstand.

Don't be gross. The toilet paper was for nose blowing. I was too cheap to buy tissues.

I grabbed the napkin and headed back into the den. With seven spins of the rotary dial, Donny's warm bass echoed through the line. "Hello?"

"Uh, hey, Donny?"

"Michael." I could *hear* his smile. "It's nice to hear your voice again."

Now I was smiling. "It's nice to be heard. Um, I mean, it's nice to talk to you too."

He chuckled at my awkwardness.

"So," I blundered. "I was wondering if you might like to grab dinner or something sometime."

"That sounds great. I have to work tonight at seven, but could grab a quick bite before."

So soon? I didn't really know this guy, and was only doing this because Dwayne and Katie had guilted me into it, but my heart still skipped a beat. Why was I suddenly sweating?

"Awesome," was all I could get out.

We chatted a few more minutes, comparing areas of town, driving distances, and where might be a good, cheap spot in the middle. We were both on tight budgets. I liked that.

As I replaced the receiver, I couldn't help but feel a bubble of giddiness grow inside my chest. It had been months since I'd felt anything there—well, other than that murderous, stabbing sensation from the Carter breakup—but that doesn't count.

Maybe Dwayne was right. I just needed a good cowboy…I mean, horse…I mean, date. Yeah, *date*.

13

BARFLY

Donny and I met at a ramshackle rotisserie chicken place around the corner from the Chute. It looked a lot like the diner, but with stained wood and the permanent smell of roasted chicken rather than coffee and bacon. They served tasty, healthy chicken, and the best vegetables in town. I loved their creamed corn, okra, and baked sweet potato slathered in cinnamon butter.

I'm not sure what I expected, having never been on a date with a bartender. The stereotype racing through my mind was of a guy whose pockets were perpetually over-flowing with the phone numbers of patrons trying to get into his alcohol-stained pants.

Donny was *nothing* like my mental image.

Our conversation started with him asking if I'd read the latest book by…I don't remember. I've never cared for books. Movies always have more action and sound—and don't involve hours of reading. Donny, on the other hand, was a voracious reader. He enjoyed a good *Lord of the Rings* fantasy, which I respected, because those books would make a great movie one day. But he also enjoyed literary classics. He boggled my mind rattling off his reading list, a Santa's register of books he wanted to read but were patiently waiting in line for the one ahead to be completed first. Most were by British or French authors, with a few Russians added for their sexy accent.

I had a magazine on my nightstand. Did that count?

To escape the cultural hole I'd dug for myself by asking about his favorites, I changed the subject. "So, where are you from? Any brothers and sisters?"

He took a sip of tea. "I grew up in Ohio on a farm. My folks still live there, but they hired someone to run the place a few years ago. They're in their seventies now and putter around the house most days. My brother owns the place next door and practically lives on a tractor."

"You didn't want to work on the family farm?"

He laughed and held up his hands like I'd threatened to shoot. "Lord no. I grew up hauling hay, mucking stables, feeding pigs, and milking cows—and most of that had to be done before the sun came up every day. That's a lot more work than I'm willing to do every day."

My eyes roamed his bulky frame and grinned. "Looks like it did you *some* good."

He flexed a bicep in his best Arnold pose and flashed his pearly whites. "Hard work does build a body, true enough."

I wanted to pull my short sleeves down to cover my guns that now felt more like pea-shooters, despite their recent progress at the hands of Herr Peter.

"It was a great place to grow up." He got a faraway look in his eyes. "The farm's where I learned to love working with animals. We had everything you'd expect: cows, horses, chickens, pigs, you name it. The nearest vet was fifty miles away, so the whole family had to learn to take care of minor wounds or illnesses. I'd delivered babies by the time I was fourteen years old." I waited as he returned to the present. "The best part about working at the zoo is I don't have to wonder when we're going to slaughter an animal I've come to care about."

My face must've fallen because he nodded and continued. "Yeah, every year, especially the cows and pigs. There were a few we'd keep for breeding or milk, but a good number would go to the slaughterhouse. Aside from the grains we grew, that's how the farm paid the bills."

Our food came and I had a whole new respect for the chicken sitting before me.

Donny noticed me staring and made a peeping sound, then said in a squeaky voice, *"I can't believe you're going to eat me, you bad, bad man."*

He was grinning from ear to ear when I looked up, and we both broke into a fit of laughter. I turned eight shades of red, which only encouraged him. Before I knew it, tears were rolling down his cheeks and he was mimicking a sad chicken voice between guffaws.

The waitress appeared, looked back and forth between us, then bolted for the kitchen to get away from the crazy clucking gays. We shared a look and the tears flowed harder.

I couldn't remember the last time I'd laughed so hard my gut hurt.

As I finished the last of my actual chicken, the waitress braved another visit to our table, grabbed our empty plates, and tossed the bill down like it carried the plague. We both chuckled as we stood to walk to the register.

"Why don't you stop by the bar later?" Donny said. "It doesn't get busy until late, and there's only so much setup I can do. It'd be nice to have a little company."

I didn't know what to say. Would visiting him at his work be considered a second date? Was that even allowed? I'd have to check the Gay Handbook when I got home.

Screw the handbook. "Sure. Dwayne and I are supposed to touch base later. Mind if he tags along?"

"I love to see that old coot anytime. He's one of my favorites."

Old coot. That made me chuckle all the way to the car.

I WALKED INTO THE CHUTE AROUND NINE O'CLOCK TO FIND Dwayne comfortably perched by the bar, Jack and Coke in hand, a tall glass stuffed full of lime wedges beside him on the counter. Donny was leaned over the bar toward him, and I thought the pair looked a little too conspiratorial. I stood just inside the doorway and watched for signs of an evil scheme. Dwayne was always up to something.

Donny's simple white tank from the night before had been replaced by a brown leather vest that hung open in the front. I was twenty yards away, but could see the definition of his furry pecs poking through. With the appearance of uncovered flesh, all fears of a conspiracy went out the window, and I made my way to the guys.

Dwayne raised his glass in greeting, his eyes twinkling with…something.

Oh boy.

Donny leaned over the bar to give me a quick hug. His vest popped fully open and my eyes widened as I lost count of the abs smiling up at me through their coating of neatly trimmed fur.

Holy mother of pearl, he was *ripped.* I hadn't seen that coming. I mean, I knew he was muscular, but not like *that.*

When he hugged me, the gay equivalent of a European kiss on either cheek, I squeezed to see if he was as firm as he looked. The muscles of his back were as hard as the bar's granite counter. I swooned a bit before letting go.

He must've noticed I'd held on longer than was specified in the Gay Handbook, because he and Dwayne shared a grin as I took a seat.

Donny excused himself to fetch another case of beer, giving Dwayne a chance to satiate his appetite for grilled Michael.

"So, how was dinner?" His voice carried the tone of someone who already knew the answer, but couldn't wait to hear how I'd respond. Yes, he was baiting me, and I knew it.

"It was good."

He waited. I shrugged. I could play too.

"Good? That's all I get? After all we've been through, that's it?"

"Forgive this one, sensei." I bowed my head formally, then looked up with a grin and rolled my eyes. "It was a nice dinner. Good food, pleasant conversation. That's about all there was."

He huffed. "Listen, *you*. You're *never* tight-lipped. That tells me as much as if you had diarrhea of the mouth, which is far more normal. Start talking before I use these limes on you right here in the middle of this bar." He grabbed the glass and pointed it threateningly.

We both laughed at the fruity gesture.

Is a fruity gesture normal in a gay bar?

Anyway.

I shook my head, then shrugged again. "I don't know what to say. He's a really nice guy. We met for rotisserie chicken, then went our separate ways because he had to work. I guess he liked me enough to invite me to the bar, so if stalking a bartender counts…"

"Let's not use *stalking* in a sentence, shall we? You have a history."

"Ha ha. Very funny. That was *one* time, and I was a virgin gay." I stuck my tongue out in the most mature gesture possible.

His brows shot up. "As I recall, there was a certain nameless flight attendant who might disagree with that assessment. I don't believe he flew on *Virgin* Airlines."

Before I could respond, Donny appeared and set a glass of icy Coke in front of me. I raised it toward Dwayne, chuckled, and said, "Point to the old fart."

He tossed a lime at me.

"Wow. I step away for two minutes and you two are throwing garnish. What did I miss?" Donny leaned over with his elbows on the table and chin in his hands.

"*Nothing*," I snapped, cutting off any smart-ass remark Dwayne might've had ready. "Dwayne was just being a snot."

"I was *educating* the boy on the meaning of the word *virgin*," Dwayne said, triumph in his eyes as he shot me a glare.

Dammit.

"Virgin? I take it we're not talking drinks, are we?" Donny quipped, suddenly appearing less confident about the quicksand on which he now stood.

"Ignore the senior citizen. Sometimes he forgets his name, where he is, all those things." I tried to laugh it off and change the subject. "So, tell us more about this zoo you work in. Sounds fun."

Donny cocked his head, thought a moment, then said, "Nope. Not gonna do it. If you want to know more, you'll have to come see it for yourself. I'll give you a guided tour."

Did he just ask me on *another* date? Holy virgin margarita. "That sounds awesome."

I glanced over to catch Dwayne's all-knowing smirk.

"You'll even get to meet some of the cats I hand-raised."

"Hand-raised?"

Donny nodded. "Sorry, I forget normal people don't know zoo-speak. Let me take care of this other guy. I'll explain in a minute. Be right back."

He darted to the opposite corner of the bar and began chatting with another customer. I'd almost forgotten he was working.

"Must've been some really good chicken. Do they serve *virgin* chicken there?" Dwayne's chirping woke me out of my daze. I'd been staring at Donny's ass…I mean jeans.

I snorted. "He's just being nice. Besides, the whole raising lions and tigers thing sounds totally cool."

"Totally cool? Since when does a Nashville boy turn valley?"

"It's, like, totally cool. Like, super cool, dude."

We giggled at our own goofiness before turning to watch Donny approach with a newly filled glass in each hand. "Can't let my boys go thirsty." His eyes locked onto mine as he smiled and set the glasses down. Tiny, adorable dimples I hadn't noticed before peeked from his cheeks.

We chatted for another half hour before the flood of gay-bar-loving patrons began streaming in. On cue, Dwayne and I synchro-drained the last of our drinks and set the glasses on the bar with a perfectly timed thud.

Even the Russian judge gave us a ten. Donny shook his head and laughed.

"Donny, it's been a pleasure, as always." Dwayne bowed in a most regal gesture.

The barkeep turned to me. "Three weeks from Sunday? The zoo is closed for cleaning and repairs. It'll just be you, me, and the staff. Oh, and Tina."

"Tina?"

He grinned. "Tina the tiny tiger. She's a Bengal weighing in at four hundred pounds, but she'll always be Tiny Tina to me. She was my first hand-raised cub. When I got her, she was the size of both of my palms put together. All fluff and massive golden eyes."

"So cool."

Dwayne speared me with an elbow.

Donny ignored him. "You should know, she's my character test. If she doesn't approve, we can't go out anymore —and she'll probably eat you."

I knew he was kidding, but he kept such a straight face the color must've drained from my cheeks. He barked a laugh and waved the rag in his hand. "You kids drive safe. I hear there's gays out on the road at this hour."

Dwayne and I giggled our way out the door, turning more than a few of the new arrivals' heads. They were clearly curious about the guy who'd captured Donny's attention. I puffed out my chest, proud to be the guy someone else was jealous of for a change.

14

ZOOLANDER

Zoo day finally arrived.

I rose early and downed several cups of coffee before struggling to decide which pair of shorts went best with tiger fur. On my best days, I struggled with choosing clothes. How was I supposed to know what to wear when going on a date at a zoo? I gave in to ratty cargo shorts and a plain blue T-shirt.

Determined not to get lost, I carefully followed Zoo Guy's directions, which led me into a residential section in the heart of Nashville. I looked around, sure I'd made a wrong turn somewhere. Who would put a zoo in a neighborhood with, I don't know, *neighbors*? It seemed odd.

A moment later, a brightly colored wooden sign appeared. Apparently, the zoo *did* like neighbors after all.

I was surprised to find the parking lot nearly empty, then remembered Donny mentioned this was a staff-only day. My favorite bartender-slash-zookeeper was standing near the public entrance, a series of tall metal gates shaded by various trees to give patrons the feeling of entering a jungle. He waved as I nestled Betty into a front-row space a dozen yards away.

He wore jeans and a green shirt with 'Nashvegas' scrawled in white script on the chest.

Damn, he was tall. I'd somehow forgotten that.

"Hey!" He trotted over to the car as I climbed out, wrapping me in a quick hug before turning back to the gate.

I'd just arrived and already scored a hug. Sweet.

"Come on. I'll give you the tour before we go see my babies. You can help me feed the lions."

Oh shit. That sounded bloody dangerous. Like, *literally* bloody.

A thrill ran through me as I followed him onto the tan cobbles past the entrance. To either side, every six feet a wooden beam rose from the ground, supporting thick, rough-hewn rope that drooped between the posts. The sounds of a thousand birds chirping—and the smell of that same flock's poop—assaulted my senses. There wasn't a fence or cage to be seen.

"Aviary is first," Donny said, a few strides ahead of me.

I had guessed that on my own.

We turned to the right and walked into a wooden building with an insanely high ceiling. Netting made of the same thick rope I'd seen outside hung everywhere above. We stepped onto a wood-chipped path that wove through clumps of trees and bushes, giving the structure a natural, jungle-like feel. The peeping and squawking was over-whelming. Everywhere I looked, wings of every size and color flapped as their owners fluttered by. They seemed utterly disinterested in the humans strolling through their territory.

I'd been so distracted by the trees and birds that I'd lost Donny. I rounded two more bends in the path before nearly bumping into my gentle giant. He had a broad smile plastered across his face and a bird perched on each of his outstretched arms. A large parrot called out "Welcome to the zoo" from his left, while a solid-white peek-a-something glared at me like I wanted her lunch. Then I looked up and noticed two tiny, bright-orange feathery balls on his shoulder. They nuzzled his neck.

OMG. Cuteness overload.

"Most of the residents keep their distance, but these are the one we've trained to be held by guests. If you stretch out your arm, at least one of them will come to visit."

I did as instructed, and the white, snarky-looking bird flapped onto my arm. I half expected her to peck my eyes out, but she simply scooted sideways up my arm until she found a comfortable spot. Donny pointed out a few special birds in the tangle above.

After a moment of nuzzling beaks and fluttering feathers, we moved on.

The building wound in a U shape connected by a narrow hallway at the U's bottom. The other side of the letter housed critters I wasn't sure I cared to see, but Donny insisted.

"We don't have to stay long, but I want you to see a few of the snakes—and their keepers."

"Their keepers?" I cocked my head.

He chuckled. "No cheating. Just wait. It'll be fun."

I couldn't decide if the mischief in his voice was more endearing or frightening. I chose to go with endearing because he was tall…and handsome…and his butt looked amazing in those jeans.

We rounded the bend and were greeted by a short, rail-thin guy with long, stringy hair I doubted had seen shampoo this decade. His grimy black hair blended into a black shirt that flowed down to even blacker pants. Beady eyes blinked in an odd, rapid rhythm as he looked up from one of the glass cases.

"Donald. Welcome. We are pleased to see you." His voice was metallic yet smooth—definitely spooky—and he referred to himself in the plural, as if he were the Queen of England.

Donny grinned broadly and patted Mr. Munster on the shoulder. "Thanks, Edward. This is my friend, Michael. He's a virgin."

I nearly tripped. Both keepers chuckled.

"A *zoo* virgin. What did you think I meant?" Donny's grin held more of that mischief I'd seen earlier.

Before I could answer, Edward spoke. "Please forgive dear Donald. He has no manners, certainly not like our pretties here." He waved dramatically at the glass cages full of slithering bodies.

I suppressed a shiver, both at the snakes and their creepy caretaker.

Donny walked me quickly through the exhibit, and I was relieved when we stepped out into the sunlight and fresh air. There was something heavy about the air in that place. It felt, I don't know, *off.*

Maybe I just didn't like snakes.

"What did you think of Edward?" Donny asked as soon as we were out of earshot of the snake pen.

"Um, he was alright, I guess." I wasn't sure if they were friends or not and didn't want to offend Donny.

He laughed at my discomfort and leaned over, whispering, "He's fucking weird. I can see it all over your face— and you're right. He's nice enough, but he makes my skin crawl. It's like he came from House Slytherin, but creepier and without a shower."

"Yeah, I kept waiting for one of his *pretties* to poke its head out of his hair."

We shared a laugh, then he reached down, grabbed my hand, and pulled me forward. I felt a tingle travel up my arm at his touch. "Come on, you're gonna *love* this next family."

As we traveled along the path, hemmed in either side by the dock-like poles and heavy rope, a large grassy expanse opened on our left and I could see several varieties of antelope. Long, curved horns formed sharp points at the tip. Groups of ten or so moved in unison as they grazed lazily. The largest among them perked up as we passed, his head shooting straight up, horns high. There was a majestic beauty to the beast, a tranquility too.

A dozen paces later, another field opened to our right, but this one was more dirt than grass. It looked like it had been heavily trodden and barely a blade had survived. Donny's pace quickened and he called over his shoulder, "We're here."

He stopped in front of a large metal gate that led into a paddock. I didn't see any animals. Then the ground trembled. And again. If Donny hadn't been standing calmly nearby, I would've jumped back over the gate.

Seconds later, three mountains on legs appeared from nowhere. The elephants stood twice as tall as Donny, and must've weighed thousands of pounds. Wrinkles covered almost every inch of their bodies, and long tusks preceded them as they approached.

A man called out, "Hey, Donny. Come to see the fam?" His voice was warm and welcoming, and carried the same low rumble I heard in the beasts' thunderous footsteps.

One of the elephants moved away from the others, revealing a tall man with thick gray-black hair and a broad toothy smile. He waved at us, then issued a command to the elephants. On cue, all three animals stopped walking and turned to him, and one let out a deafening greeting.

Then the elephant trainer made a clicking sound and each member of his herd wrapped their trunks around him in a long, nasally hug. One of them got frisky and tickled his side with its snout. His high-pitched laughter was such a contrast from his booming voice that I couldn't help but join in his amusement. I caught Donny looking between the elephants and me, and his grin broadened. He was loving showing off his zoo as much as I was reveling in its wonders. I felt the warmth of his hand on my back as he urged me forward. "Come on, let's meet the family. The keeper's name is Ken."

We spent the next thirty minutes listening to Ken explain about the elephants, their upbringing, how they came to the zoo, what they ate and drank, the toys they played with—I didn't even know elephants played with toys. The handler's smile never wavered as he talked about each beast's unique personality, and he insisted I learn their names and call them properly.

Just when I thought we'd move on to the next exhibit, Donny pushed me into the middle of the elephants. He and Ken remained a few feet away, outside the ring of wrinkles. Ken issued a command and I received the same trunk-love they'd given him earlier. Rather than tickle me, Cootie, the female, used her snout to suck up my hair, then blow snot all over it.

Awesome. I was now the elephant version of Edward, the slimy-haired snake dude.

Then Ken whistled some other obscenity, and the elephants began walking in a ring around me. One minute they were creeping along, the next their tails were gripped by the trunk of the elephant to their rear, forming a solid circle. They walked faster and faster, kicking up dust and making the ground beneath me shake. As Cootie passed in front of me, I caught a flash of her eye and a quirk of her mouth.

Great. I've amused the snotty beast.

Donny giggled like a schoolgirl.

Ken hooted another directive and the circle froze. Each elephant dropped their partner's tail, took two steps backward, then reared up on their hind legs.

I'll admit it, I was terrified. I might've piddled a little.

Eight gazillion pounds of elephant was standing on two legs facing me from every direction. Their front legs wiggled wildly in the air, and the beasts roared. I later learned it was their version of a salute, a sort of primal welcome. At the time, I was worried about getting squished.

We thanked Ken, and I said goodbye, by name, to each of the powerful creatures. They really were gentle, and there was such intelligence in their eyes. I never would've expected it, but I could swear Cootie knew what I was saying. She wrapped her trunk around my neck and pulled me into a slobbery lick.

Yes, that was gross…and kind of cool.

We'd walked a few paces before I realized Donny had grabbed my hand and intertwined our fingers. He looked down at my slobber-covered face and squeezed my hand. A shiver thrilled up my arm again.

What was it with Donny making me shiver?

Without thinking, I returned his squeeze. I could see his cheeks tighten with his smile, though he didn't turn and look.

"What do you think so far?" he asked.

"This is so *awesome*. Thank you for sharing it with me. I had no idea Nashville had such an incredible zoo—or that I would love it so much."

"What do you think of the staff?"

I chuckled. "Well, as a wise man once told me, Edward is creepy as fuck. Ken is totally cool and laidback, but has a hidden strength." I paused a moment. "It's like they're linked to their animals or something. That's so weird."

He nodded. "I wondered when you'd pick up on that. Most snake people are just like Edward. They dress like him, talk like him, even fail to bathe like him. I've been working in one zoo or another for nearly ten years, and they've all been basically the same. But elephant people are an interesting lot too."

"What do you mean?"

"Did you notice how many times Ken used the word *family*?"

"Huh. Yeah, now that you mention it. He did it a lot, even referred to the elephants as his family."

"You met Ken, the son. His parents are keepers here too. That's how elephant handlers are—*families* who go into the elephant-handling business. One family taking care of another—and they're very proud of that fact. Again, every zoo I've worked at, that's held true."

"Wow. That's…I don't know. Cool, I guess." I thought a moment. "So, you're the cat guy. What are cat keepers like?"

He turned to face me with a glint in his eye, then took an aggressive step forward, so close our bodies pressed against each other, though our faces were still an inch or two apart. His voice was a low rumble full of passion and fire when he spoke. "Just wait. *My* family's next."

He ran a hand down my cheek and my whole body flared with heat.

———

WE FOLLOWED THE TRAIL FOR ANOTHER FIVE MINUTES before reaching a side entrance marked 'Employees Only.' I had noticed little change in the fields to our left and right, other than some barrier fencing made to look like natural obstacles. Interestingly, there were still no bars or cages. I thought zoos were covered in metal bars and wire mesh.

As we crossed a thin wooden bridge, I looked over the edge and realized why Nashville eschewed traditional enclosures. Rather than building fences to keep humans and animals separated, the clever zoo builders had dug moats some thirty feet deep and twenty feet wide. Looking out at the fields from the path, I could see there was a gap, but could not really understand the depth or purpose. From the sideways angle of the bridge, it was clear they were dug to divide the two worlds. It was an ingenious design that made it appear like guests were walking through the animals' habitat, rather than viewing them through prison bars. The idea was subtle, but the impact as a viewer was dramatic.

Donny sensed I'd stopped following and strode back to stand beside me on the bridge.

"Pretty cool, isn't it? There isn't a single place in the zoo where a guest sees a bar or metal cage. We want everything to look and feel as natural as possible."

I nodded, looking back down into the gulf between field and path. "What if one of the animals got down there somehow? How would you get it out? And what would stop it from climbing up the other side?"

"They do occasionally get brave and stray too close to

the edge. There are a few openings at various points of the gully where we can let them back into their living area. As for climbing up the other side, there are electrified wires, starting about ten feet from the top, that ensure they don't get all the way up. The zaps aren't strong enough to hurt them, but they sure scare the shit out of them enough to change their mind about getting out."

Again, the design impressed me.

Donny grabbed my hand again and pulled me off the bridge. "Come on, this is what I really wanted to show you today."

We rounded the corner and were met by a wall of thick metal bars, the first I'd seen since we entered the zoo—aside from those at the front gate to keep unwanted humans out when the park was closed. The bars formed a box, with more bars crisscrossing the top. I looked through to find the box situated directly against one of the moats that separated two exhibits. There was a thin dirt bridge, barely as wide as a gymnast's balance beam, leading from the exhibit on the far side into the cage.

Donny pressed his face between two of the bars and made a whirring sound. It undulated between high and low pitches in a rhythm that was somehow familiar, though I couldn't place where I'd heard it before. In seconds, a blur of orange, black, and white crossed the bridge and skidded to a stop before the bars where Donny's head still protruded.

He never flinched. I nearly jumped out of my jeans.

A massive Bengal tiger, with a head twice the width of Donny's, peered up, sniffed the air, then pressed its head against Donny's forehead. I watched in amazement as the tiger closed its eyes and emitted a deep rumble. I didn't speak tiger; I wasn't sure if it was happy or hungry.

Donny then made a low *guff-guff* sound that started deep in his throat and rose to his lips, though they never parted. In response, the tiger mimicked the sound loudly and switched from a head-nuzzle to licking his face. If it wasn't for the beast's size, its licking and nuzzling was like the reaction of any common house cat when greeting their chosen human.

I was transfixed.

Then it hit me. Donny's head was pressed through the bars against a massive predator with sharp, pointy teeth and even pointier claws. That cat could've crushed his skull like a watermelon.

Sorry for the imagery there. That was kinda gross.

Before I could react or pull him to safety, or whatever stupid thing I was thinking at the time, Donny straightened and turned toward me.

"Come meet Tina. I hand-raised her from a cub. She was three weeks old when she came to live in my house."

My jaw must've dropped, or my face made some other cartoonish effect, because he barked a laugh. "Trust me. Tina knows me as her father, as any cat would know the human who raised them. If I approve of you, she will too."

"Uh, okay. Cool. Right. Uh…sure."

I was articulate as ever—and utterly unconvinced—but Donny's broad smile reached well into his deep brown eyes, and I couldn't resist his outstretched hand.

Shit, that tiger was big, and her teeth looked like small, curved white daggers.

When I was close enough, he took my hand and held it out before Tina's nose. Her eyes snapped up to Donny's, then narrowed slightly and shifted toward mine. Her gaze wasn't exactly hostile, but I wasn't sure she fully appreciated my presence either. Could tigers be jealous? What if she didn't want to share her human, her father?

Without relinquishing her protective position between us, she leaned her nose toward my hand and sniffed. Her eyes flickered back to Donny with one last question, then I *felt* her relax as she nuzzled my hand with the top of her head. Her rumbling purr vibrated up my arm.

Donny squeezed my shoulder and I released the breath I'd been holding. "She likes you," he said, a proud smile curling his lips.

"I'm glad *you* can tell. I had images of my fingers being ripped off and blood spurting all over your pretty blond hair."

He leaned down and pressed his forehead into mine, similar to how he'd greeted Tina. "I'm glad you survived, digits intact."

Then he laughed and stepped back, amused at his own jackass-ness.

I couldn't help but laugh too. It was a relief. Then I realized my hand was still on the head of a six-hundred-pound tiger. The only movement Tina had made was to lean *into* my touch. Maybe he was right and she *did* like me.

Then she pulled back and sneezed. Snot and spittle flew all over me, coating my hand in slime. Donny lost all composure, doubling in laughter before giving in to gravity and sitting on the grassy ground.

"Thanks a lot," I said to Tina. "What is it with me and the animals here blowing their noses on me?"

She blinked up at me, wiped her face with a paw, then craned her neck forward and licked the goo off my hand. My eyes popped wide as she gently cleaned every drop.

When I turned back to Donny, his eyes were equally wide. "Huh. She really does like you. Cats don't clean others they don't like. That's her way of apologizing for the snot, and saying she accepts you. It's a very intimate gesture I wouldn't have expected for months, if ever."

My chest puffed out. *Damn, I'm good. Like effin' Siegfried and that other guy good.*

In that moment of triumph, Tina gave me a playful nip. I yanked my hand back and let out the manliest squeal any tiger had ever heard.

Donny roared, and I swear that Tina laughed along with him. She let out a gurgling sound and her eyes turned to slits while the skin around her nose crinkled.

Damned cat.

When everyone had finished their cawing and crinkling at my expense, Donny rose and gripped my shoulders. His hands were what you'd expect on a six-four dude, thick with a wide span. His grasp was firm. He leaned into me and my heart raced as his breath tickled my nose. His lips pressed into mine. They were chapped and rough, yet somehow felt right on this strong keeper of beasts. He held me for a long moment, then pulled back and smiled again.

Tina growled, shattering the dizzying moment.

Donny released my shoulders and turned back to the cat, placing both hands on either side of her broad face. He scratched behind her ears with his fingers, and she emitted that whirring rumble again and leaned into his caress. They touched foreheads one last time.

"We can't go in there, unfortunately."

I raised a brow, unsure if I *wanted* to go in there. Tina accepting me through iron bars was one thing, but roaming into her territory was a completely different form of terror.

He grinned, reading my thoughts yet again. "She'd never *intentionally* hurt me, but think about playing with a house cat. Sometimes they get a little too rough and draw blood with their teeth or claws. They're just playing, but they get carried away. Now, replace that three-pound cat with Miss Tina's six hundred pounds."

"Right. No playing on Tina's turf. Definitely okay with that." I thought a moment. "You said she lived with you? You mean *actually* lived with you in your home? Like a house cat?"

"Yeah, that's what hand-raised means. The idea is to get the cats used to the person who will be their ultimate keeper, and to humans in general. They learn smells, tastes, sounds. Most importantly, they learn trust. There's a bond between a hand-raised cat and their handler that doesn't exist with any other keeper–animal relationship. It's special."

Why did my heart soar hearing him talk about hand-raising a cat?

His eyes drifted somewhere else as he spoke, and his smile transformed from playful to wistful. I could see him replaying memories of Tina in his home, of her as a cub nestling on his bed or in his lap.

Wait, I was not thinking about his bed—*or his lap*. I swear. We'd never talked about his bed. I'd never seen it. Really, his bed had never popped into my head.

Damn it. Now I couldn't get his bed—*or his lap*—out of my mind.

That's *your* fault!

"Did you go somewhere?" he asked.

I shook my head free of beds and laps. "No, was just imagining Tina as a cub. I bet she was adorable."

"She was just a ball of the softest fur you've ever felt. Her eyes had opened the week before I got her, but she still couldn't see very well, and she stumbled around more than walked. I bottle-fed her for over a month." I watched him drift away again. "Tigers basically sleep all the time as cubs, only waking to eat, drink, or poop. They're not really playful like other cats. She slept in my arms or lap more hours than I could count, and I loved every minute of it." He closed his eyes. "I can still feel her purr against my chest."

Tina must've sensed he was talking about her, because she let out a low growl-purr and scratched herself against the bars. Donny gave her a deep scratch, earning an even louder rumble.

We were standing in a zoo in the middle of Nashville, but I felt like I'd been transported to another planet. It's not like we went to Africa or anything exotic, but seeing all this through Donny's eyes was extraordinary. These cats were family to him in a way I'd never understood or expected. I would've thought keepers were professionals trained to feed and care for animals, but hand-raising and soul-stirring bonds? This was something special, and I was honored to witness it.

"How long did she live with you?" I asked.

"We judge that more by size and weight than time. Cats grow within a range, but can also vary widely in when they reach puberty or other key physical markers. They normally stay with us until they're around a hundred pounds, maybe a little more. A lot of that depends on breed and temperament. Our zoo gives me a lot of discretion, while others have hard rules forcing a keeper to relinquish an animal at certain weights."

"Sounds like letting them go would be hard."

"It is and it isn't. I miss having her at home, but she wasn't comfortable there anymore. She needed room to roam and hunt, to be the majestic beast she was born to be. She couldn't do that in a house or apartment. Plus, I knew all along that I'd be her keeper, so it's not like I lost her. Our living arrangement was all that really changed."

He guided me back to the main path where we wound our way around the zoo.

"Is Tina the only cat you've hand-raised?"

"No, she's my third, and I have a few other friends living with me right now."

Interesting. There was mischief in his voice, but he didn't elaborate.

We turned onto another side path and came to another box, this one with solid metal walls and bars on the front face. It was a sturdier version of the cage I'd met Tina in. On the far side was a series of two sliding panels that allowed keepers to bring in one animal at a time while closing the other panel behind them, reminding me of an entrance to a restaurant in some wintery city where you entered one door, then another as the first closed, to keep the cold out.

Donny walked up to a series of buttons that rose along the left edge of the cage and pressed the blue one. A horn sounded for as long as his thumb kept pressure on the button; a few seconds. I heard thunder as heavy paws carried something large toward the cage. Satisfied his call had been answered, Donny lifted a plastic cover and pressed a red button. It looked like the zookeeper's version of launching a nuclear missile. The nerd in me thought it was *totally cool.*

A second later, the panel facing the living area opened and a blur of tan raced in. A yellow button was pressed next to close the outer panel, then open the inner one. The mechanism timed those actions so two panels were never opened at the same time. As soon as the inner panel lifted, powerful golden eyes surveyed the cage and the lustrous mane of a male lion shook, heralding the beast's arrival. The moment the powerful cat strode into the cage, the inner panel slammed shut, triggered by a motion sensor I hadn't noticed.

The lion padded its way toward us, and I took an involuntary step back.

Donny didn't approach like he had with Tina.

When the lion was a foot from the bars, he sat on his hindquarters and looked expectantly up at Donny. His head was wider than my shoulders, and rose to Donny's chest when seated. Standing, he was monstrous. Behind his thick mane, the fur on his body laid back like a short-haired house cat, in shimmering tan waves. I could see muscles ripple every time he moved.

"Uh, Donny, that's a freakin' lion."

"You're *good*, practically an expert now," he teased.

I rolled my eyes. "Thanks, Obi Wan. What the hell are we doing with a lion? You're not going to cuddle with that thing, are you?"

"No. No cuddling Duke. I didn't hand-raise him, and lions can be less predictable than tigers, especially when it's feeding time. We're just going to give him what he wants."

"That doesn't involve a Michael sacrifice, does it?"

He ignored my jibe and walked around the side of the solid wall, returning with a bucket.

"I had Duke's keeper leave us his dinner so you could experience feeding time. Care to help?" The mischief was back in his eyes again.

"Uh, sure."

He reached into the bucket and pulled out a slab of some kind of bloody meat on a bone. It could've been remains of the aforementioned keeper, or maybe one of the antelopes I'd seen earlier—I couldn't tell. I didn't care. It dripped and oozed all over the ground, and Duke responded immediately, sniffing the air and pacing in front of the bars. He huffed excitedly.

Great. Get the lion all worked up. That's *exactly* what I hoped for.

Donny grinned as I squirmed, then tossed the gooey mass between the bars. Duke lunged. The sound of rending flesh and crunching bones echoed inside the metal box. One chomp of his mighty jaws shattered the femur that was thicker than my arm into a dozen splinters. Duke downed the smaller pieces, while larger bones fell near his paws.

When he had finished his appetizer and was again facing us, seated and staring, Donny held the bucket toward me.

"Your turn, Great Lion Tamer."

I looked down and another bone-in-rib-something poked up from a disgusting pool of blood that filled half the pail. I'd never been squeamish, but that was gross, and I really didn't want to touch it. Unfortunately, a guy I wanted to impress was standing there, waiting.

I realized just then that I *really* wanted to impress him. Interesting.

I did the manliest two-fingered grip I could muster and plucked the thick slab of bony meat out. Blood and gore splashed everywhere. Lovely. When I looked up, Duke was standing with his nose just outside the bars, his golden eyes fixed on me and the main course dripping in my hand—or did he think *I* was his main course? I didn't want to find out.

I flung the bloody hunk toward the cage and Duke swatted it down with a massive paw through the bars, then dragged his prize inside.

If I thought my heart had raced when Donny kissed me, it was running sprints right then.

Holy king of the beasts.

We watched Duke finish his lunch, then Donny reversed the button-pressing procedure to return him to the living area. For his part, Duke knew the routine and didn't argue when the metal slider lifted. He simply turned and strode through.

"They've each been trained since they were juveniles to follow this feeding ritual. They know exactly what the horns and sliding doors mean, and what's expected. On the off-chance they balk, we have prods to help them remember what to do." He pointed around the corner to a sealed plastic case mounted to the outer wall of the cage.

Once Duke was secured and the cage was reset, Donny rummaged through a metal cabinet next to the plastic container and returned with a towel. I wiped a few blood splashes and the last of Tina's slobber from my arms. He chuckled as I scrubbed at dried snot.

An hour later, we'd returned to the zoo's main entrance, having walked a complete circle around the sprawling park. Donny turned to me before unlocking the metal gate that led to the parking lot. "What did you think? Was it alright?"

"Yeah, I guess, if you're into that sort of thing." I tried playing it cool, but the twelve-year-old in me couldn't resist. "What are you talking about? That was the coolest, most exciting, craziest day I've had in forever. It was a total blast. Thank you so much. You have the coolest job ever."

Donny broke into warm laughter. His smile…wow. His smile made me swoon. He was the most beautiful cat I'd seen all day, and it was only in that moment that I realized how much I liked him.

"Can I see you again?" he asked. "I'd really like to. It might be nice to get another kiss sometime too."

Sweet baby Jesus, he sounded like a man from one of those old-timey movies asking if he could court me. Despite the blood, snot, and dust that covered us both, it might've been the most romance-novel-worthy thing anyone had ever said to me.

"I'd like that. Both. I mean, yes, I'd like you to see me, or me see you. Again. And the kiss. Yes. Well, shit. Yes to all of it. Yes!"

I really was sputtering by the end of…whatever that was.

He beamed. He leaned down and planted another kiss on my lips as his hand pressed gently against the side of my head. Strong fingers raked through my hair until he held my neck, pulling me into him.

I thought I might pass out.

15

WHO YOU BE?

Donny called the next day. I snorted when he said
Tina couldn't stop talking about me. He said she'd
growled and paced back and forth until he assured her he'd
ask me out again. He'd kept a straight face—well, a straight
voice—throughout the whole tale, and that had made it irre-
sistibly cute. I found myself grinning so wide my cheeks
hurt by the time we'd hung up.

April's on-again, off-again warmth and rain, coupled
with waves of pollen that knocked my sinuses into the last
decade, gave each day an odd bipolar mix of pleasure and
pain. Now that basketball season was over, and the rush of
AAU and summer leagues had yet to arrive, I had little to
occupy my evenings.

As we learned before, boredom is a dangerous thing.

I threw myself into working out, and my shoulders
rounded and chest filled out. T-shirts that had hung loosely
last year now fit snugly, and the sleeves strained at their
hems from my growing arms. I'd never known the feeling
of a healthy, growing body before. It was a rush—and not
just the post-workout, endorphin-fueled rush guys talk

about experiencing after a hard day with weights. It was the mental fix that came with looking in the mirror in the morning and realizing I was no longer a bean pole. The definition forming between my biceps and triceps was exciting, something I'd seen on the muscle heads at the gym and longed for.

I was, by no man's definition, a muscle head, but I was able to change my *body type* answer on my AOL profile from thin to athletic. I stared at the screen, watching the cursor blink as it waited for me to hit *confirm*, struggling to believe I was about to enter the world of athletic-bodied men. For a second, I wondered if changing that answer would impact the guys who'd be willing to respond when I messaged them. Did I need new pictures?

Hell yes I did! Before pressing the button, I raced to my closet and threw on a blue tank top that fit just right, meaning it was a size too small. Everything looked bigger in that tank top. I loved it. Then I dug in my dresser drawer for my digital camera.

Yes, kids, this was before phones had cameras. In fact, it was before cell phones were even a thing. Don't pass out.

A hundred shots later, I was satisfied with how the light from my bedroom window created shadows in the creases in my arms and across my chest.

Yes, it was a vain moment. Give me a break.

I hit *cancel* on my profile update, uploaded the new photos, then reupdated my profile with the new *athletic* body type.

Ding. An instant message window popped up.

That was odd. I wasn't in a chat room, and none of the guys on my handy friends list were online. Who could be ringing my bell?

I giggled at the song that started in my head and danced a bad white-man jig in my office chair.

RAL1027: HEY

Huh. RAL1027, wonder what that means. I sifted through my printed profile sheets, now neatly alphabetized, hole-punched, and bound in a three-ring binder.

Don't make fun. I had to keep track somehow.

MICHAELSPORTSGUY: HI. SORRY, HAVE WE CHATTED BEFORE?

RAL1027: NO. SAW YOUR PROFILE AND THOUGHT I'D SAY HI.

MICHAELSPORTSGUY: OK. COOL. HI. I'M MICHAEL.

RAL1027: RYAN.

MICHAELSPORTSGUY: NICE TO MEET YA, RYAN.

RAL1027: YOU TOO.

There was a long enough pause at this point, so I got up, went to the kitchen, and made a bowl of cereal. When I came back, Ryan had responded a few times.

RAL1027: WHATCHA UP TO?

RAL1027: STILL THERE?

RAL1027: HEY, GOTTA RUN. CHECK YOUR EMAIL. SENT YOU A PIC. FEEL FREE TO RETURN.

On a whim, I added him to my friends list. The window said he was no longer online, so, between bites of Frosted Flakes, I clicked my email and opened his pic. Blond, gray eyes, nice smile, fit from what I could tell. The pic looked like one taken for work, a headshot that only went to his shoulders and revealed nothing more than his light-blue dress shirt.

Didn't this guy know he was supposed to send a shirt-less pic so I could judge if he was worthy or not? Wasn't that the rule? AOL was a fairly new invention, but I was sure the Gay Handbook covered the topic.

Before shutting down my computer, I printed Ryan's profile and picture, then smacked it through the three-hole punch. I scribbled a note on his page, then put two stars at the top. No circle. The conversation was too brief to earn the highest distinction available.

16

LIQUID DIET

D ate night came quickly. As I rummaged for clean clothes, a task more challenging than I'd expected, my excitement grew. I couldn't remember a day more fun than the one we'd spent at the zoo, certainly not in a long time. Who gets to pet tigers on a date? I didn't know Donny well, but there was something in his childlike smile that made me want to spend more time with him.

I found a clean shirt, but sighed as I realized how badly wrinkled it had become hidden in the clean pile all week.

Yes, I know, I should've laid my clothes out when they were still warm from the dryer. Better yet, I should've put them away. Stop nagging.

I was waiting for the iron to heat up when the phone rang. I banged my shin on the coffee table sprinting across the room, but managed to grab the receiver before the caller hung up. "Hello?"

"Please don't hate me."

"Donny?"

"Yep. It's me. I'm really sorry to do this, but I need to

put off our dinner. The bar called and two guys called out sick. They need me to work tonight after all."

"Well, that sucks," I blurted without thinking. "I mean, I'm sorry they're sick. We'll have to pick another night."

I could swear I heard him let out a breath.

"We definitely will. How about I cook for you to make up for it? I make a mean pasta."

"Perfect-o," I said with a terrible Italian accent. He chuckled.

"Hey, since you don't have plans now, why don't you stop by the bar? I know a guy who's stuck working you might like."

I grinned and played along. "Really? What's he look like? I'm pretty picky these days."

"Well, he's not much to look at, but he works out, and I hear he's great with cats."

"Awesome," I feigned sarcasm. "You're setting me up with a crazy cat lady. Are you sure this dude's not a lesbian in disguise?"

He snorted. "Definitely not a lesbian. Although, he does go to Home Depot a lot. Is that a coincidence?"

We both laughed.

"What time do you work?"

"I'm headed in now. With two men down, they'll need help to set up."

"Alright. I'll grab something to eat and head over in a couple hours. Look forward to seeing you…I mean, Crazy Kitty Man."

He snorted again. "See you soon."

I hung up the phone, disappointed that dinner had been scrapped, but excited he still wanted to spend time together. I'd been blown off before, and this was definitely not a blow-off. On a whim, I dialed Dwayne. "Hey, are you working tonight? Donny had to work at the bar and asked me to swing by. You should come."

"As it turns out, I got cut tonight. Want a dinner date since yours canceled?"

"You're the best date ever. Absolutely!"

Thirty minutes later, Dwayne and I sat staring at plates piled high with rotisserie chicken, fried okra, and mashed potatoes. He looked suspiciously at the okra, but I was in heaven. What can I say, my mama raised a veggie-lovin' Southern boy.

We bantered like the two old guys in the balcony on *The Muppet Show*. Dwayne was the best friend I could ever hope to have. He grounded me. Somehow, he never took himself—or me—too seriously. Time with him was comfortable and safe, and I knew he'd be there no matter what insanity I got myself into.

Everyone needs a Dwayne.

An hour later, we strode into the Chute. There were several guys seated around the bar, and Donny was bouncing quickly between them, filling glasses and chatting. Our two regular stools stood empty, one with a Jack and Coke beside a tumbler filled with limes. A second glass with Coke fizzed nearby.

"How did he know we'd be here now?" Dwayne whispered to me.

I shrugged and grinned at Donny's thoughtfulness. My chest warmed as the tall man behind the bar turned and waved. His smile lit up the dim room.

Dwayne's elbow jabbed my ribs. "Are you going to stand here in the doorway grinning like an idiot, or can we go see him now?"

"Oh, sorry. Sure. Let's go."

Donny leaned over and hugged Dwayne in greeting,

then did the same with me. He squeezed my back with his hands and pressed a kiss into my cheek before pulling away.

I flushed and grinned stupidly again.

A guy on the other side of the bar turned to his neighbor and said, "Looks like somebody's taken Donny off the market."

I nearly fell off my stool.

"You okay?" Donny asked, either not hearing or ignoring the comment.

"Yeah, sorry. Just missed the stool."

Dwayne eyed me with a wry grin. When Donny turned to serve another customer, he leaned over and whispered, "You really like him, don't you?"

"I…uh…sure. I guess so. He's super nice, and the zoo date was one of the best ever—and not just because of the animals. He was awesome too. I definitely want to get to know him better."

"And you want to find out if *everything* is as big as the rest of him too. I know you."

"Dwayne!" I feigned offense. "I'm a gentleman. I have no idea what you're talking about."

He guffawed. "You know *exactly* what I'm talking about. Besides, I'm curious too. I bet that thing's huge. It might even give your tight little ass a run for your money."

Now I *was* blushing. "My ass—"

"Go on. Don't stop for me," Donny said, leaning over with his chin in both hands, elbows on the bar, batting innocent eyelashes at me.

Eight shades of red turned into twenty. I wanted to crawl under the bar. "Uh…Dwayne was just…I mean—"

"I was agreeing with Michael that your ass looks good in those jeans," Dwayne interjected.

I turned, eyes wide, and slapped him playfully on the arm. "I didn't say—"

"So you don't like my ass in these jeans?" Donny asked, clearly picking a side.

"No, I didn't say that—"

"So you *do* like his ass?" Dwayne countered.

I felt like a tennis ball at Wimbledon. Just when I thought I was safely across the net, someone smacked me back to the other side—and those damned royals did *nothing* to stop it, just sat in their fancy nest and watched.

Unable to string two words together, I grabbed my Coke and took a long pull.

Dwayne and Donny shared a grin while I drank. Donny turned, slapped one of his butt cheeks loudly, then crossed the bar to refill someone else's drink.

Dwayne was hyperventilating.

"Thanks a lot. Some wing man you are," I groused, unwilling to admit how funny the scene had actually been.

Dwayne stood and pointed at the restroom. He couldn't speak through the tears. His shoulders never stopped quaking as he laughed all the way to the far side of the bar.

"He's a good friend, isn't he?"

I turned back to find Donny leaning over the counter again. "I hate to admit it, but he's the best."

He chuckled. "Those are rare. I had one like him." His eyes shifted from laughter to—something.

"Had?"

He nodded slowly. "Yeah. He took two bullets."

"Bullets?"

"Yeah, we served together." His voice stilled.

I watched as he drifted far away, staring at the counter before him. His brow furrowed, and his eyes closed. I wanted to say something, but no words could bring his friend back, and they certainly wouldn't be worthy of honoring his memory, however well intentioned.

A pair of guys entering the bar brought Donny back to the present. He gave me a long look, then nodded and turned back to his work. I wasn't sure what had passed between us, but I was sure *something* had. I got the impression he didn't tell many people about his time overseas. Given what he'd lost, I couldn't blame him.

"Penny."

I looked up to find Dwayne settling back onto his stool, staring at me. I raised a questioning brow.

"For your thoughts. You look lost in them."

"Oh yeah. Donny just told me some things…from his past."

"His time in the army?"

I looked up, surprised.

"I've been coming here a long time. Sometimes he wears dog tags. On nights when he works without a shirt, they're hard to miss. He's never talked about them, but I could tell they weren't the kind you buy in a gift shop."

"How do you know the difference?"

He cocked his head. "Because I was in the navy. And because of the way he'd hold them when he thought no one was watching. I could just tell."

"You never told me you were in the navy. When?"

"A lifetime ago." Now Dwayne got that same faraway look in his eyes. "I'll tell you about it sometime, just not here, not now. Okay?"

"Sure," I said quietly.

The slow trickle of men entering the bar had turned into a full-on flood, and Donny was struggling to keep up, bouncing from one waving hand demanding alcohol to the next. He stole a moment to apologize for ignoring us.

"It's alright," I said. "We know you have to work. Why don't we go and let you do your thing?"

Donny leaned over and kissed me full on the mouth. Conversations around the bar hushed. Then everyone applauded and cheered as he pulled back. I turned crimson, earning a chorus of giggles from the gaggle. "Dinner Sunday night? I definitely won't work then, no matter who's sick."

I grinned, overcoming my embarrassment. "Kissing like that? How can I say no?"

Another wild cheer erupted around us. Dwayne ushered me out before my ears could turn any redder.

17

A COMPLETELY DIFFERENT ZOO

As I pulled into Donny's driveway, a whole zoo's worth of butterflies took flight in my chest.

I no longer wore the label *newborn gay*, having been on a number of dates and locked down my first boyfriend, even if that was only for a few months. I'd made meaningful, intimate love to a man I cared for deeply. And I'd been tied to bedposts with silk bonds.

No, I was definitely not new anymore.

That still didn't make me experienced. One boyfriend and one breakup hadn't turned me jaded or stolen my idealism. I still believed in The Dream. You know, that sappy daydream where I'd meet the perfect man, fall helplessly in love, then walk down the aisle together while rose petals and doves flew overhead.

Wait, doves poop, don't they? Scratch the doves.

Insert Disney movie music. Or Journey—*definitely* Journey. They were my all-time favorite band. I needed them on my special day.

Stop laughing. It's an awesome dream—if a bit sappy— and I still believe in it whether you do or not.

Where were we? Oh, driveway. Right.

I stared through the windshield at Donny's house. It was a nice starter home, a one-story brick box that probably had two or three bedrooms and an outdated kitchen. The neighborhood was nice too. Cars and trucks filled the driveways on either side, giving the impression this was a middle-class working neighborhood, exactly where I envisioned a zookeeper might live.

Sitting there, my mind strayed to our date at the zoo. That day had been such an incredible surprise. There was no way a simple dinner without animals or snakes could top that.

Well, unless he *actually* topped that.

My butt quivered at the thought.

I hopped out of the car and strode up to the house. With a couple taps of the clacker, Donny appeared, his towering frame consuming the doorway. He wore tan shorts and a light-blue shirt. For a moment, I thought he was still in his zoo uniform. He definitely looked like a hot park ranger, with thick, hairy legs and broad shoulders. Then he smiled, and I swooned.

"Hey you." He opened the door and wrapped me in a tight hug while planting a long kiss on my lips. I don't know what I expected from his greeting, but it wasn't *that*. I melted in his arms. When he pulled back, still holding me, his eyes sparkled, the tiny creases around them curling upward in a smile all their own.

Sweet buttery popcorn. My heart fluttered again.

"Come on. I need your help with something while I finish dinner."

Curious, I let him take my hand and lead me through his house, which was exactly what I had pictured while sitting in the driveway. Paneled walls and fixtures from the

'70s surrounded us. A few pictures of tigers and lions hung on the walls, some with Donny, others without.

We came to a closed door, and he turned to face me. "I need you to babysit for me. Are you okay with that?"

Babysit? What the hell? He never mentioned having kids.

Wait. I *loved* kids. Was he serious? Another swoon threatened, but I slapped that bitch back into place and stared up at my host. "Uh, sure. Whatever you need."

"Alright. Stay here a second. Let me get everything ready."

Um. That's weird. Did he have his child in a cage? Was this about to turn into one of those shows where the police rescue a dozen kidnap victims who'd been hidden behind walls?

"Okay, come on in." He sounded amused, not what I expected from a serial kidnapper.

I pushed open the door, revealing a small, unfurnished bedroom. A twin-sized mattress lay on the floor, and a large metal cage rested against the far wall. Donny sat with his legs crossed in the middle of the room, his back facing me.

"Shut the door behind you."

I complied.

"Now come sit with us."

Us? Oh shit.

I squatted on the floor and he turned, holding a squirming ball of pure-white fluff. He held the ball up and four paws flopped to its side. Wide golden eyes stared up at me.

"This is Roxy, our newest Bengal tiger cub." He held her out and I took her in my arms, cradling her like a baby. Her fur was softer than any puppy I'd ever petted. Her eyes held a lazy, disinterested look, and her body oozed into my lap as though she had no bones. I scratched her head and was rewarded with a rumble far bigger than the tiny body in my arms should've been able to produce.

I couldn't stop smiling. Roxy was adorable.

"She won't play or anything. At this age, what you see is what you get. She barely gets excited at feeding time. Sometimes I think she gets annoyed I'm interrupting her sleep to feed her." He chuckled.

"She's beautiful."

"Yeah, she really is. Her markings won't show for another couple months. This solid-white stage is my favorite. I'll only get to keep her for another three or four months. Bengals grow really fast."

"I don't know how you give them up. I'm already falling for this little girl."

He grinned. "It can be hard sometimes."

Hee hee, he said hard, the little devil whispered in my head.

"Let's put her to bed. She's not who I need you to watch."

This dinner date just got really interesting. I could hardly wait to see what he had in the other bedrooms.

Hey, stop that. I was thinking about furry, cuddly things.

No, not *that* furry thing, you filthy-minded beast!

Once Roxy was secured in her crate, we moved down the hallway to bedroom number two. This time we entered together, though he insisted I close my eyes and sit on the floor.

A second later, a knobby, furry head slammed into my chest, and my eyes flew open to find a football-sized cougar cub playfully pouncing into me. A blur of motion to my right revealed a brother or sister racing around to attack from the side. They were young, only a couple months old, but keen intelligence showed in their eyes as they coordinated their approach. I couldn't stop laughing.

And then stinker number three pounced on my back.

I hadn't seen nor heard the other cub sneak around my left side while number two distracted me. The pounce caught me completely by surprise. Tiny needles poked into my back as the assailant climbed up to nibble my neck.

Donny stood in the corner of the room, laughing at my dilemma.

"These are the three troublemakers I wanted you to meet. That's Simon in your lap, Alvin crawling up your right arm, and Theo on your back."

I barked a laugh. "Those are chipmunks, not cougars."

"Yeah, I know, but zookeepers have a sense of humor too. Besides, we run out of names and have to get creative." He tussled my hair as he walked toward the door, careful not to dislodge any of the cubs. "I'm going to work on dinner. Good luck."

Just like that, the door clicked shut and the cubs renewed their attack, playfully pawing and gnawing like the baby cats they were. I was amazed at how they communicated on some instinctual level, coordinating their efforts. Every time I'd get the upper hand, they'd retreat to the far side of the room and glare, then Simon would stalk toward me, his eyes never leaving mine. Simon was the instigator, the bait. Alvin was the muscle, blundering in whenever Simon's devious dance had me mesmerized. Theo was the assassin, the ninja.

The other two cats were smart, but Theo was brilliant. At one point, I picked him up and he chomped down on my hand. I let out a yelp. He released me immediately and looked up with his ears pinned back, then carefully craned his neck to lick the skin his teeth had just pierced, his version of an apology for playing too roughly.

Alvin let me hold him upside down and scratch his belly. His tiny purr was more akin to a pull-cord lawnmower starting than any cat's purr I'd heard, but I loved it. He wrapped his paws around my non-scratching fingers and pulled them into him as I worked. His mouth held an upward turn I took for a smile, as his eyes lolled back in his head in pure ecstasy.

Our moment of bliss lasted as long as it took the other two minions to get a drink and come up with a new plan. I chuckled as Theo snuck around behind me again.

"You know I can see you, right?"

He squinted his eyes in concentration, unwilling to let my teasing distract from his mission. Meanwhile, Simon pranced innocently toward me, climbed onto my lap, giving Alvin a lick on the head. My mower's engine grew louder at his brother's touch.

In a feat of magical synchronization, Theo and Simon leapt at the same moment, one pouncing on my chest, the other my back, but I was ready for them this time. I grabbed Simon, tickling his toothpick-like ribs. He squirmed and squealed, finally freeing himself and sprinting across the room to the safety of their crate.

Theo climbed my back again, locking his teeth onto my hair and yanking. I shook my head and the rascal dropped free, then bolted around for a frontal assault.

Thirty minutes flew by, and the tiny terrors never tired.

When Donny returned, he had to detach the chipmunks one at a time. As soon as he got one, the other two latched on. It was a losing battle. They squirmed and let out the cutest growls, clearly not done with play time. I wasn't sure

I wanted to stop either. That was the most fun I'd had since our day at the zoo—and that day ranked on my all-time list.

Resigned to plan B, Donny grabbed a bottle full of milk I hadn't noticed and handed it to me. He then grabbed two others and shook them in front of the cougars. The change was instant. They swarmed the bottles, tiny pink tongues lolling and licking.

Simon chose me. I guessed all that climbing and attacking had bonded us. He lay peacefully on his stomach in my lap while I bottle-fed him like an infant. As his brother had done earlier, he gripped my off-hand with his paws and held it as he drank. Every time he looked up at me and blinked, my heart skipped a beat.

I was so wrapped up in watching Simon feed that I'd almost forgotten Donny and the others were in the room. He was staring at me, smiling, when I looked up. "What?"

"You're a natural. They adore you."

My eyes drifted back to Simon. "I'm kinda falling for them too."

"Just them?"

My breath caught. If you didn't count the bar visits, we'd only been on two real dates, and I hardly knew how to respond. I was definitely drawn to him though.

I gave him a sheepish look. "The keeper's not too bad once you get to know him."

He must've liked that answer because he leaned over and planted a kiss on me that nearly made me drop my pussy.

Cat! Pussy *cat*, you rogue!

18

REPORTING IN, SIR

"Wait. You've had *three* dates and been to visit him at the bar *four* times?" Jason asked.

I shrugged. "Yeah. Maybe five times at the bar."

"The staff knows him by name, but they call him Donny's boy." Dwayne smirked.

"I can't help it if people like me."

Jason wouldn't be thrown off the scent. "Don't distract me. That's *eight* dates. You went to his bar specifically to see him. On more than one occasion, he *invited* you. Those count as dates."

"And?" I had no idea where this was going.

"And you haven't seen him naked yet? What kind of self-respecting homosexual are you?"

"Apparently, one with more self-respect than the slut grilling him at the moment," I shot back.

Dwayne choked on his coffee.

"Said the guy who bedded a sky mattress without getting his name, then became a couple sandwich because someone dangled a hot dog…I mean, hot tub…in front of him."

"Hey! It was a *nice* hot tub, and we actually used it."

"You used the hot dog too," Dwayne said.

Jason spat tea all over the table.

"Ha ha. Very funny." I crossed my arms. "I don't know why we haven't done more than make out. We just haven't. The zoo wasn't really the place to get naked, and when I had dinner at his place, he didn't invite me to stay. We cuddled on the couch and kissed, but that was it."

"Maybe he's heard about your deviant ways?" Jason jabbed.

"Or maybe he's a gentleman and wants to get to know me before we bump and grind," I countered.

"How do you know who bumps and who grinds? Have you even talked about sex?" Jason asked.

I thought a moment, realizing we hadn't. What surprised me more was that I didn't care the subject hadn't come up. I just enjoyed being with him. "We talked about pretty heavy stuff the other night. He told me about his family, then talked about—"

"What?" Jason pressed.

"…His time in the service."

Dwayne leaned in. "You don't have to talk about that if it's too personal. Those are his truths to share, not yours."

"I know," I snapped, more defensively than intended. I sucked in a breath. "I know. It was just tough for him to open up, and I was surprised he did. I'm sure there's plenty he didn't tell me, but he described a lot, including how he lost his best friend."

"Jesus," Jason said.

"I wanted to hold him, comfort him, not jump his bones. If it's right, all that will come in time. I'm honestly enjoying just getting to know him."

"He is setting a high bar for dates. Shit. Who's ever going to top the zoo or wrestling with baby cougars?"

I giggled. "You said *top*."

Jason giggled along with me as Dwayne rolled his eyes and took another sip of coffee.

"So, I hear he actually is a top, and a damn good one," Jason said.

My blood flowed a little faster. "What? Where'd you hear that?"

Dwayne smirked. "Oh honey. He's a bartender, and gays talk. Donny's got a *lot* to talk about, if you know what I mean."

Jason flopped his arm on the table with a loud *thunk* and my two best friends broke into a fit. The redder my ears turned, the louder they laughed. Finally, salvation came in the form of a Flo's Diner waitress uniform.

Katie sidled up to our table. "Hon, are they badgering you again?"

"No, we're preparing him for an incoming torpedo," Jason gasped. Dwayne had tears running down both cheeks. I looked up, hoping Katie would save me.

"Don't let them get to you, sweetie." She leaned down and whispered loud enough for everyone to hear. "I assume your plumbing works the same as mine. Just lay back and relax—and whatever you do, *don't clench*."

My jaw dropped.

Jason howled, and Dwayne, having lost any semblance of composure, was horizontal.

Katie, *my salvation*, made a dramatic gesture and a popping noise with one palm hitting the side of her other fist, then walked away laughing.

19

HOW CATS DO IT

Three dinner dates and four bar visits later, I'd still not see Donny's naked glory. If it hadn't been for Jason's ribbing, I might not have thought much about it, but now it nagged at me. I dreamed scenes of walking into an empty bar, of Donny stripping and taking me on the counter where Dwayne's limes usually sat. The little devil had evicted the angel completely and was practically stroking me into an overheated state day and night. I guess I could've turned to AOL—or to more *handy* methods—but I wanted Donny.

We'd been dating six weeks. Hell, in gay years that's practically a silver anniversary. Shouldn't he get me a punch bowl or something?

And it wasn't just that I was horny. I was starting to doubt myself. Maybe he wasn't interested in me *that* way. Maybe he didn't want to get naked. I knew I was filling out my clothes nicely now. Other guys confirmed that when they eye-licked me across the bar.

Yes, eye-licking is a thing, and it feels good to be the lickee. It's very flattering.

I hated having so many questions and doubts. They were silly. I knew it. Donny liked me, and we made out like champs. He wouldn't do that with someone he wasn't interested in, would he? Of course not. I just needed to be patient and ride this out.

Shit. I said *ride*.

Now I was horny again.

I pulled into—

Damn it, everything sounds sexual now.

I *parked* in his driveway for a planned Thursday night dinner and playdate with the pack. Donny was down to just the cougars, as Roxy had outgrown the hand-raising stage and was firmly ensconced in her new home at the zoo. It was crazy how quickly the chipmunks had grown, and Donny now used rubber nubs on their claws to keep from accidental piercings. Despite their increased size, they were still as cute as ever, and far cleverer. We played, then I fed them while Donny finished cooking dinner. The little beasts would start solid food soon, so I wanted to enjoy as much bottle time as possible.

After a dinner of pot roast and veggies—a ridiculously delicious meal, by the way—we retired to the den and snuggled on the couch. During a commercial break, Donny leaned down and kissed me. A peck grew into a kiss, then a passionate tongue-probing make-out session. We never returned to the show.

The devil stabbed me with his pitchfork, so I decided to try something. Ever so hesitantly, I reached up and began unbuttoning Donny's shirt. I got two undone before he realized what was happening and placed his hand over mine, stopping my dastardly deed in its tracks.

I looked up, a question in my eyes.

He sighed, and his eyes fell. When he spoke, his voice was quiet. "Can we wait?"

My brow crinkled. "Of course. There's no rush. I just thought—"

"I know it's probably weird that we haven't done anything more than kiss yet." His eyes flitted from mine to the floor and back. "I guess I'm paranoid about being a bartender."

Huh? I wasn't sure what reason I expected, but it wasn't that.

He must've seen the confusion, so he continued. "Everybody thinks we sleep around all the time. I work in a bar where a lot of guys go just to hook up. I mean, we do get hit on a lot. Plenty of the staff gets more than their share of sex. The reputation is probably well-earned. I leave work most nights with at least one phone number in my pocket, usually more than one. But it's not a glamorous life. By the time the bar closes and we clean up, it's three or four in the morning. We're too exhausted to hook up with anybody—and those phone numbers end up in the trash more often than not."

All those thoughts had crossed my mind when we'd first met. I'd assumed bartenders got tail pretty much every night. The thought of trusting someone so public, so sought after, made my skin crawl. Hearing him describe things from his perspective gave me pause. Had I misjudged bartenders? Clearly, I'd misjudged him, even if others acted differently.

He leaned against the arm of the couch, staring down at his hands. "I really like you—a lot. More than I've liked anybody in a long time."

He looked up, and he looked unsure or nervous, maybe even afraid. I wasn't sure, but I wanted to reach out somehow. "Donny, I feel the same. I've loved every minute we've spent together."

He smiled weakly. "I know. I get that. It's just…there's so much you don't know about me. You might not feel the same when you learn it all."

I fell back on the only thing I could think of: humor. "Did you kill someone?"

He chuckled. "No."

"How about rape or pillage? Maybe burn a village or two? You're not secretly a Viking, are you?"

His eyes rolled dramatically. "No, I'm not a Viking. No raping or pillaging."

"Oh! I know what it is. You don't have a penis and you're scared I won't like you without one."

He finally laughed. "No, that's *definitely* not it—and it works just fine, thank you very much."

"You're a bartender slut, sleeping with every old man who wiggles his wrinkles at you?"

He smacked my arm. "No! Never the wrinkles."

I cupped his cheek affectionately. "If it's none of those things, we'll face it together. I'm not scared of you or your furry family, mister."

"I hope so." He sobered and looked into my eyes. "I really hope so."

THAT NIGHT, I STAYED AT HIS PLACE FOR THE FIRST TIME. I slept with his arms wrapped around me, the rise and fall of his chest lulling me to sleep. I usually slept naked, but that night I wore shorts and a T-shirt.

You just did that to spite him. If you couldn't see his

Klondike bar, he couldn't see yours, the little devil jeered in my mind—but he was wrong.

Donny's honesty, even his insecurity and vulnerability, somehow made me like him more. The Pisces in me needed to take care of someone, and here was a man who desperately needed support.

Sign me up, coach!

I woke the next morning with Donny staring down at me. His head was propped on one elbow while his other hand gently stroked my hair. In that moment, in that one look, any doubts I had about his feelings for me vanished. This was a man who guarded his heart—but when he cared, he cared deeply, with everything he had.

For whatever reason, his heart was opening *to me.*

Was I worthy of it?

I watched him watch me, and neither of us spoke. I studied his face, the curve of his nose, the line of his jaw. My eyes traced the tiny creases forming around his eyes. There was a quiet strength to this man. Yes, there was pain hidden deep within him, I could see that in the depth of his gaze, but there was also joy and love.

A smile tugged at the corners of my mouth.

"What?" he asked.

"You feel good."

His manly face transformed into a boyish grin.

"And I don't just mean your body next to mine. Waking up and seeing you before anything else…Donny—"

He pressed his forefinger to my lips, then leaned down and replaced it with his mouth.

I melted into his arms, and visions of rose petals and doves fluttered, unbidden, through my mind. I tried to giggle at my silliness, but his tongue stifled my mirth.

Strong hands gripped my back and pressed me into him. His warmth filled me with a joy I'd thought lost.

Images of wings and roses returned.

This time I smiled and watched the petals as they drifted on the wind. They would land one day, and in that moment, I hoped with all my heart they'd land on the man beside me.

EPILOGUE

Nothing but the Truth

I know what you're thinking. Where's the sticky, steamy, sweaty romp with your protagonist's new man? Never fear, dear reader. There's plenty more where that came from . . . just not in the way you might expect.

Donny and I . . . well, let me just say this: our sexcapades didn't exactly follow the script.

But that's a story for another day. Prepare yourself, it's quite the ride.

And yes, I said *ride*. Stop it, you naughty sausage.

My
Dream
Date

Casey Morales

1

———————

PERKY PYTHON

I stopped speaking long enough to shove another bite of waffle in my mouth. Dwayne and Jason ate quietly, attentively, allowing me to, well, waffle on without interruption. Though how Jason's ever-present shit-eating grin survived each forkful of whatever hash he was devouring, I'll never know.

"I never thought I'd fall for a guy who raises tigers and cougars for a living. In fact, now that I think about it, I never expected to fall for a guy at all." I dabbed the napkin to the corner of my mouth. "My whole world had been mapped out, complete with a fancy wedding in a packed church with my mom wailing from the front row. I guess the whole gay thing shattered that dream."

"Wait. Are you saying your mom doesn't still want a wedding? I figured she'd bake a cake with a giant dil—"

"Jason, *behave*," Dwayne said, his voice indignant but his expression amused. "Let the boy talk. Can't you see he's excited?" He motioned with his fork for me to continue.

Jason made a childish face, and the two of them giggled. I cleared my throat to regain the floor.

"Are you two listening?" I tried to sound irritated, but it just came out squeaky. I was too giddy to be upset. "For the first time in a while, I'm *really* happy. I mean, I was happy with Carter and the kids, but I don't think I really knew what dating or a relationship *was* with him."

Dwayne snorted. "Dating? You moved in after *one* dinner. That was downright lesbionic of you."

"Lesbionic?" My brow quirked, and Dwayne smirked. "Never mind. I'm not letting either of you get me sidetracked today. I'm too excited."

"Lord. Is he pregnant? Am I going to be an uncle? What would that make you, a great-great—" Jason earned a playful slap on the arm from Dwayne.

"No, nobody's pregnant. But since you brought it up, have I told you how big—"

"YES!" Dwayne said, waving his fork, not realizing there was half a sausage stuck to it. Jason and I burst into laughter that grew louder when the offending sausage flew into the window. He tossed the fork down. "We get it. He's huge. Practically a python. Move on."

"Somebody's *sensitive* today," I quipped.

"When he doesn't get his morning Geritol, this happens," Jason added.

"I'm only forty-four!" Dwayne said.

I nodded conspiratorially at Jason, as if he'd just made our point for us, then continued. "Donny and I have been dating for a little over four months now, and it's been great. He's funny and sweet, but in a strong, real-man way. I love getting to play with the cougars. They're crazy, always sneaking and attacking. It's incredible how they coordinate. I never knew cats were that smart."

"Why do I sense a *but* coming?" Jason asked.

"But…well…I still haven't seen him naked, much less done anything with his…python."

"Wait," Jason said. "*Four* months? How do you know he's huge then?"

"We make out on the couch or in bed. Trust me, it's easy to feel through his underwear. That thing is—"

"Huge. Yes, yes. We know. Back to the lack of sex, please," Dwayne said.

I chuckled. It was fun to poke at Dwayne. He was the best friend I'd ever had. Come to think of it, he might've been one of the best people I'd ever met. He'd seen me through so much, and never asked for anything in return—other than an occasional shoulder to cry on when one of his twentysomething infatuations moved on to someone closer to their own generation.

Dwayne grounded me, but in a way that made me want to do better, to *be* better. Do all best friends do that? Or is that unique to best friends who are double your age?

Don't tell him I said that. He'll slap you. And me.

"I don't know what to think. There's no doubt he likes me—and when we make out, there's no question he's attracted. His perky python makes that clear enough. So why aren't we having sex? Is that weird? Am I thinking too much?"

Jason snorted again. "You're *always* thinking too much —unless you're doing stupid things because you're not thinking enough."

"You're one to talk about stupid, Mr. Rocket Scientist," Dwayne snarked, then turned back to me. "Have you asked him about it?"

I hesitated. "Well, not really. I mean…we talked a while back about him wanting to wait—"

"But you haven't talked about your concerns recently?" Dwayne asked.

"They're not really *concerns*," I said, a little too defensively. "I mean, I guess they are. I'm okay waiting for sex, but I'd like to know why. It seems very un-gay of him."

Dwayne actually spit coffee across the table. It took a couple minutes for him to stop laughing long enough to speak. "You were the most un-gay gay I'd ever met, young man. You have *no* room to talk there."

"I don't know," Jason said thoughtfully. His sudden seriousness caught my attention. "Maybe Michael has a point. Most guys get naked right out of the gate, or at least early on. They want to see if the magic is there, or if Tab A really does fit into Slot B. Not getting naked after four months is pretty weird."

Silence hovered over our table until our ever-vigilant waitress, Katie, arrived.

"You three are never quiet. My alarm bells are ringing." She turned to me with both fists planted on her ample hips. "What did you do?"

"Me? Why me?"

Dwayne and Jason laughed and avoided Katie's roaming gaze.

"Because silence at this table always revolves around something you've done or someone you're dating. Don't you read the menu?"

"The menu—" Dwayne spat through hoots. "That's the best line of the day, Katie. You win."

"Oh, shut it, *old man*," I said, turning back to her. "We're just talking about a guy."

"Shocked face," she said, scooting into the booth beside me. "Out with it. Aunt Katie is here now. Ignore whatever stupidity those two told you."

"Hey!" Dwayne feigned offense. She raised a brow and he settled back into his seat, unwilling to duel with a superior opponent.

Katie listened attentively as I recounted our conversation, sans the part about the perky python.

"Honey, you need to talk to him. Just ask him why waiting is important to him. If he really cares about you, he'll appreciate the open dialogue."

"That's what I told him," Dwayne huffed from behind his coffee mug.

"Zip it." Katie made a zipper signal with her fingers across her lips. "Michael, if you can't talk openly about everything, he's not good enough for you. Trust me. I've dealt with my share of closed-off men. They're not worth it."

There was such sincerity in her eyes. I thought there might've been a little pain in there too. As long as we'd been coming to the diner, as many times as Katie had been part of our conversations, I realized we really didn't know *her* story at all. I'd have to fix that. Later, after I'd dealt with Mr. No Sex.

"Thanks, Katie. You're the best," I said as we hugged.

"Oh, I know. Make Dwayne add a counseling fee to today's tip." She winked, grabbed our empty plates, and hustled away.

2

THE BIG GAY BUBBLE

D onny had left for a zookeeper conference in San Diego and wouldn't return until the weekend. Thanks to the bar's revolving door of employees, he was one of two bartenders available to work, so our next date was on the books for Sunday night. That gave me plenty of time to obsess—I mean, *think carefully*— about the conversation I wanted to have.

Ironically, during that same week, I finally flew the proverbial nest. After working with my dad since graduating from college, I left the family business and started a new job in the real world. It was exciting and frightening, and all the things people normally feel when they start their first big-boy job, only I was doing it at twenty-seven years old.

Let's just call the time with my dad my master's degree in running a small business and move on, shall we?

On Monday morning, I donned my cleanest, least-wrinkled khakis and a light blue polo shirt, grabbed a tumbler full of coffee from the kitchen, and drove to my new office. The company was relatively young—and small. There were only a few senior people, and a dozen worker bees like me. It felt a lot like a family business.

Apparently, the gods of employment had a sense of humor.

We sold IT equipment and computer services to companies. There were teams of salespeople, computer engineers, and software programmers, along with a few muckety-mucks who mostly drank coffee and smoked cigars out back. I later learned the mucketies were related, completing the employment gods' circle of irony.

The sales guys (and one gal) were exactly what you'd expect: type A go-getters who thrived on the hunt. There was so much testosterone in that group, even with the lone female, that their corner of our office practically vibrated with energy.

Separated by a thin barrier of scrunchy room-divider stuff—no, I don't know what that's called—were the engineers. Imagine if *Star Trek* and *Star Wars* had a baby. That's an IT engineer. The level of nerdiness on their side of the Great Wall far outpaced the testosterone on ours. They were nice enough folks, and super smart, but I half expected a game of Dungeons and Dragons to break out at any moment.

Then there were the programmers. We only had five of those critters, and they kept to themselves in a separate room. I guess it made sense to segregate them. They needed to concentrate, or one *01* might turn into a *10* and there goes the program.

But what did I know? I was a sales guy. We were tasked with finding companies who needed computers, or computer help, or a computer upgrade, or anything to do with computers. We were bred to be stupid and promise the world, regardless of what the engineers and programmers claimed was possible—and we drove those poor people crazy.

In truth, we did push the envelope, but much to their chagrin, the engineers usually found a way to make our promises a reality for clients. They might've used duct tape and paperclips, but they made shit happen.

All hail the pocket protector!

A few hours into my first day, the owner asked me to join him in his office. Gary was a rail-thin man with bottle-bottom glasses that made his eyes appear bugged out. His massive front teeth rarely allowed him to close his lips, so two Bugs Bunny teeth were usually visible, resting happily on his bottom lip. It looked like he had tried to grow a beard, but, like many nerds of the programming clan, it wasn't genetically possible. Scraggly patches of brown and graying hair looked more like a swamp on a map than a beard. He was a nice dude, but man was he a candidate for one of those makeover shows. Unfortunately for him, the original Fab Five were still a few years away from zhuzhing their way around America's most clueless straight guys.

As we entered his office, my boss, Rick, who was standing by Gary's desk, waved me in. The contrast between the two company leaders couldn't have been starker. Rick stood at six three, weighed a solid two-eighty, and had once been a strapping college football player. Now, his belly was wider than his broad shoulders, but the football-player frame was still visible. Rick was an outdoor-lovin', pickup-drivin', boot-wearin' slab o' man—and he oozed 'sales guy.'

With two enormous strides, he crossed the room and gripped my hand with a vice-like paw, while his other hand squeezed my arm. "Good to see you again, Michael. We're really happy you joined our team."

Gary shuffled around his desk and sat, adjusted his bottle-bottoms, straightened the four pens I hadn't noticed on his desk, then blinked up at me. "Right," he said. "We want to give you a welcome gift. Rick?"

Rick reached behind the desk and pulled out a shiny white jacket with *Crystalogic* scrawled in thumb-sized script across the left chest. Each letter of the company's name was shaded a different color, creating a rainbow out of the logo.

My mouth dropped open at the *obvious* gay reference.

"You like it?" Rick asked as he handed me the coat.

"Yeah, it's nice. Thanks, guys."

"Gary named the company, but I came up with the logo myself," Rick said. "Saw a bumper sticker on a car in front of me at the McDonald's drive-through that read 'Family Values' in rainbow colors, thought it sent a nice message about what we stand for."

I looked to Gary. His bland expression didn't waver. "We're a family company. We do what's right for the customer above our own interest. We treat each other right. Stuff like that."

Sweet baby Jesus, they didn't know what the bumper sticker *really* meant—and they had crafted the company's image around something they thought was more about church than, well, families with two daddies or mommies.

Like a good little rookie employee, I donned my jacket while swallowing hard to keep from laughing. When I looked up, both men were smiling.

Who was I to burst their big gay bubble?

3

AN UNEXPECTED DINNER GUEST

Friday night was a high school basketball night, and I refereed eight back-to-back AAU games on Saturday. By the time I got home Saturday evening, my legs were wobbly. The thought of visiting Donny at the bar popped into my head, but my body revolted. I ate Cheerios for dinner, watched a rerun of some '80s comedy, then passed out.

On Sunday evening, I knocked politely on Donny's door, then let myself in. The sumptuous smell of bacon frying made my stomach do somersaults.

"I'm in the kitchen. Go say hi to the kids while I finish dinner."

The *kids* Donny referred to were three cougar cubs he was hand-raising before their life at Nashville Zoo began. When I first met the little terrors, they were barely larger than a newborn infant. Now, they'd dwarf a mid-sized dog. It had been fun to watch them grow, but also sad. They were clearly outgrowing the confines of a crate and needed room to roam and hunt—and do whatever it is that frisky cougars do all day.

But for another month or so, they were our kids.

As soon as I opened the bedroom door, the playful growls and groans began. Theo pawed impatiently at the metal of the cage.

Yes, his name was Theo. The other chipmunks were Alvin and Simon. It turned out that zookeepers had an odd sense of humor that directly translated into their naming convention. Who knew?

Theo was the assassin, the incredibly intelligent, sneaky little bugger who loved to ninja his way behind me and attack my back. Alvin was the other sneak, only his attacks usually came from the side. Simon acted all sweet and innocent, lowering his head for a good scratch and purring loudly, then curling up in my lap—all as a distraction for his brothers. As soon as Theo pounced, Mr. Sweet and Cuddly's claws came out, and he'd join the assault. Those cats planned and coordinated their attacks as well as any Navy SEAL team.

And I loved every minute of it.

Except for their teeth. You know, the needle teeth every kitten has that pierces the skin no matter how light or hard they bite? Donny had rubber tips glued to their claws to protect us from their daggers, but nothing could stop those teeth. By the time my savior arrived to announce dinnertime, my hands and arms were bleeding from several tiny puncture wounds—but they were worth it. Those cats made me laugh more than a whole building full of Crystalogic engineers.

"Should I put your dinner in a cat dish and feed you all together?" Donny said from the doorway.

Simon darted toward him and nearly escaped into the house, but Donny blocked him with an expert Jackie Chan leg sweep that stopped the furball in his tracks. I stood and began loading them back into their crate, something easier said than done when there were three of them and only one of me. You know the expression "herding cats?" Yeah, that's what it was—squirming, squealing, and nipping all the way.

"You've actually gotten pretty good at that." Donny chuckled. "Come on. I made a chicken dish from a recipe for Outback's Alice Springs Chicken I found online."

I hopped to my feet and gave him a peck on the cheek. "You had me at Alice Springs Chicken."

He laughed and dragged me into the kitchen by the front of my shirt.

As with every meal I'd enjoyed at Chez Donny, the faux Alice Springs Chicken was fabulous. I didn't know how he did it, but it tasted exactly the same as I remembered from Outback, minus the buttery bread and Boomin' Onion. One can only expect so much from his home-cook boyfriend.

Donny told me about a new keeper the zoo had hired, a bird guy. I'd met the creepy snake handler, the elephant family, and was dating the cat guy, but I'd yet to meet a bird keeper. Each animal expert I'd met had mirrored the animals they kept with startling similarity. Donny's personality and mannerisms reminded me of the Bengal tigers and lions. Even the cougars and their playful mischievousness made me think of him.

The elephant family comprised overly large humans whose quiet natures somehow commanded respect merely by their presence. And the snake guy may as well have climbed into one of the glass enclosures and lounged on a rock. He was all creepy, slithery snake-ness.

He described Janice, the new bird lady, as a cross between one of the elephant keepers and Beeker from *The*

Muppet Show. We laughed as he mimicked her long, stiff neck and upturned chin, twisting sharply from side to side. She even had a peeping, high-pitched voice.

Zoo people cracked me up.

I told him about my first week at Crystalogic. We laughed over the logo and my new jacket, and I shared some of the engineers' better customer service stories.

It was a light, fun dinner, like always.

Until I said, "Hey, can we talk about something?"

"Sure," he replied tentatively.

I looked down at my nearly licked-clean plate. "So… I've been wanting to ask you about this, but wasn't quite sure how. I'm not upset or anything."

I hesitated.

He leaned forward. "You're not usually shy. Just say it. You know you can ask me anything."

I smiled weakly. "I know. Donny, I really like you—"

He leaned back. "Uh-oh."

"No, no. It's not like that. Please." I took a deep breath and covered my face with a palm. "I'm sorry. I'm making this a bigger deal than it should be. It's just…we've been dating almost four months now, and…well…we haven't *done* anything."

I couldn't read his expression. There was a flash of a smile at my stammering, then a crease around his eyes as the question struck home. I had no idea whether he was amused or pissed. Donny was a great guy. The last thing I wanted was to blow it over something as stupid as sex, but I couldn't keep my question bottled up any longer.

I gripped my napkin as my palms began to sweat.

He sighed. "I guess it's time we had *that* talk."

That talk? I had no idea what he meant.

He rose from his seat and squatted next to me, turning

my chair so we faced each other. Then he gripped my arms with both hands and looked up. This strong veteran who'd survived more than I could imagine looked like a scared little boy.

"Michael, I wanted to wait for all that because I wanted to get to know you first, for you to get to know me."

I nodded like I understood. I didn't.

"And it's been great—better than great. I'm really falling for you."

"I feel—"

"Just let me get this out." He squeezed my arms gently. "I don't date much anymore. I mean, before I met you, I didn't date much. Guys would ask. They'd give me their numbers at the bar, but I couldn't bring myself to try again."

"Donny, I'm lost. What are you talking about?"

"Michael, I'm HIV positive."

The pleading in his eyes as he said those words pierced my heart, but I had no idea how to react, what to say, what to think. Dwayne and I had talked a little about HIV and his work with the blood bank years ago, but I didn't know anyone who was positive.

Did I?

And here he sat, waiting for me to respond.

I couldn't speak.

His eyes dropped to my fidgeting fingers. "I'm sorry I didn't tell you sooner. It's just...I really like you, and I didn't want you to run away before you got to know me."

"Run away?"

He nodded slowly. "Yeah. I used to tell guys right away, practically in the same sentence with my name. I figured they deserved to know, deserved a chance to decide for themselves if they wanted to go out with someone...like me. It was the last time I talked to a lot of them. They ran as fast as they could. Some of them barely make eye contact when they come to the bar now."

There was an ache in his voice. I wanted to reach out, to hold him, to comfort him. I wanted to tell him it would all be alright, that I would never run away.

But I couldn't move.

He looked into my eyes. His were rimmed with moisture. He waited for me to do something, to say something.

I didn't.

He sucked in a breath, gave my arms one last squeeze, and stood. "I know it's a lot, and I really hope you can see *me*, not my disease, but I'll understand if you're not comfortable dating anymore."

My heart stuck in my throat.

He started to turn away, but I had the presence of mind to stand and wrap him in a tight hug, nuzzling my head beneath his chin. I felt his chest tremble as tears began to fall. This poor man. This beautiful, amazing, poor man.

He led me to the door and kissed me goodnight, then watched as I climbed into my car and drove away. He pressed a hand against the screen door and held his wave until I was gone.

4

____

THE QUILT

When I got home, I logged into AOL and searched Google for information on HIV. A hodgepodge of pages detailed symptoms and treatments—and the lack of treatments. Images of patients with concave cheeks and distended bellies spoke of early-disease medication reactions. Other pages talked of support groups and hope for a vaccine, yet none believed a cure would come anytime soon. Several were dedicated to how HIV spread and the importance of safe sex, echoing much of what Dwayne had told me years ago.

And then I opened a page discussing life expectancy. There were pages honoring the thousands—no, the hundreds of thousands—of men lost to this terrible plague. In 1993 alone, more than three hundred thousand had died in the United States. The worldwide number was unfathomable to me.

I clicked on a link titled *Quilt Project*.

The quilt stretched the heart-wrenching length of the Mall in Washington, D.C., each square lovingly sewn in memory of someone lost to the disease. There were hearts and smiles, pictures of men and women in suits and dresses, others in sports uniforms, still more playing instruments or singing—hundreds of colors and shapes; thousands upon thousands of candles snuffed far too soon. There were images of throngs of men and women visiting the quilt, holding each other through their grief as they celebrated and mourned friends, family, and lovers.

Tears were rolling down my cheeks before I thought to click out of the site. I wanted to look away, to see anything other than that eternal cloth, but I *had* to see it.

I had to see *them*. They deserved to be seen.

I grew up in the '80s, when AIDS first hit the news, but my life had been so sheltered and far removed from anything related to the gay community that I never grasped the magnitude of the tragedy. Dwayne said he'd lost several friends. I hadn't understood how that was possible at the time, how one person could know so many people to catch the same strange disease. It seemed such an odd coincidence. It didn't make sense.

The quilt *made* me see.

It made me see the vileness of a disease that struck down so many in the prime of life.

It made me see why Donny's eyes carried such fear and pain.

What it *didn't* do was help me know how *I* should feel or what I should do.

I was more confused than I had been before logging on, and definitely more so than at dinner. This was the '90s, but there was still so much unknown about AIDS. I knew unprotected sex was the primary way people got infected, but what about other activities? Donny and I hadn't done anything but kiss—and we'd done a lot of that. Could I have already been exposed? Did I need to go to a doctor? Could a negative guy even date a positive guy?

The ache of seeing the quilt fueled my fears and doubts. My breath became shallow as panic set in.

This *couldn't* be happening. I *couldn't* become a square on that quilt. My life was supposed to be more than a piece of cloth. I had no idea what it would become, but it was *supposed* to be more.

Without thinking, I logged off, sprinted to the den, and grabbed the phone. In two rings, Dwayne's sleepy voice answered. It was eleven thirty.

"Dwayne," I choked out between sobs. "I need to talk, please."

He didn't even ask why. "I'm on my way."

Everybody needs a Dwayne.

<hr>

"WHAT HAPPENED?" DWAYNE ASKED AS I OPENED THE door. I was finally breathing again, but my eyes were puffy and rimmed with red. I probably looked like hell.

I didn't answer, just pulled him inside, shut the door, and wrapped my arms around his thin frame. He didn't resist the embrace, but it took him a moment to hug me back. I think he was shocked by the ferocity of my need. I really was a mess.

After a long moment standing just inside the doorway, we migrated to the den. I'd spent the thirty minutes it took him to arrive printing pages from all the sites I'd visited. They were splayed across the floor in front of the couch like a giant Japanese fan.

Dwayne scanned the papers, then his eyes widened and shot up to mine. "Michael, you're not—"

"Oh no. Not me."

His mouth quirked in concentration. "Donny?"

I nodded. The sobs I thought were sitting quietly in the corner returned, and Dwayne grabbed me again.

His presence calmed me quicker this time. When I pulled back, he stared at me with sympathetic, fatherly eyes. "Let's sit and talk."

I told him about dinner, and how the evening had ended with Donny, then about my online search. I showed him the images of horrific side effects and peppered him with a million questions. *Is Donny in pain? Will his belly do that? What about his cheeks? Will he get those sores? How long does he have?*

When I asked that last one, Dwayne's eyes spilled over.

"Michael, listen to me. HIV isn't the death sentence it once was. I lived through that time and, thankfully, never contracted the disease." He looked away and whispered, "Too many of my friends weren't so lucky."

Now it was my turn to sit back and watch as he relived a decade of loss.

I reached down and picked up the pages filled with images of the quilt. "I had no idea *so many—*"

"Yeah, *so* many." His voice was distant.

His shoulders slumped, and his eyes tightened as he fought off another wave. He sucked in a steadying breath and returned to the present.

"It's *not* like it was back then. We have great meds that keep the disease in check, and guys are living normal lifespans. Donny isn't going anywhere, and I want you to stop looking at websites and brochures that talk about side effects. Most of those are either rare or from a time before modern meds. They won't do anything but scare you."

I nodded weakly, relieved to have permission to discard those terrible pages.

"But…" I struggled with my next question. "What does it mean for Donny…and me? I mean, for *us*? He said it's why he wanted to wait for sex, so I would get to know him as a person before learning of his disease. He thought I might run away."

Dwayne nodded knowingly. "I've heard that a lot. He didn't want you to think he *is* his disease—but HIV is just something he deals with, like any other chronic illness."

"I guess that makes sense." I wasn't convinced.

He cocked his head. "If you'd known he was positive when you met, would you have dated him?"

"Of course. I mean…maybe. I…I don't know."

He let out a deep sigh. "Exactly—and you shouldn't feel bad about having doubts or questions. HIV has been a scary mystery since the whole thing started."

"I guess." I thought a moment. "But that still doesn't answer the question about Donny and me. I mean, can we date? Could we have sex? What about kissing or, I don't know, anything else?"

His eyes were so sad. It took him a long moment to respond.

"There are no absolutes. Think of the risk of infection as a scale. On one end, the riskiest thing you could possibly do would be to mix blood with blood. On the other end, you stay on opposite sides of the city and never stand in the same room."

The absurdity of his examples made me chuckle and lightened the mood. "Well, I don't think either of those options make sense."

His lips pursed into a tight smile. "No, probably not,

but everything in between will either make you more or less likely to become infected—or, at least, exposed."

We spent the next few minutes talking through the litany of activities on Dwayne's scale of risk: kissing, licking, licking other things, kissing other things, putting other things in other places, and so on.

In the end, I knew a lot more about HIV, but was still baffled about dating Donny. My heart wanted to jump in my car, break a few speed laws, and wrap him in the biggest hug possible. I wanted to tell him it would all be okay, that we could make it work, that we could make *anything* work. I wanted to tell him I'd never run away from some stupid disease—and I certainly wouldn't ever run away from him.

I wanted all those things—at least, that's what my heart wanted.

My head, never before one to interfere with my heart— or Little Michael—was ringing an alarm bell so loudly it hurt. It wouldn't be ignored. The *risk* was too great.

Risk.

Donny was a risk.

Dwayne watched me grapple with my thoughts in silence. He was good at giving me time to process. I wish he'd just given me answers, told me to stick it out or run away, one or the other, but I knew he wouldn't do that. He was too good a friend. I needed to come to terms with everything on my own, in my own time, otherwise whatever conclusions I reached wouldn't stick. I'd just be acting on *his* ideas and *his* decisions, not my own.

God, I hated being an adult.

"Am I an asshole?"

Dwayne looked up, brow furrowed. "In general? Or for something specific?"

Stupid friend, making me laugh again.

"For struggling with whether to keep seeing Donny. I mean…it's just a disease. It's not like he's a serial killer or anything. I wouldn't run from someone fighting cancer. It feels wrong somehow, all this questioning. Does that make me an asshole?"

"You're not an asshole—at least, not for this." He smirked. "It makes you human. You said it yourself. A couple years ago, you didn't even know gays existed all around you, much less the dangers associated with this disease. Why should you feel guilty for being scared the first time you encounter it?"

"I guess. It still feels terrible. Donny's such a great guy."

"Great guys get sick too. And there are a lot of great guys out there who aren't a match for you."

My head snapped up. "Are you saying—"

"I didn't *say* anything. Donny may be perfect for you, or he might not be. You've known him for a few months. That's hardly enough time to place a lifetime bet, with or without the complications of HIV."

"Huh. Complications. That's one word for it."

He gripped my hand. "That's *exactly* what it is, a complication. It doesn't mean you can't be with him, but it does add to the list of things you need to think about when deciding who you spend your life with. It changes how you interact, how free you might feel with physical contact. Some guys will never be comfortable or get past that nagging voice in the back of their heads. Others are perfectly fine."

"I don't know where I am in all that."

"I know. Donny knows that too. It's what scares him."

Now my lips pursed. "Scared? Why would *he* be scared? I'm not the one with the deadly virus."

Dwayne released my hand and slapped it reprovingly. "Don't be stupid. You're better than that. He's scared of *getting hurt*. He told you about other guys who ran away the minute they found out, and a lot of those were men he hadn't spent much time with, guys he didn't care about yet. He *cares* for you. If you ran, how do you think he would feel?"

I put my face in my hands. "This sucks so bad."

"Yeah, it does."

After another interminable moment, Dwayne reached across the couch and hugged me. It was two o'clock in the morning, and he looked exhausted. I felt drained.

"Don't make any decisions tonight, or tomorrow. Just take time to think. And whatever you do, don't look at those medical sites anymore. They tell you everything that *could* ever happen, not what's likely—or even reasonable— to happen."

I nodded and stood. "Talk tomorrow?"

"You bet."

THERE WAS NO BASKETBALL TO BE OFFICIATED THAT Monday night, so I went to the gym after work. My heart wasn't in it, but I walked through the motions anyway. I couldn't stop thinking about everything Dwayne had said the night before. As hard as I tried, I couldn't stop seeing the quilt.

Everywhere I looked, guys pulled or pushed, trying to get fitter or bigger or thinner. If a guy had even the slightest gut or sunken cheek, my brain flashed to those images of side effects. I couldn't stop it. The thoughts kept coming.

Frustrated, I racked my weights and left.

When I got home, I called Donny. I just needed to hear his voice. I hoped he wanted to hear mine.

"Hey," I said when he answered.

"Hey, yourself."

"How are the kids?"

"Fine. Frisky as always."

There was a long, awkward pause.

"You okay?" he asked.

"Oh yeah, I'm fine. Good. Really." *Idiot.*

"That's good." He didn't believe me. I could hear it.

"I missed your voice."

"Me too."

Another awkward silence.

"I need to feed the cubs. Chat later?"

"Sure," I said.

The tone that rang in the receiver when he hung up was like a heart monitor with a flat line.

5

COLLEGE HUNKS MOVING JUNK

Donny and I never went out again.

We met at a local coffee shop one afternoon before his shift at the bar. I tried to meet his eyes, to explain how much I liked and admired him. Admired? I was such an idiot. Who says that?

Nothing made it better.

The tears clouding my eyes expressed more than any words could, and he gripped my hand. As I pulled away, he held me closer. He was such a good man. He didn't deserve my fear—but I couldn't reign it in. It had won.

In the years that would follow, I'd think back often to what could have been with Donny. What would life have held with the hunky bartender and his frisky cats? In our brief time together, he'd shown such tenderness and respect, such compassion. With each memory, I knew I'd walked away from something special—no, from *someone* special.

When had life become so serious?

It was just yesterday I was fumbling my way out of a closet, laughing as I said and did stupid things borne out of sheltered ignorance or curiosity or some juvenile naivete. Now I was coping with life-threatening diseases and life-altering decisions, choosing paths in forked roads where only moments before I'd not even seen a road at my feet.

Why did life have to be so . . .

There wasn't a word for how my heart felt.

Dwayne and I visited him at the bar, and he was friendly and attentive, as always. He even had our drinks waiting before we could reach the bar from the front door. But he never asked me out again, and I never asked him. There was a sadness in his eyes each time we saw each other. I felt it in my own too.

Weeks turned into months of monotony at the new job. Years of schlocking drugs with my part-time preacher dad had taught me decent sales skills, and I was promoted to sales manager after only four months. I honestly had no idea what I was doing, but the previous sales manager left, and they needed someone to babysit the crazy sales dudes and translate programmer speak into English. It came with a raise, so I couldn't complain.

As shades of orange and yellow filled the trees, I became restless. I couldn't explain why, it was just a feeling that crept over me and wouldn't be ignored. Dwayne thought I was still smarting over Donny and just needed to get back on the horse—again. He'd been through a breakup with me before. He always shoved horses at me, and it usually worked. I'm a guy, after all.

This time, though, it didn't work. I needed something different, something *radically* different. I needed a change of scenery; a fresh start.

The more I thought about it, the more sense it made. I'd lived in Nashville my whole life. Hell, I could visit the room at Baptist Hospital where I was born. Outside of a few hundred-mile treks with the family for holidays to visit the grands, I'd never really left the county. Peter, the most amazing ab-covered roommate on the planet, had deserted me, and I was once again boyfriend-less. The idea of moving somewhere new was terrifying but exciting at the same time.

It was time for this baby bird to leave the nest. He needed to fly!

On a whim, I grabbed a map. From years of travel with my dad, I owned a stack of gas station maps—you know, the folding kind you could *never* neatly refold? My dad even bought me a road atlas detailing every interstate, street, and dirt path in the continental United States. That sucker was thicker than the Yellow Pages I'd let sit on my doorstep for two months.

I drew a circle in red around Nashville to narrow the search to within a few hundred miles. I figured if I hated the new place, missed the pack, or just wanted to move back, it made sense to be somewhat close to home base.

I knew I wanted to live in a bigger city, to experience the hustle and bustle I'd heard so much about, and that narrowed the hunt to a few large black dots and stars. Then I narrowed the choices to cities with large gay communities based solely on representation at softball tournaments my team had played in.

Yes, folks, I was downright scientific in my search for a new home.

At no point did cost of living, the job market, the housing market, traffic, or any other *logical* element factor in. This decision was based largely on how many teams a city sent to a gay softball tournament.

The leather-clad devil on my shoulder snickered as I narrowed the finalists to Atlanta and Chicago.

The angel began to cry.

I thought about Chicago. It was a musical. They liked pizza. That's about all I knew.

Atlanta was in Georgia, about an hour from where my grandmother lived. The Braves were there. So were the Falcons, but nobody cared about them back then. I knew Atlanta had bad traffic, but had also hosted the Olympics. That's cool, right?

I remembered Chicago had the Cubs; again, not caring —possibly even less than I cared about the Falcons. Both teams sucked. Screw the goat and his curse.

Then it hit me. I *hated* cold weather.

Atlanta, here I come!

"I STILL CAN'T BELIEVE YOU'RE DOING THIS WITHOUT finding a job first. How did you get an apartment?" Dwayne asked as I handed him my coffee maker.

"There was a Post Apartment down there. Since I'm already a resident, they considered it a transfer and didn't even ask about employment."

Dwayne laughed and shook his head. "This is either fate and you're blessed, or the dumbest thing I've ever seen. I'm still not sure which."

"Oh, stop it. Just be excited for me, old man. This will be an adventure!"

"You can say that again," he muttered, loud enough for me to hear.

The true test of friendship is if they'll help you move. Dwayne had arrived early that morning, helped pack and haul every blender and box, cramming my U-Haul as fully as the sucker would allow. He'd taken several days off from the restaurant and was determined to drive down and get me settled in. He said he just wanted to see Atlanta, that it had been years since he'd visited "a real gay bubble," whatever that meant. I knew he just wanted to spend time together before our lives were irrevocably altered by time and distance. That part made me sad. I'd miss Dwayne more than any of the pack. He was my family.

Once the trailer was stuffed, we drove to do the same to ourselves at our favorite diner one last time. Katie was waiting for us as we walked in and practically threw herself at me. I almost choked on the scent of cheap perfume and bacon grease. Damn, I'd miss that too.

By three o'clock, we were on the road, Dwayne in my car and me in the U-Haul. Cell phones still weren't a thing yet, so we developed a honking and flashing lights system to let each other know when we needed to stop and stretch or pee.

Poor Dwayne and his itty-bitty bladder. The drive should've only taken four hours. We stopped six times.

By the time we pulled onto the Fruit Loop, also known as the Perimeter, it was dark. Dwayne had learned years ago never to trust my sense of direction, so I followed him into the city. Around nine o'clock, we pulled into my new apartment complex in a neighborhood called Midtown. A super-cute guard in a uniform shirt that was a size too small for his bulging arms greeted me, handed me my keys, and passed us through the gate. I caught him grinning in my rearview mirror as we drove through.

The Goddess of Delightful Dimples had definitely blessed this new land.

In that moment, I knew I'd *love* Atlanta.

6

WELCOME HOME

I was not born with decorating or nesting genes, so unpacking the U-Haul only took a few hours. Dwayne was an annoyingly early riser, so we started lugging suitcases and black trash bags full of clothes at an ungodly hour. Yes, I was a twenty-eight-year-old college student when it came to packing. My dear friend made fun of me the entire time.

Once everything was safely inside my third-floor abode, Dwayne set to work arranging my sparse collection of furniture. He spent a ridiculous amount of time scooching and scanning things in the den, rearranging the couch and cardboard box I used for a side table.

How could two pieces of furniture need that much attention? One of them wasn't even classified as furniture.

I'm a pretty simple guy in that regard. As long as I can see the TV from the couch and reach the kitchen in less than ten steps, I'm set. In the end, Dwayne moved everything back into design number seven and declared it perfect.

Around two o'clock, hunger overtook the excitement of

pulling undies out of trash bags. Dwayne had heard of a place called Roasters that sounded remarkably similar to the rotisserie chicken restaurant we loved so much in Nashville, but neither of us knew where it was. On our way down the winding metal stairs, we heard splashing and laughter mixed with upbeat dance music booming from the complex's interior courtyard. That was as good a place as any to ask for directions.

Given the splashing, we deduced that a pool would be part of the scenery. (I know, we're still awaiting our Nobel Prize for that nugget of genius. Must've got lost in the mail.) What we hadn't expected was more than a hundred men swimming, drinking, laughing, and dancing. I would've bet every quarter in the sacred laundry stack that they were *all* gay. The kissing and playful touches gave that way. One didn't need a gaydar to peg this group.

Everywhere I looked, there were slabs of abs laying out for a tan, and most of the dudes were clad in little more than a sliver of cloth covering their pronounced dorsal fins.

Wait, that would be on their back, right? What's the other one called? Never mind. The point is, I could see lots of wee-wees and butts. It was awesome.

My keen powers of observation latched on to two things immediately. First, with over a hundred guys in thongs in the pool area, there was only one woman present. I knew Atlanta was supposed to be a gay-friendly town, but did straight people even live here?

Second, and even more remarkable, was the percentage of Hollywood Hotness splayed before us.

Let me explain. There are hot guys, and then there are the elite; the "Hollywood Hot." The difference is simple. A hot guy is your average handsome man you might find in any city across America. He could be muscular or thin, athletic or…you get the idea. Bottom line, he's widely regarded as handsome *in his town.*

Now, let's take that same handsome dude and drop him into the center of Hollywood. How does he compare? Let's face it, there's a difference between most next-door cuties and Henry Cavill.

Oh, Henry. You need me. You just don't know it.

Back to the pool.

Nashville had its share of beautiful, muscle-bound men. I would even say we had the average share of Hollywood Hotties too. Every city does. What stood before us at that pool made my heart thump harder than the bass thumping from the speakers. There were more genuine Hollywood Hotties contained in that gated gathering than I'd ever seen in one location, minus the Oscars or some other meeting of the elite.

"Where are we?" I asked Dwayne, unable to stop my eyes bouncing from one chest to the next.

"This is Midtown. You've moved into the Gay Bubble. Good luck."

He seemed unfazed by the buffet of buttocks before us —until a flock of very bubbly chickens showed up and stripped down to their banana hammocks. Dwayne nearly fainted. I was *sure* I heard his ankle bracelet buzz.

One of the chickens looked up from across the pool. He was a skinny blond twink barely into his twenties—*exactly* the kind of boy to rev Dwayne's engine. He tossed us a smile and wave, then turned and bent over to remove the pants he wore over his blue Superman speedos—the ones with the *S* logo on the center of his butt.

"We need to get directions and leave before I have heart failure," Dwayne said, dabbing sweat from his forehead.

I barked a laugh, then leaned over the railing to the

nearest sunbather. A few minutes and a dozen flirts later, we were headed to the parking lot.

"Have you moved into a gay bar?" he asked. "I knew Midtown was like Boystown in Chicago, but had no idea it was all *that*."

"Don't look at me. I've never been here before."

As we drove out of the complex, he started laughing for no apparent reason.

"Do I even want to know what you're laughing at?"

"Your apartment complex is called Monroe Place," he said between snorts.

"Uh, yeah. So?"

"I heard some of the guys back there calling it Melrose Place. It all makes sense now."

I didn't know what that meant, having refereed my way through nights filled with cheesy shows, but Dwayne laughed all the way to the restaurant.

WE WALKED INTO ROASTERS AND THE MOST DELICIOUS smell drifted into my nose. It was a combination of slow-roasted chicken and every vegetable I could imagine. The place itself was quaint, an upscale version of our diner back in Nashville. The patrons, however, were entirely *unlike* anything I'd seen in our diner. We stood, gaping, in the doorway for a long moment, before a woman in her mid-sixties wearing a red-and-white checkered apron and tight bun waddled up.

"You boys here to eat or stare? You can do both at a table," she said without a hint of humor.

"Sorry, yes, we'd love a table. Thank you," Dwayne said.

There was one table open in a restaurant that seated one hundred, and it was all the way in the back by the kitchen. As we walked, weaving between tables, every head turned in a wave of glances.

Did I mention there wasn't a single woman in the place, other than Ms. Snarky Bun?

Every table we passed was filled with men. Young, old, tall, muscular, fat, thin…you name it. For every veggie on the menu, there was a flavor of gay to match it. There were athletic guys in T-shirts and tank tops who'd probably just worked out. One group of bespectacled boys was playing some weird board game with miniature dragons and knights. One of the nerds tossed a bunch of dice as we passed. They clearly represented an intellectual breed of gays I had yet to encounter and reminded me of the programmers I used to work with. A few booths held couples snuggled lovingly on the same side. They picked at each other's food. Most tables were filled with groups of three or four engaged in festive conversation.

It was all so delicious.

Uh, I mean…the food. The food smelled delicious.

Dwayne leaned across the table and whispered once Bun left, "Are we eating in a gay bar?"

I couldn't stop scanning the long room. My head was on a constant swivel, like a submarine periscope on the fritz.

The restaurant was twenty, maybe thirty yards wide, but a good Heisman-earning pass long. Booths lined either wall, and two rows of four-top tables filled the middle. Everything in the place was wooden, making it especially noisy when the gays got to gabbing. For the uninitiated, gays never actually stop gabbing. They merely pause to shove food—or other things—into their mouths.

Our table was crammed between the entrance to the kitchen and thin hallway that led to the restrooms. One particularly fit, handsome guy in a Lycra tank top slowed his stride as he passed us on his way to relieve himself. I looked up and he grinned, then continued on his way.

"I think I've died and gone to gay heaven," I said, staring after him down the hallway.

Dwayne chuckled and snapped his fingers. "I'm over here, Slutisha."

My head snapped around. "Hey! I've only lived here, what, fifteen hours? I haven't had time to earn that title. Give me a minute."

He rolled his eyes. "Based on the way you slept through Nashville's phone book, a minute is all it'll take before we'll have to move your worn-out ass to another city."

"Ha ha—"

I clamped my mouth shut, realizing a very amused, very cute young waiter was standing behind me, listening to the whole conversation. Dwayne had the nerve to wink at him. They'd conspired!

"Welcome to Roasters. I'm Jack. What looks good, gents?"

Sneaky Jack made his way to the side of the table so I could get a better look. My eyes darted between his dimples to his chest, then across his burgeoning arms.

"Uh-hum. Up here, gorgeous. I'm not on the menu tonight," Jack said with a smirk and a wink.

What was it with all the winking?

Dwayne spit the water he'd been sipping. "You'll have to excuse Michael here. He's fresh meat…I mean, he just moved here from Nashville."

"Aww. That's precious. Just a poor country boy on his first day in the big gay city," Jack said playfully, then winked again at Dwayne with a mischievous gleam in his one open eye. "Let me handle the introductions."

I stiffened. Something was coming, I could feel it.

Jack turned, made a dramatic show of stuffing his order pad in his apron, and clapped five times toward the dining room. "Everyone! Hello! Attention down here."

Someone decided to help and clanked a fork against a plate several times, scaring the shit out of the guy seated behind him. I laughed as the jumper turned and glared at the clinker.

Once everyone had quietened and heads had turned, Jack put a hand on my shoulder. "Gentlegays of Atlanta, this is Michael. He just moved to Atlanta and doesn't know a soul. And he's *purdy*." He drew out the *purr* in purdy as he reached down and squeezed my bicep. "Let's make him feel welcome, alright?"

Everyone in the place, including Snarky Bun, dropped their forks and applauded. Some hooted, others hollered, a few yelled out phone numbers.

I'd never had a gay Quinceañera. I imagine that moment was what it would feel like.

What does one do at such an auspicious event? I didn't know whether to puff my chest out with pride and wave like Miss America, or slink down the hallway to hide in the bathroom.

Then again, maybe hiding in the bathroom when that many gay men had just been told to make me welcome wasn't the best idea.

Or maybe it was. I had a title to earn.

I sat and turned fifty shades of red. Not a sexy red, like in the *Fifty Shades* pleasure room. This was plain ole embarrassed red…all the way to the tips of my ears.

And that encouraged the mob.

Jack leaned down and kissed me on the cheek. The place erupted.

Dwayne, *former* best friend and wing man, had tears streaming down his cheeks as I squirmed under the rainbow spotlight.

Following Jack's instruction, every guy who passed our table on their way to the restroom paused and said some version of, "Hi, Michael. Welcome to Atlanta."

A few were a tad more forward. One was downright lecherous. I got *his* phone number.

7

ON THE ROAD AGAIN

On my third day in Atlanta, I landed an interview for a sales manager gig at an IT staffing company. I didn't know anything about staffing, but had a decent understanding of the IT world and was pretty confident in my sales abilities. It was worth a shot.

My interviewer, Mark, was the outgoing sales manager. He wasn't leaving the company, he just didn't want to babysit the kids anymore. We laughed at that description. It was frighteningly accurate.

Thirty minutes into my chat with Mark, a rail-thin man waltzed into Mark's office. The guy was in his mid-thirties and was so pale he could've been an extra on *Buffy the Vampire Slayer*. I hopped to my feet and Mark introduced the newcomer as Ted, the company's founder and owner. We shook hands, spoke for five minutes, and he left.

In sales industry parlance, it was a drive-by. I hadn't been there an hour and knew an offer was about to hit the table.

It did. I was gainfully employed.

THE NEXT SUNRISE HERALDED MY FIRST SATURDAY IN Atlanta. We drove aimlessly, exploring my new town, pointing and chatting and laughing all the way. It was cool seeing the Olympic rings from when Atlanta played host to the world. The city experienced healthy growth before the Games, but exploded in the years that followed. Everywhere we looked, cranes towered atop partially completed buildings. Oddly, all that construction made the place feel alive, like the city itself was reaching up from the ground to spread new life everywhere.

I was surprised by how big the Braves' stadium was. They called it the Ted, for the illustrious Mr. Turner. Nashville didn't have a professional baseball team, so I'd never really been a fan, but I committed to buying some swag and learning more about my new team. When Dwayne asked if I planned to do the same with the Falcons, I laughed. I enjoyed winning a lot more than fitting in.

Margaret Mitchell's home was quaintly nestled amid Midtown's skyscrapers. I barely remembered seeing *Gone with the Wind*, but the author's house was a point on the tour I was glad we hit. Dwayne was thoroughly amused when I told him the house made me think about Carole Burnett wearing curtains with a rod spread across her shoulders.

Piedmont Park was almost as eye-popping as our first visit to Roasters. The park itself was impressively large and beautiful. On one side, sprawling, grassy fields were interrupted by softball diamonds and soccer goals. The other side held rolling hills with flat land in the center. Guys and gals cycled, skateboarded, and rollerbladed on the well-maintained walkways that encircled everything, while hundreds of other park-goers played frisbee with dogs, tossed footballs, or lounged in the sun.

The eye-popping part of our Piedmont Park drive-by was not in the number of Atlantans who'd ventured out to enjoy the fresh air, but in the makeup of the population there. Most of the guys were either shirtless or wearing skimpy tank tops. Some snuggled on blankets, others hugged and kissed. When two groups met, they hugged like I'd seen so many times in the gay bars back in Nashville. Unlike the pool at Monroe Place, there were quite a few women here. Some were in groups with the guys, but most were segregated in their own small huddles. Quite a few of the women wore some version of rainbow colors.

It was also notable that the Hottie Percentage held true. While other cities might boast a few truly beautiful among their flock, a solid plurality of those in Atlanta appeared to have broad, firm, very colorful feathers. My blood pumped a little faster, both at Little Michael's rising enthusiasm for the possibilities, and my heart's anxiety over just how intimidating all those tasty men were. How does one compete in a land of the truly blessed? The concentration of hotness was overwhelming.

That night, Dwayne took me out to celebrate getting a new job so quickly. I think we were both surprised how the fates appeared to be endorsing my move. We went to Roasters again. What can I say? We loved great chicken and veggies. The man meat on the menu didn't hurt either.

The festive gay vibe at dinner put both of us in the mood to tour a different side of Atlanta, so we grabbed one of the trusty *David* magazines from a rack at the front door and tried to guess which bar would be popular on a Saturday night. Dwayne ruled out a few places he remembered being either too seedy or aimed at a very specific niche within the gay community. I was no longer new to the rainbow world, but had yet to learn about different colored handkerchiefs and what tattoos meant when placed on the left or right arm. I made a mental note to return to the Gay Manual for guidance.

We settled on the bar with the largest ad, a place called Backstreet. Two whole magazine pages were filled with images of half-naked boys dancing on boxes or wiggling next to a bar. Every bartender pictured looked happy, hot, and horny.

No, I don't know how one *looks* horny in a magazine, but that's what I thought. Or maybe I was the one who— never mind.

Backstreet's parking lot rivaled that of the Connection in Nashville. Cars sprawled in every direction, while men poured out of them like ants headed back to their hill. As we pulled into a parking space, I felt butterflies I hadn't experienced since that first night I realized I had accidentally ended up in a gay bar.

I'd been to plenty of bars in Nashville since that night. Why was I suddenly nervous?

"Time for the big leagues." Dwayne answered my thoughts as we exited his car.

"Yeah. I'm actually a little nervous."

He barked a laugh. "That'll go away with the first shake of your booty—maybe the first grab or pinch, if I remember your record in bars correctly."

I grinned. "It's more grabbable than pinchable. One might hurt one's fingers trying to pinch my granite cheeks."

"Gah!" He rolled his eyes and laughed. "Just don't leave me alone, alright? I have a feeling you'll be very popular. Fresh meat usually is."

"Aww. Meat. That's the sweetest thing you've ever called me."

He slapped my arm and playfully shoved me toward the bar entrance.

Over the next few hours, I counted a dozen chest strokes, two bicep squeezes, and more butt grabs than my alcohol-addled brain could remember. Dwayne cackled as I nearly jumped out of my painted-on jeans with the first few flirts—but I settled in and came to enjoy the attention I'd never received as a freckled, ginger young nerd. Even some of the Hollywood Hotties gave me a respectable ogle. Who knew? I might actually have a shot in this land of lovelies!

Dwayne pulled me away from a tall, hunky, curly-haired boy whose nipples shown bright red in the strobing lights. I hadn't realized pinching nipples was nearly as popular as gripping butt-cheeks. I reluctantly gave Naughty Nips a peck on the cheek and allowed myself to be dragged out to the car. Dwayne was a blast to hang out with, but his tolerance for watching me flirt with every dude with dimples lasted only so long.

***

THE NEXT DAY, DWAYNE RETURNED HOME. AS MUCH AS WE liked to tease each other, it was a sad parting. We offered all the promises friends make when moving hundreds of miles away from each other, pledging to keep in touch and stay just as close as we'd always been, but we both knew life didn't work that way. Despite our best intentions, he would get busy chasing chicken and trying to remove his ankle bracelet, and I would start a new life exploring my new city and job.

We were about to drift, and I *hated* it.

I hugged him so long, he had to tell me to let him go. Then he did something he'd never done in all the time we'd known each other. He reached up and kissed me on the cheek, then rubbed it with his fingers. My heart stuck in my throat. I knew he was saying goodbye, being a loving, caring friend, but I didn't want to let go.

Watching him drive through the gates of Monroe Place, a part of me left Atlanta.

8

THINK!

I owned two suits. They hung, side by side, on the back of my closet's folding doors. A dozen or so ties lay scattered across the bed as I held each one up in a desperate attempt to pick my first-day-on-the-new-job outfit. I'd never been good with that sort of thing, and starting a new job hadn't magically imbued me with better fashion sense. I picked a white shirt, charcoal suit, and blue tie with tiny pink dots. I had no idea if it matched.

A mug of coffee and a twenty-minute drive later, I stood in the lobby of my new office. A girl who'd clearly had more coffee than I greeted me with a chipper smile. She sat behind a massive cherry-red unit that rose nearly to my chest. On the wall behind her, highlighted with bright spotlights, was the company's name in silver metal letters: Think!. I later learned they rarely used the second word in the name, *Resources*, because the owner liked how catchy Think! was.

When the receptionist learned I was the new sales manager, she hopped up from her seat behind the sprawling switchboard and shook my hand. Somehow, her highly caffeinated smile widened. It looked painful.

Seconds later, a towering form filled the entry to the right of the reception desk. Mark must've been walking by when I arrived because the girl hadn't had time to call for him. He smiled, stretched out his meaty paw, and gripped my hand like he was juicing an orange.

"You have no idea how glad I am you're here," he said.

I wasn't sure how to read his enthusiasm, but I tried to match the firmness of his grip and the tone of his voice. I smiled up at the giant. "I'm happy to be here."

"Come on back. I'll give you the tour, then you can get settled into your office. There's a team meeting at nine to introduce you. No pressure, but they're a tough crowd."

We strode past a small grouping of cubicles filled with programmers and clerical staff. Mark pointed to my office opposite this cluster. It was about what you'd expect, a twelve-by-twenty box with a desk, credenza, bookshelf, and two chairs for visitors. The back wall was entirely glass overlooking a grassy field. I noted the blank walls and desk, wondering how I'd make the place my own.

The office beside mine sat empty. Mark explained it was for the manager of the recruiting teams. I had no idea what that meant, but nodded thoughtfully. He explained I would have a heavy vote in who was hired for that role.

I added 'learning what the hell a recruiting manager was' to my growing list of homework.

Mark's corner office sprawled across one end of the building, taking up enough space to fit three offices the size of mine. Apparently, he was an IT staffing baller. Dennis, the head of technology, hopped up from his chair and greeted me as we passed his closet-sized space.

"Hey, you must be the new sales manager. Michael, right?"

I nodded and shook his hand. His grip was decidedly looser than Mark's—and slimier. It felt a little like squeezing a snake that wanted desperately to slither away.

"Great. We're glad you're here. Don't touch the computer until I show you how to log in and have given you the welcome speech, okay?"

I glanced at Mark. He rolled his eyes just enough for me to see.

"Uh, sure. I'm not that great with computers anyway. I could use any help you can give me."

"Great. Just don't push buttons or click anything you don't understand. Okay?"

"Deal."

Mark's paw nudged my arm, a hint meant to save me. I took it gratefully.

"Nice meeting you, Dennis. See you after the sales meeting," I said, and Mark and I began moving further down the hall. Dennis's door clicked shut.

Mark leaned down and whispered, "He means well, and he's a hell of an IT guy, but he's kind of a dick."

As the new guy, I wasn't sure how to react to Mark's frankness, but chuckled and gave him a tight smile. "Need to win him over. Got it."

The last office we visited was that of the owner, Ted, who sat glaring at one of five computer screens spread across his insanely long desk. He didn't notice when we walked in and Mark had to clear his throat twice to get him to look up.

"Oh, Michael, are you starting already?" he said, clicking a few keys before making his way around the Tajima desk.

Mark saved me a second time. "Today's Michael's first day. He meets the troops at nine. I can't wait to pass this baton."

Ted grinned and nodded, as though they'd had that conversation a hundred times. "Welcome. Why don't you have a seat, and I'll tell you a little more about our company, then you can go settle into your office. I assume Dennis beat you over the head about the computer already?"

Mark coughed a laugh from behind me.

I nodded. "Yes, he pretty much told me to wait for instruction before touching anything."

Ted smirked. "Good. Don't believe his bluster, he's a good guy. We had a bad hack a year ago and he's paranoid now. That's probably healthy for an IT manager these days."

The three of us sat at a small conference table, where Ted and Mark described the company's founding and growth. The pair alternated, often finishing each other's sentences like an old married couple, but appeared annoyed when it happened—again, like an old married couple. They were forthright and friendly, but serious about their business. Mark loved the sales side and wanted nothing more than to focus on his own personal hunt for new clients. Ted wanted to turn Think! into the largest IT recruiting firm in the country. He spoke passionately about the computers and process, how the website drove traffic for new candidates and winnowed them down for the perfect hire.

Months later, replaying that conversation in my mind, I realized the one thing Ted didn't talk about—not even once —was the *people* who worked for him.

My first week was filled largely with meetings with each member of my new sales team. I now oversaw thirty-two men and women, most of whom were in their twenties or early thirties. The one-on-one meetings were interesting. Virtually every person who walked into my office did so with an air of caution, as if unsure whether they were meeting an ally or executioner. I dedicated most of the time to asking questions about their background, interests, and goals for the future. I'd learned long ago that nothing calms a salesperson more than the sound of their own voice.

The recruiting team was slightly larger than my sales team, boasting forty-five members. I pitied whoever we hired for that management gig. My group was over-whelming as it was, I couldn't imagine trying to wrangle an additional thirteen people.

On Thursday, Ted's head popped into my office. The rest of him snaked around the wall. He was an odd man.

"We have candidates for the other manager position we'd like you to interview. You free at two this afternoon?"

I scrolled through my calendar, then nodded. "I'm free. Anything in particular you want me to look for?"

He shook his head. "No. Just trust your gut. This person will be your partner in running the teams, so we need you to be comfortable with whoever we hire."

Without another word, he vanished, leaving me staring at the empty doorway.

When two o'clock rolled around, I found my way into the conference room where the first candidate waited. He was a tall, thin, extremely pale man with tight-cropped black hair and brown eyes that bugged out like a pug's. I tried not to stare, but he blinked rapidly when he talked and made it impossible to look away. The effect was both comical and creepy.

Pug Man had never worked in sales. He'd never led a team. He had no experience with recruiting, and barely any experience working in a professional setting. I wasn't sure why the recruiters had moved him through to the interview stage, as his résumé clearly mirrored the vacant look in his far-too-pronounced eyeballs. I made a note to discuss filter criteria with the recruiting team.

At two thirty, the receptionist appeared and announced my next interview had arrived.

Next interview? I was sure Ted had only mentioned one.

Nevertheless, I thanked Mr. Pug, then asked Perky Patty to show him out and bring in the next victim.

Candidate number two was a woman with gray hair pulled into a tight bun. She wore a sharp black pant suit with a frilly white blousy thing puffing out the front.

I'm *sure* that's what it's called. Stop snickering.

As she entered the conference room, she extended a stiff, unyielding hand and pursed her lips into a taut, thin line I took for a smile. I quickly learned it was *not* a smile. Herr Hilda did not know *how* to smile. She spoke in short, clipped sentences, with the precision of a surgeon's scalpel. I felt each cut—I mean, word—deeply. Unlike Mr. Pug, her eyes never blinked, never wavered, never left mine. Strong eye contact was a great quality in a professional, but hers was unnerving. I kept waiting for the creepy music to start so I could run to safety into the cemetery or barn filled with chainsaws. Wasn't that always the safest place to run in a scary movie?

At three o'clock, my salvation in the form of the door-knob squeaking open arrived. Perky Patty appeared and announced the third candidate's turn. That was both a relief and annoying. I couldn't wait for Herr Hilda to leave, but again, I was not expecting this many interviews. How long would this day last? And how bad would the candidates get? I hoped this wasn't the quality of candidates we put in front of our clients.

I asked Patty to stall the next candidate so I could check my calendar and move any conflicts. Thankfully, all I had was another training session with Dennis on how not to break his network. He gladly rescheduled.

Candidate number three was ushered into the room roughly ten minutes past the scheduled start time. Patty introduced the woman as Constance Black, then closed the door as she left.

"Constance, I'm so sorry to keep you waiting. Today's been back-to-back," I said, stepping forward, hand extended.

"Please, call me Connie. You gave me time to grill Patty. She's delightful."

Connie was pleasant, professional, and I was immediately drawn to her easy smile.

"Hope she said nice things," I quipped.

"Oh, she did. Not about you, but about the company."

"So, she said bad things about me?" I raised a brow.

She grinned. "I wouldn't say *bad* things. Let's just say the jury's still out on the new guy."

She was teasing me, in an interview—an interview that had barely begun. I didn't know whether to be offended or impressed, but her confidence and openness was refreshing, and I couldn't help but like her.

We talked for over an hour, lobbing questions back and forth with the comfort of old friends. Connie loved working with people, developing them, finding what made them tick, and using that knowledge to help them succeed. She didn't have direct recruiting experience, but had led several teams in other industries. I was confident she'd pick up the recruiting business quickly. By the time Patty appeared to check on us, Connie and I were leaning forward across the table, giggling like schoolmates at some story about a former employee.

Ted made me interview two more people the next day, but Connie was the clear winner. She was sharp, well-spoken, endearing, and, most of all, she made me laugh. It was a match made in corporate heaven.

9
———

DEBUTANT

F riday after work, I decided it was time to find a new gym. The muscle buffet on display at the pool had made it clear I had work to do. I was in great shape for Nashville's quaint gay scene, maybe even in the top third of contenders, but I was merely average in the sea of hotness that was Atlanta.

I turned to the literary reference material that had proven most effective in guiding me thus far—*David* magazine. Using Dwayne's flawless logic, I found the gym with the largest ad. A quick three-minute drive from Monroe Place, nestled in a residential valley in Midtown, was Powerhouse, gym to the gay stars—or, at least, the boys who lived in Midtown. There were a few other options, but they weren't as close by and didn't show up as prominently in *David*.

"Welcome to Powerhouse," a deep, friendly voice rumbled as I entered. I looked up to find an enormously muscled guy standing behind a counter. He wore a white tank top with Powerhouse printed in bold red lettering across the chest. He was clearly a bodybuilder, as muscles I couldn't identify bulged out of every opening in his shirt. I swear his neck was wider than his head. I tore my eyes from his eighty-inch arms and read his name tag.

"Hi, uh, Greg. I'm looking for a gym to join."

"Awesome." He grabbed a clipboard and handed it to me. "Fill out that guest pass info. I'll give you the tour."

A few minutes into our tour, I realized I had even more work to do than I'd thought. Everywhere I looked, perfectly sculpted men pulled and pushed, stretching already rippling muscles past their limits. Rows of guys lay on blue foam pads, stretching legs and working abs. I saw more abs in that ten-minute tour than I think I'd seen in my whole life.

Sweet baby Jesus.

I followed Greg through an entryway that wound around an S-shaped wall then opened into the locker room. I nearly missed a step. A dozen naked gods strutted about the room. A few wore towels tied about their waists, but most seemed pleased with the opportunity to display their, um, hard work. And some of their, um, *work,* was definitely hard. I caught my face in the mirror and realized my mouth was open and eyes were bugged out, darting faster than a squirrel crossing a road. Greg laughed, snapping me out of my daze.

"Lockers over there. Showers to the right. Steam room and hot tub are in the back. This side is men only, so the hot tub and steam room are clothing optional."

I'd stopped listening as a particularly hot guy emerged from the shower and exercised the *optional* part of that policy. My head followed as he passed, and I stumbled into Greg, who'd stopped to show me something.

"Oh, Greg, sorry. I, uh, tripped over a towel."

He laughed again. "You're new to Atlanta, aren't you?"

I nodded sheepishly.

"You'll be fine. It takes a little getting used to. I've lived here over twenty years, wouldn't want to be anywhere else." He eyed my body. "Looks like you've been working out. Chest is filling out, arms are nice. What are your fitness goals? Do you know where you'd like to see your body?"

The hottie from the shower walked by and made eye contact over Greg's shoulder.

"I, uh, goals, well…I, uh…"

"Let's go back to the desk. It might be easier to talk out there." He chuckled to himself as we walked back up front. I felt every eye in the place follow me. Should I have been proud? Were they *liking* the new guy? I felt like I was trying out for some team and didn't even know what sport we were playing.

Greg finished the enrollment process and sent me out the door with a shiny new key fob to scan each time I worked out. I know it sounds silly, but there was something about that plastic hanging off my keyring that made me feel like I really lived here now. I was officially an Atlantan.

I GRABBED SOME CHINESE TAKEOUT ON THE WAY BACK TO my apartment, unsure what to do with my first weekend alone. After a plateful of cashew chicken and white rice, I turned to my trusty *David* for guidance. *David* and I were becoming great friends.

The bars were listed in two places. Ads were splashed throughout the magazine, displaying bartenders and bar-goers in various states of drunken delight. Some were specific in their marketing, showing guys in cowboy hats and fringe shirts, indicating the bar that catered to country-loving gays. Another showed large, hairy men in black studded leather. One guy held a chain attached to a collar encircling another dude's neck. I wasn't entirely sure what Disney theme that represented, but knew it wasn't what I was looking for.

What was more interesting than the themes in the ads was the specificity with which they advertised which night was best to visit. Backstreet and the Armory, two of the larger bars that happened to share a parking lot, stressed Fridays and Saturdays. The leather lads represented The Heretic, which noted Wednesday nights were their specialty. Other, more generally themed locations claimed Mondays and Thursdays.

Sundays were apparently all about a tea dance. I had no idea what a tea dance was. The ad even had a picture of a tea bag in a shot glass with its little white tag dangling over the side. Did gays have a special thing for tea? Were all gays now British? I was baffled—and more than a little intrigued.

In addition to the weird tea reference, that particular dance started at two o'clock in the afternoon. Virtually no one showed up to any of the bars before midnight, but that major weekly event started in the middle of the day. The whole thing seemed odd.

Tuesdays appeared uniquely devoid of bar mayhem. Even gays had to rest from all their merriment, I supposed.

Research complete, I closed the lid on my leftover Chinese food and decided to check out the bar of the day— or night, as was the case on a Friday. It was only nine o'clock, far too early to go out, so I flipped on the TV and watched *Star Trek* reruns until the witching hour arrived. As excited as I was to venture out, I forced myself to wait until twelve thirty to get ready.

One mustn't appear too eager, must one?

I squeezed into my look-at-my-ass jeans, threw on a nearly clean white T-shirt, and headed out. Backstreet called to me again, and I felt a flurry of something in my gut as I looked at the ad for the address. If the percentage of Hollywood Hot held true from what I'd seen in town so far, this was going to be eye-candy heaven, but also I worried I was out of my depth. How could a raised-by-wolves preacher's kid from small-town Nashville fit into this big city sea of hotness?

I PULLED INTO THE MASSIVE PARKING LOT A QUICK FIVE minutes later. The Armory's squatty long building sat at one end, while Backstreet's multi-floored monstrosity consumed the side perpendicular to the Armory. Scowling security guards attempted to direct the flow of cars, but were unable to prevent them from stacking up beyond the entrance. It took twice as long to park as it had to drive from my apartment.

Men in twos and threes, mostly in jeans and T-shirts or tank tops, laughed and squealed their way into the bars. As I walked past one group, a young guy with wild blond hair styled in the popular finger-in-a-light-socket motif scuttled away from his pack and pinched my butt. I nearly leapt out of my jeans, and the dumbfounded expression on my face when I turned around sent blondie's whole group into a fit of laughter. I stared, stunned, as they *skipped* toward Backstreet's doors.

The Connection in Nashville was immense. Its main dance floor held five hundred, and each of the smaller bars held many hundreds more. The first few times I went there, it was both thrilling and dizzying. To see so many gay men packed into one place was beyond anything familiar to me. While Backstreet packed in hundreds of men, probably more than a thousand, it had a completely different vibe. All the basics were there: bars at every turn with half-naked, totally hot bartenders, boxes on which scantily clad men danced, and multiple levels allowing lurkers and lurkees to do whatever it is they do in the dark. The general age was twentysomething, similar to Nashville's bar scene.

But there were also clear differences.

The Atlanta boys did not disappoint. The intimidating ratio of Hollywood Hot to Normal Hot was off the chart. I'd never seen so many muscles and pearly whites under one roof. In Nashville, I could stand in my safe, dark corner and pick out those who deserved a Best in Show ribbon. Just like in dog shows, where hundreds entered the competition, only a few walked away with the honors. Backstreet followed different judging criteria. Ridiculous hotness surrounded me, pressing and shoving, dancing and swaying. Every time I thought I'd found the vaunted Best in Show, some other stunning specimen would walk off the cover of his magazine and into the bar. It was mesmerizing.

Another difference was something we'll call the IKEA Effect. There wasn't really a conscious flow of traffic, and it was easy to lose yourself in the maelstrom as you…um… browsed. At the Connection, there were obvious wide hallways that led from one section to the next. Backstreet had none of that organization. Men squeezed and squirmed, headed in every direction. Even the entrance held that fighting-against-the-current feeling, as departing guys shouldered new arrivals in a contest of wills.

Backstreet was also darker than the Connection. Sure, when strobes were flaring and the dance floor was rocking, both bars had dim lighting, but Backstreet lacked the towering ceiling of the Connection, making it feel more closed, and somehow more intimate.

It took an hour for me to identify the final, most important difference: guys in Nashville made eye contact and were generally friendly. These newer, hotter models seemed intent on some mission—or on being the object of someone else's mission, I wasn't sure which. They rarely made eye contact, and when they did, it was often followed by a 'what are you looking at?' scowl. Did pretty people not want to be ogled? Apparently, the rules were different in Atlanta. The Gay Manual had failed to prepare me properly.

I ogled anyway. Screw them.

Not literally.

Well, maybe…

Midway through the night, I was standing in line for the restroom when a guy sidled up beside me. He bobbed a tad faster than the beat of the music, twitching more than dancing. His eyes were wide and unfocused. I took a step forward as someone left the restroom.

"Hey." Twitchy's voice was as twitchy as his dance moves.

"Uh, hey."

"You want some coke?"

I cocked my head and held up my plastic cup, half full of brown fizzy goodness. "I'm all set, thanks."

He stopped twitching and gave me that sideways head flop a dog gives when asked a question, as if he couldn't fathom the meaning of what I'd said. His eyes managed to focus and held the same confused expression as his head tilt.

I rattled the ice in my cup. "Coke. I'm still half full—but thanks."

He got it, then started laughing. I still don't know what I said that was so funny. He gave me one last look, shook his index finger accusingly, then disappeared into the crowd.

Atlanta guys were weird.

10

CURIOUS GEORGE

As the weeks rolled by, I fell into a comfortable routine. Think! didn't open the doors until eight thirty, so my anti-morning-person nature was well pleased. Connie got the recruiting manager gig, and she quickly became my new best friend. We collaborated well on projects while each learning the ropes of our new position. It was fun figuring it out together. Aside from our shared brain in working with teams, Connie had an infectious laugh—and she laughed all the time. Barely a day passed that we weren't giggling like children over some silliness.

After work, I drove directly to the grocery store to purchase my pre-workout snack, a single Fuji apple. The first time I set my lonely fruit on the conveyor belt, the checkout clerk's eyes drifted from the apple to me, then back to the apple.

"Just an apple?" she asked, her voice straddling curiosity and amusement.

I nodded, glancing at her name tag. "Yes, Miss Anne. Just the apple."

By my third visit, Anne had come to expect my odd purchase and welcomed me by name.

My workout began with fifteen minutes of cardio to wake me up from Think!ing all day, and rotated between chest and biceps, back and triceps, and the dreaded leg day. I did twenty minutes of abs after each lifting session, then another thirty minutes of cardio on the elliptical. Workouts lasted roughly two hours. By the time most workouts finished, I was mentally and physically exhausted and hungry enough to eat all the apples Anne might have stashed in the storeroom.

Cooking had never been my strong suit. Moe's, the nearby takeout Chinese place, and a Western-novel-themed restaurant called Cowtippers usually won my post-workout business. Aside from the fun name, I especially liked Cowtippers' wooden patio with dozens of outdoor tables where traffic, both driving and pedestrian, were visible. What dinner didn't go well with eye candy?

As I sat eating my sweet potato drenched in brown sugar and cinnamon goodness, I decided to find out what Atlanta had to offer beyond the bar scene. Once again, *David* turned out to be helpful, offering pages of activities run by various local gay groups. I had thought we were lucky because Nashville had a decent softball league and a pickup volleyball night, but as I flipped through page after page, I was awed by the breadth of Atlanta's community. There were groups for *everything*.

God bless the boys and girls in the Atlanta Gay Quilters and Atlanta Rainbow Chess Society. Everyone needs a home, even nerds with needles.

I circled the contact information for the softball and volleyball leagues—they had a whole volleyball *league*, not just a pickup night. After my head-spinning, scantily clad introduction that first day at the pool, I hadn't thought my love for Atlanta could deepen. I'd never known there were cities where I could be around gay people and not feel the need to look over my shoulder, to wonder who might be watching. Don't get me wrong, I loved living in Nashville —it was an amazing, growing town with some of the nicest people on the planet—but the idea of two men or two women holding hands as they strolled down Broadway was unimaginable. I was never worried about being attacked, but growing up in the buckle of the Bible Belt did give a preacher's kid a unique appreciation for the power of excommunication.

Staring at the pages of Atlanta's most colorful organizations, I realized how amazing my new home really was.

THE RHYTHM OF THE BAR SCENE BECAME PART OF MY routine. I didn't go out much during the week, largely because going to a bar before midnight was a waste of time and I needed my beauty sleep on school nights. But I looked forward to Friday and Saturday nights, and whatever mischief they might bring. On my fifth weekend in the City of the Peach, I decided to be adventurous and visit one of the darker-themed bars, The Heretic. Even the name made me shiver with excitement.

My little devil appeared in his tightest leather, a wide grin spread across his miniature face. "Dude, it's about time. You're gonna love the dark side," he said with a glee I didn't know devils could possess.

"I'm just going to visit, to walk through and see what it's like, then I'm leaving for the safety of Blake's."

The devil actually coughed a laugh, and I swear I felt

spittle on my neck. "You are not a *stand-and-model* gay. You're a *seize him by the balls and do nasty things to him gay*—or a *tie me to the bedpost with your silk*—"

"Hey!" I protested.

"Blake's is a perfectly fine place to see hot guys walking back and forth or…holding up walls."

Man, he was bossy, but he had a point. Blake's was full of pretty boys who wouldn't do much more than stand around. On the other hand, the thought of exploring uncharted territory made my pulse race—and made Little Michael tingle. Maybe I'd stay at The Heretic for a half hour. It deserved a fair shot, right?

"You bet your ass strap, it does!" The devil clapped his hands together and a puff of dark smoke wafted past my ear. "And next week we'll try The Eagle or Bulldogs!"

The Eagle? Bulldogs? I didn't remember seeing either of those particular tourist attractions advertised in my trusty *David*. I'd have to do more research before agreeing to that adventure, as something in his voice made me question the Sunday School-esque nature of those establishments.

MIDNIGHT ARRIVED AND SEXY JEANS WERE DONNED. THE time had come for my virgin voyage to The Heretic.

My nerves fluttered once again, so I hung out in the parking lot and watched the boys walk toward the entrance to get a feel for the place. This was a decidedly different crowd than the one I'd seen at Armory and Backstreet. A fair number of the guys were big—and I don't just mean tall. If the check boxes ranged from short to tall, skinny to plump, and muscular to athletic, The Heretic's crowd was weighted toward the heavier, hairier side. The median age was also older, somewhere in the thirties, versus the twentysomethings who dominated the other bars.

Even the sounds coming from the groups of men were different. Where many of the gaggles at Backstreet giggled their way into the building, deep, rumbling bass tones echoed across the paved lot here.

Backstreet had a young, sexy, hot vibe.

The Heretic felt *manly*.

While Backstreet boys begged to be worshipped, men at The Heretic looked like they'd rather shove you against the wall and make you their—

Anyway.

The Heretic also had a thing for leather. Black, brown, blue—yes, there were men in blue-tinted leather—no one seemed to care as long as you wore it. Many of the more muscular guys wore leather vests without a shirt, giving you a tasty hint of what lay beneath without fully revealing their deliciousness. Others opted for harness things I'd seen on dogs at the park the other day. A few even had a collar with a tag. Images of walking through Nashville Zoo with Donny streaked through my mind, but this was a *very* different kind of zoo. Instead of big cats and elephants, I watched a parade of bears, otters, and other critters I didn't yet recognize stroll by.

A massive guy in leather chaps—and no pants underneath—walked by carrying a silver leash attached to a studded collar fastened around the neck of a young skinny dude shuffling sheepishly behind. I wasn't sure if the follower actually wanted to be there, until he suddenly perked up, bounded forward two strides, and licked his master's ear.

I couldn't stop staring. My dog used to do that to me.

We definitely weren't in Nashville anymore.

A good fifteen minutes passed before I pulled myself up by my balls and climbed out of my car. I hadn't noticed the giant circular sign on the wall beside the door until then. It was black with the name of the club wrapped around the outer edge in white. The image of some bird of prey with ears and a long tongue stared down at me from the sign's center.

Now I really was nervous.

"Just you, precious?"

My head snapped forward. A snow-topped, rail-thin man behind a high-top table blinked and smiled.

"Uh, yeah. Just me."

"Five bucks," he said, hand extended.

A cover charge. That was new.

The guy gripped my arm with his outstretched hand and leaned over the table. "You've never been here, have you?"

I shook my head.

He chuckled. "Go on in. Tonight's on me. Just don't stop walking if you go into the back hallway. They'll eat a pretty little thing like you alive."

I nodded nervously and hurried past, but froze at a wall lined with men that forced me to go left or right. The men grinned as my head snapped skittishly back and forth. Finally, one of them took pity on the scared little rabbit and said, "Left is leather and military, right is sports."

I darted right faster than they could laugh.

The sports bar was the size of a two-bedroom apartment without walls. The only sign of sports of any kind was a lone television tuned to ESPN. I laughed at the absurdity of professional bowling playing in a seedy gay bar on a Friday night.

And just like that, my nerves eased.

I took a deep breath and looked around. Most of the

sports crowd were younger, leather-less guys, with just a smattering of leather caps and vests thrown in for seasoning. There wasn't nearly as much space here, so every step meant rubbing shoulders and chests. I said a polite "excuse me" each time I bumped into someone, until a dude turned around, ran both hands down my chest, and said, "You're excused. Now do that again."

My mouth fell open. A friend of Mr. Hands stepped around him and grinned. Before I knew what was happening, his meaty palm was rubbing up and down my jeans, hungrily hunting for Little Michael. Startled, I jumped back and nearly caused a tumbling domino effect of dudes. The guy behind me wrapped both hands around me, gripping my abs and pulling me into him. Meanwhile, Meaty Palm decided a massage was in order. Mr. Hands reappeared and reached around to squeeze my butt.

Three guys I didn't know in the middle of a bar were rubbing and squeezing me, and I couldn't stop it—didn't stop it; didn't *want* to stop it—and then a barback carrying a case of beer stepped between us and freed me from their grip.

"Coming through. Everyone back." He turned to me as the sea parted. "You okay?"

I tried to play it cool. "I'm…uh…I'm good. Yeah. Really. I'm great."

His smile was thin. "I'm Jase. Ask for me if you have any trouble, okay?" Then he stepped to the bar and heaved his case of beer through the swinging door.

When I turned back, Mr. Hands and Meaty Palm had vanished. I squeezed back to the entrance and out the door without looking back. I climbed into my car, reveling in the comfort and safety of her well-worn seats, and calmed my breathing. I wasn't sure why I was so terrified. Guys had grabbed my ass before and I'd bragged about it to Dwayne. The men in The Heretic weren't exactly ripping my jeans off, but their touch felt more like a violation. I didn't understand why.

The weirdest part of it all was the reaction of the guys packed around us. Except for my savior, Jase, none of the others seemed bothered in the least. I wasn't exactly thinking clearly in the moment, but I remembered several men glaring and grinning at the display of wanton sexuality before them—and that was in the *sports bar*. The doorman warned me about some back hallway, not the bar areas. How much more handsy would that stretch of darkness be?

Puff. The devil was back, now in a road-worn, black biker's jacket and faded torn jeans.

"Dude, you're such a *puss*. The only way to know is to go back in there and see for yourself—or feel for yourself, if the mood hits ya."

I didn't like the way he chuckled, so I flicked him off my shoulder like a wayward bug. He vanished in another puff of black vapor as his leather-clad body slammed into the car window.

"Oof! Your loss—" was the last thing I heard before starting my car and heading home.

11

VIRTUAL REUNION

My dreams were filled with images of men in leather, men taking off leather, men swinging leather over their heads, men putting leather on me, and on it went. I tossed in my sleep as hands reached from every direction. Fingernails grazed my bare flesh. Strong fingers gripped me, rubbed my back and legs and butt, stroked my—

I woke up drenched in sweat. Terror had taken a back seat to intrigue and a heart-thumping *something* I couldn't identify—but it felt exactly like the thrill I remembered from my night a few years ago with Fly Boy and his silk ties.

Fear mingled with desire wrapped in pleasure.

Yeah, that summed it up.

I'd never been a fan of cold showers, but one seemed highly appropriate that morning. Once the shock of the cold subsided, it felt good to wash The Heretic off and return my brain to some semblance of normalcy. The devil didn't reappear, but I thought I heard the tinkle of faint laughter coming from the angel's side of my brain.

Great, now they were *both* amused.

After a quick breakfast of toasted blueberry bagel with strawberry cream cheese, I refilled my mug with java and strode back into the bedroom to check email and kill some time chatting on AOL. A few new Nigerian princes were offering me large sums of money. They were really nice people, but I felt guilty taking their money for nothing, so I replied, suggesting they give it to charity.

Email complete, I remembered wanting to check out the Eagle and Bulldogs online. The devil seemed determined to expose me to every facet of Atlanta. His suggestions were usually fun, but came with some wicked twists.

While I waited for the Eagle's painfully slow website to pull up, something flashed in the corner of the screen: one of my friends was online.

RAL2027.

Huh. The screen name was vaguely familiar, but it had been months since we last chatted—and in AOL time, that was decades. I'd printed hundreds of profile sheets since chatting briefly with that dude, and my online memory sucked.

HEY, HAVEN'T SEEN YOU IN A WHILE.

I was a little surprised when he IMed me. I quickly flipped through my overstuffed notebook of profile sheets to review my notes on this mysterious candidate.

All his profile listed were the standard stats: *SWM, 31, 5'9, 170, 31w, 16a, 8c.*

Beneath the printed line, I had written, "Ryan. Seems nice. No pic."

It didn't look like we'd had much of a conversation—at least, none worthy of diligent notes—but it was Saturday morning, I was bored, and he was the only dude talking to me at that moment.

Hey. Good to see you too. Ryan, right?

Wow. Good memory.

I grinned into the screen.

I'm pretty good with names, especially online.

I really wasn't.

I see that. So…what are you up to these days?

Well, I moved to Atlanta. Got a new apartment and job. Now I'm just trying to figure this place out and make it my home. What about you?

Atlanta? Really? I live in Atlanta.

Huh. Guess I never thought to ask that when we initially spoke. I'd just assumed he lived in Nashville.

Really? How cool. We're neighbors now.

Where in town do you live?

Midtown. Right in the middle of the gay bubble.

LOL, Gay bubble is right. I'm up in Norcross— outside the beltway. Most guys consider that another country.

There was a brief pause as I watched the cursor blink and tried to come up with something else witty. We'd talked a whole three minutes with no sexual references or requests for pictures. Something was different about this guy.

Hey. Sorry to chat and run, but I gotta go. Talk to you later?

Sure.

His name vanished from my friends list. He seemed nice enough, but didn't capture my attention enough to quash the chat-fever that consumed me. For the briefest moment, I wondered if my chatting was borne out of loneliness, horniness, or curiosity surrounding the men in my new community. I wasn't in the mood for a deep philosophical debate, so I chalked it up to all three and resumed the mission at hand (so to speak).

I spent another thirty minutes scrolling through the chat rooms, looking at profiles and introducing myself to the Atlanta boys. There were more ATLM4M rooms than I thought possible. If there were thirty-one flavors of bar in town, there were hundreds of subtle tastes online. I didn't know what half the acronyms meant, but the guys in the chat rooms understood their meaning on an intimate level and they weren't shy about saying so. Holy cow, these guys were forward—and some of them had interests that went beyond what my little devil might suggest. One guy sent me a picture of him underneath a glass-top table watching another guy drop his poop on the glass. I clicked LOG OFF as fast as I could and jumped back from my keyboard as if it was about to bite me—or poop on me.

I really didn't care that Mr. Poop-N-Peek got his jollies from something I found repulsive, but *yuck*. Poop watching? Really?

I did learn some useful information though. Besides AOL, a couple of newer websites now offered dating services similar to Match.com but for the gays. Two kept popping up in conversation, usually in the form of, "What's your name on Manhunt or Adam4Adam?" After the first time or two, I noticed a pattern. The guys who asked about Manhunt were definitely *on a hunt*, and not for pheasant or elk. They wanted the all-mighty ram, and they wanted it *now*. Those asking about A4A, as they abbreviated it, sounded more like traditional daters looking to get to know someone. I'm not saying the Manhunt guys weren't nice or ultimately hoping to meet someone for conversation, but, let's face it, they were on a site with the word "hunt" in it.

We weren't exchanging recipes or inviting each other to the church social.

Curious, I opened my browser and went to the first site my lizard brain could handle: Manhunt.

Holy bejesus.

Half-naked men popped up. And by half naked, I mean *totally* naked with the naughty bits blurred out—and those naughty bits were going inside other dudes' naughty-bit holders. Bit grippers? Bit bums?

Asses. They were sticking their dicks in asses, okay?

The PK in me was shocked. The twentysomething, seriously repressed dude in me was elated.

The site made me register before I could go further, so I created a screen name that I thought described my interests. This was a dating site, wasn't it?

ATLSportsGuy. I liked sports and I lived in Atlanta. Seemed clear to me.

It, however, wasn't clear to some of the guys on Manhunt, who were into things I had yet to discover.

Have you ever heard of a golden shower? I hadn't. The second guy to message me asked if we could do that together. He wanted to do it all over my chest. He described, in great detail, how he wanted to lick it off and—

He wanted to pee on me. Really?

Unable to just walk away, I asked him why he thought I would be interested in his offer. He pointed to my screen name, thinking it was short for water sports, yet another reference to guys enjoying whizzing on each other. When I told him I meant softball and volleyball, he replied with the popular ROFL and called me a rookie.

I *was* a rookie—couldn't be mad at him for that.

I thanked him for his interest and moved on.

As I scrolled through the guys, I was again amazed by the variety and hotness of the men in Atlanta. Black, white, brown—and every color in between—and *so many* of them were ripped and sexy. Whatever flavor I wanted, it was there for the taking, and Manhunt made it easy. It was like all the NOW chat rooms on AOL bundled into one site, complete with an easy-to-use filter so a user could hunt in the most efficient way possible.

I chuckled at the idea of efficient sex. Was that even a thing? I guessed it was now.

The newness of the experience and the images of the guys, some of which left absolutely nothing to the imagination, were getting me excited. Little Michael was rearing his head, tickled further by the silky shorts I was wearing, sans undies. The Manhunt dudes were advertising their best qualities, and damn, some of them had amazing, erect, perfectly curved qualities. Uncut qualities. Qualities with the barest leak of silky white—

Shit. I had to stop.

Desperate for a cold shower, I decided to check out Adam4Adam. As promised, it was almost a mirror of Match.com, with images of guys mostly clothed. Some held dogs or cats, others wore suits (that seemed a tad weird on a dating site). Profiles were filled with hobbies and interests, places they'd visited, even detailed descriptions of their ideal mate. After the testosterone-fueled heat of Manhunt, this was refreshing.

Don't get me wrong, I loved the sexy, gritty, let's-get-to-it quality of Manhunt. My heart was still racing from one brief visit to the site, but I knew I wanted more than a hookup long term. What I had with Carter, however brief our time had been, showed me that clearly. Rolling in the hay—or, in my case, having your hands tied above your head while a hot-as-fuck flight attendant banged me into the last decade—was insanely hot fun, but that was the *icing* on the cake. It wasn't *the cake*. Icing looked and tasted amazing, but it was fattening and bad for you and devoid of any lasting nutritional value.

Making cottage cheese with canned fruit together every night had substantive value. Tucking the boys in, kissing their tiny foreheads while they gripped my hand, that had true meaning. Doing the dishes shoulder to shoulder or sitting in a breakfast café without speaking—just being together—those were the moments that made a life together beautiful.

There was no way to replace the cake with the icing, no matter how many hot and horny hookups I enjoyed.

Thoroughly cooled down by my ruminations, I checked my new A4A inbox, expecting messages of introduction or pleasantries, maybe an invitation to coffee or dinner.

COME OVER AND POUND ME was all Trevor4Love said.

Maybe the two sites weren't *that* different. We were guys, after all.

That was what Dwayne had warned me about before he left.

The thought of my old friend made me smile. I needed a dose of Dwayne, but it was still early in Nashville and he was a late riser most days. I vowed to call him later and catch up.

Another item on my checklist was looking into the high school basketball officiating associations in town. After ten years of work in Nashville, I'd built up some seniority among that group and dreaded breaking into a new one. Would they assign based on merit or would the group be a politicized, good ole boys' network? Would the basketball be any good? Would I have to drive a million miles in

Atlanta's infamous traffic to work for pennies on the dollar? Oh, and what did officials get paid down here?

I had so many questions.

A quick search found there were four or five associations that serviced schools in the Metro Atlanta area. That boggled my mind. Our group in Nashville covered surrounding counties, and it was fairly common to drive outside the city to work. That one city needed four or five governing bodies made my head spin.

I clicked on the first group and found the president's name and number listed on the home page. Ten minutes later, I'd learned all about round ball in Atlanta. Mr. Prez said he would love to have some fresh blood in his group, but explained that their territory covered areas well outside the drive I'd wanted to make during a workweek. He then steered me clear of a couple groups known for shunning new folks, referring me to the group he thought best suited to my experience level and locale. It was spring, so there was plenty of time to meet the locals and work some AAU games for exposure and experience.

Atlanta had come through again—this time with my greatest passion, something unrelated to guys or bars or anything gay. I was sure someone would eventually revoke my gay card for that offense.

12

CARIBOU SEASON

The sun rose on a beautiful spring Sunday. Only a few wisps of cloud dotted the crystal-blue Atlanta sky. A light breeze tickled the hair on my arms. I'd learn in a few months how much every Atlantan misses that breeze when the town's stifling summer roasts everything in sight.

Curious about the softball league and what it would be like to participate in a gay sport with so many other guys, I drove across town to the fields where games were played. The first thing I noticed was the sheer number of fields in play at any given time. Back in Nashville, we generally had two or three games going at once. Here, there were eight fields filled with players, with several other teams watching from the sidelines, waiting for their game's start time.

And then there was the sheer number of guys.

If each field held two teams of a dozen or more, and there were eight fields occupied each hour, by my shoes-on math, that meant nearly two hundred dudes were actively competing every hour. I don't know which surprised me more: the number of gay guys gathered in one place, or my ability to sort through that math in my head.

The presence of uniforms surprised me. Each team was decked out in unique colors and logos; just like in straight leagues, but with one subtle difference. The gay teams' names were far cleverer and often carried either a snarky or sexual overtone. There were the Head Hunters, P-Cocks, the Dangling Darlings, I'd Hit That, the Morning Wood, the Packers, and, my personal favorite, Pitch Slapped. That last one had me giggling as I walked from one field to the next.

Even the league itself had a clever name: the Hotlanta Softball League.

Jokes aside, the boys took their games seriously. I half expected silliness and shenanigans, but even the lower-level players were intent on winning; well, except for a few teams who never stood much hope of winning—ever. It was easy to spot the purely social teams. Some of them wore colorful boas around their necks, or skirts instead of shorts. There was even a team of bears wearing tutus. Lord, help me. Every time one of them dropped a fly ball (which was *every* time one was hit to them), the entire team cried out, "OOPSIE!" and tossed their gloves into the air, giggling like embarrassed schoolgirls.

The athletic ability on that field was about as low as it could get, but the entertainment factor was off the chart. I watched several innings just to see how they reacted to different Bad News Bears level plays. If a particularly loud laugh or applause came from the crowd, several of the tutu-clad clan would turn and curtsey, then give several Miss America waves as though they'd won something special. They were hilarious—and they knew it.

After a thoroughly amusing morning of softball, I headed to the gym for my daily workout, then hit Cowtippers for my usual grilled chicken and baked sweet potato. I'd eaten there so often that the waiters (no waitresses—

this was Midtown, after all) didn't even ask what I wanted. My tall glass of iced water waited on the table before I was seated, and food arrived faster than McDonald's could toss a toy into a Happy Meal box. It was tasty, healthy, and super-fast—and the eye candy was fabulous, especially on a weekend when the patio was filled with boys.

I got home around three o'clock and decided to quash my boredom with another round of AOL chatting. The warm tones of Mr. AOL greeted me with the ever-familiar, "You've got mail." Those were always welcome words. I'm sure there was a scientific explanation, some endorphin release or such. All I know is it made me giddy thinking someone had sent me a note.

HEY, AGAIN!

I was still skimming the Crate and Barrel coupon email when an IM popped up. It was RAL2027. Two days in a row? We'd gone a couple years between conversations, then months, and now he was chatting on back-to-back days? Interesting.

HEY, RYAN. WHATCHA UP TO?

NOTHING, REALLY. BORED. GOOFING OFF. U?

NADA. JUST WORKED OUT AND ATE.

We'd chatted for an hour before I realized how much time had passed. Losing an hour like that wasn't unusual when I had five or six chat windows going at once, but to spend an hour talking to only one guy was…unexpected.

Ryan read my mind.

WE'VE BEEN CHATTING FOR OVER AN HOUR AND YOU HAVEN'T MADE ONE SEXUAL REFERENCE.

IS THAT ALLOWED ON HERE? HA HA.

ARE YOU ASKING ME TO TALK DIRTY TO YOU? I was proud of that twist.

That wasn't exactly what I meant, but feel free. I'm a big boy.

Oh, really? How big?

OMG, now I'm blushing.

I'd really enjoyed our conversation to this point, but the sheer cuteness of his response made me grin.

Then I thought about our past chats. We'd never once talked about anything sexual. He was right. That *was* out of the norm. I liked to get naughty as much as the next guy, but in that moment, the fact we hadn't even mentioned sex struck me as really cool.

I'll never be sure if it was my tiny angel or devil guiding me, but I decided to ask Ryan to meet. As I started to type, I heard a ding.

We should meet—for real.

Holy shit. He'd beaten me to the punch.

I wasn't intimidated by the idea of meeting in person. I'd met plenty of guys from online, either for coffee or dinner, or just to hook up—okay, *mostly* to hook up. What can I say? Let a preacher's kid off his leash and watch out. I had years of repressed time to make up for.

"Darn right. *Repressed* doesn't even begin to describe what you were." My leather-clad demon appeared with a dramatic puff on my shoulder. For some reason, his tiny vest was splayed open and his chest looked oiled. Is an imaginary conscience supposed to lube himself up before offering guidance?

Why was I nervous about meeting this Ryan guy? Technically, we'd been chatting online for years, though we'd actually lost touch throughout most of that time. Still, it felt like we'd been chatting for a long time. His conversations were comfortable and easy, and if his stats were accurate, he was a tasty morsel. It seemed so silly for me to get the jitters now. I laughed at my own silliness and sucked in a breath before pecking at the keys again.

WE'VE BEEN CHATTING A WHILE ON HERE. SURE. WOULD BE NICE TO MEET.

NOW?

UH, SURE. WHERE?

YOU KNOW THE CARIBOU COFFEE IN MIDTOWN?

I remembered passing it dozens of times as I wandered around town, but would still need to look up directions. I didn't want him to know I was a complete idiot when it came to getting around.

YOU BET. SEE YOU IN TEN?

PERFECT. I'LL BE THE GUY IN THE BLUE SHIRT.

AWESOME. SEE YOU SOON.

I GOT TO THE COFFEE SHOP FIRST. UNSURE WHAT TO DO, I grabbed a booth and waited for a dude in a blue shirt with blond hair who was about my height. That wasn't exactly a Columbo-level description, but it would have to do. My fingers wouldn't stop fiddling with each other. The place was busy, and customers entered and exited in a blur of caffeine-induced perpetual motion. Every time the little bell attached to the door tinkled, my head snapped up, hoping to get a first glance.

Then I realized I'd broken the most sacred law of online dating.

Always, always, *always* get a picture—or several—in different settings, if possible, using different angles, and with a newspaper to verify the date and authenticity.

Yes, I was a bit of an online dating freak.

I'd done *none* of that with Ryan.

I had no idea what he really looked like and was sitting there anxiously awaiting his grand entrance. For all I knew, he could be eighty, bald, and have three horns poking out of his head. Alright, he wouldn't have the horns, but you get my drift. I knew nothing—and any self-respecting gay knows his first job *is* to judge the book by its cover. How could I do that when I hadn't ever seen the book? Ryan's profile was woefully bereft of stars, much less the special circled kind, because I'd been derelict in my AOL trolling duties.

My nervousness grew as I pondered how careless I'd been.

"Three creams and one Splenda, right?"

I jolted out of my seat, banging my knees on the bottom of the table and knocking myself back onto the booth. When I looked up, my blond blind date had an amused grin on his face and a cup of coffee in each hand. He set the cups down.

"Hi, I'm Ryan."

Yes, you are, I thought.

His online description, though sparse, had been accurate. It had, however, left out the crystal blue-gray eyes that twinkled down at me. Paired with his blond hair and broad smile, they were dreamy, almost wolf-like. I thought he was handsome; Normal Hot, not Hollywood Hot. Cover models might make great pin-ups, but Ryan's ordinary good looks were endearing, somehow more real than so much of the perfection I'd seen walking around Atlanta.

His profile had specified 16a, meaning his arms were sixteen inches when measured with tape—but that stat never sank in. I needed a visual—and his biceps gave me more than an eyeful. Sixteen inches never looked so good.

Now, stop that. Sixteen inches *down there* is unreasonable—unless you're Catherine the Great's horse.

"Uh, hey. I'm Michael. How'd you know how I like my coffee?"

Yes, that was the first thing I said to him. I am a total moron.

He shrugged and dropped into the chair across from me. "You mentioned it a while back, maybe a year ago."

Holy crap. How did he remember a detail like that from an online conversation we had a year ago? Did he have a secret notebook too?

"Do I look okay?" he asked.

I'd finally gotten over the knee-bumping incident enough to return to my smart-ass self. I scanned him up and down with an exaggerated gaze.

"Yeah, I suppose you'll do—for coffee."

He chuckled and raised his cup in salute, then took a drink. "Not bad yourself."

I blushed and ducked my head. "Thanks."

We'd arrived around four thirty in the afternoon. When the clock chimed seven times, Ryan glanced at his watch and let out a long sigh.

"I can't believe we've been here this long. I need to get home. Tomorrow's a school day."

We walked to the parking lot together and leaned awkwardly against one of the building's pillars, staring at each other.

"I can't remember the last time I talked to someone for so long and didn't want to escape halfway through." He smiled sheepishly and tiny divots appeared. The man had dimples to go with the sparkling eyes. I fought back a swoon.

"Yeah, I had a great time," I said.

"Okay, I really gotta go. See you online later?"

I nodded. He leaned forward, then pulled back, then stretched out a hand and patted my arm. Yeah, it was totally awkward, but in a weird way it was perfectly suited to our coffee date.

13

HI, BARRIER!

The next day, Connie bounded into my office, her endless energy and infectious smile overpowering my non-morning-person desire to smack the life out of her cheery disposition.

"We need to do a sales contest. My team is bored with the comp plan, and I think we can use something like this to make people *like* working here for a change."

"Okay. What did you have in mind?"

She plopped into a chair and scooted it forward so she could rest her elbows on my desk. "I have no idea. We need to brainstorm, but I have a team meeting in five minutes, and the afternoon is back-to-back."

"I guess we could get together after work. Today is my off-gym day."

"Perfect. It's a date." She winked and hopped up from her chair. "You can drag me to one of those gay bars you told me about last week."

And with that crazy seed planted, she vanished.

At five thirty, she reappeared in my doorway. "Stop working. We have brainstorming and gay gawking to do!"

I couldn't decide if her enthusiasm for this little adventure amused or scared me. Connie and I had been to lunch countless times over the month or so we'd been working together. She'd become my closest friend and confidant, but taking her to a gay bar was uncharted territory. Hell, other than Dwayne, I'd never taken anyone else—unless you counted the boys I had escorted *out* of the bars.

No, they didn't count.

It felt like I was about to expose a part of my life I'd kept carefully segregated from every other part. It sounds silly now, but at the time, that thought was terrifying. Would she still see me the same way after an hour with me in the gays' natural habitat? Would she still respect me? Would our working relationship change? Would our friendship?

Poof. "You're overthinking and not giving *her* enough credit. Go, have fun. Drool over the boys. Maybe have a drink—something *other* than a Coke for a change." The devil had changed out of his leather and donned a sharp blue suit with a crisp white shirt and tastefully patterned tie. His raven hair was slicked back and somehow his eyes sparkled the color of emeralds.

Damn, even my devil was starting to look hot to me. I really needed therapy.

Not to be outdone, the angel appeared. He now wore a Catholic priest-like robe, but in white, like the Pope. "For once, I agree with Sparky over there—except for the part about what you drink. Coca-Cola is perfectly respectable and pleasantly fizzy. Stay on the path, Michael."

Was that encouragement or a lesson?

With another poof, they vanished, and I realized Connie was still standing in my doorway watching me. One brow was raised, her lips were turned up in an odd quirk, and her arms were crossed beneath her ample boobs, both of which were staring at me with their one good eye through her white shirt.

"Alright," I said, stuffing a folder into my desk drawer and locking it. "Let's do this."

CONNIE AND I GIGGLED ACROSS THE TABLE AT COWTIPPERS, tossing out one crazy idea after another. Some were actually serious and went on her list, scrawled in meticulous handwriting that made my illegible scribble look more like the ramblings of a third grader than a professional adult. I watched her write a long description and smiled as I realized how close we'd become in such a short time. She was the kindest, most positive person I'd met in years. She smiled easily and brought laughter into every room she entered. You could *feel* her walk into a room. It was a special gift I'd only known a few to possess. On top of all that, she made me laugh so much my side hurt—and no topic was safe from her sharp wit.

I switched into full salesman mode. "We need to do something big. Ted thinks waving a stack of Benjamins around will get the team fired up, but that only works on a few of them. We've got to capture their imagination as much as their competitive spirit."

She thought a moment, then came a twinkle in her eyes that told me something amazing was about to come out of her mouth. "What's more magical than a trip to Paris?"

"Okay, I'm listening."

"Think about it. The Eiffel Tower, the Arc de Triomphe, the Louvre—even simple scenes of people eating at outdoor cafés while tourists stroll by. Everything about

Paris screams sexy and exciting. We can decorate the whole office in French flags and banners."

She propped her body up and tucked her legs under her butt, then leaned forward on the table and giggled. Thirty minutes later, we had a fully baked plan to present to Ted, complete with a budget, decoration layout for the office, and a sketch of flyers we would create detailing the rules. She let her legs drop and settled her butt back onto the booth, excitement ebbing as I paid for dinner.

"Okay, that's done. Where are you taking me now?" she asked in the eager voice of a teenage girl who was out past curfew.

I chuckled. "It's Monday at seven o'clock. The only place with any crowd will be Blake's."

"Look at you, already knowing which bar is busy when."

"Yeah. It's part of a new gay's compulsory training."

She laughed and levered herself out of the booth. "Awesome. Let's go, my knight in rainbow armor."

Arm in arm, we laughed our way to the car, then drove the few blocks to Atlanta's most famous stand-and-model bar. It was exactly as I'd expected: sparsely filled with a handful of gaggles clustered in twos and threes, either at the bar or around high-top tables scooched against walls. Connie grabbed a table while I flirted with the bartender and ordered drinks. I returned a moment later and presented her with a Sex on the Beach, then set my Coke down in front of my stool.

"Oh no you don't. Go back up to that hottie behind the bar and get a real drink. It's rude to make a lady drink alone." I followed the line of her index finger to find the grinning bartender. He gave me a wave.

"Fine. You win. Be right back."

When I returned, Jack had joined my Coke. Then the interrogation began.

"So, how did coffee go with Ryan?"

She never forgot *anything*.

We'd had to complete a form a few weeks back that required my social security number. She had written it *one* time and could still recite it. That was impressive *and* scary. I shouldn't have been surprised she remembered the random online coffee date's name.

"It was fine."

She cocked her head as she sipped her drink, then giggled at how strong it was.

"Fine? That's all I get? I ask you to take me to Paris and you drive me to Decatur?"

"Hey! Decatur has charm. Have you been downtown?"

She rolled her eyes. "Go on. Out with it. I want details."

There was no escaping her steely glare. "He's nice. I hadn't seen a pic before we met, so I really didn't know what to expect. He works out a lot—I could see that in his arms and how his chest filled out his shirt. He's blond. That's new for me. I usually like guys with dark hair, more Italian or Latino—but he's handsome. He has weird lips. The bottom one kind of pooches out." I made an attempt at mimicking Ryan's lower lip, and she cackled.

"What did you talk about?"

"Oh, wow. A lot. We talked for a few hours."

Her right brow shot up. "A few hours? For coffee?"

I nodded.

"That's a lot of talking for a first date."

"Yeah, it was—and it was easy. You know how sometimes it's a struggle to keep a conversation going with someone new, to think of something to say to fill the awkward spaces? There wasn't a single moment of dead space to fill. It felt good. He seems like a really nice guy."

She threw back the last of her drink, and I knew I was in trouble. She was getting tipsy.

"When are you seeing him again?"

"I don't know." I shrugged. "He's nice and all, but I wasn't blown away—and I'm still fresh meat, as Dwayne would say. I can't tie myself down before I see what else might be on the menu." I raised my cup. "Plus, there's something odd I can't put my finger on with him. We'll talk for hours on AOL, several days in a row, then he'll disappear for a week. Before I moved here, he vanished for over a year. By the time he resurfaced, I'd forgotten who he was."

"Everyone doesn't live on that dumb computer. You could get out and meet people in person."

"I am. I go out almost every Friday and Saturday night —haven't missed *meeting* a guy yet." I winked and stood to get us another round. "Something feels weird with Ryan, though. I don't know. Maybe *I'm* being weird."

She laughed. "That's *definitely* not a first."

We had two more rounds. Connie switched to water with lime for her third drink, but insisted I needed to keep going with the stronger stuff. She was enjoying the insanity that tumbled out of my mouth when I was well lubricated. Midway through that third drink, the lights in the bar dimmed and loud music boomed. A drag queen standing over six feet tall, wearing high heels and a headdress that added another couple feet of height, sauntered into the room with a microphone in her hand. Guys streamed in from every entrance until they were crammed shoulder to shoulder. An irreverent monologue of jokes and jibes was followed by familiar, upbeat songs that had every gay in the place singing along and waving their hands in the air.

Connie laughed the entire time. I thought she was going to hyperventilate—or piddle. My alcohol-induced giggle wasn't much better and fed off her perpetual, childlike laughter. We were a complete mess and loving every minute of it.

After the show, she drove my car back to Cowtippers. She cackled every time my head swiveled and I pointed out the next hot guy walking down the street.

"You're gonna hurt your neck one of these days," she quipped.

"Ooh, look at that one!" I pointed excitedly at a dude jogging shirtless. His chiseled chest bounced with every stride. I made a *boingy-boingy* sound in time with his foot-falls. "Daaaaaaamn."

She playfully slapped my arm. "I swear you'd think a road sign was hot."

On cue, we passed a construction crew erecting wooden horses to block pedestrian traffic on the sidewalk. I snapped my head dramatically and said, "Hi, barrier!"

She snorted, and we both fell into another tear-filled fit.

14

PUTT-PUTT IS REAL GOLF

Ted approved our proposal the next day, and we scheduled a rollout meeting for the sales and recruiting staff on Thursday. Connie could barely contain herself. We hit every party store we could find, grabbing everything in the iconic blue, white and red. By the time Thursday arrived, every desk had a miniature French flag, there was bunting draped throughout the office, and French music greeted employees as they entered our suite. I have to give her credit; Connie's enthusiasm was even more infectious than her laugh. The troops were pumped before the meeting even began, and exploded in applause and cheers as she revealed the grand prize.

Connie and I were already well liked by our teams. Ted ruled with an iron fist and didn't understand how to motivate people. Connie and I genuinely cared about them, and that made all the difference. Throw in a chance to go to Paris, and we became instant rock stars.

Each day of the contest, we passed out a different French-themed goodie. One day it was cookies, the next croissants, then buttons with French colors. It generated so much buzz that groups would gather in the mornings to await whatever the day's surprise would be. Connie insisted we sing our surprise one morning. I'm pretty sure the troops wanted their money back from that concert.

We also crafted daily prizes so everyone could win something, even if they fell behind in the main horse race. Those contests became the backbone of growth for our sales campaign, with the bulk of my salespeople clearly out of the hunt for Paris.

In a matter of weeks, the monotonous rhythm that pervaded the office had been replaced by playful French accents and shouts of "Oh là là" when someone made a sale. It was silly and crazy, but brilliant. Connie was a miracle worker, and we were great partners.

We were so busy that first week that I hardly thought about Ryan. I barely even logged on to AOL.

Friday, after a painful workout, I flopped into my wobbly office chair and powered up my PC. AOL's normally friendly voice seemed annoyed at the volume of emails stacked up in my queue, growling "You've got mail" as the hourglass flipped.

Deep in the pile were two emails from Ryan.

TUESDAY 9:47 P.M.

HEY. JUST WANTED TO SAY I REALLY ENJOYED COFFEE. HOPE YOU'RE HAVING A GOOD WEEK.

RYAN

I MOVED DOWN THE LIST AND OPENED THE SECOND.

·　·　·

Wednesday 9:29 p.m.

Hey again. Just realized I never sent you a pic. Enjoy.

R

The emails were innocuous enough, and I was flattered he'd thought about me. It was more than I could say. I liked him fine, but just didn't feel that burning passion after we'd met. Maybe that was a good thing. Maybe we're supposed to be a little less *enthused* and more intellectually intrigued. I don't know. After my introduction to gay intimacy by Fly Boy and his silk ties, I knew I wanted passion, but I also wanted to be challenged with good conversation.

Was it too much to ask for both?

"Yes, moron. Just let Little Michael drive the car, and we'll all be fine." The devil appeared, in fishnet stockings and a pink leotard. That was new. How could I take his counsel seriously when he dressed like that?

"You're growing, Michael. I'm proud of you." The angel's soothing voice flowed into my other ear. He materialized on my shoulder in a shimmering white three-piece suit with a golden tie. He looked like he was ready to host a game show, but maybe that's what heaven really was—one big, cosmic game show.

I shook my head free of the lace and glitter. "Guys, I'm not really interested in Ryan, okay?"

The devil huffed something inaudible, then vanished. The angel actually laughed as he winked out. Weird.

I clicked the little paperclip, and a headshot of Ryan filled the screen. It looked like his work ID picture. He was handsome enough, even if his lower lip pooched out oddly.

I stared at it for a second, rotating the pic ninety degrees to see if it changed. Nope. It was still poochy. For a successful dude, he really didn't have any online dating game. Who sends a stiff, fully clothed pic that doesn't extend below the shoulders? I closed his pic and moved on.

When the rest of my overstuffed inbox proved as disappointing as Ryan's pic, I decided it was time to see what other fish the Atlanta sea might have to offer. I pulled up the list of rooms, beginning with AtlantaM4M, and searched for one I hadn't entered before.

Ding.

Hey. You're back.

He had a quick trigger finger—and his IM let me know he'd added me to *his* friends list too. That made me smile. Who doesn't love a little flattery?

Hey, yourself. How was your week?

Good. Busy at the office. I worked until 8 or so most days.

Ouch, I said. That sounds painful.

I'm used to it. We have people overseas, so I have to do calls during their workday hours. It makes for a late night.

I scrolled through chat rooms, not really paying attention to our conversation.

I have an idea.

When he didn't elaborate, I typed, Okay, fire away.

When's the last time you played putt-putt?

Well, that was random. I clicked the chat rooms closed. Now he had my attention.

Umm, I don't remember. Years. Maybe since I was a kid.

You're still a kid.

Ha Ha. Smart ass, Grandpa. How old are you anyway? You never told me.

That's me, a smart ass;) So, putt-putt with me tomorrow?

When I didn't answer right away, he added, I have to warn you. I used to play semi-pro golf. You won't win, but it should be fun watching you try.

That little bitch.

Oh, it's on now. Bring your clubs or whatever you need, old man. You're going down.

I was hoping you'd say that eventually.

Ha. I'm talking putt-putt.

Yeah, right. Just don't get your hopes up. You're still going to lose.

We agreed on a time and place, then he logged off, claiming he had another work call or something—on a Friday night. Something still felt weird, but I loved a challenge, and his playful banter was on point. I had to admit, Ryan made me smile.

"Told ya," my white-suited friend said as he puffed into existence, hands planted firmly on his hips in the teapot pose. "Keep an open mind. I have a good feeling about this one."

The devil, back in his black biker leathers, leaned in front of my chin and stuck his tongue out at the angel. "Just get some dick and move on. You're too young to get tied down—unless you're getting *tied up*."

Those two really needed therapy.

The next morning, after a tumbler of coffee and two packets of cherry frosted Pop-Tarts, I tossed on my Nashville Rocks T-shirt and a pair of khaki shorts and headed to the course—okay, the putt-putt place. I'd never been on a real golf course, but I was pretending this was the Masters, complete with a green jacket waiting for me after I nailed the clown face on the last hole.

I didn't have any expectations built up for the date. My recollection of Ryan was of a nice, handsome-enough guy who held down a good conversation. I hadn't been particularly smitten, and looked at the day as a fun time with a friend more than a date. The thrill of competition against a cocky opponent was more rooted in my mind than, well, his root—or anything else about him.

I pictured the end-of-day scene in my mind:

Park attendants wearing green polo shirts were lined up and clapping, while the nerdy, bespectacled manager helped me put the winner's jacket on for the first time. Thousands of fans lined the green—okay, tens and tens of people lined the game room—all smiling and applauding, amazed at my unparalleled golfing prowess. They'd even play 'Eye of the Tiger' in the background. Nothing said crushing victory like a *Rocky* theme. Ryan was standing off to the side, a mix of jealousy and disappointment on his face as his embarrassing defeat sank in.

It was a beautiful scene. I might've even shed a tear at the end.

Who needed therapy now?

I pulled into the parking lot, surprised to find it nearly empty on a Saturday. So much for my poetic scene with the dozens of applauding fans. I parked beside Ryan's silver Honda and walked through the main gate to the hut where guests purchased tickets for golf or go-karts. Ryan was standing a few feet from the hut. He waved, and I nearly tripped over a curb.

When we'd first met at Caribou, Ryan wore sensible, business casual clothing; a polo shirt and khaki pants. I don't know what I expected that day at putt-putt, but it wasn't a neon yellow tank top—you know, the kind the muscle heads at the gym wear with the stringy shoulder straps and deeply cut sides? The wind was blowing lightly, billowing his shirt so I could see his perfectly cut abs and protruding chest through the sides. He smiled, beaming perfect pearly whites at me. His blond hair, something I'd never found terribly attractive, blew in the wind—yes, like Marilyn's dress—and I swear the sun behind him cast a glow.

In that sun-blind moment, I knew I was in trouble. My heart raced, and I immediately worried English would be my second language if I tried to speak. What was happening? I wasn't even that interested in this guy.

I looked up and *holy shit*, he was beautiful. No, he was stunning. Striking? Fucking hot.

Where had *that* come from? My brain, heart, and Little Michael—all of them—were rebelling and going in a direction I hadn't anticipated. Today was about crushing the opposition, not ogling him.

"Hey, you okay?"

Ryan gripped my arm to help me from my near-tumble. His skin against mine sent a wave of fire up my arm and into my already turbulent chest. I glanced up and our eyes met.

"Yeah, I, uh, thanks. I tripped. I'm good."

He smiled and kept his hand on my arm as we walked to the hut—long after I'd righted myself and no longer needed help. I reveled in his touch, in his hand staying connected. My mind spun.

"Grab your balls," Ryan said, pulling me out of my—whatever that was.

"What? My—"

He rolled his eyes and chuckled, then grabbed a club and pretended to swing it, measuring the balance or something. I watched the way he gripped and swung with practiced ease and knew my dream of a green jacket was in as much jeopardy as any thought of not being attracted to Mr. Sexy Chest. I grabbed the first club I saw and a blue ball.

He started laughing.

"What?"

"I'm not sure which is funnier, you picking the kids' club or declaring your blue balls in public."

I looked down. The club was short. No, it was *tiny*, sized for a child of six or so. Then I glanced at the ball in my hand and caught on to his joke.

"Just don't want you feeling overconfident," I said, then quickly replaced the club with an adult version. On a whim, I grabbed a black ball and held it up for him. He raised a brow. "It's symbolic of the death of your pride, Mr. Semi-Pro."

He barked a laugh. "We'll see about that. You don't know what you've signed up for today."

He had no idea how true that was.

ON TWO OUT OF THE FIRST THREE HOLES, RYAN PUTTED A hole-in-one. If he hadn't been so cute, the smug smirk twisting his poochy lip might've been annoying. He clearly knew his way around a golf club, and I was beginning to think all my smack talk was going to bite me in the butt—and not in the fun way.

By the midpoint, which Ryan proclaimed "the turn," he was ahead by more than ten strokes.

"You can concede at any point. I won't think less of you."

I rolled my eyes dramatically and pointed my club at him. "I'm about to get a very different ball in with this club, mister. Your turn."

He snickered. "Testy, testy."

"Testy-cle is what you risk by not taking your turn."

He laughed, eyeing me for a moment before turning to line up his next shot. Hole ten was based on blind luck. There were two tunnels on the side of a faux mountain. One dribbled down to a very likely hole-in-one. The other took the ball into a hellscape of obstacles, including a water trap that was clearly marked "three-stroke penalty" in creepy Halloween font. The real twist in this guessing game was that the paths through the mountain were hidden. There was no way to walk the course and see which hole led where.

I see you snickering. Get your mind out of the gutter!

Like the unfortunate dude in *Indiana Jones and the Temple of Doom,* Mr. God-Given Golfer chose poorly. He stroked his putt and the ball *swooshed* through the right-side hole without hitting the sides. We ran around the mountain, giggling like five-year-olds, then waited impatiently as the ball rattled around and plopped out into the desert of doom, bouncing off several obstacles, then creeping its way to the edge of the water hazard. Ryan bent over and pretended to blow on it, desperate to keep it dry. I called foul at his antics and hopped with glee as the ball finally splashed into the water.

"Plus three! I need the judge to mark that down." I did a happy dance to rub it in.

He play-shoved me. "You're still *way* behind, young man. Go take your turn."

"Yes, Dad."

His shove became a tad less playful at that.

"Now, now. No abusing your far younger companion."

I hopped away before the next shove could land.

Going second on that hole was a huge advantage. I tapped my ball down the left-side path and danced a jig as it fell out of the mountain and rolled directly into the cup.

"One!"

He gave me a mini-clap, tapping his fingertips primly against his other palm like an aristocratic lady. "Bravo. About time you got one."

"Oh, I'm just warming up. All those other holes were just to make you feel good."

And another shove, this time with a squeeze of my bicep. I looked up from his hand to find him smiling appreciatively. I couldn't think of a single smart-ass thing to say.

"Alright, let me show you how to get out of a mess." He turned to retrieve his ball from the drink.

Five strokes—and one more trip to the pond later—the overall tally was dead even.

"I believe we now have a race, good sir." I smirked and squeezed his bicep like he'd done mine. It didn't budge.

Damn. Like, really. *Damn.*

"Don't hurt your hand," he said with a grin.

Again, my brain and mouth failed to communicate. I stammered something unintelligible and released his arm —reluctantly.

By the time we reached the final hole, Ryan was no longer laughing and shoving. He was all game face. I was giddy just to still be in it. We had traded holes-in-one following the mountain, leaving the score tied going into the dreaded clown face. Despite my big talk, I'd fully expected Ryan to wipe me off the course—but I actually had a shot at winning. He'd *never* live that down.

He squatted down and raised his club, taking in the lay of the land.

"This is mini-golf, not the Masters," I chirped from the side.

"Hush. I'm working over here." His head never turned, but I could see a hint of a smile crack his serious composure.

After the longest non-caddie-assisted pre-putt in the history of golf, his club struck. The ball rolled perfectly down the center of the turf, expertly missing the windmill's sails, and directly into the clown's gaping jaw.

"Hole-in-one! Top that," Ryan hooted, club raised in salute to the crowd that hadn't gathered.

I ignored the obvious sexually laced quip dying to fly off my tongue, and tried to act confident as I strode up to the tee. He brushed his shoulder against mine as he moved to watch. A hint of sweet cologne added a heady sensation to the thrill of his touch. I fought back a swoon and focused on the spinning windmill.

Just to be a smart ass, I squatted down and mimicked his lay-of-the-land thing, having no idea what I was looking for. He grunted—or laughed—I couldn't tell. I straightened, took a slow draw, and struck. He raced up beside me and watched as my ball followed the same perfect line his had traversed moments before—then smacked into one of the windmill's sails and bounced to the side. It dribbled back up the green to stop a foot in front of us.

Stupid traitor ball.

My head dropped dramatically, and Ryan rubbed my shoulder in consolation.

"There, there. You put up a great fight."

"Down to the last hole." I grinned up. "Bet you didn't think it would be that close."

He shook his head. "I really didn't."

We walked around the evil clown and his dastardly windmill to the hut to return our clubs. The sun was shining brightly above in a crystal-clear sky. We squinted in the glare.

"So…" he started.

We walked away from the hut toward the parking lot. I waited to see if he'd continue.

"That was a lot of fun."

"Yeah, it was," I agreed.

He stopped walking. "Want to grab lunch? I think there's a restaurant inside."

"Sure. Who knew golf could make ya work up such an appetite?"

"It's an athletic sport," he said.

I rolled my eyes and grinned. "Right, especially with clowns and windmills."

"Just 'cause you came in second—"

"Lord, you're going to remind me of that for years, aren't you?"

"If you're lucky." He grinned.

My head snapped up. I didn't think he meant what came out. He was just bantering and teasing—but he'd said it. His eyes told me he knew what he'd said, and he wasn't apologizing for it.

Unable to think, I said the only thing that came to mind. "Lunch?"

15

POOL PARTY

We wandered inside the entertainment complex's entrance, greeted by the bings and bongs of the video arcade at the far end of the massive room. A left turn led us into a restaurant decorated like a 1950s café, complete with slick, faux-leather booths framed in highly polished silver. Bouncy music played over crackly speakers.

The lights were dimmed, except for one tiny section of four tables brightly lit by neon wall decorations. The only sign of life in the place was a lone server bent over a dog-eared book at the counter. She didn't notice us walk in, and Ryan had to stand in front of her to get her attention, a move that startled the poor woman. His shoulders shivered with laughter as she nearly jumped out of her pink apron. Her book flew across the floor, and I grinned when Ryan knelt to retrieve it—both because of the way his lats and triceps flexed in his skimpy tank, and at his simple act of chivalry.

Chicken sandwiches and fries appeared to be the safest things on the menu, and despite being the only customers, they took a painfully long time to arrive. We barely noticed. Conversation flowed as if we'd known each other for a lifetime. One story led to a memory or snarky jibe, then streamed directly into some other tale or question or thought. Being with Ryan was easy and felt…good.

Did that even make sense on a second date? Was I *completely* insane?

"Yes, you are," the angel said on my shoulder, this time dressed in a white polo shirt with white-and-tan checkered golf pants popular in the 1930s. "But falling in love *is* insane, Michael. It's beautifully insane, and you'll never make sense of it. Just enjoy the moment, and follow your heart."

I was shocked to hear encouragement from the one usually yanking hard on my leash.

Then the devil appeared on the other shoulder dressed in tight, shiny faux leather and high heels. His whip cracked against my neck.

"Hey!"

He grinned. "Shut up and listen. For once, that angelic windbag has a point—but there's more to this dude than hot tits and arms. Something feels *off*, and I like that. Let's get him naked."

"Easy," the angel said, poking me with a tiny golf club I hadn't seen. "Take your time. If he's right, he'll be right tomorrow. Just enjoy the ride."

"Ha. He said 'ride.' That's *exactly* what I want you to do."

I shook my head clear, and the annoying little trolls vanished. When I looked up, Ryan was staring at me with a bemused set to his poochy lip.

"Penny," he said.

"Huh?"

"For your thoughts. I lost you there for a second. First time today."

My lips curled upward at that.

"Sorry, the voices in my head get into arguments sometimes, and I have to break them up."

He laughed at what he assumed was a joke. Somewhere in the back of my head, I heard the devil laughing too.

Ryan reached across the table. A bolt of lightning streaked from my fingers to my soul at his touch—his first real touch. He took my hand in both of his.

"I like your voices, Michael Reed. All of them." His crystal eyes stared into me, and I felt the café tilt.

What did one even say to that?

I smiled weakly and looked down at our hands. "Thanks. Me too. I mean, I don't like my own voice, or voices. Well, I do. They're funny sometimes, but that's not what I meant. I like your voice. That's what I meant."

His lips parted wide, and his eyes smiled even wider, if that was even a thing. I couldn't tell if he was more amused at my stammering or pleased that we seemed to be on the same page. I hoped it was the latter.

He sat back, stealing his hands from mine. It felt like the world had been pulled from my grasp.

The server arrived, and Ryan insisted on paying for lunch. It was about two o'clock now, and I figured this would be when we said our goodbyes.

I wasn't ready for goodbye.

"You like pool?" he asked with mischief in his voice.

I cocked my head. "Uh, sure. I guess."

He pointed across the café. "There's a table over there. I'm pretty good, but who knows? You might get lucky. Want to try for a little post-golf revenge?"

He wasn't saying goodbye.

I felt like a ten-year-old walking into a toy store. It was awesome.

"Bring it. I owe you *and* that clown."

He laughed. "Oh, so now I'm colluding with the clown? Is that how it went?"

"The clown, the kid with the clubs, pretty much everyone over there was on your side. I was lucky to keep things close. Now you're on your own, bucko. Just you, me, and the balls."

He barked another laugh as I turned four shades of red.

"The *pool* balls, dirty man."

"Don't forget my massively long cue. You can chalk the tip if you want."

I missed a step, and the crimson deepened. What the hell? I'd been tied to a bedpost without blushing. Why were this guy's terrible innuendos turning me into a bumbling schoolboy? Every time I blushed, it *encouraged* him, like a vampire smelling blood.

Over the course of five games of eight-ball, the sexual references flew faster than the cue ball. I'm pretty sure I laughed—and blushed—the whole time.

But I won.

"That's three out of five, good sir. Do you concede defeat or shall we continue?" I bowed dramatically like some vassal greeting his lord.

He racked his stick and glanced at his watch. "Wow."

"What?"

"It's five o'clock. We've been here almost since this place opened. I probably should head home."

There was an odd hint in his voice, the same one I'd picked up in his instant messages. He wasn't saying *something*—and it felt important.

"Got a hot date later?" I prodded playfully.

He grinned and shook his head. "No, just some work to do around the house."

We racked the balls and walked past the cacophony of sounds blaring from the arcade out into the fresh air of the parking lot. When we reached our cars, Ryan leaned against his and shoved his hands halfway into his pockets.

One perfectly pink nipple peeked out of his tank top. I couldn't stop staring at it.

He glanced down, and realization dawned. With a smirk, he pulled his tank top back just enough to show half his ridiculously rounded pec.

I still couldn't look away. *Damn.*

His smirk turned into a chuckle. "This was one of my best dates ever," he blurted out.

I finally tore my eyes away—reluctantly. "Mine too. I had a blast."

"Even in defeat?"

"Hey, I won pool. That's far more challenging than some fake golf game."

He laughed. "We can take our golf onto a real course, if putt-putt wasn't to your liking."

I shook my head. "Nah. I'm good. I might make a good bag kid for you, but that's about it."

"Bag kid? You mean caddie?"

"Oh yeah, caddie. Right." *Idiot.* I blushed again.

He reached out and brushed my arm lightly with his fingers. My skin pimpled, and I shivered.

"I'd like to see you again. Is that okay?"

"I'd really like that too."

"I would kiss you, but we're in a public parking lot." He looked around meaningfully.

For you liberated gays who enjoy holding hands and kissing in public, that wasn't always an option. One might find himself on the receiving end of an egg, or worse, a baseball bat; at the very least, some harsh words. Even Ryan reaching across the table and taking my hand would've raised more than a few eyebrows in most parts of town. We were lucky our bored server sported a rainbow tattoo on the inside of her wrist and barely gave us a second glance.

Our eyes held each other for a long moment. It felt like an embrace, the intimacy of that gaze.

"Alright. See you online later?" he asked.

"Sure. Drive safe," I said as he climbed into his car.

His door slammed shut, then his window rolled down. "Worried about me already?" he asked with a poochy smirk.

I tried to say something witty, but my mouth wouldn't work, so I grinned and waved like a dork. He winked, and I watched him drive away until his car vanished beyond the building.

16

AFTERGLOW

When I got home, I tried to be productive, making it as far as wiping down the kitchen counters. An hour later, dishes were still stacked in the sink, and dirty laundry was still piled in the corner of my bedroom.

My cheeks were getting sore from the unbearable grin that had only grown throughout the evening. I could barely contain myself. The poor den carpet, desperate to avoid my frantic pacing, lay flatter than a dog's ears. All I could see when I closed my eyes were Ryan's lips, his perfect teeth, his nipple teasing me as it snuck out of his tank top. That made more than my heart stir.

Completely distracted and unable to focus on even the simplest task, I tossed the rag on the counter and bounded across the room. Dwayne answered my call after one ring. I told him to hang on a second and, without waiting for his response, pressed the button to add a third person. I'd never done a three-way call and I hoped I hadn't just lost him. It took Connie three rings to answer. Then I held my breath and clicked the button again to unite all of us in telephonic bliss.

I sat on the couch and took a long breath. "Dwayne, you there?"

"I'm here."

"Connie?"

"Hi, barrier," her perky voice sang through the receiver.

"Very funny. Connie, meet Dwayne. Dwayne, Connie."

"Hi, Connie," Dwayne said. "This is either really good or really bad for him to need us both."

Connie giggled. "He's way too bubbly for it to be bad —which means this should be juicy."

Dwayne snorted.

"Are you two done?"

"Sorry, forgot this was all about you," Dwayne chided playfully.

"Go on, little one. Out with it. What have you done?" Connie took on a slightly sarcastic, motherly tone.

"I'm very much *in like*. This one's special. I mean—"

"Hang on. Back up. Who are we talking about here?" Dwayne asked.

"Did you go on your golf date with Ryan?" Connie's voice was all bubbles and excitement, pretty much her norm.

"Ryan is his name, and yes, I just got home from our date."

"Just got home? Weren't you meeting him around eleven this morning?" I could *hear* Connie grinning.

"Who's Ryan?" Dwayne asked.

"I feel like a ping-pong ball," I said.

"Wait, I thought you said you played golf with him." Dwayne now sounded baffled.

Connie giggled.

"Alright, you two. Let me tell you my story and then

you can pummel me with questions. I knew getting you both on the phone was a bad idea."

Connie laughed again. "I think it's the best thing you've done all day—unless you got laid. That would definitely be the best thing, especially considering how big you thought Ryan's—"

"There was no getting laid!" Connie let out a mocking whimper at that declaration. I felt out of breath, and I'd hardly spoken.

"But he has a big cock?" Dwayne chimed in, no doubt realizing how flustered I was and loving every moment.

I let out a huff. "I have no idea how big his cock is. I've never seen it, except through his exceptionally tight jeans."

"Told you!" Connie perked back up.

"Yes, you did." I couldn't repress the smile she ignited. "Here's the short version. We met to play putt-putt. That was fun, even if he won on the last shot. Then he suggested we get lunch at the complex's café. After an hour or so, he challenged me to pool, which we played for a couple hours. He realized we'd been there all day and had to leave. We said goodbye in the parking lot, and I watched him drive off. That's it."

"Didn't you start this whole conversation with 'I'm going to marry him?' or some other nonsense?" Dwayne asked.

"Yeah, did he propose in the parking lot? When's the wedding? And when do we get to see

his—"

"Connie!"

"Wait. Did he get you a ring? I can't wait to see it! Is it huge? Or do you get a diamond-studded cock ring instead? I'm unclear on gay protocol for a proposal. I might enjoy seeing you try that on too."

"CONNIE!"

Dwayne was giggling uncontrollably now. This was hopeless.

I stood and began pacing, testing the limits of the phone's scrunchy cord.

"I don't know how I know. I just do. Ryan's amazing. We talked and laughed for hours without there ever being an awkward pause or anything. It felt like we'd known each other for years, like we were *supposed* to be together. I know that sounds nuts, but I can't remember ever feeling this before."

"Even with Carter?" Dwayne ventured.

A week ago, that name would've doused any possible exuberance. Following our breakup, it had taken weeks for me to talk about Carter and the boys without breaking down. He'd been special in a way only a first love could be; and those boys, they were *everything*.

But today, in the afterglow of the most magical, dreamy date ever, there was no blanket wet enough to douse my excitement.

"Carter was different. He was my first, and I didn't know what I was doing."

"And you do now?" Dwayne prodded.

"No, not really," I admitted. "But I *know* this is differ-ent. Everything about it *feels* different. I just left Ryan, and all I can think about is talking to him again."

"Huh," Dwayne grunted.

"Huh, what? That's never good."

"Talk? That's what you want to do with him again?"

"Yeah, I feel like I know so much about him from all our online chats, but every time we talk, I still learn so many new things. It's like unwrapping the sexiest, funniest, snarkiest present again and again—and each time it's a little different, and better."

"Dwayne?" Connie finally spoke again.

"Yeah?"

"This is bad. You know that, right? We might need an intervention," she said.

"Intervention? What are you talking about?" I asked.

Without missing a beat, Connie said, "He wants to *talk* with another gay man, and he hasn't even seen how big his—"

"Connie!"

"—cock is." She would *not* be deterred. "This coming from the guy who needs to oil the bearings in his neck from all the swiveling. Have you ever driven anywhere with him?"

Dwayne laughed.

I couldn't find words.

"I mean, really—if it's male and showing even a hint of skin, Periscope Michael is on it, locked and loaded. We can barely go fifty yards without him yelling, 'Ooh, look at that one,' or 'Did you see him?'"

"I can't help—"

"Zttt." She silenced me. "Let the grown-ups speak."

Dwayne fell into a fit of laughter, snorting through the phone.

"Something suspicious is going on with this Ryan guy." Connie went on. "Not once in this conversation have you talked about his arms or chest or butt—or anything physical. That's *very* unlike you, Michael Reed. In fact, I didn't think it was even possible. If I didn't know better, I'd suggest we drive to the emergency room right this minute to have your head examined. I'm afraid you may be *smitten*, and that's a very serious condition."

I let out an exasperated, slightly amused sigh. "That's what I've been *trying* to tell you."

17

LET THE GAMES BEGIN

I hung up the phone, torn between the giddy feeling that lingered from my date and the perpetual chuckle from the conversation with Connie and Dwayne. Either of them could plant a smile on my face. Together, they were a force of nature. But they both loved me and only wanted me to be happy. In Dwayne's case, paternalism might take that a step farther into 'what's best for me' territory, but the principle was the same. They were the best friends—no, the best *family*—I could ever imagine. I was lucky to have them in my life.

My stomach rumbled, and I realized it was well past dinner time. After a depressing search of my sparsely stocked kitchen, I drove to pick up some well-earned Chinese takeout. Nothing said "amazing date" like crab Rangoon.

Thirty minutes later, I was sitting in my den, oblivious to whatever show was on TV, lost in the bliss of cashew chicken and daydreams of Ryan bending over to putt. I closed my eyes, savoring a bite, and the curve of his taut lats peeking out the side of his tank top gave me a shiver.

My mental eye roamed up to his exposed chest and the glistening sweat my conscious mind hadn't registered earlier. Apparently, my unconscious mind had a better eye for detail. I wanted to lick that sweat so badly. I could taste the salt.

Wait, that was a cashew.

I threw myself back on the couch and realized I'd become hard just visualizing Ryan. That *never* happened. My motor needed to be primed—and touched—before it roared to life. The idea of an image, mental or otherwise, bringing Little Michael to full attention was unheard of. Out of stupid lizard-brain curiosity, I unbuttoned my jeans and pulled the zipper down. Lo and behold, Little Michael popped up faster than a Jack-in-the-Box. I chuckled at that thought, then realized the double entendre of *Jack*.

That made me harder.

Getting harder made me think about Ryan.

My hand, still greasy from the Rangoon, grazed the tip of my penis. It quivered. I closed my eyes and replayed every hole, imagining Ryan walking, bending, stretching, and flexing. His tank top blew in the breeze. A gust came along and somehow—in the way unexplained things happen in dreams—it vanished, leaving him standing bare chested, putter in hand.

I had my putter in hand too. Stroke after stroke.

I watched him squeeze the shaft of his club, gripping and releasing, sliding his hands up and down. He knelt to line up his shot and his jeans cupped his perfectly round ass. Blond hair blew in the breeze, and I could smell his musk, a delicious mixture of sweat, heat, and Irish Spring. Damn, those leprechauns knew how to make soap.

Satisfied, he stood, fiddling the club with his fingers, rubbing it, making it his. He *owned* that club. I felt him own it. I felt him own me, want me, love me. He needed me. I knew it. He had to have me, to stroke me, to stroke—

Then, without warning, he putted, and the ball shot through the clown's mouth—I mean, face—I mean, into the hole.

Dammit.

I had shot all over my cashew chicken.

If I hadn't been so turned on by the scene in my mind, I would've been horrified by the desecration of my favorite meal, but it was worth it. Ryan might not have realized it, but we'd just come together for the first time.

Alright, it was in my head, but in my own weird way, I was admitting to myself just how bad I had it for this guy.

Connie was right. I was *smitten.*

Spent, mentally and physically, my mind returned to the present. I stared up at the ceiling, grinning like an idiot, wishing Ryan had been there to take his shot for real.

Pick your entendre. I wanted them all, as long as they were his.

Saturday 9:51 p.m.

Hey you. I really had a great time today. That was supposed to be a quick round of putt-putt, but I couldn't stand the idea of going our separate ways so quickly. Thanks for giving me a whole day. You looked super sexy, by the way.

I have to go out of town tomorrow for work and will be gone all week. Can I see you next weekend?

Dinner, maybe? Pool rematch, since you crushed my hopes and dreams?

Let's talk online this week while I'm gone.

Thinking of you (and smiling).

Ryan

I really don't know how long I stared at the monitor, drinking in every word of that email. The goofy grin never left my face. Ryan was thinking about me—and wanted to see me again. That made my heart go into hyperdrive. This was real. I wasn't imagining things. This amazing, funny, smart, successful, insanely hot guy—with poochy lips—liked *me*.

I grinned wider, thinking about his lower lip protruding before him. It had seemed like such an annoying flaw when we'd first met, something that distracted from his other, more delicious qualities. Now, as I saw that lip in my mind's eye, my chest warmed. It was cute. It was part of him, something no one else had. I wanted to kiss that lip.

"Shit, you're sappy," I said to myself, chuckling at my own schmaltziness. "But you can't leave him hanging on such a great email. How does a smitten puppy respond without sounding so…smitten?"

Saturday 10:02 p.m.

Hey you back.

Today was one of the best dates I've ever had. Really. Putt-putt was a blast (even if you cheated on that last shot *chuckle*), and all the other stuff was fun too. I still can't believe we never run out of things to talk about. Is that normal?

What kind of business trip are you going on? Where will you be? Inquiring minds...

Yes, let's do dinner next weekend. And yes, let's IM and email. You make me smile.

Oh, did I mention that tank top was inducted into the Dating Hall of Fame? I was having naughty thoughts all night thanks to you. *Really* naughty thoughts. Way to ruin this righteous PK, mister *grin*.

Enough of that. Have a great trip. Can't wait to see you next week.

M

. . .

As I was rereading my email for the third time after sending it, giggling at my own cleverness, Mr. AOL announced, "You've Got Mail."

Ryan had replied.

I turned into a thirteen-year-old girl with her first school crush, hopping out of my chair and wiggling in a weird white-man happy dance before plopping back into the chair. I sat with my feet tucked under my butt and leaned toward the screen—as if his message would hop out and kiss me or something.

Saturday 10:03 p.m.

You had naughty thoughts about me? I love that. Why don't you do something about it? Unzip and take care of yourself thinking about me. That would be so hot.

I'm a Scorpio. I like it hot and hard. What can I say?

Enjoy yourself.

Ryan

I laughed as I read his message. If he only knew what I'd already done to my poor Chinese takeout in his name…

18

STOP THINK!ING

As the leaves of Atlanta began to turn, days at Think! started feeling like one long battle. Ted was an irritable boss, and his cadre of yes-men rarely challenged his holy word. Connie and I had been hired to change the culture within the sales and recruiting teams, but Ted undermined our progress by issuing ridiculous edicts born out of bad information or knee-jerk reactions.

"You're not going to believe what His Majesty did today."

Connie covered her mouth with a finger. "Shh. Not so loud."

"Sorry," I whispered. We were sitting in my office, but she had a point. The walls were thin.

"He made my entire team stand."

She quirked a brow. "Stand? You mean stand up?"

"Yeah, and *keep* standing. He said he'd been looking over the outbound call numbers and wasn't happy. He thinks the team's been lazy about making their dials."

"So he made them stand up? That doesn't make any sense."

"He didn't just make them stand up. He took away their chairs for the entire morning—from eight o'clock until lunch. They had to dial and talk while standing at their desks."

Her jaw dropped. "You're kidding."

"Nope. You want to know when I learned about this little exercise in idiocy?"

"Uh-oh."

"Traffic was a mess this morning, and I was a few minutes late. When I walked in, everyone was already on their feet. You should've seen the looks I got when I walked onto the sales floor."

"They're blaming *you*? You weren't even here when he did that."

I shrugged. "I don't know if they're really blaming me, but they look to me to shield them from him, to talk sense into him before he pulls shit like this. Before you and I came along, he'd do things like this almost daily."

She put her head in her hands. "He can't do this. It undermines everything we've been working for."

"Yeah, I know."

"Have you talked to him about it?"

"I tried. He blew me off, said he had appointments this morning. He suggested I join him and the boys for lunch."

She snorted. "You mean the daily lunch where they make all the decisions? The one I'm never invited to?"

"You and me both. And yes, *that* lunch." I blew out a breath. "I've been here, what, five months? Six? We haven't had a single management team meeting. Everything gets decided at lunch where neither of our teams are represented. We find out our marching orders later and have to clean up their mess."

We sat in silence staring at the surface of my dusty desk.

"I don't know how long I can keep doing this," I whispered, more to myself than to her.

She stood slowly. "Go to lunch. See if they'll listen. You've got to at least try."

I nodded. She was right, but I failed to see what difference it would make. Ted didn't listen to anyone other than Mark and Dennis. As Connie left my office, I realized how awkward that conversation must've been for her. She'd only been with the company for a couple months, and I was the person who brought her into the fold. We were equals, partners in leading the bulk of the company's employees, and she'd never seen me show anything other than an upbeat and positive attitude. What would she think now? The idea of my team suffering under Ted's stupidity drove me crazy, but the thought of letting Connie down stung deeper.

Mark's giant form darkened my door and snapped me out of my thoughts. "Hey, you look too serious. Come to lunch. I think the boss is buying barbecue."

Mark was a good guy. He rarely said a negative word, and was an incredible salesman. I had thought he'd take a back seat when he stepped out of management to focus on his own sales efforts, but Ted insisted he continue going to lunch every day. Not only was Ted making critical decisions at those lunches, but he also sought the input of his *former* sales manager rather than his current sales manager.

The last thing I wanted to do was to stink like barbecue, but I smiled and stood. "Sounds great, especially if it's on Ted."

Mark chuckled. "Absolutely. Come on. You can ride with me."

A LITTLE AFTER FOUR O'CLOCK, CONNIE STRODE INTO MY office and plopped into a chair.

"So, how was lunch? Love that new cologne you're wearing. What is it? Aux de Piggy?"

"Ha ha. Very funny." I sniffed my shirt and wrinkled my nose. "Argh. That's terrible."

She snorted.

"Lunch was about what you'd expect. The guys talked about nothing until the food came, then Ted launched into the numbers. He was *pissed* about the call stats. I tried to point out that our sales and net revenue numbers were breaking all-time records, but he wouldn't hear it. All he cared about was how many dials per day each salesperson made. At one point, Mark tried to back me up, but Ted blew him off. He threatened to make the entire team stand until every salesperson hits a hundred dials in the same day."

"What?" She sat back. "He can't do that. If we had an HR person, they'd go nuts. Besides, is that even possible, every person hitting a hundred?"

"Of course it's not. If they get a hot lead on the phone, that one call could take thirty minutes. The better sales-people spend most of their time on the phone, but only talk to a dozen or so people per day. If someone makes a hundred dials, they're either not reaching anyone, or they suck at closing. More dials won't fix either of those problems."

"What are you going to do?" she asked.

"I don't know." Without thinking, I started fiddling with a pen, clicking it over and over. "You've been here long enough to see how things are. Do you think he'll ever change?"

She thought a moment. "I don't know. Probably not. He built this place from scratch. He's proud of it—hell, he's just proud."

"That's an understatement." I rolled my eyes. "He deserves credit for getting this place to twenty million, but he'll never take it to the next level pulling crap like this. I had three of my team threaten to quit today if he made them stand again."

"Really?"

I nodded.

We both jumped at a knock on my door. It was Evan, one of my sales guys.

Connie craned her neck, then stood. "I'll let you deal with Skippy." That was her nickname for Evan. He was a strong closer, but had a quirky personality that always left me wondering if he'd stood a little too close to the microwave as a kid.

I chuckled. "Okay. Thanks for listening. Sorry to dump on you like this."

She waved me off and opened the door. "He's all yours," she said to Evan.

When Connie vanished down the hallway, Evan closed the door, sat on the edge of the chair, and leaned forward.

"I'm giving you my notice."

Shit. "Evan, you're one of my best guys, and you've only been here a few months. Why would you want to leave?"

He sat back and crossed his arms. "I won't stand and dial, or whatever lunacy Lord Think! comes up with next."

I raised my palms in surrender. "I know—"

"Everybody out there knows *you* didn't do this, that you would never do this, but we also know you can only talk so much sense into Ted. Those who've been around a lot longer than me say this is how he's always been. They don't think he'll ever change. I wouldn't be surprised if half the sales team left over the next few months." He sucked in a deep breath, then lowered his voice to a whisper. "Look, I didn't come in here to discuss this. My mind's made up. I'm leaving. The only question is whether you're coming with me or not."

I might've been raised by wolves, but I wasn't easily shocked—well, unless you counted the acrobatic positions and fetishes I was learning about on Manhunt or AOL—but those weren't on the agenda for this meeting. My jaw must've dropped to my desk because Evan was grinning from ear to ear.

"What, uh, you want me to—what?"

"I want you to come with me. Get out of this place. The old crowd is right. Ted's never going to change, and we can do better without him."

I barely knew what to think, much less say. "What are you talking about?"

"I found this company out west. They teach people how to be computer engineers, help them get their Microsoft certification. They're willing to give me the rights to sell in the eastern US. I'm a decent sales guy, but I don't know how to run a business. I need someone like you to make this work. I want you to be my business partner."

I stared at him, trying to see if he was pulling my leg— or setting me up. Ted had been known to test people like this. He called it "checking their loyalty."

Ted was such an asshole.

"Evan, I don't know what to say. I mean, I'm flattered you'd think of me, but—"

He threw up a hand, staving off my objections. "I get it. It's a lot to take in, and I caught you off guard. You don't need to make a decision right now. Let me get you the information on the company and the business plan I came up with. If you like what you see, we can talk more. We're not doing anything but talking about a hypothetical business transaction. Are you okay with that?"

I hesitated. What was I doing? This was nuts. Ted might be an ass, but he ran a successful, stable company. He'd given me a job the same week I'd moved to Atlanta. Hell, Think! was the reason I had a comfortable life in a new town I absolutely loved. And Evan was asking me to throw all that away, for what—a startup?

Then again, my time working with my dad taught me how much I enjoyed the independence of working for myself. Maybe owning a company with a partner would be a good thing.

Despite the churning in my gut, I looked up at him and nodded once. "Alright, but you can't give me your notice today. Don't do that until you're ready to leave and start this new thing. If I decide to join you, we'll have to figure out how to time things."

He smiled. "I'm good with that. Consider my resignation rescinded." He stood. "This is gonna be awesome. You'll see."

As soon as he vanished from my doorway, I grabbed the phone and dialed Connie's extension. "Emergency dinner. Now."

She laughed. "Did you see another barrier? Are we going to say hi to it?"

I couldn't hold back my own laugh. "Yeah, a big one— just not the kind you're thinking."

———

"Are you really considering this?" Connie asked between sips of pinot grigio. Why she put ice cubes in wine baffled me. I wasn't an expert on alcohol consumption, but that offended even my rookie sense of liquor honor.

"I don't know." I set my fork down and leaned back, staring at the ceiling fan as it spun lazily above. "I love working with you, and I really like our teams. We've done some great work."

"Chez Paris!" she said with a terrible French accent and a wave of her hand.

"Oui, Paris." I said in my best Tennessee-drawl-infected French accent. "The idea of leaving you makes me sick, but Evan's right. Ted's a raging prick, and that's never going to change. They do their lunch every day and make decisions for our teams without including us, then he pulls crap like the standing calls. I can't blame the troops for looking at the door with that shit going on."

"Yeah, the recruiters were talking, wondering when he'd do it to them."

"If we start losing people, you know who Ted will blame, don't you? Mr. High Holy created this company and shits gold. He'll pin it all on you and me. Then where will we be?"

She eyed me over her glass, one brow raised. "Are you venting or trying to convince yourself of something?"

I sighed. "I don't know. Connie, he's *terrible*. I can't see myself at Think! in three years. If I'm honest, I couldn't see myself there in a year, with or without Evan's deal. I haven't seriously looked for something else, but when sales manager jobs have posted for clients, I've caught myself wondering if I might be a good fit for them."

"Well, it sounds like you've decided, at least about leaving. The only question is where you'll go."

This was usually the time Connie made a joke or used a silly voice to lighten the mood. She did neither. She just sat across the table waiting for the lightbulb to go off in my stubborn, thick skull.

I lowered my head. "I guess. This really sucks. I was looking forward to doing more things like Paris with you. We're a great team."

She beamed. "No, we're the best. Ted's lucky to have us, even if his head's too far up his ass to see it."

"Ms. Black. Language, please," I mocked.

"Oh, forgive me, kind sir. I will watch my fucking language for you in the future."

Just like that, the tension broke and we were giggling like children again.

A FEW DAYS LATER, EVAN RECEIVED A PACKET OF information from the owners of the training company in Utah, two guys who started the business out of one of their garages and now boasted several million dollars in annual sales. The only small business I knew by comparison was my dad's wholesale drug distributor, which barely sold half a million dollars of product each year. Ted claimed Think! brought in roughly twenty million each year. If Evan and I could get this thing off the ground and generate revenues somewhere in the middle of those two extremes, I'd be thrilled.

Over the weeks that followed, Evan and I held dozens of clandestine meetings, usually over lunch so we wouldn't raise suspicion among the Think! crowd. I told Connie what was going on, but no one else knew anything was amiss. Part of me hoped Ted would take the advice of everyone and stop the tyrannical shenanigans, but he never did. Chairs went missing on occasion, and call stats were posted several times each day to humiliate those with lower numbers. Morale among the troops, which I had doubted could get any lower, found a way to limbo under even those minimal expectations.

People were miserable.

Four weeks following the Great Chair Removal, the first salesperson resigned. Two more left the following week.

Ted was incensed. He couldn't wrap his head around why people would leave his blessed company. Behind closed doors, he ranted to his inner circle about how those leaving were betraying him, after everything he'd done for them. Never once did he look in the mirror and ask, "What is really causing people to leave?"

He took his anger out on anyone nearby, either with snide remarks or outright attacks on their performance or professionalism. Even Mark, Ted's most loyal and long-standing employee, fell prey to his biting barbs.

Morale went from poor to pathetic. The rumor mill predicted a wave of resignations in the coming weeks. Connie and I did all we could to encourage people, but we could no longer buffer the troops from Ted's tantrums.

Late one Thursday afternoon, Evan walked into my office and closed the door behind him.

"I can't do this anymore. Ted's an ass, and we have all we need to start the new company."

"We need capital. We can't start a company without cash. I can't afford to go without a paycheck right now." I had less than a thousand dollars in my bank account. I might've been a good sales manager, but I was a terrible saver.

"I have some money saved up. I'll invest twenty thousand to get us started. The company can pay me back when we turn a profit."

I gaped at him. He was offering to fund our startup out of his own pocket. I knew Evan's family had money, but I didn't think he enjoyed any of it yet. Then again, I wasn't exactly an expert on trust funds. All I'd likely inherit from my family was debt.

"Evan, I can't—"

"Yes, you can. Please. I can't do this without you. Cash or no cash, without someone to run the business, to connect us to lenders and handle the day-to-day, I'll be lost. I need you."

I stared down at my hands for a long moment, barely breathing. It felt like one of those life moments where I could see the fork in the road stretching for miles before me. Neither path showed any hint of the destination or ease of travel. I begged that vision to offer some message, some hint, but nothing came.

"Can I sleep on it and give you an answer tomorrow?" I finally asked.

He grinned and bounced toward the door. "Sure. Bring your resignation letter."

I sat at my desk for another hour, staring but not seeing. One coworker after another trailed past, waving goodnight but not waiting for the reply that wouldn't come. My stomach clenched as I thought through my options for the thousandth time.

One: I stay the course with Think! and try to make things better with Ted. That wouldn't be an easy road, but it offered stability and a paycheck. More than that, Connie was there, and I loved working with her. We'd be friends no matter where I worked, but I'd miss seeing her every day and collaborating on crazy contests and whatnot.

Two: I leave and find a new job. I hadn't even looked at the job market, and the thought of starting over scared me. Plus, in the time I'd been at Think!, I'd learned a lot about résumés and the impact that single sheet of paper had on an employer's decision. I might be able to explain having a rough start in Atlanta with my first job, but I'd still have to explain it in *every* interview. That sounded terrible.

The third option was to take Evan up on his offer and start a new company. That was the scariest of all, but also the most exciting. It got me away from Ted and made me my own boss. I liked Evan well enough, and the Utah company had checked out. They even offered to help support us in the startup phase. All the proverbial ducks were lined up and waiting for me to have the balls to lead them.

THE NEXT MORNING, I WALKED INTO THINK! FOR THE LAST time, gave Evan a nod, and took my resignation letter down to Ted's office. He blew a total gasket and refused my offer for a transition period. He even forced Mark and Dennis to escort me out the door, like one of those perp walks you might see on TV murder shows. I held my head high as the troops gathered and applauded my exit. Evan had told them what I was doing in Ted's office.

I hated thinking about what spite-filled punishment Ted would hand out for that little display of disloyalty.

But I was free.

SLUTISHA, PARTY OF ONE

With one job over and the other yet to begin, I found myself with a little time on my hands.

While I kept my daily evening ritual of purchasing a singular apple, working out, eating Chinese or grilled chicken at Cowtippers, then heading home, my days were free for other important pursuits: the men of Atlanta.

I checked my email each night and was disappointed there was nothing from Ryan. He hadn't called, but that wasn't unusual. He was an emailer. It was strange he'd just vanished without even a quick note after the fantastic day we'd had, but I shrugged it off as a busy man on a work trip.

At least, that's what I hoped it was.

Could he not have had the same post-date euphoria I'd had? It wouldn't have been the first time I'd misjudged a guy's reaction. Hell, I was usually so optimistic after a date, I assumed the dude was picking out rings or picket fences. Wait, that's lesbians. Maybe he'd just be thinking about me and our next date. Yeah, that's more like it.

Despite my newfound hope for something more with

Ryan, experience had taught me to hedge my bets. The odds of any one date turning into a long-lasting love affair were slim, especially when you slammed the egos, stunted emotions, and general horniness of two men together.

Given that world-class rationalization, I turned my free time toward mastering Manhunt and Adam4Adam, while not shirking my fans on AOL. One must care for one's followers, after all.

Yes, I was a bit of a slut.

And I loved Atlanta.

With a few clicks of my mouse, a horny, half-dressed man would show up at my door faster than a pizza from Domino's. Over the past few months, I'd learned to weed out those who lived in Monroe Place, my home. I'd made the mistake of hooking up with a *homer*, and was thoroughly embarrassed when we ran into each other at the pool or laundry room. That was a shame, really. The convenience of having so many men within walking distance was appealing.

As you might imagine, the little angel and devil appeared each time I "ordered in." They fought like an old married couple, or like the two old guys on the balcony from *The Muppet Show*—yeah, that's more like it. The angel played the Ryan card, begging me to be good and have faith that he'd show up and sweep me off my feet, but the devil made a more compelling, immediate argument. Little Michael had an itch and might fall off if I didn't scratch it.

That was probably not medically possible, but it worked in the moment. My entry into slutdom was pure self-preservation. I couldn't exactly let Little Michael wither and drop, could I?

On Thursday night, as I scrolled through the menu—er,

I mean, the men online—my PC let out a familiar ding. I closed the Manhunt browser, then minimized A4A, revealing a lonely, untended AOL screen beneath. I'd pretty much abandoned the chat rooms for the pictures and profiles of the dating sites. They contained the same guys, just with different goals and timetables. How's that for rationalization?

RAL2027: HEY YOU! HOW'S YOUR WEEK BEEN?

Wow, that was fast. He'd logged on and messaged me right away. I felt a little flutter.

IT'S BEEN OKAY. HOW'S THE TRIP? YOU'RE IN LA?

SAN FRAN. IT'S OKAY. SAME OLE.

San Francisco? The gay Mecca? I'd never been there, but every movie I'd ever seen depicted the city as one massive orgy, with hairy, muscular men pounding each other in rapid succession. While the mental imagery might've thrilled me a moment ago, my heart sank at the thought of Ryan being there all week.

OH, NEVER BEEN THERE, I replied, unable to leave it alone.

IT'S OKAY. OUR OFFICE IS DOWNTOWN, AND MY HOTEL IS RIGHT ACROSS THE STREET. IT'S CONVENIENT, BUT I DON'T DO MUCH MORE THAN WORK, EAT, AND SLEEP.

That was a little reassuring. Ryan being bored and a workaholic was good, right?

OH, COOL, I GUESS.

YOU ALRIGHT? YOU SEEM A LITTLE…I DON'T KNOW…*OFF*.

YEAH, I'M GOOD. JUST BEEN A LONG WEEK. LOTS GOING ON AT WORK.

Why was I *off*, as he put it? I felt it too. Talking with Ryan had never been uncomfortable or awkward. In fact, he might've been the easiest person I'd ever talked with. Tonight, I felt like a sputtering idiot.

Poof. "It's because you've been hooking up with other guys while he's away on a work trip. You're a trollop, Michael. Face it." The little angel wore a black pilgrim outfit with white lace crawling up his neck. Since when did male pilgrims wear lace?

"Don't listen to that prude. You and Ryan have been on exactly *two* dates. You don't owe him anything. Have your fun." The little devil, wearing brown chaps without underwear, wagged a finger at me. "You don't want Little Michael falling off, remember?"

The angel sighed.

Was I feeling guilty? That was a stupid question. PKs were always feeling guilty about *something.*

The angel was right, I had been slutting my way around Atlanta while poor Ryan was working.

Shit. Now I *knew* I felt guilty.

STILL THERE?

The cursor blinked impatiently.

OH, SORRY. RAN TO THE KITCHEN. SO, WHEN ARE YOU HOME?

FRIDAY. I WANTED TO SEE IF YOU'D HAVE LUNCH WITH ME SATURDAY. I CAN'T MAKE IT A DAY LIKE LAST TIME, BUT I CAN DEFINITELY SQUEEZE IN A LUNCH.

Squeeze in a lunch? Was his social secretary keeping him that busy? Sheesh.

SURE. I'D LOVE TO. NAME THE TIME AND PLACE.

He suggested a Thai place I hadn't heard of. I looked up the address and agreed on noon, then he said he had to take a phone call and logged off.

It was 10:15 p.m. Who was calling him at ten fifteen on a Thursday night while he was on a work trip? I wasn't exactly hearing an alarm bell, but there was an uncomfortable feeling creeping up my spine. Then I chided myself for being jealous of a man I had no claim over—as if anyone ever has a claim on anyone else. Then I scolded myself for that notion.

Wow. I'd just completed a guilt hat trick.

I was a damn good PK. My father would be proud.

THAI FOOD HAS ALWAYS BEEN ONE OF MY FAVORITES. There's something comforting and rich in the flavors and aromas that makes me happy.

As I sat across from Ryan, my stomach rumbled at the thought of pad Thai. Nothing said love like peanuty goodness.

"How was San Fran?" I asked between chews of veggie spring roll.

"Fine," he said, brushing the crumbs from his fingers. "It's always the same: corporate bosses asking questions about reports, a steady stream of issues with our travel vendors, and some new vendor banging on the door wanting our business. That pretty much sums up every day, now that I think about it. Oh, I can't forget dealing with employees. It's a rare day that I don't have at least one employee calling to complain about Delta or American—or Amtrak. I catch more flack about them than all the others combined."

"Amtrak? The trains?" I was travel-challenged and had never been on a train.

He nodded. "They're comfortable if you're in a room with a bed, but for the average traveler stuck in the front, it can make for a really long ride—and anyone who tells you those trips are smooth is lying. Trains rattle and sway, especially if you're on the top car."

"Huh. People complain to you about that? What do they want you to do?"

He chuckled. "No clue. Mostly, they want to vent, for someone to listen. I do that, then tell them I'll talk to our corporate rep about their concerns. That calms most down. They don't really expect me to work miracles."

Corporate America. I envied the stability and fat paycheck that came with Ryan's high-end white-collar gig, but parts of it sounded like a real pain. I thought about all the issues I'd been dealing with at Think!, a small company basically run by one man, then I tried to imagine answering to thousands of bosses and coworkers, a board of directors and investors, and I realized his fat paycheck came with some sharply barbed strings.

"How was your week?" he asked.

"Ehh. It was okay."

He cocked his head. "Just okay? You're usually more upbeat than that. Did something happen? What did Ted do now?"

I nearly spit the hot tea I'd started to sip. How had he known Ted was at it again? Then I remembered all our online chats and realized he knew more about me than most third dates. Hell, he knew more about me that anyone I'd ever dated. That realization slapped me in the face. I thought it was a good slap, the kind you get on your butt right before—

"How did you know?" I gave him a wan smile. "I don't know how much more of his nonsense I can take. He made my whole team stand while they did calls. He actually took their chairs, moved them into the conference room until his little object lesson was complete."

"You're kidding?"

"Nope. Sad but true."

"Wow. He's a real ass."

I nodded. "My exact words to Connie."

His face lightened at the mention of my new bestie's name. "How is dear Connie? Any more French flags flying about?"

Damn, he didn't miss anything, did he?

"No more flags. She's good. Chipper as ever, though Ted's stunt burst her usual bubbliness for a hot minute."

He sobered again. "If Ted's so bad, why stay? You're a bright guy. You could find something else."

He thought I was bright. My cheeks colored at his flattery.

"So, it's funny you say that. One of my sales guys came to me with an opportunity." I took a sip of tea to give myself time to think. Ryan was a successful business guy. Would he think I was crazy considering a startup? Would I look unstable? The last thing I wanted was for him to think I was a flake or didn't know how to stick to things.

He raised a brow as I struggled for words.

"There's a guy at work, one of my sales guys. His name's Evan. He has a connection to this company somewhere out west that provides Microsoft certification training to engineers."

"So it's a school? Or a for-profit educational institution?"

"Right. It's definitely a company, not a school. Evan's supposed to get more details next week. All he had when he approached me was an overview and the offer to take the eastern US. They're not even asking him to buy the rights."

"Huh." Ryan leaned back and one hand drifted to his mouth.

"Okay," I said. "In sales, we call that gesture a *stop sign*, and it's usually used by prospects when they don't like something. What are you thinking?"

He grinned at my grilling. "IT is a hot field, that's for sure, but we still don't know enough to get a handle on the business. I'd be interested to hear what Evan comes up with this week. Until then, it's just an idea. We can't make a plan with just an idea."

Ryan was a good dozen years older than me. In that moment, I felt our age difference for the first time. He sounded so intelligent and experienced, so stable. I could see his mind working as his eyes drifted upward, then back to me. He was trying to puzzle out the scraps of information I'd given him, trying to find a way to make things work.

And then I realized he'd used the word *we*. Sure, he was just talking about an idea someone had presented, but he talked as though *we* were making a decision together.

That made me smile.

Ryan noticed the change. "What are you grinning at, mister?"

"Oh, nothing." I decided to play it cool. "I just appreciate you helping me think through all this. It's a big decision to leave a company and do something new."

"It is, but I admire you for considering it."

"You do?" The flutter grew stronger.

He nodded. "It takes a lot of guts to leave the safety of a company and start something. Most people fail when they start a business, but you won't be one of them."

Sweet mother of pearl. He *believed* in me. I had to fight the urge to do a happy dance. My guts were already doing one.

"Thanks," I squeaked, before taking a quick sip to wet my suddenly parched whistle.

We spent the rest of dinner talking about little things. The Atlanta fall softball season was kicking off, and I was excited to get back on the field. I'd been assigned to a team called the Slippers. Ryan teased that I'd have to play in heels. When he asked what position I played, his brows rose again.

"Pitcher, eh. I had you pegged for another position."

I chuckled. "Really now? Are we still talking softball?"

He raised his glass. "You tell me. I love a well-rounded player."

"Let's just say I'm a *team* player."

"So, you'd let me change your position, if I wanted?"

"Put me in, coach." I saluted with my own raised glass.

His eyes sparkled, and his smile broadened as he held my gaze.

20

THE CHRISTENING

The next few weeks were a flurry of activity. Evan and I scouted new office space, settling on a building owned by a bankruptcy attorney who had a few offices to rent. We took the bottom floor, which consisted of two offices, a small conference room, a storage room for files, and a restroom. The attorney was an older lady who loved gold gilding, so the place was decked out like a French palace. There wasn't much elbow room, but it was fancy. My office contained an elegant cherry-wood desk that reflected lamplight like a mirror, along with high-back armchairs with ball-and-claw feet. It made me think of an episode of *Antiques Roadshow*, in which the blond twins had shown off dining chairs with the same feet. They were really cool.

The Utah guys put us through our paces, which included studying software loaded onto laptops and four-inch-thick binders. My head hurt after the first day. I'd never been rocket-scientist-smart, but was brighter than the average bulb. Something in the monotony of those sessions made me wonder how dim a bulb could get. Mine was flickering like it wanted to give that lasts pop and never shine again.

I was glad Evan was handling sales because I would've thrown that binder through the window before finishing it. All I needed to know was the basics and how to explain our business to banks and other businesses.

Throughout the craziness, I maintained my post-workday ritual of stopping by the grocery store for a lonely apple, then heading to the gym. Ryan and I emailed and IMed several times each day. He was all about meeting for lunch on Saturday or Sunday, but always had some reason he couldn't do dinner. It was odd, but I was too busy to give it much thought.

On the fourth Saturday following my resignation from Think!, Ryan and I met for lunch at a diner near the new office. I was proud of our little venture and wanted to show off the fancy digs to my…what was he at this point? Date? We'd been on a dozen dates, all either lunches or coffee. We'd never been physical, though he had kissed me a couple of times. Why was that?

For once, my Pisces mind let a subject rest without hammering both sides into submission. I liked Ryan, and I was pretty sure he liked me. His *eyes* said he did. We'd been dating a couple months, that's all. It wasn't more than that. I wanted it to be, but wouldn't let myself think of it as more until it happened.

Calm down, Michael. Breathe. It's just a date.

"I can't wait to see your new place. It sounds swanky," Ryan said between bites of eggs Benedict. The diner was new to both of us, a little breakfast place called Le Peep. The sign out front pictured a fuzzy yellow chick just peeking out of a newly cracked egg. That's what drew us in. It was cute. As it turned out, the food was fantastic, and the servers were a hoot. Our server, Betty (yes, also the name of my all-time favorite Saturn), literally threw packets of sweetener at Ryan when he asked for more, then stormed off like she was mad at his insufferable request. It was all an act, part of the charm of the place, and we loved every minute.

"It really is. There's not much room, but it's enough for the two of us."

We talked about the first few weeks of training, the Utah guys and their outlook on the business, and how Evan and I planned to kick things off. Ryan listened attentively, asking questions and making suggestions throughout. It was like having my own personal business coach—a really hot coach with a tight powder-blue T-shirt that nuzzled his biceps just right.

I took a sip of iced water to cool down.

Betty eventually strode by, scolded us for not cleaning our plates more effectively, then threw the bill at Ryan. We laughed all the way out the door. Betty flicked us the bird and a broad smile.

Le Peep just became our new favorite breakfast joint.

The office was a quick five-minute drive from the restaurant, and the attorneys rarely worked weekends, so we found the place dark and locked up tight.

"Holy shit. You weren't kidding when you said the boss likes fancy gold." Ryan's head rotated, taking in the high ceilings and gilded trim. He walked across the entrance toward a graceful painting that consumed the entire far wall, then whistled. "This is an *original*. I bet she paid at least twenty thousand for it."

"Dollars?" I almost stumbled.

He turned back and nodded. "Yeah. This thing's stunning."

I showed him the conference room, then Evan's office, then took him upstairs to see the fanciest room in the building, the old attorney's private conference room. Cherry wood and polished silver gleamed throughout. A buffet held court on the far wall, donned with several massive candelabras holding tall, white, never-been-lit candles. Twenty elegant chairs lined the table at the center. Before each high-back chair sat a crystal water glass, writing pad, and pen. A faint leathery smell drifted throughout the room from the rich mats on which those items rested.

Ryan whistled again, walking to the far side to examine a vase. "Is this thing real?" he asked, kneeling down to look under it.

"No idea. Knowing the owner, probably."

He glanced around the room one last time, then we went back downstairs to my office.

"This is my little corner." I waved my hand in a flourish.

"Very nice." He skimmed the bookcase, then walked around my desk and dropped into my leather office chair. "This is comfy. Kinda bouncy."

I chuckled. "That it is."

"Does your door lock?"

"Uh, sure."

I didn't know why, but my heart started racing.

"Lock it and come over here. I want to kiss you, and I'd rather not be disturbed."

I grinned. "Yes, sir. Though I doubt anyone will come in today."

"Just do as you're told, young man." He motioned to the lock.

My grin widened.

He grabbed me around the waist when I got within

arm's reach and pulled me onto his lap. It took an awkward moment of flailing legs to get me fully situated. I'm not sure how we did it, but my legs flowed over the top of the chair's arms as my butt ground into his lap. It wasn't comfortable, but I didn't dare move.

He reached up with both hands and pulled my face toward him, pressing his lips against mine in our most passionate kiss to date. His poochy lower lip devoured mine as he went from zero to sixty in two-point-three seconds.

His embrace was aggressive, but the first tickle of his tongue was tentative, questioning. It sent a shiver of warmth through my chest, and I answered with my own, exploring the underside of his.

He groaned.

All questions vanished. I'd wanted this so badly over the previous weeks that I lost myself in his embrace. My hands found their way to his chest, tracing the definition, gripping its firmness. His fingers rubbed my back, tickled my neck. The chair squeaked as he shifted, and I realized he'd hardened under the weight and grinding of my butt. I pressed myself against him, making him squirm even more.

"I want you, Michael."

"You can have whatever you want."

"I want to be inside you. Now."

I pulled my head back and quirked a brow. "Now? Here? In my office?"

He grinned and nodded. "Right here. Right now. You said it yourself—no one's coming in."

He reached down and began untying the string on my shorts.

I fumbled my way to stand before him. "You're serious?"

The only answer was the sound of my pants hitting the floor. I rarely wore underwear, so Little Michael stared up at him with curiosity in his one good eye.

Ryan gaped, then his gaze rose to meet mine. "Damn."

I helped him with his pants, amused to find he wasn't wearing undies either.

"Holy shit, that's big," I blurted out.

He chuckled. "And it's all yours. Want it?"

"Hell yeah. Although it may take me a minute."

His cock was perfect. Eight and a half inches of thick, veiny manhood, curved slightly upward and crowned with a pink, cut mushroom tip that begged to be licked.

I never got the chance.

Ryan gripped my hips with both hands and pulled me into his mouth, taking Little Michael all the way to my balls before I knew what was happening.

Damn, he didn't even gag.

My whole body convulsed.

Ever so gently, he pulled back, running his lips along my shaft and his tongue around the rim of my head. He kept the tip in his mouth and toyed with it, alternating between his teeth and his tongue. Despite his iron grip on my hips, I had to brace myself on the desk. My office was spinning.

When I stiffened to my limit, he switched to slowly swallowing my dick, tracing it gently with his teeth, taking all of me with each motion.

Then he stopped and leaned back. "Take off your shirt."

In one perfume-commercial-like movement, I gripped the bottom of my shirt, yanked it over my head, and tossed it into the corner.

Ryan's eyes widened appreciatively as he reached up to trace my still-forming abs. "So nice."

I blushed. "Thanks."

He chuckled. "I like that you get embarrassed. It makes me want you more."

The reddening deepened. "And *your* shirt?"

He leaned forward in the chair and removed his tee, revealing the most beautifully sculpted chest and shoulders I'd ever seen—and I'd seen some beauties in my short little slut-life. His pecs were full enough to actually cast a shadow. I couldn't speak. I just stared.

"You can do more than look. It's all yours."

I couldn't believe this was happening. Ryan was amazing: smart, hot, successful, and he wanted *me*—in my office. I kept waiting to wake up from the dream or for someone to knock on the door, but neither happened. Then my eyes shot toward the door and a thrill ran through me at the possibility of getting caught. What were we doing—in my office? What if one of the attorneys or their staff walked in? What if Evan showed up? *He had a key.*

Excitement at dancing with danger overrode good sense, and I turned back with hunger in my eyes.

Ryan reached down and stroked himself. Any remaining control I had vanished.

His other hand gripped the small of my back and pulled me onto his lap like we'd done before, but this time felt entirely different. There were no shorts between my butt and his cock. He pressed against me, and I felt how much he wanted to be inside me. He pulsed and twitched. I ground against him, and he pushed me down.

"Do you have any lube?"

I couldn't stop the laugh. "At my office? Uh, that would be no."

He chuckled. "Guess we'll have to do this the old-fashioned way."

I cocked my head, having absolutely no idea what he meant—until he spat on his palm.

"You're not serious, are you?"

He moistened his cock beneath me, never losing eye contact—and never answering.

He filled his palm again. I watched in fascination, unsure if this was still a good idea.

This time, his fingers traced my hole, slickening it, brushing against its opening with only the slightest pressure. I flinched, then shivered again. The tip of a finger slipped inside, and he swirled it slowly around. Another shudder ran through me, and I squeezed his shoulders.

He pulled his finger out, wet it again, then returned it. This time deeper.

I felt his knuckle. Then it slipped past. He retreated, then pressed in once more. In and out as my hole began to trust his touch.

When a second finger snuck in, I clinched.

"Easy, baby. Just relax." He wet his hand again, then two fingers broached the entrance as he kissed my chest. I shut my eyes and let my head fall back. His kisses and fingers pressed and probed, no longer gentle, now insistent with need and desire. I found myself levering up and down, urging his fingers onward, inward.

He pulled them out, and I heard him wet his hand again. I dared not look.

This time, fingers didn't return to my hole. His dripping cock pressed against my rim, soft and stiff at the same time. I thought I felt more than spittle, a slickness no water could provide. I reached back, thrilled to feel the oily smoothness of pre-cum, and pressed down, but he held me up, teasing my desire with his, taunting my hole with his hardness.

Then he pressed himself into me.

"Owwww!"

God, that hurt.

He pulled back. "Are you okay?"

"Don't you dare pull out. Just go slow. Give me a minute. You're ramming a Mac truck up my ass."

He laughed. "You're *so* romantic."

"Just shut up and fuck me."

"Now who's bossy?" He grinned.

Without warning, he slid all the way into me. The weight of my body straddling him pressed his cock so deep he hit some inner wall to a chamber I never knew existed. I groaned as the pain became wrapped in ecstasy. My back arched.

He stilled, wrapped his arms around me, and held me tight.

I looked down, confused.

"Don't move. Just let me be inside you."

One hand gripped my back while the other cupped my cheek.

We didn't grind or screw or fuck. There wasn't even another thrust.

We simply sat—joined as one person—and kissed.

21

THREE-WAY CALLING

"So neither of you *finished*?" Dwayne asked.

I described our lunch, then the office tour, without leaving out a single detail. The passion I'd felt in that moment poured out of me. Smitten no longer described what I felt for Ryan. I was seriously falling for this one. Connie was on the three-way call again, and my sheltered PK sensibilities were embarrassed by the explicit discussion of our escapade. Yes, she and I shared everything, and had talked about more butts, boobs, and wieners than I could count, but something about sharing my own private experience turned me into an awkward teenager.

"Well, no. He said he wanted to save that, that he only wanted to be with me in that moment as one person."

Connie sighed loudly into the receiver. "That's the most romantic thing I've ever heard."

Dwayne snorted.

"I thought so too," I said. "The kissing was incredible, especially while he was, you know, *up there*."

Connie giggled.

"After all this time, you still turn bashful just talking

about sex. We have so much work to do, Connie," Dwayne said.

She giggled again. "I don't know. Our little chick seems to be growing new feathers every day."

"Uh, you two know I'm on the phone, right?"

That drew another round of amusement from the peanut gallery.

"I still can't believe you did that *in your office*. How will you ever sit in that chair and not think about that day?"

Huh. I hadn't thought about that. Now she'd planted a seed.

Dammit.

"Yeah, you'll be sitting there crunching numbers or working on some spreadsheet and your butt will tingle every time the leather squeaks." Dwayne was loving this conversation.

"Ha ha. Very funny. I'm a professional. I can handle it."

He snorted. "Professional who just bonked his boyfriend in his office chair."

"He's not my boyfriend. At least, I don't think he is yet. We haven't talked about it." We'd been dating for nearly two months, having lunch most Saturdays and Sundays, chatting online or on the phone several times each day. Did that make us boyfriends?

"So, how did you leave things?" Connie asked.

My mood sobered. "That's more the part I wanted to ask you two about. It was weird. There we were, peg-in-hole in my office chair, and his watch chimed. He looked down and got this look on his face. It wasn't fear, but it was *something*. He looked back up and gently pulled us apart, then told me he had somewhere to be and needed to go. It was all so...I don't know. Abrupt."

"Did he tell you where he was going?" Connie asked.

"No, just that he had somewhere to be. Even the way he phrased it made my hair stand on end."

Dwayne grunted. "I'm not sure you'd know what was standing on end in that moment, but we'll go with it. You've said things like this before about Ryan, how he won't do dinner during the week and logs off chats a little too quickly sometimes. As much as I like to tease you, your gut is solid. You should trust it."

"What does that mean? What are you saying?"

Dwayne's breath came in rasps down the phone line as he thought. "You know Ryan. We don't. From everything you've told us, he's a great guy worth getting to know. Just be cautious. You've sensed red flags; they could be nothing, but they could be something. Keep your eyes open and guard that last bit of your heart you haven't given him yet."

"I haven't given—"

"Uh-huh. You have. Don't even try to deny it," Connie cut in. "And that's amazing, but Dwayne's right. If you smell something off, just step carefully."

22

THE GOLDEN GATE

When Ryan's monthly trek to home office called, he invited me to join him.

I was stunned. No one had ever invited me on a trip, certainly not across the country to the Holy Land o' Gays. I'd also never been to San Francisco, and he said he wanted to show me what his trips were like.

He said he'd racked up so many frequent flyer points from all his work trips that he'd never be able to spend them all. The whole trip, minus meals, would be paid for by vendors and points programs. He described a luxury hotel, elegant meals, black car service, and loads of free time to explore and play tourist. It sounded like a four-day Michael-spoiling-in-the-making.

Like the wise woman said in *Pretty Woman,* "We need a little sucking up over here."

After a few minutes of appropriate, "Oh, I can't accept that," being countered by, "Oh, but you can," my defenses crumbled, and I agreed to go. There was never a question, I was just being polite with the mock refusal—and he knew it. Sneaky bastard.

Two days later, the lovely people at American Airlines ushered us to our first-class seats and offered a complimentary glass of champagne. Was that normal on flights? Ryan grinned broadly as he took a flute from the flight attendant and passed it to me. I was already putty in his hands. Add alcohol and it was a merry flight indeed.

A black SUV pulled up to the curb as we exited the airport. LOWELL was printed in neat lettering on a sign in the window. I'd expected a car, but this decked-out SUV was pretty hot.

Ryan hadn't lied about the hotel. Holy crap, his company put him up in fancy digs. Our room was nosebleed high in a skyscraper, offering views of the city and bay I thought only came in postcards. I set my roller bag down and flopped onto the bed. It swallowed me up. Between the plush comforter and the heavenly mattress, I wasn't sure I'd ever want to move—until Ryan leapt on top of me and started tickling.

"If I pee everywhere, you'll have to get us a new room," I called out between gasps.

He howled with delight and pressed his evil digits harder into my ribs.

We wandered down to the lobby sports bar for lunch, then my guide took me on a walking tour of downtown. That was the first time I'd ever held hands with a guy while walking down crowded streets. My eyes darted from one passerby to the next, anticipating a snide remark or snarly look, but no one gave us a second glance.

When we returned to our room and the door clicked shut, Ryan grabbed me around the waist and tossed me onto the overstuffed chair in the corner. He wrapped his arms around me and kissed my neck. Between pecks, he rattled off our agenda for the week.

"We have to do the Golden Gate Bridge."

"Are we going to walk across it?" I asked.

"Nah. It's a really long walk, and that would kill too much of our time."

"Okay. What else?"

"Let's see, there's Chinatown, the Castro District, Alcatraz—"

"Alcatraz? As in *the* Alcatraz? The prison?"

He chuckled at my enthusiasm. "Yep. It's been closed as a jail for years, but they do tours. Better be good or I'll lock you up."

"What if I want to be locked up with you?" My eyes were suddenly sparkling with mischief. "Maybe we need to check out the showers so I can drop the soap. I hear that leads to interesting encounters in prison."

"You're bad." He kissed my neck again. "Besides, if you want to drop the soap, there's nowhere around with a more comfortable shower than this room."

"Mr. Lowell, are you propositioning me?"

He grinned. "I'll knock the soap out of your hand if I have to. You're mine this week."

I craned my neck to nibble his earlobe. "Yes, sir. Anything you want, sir. I'm all yours, sir."

"Finally, he shows me proper respect. This may be a great trip, after all."

That earned him a playful punch on the arm.

RYAN TOOK THE NEXT DAY OFF, AND WE HIT THE aforementioned tourist destinations. As promised, the views from the Golden Gate Bridge were stunning. I'd never realized how wide San Fran's bay was. A tourist marker we passed estimated the bay's total surface area at sixteen hundred square miles. The ever-present breeze kept white-capped water churning in every direction.

The Castro was eye-opening. Rainbow flags fluttered everywhere. Even the sidewalks shed their monotone in favor of festive colors. Bookstores, of both the peep and literary variety, sat shoulder to shoulder with restaurants, gift shops, bars…you name it.

Then there were the open displays of affection. Hell, that's gentle. Guys were practically naked and doing it on the street. Other than the one homeless man peeing on the sidewalk, I didn't see anyone *actually* naked, but they were darn close, and I got the feeling that all bets were off after dark. San Fran just had that vibe. It was thrilling and terri-fying at the same time.

I felt like a newborn gay with wide eyes and jaw agape.

Chinatown turned out to be my favorite area. I'd always had a fascination with all things Asian, and this neighbor-hood did not disappoint. Shop after shop offered foods I couldn't identify, and antiques dating back to periods in Chinese history I'd read about in college classes years earlier. It felt like walking back in time.

I met a group of Buddhist priests strolling from their temple to a local restaurant. They gave me a primer on Chinatown's history, and suggested the best shops and restaurants that most tourists would never notice. Before we parted ways, one of the priests reached into a pocket of his robe and pulled out two coins with centers that had been hollowed out in a square. Faded Chinese characters were embossed in the bronze metal.

"Take these to remember us." He pointed to one of the symbols. "This is Kangxi. He was emperor during the Qing dynasty in the seventeenth century. I feel his spirit in you."

I stared at the coins in my hand. "I can't take these. They're so old. Aren't they valuable?"

He chuckled. "Everything is old in China. These coins are common. Take them. I hope they bring you luck."

I thanked him and we said our goodbyes. I didn't understand how coins could bring luck or how Kangxi might be lurking in my spirit, but it was the coolest souvenir I could have hoped for.

Ryan had to work during the other days of the trip, so I wandered around town and enjoyed exploring more of Chinatown's shops. Most nights we ordered room service and watched movies on the wall-sized flat-screen.

On Valentine's Day, we fed each other chocolate-covered strawberries and sipped champagne. Ryan insisted the first sip occur while our arms were interlocked. We proved just how uncoordinated we both were with that maneuver, laughing like schoolboys the whole time.

It was one of the most romantic weeks I'd ever experienced.

23

____

SHOCK AND AWE

Ryan and I were supposed to have lunch the next day. As I was getting dressed, the phone rang.

"Hey." Ryan's voice sounded strange.

"Hey you. Everything okay? Still on for lunch?"

He didn't say anything for a long moment. When he spoke, it was clear he'd been crying. "I don't want to lose you."

What the hell?

"Ryan, what's going on? Talk to me."

"You might, when I tell you…"

I waited while he gathered himself.

"Michael, I'm married."

My mind couldn't register what he'd said. All my circuits overloaded at the same time. I couldn't move, couldn't breathe. Words wouldn't form.

"You're…what?"

"I'm married. Her name is Diane. We've been married for eighteen years."

I don't remember sitting on the couch or turning the TV off.

"We have two children. An eight-year-old boy and a five-year-old girl."

I wanted him to stop talking, to stop telling me all this. We were supposed to go to lunch. We were supposed to be falling in love. He was supposed to be…so much.

The walls of my apartment began to close in, and I wiped tears from my cheek.

"I'm so sorry I didn't tell you. I never thought I'd meet a guy who…made me feel like this. I thought it was all just fun, that it didn't mean anything, like experimenting."

Anger bubbled up. "You thought we were an *experiment?*"

"No, of course not. I mean, at first, but not now." He blew out his exasperation. "Michael, I've fallen in love with you. That wasn't supposed to happen—with anyone. I didn't mean for it to happen. Now all I can think about is being with you."

"But you're married—*with kids*. How do you think that could work?"

"I don't know. All I know is I don't want to be without you."

What was I supposed to say to that? I wanted to be with him more than anything, but the Ryan I was falling in love with wasn't the man I thought I was getting to know. The *real* Ryan had been married for *nearly twenty years* and had two kids. What was he doing online, meeting guys, dating? Did he have so little respect for his wife and the promise he'd made to her? How could he betray his family like that? Now he talked about us like we were a couple, like we had a future. How could I ever trust him? If he'd play around on his wife and kids, would he respect any promise he made to me? Did his promises mean anything?

And then my father's voice echoed in my head with one word.

Adultery.

I'd had sex with a *married man*. That violated so much of what I believed, what I was taught. Set aside the whole gay thing, we'd trampled all over something I'd always held as precious: a marriage between two loving people.

My anger morphed into misery, then frustration, then guilt.

Always guilt.

My mind was spinning so fast I'd nearly forgotten the receiver was still pressed to my ear. Then he spoke again.

"I get it if you don't ever want to see me again." There was such pain in his voice. It broke my heart. I wanted—no, I *needed*—to comfort him.

"Ryan, that's not what I want, but…" I struggled to form a coherent thought. "I don't know how I feel or what to think. I need some time."

"That's fine," he responded quickly. "Take all the time you need. I'm here."

"Okay. Yeah, I know. Thanks."

I ran out of words and hung up the receiver.

24

—————

WHIPLASH

I sat across the table from Connie in the seat Ryan was supposed to fill. She ate her chicken and veggies, quietly observing me push Brussels around my plate without ever tasting one. Roasters was one of my favorite comfort-food places in town, but my appetite had disappeared faster than my trust in Ryan.

"This sucks," I said, unable to meet her eyes.

"Yeah. It does."

I slumped back in my chair and continued playing with my food.

After several minutes, she broke the silence. "Are you going to see him again?"

I looked up. "How can I? He's *married*. I've abandoned a lot of what I believed growing up, but I've never lost my faith in a promise. Marriage, religiously blessed or not, is a sacred oath. We pretty much shattered his last weekend."

"I'm pretty sure he shattered it before he met you."

I folded my arms. "What do you mean?"

"You don't think you're his first, do you? He knew his way around your body and mouth like he'd been there before. At least, that's how it sounded when you described your little office visit." She cracked the slightest smile to lighten the mood.

My frown didn't budge. "Yeah. He knew what he was doing. That doesn't make my part in breaking his word any better. I feel terrible for his wife—and kids. He has two kids. What would they think if they knew their dad was running around on their mother with men?"

"Probably no worse than if he cheated with women."

I gave her a solid eye roll.

"Okay, we are in the South. You're right," she admitted.

"What am I going to do, Connie? I know I should just tell him I can't see him anymore, but—" My voice caught in my throat.

"You've fallen in love with him, haven't you?"

I looked up with watery eyes and nodded.

"Oh, sweet pea."

The server appeared and asked if something was wrong with my uneaten food. Connie saved me from trying to speak. "He's just not feeling well. Can we have a to-go box?"

The server gave me a sympathetic look, nodded back to Connie, and strode away.

She leaned forward and took my hand. "Look at me."

My head rose slowly.

"You don't have to make any decisions right now. You just learned about this. Give yourself a day or two to let everything sink in, to figure out what you really feel."

"How will a couple days change the ring on his finger?" I asked. "Oh, wait. He didn't wear one. That was all part of the deception."

The more I talked, the angrier I got. Ryan had not just cheated on his family, he'd also lied to me, over and over.

His profile lied. His words about feelings for me lied. Even his empty ring finger lied.

Had he ever been truthful?

I seethed as the server brought the check. Connie handled things, probably fearing the eruption she sensed was coming. If there was ever an empath in this world, it was Connie. She could feel a twitch across a room and know how everyone was feeling. Like her memory, it was creepy.

"Listen to me. Everything you're feeling right now is normal. I'd be worried about you if you weren't bundled up with anger and hurt, maybe with a decent serve of guilt thrown in. You're good at that one. Just don't be too hard on yourself—or Ryan—until you know the whole story. If he's the guy you thought he was yesterday, he deserves that much. You deserve it too."

I glared at her, then my gaze softened. She was right. Ryan might be a lying cheater, but I knew he was a good man, a great guy. Shit, that even sounded terrible in my head. Why did this have to be so hard? Why couldn't I just meet someone like Ryan, fall madly in love, and never have to worry about dating or cheaters—or anything—ever again? The longer I sat and stared at the rugged wooden tabletop, the more confused, angry, sad—and guilty—I became. I hadn't even noticed Connie stand. She'd been waiting for me to get up for a couple minutes.

"Up. You can sulk at home."

I finally cracked a hint of a smile. "Yes, Mom."

She slapped my shoulder playfully as I stood. "I'll take ma'am, but I ain't yo mama."

She giggled, and my smile broadened. God, I loved her.

I LEFT LUNCH AND DROVE TO THE GYM. MY HEART WASN'T into working out, but I hoped the rush of a good body pump might lift my mood. It usually did.

The gym wasn't very busy, but there were always a few hotties strutting around. Most took their workouts seriously, but some clearly viewed the gym as more social than physical. The preeners were in full force that day.

Ten minutes into my treadmill warm-up, I mashed the *stop* button and dragged my sorry ass home. I was on the verge of tears. No amount of endorphins could wash them away.

When I got home, I logged into AOL and Ryan was waiting on my friends list. He IMed me immediately.

HEY.

I logged out as fast as I could.

Yeah, I was a wuss. Avoiding him like that was probably childish, but I wasn't ready to face him. The jumble of emotions in my gut were doing their impression of a Wide World of Wrestling bout, and I couldn't figure out how to end the round. The last thing I wanted was for him to ask how I was doing—or say he wanted to see me again.

My conscience, with its smoothly filed corners that barely registered any pain these days, found ways to prick my heart at the thought of dating a married man, even one as amazing as Ryan. I wanted to find some way to justify everything, but the moral compass instilled in me years ago wouldn't allow it. I doubted even my little devil would tread on that ground.

Then the phone rang.

I figured it was Dwayne. Enough time had passed since lunch for Connie to call in backup. She'd never seen me like this, and I felt sure she'd loop Dwayne in before I had the chance. I grabbed the receiver and pulled the scrunchy cord over the couch.

"Hello?"

"Hey."

It was Ryan.

My throat became suddenly dry. My heart turned into an Olympic sprinter. I opened my mouth to say something —I had no idea what—but Ryan spoke first.

"I told her."

What? Who was *her*? And what did he tell her? He sounded miserable, but there was a twinge of something else in his voice I couldn't identify. Hope? Fear? I wasn't sure.

"She didn't throw anything, but there was a lot of yelling. She told me to leave."

My heart begged to reach out and hold him.

"Ryan, what are you saying? I'm not following."

There was a long pause.

"I told Diane I'm…gay. She asked if I'd acted on it, so I told her about hooking up with guys when I was on business trips, and a few times here."

Oh shit.

"I told her I'd been doing that once a month or so for the last five or six years. I can't blame her for screaming or being upset. I get it. What I did was terrible—for both of us."

I barely knew what to say. Ryan started crying.

"Why?" My voice croaked out in a whisper. "Why did you tell her?"

It took him another minute to stop crying. As long as I live, I'll never forget the words he spoke next.

"Because I'm in love with you."

I didn't think my heart could beat any faster, but it did.

What I couldn't tell was whether that was from fear or anger—or the thrill of being told the man I'd fallen for was also in love with me. I wanted to scream at him for lying and deceiving me, for cheating on his wife, but my heart craved falling into his arms and sharing his warmth again.

An overwhelming sense of guilt doused that ember before it could spark. What kind of guy has such mixed emotions about betrayal? Who was I turning into? I wasn't sure I liked the answer that echoed in my head.

"Michael, please say something."

How long had I been silent? I could barely think.

"I'm in love with you too," slipped out.

What the literal fuck had I just said? The receiver dropped into my lap as my hand flew over my mouth.

I tried to grab the words and shove them back down, but they'd flown into the phone and refused to return. I knew it was true, that I *was* falling for him, but given everything, it was the *last* thing I should've said. I was supposed to be walking away, standing up for my principles, refusing to take part in his lie.

Was it still a lie?

He'd come clean. Sure, he'd broken their vows—and a few Georgia laws— but he wasn't *lying* to Diane anymore.

I heard him release the breath he'd been holding. "Really? Seriously? Even after—"

"Yeah, seriously." Shit, I was sinking fast. Why did I just confirm the thing I shouldn't have said in the first place?

Fuck. Fuck. Fuck.

I had to fix this. "I still don't know how I feel about everything, though. You're married with kids—and you never told me any of it. You weren't just lying to her. You were lying to *me* the whole time too."

"I know." His voice was so small, so riddled with pain. "I'm so sorry. I didn't want to, but I didn't know what to do. The more we got to know each other, the more I knew my life was about to change, and I couldn't figure out how to navigate between the two lives I was living."

Shit. That would be hard.

Growing up, I didn't know I was gay, didn't have a clue. Given the right planets lining up, I could just have easily been Ryan, married with kids and struggling with my true feelings. My heart shifted again.

"How have you lived like this for so long?"

"It was easy at first. Diane really is great. We were happy, and I thought my attraction to guys would just go away once we got married and had kids."

"Did it? Go away, I mean?"

"I guess—for a while. Maybe I was just so distracted with life to pay attention. Looking back, there were men at the gym, or at work, really handsome guys. They caught my eye in a way that was different, but nothing I understood. I never acted on anything."

"When did that change?"

He thought a moment. "We had Alan, and everything was amazing. Diane bounced back from that pregnancy like a champ. He grew so fast. There really wasn't time for anything other than taking care of the house and chasing his squirmy butt."

I could hear the smile in his voice as he recalled happier times. Then it sobered again.

"When we had Elaine, a lot changed. That pregnancy was really hard on Diane. After Elaine was born, Diane was bedridden for weeks, and couldn't do very much for months. Alan was a toddler. That didn't help. When my company insisted I start visiting home office twice each month for a week, Diane took the brunt of everything, taking care of the kids while still not feeling one hundred percent. I felt terrible for what she went through, but didn't know how to help.

"When she'd finally recovered…I don't know…we were different; distant. Everything felt like we were just going through the motions, doing everything we needed to do, but neither of us was happy to be doing it. We went to counseling, talked to friends, went on vacations together. We really tried. Nothing seemed to help. We didn't mean to drift. We just did."

He was silent for a time. Then his voice crept out, quiet and strained.

"Five years ago, almost to the month, I was in San Fran on one of those trips. It had been a long day, and I got back to my hotel late. I was starving and exhausted, so I headed downstairs to the hotel bar. While I was waiting for my dinner, this guy in shorts and a T-shirt walked in. He'd just finished a workout in the hotel gym, and he was sweaty. His shirt stuck to his body in all the right ways. I didn't mean to stare. My eyes just wouldn't look away. Neither did his.

"He was my first."

25

———————

BENDS AND FORKS

Ryan and I talked for over an hour.

He told me more of his journey, how the random first encounter in San Francisco bloomed into other encounters. Then he discovered AOL, and finding occasional companions on his travels became easier. He said he only hooked up a couple times a year, but my gut told me it happened more often. My heart ached as he fought tears and talked about Diane and the kids. While he'd continued to explore his sexuality, his relationship with them—especially with Diane—weighed heavily on his conscience.

From the anguish in his voice, I could tell it was crushing him—and had been for years.

My uptight PK brain wanted to be offended, to be angry and stand up for Diane. He *had* broken his vows, repeatedly. He *had* lied for years, hidden his truth from her—and himself. I understood the journey, the battle of identity that tore your soul apart, and empathized with his searching and questioning. Hell, I'd followed a similar path; virtually every gay person does. The self-doubt and self-loathing were familiar, like a second skin I'd learned to shed when necessary. Eventually, we grew past those scars—at least, that's what I hoped would happen. Mine still felt fresh some days. I'm sure his were raw and painful.

But I hadn't committed my life to someone else or fathered children who depended on my guidance and faithfulness. His discovery of himself would shatter their world. It would forever alter the trajectory of their lives. Alan was old enough to understand, but Elaine wouldn't. All she would know was the loss of a father she loved.

My heart ached for those little ones.

It was hours later, and I'd thought of nothing else since our phone call ended. I hadn't eaten; I had barely moved. Every time I thought I'd reached a conclusion, my head would argue the other side.

As quickly as I steeled myself to be righteous, I remembered how it felt to just talk with Ryan. There was a freedom, an openness, a fluidity to our conversations. That was something I'd never experienced with anyone, not even Connie or Dwayne. I'd never thought of conversation as an intimate act, but even our first date—the one I didn't think was that special—was filled with hours of intimacy through words and the simplicity of being together.

Sure, Ryan was hot as fuck. I now knew his fuck was hot too, but that wasn't what flooded my mind as I considered walking away. It was our chats. It was lunch at Cowtippers or breakfast at Le Peep. It was watching him get sugar packets dumped in his lap, and the way his poochy lip would try to curl but fail.

His eyes never failed. They smiled as wide as any mouth. They positively glowed when he was happy.

I would miss all that. I didn't just crave that level of closeness; I *needed* it.

What was I supposed to do now? Could I stay with him

given what he was doing to his family, what he'd already done? Could I trust he wouldn't do that to me?

Was that even a fair question?

He was facing his sexual identity. It was probably the first time he'd been fully honest with himself in four decades of life. Despite all the lying, he was actually seeking an honest answer.

The irony of that made me pause.

In the silence of my tortured thoughts, the phone rang. It was Dwayne.

"Just checking in. How did lunch go?"

Shit. I have to go through this all over again, I thought.

"Hang on. Let me get Connie on the line. I'd rather not have to repeat the whole show."

"That doesn't sound good," he said as I clicked the three-way call button.

"Hi, sweet pea." Connie's singsong warmed me through the receiver.

"Sweet pea?" Dwayne barked a laugh.

Connie went in mama lion mode. "It's my nickname for the sweetest pea in Atlanta. Don't you dare make fun of it."

"Easy, tiger. I'll call him pea from now on."

I gave them a halfhearted laugh. "Very funny, you two. Connie, would you mind giving Dwayne the *Reader's Digest* version of today? I don't think I can go over it again."

"Aww. You really are down, aren't you?" she said sympathetically. "Bottom line: Ryan's married with two kids. He's been playing around on the side while on business trips. He told Ryan all this, then—without warning— told his wife. She kicked him out. Now Ryan is homeless and sad, and Michael is miserable and confused about what he should do."

"Well, shit." Dwayne was never short for words, and he rarely cursed. This was bad.

"Can you give me a little more than that? I need my sherpa today, more than ever. Give me pearls of wisdom."

He grunted a laugh. "I'm not sure how wise I can be in this situation. What do you want advice on?"

That was frustrating. Wasn't it obvious?

"Ryan cheated and lied—*for years*. He's breaking up a wonderful family. I need to tell him to take a hike, right? The last thing I should do is date a liar and cheat, a wounded man who's just now finding himself. Right?"

Connie kept quiet, and Dwayne took forever to respond. By the time he spoke, I was off the couch and pacing.

"Do you love him?"

Fuck. That wasn't an answer, and it definitely wasn't on my list of things I thought he'd ask. I wasn't even sure I knew the answer.

"Maybe. I think so. I don't know. I'm falling in love with him. Is that the same thing?"

"Yeah, it counts." Dwayne's deep sigh blew through the phone line. "Look, Michael, I know you want this to be black and white, for there to be a *right* answer. That's how you were raised, to follow the one true path. Unfortunately, life isn't that clean and neat. Most paths bob and weave, probably fork a hundred times, and they're rarely free of obstacles or debris."

"I'm not following. Are you comparing Ryan's cheating to a bend in the road?"

"Don't get impatient. Hang with me." He had steel in his voice I'd never heard before. I recognized it as the steel of a father teaching his son. I'd never loved Dwayne more than I did in that moment.

"You should know better than anyone what it feels like

to come out later in life. You grew up thinking you were straight. Hell, the night we met, you practically preached a sermon about it. I seem to recall us sitting in a gay bar while you did that, but whatever."

Connie snorted.

"My point is this: if Ryan's family is anything like yours, he was taught, from the time he could understand, that his job in life was to grow up, get married, have a family, and carry the family name into the future. Based on what you've told us about him, he never questioned that. He did as he was raised to do. He got married. He had kids. Somewhere along the way, like you, his true nature found the surface and demanded to be acknowledged. While his actions were his own, and I understand how you would see them as cheating, it sounds like he felt trapped in a life that didn't fit. It might've been a good life, but was it truly the one meant for him? I actually feel sorry for him."

For the second time that day, a conversation held so many conundrums that my head hurt. My pacing was furious. I wanted to throw the phone. "That doesn't help me know what I should do."

Dwayne switched to a soft tone. "I can't give you the answer. It has to be yours."

With those words, my heart sank even lower. I hadn't thought that was possible.

How was I supposed to come up with the answers? My heart was in my throat and pounding. I wanted to cry, but tears wouldn't even cooperate. Now the two people I knew could guide me through this mess—

"Let me ask you this," Dwayne said. "Based on your conversation today, how does Ryan feel about all this?"

I didn't have to think about that one. "He's miserable. He knows he just shattered a family he's spent two decades building, and that damage will continue for the rest of his life—of all their lives. I can't tell whether he's more angry with himself or guilty. If I didn't know how much he loves his kids, I'd be worried about him hurting himself."

"What about how he feels toward Diane now?" Dwayne asked.

"He talked about her a lot today, told me how they met, the early part of their lives together. He loves her, and that's making this so much harder. He said the hurt in her eyes when she kicked him out felt like a sword in his gut. He said they'd never really had a fight in all those years—and then this happened."

No one spoke for another painful moment as I replayed our conversation in my mind.

"He said he knows she'll come around and accept him for who he is, that she's hurt and feels betrayed. He broke down crying several times as he talked about what his confession had done to her."

"That actually makes me feel better about his situation," Dwayne said.

"Huh? How?" I asked.

"If he didn't feel that guilt or understand clearly what his actions were doing to his family, he'd be a lot worse than a liar and cheat in my book. Nothing will ever make up for the damage he's causing right now, but I can at least understand him. He doesn't sound like one of those guys to just walk away from his obligations, especially those he loves."

"No, he's not like that. He'll never turn his back on Diane and the kids."

Where was Dwayne going with all this? The last thing I wanted to do was rationalize away the gravity of Ryan's actions. He might make my skin tingle, but I dreamed of a lot more in a relationship than just a hot body by my side. I wanted a guy with character and the strength to back it up, even when things were hard—*especially* when things were hard.

Then it hit me. That's exactly what Dwayne was getting at. Could Ryan honestly be expected to live a lie for the rest of his life? That's what his marriage to a woman was. He knew he was gay, especially after all the years of experimentation. Was a man in that position expected to live with a commitment he'd made before he truly knew himself? What kind of tortured, lonely life would that be?

The stubborn, conservative PK in me answered harshly. *Yes, absolutely, he should've lived with his decision and suffered like the sinner he was.*

God, hearing my own voice, how I would've answered a few years ago, I cringed. Had I really been that cruel; possessed so little compassion? Weren't religions supposed to uplift people, especially those hurting or in need? Had I only learned the part of the Good Book that condemned?

In that moment, I hated who I'd become—or who I had been. I wasn't sure. Everything was so confusing.

"Michael." Connie's voice cut in.

"Yeah?" I croaked.

"If you love him, don't give up. If you leave now, you'll never be able to go back. Everything you've told me about Ryan makes me think he's special. Most people never get a shot at that. There's always time to walk away later if you think that's the right thing."

"Just keep your eyes open and take it slow, alright?" Dwayne cautioned.

"So…you're saying I *should* stay with him?"

"I'm saying we won't judge you—or him—if you do. He'll have to face what he's done. Like you said, he'll be facing it for the rest of his life with his family. What *you* do with him in his next chapter has yet to be written. You have an opportunity to find out what those pages hold —*together*."

Did Connie really want me to give him a chance?

My heart lifted for the first time all day.

I still wasn't sure how my conscience would react tomorrow, but I *was* falling in love with him, and Dwayne was right. He'd never had a chance to know himself, to find himself—whatever that meant. Maybe I was put in his life to help him do that.

Or maybe I was justifying what *I* wanted.

Dammit. Why does life suck so hard sometimes?

"Thanks, guys. I love you both so much."

"We love you too, sweet pea." Connie sounded chipper again.

"Yeah, sweet pea. Me too." Sarcasm dripped from Dwayne's voice, but it was full of warmth too.

We hung up, and I flopped back onto the couch and stared at the ceiling. My heart might've settled, but my stomach was still doing somersaults. There wouldn't be much sleep tonight.

26

A NEW BEGINNING

Ryan and I sat across the same table we'd sat at when we first met. Caribou was special to us. The irony of returning here for this conversation wasn't lost on me as I looked into his deep, troubled eyes.

A week had passed. Ryan and I had chatted every day online, but had only spoken once over the phone. The strain in his voice on that call broke my heart.

As I cradled a coffee mug in my hands, he spoke quietly about the conversations he'd had with Diane, and the couple times he'd gone to see the kids. They had asked a thousand questions, all the ones you'd expect confused and frightened children to ask in their situation. Ryan's voice trembled.

I'll never know how he got through that first week—or how they did.

The bedrock of his emotional stability, his family, had been irrevocably altered—possibly shattered—and there was no way of knowing if he would forge relationships built on new truths or lose them entirely.

His watery eyes told me he had resigned himself to losing me as well.

I couldn't take the anguish on his face anymore, so I reached out and gripped his hands in mine.

His eyes widened.

I'd had a speech planned, but every word of it fled when my mouth opened. What came out was a stream of consciousness driven from somewhere deep inside, and I couldn't stop it.

"Ryan, I've thought about you a lot this week. Shit, you're all I've thought about." I was fumbling, but had to press forward. "I can't understand what you felt when you married Diane, or how your loyalties were strained as you realized your true nature. A huge part of me struggles with your vows, and the commitment you made to your kids, and how all that will change going forward—but just as I ask you to be honest with yourself, I have to do the same."

He was holding his breath.

"I'm in love with you."

There, I said it. Fuck, what now?

I blundered on. "I've tried to walk away from you. I've done it a million times in my mind, but every time you return. Ryan, I can't imagine my life without you in it. I know we just met a few months ago, and that sounds totally crazy, but it's the truth. It's my truth."

The death grip he put on my hands told me all I needed to know. Then he spoke.

"I'm so in love with you it hurts," he said. "When I'm not obsessing over how I hurt Diane or what will happen with the kids, I'm missing you. All I want is to be with you, to talk with you, to feel safe next to you. I've never felt that with anyone."

I made him feel safe? This man, twelve years older,

who ran a massive business and was more confident and surer of himself than anyone I'd ever known, found shelter in *my* arms?

A tear escaped his eye. I reached up and wiped it with my thumb. He leaned into my touch.

"I want that too," I whispered. "More than anything."

We'd run out of words, so we sat clutching each other's hands on the table, our eyes never leaving the other's. Lord knows what the people in that coffee shop must've thought about the two gays holding hands and crying in the corner. For the first time in my life, I didn't care.

"So what do we do now?" I asked.

The happier version of the man sitting before me peeked out. "I don't know about you, but being miserable makes me hungry. Can we go to Le Peep and get stuff thrown at us?"

I grinned. "That sounds perfect."

BETTY GREETED US AT THE DOOR. SHE GAVE RYAN AN ODD look, apparently having some diner-waitress-Spidey-sense that picked up on the mood of our day, then led us to a lonely table in the corner of the restaurant.

As we sat, she pointed an accusing order pad at Ryan. "Honey, you look terrible—and you're too cute to look terrible. What's going on?"

Ryan shrugged and gave her a weak smile. "Rough week. We're okay, though."

He glanced sideways at me when he said "we." I couldn't stop the warmth that swelled within.

Betty missed nothing. "Yeah, you two are bookends, alright. Best matched set I've seen in a while."

Ryan turned to me, and I melted into an inarticulate, babbling mess of rainbow glitter. "Yeah, he's dreamy. I mean, we're dreamy. No. We're good. I mean great. Matched. You said matched set. That's perfect. Oh, never mind."

Ryan grinned. "What he said."

She barked a laugh and waved her pad. "Told ya. Now, what's for breakfast?"

We ordered our usual. Ryan got eggs Benedict, and I ordered wholegrain pancakes with bacon and over-medium eggs. Le Peep had the fancy flavored creamers on the table, and our hands were a jumbled blur as we raced to grab the last of the hazelnut. There was a normalcy to ordering breakfast, something soothing I didn't fully understand. We both needed it.

"Where did you leave things with Diane?" I'd wanted to focus on lighter subjects, but needed some idea of what the future held.

He sighed as he stirred his coffee. "She wants me moved out by the end of the month. Guess it's time to find a place of my own."

"You could stay with me," I blurted out.

Where the hell had that come from?

In all my ruminations, that idea had never crossed my mind. Dwayne and Connie were going to shit a brick. Don't get me wrong, the idea of waking up beside Ryan every day made my heart skip a beat, but it was far too soon for that step. My rational brain scolded me as soon as the words flew out of my mouth.

He looked up from his mug and quirked a brow. "Really?"

I was in it deep now. *Shit.*

I nodded. "Sure. My place isn't fancy. I don't even have

end tables in the den, just cardboard moving boxes, but you can stay at my place as long as you need."

"It couldn't be long term. Diane would lose her mind if she knew I was living in your apartment."

I shot upright. "She knows about *me*?"

He nodded slowly. "I promised to tell her the whole truth, no more lies. She, uh, thinks you *turned* me."

I coughed. "Turned you? What am I, a vampire?"

"Something like that. 'Blood-sucking evil bastard' is probably closer to her description. You're the guy who stole my heart away from her." He raised his mug in salute. "It's not about you, really. She doesn't even know you. But she's looking for someone to blame, some explanation to ease the feeling that she failed, and you're the easy target."

"Wow." I leaned back. "I guess that makes sense. She knows she didn't do anything wrong, doesn't she? God, she can't carry guilt along with everything else. That's our job."

"Guilt is probably one of a hundred emotions she's feeling. And yes, I told her she's not to blame. It'll take time for her to understand that."

"Until then, I'm public enemy number one."

"Yeah, I'm pretty sure you won't be invited to Thanksgiving."

I knew he was trying to lighten the mood, but I couldn't pry myself out from the pile of shit he'd just dumped on me to acknowledge his attempt.

"I'll still need to find my own place." His eyes drifted back to his mug as he spoke his next words. "Maybe you could help me look?"

Was he asking me to help him find *his* new home, or a place for *us*? My brain danced between disbelief, elation, and complete shock. Was this even something I *should* consider? I mean, I had just asked him to move into my apartment. That was basically the same thing, just with cheaper furniture. Wasn't it?

He saw my mind whirling and grinned. "House shopping is more fun with somebody. Besides, it'll be fun to compare notes on what we both like and don't like. You know, for if we get a place together one day."

Guess that answered that.

My shoulders slumped. Why was I so disappointed? It was insane to even consider moving in together right now. He wasn't even divorced yet. Holy cow, had I shoved my head all the way up—

"Where'd you go?" He saved me from a terrible mental image.

"Sorry, house shopping sounds fun. Where were you thinking?"

"I work out of my house most of the time, so that makes things a little easier. Being close enough to help with the kids is the only real consideration. Maybe start with the Roswell area?"

"That's near my office."

He grinned and nodded.

He knew that. No freakin' way. He'd factored that in. That sneaky—

"I thought it might be nice to grab lunch during workdays."

I lit up. "If you're lucky, there might even be some lunchtime dessert. We can't exactly do a repeat in my office during a workday, but if you lived close, I could use my lunchtime for more…athletic adventures."

"Acrobatic is more like it, based on how your legs bent over that chair."

We both froze as Betty's voice cut through. "And just what were Michael's legs doing?"

Ryan actually turned redder than I did. I didn't know that was possible.

Proud she'd thoroughly embarrassed us, Betty leaned over and planted her palms on the table. There was very little of her cleavage we couldn't see. Gravity is an unforgiving force. "When I was your age, I could bend my legs—"

"And, we're done with breakfast," Ryan said, saving us once again. "Thank you so much, Betty."

She cackled. "Why do you think I always wear hoop earrings? Gotta be prepared for anything."

She tossed the check at Ryan's chest and laughed all the way back to the kitchen.

AROUND EIGHT O'CLOCK, THE SUN WAS STARTING TO SET, and Atlanta's skyline was framed in brilliant hues of orange and yellow.

I greeted Ryan as he stood outside my apartment door. He had a duffel bag slung over his shoulder and a sheepish look on his face. "Still willing to take in a stray?"

I chuckled, gripped his face with both hands, and pulled him toward me for a kiss. "Strays are kind of my thing, especially hot ones."

"You think I'm hot?" He grinned.

I rolled my eyes. "You're far too vain to ask me that. No one with abs on his toes has the right to ask that question."

He looked down at his flip-flopped feet and cocked his head. "Huh. Washboard pinkie. Never noticed that before."

I slapped him playfully. "Just get in here."

He eyed the sparseness of my apartment but had the good grace not to say anything.

"I know. It's pretty lame, but I haven't had time to furnish the place yet."

"It's…minimalist."

I laughed as we entered my bedroom, the only room with a full complement of furniture.

"No, it's *empty*, but thank you. Just drop your duffel over there in the corner. I've cleared a couple drawers in the dresser for you." I motioned to the 1950s dresser my mom gave me when I went to college. I think she'd used it when *she* went to college. It was functional, but not very fashionable. I'd never cared until Ryan showed up. Now I was embarrassed.

"You cleared drawers for me?" he asked from the doorway.

"Don't get all mushy. It's a practical thing. Your clothes will get all wrinkled if they stay in that bag."

He shook his head, grinning ear to ear.

I knelt to open the two bottom drawers. As I rose, Ryan's strong hands wrapped around me from behind and pulled me tight against his body. I could smell his salty-sweet musk; his breath was hot against my neck. I surrendered completely and leaned my full weight against him.

"The clothes can wait." His voice was raspy and full of hunger.

Warm lips pressed against my neck. I felt the gentle nibble of teeth on my ear, sending a jolt down my spine. I tried to turn to face him, but he held me fast.

"Oh no. You stay where you are."

I was powerless to resist.

His hands gripped my chest, caressing and kneading,

then slid down my stomach. Gentle fingers traced the outline of my abs through the fabric of my shirt before sneaking under and uniting our flesh.

His hands were warm, almost hot. His fingers tickled the tiny hairs trailing down my stomach, and I squirmed. He squeezed his arms tighter, gripping my body against his, and I felt how hard he'd become as he throbbed and pulsed.

Damn, I could feel it through my shorts. He ground against me, growling in my ear with each twist and turn.

Now *I* was pulsing. I moaned again, and he growled louder.

His hands traveled up my shirt until his fingers gripped my nipples. He teased, circling the base then grazing the tips. They'd never been sensitive before, but fire lit within them at his touch. What was this man doing to me?

Without warning, he pinched them between his thumb and forefinger, and my whole body lurched. In his grip, there was nowhere to go, and the blissful pain of his grasp shook us both. I tried to cry out, to say it hurt, but no words came, just a guttural howl. He twisted his pincers as his tongue rimmed the outside of my ear.

My cry deepened.

His tongue vanished and teeth began nibbling up and down my neck. His hands descended until they pressed the waistband of my shorts. When they fell to the floor, I stepped out of them as Ryan's palm wrapped around my hardened dick. It spasmed at his touch.

"There are so many things I've wanted to do to you," he whispered in my ear.

"Uh-huh," was all I got out.

He lifted my arms above my head and ripped off my shirt. Again, I tried to turn, but he gripped my shoulders to hold me in place, facing away from him.

"You're being a very bad boy. Keep that up, and I might have to punish you."

Punish? Oh, God. Please punish me. Punish me into the eighteenth century.

That was my inner voice. "Yeah?" was what squeaked out.

His hands drifted down my arms to rest on my hips. I heard him settle on his knees. He kissed the small of my back, then licked it tenderly. His tongue ventured lower, teasing my crack as it edged ever closer. When his hands left my hips and parted my cheeks, I stumbled forward. He laughed as he caught me.

"So jumpy," he said as he turned me to face the bed then shoved me face down onto it. A second later, my legs were spread wide and his face was buried in the fold of my buttocks. I tried to lie still, but every time his tongue edged my hole, I squirmed. I lost track of time—hell, I lost track of everything. I'd only had one guy do that to me, and Ryan's passion blew the other dude's effort out of the water.

He lifted my butt up to get a better angle. My dick slid against the bedspread with each thrust of his face. The friction was driving me crazy.

He finally came up for air.

I glanced over my shoulder, then turned and sat up facing him. He cupped my cheek tenderly and stared with the most intensely passionate gaze ever pointed my way. I looked down after a moment, suddenly awkward and unsure, but he lifted my chin, forcing our eyes to lock once again.

"Thank you," he said.

My brow furrowed. What had I done?

"I know what it meant for you to give me a chance

after…everything. I don't deserve your faith or trust, but I hope to earn it one day. You make me want—"

I leaned forward, grabbed his face, and pulled him into an unrepentant kiss. A salty tang dribbled into my mouth from the fresh tears he'd shed, and his body trembled. The change from overheated passion to tender vulnerability kicked my caretaking senses into overdrive. I wrapped my arms around him and pulled him into me, holding him as tightly as he'd held me before.

After several minutes, his trembling and tears ceased.

His hand drifted back to my head and stroked my hair as his eyes explored every curve of my face. In that moment, I saw a different man; no, not different, deeper layers of the man I already knew. His leathery shell had peeled away, and the frightened, exposed, hopeful little boy beneath begged for acceptance and forgiveness.

My heart lurched as I leaned forward and kissed him again. "We're in this together now. You'll never be alone."

Ryan's last wall crumbled. He buried his face in my chest and heaved again.

I don't remember how long we lay there. Time didn't matter. Nothing did, other than holding Ryan and making him feel loved. As sad as his tears were, my need to care for someone filled my heart with a joy I hadn't known in years. I was still amazed that this wonderful man wanted to be with me, wanted me to be the one holding him in his times of happiness or pain.

He finally stirred. I turned so my back was upright on the headboard, and he found his knees and straddled my legs. With one hand, he brushed fingers lightly across my chest until they found a nipple. This time, rather than teasing or rough, he caressed it as one might the most fragile glass.

"You're so beautiful," he said.

When I blushed and looked away, he leaned down and kissed me deeply.

"I'm in love with you, Michael Reed."

His mouth stopped any reply. A heartbeat later, his tongue was caressing mine with the same gentleness it had my nipple. I think that sensation, more than any other, sent my heart and mind spinning.

As we kissed, I reached down and pulled the bottom of his shirt upward. With a toss, we'd moved on to his jeans. Why had Wrangler invented the button fly? One button was bad enough, unfastening four while trying to maintain tongue-lock was nearly impossible. After several failed attempts, Ryan pulled back and laughed, then reached down and flicked the damned things free like it was nothing.

"You should see me do that with my teeth." He smirked.

I'd seen his cock before, but here, in the light of my bedroom, it was a wonder to behold. He noticed my widened eyes and laughed again as he stood on the bed, craning his neck to avoid the ceiling fan, then peeled off his jeans.

As God intended, he wasn't wearing underwear. Let the angels sing.

"You're so going to hell for that," the little angel's voice whispered in my head.

"Not a chance. Look at that thing. Angels should *sing about it,"* the devil rebutted.

"You really have to stop being amazed. I mean, I get it. It's glorious." He did his best Vanna White hand wave at his very large letter D. "It's all yours. No need to be intimidated."

I grunted a laugh, leaned forward, and took his cock in my mouth all the way to his balls.

Yeah, I overreached.

The gag that ensued sent Ryan into a fit of laughter that totally blew any sexy mood we had going on. For the first time that day, his tears were borne of happiness. The fucker took that moment to reach down and tickle my ribs—which are, like the rest of me, highly sensitive. I curled into the fetal position and howled like a newborn being slapped on the rump that first time. Ryan took that as encouragement, sat his weight on my legs to hold me down, and intensified his attack.

Right there, in the middle of my own goddamned bed, with the man of my dreams naked and erect, I peed all over everything. Not the demure little dribble one might mistake for sweat or something, a geyser of gold to rival the tallest of McDonald's golden arches.

If I live to be a hundred, I will never turn that deep crimson again. It's not possible.

Ryan practically fell off the bed, he was laughing so hard.

I leapt up, retrieved a towel from the bathroom, and stripped the bedding. Ryan helped, though I avoided making eye contact as he cackled throughout our first domestic activity. Once the sheets and comforter were on the floor and the mattress pad was wiped down, I looked up.

"That's my only set. I'll need to go to the laundry room before we can sleep in this bed."

We were both still naked. In the embarrassment of the moment, I'd forgotten that. Ryan hadn't.

He stepped forward and shoved my chest with both hands. We tumbled together back onto the bed.

"There's no way you're putting clothes back on. We have unfinished business."

His hand found my now-flaccid penis and went to work. His mouth did the same, and we were soon locked in a tongue dance for the ages.

"Where's your lube?"

I pointed to the side table drawer. When he leaned across me, stretching to his full length, I took him in my mouth again. The sound of a drawer opening was drowned out by the snap and pop of vigorous sucking and slurping. The salt of his sweat was nothing compared to the tang of his pre-cum. I ran my tongue over his opening and licked him clean. When his body quivered, I redoubled my efforts, gripping his balls in one hand, while cupping the base of his shaft with the other and sucking him vigorously.

He grunted, dropped the lube, and rolled onto his back so I had a better angle. Over the next several minutes, he pulled my head up, urging me to stop lest he finish before we ever got started. I ignored him and dove back down, desperate to give him half the pleasure his kisses had given me. A dribble of pre-cum became pulses of tang as he filled my throat.

Still, I didn't stop.

His back was now arched, his chest taut, his abs clenched in chiseled splendor. I ran my hand over them, feeling every crease, the hardness of his muscles. I thought he would soften, having fed me his load, but his cock only stiffened further. I looked up, dick in mouth, to find him staring down the length of his shaking body. I let him fall from my mouth but kept my hand gripping his base. He was so fucking perfect.

I swallowed the last of his contribution as I reached down for the fallen bottle. The pump had cracked. When I raised it from the floor, slippery liquid spilled across Ryan's chest and stomach.

"Shit, that's cold." He started to sit up. I pushed him back down and set the bottle on the night stand.

"You, stay still." He quirked a grin, enjoying the evil glint in my eye as I took both hands and smeared the lube across his pecs, over one arm then the other, then his abs. Finally, when he shone like a Roman statue in the rain, I slicked his cock. He threw his head back and moaned as I rubbed his head with one palm while my other hand stroked the length of his shaft. Despite his orgasm, he was still fully aroused.

I took one hand and moistened my hole, slipping a finger in to ready myself. Then, with his head still back and eyes closed, I lifted myself and guided him inside me. His hands reached up to grip my hips, but I grabbed them and leaned over his body to hold them above his head. Our lips were inches apart. I could taste his breath. I pressed my butt down and drove him deeper inside me as our bodies pressed together, smooth with oily wetness. There was no friction, but there was definitely heat.

Fire.

Holding his hands in place, I ground him in and out. His kisses became a torrent of hunger, of need, of desire.

I released his hands, and he wrapped his arms around me, pulling him into me. His cock found my prostate and I cried out, arching my back. Driven by my pleasure, Ryan's strong arms flipped me onto my back, careful to keep his pulsating cock deep inside me. Oil dripped from his chest as he rose above me. His hands squeezed my shoulder, then my chest, coating my body like I'd done his. He grabbed my dick, but I pushed his hands away, unwilling to let this end.

"Fuck me harder, faster," I begged.

He grunted and slammed himself forward. Our skin slapped, his balls ground against my butt. The bed squealed in protest. Every thrust sent an echo of something—something primal—screaming through my body.

He pumped faster, and his moans grew louder. Then he stopped, and I felt his hands grip my shoulders. Again, without removing himself, he flipped me over and spooned me from behind. I hadn't thought he could go any deeper, but now learned how wrong I had been. I tried to relax, but the thrill he sent through me caused my whole body to tense. He hardened more each time I clenched.

"Oh, God. I'm so close," he said through gritted teeth.

"Don't stop. Please."

He didn't.

With one last maneuver, he pressed me face down and spread my legs, arching my butt toward him again. I gripped the corners of the bed, my arms stretched as wide as my legs. Every muscle in my oil-slicked arms and stomach flexed, and my ass clutched his dick like a vise. I felt his pulse quicken through the throbbing of his cock. I couldn't believe he lived in my body. My mind raced. My heart danced. My body shook.

His thrusts were now so fast I could barely take a breath between them. He grunted with every push, loud and deep, somewhere between growl and groan. His sweat dripped hotter than the lube. He interlaced our fingers as he bent over me, thrusting, until he released one last cry in time with his body's explosion.

I could feel the heat of his life within. It was his second time, yet thrust after thrust sent more of him inside me. I reveled in the thought of us becoming one.

He started to pull away, but I reached back and held him. "Don't pull out."

"It's your turn."

"I want you inside me when I cum."

He bit my ear, and my butt squeezed. "Ahhh," he called out.

"That's what you get for biting. Now do your job, mister."

He grunted, then reached around and began stroking me. I'll never know how he stayed hard, but as he rubbed my dick, his own began thrusting once more. I didn't last long. Every part of my body cried out for release. Ryan's hand obliged.

Sticky, sweaty, and slick, we lay spooning, Ryan inside me.

Neither of us dared move.

We fell asleep as one.

27

HOME SWEET HOME

I woke the next morning to the warmth of Ryan's body pressed against mine. One arm still held me close. I could hear his slow, steady breathing as he slept. We'd fallen asleep with him inside me—the thought of which made me giddy—but sometime in the night, he'd popped out. I guessed even his eternal erection had to subside at some point. Little Michael was jealous of his staying power.

After a delicate un-sticking, I watched Ryan for a few moments. His normally perfect hair was thoroughly mussed. I reached down and moved it out of his face, and there were those lips—one normal, the other slightly puffy. It reminded me of a model who'd gone to the wrong plastic surgeon. How had I seen it as a flaw, a reason to strike him from the list? Staring down at his sleeping form, I couldn't imagine a more perfect feature on a man. I loved how that lip felt as it pressed tenderly against mine, how it tasted when I swirled it with my tongue or nibbled it with my teeth.

It was part of Ryan, and I loved it.

He didn't stir, so I rose and walked into the kitchen to make coffee. The air conditioner had been on full blast and, without clothing or Ryan's arms to keep me warm, I regretted not throwing on a T-shirt and shorts. The coffee maker took several minutes to heat water, so I did what everyone did when boiling water—I leaned back and watched it intently.

"You know that doesn't make it heat quicker."

I nearly jumped out of my shorts—well, I would've if I'd had any on.

Ryan wrapped his arms around me and, despite his chuckle at my jumpiness, I leaned into him.

"Good morning." He kissed my neck.

I turned to face him, wrapping my arms around his back. "Good morning to you too."

"So, it's Sunday. Pretty good day to look at houses."

I pulled back.

He raised his palms. "I need a place to live, and you volunteered to help me find one, remember?"

"Right, sorry. Guess I need this coffee more than I thought." I let out the breath I'd been holding.

I poured each of us a mug, then added three hazelnut creamers and one Splenda. We liked our coffee the same way. Try not to gag at the sweetness of that.

Thirty minutes later, we'd both showered and thrown on clothes—something I was disappointed to see as he walked back into the den in faded khaki shorts and a green Journey T-shirt.

"Journey?" I pointed at his chest.

"Yeah, my all-time favorite band."

"No freakin' way. They're my all-time."

Yes, another saccharine-soaked moment. Get used to it.

We scanned the newspaper for townhouse listings, then

logged into AOL and pulled up a couple realtor sites. Once we had a list of ten potential townhouses, we set our mugs in the sink and headed out.

There was a comfortable normalcy in that morning. We weren't doing anything earth-shattering—just waking, having coffee, and driving around town—but it felt right. I remember staring out the window of his car as we drove past the first few possibilities. He ruled them out from the street—but the simple act of us discussing their pros and cons struck me. He wanted my opinion. He cared what I thought, what I liked and disliked about each home.

We really were doing this together.

And it was the most natural thing in the world.

If my twenty-two-year-old self could see me then, he would've scoffed at the idea of two dudes holding hands as they drove around town, looking at houses and talking about landscaping. He would've ridiculed the sinful nature of their union. He would've been sickened.

That guy really was an ignorant asshole. I might've made a million mistakes since then, but I'd learned to love more than hate, to respect rather than scorn. I'd come a long way in only a few years. A spark of pride bloomed at that thought.

Now there was a *we* in the conversation.

THE BED WAS NEATLY MADE WITH FRESHLY CLEANED SHEETS by the time Ryan got back to my apartment the next day. He'd spent much of his afternoon at his company's local office, going over pitches submitted by travel agencies vying for their business. I was in the kitchen cutting carrots and onions when the key rattled in the lock.

God, that was a beautiful sound.

"I'm home."

Home. He'd called my apartment *home;* he called *being with me* home.

Every ounce of sappiness in me welled up and I had to fight back the tears. The last thing I needed was to let this incredible man think I was a perpetual puddle of mush.

"It feels so good to call this place home and see you first thing when I'm done with my day." He'd out-mushed me.

A tear slipped free. I tried to recover. "Darn onions."

"Come here. Let me get that." He spread his arms wide. I raced around the counter and fell into them, nuzzling my nose into the space between his neck and collarbone. I'd found that spot last night during one of our flips and knew instantly it would be my favorite place in the world. I sucked in a long breath, drawing in as much of his scent as I could hold. He held me close and kissed the top of my head.

"I missed you today," he whispered.

When I pulled my face out of his neck, tears were flowing freely. He reached up and wiped them.

"What's all this?" he asked.

I beamed through my leakage. "This doesn't feel real yet. It's everything I want, but feels a little overwhelming. I don't think I've ever been this happy."

His lips held mine for a long moment, then he drew back.

"I found another townhouse we need to look at."

That wasn't what I expected—not that I had any particular conversation in mind in that blissful moment.

"Oh, where?"

"Roswell. It's a two-unit building. From what I can see

in the ad, all the houses around it are single-family. The best part; it's on a cul-de-sac, so the street's quiet and there are only a handful of neighbors. It's two streets off the main strip, so we'd be close to everything."

There was that *we* again.

We were looking for a home for *him*. When had this become something else? Was I reading too much into his words, hearing what my heart hoped to hear? I did that sometimes. It's a Pisces thing. We daydream and sometimes blur the line between reality and what we wish reality would be. I rather liked living in my daydreams, but they could impede clear-thinking at times.

"I want you to move in with me when I get my new place."

I stumbled back a pace. "You want…what? Really?" Did he seriously just ask me to move in with him? "What about Diane and the kids? What will she think? We've only known each other a few months. Is this smart? Are we rushing things? Dwayne would kill me. Connie…she adores you. Never mind her. Are you serious?"

He chuckled at the torrent of questions. "Yes, I'm serious. Diane will be fine—in time. I'll continue seeing the kids at her place. She'd prefer that, even if I lived alone. You'll have to be patient with everything. It's going to get rough before it gets better, and I'll probably be hard to handle some days. Are you okay with that?"

My smile became a serious line. After a moment's thought, I nodded. "I'll support you, no matter what. I can't imagine what she's going through, what the kids will go through—and you'll need to be there for them—but you are *my* priority, and I'll be there when *you* need me."

His brow furrowed, then his mouth set as he cupped my cheek. "Michael, listen to me. Yes, we're still new—and yes, this *is* crazy—but I know what I want. I want *you* to be the last thing I see before I fall asleep, and the first thing I see when I wake up. Every day."

I don't remember if I spoke. The next thing I knew, he'd stepped forward and held my head firmly in both hands, forcing my eyes to his. It would be the first time I ever saw his lip quiver as he spoke.

"I love you, Michael, more than anything. We'll face it all together." His thumbs stroked my cheeks. "Will you live with me?"

My voice was a pitiful squeal, but I managed a "yes" before the cutest lip in the world pressed passionately into mine.

That was the moment I released all control and surrendered the last of my self-protective walls. That was the moment I gave myself fully to Ryan.

Carrots and onions forgotten, we found ourselves naked and filling each other with love—and everything else.

Fuck, there went the sheets again. We'd be spending another night naked without bedcoverings.

I really needed to buy another set.

28

———

STRAWBERRIES AND CHAMPAGNE

Three weeks later, Ryan made an offer on the townhouse in Roswell. We closed two weeks after that.

Our new home was exactly as he'd described it: half of a large, two-story house on a secluded cul-de-sac with ten other single-family houses. Yards were neatly tended, but not pretentiously so. Massive oak and pine trees towered over everything, casting dancing shadows on the street. Most of the houses were several decades old, and there was little uniformity to their construction, giving the neighborhood an eclectic, cozy feel. The front porch of the neighbor immediately across the street was littered with colorful plants and ceramic statues of animals and gnomes. A rainbow flag fluttered on a pole above the front door. The lesbians-in-residence, a couple who'd been together for more than thirty years, were the first on the street to welcome us.

Ryan rented a truck and retrieved what few things he was taking from his marriage. He felt strongly about his role in supporting his family. As he put it, he was the cause

577

of their marriage ending, so he should support them, no matter what. Diane offered to sell the house and split the proceeds. He refused, insisting she stay, and offered to sign the deed into her name. He argued that the kids needed stability, and that was *their* home. It was hers too. With the exception of a bedroom suite they'd used in a guest room, a recliner, and a coffee table from their game room, he relinquished all the furnishings as well.

In the end, he volunteered to pay more in child support than was ordered, and agreed to alimony above what the law required. He was determined Diane and the kids would not suffer beyond the emotional toll that was unavoidable.

He never wavered in putting them ahead of himself, and my respect for him grew with each decision.

Despite the two-month notice period with my apartment, we moved my things into the townhouse the week after closing and quickly fell into a comfortable routine. Ryan joined my gym so we could work out each night together. Aside from getting to spend more time together, he was a fantastic training partner, never giving me more than a moment's rest, no matter how much I grumbled. I cooked most nights. There was something in the simple act of making dinner for us that gave me satisfaction I hadn't known before. It felt like I was doing something special for him with each meal—and that man could eat.

Even the act of going to bed became a ritual I found endearing. By the time we finished our workout, then finished dinner and cleaned the kitchen, it was dark outside and we were both exhausted. We would read in bed before shutting off the lights, Ryan some business or self-help book, me an epic fantasy.

Ryan loved to be touching, almost as much as I craved it. He would hold me as we drifted to sleep. But even in the middle of the night, when one of us would roll away from the embrace, our hands would touch, or his foot would find mine and remain in contact until we woke. I barely remember a night when I woke without some part of us connected. I had never felt so loved; had never loved so deeply.

OUR NEIGHBORHOOD TOOK THEIR HOLIDAYS SERIOUSLY. When Santa was a month from his big ride, colorful lights, shimmering angels, fanciful reindeer, and enough tinsel to bury Tinsel Town in silver splashed across the lawns surrounding us. Our tiny patch of grass, which was more brown than green since fall had surrendered to winter, was a pitiful reminder that we needed to get into the holiday spirit—and fast.

We spent one Saturday tree shopping, stopping at Caribou for some pumpkin-flavored foo-foo drink Ryan swore would change my life. I'll admit, it was tasty, but there was nothing life changing in that cup, no matter what he said.

We decided to go the tasteful route, one that would meet with Ryan's mother's approval. Strings of steady clear-white lights outlined our roof, while netting with matching lights stretched over the hedgerow. A lone holly bush rose from the ground about twenty yards in front of our house. Ryan couldn't resist shaping it like a Christmas tree and putting a blinky star topper on its tip. It was *sort of* classy—probably over the line for his prudish mom— which meant I loved it.

When the actual holiday week rolled around, we cele-brated apart. It was Ryan's holiday with his kids, so they drove north to spent time with his parents. I drove back to Nashville to celebrate Santa with the pack. Both trips proved uneventful—unless you counted us ducking away from our families to talk on the phone several times a day. We were young and romantic as hell. I'd say we were hopelessly romantic, but we were actually quite hope*ful*.

Life returned to its relaxed routine once Santa found his way back to the North Pole. Basketball was again in a mid-season frenzy, and I officiated five or six nights each week. That stole from our time together, but made the moments we shared that much sweeter. Funny how it works that way, isn't it?

29

DID SOMEONE ORDER LIMES?

I was born on my mother's birthday, the twelfth of
March.

That meant two things.

First, it wasn't just a celebration of my birth, it was
"our day," as my mom called it. Before the whole *gay thing*
happened—yes, that's what she called *that*—we were close.
Our day would spark personal celebrations, usually
involving the two of us escaping the rest of the pack to
spend the day doing whatever we fancied in the moment.
I've often missed that closeness with her.

Second, according to astrologers, when one is born on
his mother's birthday, all the attributes ascribed to his birth
sign—and the rising and falling moons and suns and whatever else they say counts—are doubled. Double is my inter-
pretation. The astrology books I half-mockingly read used
terms like "exponential increase" or "multiplication factor."
I've never fully believed in all that, but I can tell you one
thing. Every description of a Pisces I've ever read fits me
perfectly, and the whole psycho Pisces addendum due to
our day also makes some weird cosmic sense. We both

share a creepy intuition, as well as an empathic sense that would make Miss Dione jealous. More importantly for our conversation, it made me feel *everything* deeply, especially emotions related to sentiment.

Let's face it. I was a mush pit.

Stop snickering. It's endearing. Right?

When my birthday rolled around, the psycho Pisces in me anticipated grand gestures of rose petals and incense, gifts wrapped in silk, and champagne bubbling out of gold-rimmed flutes. When Ryan left for work without so much as a birthday kiss, I was disappointed. When lunch rolled around, and he didn't come home to surprise me with naked goodness—or at least a cheesecake—I was disheartened.

By two o'clock, I hadn't received a single birthday phone call or email.

Not from Connie.

Not even from Dwayne.

I called Dwayne. He *never* forgot.

His phone rang until the machine picked up.

Yes, kids, it was an actual machine, not the built-in voice thingy we have these days.

Anyway, I left a quick message, not mentioning that it was my birthday. Every Pisces will understand this: it was *their* job to remember, not my job to remind, otherwise, it wouldn't mean anything.

Can I get a Piscean amen? Anyone?

I needed a pick-me-up—badly. So I dialed the one person who *always* made me smile: Connie.

"Hey, sweet pea."

"Hey, Con."

"Oh, honey. Why do you sound down? What did Ryan do now?"

I chuckled. I loved that mama bear.

"He's wonderful, hasn't done anything. Guess I'm just a little blue."

"Isn't it your birthday? You're not allowed to be blue on your birthday. It's the law."

I was grinning already. She remembered. "Yeah, I know. Guess some people are just rebels."

"Well, happy birthday." There was commotion in the background, probably Think!ers making a muck of something. "Hey, I need to run. Ted's at it again. Don't you miss this place?"

I laughed. "Not even a little. I miss you tons, though."

"Aww. Miss you too. Let's spend Saturday together. Do a tour of barriers in town or something."

I chuckled at our old joke, but couldn't hide my disappointment with her inability to spend time with me on *my* day.

"Sounds great. Looking forward to it."

I hung up. Woe-is-me wasn't my normal color, but I was wearing it with pride that day.

Then, for a brief moment, there was a glimmer of hope. Ryan called from work around four o'clock and told me to dress for dinner. He'd made a reservation at some swanky place I'd never heard of. It sounded expensive. My heart danced a little jig.

"This'll be beautiful, just us, babe. I want to make you feel special."

By the time I hung up, my heart was full, warm, and fuzzy—and that's a hard combination to hold in one's chest at the same time.

Two and a half hours later, we drove into the lot of the Hilton. Nikolai's Roof was the legendary restaurant on the hotel's thirtieth floor, offering breathtaking views of the city and a mouthwatering menu that featured house-infused vodkas, caviar, and a dessert menu to make the czar's toes curl. I'd heard about the place a thousand times, but never dreamed of eating there.

Ryan wore black slacks with a crisp white button-down. I settled on my best jeans, a forest green long-sleeve shirt, and a black leather jacket. As the elevator doors opened and we got our first peek, Ryan leaned over and said, "I think we're a tad underdressed."

I thought we looked like a million bucks. Screw all those stuffy folks in their ties and dresses.

He nibbled the top of my ear, and all thoughts of clothing evaporated.

"May I help you, sir?" the maître d' asked, his thick Slavic accent purring with each word.

Ryan stepped forward. "Yes, thank you. Reservation for Lowell. I believe Lina has the room prepared."

The maître d' scanned his book, then looked up meaningfully at Ryan. "Of course, Mr. Lowell. Follow me, please."

We followed the man who was dressed—and waddled—like a penguin.

I elbowed Ryan and leaned in to whisper, "Did you slip him a twenty? What was with that look he gave you?"

Ryan shrugged.

My Pisces Spidey sense stirred. *Shit.* He was up to something.

We walked all the way around the circular floor, past dozens of tables. The food was as elegant as the guests. Every server we passed smiled in greeting and bowed at the waist. Their gestures of respect, along with their deep maroon waistcoats with tails, made the whole affair feel like traversing the court of Czar Nicholas—before that pesky revolution took it all away from him.

As we made the final turn in our circle, the maître d' turned sharply to his left and waddled into the center of the column. A stylized door covered in gilding and deeply carved Russian lettering barred our way. Our guide rapped one white-gloved knuckle against the door, then turned the knob to allow us entry.

The first thing I saw was a wall of flowers. On the far wall hung hundreds of glass vials, with a fresh flower protruding from each. The effect of hundreds of flowers of every variety and color splashed across a black wall and lit by strategically placed spotlights was stunning. Equally beautiful flowers overflowed from ornate vases displayed at precise intervals on the table. Even the buffet against the near wall was etched with gold and laden with flora.

This was a private dining room, designed for no more than twelve, but the room *felt* massive.

Ryan's hand on the small of my back guided me forward toward the table. I was so distracted by the ambiance that I'd yet to look at the table—specifically, at how many places were set. In a world-class restaurant with an eye for detail such as this, nothing was done without purpose. Why was the table set for four? And why were two of the chairs already filled?

My eyes raised from the tablecloth and caught on a crystal tumbler filled to the brim with limes.

Something felt *so* familiar about that.

I looked up. My head cocked to one side, trying to process what my eyes were seeing. I was baffled.

"Dwayne?"

My gayfather, the greatest friend and sherpa to ever wear the rainbow robe, smiled up at me.

I still didn't get it.

"Connie?"

She was sitting next to Dwayne.

She giggled and waved.

I turned to Ryan. He was beaming.

"We're here for your birthday, dummy. Ryan flew me down," Dwayne said.

My breath caught as a hand flew to cover my gaping mouth. I knew what was happening, but I couldn't believe it. At thirty years old, no one had *ever* thrown a birthday party for me. The pack never had much money, so there was little joy there. I was a band nerd in high school, so popular kids coming over to wish me well wasn't in the cards either.

Ryan had arranged my first birthday party.

He'd kept it secret, coordinated with the people I loved most, even flew one of them hundreds of miles just for dinner. I knew how amazing this was, but my brain struggled to accept its reality.

"What do you think?" Ryan asked, his husky whisper tickling my ear.

"I...Ryan...that's Dwayne...and Connie. Why—?"

He laughed, one of those deep-in-the-belly rumbles that made a whole room feel merry and bright. Connie and Dwayne joined him, adding a tenor and soprano to his baritone.

It was the most beautiful melody I'd ever heard.

I looked from Connie to Dwayne, then to Ryan, each of whom was smiling broadly. One of the servers pulled my chair back and motioned for me to claim the table's head as Ryan walked around and sat in the seat opposite.

We dined on the finest filet, sampled exquisite vodkas, savored the deepest, most aromatic wines—and laughed like there was no tomorrow. Connie's perky, sometimes snarky jibes, mixed with Dwayne's dry attempts at humor, had Ryan and me practically peeing our pants at the table. At one point, I noticed two of the ever-present servers hiding chuckles of their own. The evening was as delightful as it was delicious—and Ryan had done it all for me.

That just blew my mind.

For me.

Midway through dessert—the *fourth* course of the evening—I had one of those *Matrix* moments. The room froze. Everyone's motion stilled. Even the sounds of the diners outside halted. I was the only one able to move and see and feel. Connie was frozen mid-giggle, Dwayne had his drink halfway to his mouth, and Ryan was—Ryan was staring at me. His gaze was intense, his eyes curled upward. His mouth was set, not in a frown, but a pose of deep consideration. There was such depth to his gaze, such warmth—and *love*. I could've stared into that gaze for a lifetime.

Unfortunately, the maître d' found the pause button, and everyone started moving again. Connie coughed and held a linen napkin to her mouth as her giggle died. Dwayne downed the last of his Jack and Coke. The servers finished clearing our dessert plates. And Ryan—

Ryan's gaze remained.

His gaze at me.

Right there, across a table in one of the fanciest restaurants around, I saw the depth of his love. I saw it in his eyes, in the set of his jaw. I saw it in the thoughtful tending to *every* detail the evening offered.

I'd always said I'd know when the right man came along because everyone in the room would disappear when our eyes met. I would forget anyone else existed. He would consume my attention, my desire, my need.

In that moment, lost in pools of steely gray, everyone around us faded into the background. The scurrying servers vanished. Connie and Dwayne became blurs in the periphery. But Ryan—my beautiful, strong, amazing Ryan—he sharpened into focus. His poochy lip quirked into a lopsided smile, and my heart soared.

A life flashed before my eyes. Not a life lived and passing, but one yet to come. I saw lunches and dinner parties, vacations and quiet evenings, adventures and trials. Woven throughout every chapter, every scene played out on the stage of my mind's eye, was the man sitting before me. I let my inner Pisces take control and dream with unfettered abandon.

And Ryan's gaze remained.

EPILOGUE

My Dearest Reader,

Thank you for sticking with me through our latest adventure. This period of my life wove together challenges and lessons for which I am thankful.

I sincerely appreciate your trust and support as we journey together. Topics such as HIV or men and women coming to terms with their identity later in life are delicate and challenging—and often messy. Yet they are *real* life for so many of us. We all struggle with internal doubts and regrets, successes and failures, triumphs and tragedies. I tried my best to weave in cheeky humor while remaining true to the beautiful people and experiences I was privileged to encounter.

I also understand that MM romance generally involves the ever-popular Happily Ever After ending. Let's call the end of this book Happily for Now. Ryan was truly amazing. He still is. We remain distant friends and chat online occasionally. I loved him with my whole being, in a way that comes to us only once or twice in a lifetime, if we're very, very lucky.

Once a heart is given freely, it can never be fully reclaimed.

I will always love him that way.

It would've been easy, as an author, to write this series with one Disney-esque ending after another, but I wanted to be honest to that truth, even if it strayed from literary norms.

Thank you for understanding and enjoying the ride.

And yes, I said *ride*. Stop it, you naughty sausage.

Get your copy of My Last Date to continue Michael's (my) journey.

My
Last
Date
CaseyMorales

1
____

HAPPY TWO YEARS

Ryan bounded down the stairs into the den. He wore little more than a broad grin and white cloth held together by a purple cord tied around his waist.

"What do you think?" He walked the length of our cozy den, turned, and struck a manly pose. "Roman enough?"

How did he manage to make his chest and arms look meaty in a makeshift toga? I swear his abs even poked through. Some people really had won the genetic lottery.

"You're a regular Caesar salad."

He grabbed a pillow off a chair and hurled it at me.

"Hey! No abusing the palace staff."

He laughed. "This is gonna be a blast. I've never done a murder mystery party before."

"Me either." I held up a thick binder. "I've been studying the case all afternoon. There are so many details I have to tell one character, but not another, and at seemingly random times I have to pass secret notes to players as they *discover* clues or hints. Most of those notes are cued off whatever crazy things the players say throughout the game. This narrator gig is real work."

He leaned down and gave me a peck on the cheek as he headed into the kitchen.

"You'll do great. You love telling stories," he called out between test bites of marinara. "Damn, this is really good, babe."

I'd started the made-from-scratch lasagna hours earlier, determined to let the sauce simmer for as long as possible before assembling the layers of Italian goodness. In addition to the traditional sauce, meat, cheeses, and pasta, I added mushrooms and spinach. This was one of Ryan's favorites and I wanted it to be perfect, both for him and the gaggle of gays about to assemble for our mystery mayhem.

THE PAST YEAR AND A HALF HAD PASSED SO QUICKLY.

During that time, we'd fully nested in our townhouse and established ourselves as a couple in the neighborhood. The lesbians across the street had latched onto us immediately, but others had approached with a bit more caution. There was a keen difference between living inside the gay bubble that was Midtown and living near it. We were clearly outside the cozy gay sanctuary, but close enough to feel its glow on our faces when we walked outside.

The relationship between Ryan and his ex, Diane, had evolved from confusion and bitterness into friendship and partnership. That had required time and countless hours of venting, crying, and a million questions anyone in her position would ask. I was so proud of how patient he'd been with her, but was even more impressed with her compassion and willingness to be open to the man who'd hurt her so deeply. It took such strength for her to accept this new person she was getting to know. At least, I guessed that's how it felt for her. We never spoke.

There were a few times Ryan came home exasperated by some of her questions. It reminded me of facing the inquisition by my parents every time I went home. I wanted to scream, "We've been over this a thousand times," but compassion drove me to follow a different path with those conversations. Ryan loved Diane, and she loved him. Their realities were intertwined, and only through love and understanding would their family survive and grow stronger.

Again, compassion reigned.

It's funny how often that word came to mind—and how critical it was for all of us.

Ryan and Diane remained a unified team in raising their kids, and while I didn't think she would ever truly understand Ryan's journey, she finally came to some healthy conclusions. She called one Saturday afternoon while we were cleaning the living room. I knew something was up, because Ryan's voice bounced from friendly to curious to concerned. He dropped his dusting rag and sat on the couch, staring into nothing, as she spoke. I continued cleaning the kitchen, trying not to hover—or, at least, to not *look like* I was hovering. Midway through the call, his tears began. I couldn't take it anymore, so I tossed my own rag and sat beside him, my arm around his quaking shoulder. I could just make out her voice in the receiver. She sounded strong, resolute, yet warm.

She started by announcing she now knew their divorce wasn't her fault. She hadn't done anything wrong and had given herself permission to stop blaming herself. It was the Mount Everest of emotional victories, and I was thrilled to hear her conquer that climb. To lose one's family and their white-picket-fence future was hard enough. Add a thick layer of guilt to the equation and anyone would suffocate under its weight. No one deserved that, especially not the mother of Ryan's children, a wonderful, caring woman who'd unfortunately married a man eighteen years before he fully knew himself.

She went on to tell Ryan to give himself a break, that their breakup wasn't his fault either. He was living his truth, and as painful as that might've been for all of them, she respected his courage to face it.

Alan and Elaine were growing up quickly. Ryan spent every other weekend with them at their house. Diane might've accepted Ryan, but she'd likely never accept me. As he put it, I represented everything that tore her marriage apart. Deep down, she didn't really believe I'd turned Ryan gay—like some rainbow-colored vampire with fairy dust dripping from my fangs—but for her, it was painful to think of me, the guy who now made Ryan smile. That had been her job for nearly two decades. As much as I wanted a relationship with the kids, I couldn't blame her for being protective of them—and of herself. She'd been through enough.

Ryan and I had become *that* couple. You know, the one others ogle over how they look at each other? That ogling came with admiration, a hint of jealousy, or the desire to visit the nearest dentist from the saccharine dripping from our mutual gaze.

Yeah, we were hopelessly in love.

Actually, that's inaccurate. We were hope*fully* in love.

Ryan wouldn't sleep without some part of us touching. Most nights we drifted off with my arm wrapped around him, our bodies pressed tightly together. His hands clutched mine until sleep overcame him. Even when the room was too hot to spoon, he pressed his toes against my leg. Somehow, we were always connected.

I'd never felt so safe, so loved.

And I'd never loved so freely and deeply.

In every prior relationship, I'd held a part of myself back, maintained that last wall to protect my heart in case things ended. The only exception prior to Ryan had been Carter, my first, and that was only because I had absolutely no clue what I was doing. After that gut-wrenching breakup, I vowed never to give up that last line of defense against heart-crushing pain.

Ryan made it past that wall.

He scaled it—or smashed through it, I'm not sure which.

I couldn't keep him out, and I didn't want to. A little over a year into our relationship, I felt that defense crumble. We were on another of his work trips in San Francisco. He'd just locked me up in an Alcatraz cell, one of our favorite tourist destinations in Rice-a-Roni town. We laughed as we walked out of the prison. Other tourists glared and smiled at our silliness. The sun was setting on the bay. The breeze carried a tickling tang. As we reached the dock to board the ferry, he ignored the assembled masses and tenderly brushed the hair from my forehead. His gaze was intense, like peering into a bottomless well and finding no end to its depth. My breath caught when I looked into his eyes.

In that moment, I knew he was forever. He was *my* forever.

And the last wall fell.

IT FELT LIKE ONLY DAYS OR WEEKS AGO THAT RYAN AND I had met for the first time in Caribou, then made a day of putt-putt. But it had been years. Two of them, to be precise. Time moved so fast.

This gathering was our way of including our closest friends in the anniversary celebration. We'd seen so many gay couples break up in recent months that we wanted to give encouragement to those giving a serious relationship a whirl. We wanted to show them that two men really *could* make it work.

Ryan took another bite before tossing his spoon in the dishwasher.

"Dinner's in good hands. I'm going upstairs to finish getting ready. Need me to do anything?"

"Mind setting the table? There are place cards with each character's name and a seating chart on the table. I need each player seated in specific order. Everyone's supposed to arrive in character, and stay in character until the game is over."

His brows rose. "Wow. You really have been working."

"Yep. Now, Caesar, out of my kitchen before I beat you with dried pasta."

"Don't threaten me with a good time, Brutus. A pasta beating sounds fun, especially if it's your big noodle doing the spanking." He swatted my butt and scurried out of the room, his toga fluttering dramatically behind.

I tried not to smile, but Ryan knew how to push my buttons.

God, I loved it when he pushed my…

Never mind.

2

MURDER MYSTERY PARTY

Fin and Rob were the first to arrive. Rob wore a tight-fitting toga trimmed in purple; Fin was decked out in full Roman soldier regalia. The light of our lamps danced in the golden sheen of his breastplate, shin guards, and helmet. Atop the helmet was six inches of maroon plumes, marking him as a high-ranking officer. They had clearly visited a costume shop and were determined to be the evening's best-dressed guests.

"Hail Caesar!" Fin declared with a closed fist across his chest. He smacked it a little too hard and winced as he shook out his knuckles.

Rob and I giggled.

"Welcome, soldier. Who have you brought to my humble home?" I asked in character.

"May I present the Honorable Senator Velum Pendulum." He motioned with his hand, then leaned over and whispered conspiratorially, "He swings both ways, if you get my meaning."

I spit a laugh. Rob rolled his eyes theatrically.

This was going to be a fun night. There was no one in town with a sharper wit—or dirtier mind—than Fin.

"It is an honor, Senator. Please, come in. Enjoy some refreshment. The others should arrive shortly."

I bowed and extended a palm toward the dining room table. Ryan had found an ancient-looking jug at an antique shop and had dutifully filled it with wine for the evening. The glasses were plastic goblets he'd found at a party store. Ryan was definitely feeling the spirit of our Roman adventure.

The Senator and his guard were pillaging the charcuterie as I walked back to the kitchen to check on the lasagna. Before I could lift the Magic Spoon of Goodness, the doorbell rang again.

"Coming. You two keep eating," I called out.

I pulled the door open to reveal the last of our murder mystery cast. Abe, the only player assigned to an opposite-gender role, gave us his best Miss America pageant wave, completely ignored me, and strode into the room with his chin held high enough to catch rainwater in his nose.

Where Fin and Rob were relatively masculine—at least, relative to the more flamboyant of the gay species—Abe's flame burned brighter and more colorfully than the aurora borealis. He relished the opportunity to dress up and fan that flame. His foot-high blond Marge Simpson wig was paired with palm-sized, bangle-style clip-on earrings and a gaudy set of faux-gold neck chains. A silky cloth was wrapped around his waist, attempting to replicate a flowing white dress trimmed in gold. I'd seen that cloth on his dining room table not long ago. The faded mustard stain near his crotch gave it away.

Invoking the spirit of Monty Python, two halves of a coconut—the white meat still intact—covered his less-than-ample bosom, but did nothing to part the pelt of thick, wiry brown hair that blanketed his chest, shoulders, and back. Neon-pink lipstick was the icing on the very furry cake.

He looked like a Wookie with fruity boobs leaping out of a marshmallow.

"Hey, ya'll Roman hotties. The most voluptuous maiden the gods ever made has arrived. You may worship me now," he said in his most un-Roman accent.

Fin guffawed. Rob waved back with the floppy slice of salami he was holding.

"You know I love a man who knows how to wiggle his meat. Maybe I'll just sit in your lap all night, let you play with my coco-nips." He lifted his half-shells with his palms and tossed back his flowing hair.

Before I could react, Ryan appeared at the foot of the stairs. He'd added a wreath of golden leaves, apparently claiming the title of champion for his character. His arms bulged nicely out of his sheet-turned-toga, so I didn't call foul on his straying from the character sheet. After all, if coconuts were in play, who was I to question a few leaves on his head?

"How wonderful," Ryan opened his arms wide. "Our dearest friends together in our home. Oh, and you, Senator. You're here too, I see."

Ryan really was in character. His role, Flavius, absolutely hated Senator Sweet Cheeks, and wasn't shy about saying so. The good senator felt even more animosity toward the evening's host.

"Yes, Flavo, so good of you to invite me. Your home is so…quaint." He waved his salami about the room.

Satisfied the players were sticking to their scripts, I slipped out of the room to rescue the lasagna from the now-beeping oven. Ryan would never let me live it down if I burned his favorite dish on party night.

From the safety of the kitchen, I chuckled as everyone introduced their characters to the others. It was awkward at first, almost mechanical, as they recited lines from their character sheets. Ten minutes in, they'd caught the fever and were ad-libbing liberally and breathing life into their Roman alter-egos.

Flavius was stoic; the good senator grumbled and groused; while Gladius, our six-foot-four body-of-death Roman guard, let coconut-crusted Leesha nest in his lap and play flirtatiously with his plume.

IT TOOK OVER TWO HOURS TO MAKE IT THROUGH SALAD, lasagna, and tiramisu. When the fourth bottle of wine emitted that satisfying *pop* of a cork-pull, we skipped pouring its contents into the Roman jug and liberally refilled glasses around the table. Everyone stayed in character, but decanting the grape juice delayed the process of getting naughty Romans more drunk.

Hail Caesar!

The mystery revolved around a murder that had taken place the night before our gathering in the home of the host, Flavius. Each member of the cast was a suspect in some way, and the players' goal was to unmask the murderer with the information gleaned from the other players throughout dinner.

I stood and walked around the table, clearing the last of the plates, and handed a sealed note to Gladius as I passed into the kitchen.

It read, *Last night, while you were on patrol around the*

manse, two voices pierced the darkness. One spoke of "eliminating" the poor murdered Roman, while the other grunted in agreement. The conversation cut off mid-sentence as you rounded a corner near where the speakers were hiding. You didn't see them, but think one of them was Flavius, the owner of the manse.

We were getting down to the end. The clues were becoming pointed. What remained the most interesting mystery was how the players handled their information. These weren't seasoned actors, but they had to tie off loose ends while keeping their game face intact—or, in the case of Leesha, keeping her coconuts from falling off.

I looked back over my shoulder from the kitchen and caught Ryan staring at me. He smiled, and his eyes glittered in that way that told me I was the only man in his world. Two years into our relationship, his gaze still made my heart flutter.

I winked and disappeared into the kitchen, wondering if that gaze would change when he learned his beloved character, Flavius, was the murderer. A stage knife, complete with a squirter and vial of catsup, was prepared for his eventual execution.

His crime would forever be a stain on our house.

Fin drained the last drops of wine into his open mouth, nearly hitting the ceiling fan as he tipped the bottle.

Tall people suck.

Ryan and Rob were dousing and scrubbing the catsup stain on Ryan's toga. His execution had been epic. Fin took great pleasure in drawing the faux knife across his neck and emptying every last drop of condiment onto his chest and lap. Red splattered more than it shot, coating him and the nearby dining room table. Abe giggled and applauded, using his best golf clap, the fingertips of one hand lightly tapping the meaty palm of the other in a most delicate and feminine way.

As he clapped and mocked the dearly departed, one coconut lost its grip and clanked to the floor.

Uni-boob was horrified.

I laughed so hard my side hurt, and I nearly piddled on the spot.

"How can you laugh at a lady in distress?" he squawked, hastily retrieving the half-shell that was rolling in lazy arcs across the floor.

"Blood and broken boobs. What could be funnier?" I quipped.

Rob sucked in a breath and looked up from his dabbing. "That gives me an idea."

He waited for us to settle and look at him.

Oh shit. He was up to something.

He turned to Ryan. "You and Michael should come to Decadence with us."

Ryan cocked his head at me. I shrugged, utterly lost.

"Decadence? The holiest of holy gay holidays?" Rob gaped. "You two are hopeless. Just say yes. We're renting a house just off Bourbon Street. All you need to do is book a flight and go shopping."

"Shopping?" Ryan asked.

Rob looked between Ryan and me with pity. "Oh, sweeties. Have you seen your wardrobe? You look like lesbians headed to Home Depot for fashion week. You'll need something much tighter, and preferably easily removed."

He winked up at Fin. The giant grinned conspiratorially.

Ryan looked to me again.

I shrugged again, nodding once. "Why not?"

"Awesome! It's in two weeks," Rob said. "Oh, one thing. You'll want to take a day off, the one after we get back. You might need to recover a bit."

3

———————

BREAD PUDDIN'

R yan was in charge of travel for a large corporation. He negotiated preferred vendor arrangements with airlines, hotels, rental car companies, as well as a dozen other modes of travel or vital links in the moving-people chain. He had so many frequent flyer miles and free hotel nights that we rarely paid for travel or lodging.

Travel perks were seriously cool.

He turned toward me and leaned across the thick leather first-class recliner.

"So, babe. Do you have any idea what we're getting into down here? Rob had mischief in his voice when he invited us."

I snorted through my vodka-heavy Screwdriver. "Mischief? More like pure evil."

He grinned and raised a glass in salute. "What did Dwayne say about this trip? Did you tell Connie?"

"Oh yeah. Dwayne warned us away from dark corners. I asked if he'd been to a Decadence before, but he refused to answer. I'm pretty sure he's been a bad little boy in New Orleans at least once."

"And Connie?"

"She didn't really know what Decadence was. Just told us to have fun and stay safe. Oh, and to take pictures of any hotties we find. She's all about some man meat."

A little of Ryan's drink dribbled down his chin as he coughed a laugh. "She's a mess."

I rolled my eyes and nodded. "Thank you, Captain Obvious. I did look Decadence up online. It's basically a gay Mardi Gras. Street parties, private parties, alcohol flowing in the streets, beads flying faster than gay slurs, that sort of thing. It looked like a menu of deliciously debauched activities. We can choose to participate in some —or none."

"Huh. Okay. See anything you want to do?"

"Oh yeah. We can't come to New Orleans and skip the street parties. We both need to hobble back to the house with hundreds of beads weighing us down."

He chuckled. "Okay. What else?"

"I've never been to New Orleans. I'd love to do some touristy stuff, maybe while the boys are sleeping off—or on —whatever they do in the wee hours." I thought a moment. "They have these graveyard tours. They sound spooky scary—and a lot of fun. Oh, and everyone says the food there is the best in the world. We have to find some places where locals eat, outside the Quarter. I want to taste *real* New Orleans."

"Was there—"

"Oh, and there's a casino." I turned my whole body toward him, as much as the seat belt would allow. "I *love* casinos, and I'm pretty lucky."

He nodded. "Alright. Casino, check. You mentioned private parties. What did those look like?"

The little devil had been quiet for nearly a year. Something about being in a stable, loving relationship seemed to bore him. His sudden puff of smoke nearly made me drop my drink.

Michael, Michael, Michael. Are you going to be lame for the rest of your life? You used to be so much fun. Do you remember the silk ties?

"Hey—"

Oh, shut up and listen. You're only young once, and with Ryan's body and your ass, you two should be very popular in New Orleans. Promise me you'll go to at least one of the private parties.

"Fine. Whatever. Can you go away now?" I blew on my shoulder.

Vodka dispels demons. Who knew?

Ryan was staring intently. "You okay?"

"Yeah, sorry, was just thinking through what I found online." He was an understanding guy, but witnessing me chatting with imaginary voices might be a stretch. "So, there's a few parties that look like ads to the bars in Atlanta, straight-up dances. Other than being around new people, I don't think they'd be different from going to any other bar."

"Um, you forget. I've never been to a bar."

My mouth opened but nothing came out. I'd forgotten he was a newborn gay on many levels. It felt really weird to be the guy with experience. Did that make me his daddy? Shit. I was twelve years younger than Ryan. I *couldn't* be his daddy, could I? What were the gay rules on this? I'd definitely have to check the manual when we landed.

"Oh, babe. Okay. We can keep one of those on the list. My little virgin." I caressed his cheek.

"Oh, fuck off. What else?" He couldn't keep the wide smile away.

"There was a party for every flavor. The bears were popular with several nights. Leather and bondage found their way into almost every event. There were a couple bareback parties. The pictures in the ads were pretty clear on what would happen there. Let's see. There were parties every night at every bar, but they sounded like normal bar nights with a promo. There's a foam party one night. No idea what that means. There weren't any pictures, just an ad full of bubbles and words. One of the big paddle boats is hosting a dinner cruise with a show, probably cheesy musical theater in honor of the gay hoard visiting town."

"Sheesh. This sounds crazy. We've only got three days."

"That's not even half of it. When we get to the hotel, we should see if there are programs or a local newspaper or magazine, like *David* back home. We can pick from the menu easier if it's sitting in front of us."

"Makes sense. At least we won't get bored."

I chuckled. "With Fin and Rob around, you think that's even possible?"

His glass shot into the air for another salute. "Throw in Abe, and we're playing out of our league."

I clinked his glass, then lowered my voice. "I'm a little nervous."

"Aww, babe, it'll be okay. I won't let the big bad bears get ya—unless…"

I smacked his shoulder and laughed. "I have all the wild animals I can handle sitting next to me. Something tells me I might even be out of my depth with him."

He gave me a lecherous grin and Groucho Marx-ed his eyebrows. "I am a Scorpio. Fear my tail."

"I'd rather tap it."

"Promises, promises."

WE LANDED IN NEW ORLEANS AND WERE DRIVEN TO OUR rented home in the heart of heathen heaven. Pride flags flapped nearly everywhere we looked: on poles in front of public buildings, beneath the American flag at McDonald's, even draped above the entrance to the massive casino. It was as if some gay Tinkerbell had sprinkled fairy dust all over the city.

Wait, Tinkerbell was inherently gay, right? Or was that just Peter?

Anyway.

More abundant than the flags were the fags.

Sweet Mother of All Things Gay and Good. They were everywhere.

As we approached Bourbon Street, the driver craned his head and said, "We'll have to go several blocks around Bourbon. The main street is blocked off, but even side streets nearby are clogged. Can't remember a Decadence this big before."

Ryan grinned and gave me a wink.

We got to the house and unpacked. At the airport, Ryan had grabbed a copy of a newspaper-looking circular called *Southern Decadence Deep Dive*. It was the official order of events and advertisements for the weekend's festivities. By the time I strode into the bedroom, he had it fully splayed across the bed.

"The boys won't get here until late tonight. Why don't we do non-gay things on our first day, then let the guys guide us the rest of the way?"

"Sounds good," I said. "We have a few hours until dinner time. Should we do a little exploring? Maybe do something touristy?"

He folded up the paper and stood. "Whatever you like, babe." He gripped my shoulders and kissed me.

I melted. God, I loved this man.

His hands shifted to my back and he gently guided me down onto the bed, our lips never parting.

An hour later, I finished washing Ryan's sweat off my body and we walked out the door. The sun was beginning to set, but New Orleans still shone brightly. I had no idea it would continue all night. During festival weeks, New Orleans never dimmed.

We took a cab around the mass of partygoers to a quieter section of town where there were shops and restaurants. It was Labor Day weekend, and the Big Easy was a sweltering pot of heat and humidity. I'd thrown on a royal blue tank top and shorts, while Ryan wore my favorite outfit he owned: that stringy, flimsy neon yellow tank top he wore on our second date, the day I fell in love with him. That shirt barely covered his chest, and any decent wind let at least one nipple escape. He caught me staring and shoved me playfully.

"No peeking. We're in public," he teased, then reached down and grabbed my hand.

I couldn't stop myself from gaping down at our clasped palms. When I looked up, he gave me a squeeze and smiled, then turned and pulled me down the street.

For the first time in my life, I walked hand-in-hand with *another man* in public. As gay-friendly as Atlanta was, it was our home. Our coworkers lived there. Our lives were there. Neither of us had been brave enough.

I know, it sounds silly. We weren't scaling a mountain or fighting a war. It was just holding hands, but something about it was terrifying. It simply wasn't done. Society wasn't there yet. *We* weren't there yet.

That day, that beautiful day, we found our way there.

My heart filled and raced—and those are *very* hard things for a heart to do at the same time. I fought back the annoying watering in one eye. Ryan stilled my sappiness with a snicker and snarky grin. That earned him a punch in the shoulder, but I immediately regripped his hand after delivering his well-deserved punishment.

Antique stores outnumbered shops filled with tourist merchandise, and Ryan was giddy. He loved anything old, especially pieces with interesting histories. Most of the shops aimed at tourists displayed T-shirts with humorous sayings plastered across the chest. We bought a matching pair with *Thing 1* and *Thing 2* on them, a reference from the holy works of Dr. Seuss.

As we passed another shop with shirts, Ryan giggled and left me on the sidewalk with instructions to stay where I was. He returned a moment later with a bag in one hand and his poochy, snarky grin stretched across his face. He giggled like a three-year-old as he unfurled a neon yellow tank top with stringy shoulders and script that read, *Don't Make Me Go All Cajun On Your Ass!* He held it over my favorite shirt he was wearing, confirming their color and cut were nearly identical.

The little shit. I loved it.

A voodoo shop caught Ryan's eye and he dragged me across the street like a kid hauling his parent downstairs on Christmas morning. We entered to the jingle of a tiny golden bell attached to the top of the door, and a woman with straggly black hair that fell below her bottom greeted us. Her eyelashes were black. Her lips were black. She'd even outlined the edges of her ears black. She was one creepy fucker.

The tinkling bell was a merry contrast to the eerie sternness of the shopkeeper. "You." Without hesitation, she pointed directly at Ryan. "Come here, boy."

Ryan squeezed my hand then stepped forward. He moved so slowly, walked so stiffly, in a way I hadn't seen all night. The woman's eyes widened as he came closer. I was a little freaked out.

Dozens of intertwined metal and bone necklaces and bangles hanging around the woman's neck clanged as she took two overly dramatic strides forward. Her bony palm flew out to land in the center of Ryan's chest. His body convulsed at her touch. It looked like he'd gone limp and only her hand was keeping him from falling over.

My skin tingled, but I dared not move.

"Your heart is strong. Your will is stronger. You have much, yet you seek still. You yearn. Your yearning will undo you. It will undo you." Her last words rasped out like the hissing of a snake who'd smoked too much.

She yanked her hand away as if his touch burned her, then leaped back a step. Ryan sucked in a breath and regained control of his limbs. I stepped forward and placed a comforting hand on his shoulder.

The woman's head snapped to me and her black-framed gaze locked onto my eyes. I couldn't suppress a shiver. It felt like she was looking inside me; *through* me somehow.

She never spoke, simply shook her head once and lowered her eyes. In a blink, she'd disappeared beyond our view to some back room where black mascara must've been stored in bulk.

Holy shit. Ryan was *shaking*.

When he turned and looked at me, his eyes were, I don't know, distant.

We left and continued our stroll in silence. We passed four shops before he clutched my hand again, his palm and fingers slick with sweat, his pulse still racing. Where before his grasp was full of affection and pride, now it felt more like the desperate act of a drowning man. The Jaws of Life couldn't have pried us apart in that moment.

After another ten minutes of silent searching, neither of us really sure what there was to search for, we passed a restaurant with outdoor seating and industrial-size fans to keep diners from melting in the heat. It emanated the smell of sausage and seafood mingled with spices, which nearly made my eyes water—in the best way possible. Without speaking or looking at each other, we veered off the sidewalk and through the ancient door. What little paint was still clinging to its wood was green, I think. La Boucherie, faintly visible, had been painted in elegant script. That paint might've originally been white or yellow. After an eternity under the New Orleans sun, it was invisible ink given a drop of moisture.

As we entered, there were no tablecloths covering rickety wooden tops. No maître d' greeted us, and no white-festooned servers scraped or bowed. One lonely woman who looked older than the door waved from across the dim dining room. She wiped her hands carelessly on her apron that was splattered with tomato sauce and whatever else might've been on the menu as she motioned us forward, sparing herself the extra steps to greet us in the doorway.

Our hands were still clasped.

"Come in, boys. Don't be shy." Her Cajun accent was as thick as her wintery hair. She eyed me up and down, then inspected Ryan, her eyes lingering on our clasped hands.

I self-consciously pulled mine free.

Her bony fingers shot forward faster than I'd thought possible, gripping my wrist, pushing us back together.

"None o' that nonsense, boy. It's clear you two belong together. Don't be 'shamed of it."

My head lowered, embarrassed by her reprimand, then ashamed by my own lack of courage. Staring at my feet, I obeyed, entwining my fingers with Ryan's.

"There. Better. Now, pick a table. Nobody here 'til dark, so ya sit anywhere ya like."

We sat. Ryan reached across the table's rough surface and pulled my hands into his again. That voodoo lady must've really shaken him. When he looked into my eyes, there was something there, something odd, but I never had the chance to explore it—the woman returned from the kitchen with a basket of bread and two glasses of water.

She paused a few feet from our table and sighed loudly.

"Cup 'n' saucer, I swear." There was more warmth in her voice than in the spices I'd smelled earlier. A crooked, toothy smile lit her face. I swear she was the most beautiful woman in the world in that frozen instant.

Ryan's smile finally returned, and his eyes breathed life once more.

I squeezed his hands and suppressed…something.

Ma (that's what she insisted we call her) refused to bring us a menu. Instead, she brought us one course after another. By the end of the night, there were platters of food on neighboring tables and we were ready to waddle back onto the streets. Ryan pulled out his wallet, but Ma materialized and the same claw that had seized my wrist descended on his.

"Oh no. Ya don't get t' leave without eatin' my special bread puddin'. Best in town. Ever'body say so."

Ryan started to object, but she waved him off and vanished into the kitchen. I was chuckling when he turned back to me. All I could do was shrug and grin. There was no refusing Ma anything, that was clear by now.

And there was no denying her unmatched skill in the kitchen either.

The bread pudding was more than a dessert. It was an experience.

No, it was a *sexual* experience.

I might've had a pudding-gasm right there at the table as Ryan's eyes rolled in the back of his head. It had been years since I'd eaten that much, but we weren't about to leave a crumb of that bread pudding or a drop of its criminally delicious, sticky-sweet, cherry vanilla caramel bourbon sauce in the bowl. Ma caught Ryan using a finger to dig the last of it out. She cackled and hugged him. When he leaned into her ample bosom, she squeezed him tight and kissed the top of his head.

"Ya make t's old woman swoon, young 'un."

Ryan smiled up. "This has been the best first night in New Orleans we could've hoped for. Thank you, Ma. Could you bring our check? We'd better walk some of this off before it gets too late."

"Pshaw." She waved her hand again. "Twenty bucks should do it."

"Twenty dollars?" Ryan's wallet dropped to the table. "That bread pudding alone was worth twenty bucks!"

"And seein' you two look at each other like ya do was worth a hell of a lot more. Now, give me that twenty and get outta here." She held out a palm and playfully smacked the back of Ryan's head. There was no arguing with this woman.

He dug out a twenty and handed it to her. "Can I at least tip my server? She was amazing."

Ma barked a laugh and blushed. "Young 'un, you's a mess. Do what ya like."

It took her a minute to stop laughing, then she wheeled toward me and stabbed a crooked finger in the air. "And don't *you* be lettin' go o' him again, ya hear?"

"Yes, ma'am." I grinned and grabbed Ryan's free hand.

Ma's smile somehow widened, and she clutched her hands to her chest, then tottered away. Ryan pulled out two Benjamins and hid them under the dessert bowl.

"Mr. Big Tipper," I teased.

"Her food was amazing. Her service was amazing. Even her advice was amazing."

"Her advice?" I asked.

"Yeah. She told you not to let go of me again. She's a wise woman."

I laughed and tossed my napkin at him as we stood to leave.

He grabbed my hand and raised it to his lips as we ventured back into the New Orleans heat.

4

THE FOAM FAIRY

We hadn't planned on doing anything decadent that night. We were determined to enjoy the city, its food and culture, without the clamor of dance music and pulsating bodies—at least for one night. But, as we walked back to the main road to hail a cab, Ryan turned to me with a glimmer in his eye.

"Uh-oh. I know that look," I said with a grin.

He usually held himself with confidence, near cockiness. In that moment, he gave me the most sheepish look I think I'd ever seen cross his face.

You know that means you're screwed, right? The little angel's voice whispered in my head. My bicameral conscience hadn't spoken to me in months, maybe a year. For some reason, it was a welcome sound that made me grin.

Wipe that goofy grin off your face and agree to whatever he's about to say. I like the look in his eyes. He's definitely up to something, and I bet it's naughty. The devil materialized on my shoulder, wearing the same green-and-gold outfit the marshal of last year's Mardi Gras parade had worn, complete with a tall, feathery top hat. He spun his cane and shook the tails on his long coat.

Now I was nervous. Those two wouldn't show up for any random recreation.

"So," Ryan continued. "There's this event you mentioned a while back, when we were deciding whether or not to come on this trip. It sounded, um, intriguing, something I've never done, and it's only happening once during Decadence."

"Okay. I'm listening."

"The foam party."

"Foam party?"

He stopped walking and faced me. "Yeah. I'm not completely sure what it is. I think it's like a pool party, but instead of wading in water, you're submerged in bubbles of some kind. Don't ask me why I'm so curious about it. I just am."

Before my counselors could chime in, I grinned and nodded. "If my baby is curious, we have to check it out. Do we need to go back to the house for anything?"

His grin widened. "Nope. The paper said they have lockers for our clothes."

My brows shot up. "Our clothes? *All* our clothes?"

His grin turned downright lecherous. "Yep. Every last piece. You don't get to wear anything, mister, only bubbles."

The angel gasped. The devil cackled. I smiled weakly, nodded, and followed Ryan toward a waiting cab.

A QUICK CAB RIDE LATER, WE WALKED INTO A LARGE warehouse. The event organizers had installed tall screens and lockers, creating two dressing rooms to either side of a large, open expanse. The entrance was fully walled off from the main area, so we still had no idea what we were getting into as we paid the fee and accepted a folded towel from the doorman.

The familiar heartbeat of dance music vibrated through my chest as we entered one of the dressing rooms. A few other guys were disrobing, wrapping towels around their waists and locking their belongings in metal lockers. I noticed most of them still wearing underwear beneath their terrycloth wrap. Ryan rolled his eyes, reading my mind, and stepped out of his underwear. Everyone in the room stilled and stared. He was glorious—and nearly hard.

Holy shit. When had that happened?

He motioned for me to follow suit, so I self-consciously slipped out of my undies and donned my towel.

"Tsk, tsk, tsk," Ryan hissed in my ear as one hand reached around from behind and rubbed my cock through the towel. His teeth and tongue teased my earlobe. "This is *my* fantasy, remember. My rules. That towel goes in a locker."

I looked down and his hard-on twitched.

Sexy, sneaky, *bossy* bastard.

But who was I to argue?

My towel flew across the room into a locker, quickly followed by the rest of my clothes.

I'm not sure either of us were prepared for what we saw as we rounded the corner onto the main floor. A sea of bubbles, a veritable ocean, spanned the full length of the warehouse and rose to our chests. A couple hundred guys stood around the perimeter, only their heads and shoulders fully visible. Most were chatting and laughing in small groups. A few brave souls danced in the center of the room.

Ryan, ever fond of a stage, grabbed my hand and dragged me to the heart of the bubble bazaar, where everyone in the place could see us. At this point, our nakedness was masked as much as everyone else's. They had no idea Ryan was fully erect, or that he was pulling me forward by my dick rather than my hand, stroking me as we waded through suds. If they had been closer, maybe they would've recognized the shivering of my shoulders or the faraway look in my eyes each time his fingers ran the length of me, but they were a good twenty yards away.

The moment we reached the room's center, Ryan turned, wrapped his arms around me, and pressed his hard, muscled body against mine. Soapy goodness squished between us, and my dick leapt to full attention.

We held each other close, swaying to the music, our bodies slipping and sliding, our abs grinding. I could feel his pulse through his dick. It raced. It pounded. Every time it twitched, my body spasmed and my own twitch sent lightning down my spine. I remembered where we were and glanced around. Everyone else had left the dance floor and were staring from the safety of the sideline. Some gaped with intrigue, others grinned, a few whispered and pointed. Before I could whisper a protest, Ryan gripped my head with both hands and pulled my face into his, into a deep, passionate kiss.

The staring men vanished. The warehouse disappeared. Only Ryan and his mouth and tongue remained.

Oh, and his throbbing cock.

We kissed through the next song, and the next. By the third song, Ryan's hands had fallen from my head and were rubbing and caressing my shoulders and back. My fingers traced the outline of his chest, then teased the ends of his nipples. I felt his body quake at my touch, and my world spun. Then my body spun as he turned me away from him and pressed his hardened cock between my cheeks, grinding it up and down, brushing my hole each time it passed. My head fell backward to rest on his shoulder and his hand wrapped around and gripped my chest. He ground in time with the music.

George Michael's voice boomed through the speakers, and one of our favorite old-school anthems rang out. Cheers rose from around the room, and guys sang along, yet none ventured onto the floor—onto *our* floor.

The first chorus began, and hundreds of voices cried, "Freedom," as Ryan finally slid inside me. He used his hands to pull my body against his, forcing his full length into me. The bubbles or suds or floaty lube—whatever that stuff was—worked to perfection, and he slid effortlessly in and out. My back arched. I couldn't open my eyes. I wanted him to live inside me forever, to never pull out, to find a way to plant his whole being in my soul.

The singing stopped as someone noticed Ryan obviously fucking me beneath the bubble sea. I heard the murmur of the crowd, but didn't care. Let them watch. The thrill of being watched added to the thousand other sensations, nearly overwhelming my mind. Ryan's hand reached down to stroke me, but I pushed it away. I didn't want this to end.

Two songs later, Ryan was thrusting slowly, then holding me without moving. I felt his pulse inside me, and thrilled at the idea of his heart beating within my body. We didn't move. We couldn't move. Then I felt his lips kiss my ear and he said, "I love you so much."

I reached back with my hands and gripped his head, twining my fingers in his hair. He kissed my neck, then turned my head to kiss me awkwardly. His hips pressed again. Slowly. Softly. Then a beat faster. Then harder. By the time George Michael was a distant memory, Ryan was pressing himself into me with hunger and need. His body tensed, and I knew he was getting close. When his hand reached down a second time, I gladly gave myself to his touch. He stroked and thrusted; we both ached for release. Seconds later, I felt him fill me and I spilled across his hand and into the sudsy sea. I swore he'd been saving up because that was the most I'd ever felt from him—and I loved it. It felt like the most I'd ever shot too.

When his thrusting stilled, we resumed our swaying to the music, him inside me, for another two songs. I finally opened my eyes and caught one group of a dozen guys clapping politely, fingers into palms. They giggled and grinned appreciatively. Ryan just growled into my ear and licked it.

Holy shit. He was getting hard again.

At that moment, the event organizers decided to enforce the No Sex on the Dance Floor sign we'd clearly missed. Our faithful fans groaned as a staffer motioned for us to move off the floor. We giggled when the staffer winced as Ryan pulled out and I shivered.

Served him right.

Who knew we loved bubbles so much?

THE DAY PASSED IN A BLUR. FIN, ROB, AND ABE WERE determined to visit every gay bar in the city, even creating a list they checked off as we hit each one. We started midday Saturday on the main strip. Fin had accidentally trashed the page with parade details, so we weren't sure if the main event was to be held on Saturday or Sunday. Either way, we wanted to see the show, so we strolled one block to check things out.

Bourbon Street was packed. Thousands of men and women—who am I kidding, they were almost all men— flooded the party district. I'm not sure why that surprised me, but we could barely squirm our way through the throng of thongs, and more streamed in from side streets every minute.

As with Decadence's straight cousin, Mardi Gras, music blasted from speakers hung from balconies where the privileged few gawked, waved, and tossed beaded neck- laces. Newcomers flashed their tits in exchange for beaded necklaces, but quickly learned the stakes for prizes at Deca- dence were significantly higher than at Fat Tuesday. Most were already sweaty and shirtless, so the better necklaces were only earned by a quick drop of a dude's undies—and a remarkable number of men were *only* wearing undies or Speedos.

Yes, sports fans, we saw flesh flash faster than wieners at a dog show.

In addition to the mostly naked men waving their, um, pride, others in flashy and flamboyant feathery outfits danced and paraded about. The costumed wonders mostly floated on the outer edges of the crowd to avoid crushing their precious wearable art. Ryan pointed at one particularly crazy outfit, then I directed him to a hedonistic hottie who was simulating a sex act with his bodybuilder buddy. We laughed as our heads snapped about in a constant blur of sensual sensory overload.

It was people-watcher heaven, and we weren't going to miss a single thing, even if our neck muscles hated us the next morning.

When the heat of the sun and sweat became too much,

Fin or Rob would motion to the next bar on the magical list, and our conga line of friends snaked our way to its entrance. I'd been to a number of gay bars in Nashville and Atlanta, but there were few places that competed with the outright opulence of New Orleans.

As we entered the first bar, a three-story joint on the corner of Bourbon and they-sell-alcohol street, my eyes darted up toward a flash of motion—or should I say a *flesh* of motion? Go-go dancers in Atlanta were common, but they wore swim trunks or thongs that covered their things. The law—and Southern sensibilities—demanded it.

But holy shit, Dorothy, we weren't in Atlanta anymore.

The dancer above me wore a *sock* zip-tied over his snake—and it was a freakin' barracuda. The sock was one of those knee-high kinds I wore in high school gym class.

Dude, respect the stocking! the little devil's voice cackled in my head.

The snake's eggs dangled and flopped freely as he danced. His ass was completely exposed—unless you counted the dollar bill athletically clutched between his cheeks as cover. I'd never seen such a public display of nudity—well, unless you counted the dedicated bead-earners in the street, but they weren't on-the-clock working stiffs (excuse the pun).

Ryan punched my shoulder to wake me out of my ball-induced trance. His eyes danced with mischief and mirth as he grabbed my hand and pulled me through to where the others stood, drinks already in hand. Abe handed us bright yellow twisty plastic cups. The necks were thin and stretched a good foot or more long, I guessed simulating a hurricane's funnel. Inside was the most devilishly delicious fruit-punch concoction I had ever tasted.

Ryan beamed as he watched me take my first sip. My

eyes bugged out a bit before settling on his. Damn, it had a lot of alcohol—but I knew showing weakness meant death in this jungle, so I took another long pull and resisted a visible wince with every fiber of my being. By the third sip, I couldn't feel my lips, and I wasn't sure my body was capable of wincing anymore.

Fucking Ryan laughed and clanked his plastic against mine.

Why did I love the bastard so much? Please explain that to me.

***

AS THE SUN FINALLY BEGAN TO SET, HUNGER OVERCAME drunkenness. Our little gaggle wandered two blocks off the main drag to a restaurant Rob had found on their initial drive from the airport. It was one of those places decorated in gaudy green-and-gold drapes with equally colorful masks glaring down from the walls. The wait staff all wore Mardi Gras themed camouflage, swirling patterns of black, green, and gold. The place reeked of tourists, but we were too drunk to care. Ryan had mediocre jambalaya, while I ate an equally adequate steak with bourbon sauce.

"So," Rob started before draining half his glass of water in a weak attempt to stave off a headache. "There's this party tonight."

Ryan perked up. "Yeah? What kind tonight? We found one last night." He gave me a sneaky sidelong grin with one raised brow.

"Oh sweet Jesus. Did you two find a prayer service before your weekend of wildness?" Fin teased.

"Something like that. Michael did call out for God a few times, if that counts," Ryan said seriously.

I turned forty shades of red, covered my face with a palm, and heard Ryan bark out a laugh.

"Lord, we don't need to hear about your marital bliss, Dad. Let us kids have our innocence a little longer," Rob said.

Ryan dribbled wine as he laughed. "Innocent? You three? You're the most corrupting influence in our lives, thank you very much."

"And you love us for it, dear." Fin leaned across and patted Ryan's hand with his meaty palm.

We all laughed and raised our glasses in salute.

Ryan's hand found my leg under the table and squeezed affectionately. The shiver the hurricane had numbed returned and I felt warmth trickle through my chest.

"Here are your choices tonight, people. One: the street party on Bourbon. It's more of what we did today, but with a bigger crowd, more beads, far less clothing, and a stage with live bands. The other option is a place called Rough Riders."

"Rough Riders? Is that a country bar?" I asked.

Rob laughed. "Not exactly. It's a sex club."

I remember dropping my fork, but little else.

Ryan's grip on my leg tightened.

"Sex club?" Ryan asked. I wasn't sure if his tone held more confusion, aversion, or intrigue—probably a little of each.

Fin flexed a bicep. "You'll get to see more of this in action. Hell, you might even *get* some action. I've been there before, but never during Decadence. It's going to be wild."

Ryan looked to me, but I sat frozen. My mind couldn't process the idea of watching other men surrounding him, naked with him, or—no, I couldn't even think that. I looked down at my plate.

"I think we'll do the street party with the bands," Ryan said, much quicker and with more steel in his voice than I expected. I looked up and he was watching me. He rubbed my leg gently and offered a tight smile.

He knew what I was thinking. The sex-starved Scorpio in him wanted to find out more about Rough Riders. Hell, a part of me was curious. But if we went there, other guys would want to touch Ryan, to do more than just touch him. God, I hated always being that guy, the wet blanket on Rob or Fin's wild ideas. I wasn't ashamed of only wanting a life with Ryan, of not wanting to share him, but they sometimes made me feel small for having such simple, old-fashioned dreams.

This time, I didn't have to object or look like the prude at the table. Ryan protected me.

That's why I loved the bastard so much.

My hand found his.

Abe, our most festive friend, stepped in. "I think that sounds perfect. There will probably be more passed around than men at that sex party. We'll see more dick on the street anyway. Yay, dick for everybody!"

And yes, I loved Abe too, the fruity fucker.

I thought I caught a slight evil-eye from Rob, but it vanished as quickly as it had appeared. Fin looked disappointed, but didn't say anything.

After dinner, we returned to the house to shower and change. Ryan donned tight blue jeans and an even tighter-fitting white Ruel shirt. His arms bulged out of the bands meant to contain far less meaty men, and his chest…fuck, how was I supposed to look at his nipples spearing the sheer white fabric of his shirt all night and not want to lick or bite them?

He caught me staring. "Like it?"

"Damn, babe. You're killin' me and we haven't even left the house yet."

He grinned and traced his index finger around a nipple. "Is this what you want? You like these old things?"

I couldn't take it anymore, and shoved him back onto the bed. My hands flew up under his shirt and gripped his chest like I was juicing oranges. When my body pressed against his, I felt his arousal—and he could feel my excitement just as much.

"Now, now," he said, gently lifting me off him. "Don't get me all wrinkled before we go out. What would the boys think?"

"They'd think you needed to take that damn shirt off, same as what I'm thinking right now."

He growled and nipped at my neck. "Later. I'm going to make you beg when we get back."

"Please? Really? I'll start begging now if it'll help."

He laughed and tossed me onto the bed where he'd just been. "You're hopeless. Get dressed. The guys want to leave soon."

I jumped into my favorite come-fuck-me jeans. It took several minutes of wriggling and bouncing to get them over my hips and fastened, but they looked like a fantastic outer layer of blue skin when I was finished. They gripped my ass so tight my crack was visible. Ryan was gonna die. He hadn't seen me wear those jeans since our first few months together, back when I was still trying to win him with my, um, more impressive qualities.

When I strode into the den, he eyed me up and down like I was on the menu of the restaurant we'd left an hour before. He hopped off the couch and ran his hands over my quads, then reached around and played my ass like a piano.

"Fuck. I can't even make an impression. When did your ass turn into stone?" He poked at a cheek with two fingers.

"Stick with me, old man. You might get some of that later if you're good." I leaned in and bit his poochy lower lip.

"Oh shit. Now you're not playing fair."

"Nope. And I never will. Deal with it." I grinned up at him and was rewarded with a broad smile of his own.

"You two are going to make me puke, and I just changed into clean clothes." Rob made a gagging sound. Fin, never one to be left out, joined in the mock vomit.

Abe sighed loudly. "I could watch them all night."

"Ha. I knew you were one of those perverts who liked to watch!" Rob said.

"If we'd known you liked to watch, you should've joined us for the foam party on Friday night," Ryan said.

"Hey—" I gave Ryan a wide-eyed glance.

"Foam party? And just what were you doing in this foam our dear little Abe would want to watch?"

"Enough to get kicked out before we could start a second round." Ryan stroked my cheek with mock sincerity.

He loved watching me squirm sometimes, and he knew this subject was doing it. We might've had sex in front of hundreds of dudes, but there were layers of foam protecting our pride. Here, there was nothing between us and the judgment of jurors one and two.

Abe scooted to the edge of the couch and leaned forward. "We really need to hear details."

"We need to get going. I heard some guys talking earlier. There's a surprise guest singer coming, and some thought it might be Deborah Cox. We can't miss her," Fin said.

"Deborah Cox? As in, 'Mr. Lonely' Deborah Cox?" I asked.

"Hey, choir boy knows his anthem queens," Rob snarked.

"Ha ha. Very funny. I know how to shake my booty as much as the next bad-dancing white guy." I turned to Ryan. "We can't miss Deborah Cox. I might die."

He snorted. "Alright. You heard him. We have a life-and-death dance situation here. Move, people."

And so we moved.

Deborah Cox indeed graced us with her royal presence. She was the queen of the gay dance stage and didn't disappoint. After two songs, she started to leave and the crowd erupted. She gave in and sang another three songs. By the time she started 'Absolutely Not,' we were screaming at the top of our lungs. Thousands of hands flew into the air and a sea of half-naked men hopped in time with the heavy bass.

Abe, never to be out-queened, even by the indomitable Ms. Cox, drag-synced every word, his index finger flying in accusation and sass the whole time. Each time the lyrics hit the words "Absolutely not," he put a palm into Ryan's chest and pushed him back against the crowd behind us. They were annoyed the first time, but quickly caught on and swayed back to let him fall before catching and pushing him back up. Before I knew what had happened, Abe had dozens around us wrapped into his act.

And our dear Deborah led thousands as they screamed "Absolutely not!" into the steamy New Orleans night.

ROB AND FIN VANISHED INTO THE CROWD AFTER DEBORAH left the stage. Abe hopped to look over the heads of the much taller men around us, but was not able to see where they'd gone. He turned back to us and yelled over the music, "What are you guys doing now?"

Ryan, without even looking at me, shouted back, "I promised Michael something. We're going to head out soon."

My brows rose. He smirked and winked, then mouthed, "Beg for it."

I missed a step in our dance and nearly knocked us all over.

Abe steadied us and shouted, "I can't compete with whatever that was. You kids have fun. I'm going to stay here and find a boy to ravage. If I'm not back by Christmas, send the National Guard."

We laughed and watched as Abe wiggled his way through to a pack of shirtless, sweaty men who had clearly taken more than aspirin to enhance their evening of entertainment.

Ryan grabbed me around the waist and pulled me into him, pressing a deep kiss to my lips. When his mouth opened and his tongue pried into mine, I felt all of New Orleans light up with fireworks. Before I knew what he was doing, my shirt was flying off over my head to the applause and cheers of those around us. I opened my eyes to catch him doing that crossed-arms shirt-pull thing models did on TV. Damn, it was a hot move. The guys who'd cheered for my striptease erupted in squeals and hoots for Ryan's Adonis-like physique. He was hard and sweaty. In the lamplight of the street, his chest and abs glistened. I nearly jizzed my jeans.

Thank everything holy they were too tight to allow blood flow—or any other kind of flow.

He tucked our shirts into a belt loop, then held me tight against him as we danced. The heat of his body, combined with the constant slipping and sliding of our sweaty skin, made me harder than the street we danced on. His erection kept bumping mine through our jeans, sending jolts through my soul.

And the fucker saw it. It was in his eyes. He knew exactly what he was doing, and he redoubled his efforts, grinding into me, dragging his hardened nipples against mine, licking the sweat off my neck before devouring the tender skin above my collarbone.

Hands reached out from every direction, teasing and touching, rubbing us, pressing us together. Ryan's mouth enveloped mine, and he didn't allow me a breath to look up and see who was touching us. Two, then three, then more men surrounded us, their hands no longer gentle, rubbing and stroking my back and neck, some drifting to feel the tautness of my ass in its painted-on jeans. Then bodies pressed into my sides and back. They must've done the same to Ryan because he squeezed tighter against me. My pulse raced with excitement and a hint of terror, but just as I began to feel walls closing in, Ryan's hot breath blew into my ear.

"You want to get out of here?"

"Yes, please."

"Told ya you'd beg."

"Fuck you, asshole." He squeezed my dick through my jeans and I moaned. "Take me out of here *now*. I want you inside me all night."

"That's my boy."

———

It was noon on Sunday before the entire clan rose from their slumber.

After Deborah Cox's inspired performance, Rob and Fin had slipped the crowd and attended their sex party. Fin, a monster of a man who rarely lost control—and was supposedly a total top—was walking bowlegged and looked like there wasn't enough coffee in the city to rouse his bleary brain. He winced slightly as he sat at the table.

"Uh, Fin, did you let a city bus park up your ass last night?" I teased.

"Shut the fuck up. Why are you yelling? Why is everybody yelling? And why is my ass raw?"

"Oh, honey, it's not nearly as raw as it was last night." Rob glided into the room as if he'd gotten a full ten hours of rest. "I saw at least four men fuck you on that Ping-Pong table. I got distracted and missed how your game of pool went."

"There was this cue—"

"And I'm officially too young to hear any of this," I cut him off, then winked at Rob.

"Oh no, dear, you're exactly the right age to learn from your Aunty Fin."

"Aunty?" Fin protested.

"Nobody who gets gang-fucked like you did last night gets to be the uncle. Just deal with it, sweetness."

For once, Ryan couldn't think of anything to say. I was staring, mouth open again, unsure whether to look at Rob or Fin.

"So, basically, you guys either fucked or got fucked all night? By a bunch of random strangers in a bar?" Abe asked.

Rob grinned and nodded. "Yep. It was fabulous. Hottest orgy I've seen in years—and I've been around, honey."

"Oh, we know," Abe said.

"Shh. Respect those with more experience."

"I'm not sure respect is what you get when you let a football team of strangers pound you all night," I said.

"Oh, Michael, it's exactly what you get. Oh, and the skanky-ho test regime at the doctor. That's a necessity too."

Ryan shook his head and laughed.

"So," Abe said, looking between Ryan and me over his coffee. "What did you two love birds do last night? You were getting pretty steamy when I left you."

"Oh, we danced a while longer and came back here, got a good night's sleep. You know us, just an old married couple." Ryan nudged my knee with his under the table.

In reality, we *had* come back to the house after a few more songs, but I doubted we got any more sleep than Rob and Fin. Ryan hadn't been kidding when he said he wanted to do an all-nighter. Foreplay lasted so long I thought I was going to explode. Every time he got me close, he'd slap my hand and pin my wrists above my head, careful to keep his body from even touching mine.

"All night means *all night*, mister," he said, over and over. His voice was rough and low, almost a growl. The sound of it nearly made me come—but I resisted. If he wanted an all-nighter, I was darn sure going to try.

In the end, we fell asleep with him inside me, much like when we'd first met. I still have no idea how he kept himself up there all night, but when I woke to his lips roaming up and down my neck, we were still one person. That's what he liked to call it.

Fuck. One person. This guy was destroying me.

In what world did anyone deserve that much happiness? How did I deserve it?

I still shiver thinking back on that morning.

"You guys fly out tonight?" Rob's voice shattered my vision of our waking moments.

"Yeah, unfortunately. I wish we'd taken a few extra days off so we could stay longer," Ryan said. I nodded in agreement. New Orleans had been a blast.

Just then, somewhere in the city, a church's bells tolled twice.

"Shit. Two o'clock. We'd better get showered and packed," Ryan said. "Our flight's at six."

And just like that, we said goodbye to our friends and the City of Brotherly Sin…I mean, love…uh, that's a different town.

New Orleans. We said goodbye to New Orleans.

5

____

THE HUMPBACKED CAT

The holiday season packed a punch in our house. Our two-year anniversary was followed by Thanksgiving, then Ryan's birthday, then Christmas. By the time January rolled around, I was ready to *not* celebrate anything. Who knew merriment could be so exhausting?

And yet, with the winds of winter came that accursed holiday when any self-respecting Irishman wore head-to-toe black and mourned. Yes, I speak of Valentine's Day.

It was a massacre, people, not a day of chocolates and roses. Good people died many years ago—at least, I think they did. I never was good with my Valentine's Day Massacre history. It was just a fun story to tell people when I was single and bitter and would not participate in their stupid ritual.

Fucking Ryan changed all that.

Asshole.

Valentine's Day fell on Saturday. I woke to the smell of eggs and bacon. Fresh coffee followed. Ryan called something in a chipper, cheery voice that would normally get him jailed, but I dragged my ass downstairs anyway. The table was set with white linen and red roses scattered about a centerpiece of brilliant irises. Purple and red might not be the chicest combination to a designer, but for a boy from Tennessee who didn't know his man even knew the state's official flower, I was overwhelmed.

"You, sit." He made a bossy motion with his spatula.

The moment my butt hit wood, coffee was poured. Wave after wave of breakfast foods followed. Ryan must've been at this for hours. I got a little misty sitting there watching him scurry about—*for me*.

"Eat up before it gets cold. I'll be there as soon as these eggs are ready. We have a full day, so don't be shy with your breakfast."

"A full day?" I mumbled through a bite of buttery biscuit.

"Yep, and don't ask, I'm not telling you anything." He sounded very proud of himself. I had no idea why, but in that moment, I knew I was toast. That thought proved prophetic a moment later when Ryan handed me an actual piece of toast.

<hr>

AN HOUR LATER, WE WERE ON THE ROAD. RYAN'S ONLY instructions were to dress comfortably in shorts and tennis shoes—no flip-flops. He said we might be on our feet all day. There was a gleam in his eye I couldn't quite recognize, similar to when a little boy is up to something he thinks is the coolest thing in the world. It was mixed with— I don't know—something *more*. I wasn't sure I'd seen that exact look from him before. An overriding sense of excitement and giddiness wafted off him.

We drove beyond the safety of the Perimeter, known to

the gays of Atlanta as the Fruit Loop. I'm sure somewhere there were guys shivering at the thought we'd left the motherland. The houses thinned, replaced by sprawling fields with tightly packed rows of some grain or vegetable. I wasn't a farmer. If it didn't come in a plastic package, how was I to know what it was?

Out of the agricultural nothingness of rural Georgia, a small town square rose. It was as if someone had planted a courthouse, pharmacy, and several storefronts back in the 1800s and they'd only recently sprung from the earth. As we neared, I noticed dozens of shops, mostly antique stores, flowing from the town's center. Beyond the square, side streets flowed in every direction. Old white houses with tall columns and wraparound porches dotted the landscape. It was picturesque, in a lost-in-time and totally-too-far-from-civilization sort of way.

Ryan drove purposefully into the heart of the square and parked in front of one of the antique shops. He reached over, squeezed my hand, then climbed out of the car. I took a deep breath before following. My Spidey sense was tingling its ass off.

A perfectly manicured sign with golden cursive lettering read, The Humpbacked Cat.

Bing-bong-bing. The door chime rang as we entered.

The smell of old wood and leather tickled my nose. Everywhere I looked, there were desks and dressers, tables and chairs, mirrors and artwork—and there couldn't have been a single piece younger than one hundred years old. I had died and gone to antique heaven.

I trailed my fingers across a rolltop desk that made my heart quiver. It was cherry and elegant; its placard placed its making around 1700. My hand yanked back, as if a simple touch could damage the work of art before me.

"See anything you like?" Ryan asked from across the shop. He stood next to a long, glass-topped case. A black cat was nuzzling his hand, curling its tail around his arm as he scratched its ear. I walked over to them and saw an odd deformity. The cat was indeed humpbacked.

"Everything here is incredible. I can't get over how new so many old things can look. It's like traveling back in time to when they were made."

He nodded, but didn't look up from the cat.

A moment of silence stretched. I continued gawking at the surrounding antiques, unaware of Ryan's sudden movement. When I turned back, the cat was alone on the case, and Ryan was down on one knee.

I took an involuntary step back.

"Babe." Ryan's voice shook in a way I'd never heard before. "I love you more than anything in the world—except maybe your lasagna." He actually winked. The fucker. "I can't imagine my life without you; without us. Spend the rest of yours with me. Please."

I couldn't believe what I was hearing. My heart was racing so fast I thought it might leap out of my chest. Moisture beaded at the corners of my eyes. My hands were shaking when he took them in his and looked back up. His crystal-gray eyes were so clear, so unwaveringly pure—and they were also filled with moisture.

"Ryan…I…Do you…Are you actually…"

"Please. Just say yes."

"Yes! Oh, God, yes. With all my heart, yes."

He leapt to his feet, wrapped his arms around me, and kissed me with a gentle fervor reserved for the gods of Olympus. The moisture teasing my eyes turned into a salty, messy stream, and we both started giggling at the dribbling mess we were making on the store's floor. I took his face in both my hands and pulled his gaze back to mine, searching for any sign of doubt or fear or, I don't know, something. There was nothing in his gaze but unrelenting love.

I'd thought the last of my protective barriers had fallen some time ago, but that was the moment I became truly vulnerable and exposed. I couldn't hold back. This man whom I loved with all my being— this beautiful, kind, obnoxiously funny man—he wanted me. Forever. *Me.*

Somewhere between amazement, disbelief, and abject joy, I felt my heart unfurl the last of itself to him. It was his completely, without reservation, now and forever.

I was his.

The sound of a nose blowing turned both our heads. Behind the counter, stroking the malformed kitty, was a spindly elderly woman who rose no taller than Ryan's chest. Her wispy gray was dappled with brackish strands. Her horn-rims dated back to the '60s. And yet, the only thing I saw in that moment was her smile. It was brilliant. And she was crying.

No, she was *ugly* crying.

And that made me cry even harder. Then Ryan joined in.

We were a blithering, blubbering mess.

When tears turned back to laughter, it took a long moment for any of us to catch a breath. It was the most beautiful moment I had ever experienced.

"Michael, this is Ruth. She owns this shop." The cat darted from Ruth to Ryan. "And this is Q."

I cocked my head.

"Q, for Quasimodo, the Humpback of Notre Dame."

When my blank stare turned into, well, nothing—it stayed blank—Ryan and Ruth chuckled.

"The original 1939 movie with Charles Laughton is my

favorite. I love old movies," Ruth said. "Oh, bugger me, I love anything old."

Her voice was scratchy and warm at the same time, like an old robe whose softness had faded but was still somehow the most comforting wrap in the world.

"Do you know why we're here?" Ryan asked.

I looked around, baffled, then shook my head. "No. I'm all about what just happened, but this isn't where I would've ever expected that. I didn't expect...I mean—"

Ryan laughed again. "We're here to find rings."

My mouth turned into a small O, but wouldn't cooperate with anything more complicated. *What the actual hell?* He'd planned this all out. He wanted to buy rings. This was really happening.

"We can't get married, so I figured the next best thing was to get rings. Screw the state. Let's tell the world we belong to each other."

Well, fucking fuckety fuck. I was crying again.

I'm not a crier. I don't cry. But damn it, I was blubbering.

Ruth darted around the counter faster than I had thought she could move. Before I knew what was happening, her arms held me snugly, and I was being guided to the glass-topped case. Through the watery haze, a sea of silver, gold, and platinum spread before me. I looked up at Ryan. He was grinning from ear to ear. He nodded and motioned for me to peruse the options.

Holy shit. This was happening.

I remember Ryan's hand gripping mine as we leaned over the case, examining each ring as though we sought the Holy Grail in a cave full of replicas.

One must not "choose poorly," as the old man had said to Harrison Ford.

After twenty minutes, we hadn't found anything we liked—and liked was not even the standard. We had to freakin' *love* these rings. These were forever rings.

"Oh, honey, I can have something custom made, if ya don't see anything ya like." Ruth stroked my hand almost as much as she did Q. It was oddly soothing.

Ryan tugged at my elbow in the *I want to tell you something private* signal we'd cooked up a year ago.

"Can I look around a bit, then come back to the rings?" I asked Ruth.

Her eyes lit up. "Of course, honey, take all the time ya like. I'll make sure you two get a good deal on anything in the shop." Her calloused fingers patted my cheek before I could escape.

I wandered slowly to the corner where Ryan studied a tall armoire that looked to be colonial or Victorian.

What am I saying? I had no idea. It was old.

He leaned down and whispered, "I have a bunch of other places to visit next. If you don't absolutely love any of those rings, let's keep looking."

I had to kiss him. His cheek was too close not to. He pressed his head against mine and nuzzled me like Q had done to him earlier.

"Let's keep looking."

He nodded, then walked over to the counter. "Ruth, we're going to see the town, maybe get some lunch. We'll be back later."

"I'll be here, Ryan. Won't close this place 'til ya get back."

"Thanks, Ruthie." He leaned over the counter and gave her a peck on the cheek. She giggled and shooed him away with a wave.

When the door clicked shut behind us, I turned toward him. "Ruthie?"

He chuckled. "I've known her for years. She's practically family."

"You little sneak."

He beamed, but just pointed across the square at our next destination. The sign read, McGuinnes Jewelry.

Everything in McGuinnes was sparkly and new, a stark contrast with the historic feel of Ruth's collection. Nothing suited our fancy.

Two shops later, our stomachs were growling. Ryan led me two streets off Main to a house that had been converted into an Irish pub. I had my favorite—shepherd's pie—and Ryan ate bangers and mash.

"Go figure, the big queen chose the giant wiener," I teased after the waiter dropped off our food. Ryan's meal was more appropriately titled Banger and Mash, as there was only one sausage. It was long, thick, and covered the length of his platter-style plate. One end of the meaty schlong rested on a bed of mashed potatoes. Because of the way the chef had laid the sausage, the potatoes looked more anatomical than gastronomical. I made pained groans every time he cut into his meat.

"Don't be jealous of my meat. I can't help it if I bang with the best o' them." His Irish accent was terrible, coming out more drunk Chinese than Irish.

"Can't argue with you there. You are a top banger."

He saluted with a piece of sausage stuck to his fork.

After lunch, we hit three more stores, but didn't find anything to match our marital mood. As if the feline fates guided our steps, we found ourselves back at the door to Ruth's Humpbacked Cat. Ryan raised a questioning brow, and I shrugged, opening the door to be greeted by a loud meow.

"I knew ya'd be back. This day's too special to go anywhere else." Ruth hooked a hand through each of our arms and escorted us toward the counter. "I expect we'll be making rings for you two, but take another look at the case anyway. Ya never know."

We did, and quickly realized she'd been right about the custom job.

"How does this work?" Ryan asked. "I've never had a ring made before, especially one this important."

My heart thrilled just hearing him say things like that. He wasn't cold by any means, but he tended toward the reserved side of expression. For Ryan Alan Lowell to speak so openly and with such affection…I barely knew how to breathe.

I really was toast.

In the end, we chose a platinum band for the base, but didn't want plain rings. One of the samples in the case had intertwining gold of different colors, like ropes twisting across the ring's base. We chose to replicate that pattern, but with a strand of green gold interlaced with yellow gold. The green represented my Irish heritage, while the yellow highlighted Ryan's German ancestry. Ruth suggested a dimpled border across the top and bottom, something she called a 'rope,' that tied it all together.

Once Ruth was satisfied with her handwritten notes, she vanished into the back of the store, leaving us to browse a bit more. She returned a few minutes later with a computerized image of what our rings would look like. Who knew our little Ruth could work a computer?

Our rings were stunning. Ryan ran a finger over the

image, as if touching his ring. I couldn't stop smiling. He cupped my cheek and said, "I love you."

I melted into his arms. Again, the non-crier was blubbering.

Ruth watched from behind the counter. When I finally emerged, she was still standing with both hands over her mouth, her own tears dribbling down her cheeks.

"Boys, I have a lot of people come through this shop, and no small number of folks gettin' married. I sell a lot of rings. You two are about the most perfectly matched couple I've ever seen—and I'm not just sayin' that. You two are beautiful."

Ryan and I shared another look, then he kissed my forehead.

"Thank you, Ruth. You helped make this day more special than I could've hoped." Ryan rounded the counter and lifted the old woman off the ground. She giggled and wiggled her legs in his embrace, once again a young girl in the arms of a handsome man. When he set her down, she beamed.

"You get outta here before I start cryin' again."

I gave Ruth a quick hug, scratched Q's head, gave the rolltop desk one last wistful glance, and then we headed home.

6

THE BEACH

A couple months later, the blessed man in brown delivered two small boxes addressed to Michael and Ryan Lowell. We hadn't discussed taking the other's name, and certainly hadn't ordered our rings to arrive that way. I felt Ruth's guiding hand in the ether. However it happened, I couldn't stop grinning like a goofy cartoon character as Ryan took his box and ripped the packaging up.

"Oh…my…God. It's gorgeous," he said, holding the ring up to the window for better light. For a moment, I thought he'd gone a little *Lord of the Rings* on me and worried he'd snap if I tried to touch his 'precious.'

I pried open my box and struggled to bring myself to lift the band. It gleamed against the sunlight in its dark blue velvet cushion. The green and yellow gold leapt off the platinum base, giving the whole thing a sense of life—of our lives—intertwined on the most precious symbol possible.

Precious.

There was that word again. I had to get Gollum's voice out of my head. He was ruining my ring mojo.

Ryan cleared his throat. As I looked up, he placed the ring on his right hand with a dramatic flourish.

"Uh, your right hand?" I asked.

He shrugged. "We can't officially marry until the nine grow a pair."

"What about RBG?"

"Her balls are bigger than any of the boys, but she's only one vote."

I nodded in agreement.

"Besides, isn't the right hand where gays wear a wedding band? Europeans do it that way. It *has* to be right —and gay."

My laugh turned into a snort. "Are you saying all Europeans are gay?"

"If they're not, they want to be. Everybody's doing it." He snuck in a peck on one cheek, then the other, in classic Euro-style. "See if yours fits."

I hesitated.

"What's wrong? Did they mess something up? Ruth will—"

"No, it's perfect," I said. "It's just...I always promised myself I wouldn't put *this* ring on my own finger. Ever."

His eyes widened in understanding, then both of his hands gripped my head and pulled me into a long, soft kiss. "I'm going to love you for the rest of your life—and mine. Would you allow me to put it on for you?"

I swooned. "How could a guy say no to that? But only to check the size. I don't want to wear it until we have a ceremony."

He pulled back. "Ceremony?"

"Well, sure. I know we can't legally marry, but I still want to celebrate it with our closest friends. They're our real family anyway. I want to write my own vows, to promise myself to you in a way that both makes you proud and turns you into a puddle of blathering mush."

Now it was his turn to snort. "You know snot isn't romantic, right?"

"No sinus drip required—just a good, old-fashioned emotional breakdown in front of witnesses. That's all I need. Oh, and this ring shoved on my finger so it can't ever come off."

He wrapped his arms around me. "Whatever you want, babe. I'll snot for you."

"Eww."

He dug his nose into my neck and rubbed it back and forth until I felt goo.

"Ugh, that's so gross."

"You wanted it all." Then he actually blew his nose on my neck. "There you go, babe. All yours."

I pulled away. "You are the vilest form of human. Why do I love you? Remind me."

He grinned as he reached up and cleaned my neck. "Because not only do I give you my snot, I clean it afterward."

"Is that supposed to be sexy? A turn-on?" I asked.

"Whatever it takes, babe. Whatever it takes."

The rings went back in their boxes. Ryan placed them reverently on the mantel, like some prize we'd won for all to see. He bent over and kissed each box before walking away.

My Ryan was a mush pit—and I loved it.

As our minds turned to dinner options, I realized something.

I had never tried my ring on.

THE WEEK BEFORE MEMORIAL DAY WEEKEND, OUR townhouse was a blur of activity. Rob and Fin had talked us into joining them on their annual trek to Pensacola, Florida. Apparently, there was some sort of gay ritual that involved thousands of our festive flock flooding the beaches to shake their tail feathers. Rob was especially excited about one event on Saturday night, a circuit party. This year's party was being held on the beach, and a giant stage had been erected for live performances and the requisite DJ booth.

"So, a circuit party? What do you think it'll be like?" I asked.

"No clue," Ryan said as he handed me two different pairs of Speedo. Between his chiseled Adonis belt and the tiny pieces of fabric he'd just handed me, I was sure we'd get plenty of attention on any beach, even one filled with deliciously decked-out gays.

"Should we bring anything? I could make lasagna. Maybe some kind of snack food? I mean, I hate to go to a party empty-handed."

Ryan looked up and thought a moment. "That's not a bad idea, but let me call Rob and ask. The fee to get into the party is fifty bucks. For that kind of money, they should have food there for us. They might not let us bring anything in."

Two minutes later, Ryan held the phone receiver away from his ear as Rob's hysterical laughter rang through. "Michael wants to cook? To bring lasagna to a circuit party?" He barely got the last words out before another round of hyperventilation blared through the line again.

"Uh, yeah. Is that not a thing?" Ryan asked.

We heard Rob call out to someone on his end. "You're not going to believe this. They want to know if they should bring food to the beach party."

Fin's unmistakable bass rumbled as he broke out in fits of laughter.

Ryan held his hand over the speaker. "I think we stepped in something. No cooking."

"No need to cook," Rob said, as if reading Ryan's thoughts. "Tell Betty Crocker we'll have a whole different kind of snack waiting for him."

More laughter from the obnoxious other end.

Ryan just shrugged.

I kept packing with eyes downcast; I felt as though our friends had just chastised my good nature. All I wanted was to be a good partygoer. Was that so wrong?

RYAN OPENED THE DOOR TO THE BOYS' RENTAL BEACH condo, and we were greeted by squeals of, "Daddy's home!"

Ryan grumbled something sarcastic that didn't match his grin.

"We can't help that you're so much older and wiser than us," Fin bellowed from the kitchen.

Abe darted from nowhere and wrapped the two of us in a tight hug. His teal Speedo barely covered his kibbles 'n' bits, which he promptly rubbed against us.

"You trying to start a fire with that thing? Jesus, I can tell what religion you are. Don't they come in your size?" Ryan was ready to rumble.

Abe slammed his shoulder playfully. "I'll have you know, old man, if it fits, it's too big. The Gay Manual is quite clear on that point."

"The author would know," Ryan countered, earning another slap.

"If only the gays would follow my lead, this would be a much more festive world." With that pronouncement, he gave me a peck on the cheek, twirled a pirouette, and vanished back down the hallway. The only thing missing was a puff of gay smoke in his wake—or would that be a cloud of glitter?

Anyway.

We quickly settled into our room, ate a bite of lunch, and joined the boys for our first tour of the beach. The condo was only one block from the shore, so we were never far from the action.

Boys were everywhere. Even before our toes hit the sand, Ryan and I were nudging each other, pointing at one hottie or another.

When we stood within a few yards of the rippling waves, we looked up and down the miles-long beach. Rob had told us there'd be a lot of people here, especially for the party, but we were unprepared for the sight. Butts and boobs crowded onto the sand as far as we could see. Tens of thousands of men and women, many wearing or waving rainbow flags, strolled and played in the sand. They came in every color, flavor, shape, and size—and so did their clothing. There were Speedos, of course, but there were also trunks with every print imaginable, and even some Speedos whose trunks were more exposed than was likely legal. Bright T-shirts with equally bright images or expressions covered the melanin-challenged, while bronzed, sweat-coated skin made the sun-touched look even more godlike.

The bay was huge, but the sea of men and women was unending.

In addition to the people, colorful tents and umbrellas dotted the tan landscape. Some were what we expected—

space for groups to escape the sun—but others were more commercial. Vendors sold drinks, food, T-shirts, swimwear, and anything else one might want while baking on a beach. We passed a number of walled tents with the word "Massage" painted on one side or scrawled on a sign above the entrance flap. A few of those had more explicit images beside the wording, and I gathered those rub-downs came with a happier ending.

We strolled for over an hour just to get acclimatized, then found an unoccupied plot of land and planted our flag. Yes, Abe actually planted a flag, making a mock ceremony out of the gesture. We were quite official in our land grab.

Rob surprised us by unpacking a battery-powered blender and mixing frozen margaritas. He produced flavor packets with coloring that matched the gay rainbow flags. Grape was my favorite, though I caught shit from the group for preferring a slushie to a true margarita.

That night, fully baked and drained from a day under the sun, we grilled chicken and baked tater tots as a family, then passed out on the couch as Fin watched some military action movie none of the rest of us cared about. Ryan's head rested in my lap, his breathing heavy and slow as he slept. I brushed a few strands of stray hair out of his face.

"Aww. You two make me so happy." I looked up to find Abe staring, a glassy look in his eyes.

I blushed and continued stroking Ryan's hair.

SATURDAY BROUGHT MORE BEACH AND SUN, THOUGH WE were careful not to spend too much time exposed to Florida's harsh rays. Rob insisted we needed to pace ourselves if we were going to truly enjoy the party later that night.

Around two o'clock, he packed up the blender and began folding his beach towel.

"What are you doing? Are we done for the day?" Ryan craned his head back toward him.

"We need our party nap. Come on, you two. Everybody up."

I rolled over to face Ryan. We were lying on a massive beach towel. "Party nap?" I whispered.

He gave me the universal, "I have no idea," eyebrow raise, then stood and offered me his hand.

Such a gentleman, even on a beach.

We napped until Mama Bear woke us up around six. Fin had dinner sizzling, and the whole condo smelled like Jamaican spices and beans. Rob was sitting in front of the coffee table in the den when we wandered out from our bedroom. There were several tiny plastic ziplock bags splayed out before him, each with a handful of blue and pink pills in them.

"What's all that?" Ryan asked.

"Party favors," Rob said cheerily.

Ryan and I shared a confused glance.

"It's X—ecstasy to you rookies," Fin's rumble sounded behind us.

I'd never done any kind of recreational drug. Neither had Ryan. In fact, we'd never even thought about it. Hell, I'd only tried alcohol a few years ago, and that first sip occurred purely because I'd been dragged, unsuspectingly, into a gay bar when I still thought I was straight.

"Uh, we're good, but you guys have fun," Ryan said, then turned to me with a questioning gaze. I nodded in agreement and gripped his hand for support. Something about all this felt strange. For the first time, it felt like we didn't belong in the same room with our little family.

Rob scowled up at Ryan. "Don't be a puss. You two didn't drive all the way down here from Atlanta to not enjoy yourselves. Besides, if you don't do anything, you'll be the only sober guys on the beach, and the whole thing will get really boring really fast."

Ryan sat beside him on the couch and stared at the packets. Superman's crest stared up at him from its embossed place on each pill.

He glanced back up at me. "I guess—"

"Yes, you can, and you will," Rob said, handing him a bag with two pills. "One for each of you. No more. You may even want to cut those in half and pace yourselves until you know what it feels like."

Ryan stared at the bag in his hand as though it was a snake about to strike.

My mouth wouldn't work. I'm not even sure I would've known what to say. The whole scene felt surreal. In the two years we'd known the boys, they'd never even mentioned doing drugs. Yet here they were, looking like experts, like guys who did this regularly.

"Do you guys do these often?" Ryan asked, reading my mind.

Rob shrugged. "Pretty much every time we go out. That's, what—every Saturday night?" He chuckled and Fin grunted over the sound of chicken searing.

Ryan couldn't take his eyes off the pills in his hand.

I squeezed onto the couch beside him and gripped his leg.

"What do you think?" he asked quietly.

"I…uh…I don't know. I mean, I've never—"

"Me either." He turned the package over. The back of the pills was smooth and unadorned. "I am kinda curious, and we *are* here with friends."

Holy shit. He wanted to try this. My head spun.

Michael, no, absolutely not. Don't you even think about it. What would your father say? He's a preacher, for God's sake. Forgive me, Father. I didn't mean to curse. My little angel appeared in an angry puff wearing a brilliant white robe and shimmering golden halo, just like my mental image from childhood—minus the wings. His itty-bitty arms were crossed, and his head was tilted with emphatic judgment.

Puff. The angel's counterpart appeared on my other shoulder, wearing nothing but a sheer red Speedo that revealed more of his massive, uncut cock than it covered. I'd never seen my little devil's, um, devil. Hell, he was hung—and this iteration of him was muscular, bronzed, and ripped. He looked like a cross between Ricky Martin and Marky Mark, two of my favorite lust objects.

You aren't seriously going to listen to that righteous windbag, are you? You're at a beach party with the love of your life and your closest friends. There's never going to be a safer time to experiment and let go. Loosen that collar a little, kid. You've been good your whole life. It's time you unpuckered your ass and had a little fun.

No, no, no. There will be no unpuckering. Your ass is just fine all puckered up. It's hot, really. I swear the angel blushed. *You know what I mean. You don't need drugs to enjoy yourself. Being with Ryan gives you all the high you'll ever need.*

But think about it. What if you could get high with Ryan? How much better could sex with him get? Damn, it makes me hard just thinking about it. Fuck me. He actually got hard and poked out the top of his Speedo. Was I actually lusting over my imaginary conscience devil?

I needed serious help.

"Babe? You okay?" Ryan's voice made both images vanish.

Rock-hard Ryan on X. That puckered asshole would never be the same. The devil's silky voice slithered inside my head. I shivered.

"Yeah, I'm good. Uh, I don't know. What do you want to do?"

"I kinda want to try it. I mean, we're here and all."

I looked down, unsure. "Can I think about it? It's just… a lot."

He gripped my hand. "But you're okay if I try it?"

That surprised me. We'd always done everything together. All for one, that sort of thing. He wanted to try this without me? Whether I did it or not?

I didn't know what to think about that.

"We'll be there. Fin and I won't let anything happen. Besides, Abe will be hovering like Mother Goose." Rob was really trying to sell this.

"Uh, sure, okay. If you want to," I said. "I just…I just need to think about it a little, okay?"

Ryan's face brightened. "Take your time. We won't leave for the party before eleven anyway."

At eleven o'clock, Ryan, Rob, Fin, and Abe each popped a pill.

I couldn't do it.

Thirty minutes later, we marched onto the beach where three thousand shirtless men bounced to booming bass that was blasted through massive speakers on either side of an equally massive stage. Colorful lights bounced off a dozen mirrored balls that hung on scaffolding above the sandy dance area. I scanned the crowd and was stunned to find virtually every body ripped and muscled. Every guy was hot. We'd apparently entered some alternate reality where only Hollywood Hotness was allowed. It was sensory overload.

We wove our way through to the center of the throbbing mass. Our shirts flew off. Ryan's hands found their way to my chest, like magnets drawn to metal. He stroked and kneaded, teased my nipples, then reached up and gripped my shoulders, each squeeze matching the pulse of the music. I looked into his eyes to find them wide and dilated. A broad, overly toothy grin was plastered across his face as his head swayed back and forth. He pulled me into him and held our bodies tightly together as we bobbed to the bass, then he planted his lips on mine in a long, hungry kiss.

But it didn't feel like my Ryan.

Sure, his lower lip was still poochy. And yes, I knew it was him, but it felt different—somehow foreign—like he wasn't kissing *me*, but whoever happened to be in front of him.

I know, that sounds dramatic and crazy. He *was* kissing me, and it felt amazing, but it also felt weird. It's hard to explain.

Three songs later, I was thirsty. The guys were now rolling harder than a bad skier tumbling down a slope, and Ryan barely acknowledged me as I slipped free of the dance floor in search of a vendor.

Jack and Coke in hand, I stood outside the mass of men and watched.

The later it got, the louder the music blasted. The night was cool, in the upper seventies, yet every muscle glistened with sweat. Many of the men no longer danced near their neighbors. They danced against them, bumping and rubbing and grinding. Skin flowed to skin. Hands reached and brushed in every direction. Everyone was connected in some way. Lips found their way to other lips, to shoulders, to chests. It was like watching a sea of sexual sensation, rippling and writhing on a bed of sand.

There was only one mood among that mass, only one emotion.

Thousands throbbed with need and desire. Thousands caressed and careened. Thousands stiffened and stroked. It was the most erotic thing I'd ever seen.

And yet, I was outside looking in. I wasn't a participant, merely an observer.

I hadn't taken the pill.

BY TWO THIRTY, I WAS EXHAUSTED. WHATEVER FUEL THE Jack and Coke had given me had long since worn off. Now all I wanted was a tall glass of water and a bed. The bouncing bodies showed no sign of slowing. Ryan and the guys were laughing, hands high in the air, as one favorite dance song after another played. We always like the dance tunes with lyrics, something we could sing along to. Wordless techno from Europe had just arrived on America's shores and was all the rage, yet tonight's DJ offered a refreshing mix of old and new.

Ryan was floating on a cloud, and despite my bleariness, I didn't have the heart to ask him to leave. I found a quiet boulder on the edge of the sandy beach and sat with my back leaning against it. The music wasn't so loud, and I had a clear view of both the stage and the undulation of the bay's waters as they rolled onto the sand.

Even the bay was rolling. I was literally the only one not rolling.

That made me laugh.

A voice barked over the speakers, announcing the end of the evening's festivities. The DJ would play one final song to allow everyone to wind down, something like a cool-down at the end of a workout. It was odd that the party's cool-down was even faster and more heavily bass-laden than the rest of the night's music. I would've thought they'd want to cool the guys off as they closed shop. They were only revving them up.

As the last notes rang out, the crowd began to disperse. Guys, mostly in twos and threes, most holding hands or with arms draped about each other's shoulders, slugged their way through the sand toward town. The massive orgy disintegrated into thousands of smaller, more intimate ones. Hands and lips never stopped roaming. It was clear babies would be made that night. Well, the gays would give it their best shot—so to speak.

I found Ryan and the guys lingering in the dance area. Abe was throat-fucking some twink with long sandy hair, while Rob tried desperately to unpackage a bodybuilder he'd acquired. Ryan and Fin swayed to music that only played in their minds. Each of them sucked on the remains of a lollypop—the white stick

"Hey, boys," I said as I approached them.

"Hey, babe." Ryan's voice carried an unnatural drawl. He pulled his sucker out and unconsciously chewed the side of his mouth.

I later learned that move was called Chewy Chewbacca. Apparently, there was something about X that made you chew or suck anything nearby.

Abe was proving that point with his twink. They seriously needed to get a room.

"I'm coming down now. You ready to go?" I turned back to see Ryan tossing his sucker stick in a nearby garbage bin. He ran a hand through his hair. "Shit, I need a shower."

"Hot water's gonna feel like fire," Fin said. "Maybe sober boy should join you."

Ryan grinned at me. "What about it? Care to wash my back?"

I didn't mean to be a wet towel, but I was drained and sick of being bored on the sideline. "We'll see. I'm pretty beat."

"Suit yourself," Fin said, turning to Ryan. "I'll scrub whatever you need. I've wanted to do that for years."

I could barely believe what I was hearing. Fin was hitting on Ryan. No, he was outright propositioning him.

Ryan let out a low growl. "Hmm. That sounds amazing. I bet your fingers would make my whole body tingle."

What the fuck?

"Come on, guys. Let's go." I bit back my rising anger as we left the beach. They were just high. They probably didn't even know what they were saying.

ON SUNDAY, RYAN AND THE BOYS SLEPT UNTIL NOON. I'D had breakfast, strolled the beach twice, and souvenir-shopped in the town surrounding our condo by the time they stirred.

"Well, good morning, sleepy head," I said as Ryan appeared in the hallway entrance.

"You're speaking to me. Why are you speaking? Why is anyone speaking?"

I laughed as he squinted his strung-out, still-dilated eyes. None of the window shades were open and only one lamp was on, but he still struggled to adjust. Ah, the joys of the morning after.

"Here, drink this." I handed him my mug I'd just filled with fresh coffee, then turned to the kitchen to pour myself a new one. "Want anything to eat?"

"God, I'm starving. I'll be yours forever if you make me an omelet."

"Last I checked, you're already mine forever. So what's in this omelet thing for me now?"

He let out a weak laugh. "I'll rub your feet, but only after my strength returns."

"Feet for frittata. I like it. Need some toe jam for your toast?"

"I can't decide if I love or hate you more right now." He grinned, both hands pressed to his temples.

"I'll take that," I said in the most annoyingly chipper voice I could muster. He deserved a little torture after his night of frivolity.

The rest of the day was dedicated to recovery. Ryan and the boys laid around on the couch, then took naps. When we finally wandered out to the beach, they clustered under an umbrella with sunglasses glued to their all-too-sensitive eyes. At one point, I caught Ryan with a towel draped across his face to further shield his irises.

We ordered pizza that night. I was the only one not knocking on death's door, and I wasn't up for cooking for my messy men. Four extra-large pies vanished in a blink as the last of the drug's sketchiness dwindled away, replaced by ravenous hunger.

I asked Ryan about his night on the dance floor—dance beach, whatever you called it. He merely grunted and said he'd had fun. He and Rob shared a couple of glances I thought carried more meaning than usual, but I let the subject drop.

Sometimes we Pisces can be too sensitive for our own good.

The next morning, at the butt crack of dawn, we packed up the car and said goodbye to Florida's sunny shores.

7

THE SKY IS GREEN

In June, a simmering pot boiled over.

As you might recall, I'd left my stable, well-paying job at a prominent recruiting firm to start a business with one of my sales guys, Evan. We were both frustrated by our former employer's management style, and Evan had found an exciting opportunity with strong upside and limited upfront investment. I didn't know him well at the time, but he was a decent salesman and a nice enough guy.

What a year in business together taught me was that Evan liked to overanalyze and overthink things more than any human I'd ever met. There was something in the way his brain was wired that required him to examine every conceivable outcome of an action before even leaning in that direction. Don't get me wrong, I'm thoughtful and cautious about decisions, especially if they have broad or long-term consequences, but to battle over minor things made me crazy. If I said I wanted to order a box of pens, we'd spend an hour debating the merits of blue versus black ink. If I looked outside my window and commented on how blue the sky was, Evan would crane his neck, then pronounce it green instead. The constant back and forth, our inability to just make decisions and move forward, was insufferable.

In addition to all that, Mr. Amazing Salesman proved to be fairly lazy when it came to prospecting for new business. He was great if I served leads on a platter. He could close anything handed to him. Ask him to go hunt and gather, to find new leads and bring them to the party, and there was a litany of reasons—excuses—why it couldn't be done. As a result, our sales numbers dropped from a healthy flow that paid the bills and allowed us both a comfortable lifestyle to the point where I was juggling which bills would involve loss of power or water if not paid first.

The whole thing was painful and going nowhere fast.

Ryan never said anything, but I could tell my inability to help pay for things was bothering him. He said he understood, but snide comments here and there made me think otherwise. When Rob asked about my job, intimating my business was struggling, I knew my concerns were well founded.

So, in the second week in June, I filed for divorce from Evan. Okay, I quit our company and gave him my half of the ownership, but it felt more like a divorce. Evan was bitter and angry, and I snapped in unprofessional ways that were completely out of character. Going our separate ways was a very good thing.

Ryan said he understood and supported my decision, but immediately asked what I had planned next for employment.

The truth was simple: I had no plan.

The look in his eyes told me he knew it too.

<hr>

Over the next week, we scoured the newspaper and online job listings. I wasn't sure what I was even looking for. Sales and sales management had been my role in each prior job, but I wasn't passionate about it. In fact, thinking back, I wasn't passionate about anything I'd done to date. They were just jobs, something to do to pay the bills so I could go out on the weekend or just enjoy life.

What would I love to do if I could do anything?

Ryan asked me that question as we started our search. A week later, I still couldn't answer it.

I could tell his annoyance was growing in direct inversion to his level of patience. The warmth I'd come to expect in his voice was nowhere to be found. I'd heard his businesslike tone enough with his employees over the phone to know he was *managing* me. It felt awful.

Worse, I knew it probably felt awful for him too. He made good money, but with alimony and child support, carrying our entire household was like a lead weight around his neck.

Guilt wove its way in with disappointment and shame.

On Monday of the second week following the break from Evan, I landed an interview with a tech company. I wasn't completely sure what the company did, but the job was managing salespeople, and I knew I could handle that. They could teach me the products or services.

Ryan gave me a halfhearted peck on the cheek as I left our townhouse. He didn't even comment on my suit and tie. The tie was one of the first things he'd ever given me. I tried not to read too much into our lackluster parting and focused on my talking points for the interview.

My meeting with the company's managing partner was

to be held in one of those sprawling convention hotels with ballrooms at one end and meeting rooms at the other. I'd never been there before, so I parked at the end with the meeting rooms. Naturally, my interview was in a ballroom.

Ryan always teased me about my sense of direction—or, more accurately, my *lack* of any sense of direction. He quipped I could get lost leaving our driveway, and we lived on a dead-end cul-de-sac.

He wasn't wrong.

The interview went well enough, though I was pretty sure I'd hate working for the asshole who quizzed me. He talked like some Boston elite whose nose was stuck up so high he caught rainwater when he walked outside. He made a snarky comment about my "pleasant" tie, though his voice held only derision as he offered the compliment.

But I needed a job, badly. If it was offered, I'd resigned myself to taking it. I could look for something better while gainfully employed.

As I trudged the length of the eternal series of buildings, I passed through a massively wide hallway where booths had been erected. I'd been so wrapped up in my own head earlier that I hadn't noticed them before. Besides, they'd been empty. Now, they were filled with sharply dressed men and women handing out pamphlets and talking with other sharply dressed people who sat in uncomfortable-looking chairs situated on the opposite side of the booth. I figured there was some convention going on and returned my focus to the pamphlet Mr. Rainwater had given me.

"Are you here for an interview?" A deep voice rumbled behind me.

When I didn't turn, the voice said, "Excuse me, sir."

I turned with a raised brow.

"Yes, you. Thank you." A tall, portly man with a terrible comb-over speared a meaty paw across his table. I shook it, then wiped his sweat on my suit pants.

"Are you here for an interview?" he asked again through a smile filled with crooked, tobacco-stained teeth.

"Uh, yes, well, I was. I had an interview, yes."

I was eloquent.

He chuckled and his whole body rippled. For some reason, I couldn't help liking this man. An involuntary smile snuck onto my face.

"How would you like another?"

Now I was baffled.

"Uh, okay. Sure."

He motioned to a chair and we both sat. Over the next hour, he introduced me to his financial firm, Waddell & Reed, and how they focused on financial planning for families. He beamed as he spoke about helping people send kids to college, or live well in retirement. He'd been a financial adviser for nearly twenty years and sounded as excited about his work today as he likely did when he'd first started. His enthusiasm and earnestness were infectious.

After a flurry of questions about me and my background, focusing mostly on my sales experience, he explained that he wasn't normally the one conducting interviews, but his boss was short-handed and had asked him to help recruit some talent. He gave me his business card and asked me to call the office and set up an interview with Brad, the branch manager. I smiled, shook his sweaty palm again, and thanked him for accosting me in the middle of a hotel. He made some reference to "mugging for dollars" and we both laughed.

As I finally found my way out the other end of the center, I stared down at the business card in my hand.

Financial adviser. Huh. I hadn't even thought of that possibility.

Two weeks and three interviews later, I had a card of my own—along with two insanely large textbooks. The series seven and sixty-six were required industry licenses, and I had to pass those exams before Waddell would start my salary.

Ryan found me buried in the series seven book when he got home that night. He flipped through one of the books, then asked when I had to take my exams.

We didn't celebrate. He never even congratulated me on landing a new job.

8

———

I'LL COME BACK

On July 2, I passed the series seven. Three days later, I passed the sixty-six. Brad, the branch manager at Waddell, said it was the fastest he'd ever seen anyone pass both exams. I was proud, excited, and slightly terrified. The prospect of starting a new career with a salary that vanished after the first year felt a bit like running a marathon where the track ended on a cliff every runner had to leap off.

Ryan congratulated me on passing with a hug.

The townhouse felt cold and clammy, like some foreign cave I'd wandered into and didn't know whether bears or tigers might dislike my presence in their den. It definitely didn't feel like the home it had been only a few months earlier.

A part of me was dying inside, and I didn't know how to stop it.

On July 6, I walked into the townhouse following a long day of cold calling. Everything was quiet.

"Ryan? You here?" I called out.

"Upstairs."

I climbed the steps and followed his voice into our

bedroom. My gut was tight. I didn't understand why, but this moment felt significant; weighty.

Ryan was lying on our bed staring up at the whirling fan. He was still in his business-casual work clothes. He hadn't even taken off his shoes.

"You okay?" I asked from the doorway, unsure if I should even enter our own bedroom.

He didn't even sit up, just turned his head. His eyes were rimmed with red.

I was on the bed in a heartbeat. "Babe, what's wrong? Talk to me."

He stared back at the fan. "I'm sorry."

My gut clenched harder. "Sorry for what? What are you talking about?"

"I can't do this. I'm not ready for forever."

My heart stopped. I couldn't breathe.

His eyes finally met mine, and he took my hand. "I love you, but I'm not ready for forever. I know I'm twelve years older than you, but I'm still new to the gay world. I've never even seen most of it."

I mutely sat for a minute. Then it hit me. "The party. All the men. You were the center of attention most of the night."

He looked away again. "I've never felt that…I don't know…acceptance. Not from a group like that."

"Ryan, you'll always get attention. You're beautiful. Men will flock to you no matter where you are."

"I didn't know that. I'd never been around more than one or two men at a time."

I leaned back, getting as far away from him as I could while still on the bed. I just couldn't take the closeness in that moment.

"I was married for eighteen years. Diane and I had been

together for five years before that. All I've ever known was family and commitment and—" His voice became quiet; small. "There's so much I never got to experience. I didn't get to be young and gay, to go to bars, to just be—"

"To be single." I finished the words he would never have said.

He nodded. "Yeah."

The longest moment I've ever experienced stretched before us. I felt the room widen, a gulf opening between us that had never existed—at least, that I'd never seen or recognized.

I saw it then. It was wide and deep—and insurmountable.

"I need to know what it's like. I can't give my forever and always look back wondering. It'll eat at me until…"

He didn't have to finish that sentence.

"Michael, I'm so sorry. The last thing I would ever want is to hurt you. You have to believe me. I love you so much."

I saw the agony in his eyes. It mirrored the writhing in my gut. My heart was breaking, yet seeing his torment, I couldn't stop myself from reaching out, from putting him first.

"I know you do."

I closed the gap between us and gripped his hand with both of mine. It felt like holding onto a life vest in the ocean. I knew I was drowning, but there was nothing else I could do. It was there. I had to grab it. I had to pretend it would be alright.

"Babe, I get it. I hate the idea of losing you, but I do understand. I might've been sheltered as a kid, but at least I got to have something of a gay adolescence in my twenties. If I had to do it over again, I don't think I could give that time up, that exploration. It helped me know who I am and what I want."

"I don't want to lose you."

His words stabbed my heart. Anger warred with grief.

How could he say he wanted to see the gay world, to play the field, or whatever the hell he was saying, and then tell me he didn't want to lose me? Those two things couldn't coexist. Could they?

I bit back the bile in my throat and clammed myself. "You're determined to do this?"

He nodded slowly.

"How long have you been thinking about it?"

"Since before Memorial Day. That weekend really put it all into perspective."

Shit. He'd been thinking about this for months.

My head spun through the past few months, like watching a movie on fast-forward. There were so many signals I'd missed, so many conversations—or *lack* of conversations. How could I have been so blind?

"I want you to keep your ring."

My head snapped up. "What?"

"Your ring. Keep it."

Our rings hadn't even crossed my mind. Physical things, our townhouse, next steps—none of that mattered in that moment. Why was he bringing up our rings?

"I don't understand."

He finally sat up and faced me. "My plan is to spend a few months going out with Rob and Fin, experience what Atlanta has to offer a new gay, then come back to you."

I pulled away and stood. My mouth was as wide as my eyes. "Ryan, that's not how this works."

He cocked his head like a confused dog.

"You're breaking up with me. You're going to go

explore the scene, date, have lots of sex, and likely meet someone new who captures your interest. Even if you don't meet someone special, you'll be focused on what's ahead, not what was behind. I'm behind you now."

He scooted closer on the bed. I took a step back.

"Please, babe. No. I'll come back. We'll come back together. Keep your ring so we can wear them together one day."

I couldn't decide whether I was more amused, confused, hurt, sad, angry—or any of a thousand emotions that raged through my body and mind. I wanted to vomit and run and scream all at the same time. My whole being felt like it was coming apart, yet I was paralyzed.

"In fact, don't move out. I'll take the guest bedroom for now. You won't have to spend money on an apartment, and we'll still be close."

Staring down at Ryan, I realized just how naive he really was about gay life.

"You want me to live here while you explore the gay world, while you date other people? You want me to be here when you bring other men home and have sex with them in the next bedroom? You want me to *see* all that? Seriously?"

I balled my fists to keep them from shaking. The war between grief and anger was taking a decided turn. To end what we had was one thing; to expect me to hang around and watch what followed was beyond rational thought. How could he?

How *dare* he?

"Well, I could—"

"No."

"No?"

"We can look for an apartment. I'll need your help with the first and last month of rent they'll require."

"Of course—"

"Ryan, I *can't* be here. I can't see any of that. The thought of other men—" My voice broke, but I steeled myself for what *had* to be said next.

"Keep the ring. If you ever offer it to me again, please mean what it stands for in your heart. Until then, it's just a pretty scrap of metal in a box to me."

I turned and walked out of our bedroom.

9

THE NEW APARTMENT

R yan slept in the guest room that night. I didn't ask him to. He just did.

The space next to me felt so empty, a void where such love and warmth once emanated. Now, it held nothing; no one.

I couldn't sleep. When I wasn't crying, I was staring at that damn ceiling fan, the same one that had captivated Ryan so much earlier. Like the anger and pain roiling inside me, it kept spinning and spinning.

Sometime in the middle of the night, I couldn't take the emptiness of our room anymore. Like an idiot—or a man dying of thirst on an island—I found myself crawling into the guest bed beside Ryan. I needed his presence, his warmth, his touch.

Before I knew what I was doing, my lips were pressed to the back of his neck, and my hands were snaking their way around to graze his bare arms and chest.

He didn't move. He didn't even acknowledge that I'd joined him.

Like an idiot, I rubbed up against him, tried to feel excitement—tried to feel *his* excitement.

He remained still.

Eternal moments later, I lay back and stared into the guest room fan. Ryan didn't stir as tears flowed down my cheeks again.

<hr>

I WOKE THE NEXT MORNING TO THE SOUND OF A LOUD motor outside the window. Peeking through the shutter slats, I saw Ryan exit a small U-Haul truck. He slammed the door, and my heart's walls clanged back into place, the same walls I'd let fall completely when Ryan—

Tears. Why wouldn't they stop?

I ran into the bathroom, locked the door, and turned on the shower. He couldn't see me like this. I wouldn't let him see me turn into a complete mess. I wouldn't.

"Hey, everything alright in there?" His knock made me jump from my place on the floor by the sink.

"Uh, yeah. Just cleaning up. Be out in a minute."

The shower had been running for at least thirty minutes. There was some comfort in the sound of its water, in the safety of the bathroom's privacy. I know that makes no sense, but nothing made sense in those moments.

"I got a moving truck. We can load your stuff and then go apartment hunting."

What the fuck? Who does that?

It was literally the *next day* following his bomb-drop, the one in which he offered to let me continue living in his romper room while he, well, romped. Now he wanted me out immediately? So much so, he'd rented a U-Haul first thing in the morning?

God, could this get any worse?

In every previous move I'd made in life, packing the moving truck had been a challenge. There was never enough room, and getting couches, chairs, and other non-Tetris shapes to fit neatly was nearly impossible.

We didn't have that problem.

By the time the last of my meager collection was loaded and Ryan slammed the metal door shut, half the truck remained empty. Almost everything we'd bought over the preceding two years had meaning. It was a vase from a trip we took to New York, or an antique dresser we found while in San Francisco. I walked through the townhouse and realized there was very little that didn't tell part of our story. I didn't want to restart life in an empty, lifeless apartment, but I couldn't bear the thought of seeing things that reminded me of Ryan—and our life together—every time I walked through my new home.

Unpacking took even less time than packing.

The Post Apartments had been my home for seven years before meeting Ryan, and they were happy to welcome a wayward son home. Ryan wrote a check for the deposit and first month's rent, then helped me lug my couch and few other belongings up three flights of stairs. When he left, I sat on the floor and leaned back against the couch's leather front.

The apartment was so quiet. I didn't even have a television.

Two moving boxes served as side tables. I was back to using my college silverware and plates, most of which carried at least one chip. My mattress dated back to when my oldest sister still lived at home with my parents. It must've been over twenty years old now, and had more lumps than curdled milk in coffee.

Did I mention the place was quiet?

Well, it was until the world folded in around me and I began crying again. I curled into a ball on the floor of that empty apartment and cried until my throat hurt and eyes burned.

As the sun set, I forced myself to wander aimlessly into the bedroom and unpack a little. Clothes went into the closet or my mother's old dresser. My one spare pillowcase and set of sheets dropped into the bottom drawer. I'd never been much of a shoe guy, so my one pair of sneakers and dress shoes landed on the floor of the half-empty closet under two lonely suits and three white dress shirts.

I glanced in the closet, then at the dresser's open drawers. My life, such that it was, glared back.

I curled up on the bed, not even bothering to get under the covers. I lay there all night, bouncing between restless sleep and tears I thought had dried.

SUNLIGHT STREAMING THROUGH THE UNCOVERED WINDOW woke me at some ungodly hour the next morning. I drifted into the kitchen for the requisite two cups of coffee necessary before conscious thought could occur. I pulled my lone mug out of the cabinet. A set of embossed jail bars stared up at me. Ryan had bought it for me on our tour of Alcatraz. It reminded me of what I'd just lost.

Before my emotions could kick in, I turned to make coffee. The empty space on the counter reminded me I didn't have a coffee maker either.

The mug slipped out of my hands and shattered. That's all it took.

I dropped to my knees, scooping up pieces of broken

ceramic, begging them back together as if binding them again could repair more than a simple mug. The pieces wouldn't fit back into place. They were too broken. I became frantic, desperate to make them fit. When they refused, I tossed them on the linoleum, slumped against the cabinets, and wept anew.

Sometime later, with the shattered pieces of Alcatraz still littering the kitchen floor, I mustered the courage to call Brad at Waddell.

"Hey, Michael. Are we going to see you today? We've missed you in our morning sessions."

Every morning, the new financial advisers gathered in the conference room for a "murder boarding" exercise. Anyone who had a new client case would put every piece of information they'd gathered about the prospective family on the whiteboard. The rest of us would poke holes, asking questions in an attempt to discover missing information or determine what more the adviser needed to ask his new client. It was a great training exercise and was mandatory until an adviser's second year in production. I'd missed two mornings in a row without so much as a phone call.

"I'm sorry, Brad. I've…had some personal issues this week."

"Are you okay?" The genuine concern in his voice made my resolve crack.

"I…yeah…no. No, I'm not really." I gasped for air. "My partner ended things. I'm not…Brad, I can barely…I can't—"

"Michael, listen, take all the time you need. This place will be here when you're ready."

"Thanks, Brad. I'm sorry. I need to go."

I hung up and sank into my couch. At least work wasn't pressuring me. That was something.

My next call was one I should've made two days ago.

"Hi, hi, hi!" Connie's ever-chipper voice sang through the receiver.

"Hey."

"Uh-oh. I don't like that tone. What happened?"

"Connie—" I couldn't finish whatever was about to tumble out. I broke down in hysterical tears that felt like they would never end.

"I'm on my way. Don't move."

I gave her my new address, and fifteen minutes later, she knocked on my door. She didn't say a word, just wrapped me in a tight hug and held me as her shoulder became soaked with my tears.

We stood like that for ten or fifteen minutes. I don't remember. At some point, she gently moved me to the couch. The crying ran its course a short time later, but we still didn't speak. She just held me and stroked my hair.

"He said this was forever."

Those were my first words to her.

"I know, sweet pea. I know."

I pulled back, about arm's length, and looked into her eyes. "I get he hasn't been out and seen the gay world. He hasn't done the parties or dating or, I don't know, any of the other gay life stuff. But is all that worth more than a life with me?"

"Oh, Michael, no. Don't say that."

"But that's what he's saying to me, isn't it? How else should I take this? He had a choice, and he chose exploration over love. He chose to be a gay teenager over a married adult—with me. I came in second to parties and drugs—"

"Drugs?" She sat up straight.

My eyes lowered. "Yeah. Guess I didn't tell you about Memorial Day weekend, did I?"

"You talked about the beach and all the men, but never mentioned drugs."

I hadn't told her. I hadn't known how.

Sitting on the couch in the middle of my empty apartment, it all tumbled out.

"Do you think he's using drugs regularly now?" she asked.

"Regularly? Like an addict?"

She nodded.

I shook my head. "No. It's not like that. At least, I don't think it is. His job is way too intense and high profile for him to use and stay on top of his game. That was his first time. I'm pretty sure."

She let out a breath. "That's a relief, I guess. I was worried he'd gotten himself mixed up in something bad."

I half laughed. "I think that's what's next, not what he's already done."

The pity in her eyes was worse than the silence.

<hr>

WE ORDERED CHINESE DELIVERED TO MY APARTMENT. SHE ate chicken with string beans while I pushed cashews around the container without tasting a single one. We put the leftovers away. I stared blankly into the open door, cold air blowing across my bare feet. The white cartons with their wire handles were the only items in my new fridge.

Connie left shortly after.

Then the phone rang. Ryan was the only person who had my new number.

"Hello?"

"Hey, baby doll. How are you doing?" It was Abe.

"Guess you heard?"

"Yeah."

I didn't know what else to say.

"I'm sorry." He was never at a loss for words either. Tonight he had so few.

"Me too."

When silence lingered again, he said, "Well, if you need anything, call me, okay?"

"Thanks, Abe." I started to hang up, but couldn't resist asking, "How is he?"

Another pregnant pause. "He's fine. Don't worry about him."

"Is he—"

"Michael, please don't ask."

"Sorry. I'd never put you in the middle, it's just—"

"I get it. You're hurting and want to know what's going on. You want to know why, to understand."

"Yeah."

"There's nothing that will help you understand at this point. Trust me. You just have to get through each day. At some point, they'll just get easier. They'll get better."

I choked a sob back. "Thanks, Abe. I gotta go."

I hung up before the sob took control.

None of our other friends called. Not once.

10

———

HORSEPLAY

I t took me another week to go back into the office. I was
numb, staring blindly at the whiteboard as others
dissected the willing victim's work. They laughed and
teased. The senior adviser at the front of the room egged
them on, guiding the discussion through questions and
answers the group had missed. I usually loved the banter
and exchange of ideas. That morning, I barely blinked as
the whiteboard filled with facts and figures.

I'd never felt so dazed.

After work, I forced myself to return to the gym. Guys I
hadn't seen in a while waved and shouted greeting. When
Ryan and I had moved up to Roswell, I'd dropped my
membership in Midtown in favor of a chain warehouse-
type facility near our townhouse. While the equipment had
been newer, and the building larger, that place had never
felt right. The other folks working out weren't as friendly.
They definitely weren't as gay (as if that was possible
outside the Gay Bubble). I missed the warmth of the
muscle-heads who never failed to encourage that extra

push, and I missed the eye candy. Damn, the men of Midtown were hot.

I know, I know. I'd been hopelessly in love. What did I need with eye candy?

Just because I was set to walk down the aisle (at least, I thought I was), didn't mean I was dead. I still had eyes. I still liked craning my neck and checking out a hottie strolling by. I'd never even thought about acting on my unabated lust, but I enjoyed a good drool as much as the next guy.

Plus, smaller gyms were like a family. You might never see the guys who worked out next to you in any other setting, but you felt bonded, joined in a common—and very painful—purpose.

It was good to be back.

Unfortunately, my muscles rebelled at the thought of experiencing strains they hadn't known for weeks, and I had to drop my weights down a few notches just to get through all the sets. I might've been embarrassed if I'd had the capacity to care what anyone else thought right then. I just didn't.

One of the most consistent, friendliest meat-heads swaggered over next to me.

"Hey, stranger. Good to have you back. Where've you been all this time?"

His name, ironically, was also Michael, though he went by Mickey. His neck was bigger than his head, and his legs were thicker than my waist. I wouldn't say I was jealous— that's not a look I'd ever aimed for—but he had muscles layered on muscles, his face was striking, and his smile was infectious. It made for a very pleasant package.

Oh, his package. That was…unfortunate. An itty-bitty wittle wabbit, as Bugs might say.

Steroids might've paved the way to bigger bodies, but they clearly had their side effects.

"Shit, Mickey. It's been, what, a year?"

"Two. You vanished without a trace. We figured you either died or got married. Pretty much the same result either way." He laughed, proud of his own joke. Despite hitting a painful mark, I couldn't help but smile. The dumb ox was just so damn pleasant.

"Yeah, something like that. Kinda got left at the altar. Now, it's just the dying part without the marriage."

I was trying to be funny, to mirror his mood, but it just came out bitter and sad.

Mickey's meaty palm found my shoulder. "I'm sorry, man. I'm here if you want to talk about it. Really."

"Thanks, Mickey. I'm kinda talked out at this point, but I appreciate the offer."

"Anytime. I mean it." He leaned down and whispered in my ear. "Michael, you're hot as fuck. I don't know the guy who left you, but he's an idiot. It won't take you two minutes to find someone else who actually appreciates how amazing you are. Give yourself time, but don't be afraid to get back out there on the field."

My mouth opened, but nothing came out. Mickey had never talked to me about anything other than weights, muscles, and nutrition. When I looked from his hand on my shoulder into his eyes, the sincerity and depth I found threatened to open my wounds right there on the gym floor.

He must've seen the change in my expression and saved me from an embarrassing scene, reaching down and picking up one of the dumbbells at my feet and offering it to me.

"Now, are you going to lift these or just stare them back into the racks?"

A rebellious chuckle escaped the bonds of my despair. "Right." I grabbed the weight from his hands, then heaved the other one and resumed my curls.

Fuck, that hurt on *every* level.

Please remind me why I liked the gym so much?

TWO MONTHS AFTER THE BREAKUP, I CAVED. ABE AND several of the guys at the gym had been hounding me to "get back on the horse," as though getting over a relationship was as easy as jumping into a saddle. I wasn't exactly an expert horseman…horse rider…jockey…whatever, but I knew a thing or two about breakups. It was never that easy.

But Abe was hard to ignore, especially when he went into full pest mode.

It was Friday night. I'd left work early so I had time to hit the gym. If I was going on a date, I wanted to have that good post-workout pump.

Stop smirking! It looked good in a tight shirt.

My dinner date was none other than Mickey from the gym. We'd been chatting a lot lately. He was diligent in checking on me every day when I was working out. His usual opening line of, "What are you working today?" had been replaced by, "You feeling okay today? Anything you want to talk about?" It took a time or two for me to notice the change in pattern, and I wasn't sure if it made me more or less comfortable, but I appreciated his effort and concern.

There was also an element of safety involved. I knew Mickey. He was a good guy. He wouldn't pressure me or ask for more than I could handle. If I had to mount a new horse, I liked the idea of it being one I knew well.

Oh, and he was hot. I'd never ridden a bodybuilding stud before…er, I mean, horse. Yeah, horse.

We met at Cowtippers. It wasn't fancy, but it was close to home and, again, was comfortable. Every waiter in the place stopped by our table at one point in the night and gave me a warm hug. After the third drive-by, Mickey made a joke about me doing a lot more than tipping cows in that restaurant. His easy smile and quick laugh calmed my jittery nerves.

His steak arrived shortly before my regular Cowtippers meal of grilled chicken and baked sweet potato.

"Look at you being Mr. Healthy Dinner."

I grinned and picked up the two plastic containers crammed with butter, brown sugar, and cinnamon. He watched me dump their contents onto my potato.

"You spoke too soon, my friend."

He chuckled. "So I did. I'm so disappointed now."

"Hey!" I threw my hands up in mock offense. "Kinda harsh there, aren't ya, Ryan?"

Mickey cocked his head. His eyes were…inquisitive? No, that wasn't right. What was that look?

"Michael, it's okay."

Now it was my turn to look bemused. "Um, sorry? I really was teasing about the butter and brown sugar. I know I should be better, but—"

The grin he gave me held no amusement. He had that expression my father used to give me when I was little and got caught doing something, then tried to make up a really stupid, unbelievable story to cover my tracks. It was a knowing look, filled with understanding and a hint of pity. Why was Mickey giving me a piteous look?

"It wasn't the butter, although you really should watch that stuff. Your abs will thank you if you eat your veggies plain." And that smile crossed his face again. "You called me Ryan."

"What? When? Seriously?"

He nodded slowly, his eyes never wavering or leaving mine.

Fuck. Seriously, fucking shit.

My eyes plunged to my plate.

A thick, meaty hand covered mine. "Michael, it's okay."

"No, it's not." I was close to tears. "I'm sorry. I shouldn't have—"

"Should, shouldn't…there's no such things. You feel how you feel, and you've been through a lot. I'm just glad we had dinner together."

I looked up and tried to smile through blurry eyes.

He went on. "Someone told you to 'get back on that horse' or 'nothing heals a breakup like finding another man,' right?"

I nodded, once again that little boy unsure how to speak.

"That's shit advice." My head snapped up. He sighed and sat back as his eyes became distant and he traveled to some faraway place or time. "When my partner and I broke up, I cried for a year. It took me another year to date without comparing every guy I met to his unreachable standard. I sat across the table, like you are now, and compared how they ate, held their hands, talked—everything. It wasn't fair to them, and it certainly wasn't fair to me.

"I needed more time. I needed to heal, to remember—and to forget. I know my friends were just trying to help, but that wasn't the right way. If only I'd known that at the time."

Our eyes finally connected again.

The hulking bodybuilder who intimidated so many with his good looks and bulging muscles, the guy whose intense, stern gaze made even the stoutest look away, held only kindness and empathy.

Dammit. He was one of the good ones, and I was fucking it up.

"I wish our timing was better, Michael. You're one of the good ones." He stole my thoughts. "Life doesn't always cooperate, does it?"

He was right. Our timing was terrible.

"Yeah. I know. It just sucks, because…I don't know… I've always liked you, and now—"

"Hey, none of that." His trainer voice was back, strong and commanding. "You don't deserve that and neither do I. Take your time. Get your head and heart back together. Life will offer you whatever it has to offer when the time is right."

His eyes didn't match his stern voice. They were deep pools of gentleness and warmth.

"I think I'd better go now."

I fled to the safety of my car. By the time the door slammed shut, I'd lost any semblance of control. There, in the Cowtippers parking lot, I hunched over my steering wheel and wept.

There would be no more horses for a while.

11

A WALK IN THE PARK

S ummer dragged.

Atlanta was hot far longer than was necessary. When Labor Day rolled around, there was no relief. The only saving grace of the month of September was that it heralded the beginning of the basketball preseason, the time when officials began their training meetings in preparation for the upcoming season. I loved being a referee. It was athletic and required a focus that forced me to shut everything else out. It was impossible to start a five-second count, watch for off-ball illegal screens, and think about Ryan at the same time. Who knew wearing stripes was the cure for breakup agony?

Around four o'clock on the last Thursday of September, as I was reviewing my rulebook in anticipation of a pop quiz at the evening's meeting, my phone rang.

"Hello?"

"Hey."

My heart leapt into my throat at the sound of his voice. Ryan.

He hadn't called me since the breakup. I'd called to

hear his voice on his answering machine, like some pathetic loser who couldn't just move on, but we hadn't spoken.

I stood from the couch and paced as far as the scrunchy cord would let me.

"Hey," I said. Idiot.

There was a long, uncomfortable silence. "You want to take a walk?"

Well, that was weird. Out of the blue, he wanted to take a walk?

But I was desperate for his attention. I longed for it. The idea of him calling to take a walk, as insane as it now sounds, gave me hope.

"Sure. When?" I asked a little too quickly.

"Uh, now, if you're free. I've over at Piedmont."

"I can be there in five minutes. Where are you in the park?"

"Sitting on our bench."

Our bench. He wanted to meet at our bench. He even called it that.

We actually had a bench when we were together. It's where we'd sit and feed pigeons while pointing out hot boys riding by on rollerblades or throwing footballs. It was a bit voyeuristic, but fun.

Oh. My. God. He wanted to see me, to sit on *our* bench again. Did this mean—?

"Okay. See you in a few."

I was jumping on the couch in my socked feet, hands waving in the air, as the receiver dropped to the floor.

This was really happening. Holy shit.

I had to calm down. Just breathe.

Instead, I giggled and sprinted into my bedroom. I changed into a tighter, cleaner T-shirt and shorts that should likely have been worn by an eighth grader rather than a grown-ass man, but they made that man's ass look amazing, and that's all that mattered.

Ryan looked good. Really good. I watched him for a few minutes before heading over.

He looked up and smiled. For some reason, his smile didn't reach his eyes. It *always* reached his eyes.

Alarm bells sounded in my head, and I immediately went into Pisces mode, dropping onto the bench and grabbing his arm. "Are you okay? What's wrong?"

He gently freed his arm and scooted over so I could sit beside him with some space between us. "I'm okay. Why do you think something's wrong?"

"Ryan Alan Lowell. I know every expression your face makes. I knew them when we were together, and I'll know them twenty years from now. What's wrong?"

His smile finally reached his eyes. He shook his head and chuckled. "I suppose you do—and always will."

I crossed my arms impatiently. He was stalling something.

"So, I need to tell you something, and I think you're fine—"

"You think *I'm* fine?"

"Please, just let me get this out."

I nodded and leaned back, arms now crossed more tightly than before.

A pair of guys strolled slowly by, chatting about some reality television show. Ryan waited until they passed to continue.

"A few weeks ago, we went to Decadence again. We

were, well, decadent. You remember what it's like down there?"

I nodded and tried not to react. It had to be above ninety outside, but I was suppressing a shiver.

"I tested positive."

The whole park tilted on some unseen axis.

"I think you're okay. I'm almost sure it happened in New Orleans, but I wanted you to know so you could get tested, to be sure."

I forgot how to breathe.

He leaned forward and took my hand. His touch was clammy, his eyes indifferent.

Then it hit me. He was there—no, *we* were there—because he felt obligated, not because of any concern for me or my safety, and certainly not because he wanted—

I tried to say something, anything. As much as I'd craved his touch moments before, it now felt like that of a stranger, unwelcome and invasive. I pulled my hand away. He stared down into his empty palm.

"When we were together, did you—"

"No, never. Absolutely never. You were the only man I was with during that time. I would tell you if that weren't the case."

"I would hope so." My voice carried far more accusation than he deserved.

We stared at each other, neither of us knowing what to say. I was trying to figure out who the stranger was sitting on our bench. It couldn't be the Ryan I knew, the one with whom conversation flowed like a river, easy and free. This guy barely made eye contact with me. He stumbled and stammered, grasping for anything to say. This guy didn't even want to be there.

It couldn't be the same Ryan.

He finally found words, just not ones I wanted to hear. "You really should get tested, just to be sure."

"I will." I nodded absently. "But I know I'm positive."

His head snapped up.

"Ryan, if you are, so am I. I feel it in my gut. Don't ask me to explain it; I just know."

"Still…"

"Yeah, I know. I'll get tested." I sucked in a breath to steady myself and stood. "Thanks for telling me."

I didn't wait for him to respond. I left him sitting on *our* bench.

12

IS THAT ALL?

I didn't even have a primary care physician. I was that lucky guy who *never* got sick. So, as promised, I made my way to the county health department later that afternoon. They conducted free HIV screenings, and were supposedly very discreet. I jotted my initials and arrival time on the clipboard where instructed, then took a seat in the waiting room where seven other men and one woman sat. Nine people tried not to look at each other, while curiosity drove their eyes around the room. They were decidedly different: different races, different clothing, different styles, and, in the case of the woman, different sexes.

Yet each wore the exact same expression. We were numb with an undercurrent of terrifying trepidation. Each shared the same questions: Am I? Will I be okay? How long do I have—?

"M.R." a nurse called through the glass divider. It was my turn.

The woman reached out and gripped my arm as I passed. Startled, I looked down. She gave me a tight smile and shaky nod that communicated more than any words ever could.

The nurse led me to a sterile white room with one large chair that had arms outfitted with school-desk-type attachments where a patient could rest an arm.

"You are Michael Reed?"

"Yes."

"Why are you here, Michael?"

My face must've shown surprise or annoyance. I felt both at that question. Why the fuck did she think I was there?

Her voice softened. "I'm sorry. I have to ask."

"For an HIV test," I muttered, as though ashamed of some crime I'd committed.

"Do you have reason to believe you have been exposed, or are you just getting a routine test?"

Sweet Jesus. How many questions would she ask before just doing this?

"I…my partner…*former* partner…he just tested positive. He said he thought he got it after we broke up, but suggested I test anyway."

She nodded. Her eyes carried sympathy. The assembly-line nurse was now human. "Michael, I'm sorry, both about the exposure and, well, the breakup."

I glared at my shoes and whispered, "Thanks."

Her hand rested on my forearm. "It's going to be okay. No matter what. Look at me."

I looked up.

"You're going to be okay."

I gulped back whatever was trying to escape, but couldn't stop a furtive tear. She reached up and gently wiped it with her thumb, then wrapped her arms around me and let me cry into her shoulder.

When I'd gathered myself again, she reached for more vials than I'd ever seen in one doctor's office. My eyes went from red slits to saucers.

"Do I even have that much blood?"

She chuckled, caught off guard by my transition from tears to teasing.

"I'll try not to take it all, but you know how we vampires are. Once we get a taste—"

She stretched her lips back and tried to show me fangs that weren't there, then bit the air comically. A laugh escaped my lips. She smiled.

Moments later, blood drawn, I exited through a hallway that didn't allow me to see the kind woman who'd offered me support as I went to visit Nurse Vamp. I never saw her again. I never knew how she fared.

TWO DAYS LATER, I RECEIVED A CALL FROM THE FRONT desk of the health department. They had my results, but would only release them in person. The woman explained the policy had nothing to do with what the results contained. Positive or negative, everyone had to come in to learn their fate.

I hadn't told anyone about my conversation with Ryan or the test that followed. Dwayne and I had drifted apart, time and distance doing what they did best. I couldn't bring myself to tell Connie, either because I was ashamed or because I didn't want to worry her until I knew my results. I wasn't sure. It was probably a mix of both.

So, on a cloudy afternoon in September, I drove back to the health department and was ushered down a hallway into a doctor's office. Unlike the sterile exam room where my blood had been drawn, the doc's office held a large wooden desk, and walls covered with certificates and pictures. It had a decidedly personal feel. When the doc appeared in the doorway, I realized the kids in the pictures had to be his. They were miniature clones of the man in the lab coat.

He looked down at a folder in his hand as he rounded his desk and sat in his oversized leather chair.

"Michael?" He looked up through spectacles without raising his head.

I nodded. "Yes, sir."

He read the file a moment, then set it on his desk and locked eyes.

"The test shows the presence of virus in your blood." His voice wasn't cold, but it sounded like a verdict he'd rendered many times before.

"So, I'm—"

"Yes, you have tested positive for the presence of HIV."

He waited for me to say something. I didn't. I didn't even offer a reaction.

"Are you alright?"

Oddly, I was. With a confident, almost snarky voice, I answered. "I'm fine. Are you?"

He snorted. "No one's ever asked *me* that after receiving this news."

"I knew it before we did the test. In my heart, I knew."

He leaned back. "Why do you say that?"

"Because Ryan was positive. For two years, we shared everything."

I thought it was a statement of fact, as clear as the sun rising in the east. The doc's expression said he wasn't sure what to make of the patient sitting before him.

"Do you have any questions for me?" he asked.

I thought a moment. "What do I need to do now? Please

just tell me what I need to know in this moment. I don't want to know about things that might happen down the road. If there are decisions I need to make today, I'd like to be fully informed. Otherwise, ignorance is bliss."

The corner of his mouth quirked at my businesslike tone.

"Well, you need to find a doctor who specializes in working with infectious diseases. He or she will run some tests, likely try to determine which strain you have, then suggest a treatment regimen." He leaned forward again and removed his spectacles. "Michael, you're going to be fine. The medicines these days are fantastic, and new ones come out all the time. The vast majority of patients live long, healthy lives, as long as they adhere to their doctor's instructions."

My confidence shattered. "Long, healthy lives?" I muttered, more to myself than to the doc.

He nodded.

"How long?" I asked.

"I'm sorry?"

"How long do I have?"

He scanned the file, then closed it, as if I'd exhausted my question time.

"You're thirty-two now. If you adhere to your doctor's orders, I'd give you another fifty, maybe sixty years, give or take." His warm smile curled the deep lines around his eyes, and I knew he wasn't just trying to make me feel better.

He was telling me I'd really be okay.

13

PURE INTENTIONS

W ork was something of a bright spot in the midst of
a dark summer and fall. Once past all my exams
and initial training, I'd fallen in love with helping clients,
hearing about their lives, and working with them to secure
a better future. It felt unlike anything I'd ever known.
These people, these families, depended on my advice to be
able to retire—and to not outlive their savings once they
did. When I stopped and thought about it, the weight of that
responsibility felt immense, but was also immensely
satisfying.

My first client was Mrs. Betty Walker. I'll never forget
her. Brad had an adviser leave the company and had to
reassign his accounts. Clients with more assets or who
generated more revenue were assigned to his best advisers,
while we rookies were tossed smaller fish, often clients
who were unresponsive to their previous adviser.

Mrs. Walker was one of my "orphaned account" assign-
ments. She had nearly one hundred thousand dollars in a
retail account, all in cash. Our records showed the previous

adviser only called her once, and she never returned his call.

Batter up!

It took four calls to get her to answer the phone. She sounded four thousand years old and terrified to talk to strangers. When I finally got her talking, she refused to acknowledge she owned an account with Waddell or to discuss any investment ideas we might have. She actually hung up on me.

The next week, I called her again.

"Mr. Reed—"

"Please, Mrs. Walker, call me Michael."

"Mr. Reed, I don't understand why you're calling me again. I told you I don't want to talk to anyone about any investments."

"Yes, ma'am, I understand, but I'm required to keep calling until we discuss your account. Our company—and the folks who regulate us from the government—won't let us have accounts without knowing our clients. I'm really sorry to bother you, but we really do need to talk. Besides, you have quite a lot of money here, and it's all sitting in cash doing very little for you."

"A lot? How much is a lot?"

Holy shit. She didn't even know how much was in the account.

"Nearly one hundred thousand dollars."

Silence.

"Mrs. Walker? Did I lose you?"

I heard heavy breathing, then sniffing. She was crying.

"Mrs. Walker, are you okay?"

"I didn't know she'd left me so much."

I waited, ignoring the dozen questions threatening to spill out.

"When Judith died—she was my little sister—she left me that account. I haven't had the heart to even look at it."

"I'm so sorry, Mrs. Walker. When did Judith pass?"

"Six years ago."

Now I really didn't know what to say.

"She was my best friend in the world. My husband died twenty years ago of cancer. Judith moved into my house that week and wouldn't leave. I tried to be nasty, to make her go, but she was more stubborn than I'll ever be. Without her, I don't think I would've survived losing Ben."

Now I was misting up. All thoughts of accounts or investments flew out the window. All I could think of was this poor woman and what she'd lost, how lonely she sounded.

"Her daughter is all I have left, and she lives out in California. She's seven now. Beautiful little girl."

Seven. Her mother died when she was one year old. My heart shuddered.

"What's her name?"

"Marie."

"That's pretty."

I could almost hear her smiling. "She is pretty. I fly out to see her every few months. She calls me Nappy. It's a terrible name, but she couldn't say Nanna when she was little and it stuck. Now everyone thinks I'm a big napkin or some such."

We laughed together for the first time. God, that felt good.

"You sound very proud of her," I said.

"Oh, I'm more than proud. She's my world now, even if she lives all the way across the country. That idiot father of hers—I never liked him—moved out there to find himself or something." She made a spitting sound. "How do you find yourself? Hell, how do you lose yourself to even have to find your own damn self?"

Her sudden cursing caught me off guard and I snorted a laugh, then caught myself and covered the receiver.

"Oh, now you got me cussin'. Sorry about that."

I couldn't stop grinning. "It's alright. You're supposed to be able to tell me anything, kind of like a lawyer but without the legal protection. A judge can still make me rat on you if you commit a crime."

She laughed. "I'm a crazy criminal, that's for sure. You rat on me all you like."

"So—"

"How old are you, young man? You sound about twelve."

I couldn't decide whether to be offended or laugh. She had that effect.

"I'm thirty-two, but I look like I'm about twelve. We gingers don't age much."

"Ha. Don't I know it. I was seventy-five, maybe seventy-six, before my pepper turned to salt. We reds are alright."

"Yes, ma'am. That's what I think too."

"I like you, Michael Reed. I don't think I'm supposed to, but I do."

I laughed. "I like you too, Mrs. Walker."

There was another pause.

"What did you want me to do with that money?"

I was startled. We'd been so lost in each other's stories that I'd almost forgotten why I called her.

"Well, honestly, I don't know."

She cut me off. "What do you mean? Didn't you call wanting me to invest or something?"

My grin returned. "I called to introduce myself and get

to know you. It's pretty hard to give advice without knowing my client and what her goals are."

"I guess that makes sense."

"How would you feel about meeting? I wouldn't want to work with a financial professional I hadn't actually met. Besides, I'd like to hear more about Marie. You could bring pictures."

"Oh, I don't know about meeting. Can't we just talk about all this over the phone?" She retreated back into her shell.

"We could, but it would be easier for me to show you ideas and proposals in person. Investments can be confusing when we can't look at the same sheet of paper."

"I suppose." She thought a moment. "But I don't want to come into some office. You buy me a coffee down at Starbucks."

I chuckled. "It's a date."

"Oh no it's not, young man. Don't go gettin' crazy ideas." She cackled at her own joke. I laughed with her.

"Yes, ma'am. My intentions are pure, I assure you."

TWO DAYS LATER, I ROSE FROM A TABLE IN THE MIDDLE OF Starbucks to greet Mrs. Walker. She looked every bit the ninety-four years her profile claimed she was. What surprised me was the man holding her hand as they approached the table. His hair still held some darkness, though the battle with gray was clearly in its latter stages.

"Mr. Reed?"

I smiled. "Mrs. Walker, I'm Michael, remember?"

Her smile was brilliant, that of a girl in her twenties

whose heart and mind shone through like the sun. I liked her immediately.

"Michael, this is Pete. He's my boyfriend."

It took everything I had not to gape at my nonagenarian client.

"He's here to…" She fumbled for words.

I grinned. "To keep you safe from the man you're meeting for the first time?"

She nodded. "He'll whoop your ass."

I laughed—one of those out-of-control belly laughs that shakes every part of your body. It just tumbled out, and was the first truly free expression of joy I'd felt in months. Her smile widened as she watched me.

During our conversation, I learned just how wealthy Mrs. Walker was. She hadn't forgotten about the money in her account at Waddell. She hadn't cared about it. It was a tiny portion of her estate and, as she put it, she didn't need a penny of it. With that declaration, Brad's suggestion of investing for the future flew out the window. That was a dumb-ass idea anyway. At what point in a person's life did that conversation become moot?

As my mind spun for other ideas, Mrs. Walker dug through her purse. Her hands surfaced a moment later with a thick stack of Polaroid pictures. We spent the next ten minutes flipping through images of her niece, then her sister, and even one of her late husband. As we reached the bottom of the stack, I hopped up.

"I'm so sorry. We're in Starbucks and I forgot to get you something to drink. What would you like?"

I returned a moment later with two steaming cups.

"I had an idea while I was standing in line," I said, handing Mrs. Walker a mocha latte and Pete his black coffee.

She took a sip and sighed. "Okay, let's hear it."

"What about sending Marie to college?"

She set her cup down and stared up at me. "What do you mean?"

"Well, from what you told me about her father, he's probably not the most financially stable adult. Your sister passed before she could really build wealth. Have you thought about how Marie would pay for college when she's older?"

Mrs. Walker shared a look with Pete, then turned back to me. "No. I'm ashamed to admit it, but I haven't even thought about it."

"That's why you have me, right?" I gave her my warmest "I'm not a used-car salesman" smile.

She chortled. "I like you, dear, but how can I help send Marie to college? She won't be going for another ten or eleven years. I'm afraid I won't be here for any of it."

The reality of that statement was a two-by-four between my eyes.

"I…uh…yes. Well, I think I have a way you can use the money your sister left you and take care of Marie's college. Your legacy will live on with your niece."

For the next twenty minutes, we discussed how 529 Plans worked. In the end, I told Mrs. Walker that I needed to do some homework and get back to her. Coming up with the idea in line at Starbucks was very different to creating a financial plan with well-crunched numbers to ensure the greatest probability of success.

Who the hell are you? And what have you done with Michael? And who talks like that? the little devil snarked in my mind.

Oh, shut up, Toasty. He's doing the Lord's work here. Leave him be, the angel retorted.

As strange as having warring voices in my head was, it was good to have them back. They'd been silent since the breakup.

"I'll call you tomorrow and we can go over the numbers. If this works, Marie will never have to worry about paying for her education."

Mrs. Walker's eyes were moist. She rose with Pete's help, then tossed off his hand and bounded around the table to wrap me in a bony embrace. I fell into her arms, returning the hug.

"Thank you, Michael. Thank you," she whispered. "You're a good boy."

AS PROMISED, I CALLED MRS. WALKER THE NEXT DAY. Everything worked out. With another eleven years to invest the initial hundred grand, Marie should be able to attend any number of excellent colleges without ever opening her own wallet. Through the most beautiful tears I'd ever heard, Mrs. Walker agreed to the plan.

The next morning, the receptionist interrupted the morning murder board session. "Michael, sorry to interrupt. You have a client in the lobby."

Surprised, I glanced at Brad. He grinned. "Go. Clients before training."

I nodded and gathered my notebook, then headed up front. Mrs. Walker sat in one of our puffy leather chairs, mocha latte in one hand and a box wrapped in two kitchen hand towels resting in her lap. I shot forward to brace her as she struggled to her feet.

"Don't ever get old, Michael. Everything hurts when you're old." She gave me the chortle I was coming to love.

"Yes, ma'am. Although, I'm not sure I like the alternative." I winked dramatically.

She cackled again and slapped my arm playfully.

"What brings you into the office? I have to say, I thought Starbucks was our place. You cheating on me with these fancy digs?"

She giggled. "No. I brought you something." She handed me the box. "Go ahead. Open it. I'll take those towels home with me though."

Buried within were homemade oatmeal raisin cookies. They were still warm and gooey.

"You told me you like these, I think. Or it might've been Marie. I can't remember. Anyway, I hope you like them. I just wanted to say thank you. You kept calling when some old lady ignored you, and my baby will go to college because of that. You changed a life this week—two, if you count the old woman who is truly grateful."

My mouth opened but refused to work. I looked down at this beautiful, bent elder and saw such warmth and love in her eyes. One eye couldn't hold back its tear—and that was all it took for my own dam to burst. In seconds, we were wrapped in each other's arms, blubbering like babies. She finally released me, took her towels back, and left the office. I stared at the door for a good minute before breathing deeply and turning to resume training.

The receptionist was staring from behind her desk. Her cheeks were moist.

Brad was leaning in the entryway to the office. He nodded and gave me a proud smile.

That was the day I fell in love with the business.

14

SEASONS OF CHANGE

Months rolled by and life's routine seized control. Days were spent searching for new clients, while most evenings involved either a workout or officiating. I was thankful for the predictable monotony. It kept me busy and unable to be alone with my thoughts too much.

Thinking is overrated when your heart is in pieces.

I worked with a team of thirteen other rookies. We shared a long conference room that had been converted into a bullpen. We called it "the incubator." Card tables lined each wall, and folding chairs spaced every few feet marked out personal space. There were no computers or equipment other than a telephone. It wasn't plush like the senior advisers' offices, but it was all we needed.

I was in my thirties, so I was the old man of the group. That set me up as the natural go-to guy in the bullpen, the one all the twentysomethings thought knew more than they did because I was older and more mature. That made me laugh, but I accepted the role and mentored as many little chickens as would fit under my wings.

Apparently, Brad noticed. He saw everything.

"Michael, can I borrow you for a minute?" he asked from the incubator's open door one morning.

"Sure."

I followed him into his office. He closed the door behind us—something he never did. My stomach did a tuck and roll. Something was up.

"I have something I want to ask you; more of an opportunity, really," he said as he settled into his plush leather chair behind his sprawling oak desk. I sat down opposite.

When I didn't respond, he continued. "You've shown a lot of initiative with the team, coaching and training where possible."

"They're a good group," I said. "Most of them just need a little guidance. I like helping them."

He nodded. "That's why I wanted to talk to you. There's an opening for a branch manager in Florida. I want you to get your supervisory licenses and take over that office."

I nearly fell out of my chair. "But all my clients are here. I've only been to Florida once as a kid. I don't know anything about the place." My head was reeling. "Besides, I've never led a team or run a branch. Well, I did run a sales team for a while, but that was different."

"It's not different. Same principles, different products and services." He smiled knowingly. "You're good with advisers, especially newer ones. Most managers aren't. I think you were made for this."

"Thanks, I think." I still couldn't believe what I was hearing. "What about my clients?"

"We'll have to find them a new adviser. Branch managers don't produce. Are you okay with that?"

"I guess. Sounds a little like giving up my safety net though."

Another nod. "That's one way to put it. I've lived without one for two decades now. It's scary at first, but you get used to it. Being in leadership lets you have a broader impact, do more good through more people. If you enjoyed helping that client I saw in the lobby a while back, just think how it would feel to impact hundreds or thousands of families through your team."

Damn, this guy was good. He was pressing all my preacher's kid buttons, hitting me in my soft spot.

"You said Florida. Where, exactly?"

"Sarasota."

"Huh. Never heard of it."

"You don't get out much, do you?" He chuckled. "It's about forty minutes south of Tampa, so you'd be close to a major city, if you like that sort of thing. The office is nice, right on the bay. I'm a little jealous, really."

He pecked on his antiquated computer, then spun his monitor around. The view out a window of a ten-story office building showed crystal blue water spread beyond the camera's vision. The sun was setting, lighting the sky in brilliant hues. The water below reflected that brilliance, like a prism scattering every color of a rainbow. It looked amazing.

No, it looked like home.

I don't know why, but I knew from that one image that Florida would be where I called home for the rest of my life. I felt it. It called to me.

Brad was also right about me loving to coach. I'd always loved coaching and training more than being a player on the field. In my current role, I got to do that without any responsibility for the trainees' performance. That would change, but the idea of spending my days helping others succeed appealed to me.

More than anything, this felt like a fresh start—the fresh start I *desperately* needed. There would be no way to run into Ryan at a bar or the gym or the grocery store if we lived hundreds of miles apart. It seemed the Atlantan fates tried to bump us into one another almost daily, constantly picking at the wounds that refused to heal.

Yes, this sounded good. It sounded right. It *felt* right.

Without thinking further, I looked up and met Brad's eyes.

"If the numbers work, I'm in."

CONNIE WRAPPED ME IN A TIGHT EMBRACE, THEN SHOVED me into my overstuffed car. We shed a tear or two, but her infectious laugh stopped us from becoming blubbering messes in the Post parking lot. I'd miss her. That made this transition bittersweet, but I knew I needed the change.

Sarasota was in the midst of "the season" when I arrived. Locals explained how the population doubled during peak months, as snow birds who lived there half the year arrived and nested. It was a small town, especially compared to a sprawling metropolis like Atlanta, but the slower pace helped me settle in and not feel overwhelmed.

That more relaxed vibe translated into the office environment too. In Atlanta, if you arrived at the office after seven thirty, Brad would greet you with, "Good afternoon. Thanks for making it in." In Sarasota, we were lucky to see some of our advisers before the market opened at nine thirty.

Another contrast was the dress. Back in the big city, suits were the norm. In Sarasota, suits were nearly akin to religious blasphemy. I tried influencing the dress of my new troops, encouraging them by setting the example, but they just watched me sweat and laughed at the newcomer who was too thick-headed to listen to reason. The teased me, promising my attitude toward ties would change once summer came.

Clearly, I had a lot to learn.

A few months later, I'd established a comfortable routine in my new home. Ten-hour workdays kept me out of trouble. An evening workout at a gym around the block from the office helped me sleep well each night. There was only one gay bar in town at the time. I visited it on my first weekend in town. Of the seven people in the place, six were over the age of sixty. The seventh was nineteen. The bartender gave me a sympathetic look as I scanned the scene, then gave me a shot of something for my trouble. At least the shot was fruity and closer to my age than any of the guys in the bar.

At a loss for where to meet guys, I turned to my most trusted sources: AOL, Manhunt, and Adam4Adam. Their pages were almost as desolate as the bar had been. I would love to tell you I spent hours scrolling through profiles, creating a whole new binder filled with stars and possibilities, but the bounties of Sarasota eluded me. Well, the single men eluded me. Bounties might be a bit dramatic.

I found a local gym and promised to be diligent in working out. Somewhere in the back of my mind, I held out hope my gaydar would buzz as I watched hotties roam from one bench to the next. Alas, hotties were few and far between, and none of them set off any alarms. One guy who'd obviously enjoyed far too many party drugs in his youth twitched his way over one evening. He used his best pickup line and tried to be witty, but I couldn't see past his hollowed-out eyes and stained teeth. On another night, a man old enough to be my grandfather made a pass. He was handsome and well-spoken, but I had a simple rule: If the wrinkles on the skin make me want to iron, they're too old.

He failed that test.

Sarasota's sad gay newspaper boasted of a softball team filled with athletic hotties ready to pitch and catch. I called the number in the ad and spoke with the captain. They indeed needed a good pitcher, but the season wouldn't start for months and there was no off-season ball to be played. I'd hoped to make some friends, maybe even find a date or two from the team, but that grape died on the vine.

There was this one guy who lived in Palm Beach. His name was Pedro, and he'd immigrated from Cuba when he was two. We met on AOL, chatted a few times, then I drove three hours to meet him and his two greyhounds. Pedro was hot and spicy, and I liked him well enough, but the idea of driving three hours for a date got old quickly. After three weekend visits, I called it quits.

After Pedro, I gave up on the dating scene and turned to my favorite pastime: basketball officiating. There was a local officials' association, but the territory they covered was ridiculous. There was no way I could work a regular day in the office and make it to a high school basketball game in time. I was eighteen years old when I stepped onto a court in stripes that first time. After a twenty-year career, the last thing I wanted to do was hang up my whistle, but I didn't have much choice. The distance and timing wouldn't cooperate.

Now I really was at a loss.

And I was lonely.

Ten-hour workdays turned into twelve. Healthy, home-cooked meals morphed into Chinese takeout and order-in pizza. I tried getting into *American Idol* and other shows the folks at work talked about incessantly, but none of it charged my batteries.

That's when it hit me.

I needed a friend, one who would be there no matter what, who would love me and welcome me home with open arms.

Dammit. That made me think of Ryan—and I hadn't thought of him once since moving. There endeth the streak.

No, I actually wasn't thinking about dating or men at all. I needed a dog!

The internet provided an endless stream of advice on which breed was best for apartment living, so I did what any self-respecting guy would do—I ignored all of it. When my eyes fell on a black lab, my heart soared. Black lab it would be. It *had* to be. I'd name him Smoky or Jet. If she was, well, a she, I'd name her Blanca.

You know that means "white," don't you? The angel appeared in white shorts and a white T-shirt holding a red leash in one hand, as if ready to walk my soon-to-be pup.

"Yes, I know that. It's ironic—and that's a very gay thing to be," I said out loud, suddenly self-conscious to be talking aloud to my conscience.

You need therapy, not irony.

"Ha ha. I'm not the one holding an empty leash for a dog we don't have yet."

This leash is for you. New town, new rules. No more wild Michael. You've sown your oats. Now you need to be a good boy like your mama raised you, young man.

"You've gotten so bossy in your old age."

Old? You have no idea how old I am. Angels—

Oh, shut it. You're ancient and wise. We get it. If you'd stop badgering the boy, he might get laid. I think we can both agree he would be far more enjoyable after a good pipe fitting. The devil made his dramatic entrance in red leather riding breeches and red boots. Oddly, he was shirt-less and bore rippling muscles and sculpted abs. Holy shit, he looked hot.

Did you just ogle your imaginary friend? the angel mocked.

He sure did, the devil said, flexing like Arnold. *Look at these guns. You know you want some, wing boy.*

"Are you two done? Jesus."

Easy with that name, the angel scolded.

"Fair enough. Now, go away. I'm heading to the shelter to find Smoky or Inky or Blanca."

That poor animal, the devil said as he vanished in a puff of red mist.

HOURS LATER, I'D SEEN EVERY DOG THE TWO SHELTERS IN town had to offer. It broke my heart to leave them in cages, but there weren't any black labs and I was committed to Licorice.

Okay, that would definitely not be his name.

The next weekend, I visited the same shelters. They'd told me to check back regularly, and we PKs were good at doing what we're told.

Ha, who was I kidding? We're good at *being seen* doing what we're told. Watch out when you're not looking.

Anyway. Round two was also a bust. But, as I was leaving the second shelter, the woman who'd escorted me through and introduced each dog recommended I drive a little south to the shelter near the county line. Sarasota was a long county, much like its beaches, and there was a whole other world at the southern end of town. My dog search was turning out to be educational. I thanked the helpful herder and drove twenty minutes to the last stop of the day.

The SoCo Animal Shelter was small but very tidy. It only took a few minutes to see every dog and puppy, even a few cats. I didn't want a cat, but they were fun to play with if I couldn't find a dog. As I was leaving, shoulders slumped at another weekend's failure, a voice called out behind me.

"Michael?"

I turned to find a young woman in her twenties, hair pulled back in a ponytail, wearing the tan pants and light blue shirt of a shelter worker.

"Hi. Yes, I'm Michael."

"I'm Deena. I know you were looking for a black lab, but did you get a chance to meet Jesse?"

I cocked my head. "Jesse?"

"Yes. She's a retriever/chow mixture, reddish tan with the shadow of a black diamond on her head and black liner around her ears. She's beautiful and really sweet."

"No, I don't think I saw her, but I'm—"

"I know. You want a black lab. Would you at least come meet Jesse? She's been cooped up all day and I'm sure she'd enjoy a visitor."

I didn't have anywhere to be, so I acquiesced and followed Deena back down the hallway to the kennels.

"Go into that greeting room. I'll bring Jesse through the staff door." She turned toward the kennels, then turned back. "One thing—Jesse was brought here by a family who couldn't keep her. The parents divorced or something. We never got the full story. She's been sad and hasn't liked many people. Don't be offended if she doesn't let you pet her."

"Okay," I said, even less interested in this visit than

before. That was all I needed—a dog who didn't want me back. Sounded too much like my dating life.

Ooh. Bitter, party of one. Your table is ready. The devil's silky voice chided in my head. The angel actually snickered.

Rotten, disloyal conscience.

The greeting room was simple and plain; the walls painted white, with dusty white tiles on the floor. Two rickety-looking chairs sat facing each other about six feet apart. I sat in one and waited.

Moments later, the door handle rattled and Deena walked through and sat in the other chair. Jesse sat politely in front of her, still tethered by a leash to Deena's hand. She was a beautiful dog with bright, clear eyes, a keen intelligence shining through. She eyed me, weighing and assessing.

Deena didn't speak, just looked at me, then down at Jesse.

Jesse didn't speak either.

This was going great.

I did the only thing I could think of. I sat on the floor in front of the chair and looked up.

In a flash of fur, Jesse bounded free of Deena's grip and tumbled into my lap. She sniffed my chin a moment, then fell onto her back and nuzzled into my stomach. I was so caught by surprise that I started laughing. That encouraged the pup. Before I knew what was happening, a slobbery black-and-purple tongue was slathering my face. It took a couple minutes for the two of us to calm, but Jesse eventually drew back and sat dutifully by my side, staring up with deep golden eyes. My heart lurched at her unerring gaze.

I'd wanted a black lab, but sometimes what I wanted

and what I *needed* were very different things. Life had a funny way of sorting all that out, if I'd just listen.

When I turned from Jesse to Deena, she said six magic words that I'll never forget:

"I think Jesse just adopted you."

15

MERGERS AND ACQUISITIONS

Two years in Sarasota flew by. When I wasn't working eternal days, Jesse and I were walking through downtown or along the bay. She was my constant companion. She also proved to be one of the most well-trained furry friends I could've found. According to the pound, her previous owners raised her from a pup. They guessed her age around two. What the shelter couldn't have known was how much effort they'd put into her training. She knew commands for everything one might imagine, and her keen intellect craved more training and knowledge. With only a few attempts, she quickly picked up on hand signals to accompany the verbal commands she already knew.

There was something in the training process that bonded us in a way I'd not experienced with a dog before. She looked at me differently. It's hard to explain. I'd fallen in love with her the day we met, but when she looked at me with her unfettered, unlimited emotion, I melted. Jesse enjoyed attention and affection, but generally wanted her own space when it was time to stretch out for a nap. The only time she'd break that pattern was when she sensed I was down. Nothing could separate us in those moments. She'd crawl onto the couch and lay her head in my lap until she knew I felt better.

How can animals move our hearts so?

As a tourist town, most restaurants featured outdoor seating that allowed for pets. We became regulars at the dozen or so shops situated within walking distance from my condo. Every server and owner knew Jesse and greeted her by name, usually with a treat from the kitchen or bowl of clean water. People at nearby tables marveled that I never had to give her verbal commands. A quick gesture had her sitting or finding a comfy spot to stretch out.

I might not have had much of a dating life, but I definitely had a best friend.

THE DAY BEFORE MY SECOND ANNIVERSARY IN SARASOTA, I got a call from the corporate office. A position had opened to run a nationwide business for the firm based in Tampa, just up the road. They thought I'd be a good fit and wanted me to post for the role. It was something of a hybrid between running a branch and a massive call center. Brad, my former boss and now mentor, told me I was crazy to even question the opportunity.

Two weeks and six interviews later, I got the job.

Four weeks after that, Jesse and I said goodbye to Sarasota. We'd enjoyed our time in a small beach town, but I was looking forward to living in a bigger city again.

At thirty-five years old, my gay biological clock was

ticking. Online, guys were already filtering me out in their searches. A twentysomething viewed anyone with a three in front of his age as ancient. Heaven forbid that number started with a four! It was like I was aging out of a dating game show. The same guys who'd hit on me at a bar would avoid me online because I fell outside their age search criteria. It was definitely a new wrinkle I hadn't expected.

Being HIV positive hadn't exactly made things easier either. I'd been lucky, never once experiencing any symptoms or variations in blood counts, something my doc credited to clean living and good genes. He said there was something in Irish genes dating back to the potato famine that gave us a sort of resistance to certain things. I never fully understood—or bought—that explanation, but two different docs pointed to studies in the *Journal of the American Medical Association.*

Bless my lucky charms.

Despite being healthy, some guys couldn't wrap their heads around dating a positive man. Honestly, I knew how they felt—I'd been there with Donny. The fact I was experiencing the same fear and rejection that I'd given him weighed on my heart. But I was kind to myself, and the guys, as well. HIV *was* scary if you didn't have the knowledge and life experience. And me, old man that I was, had racked up plenty of each.

I made it a practice to always tell someone up front, before we ever went on a date. There were two reasons. First, it was honest and felt like the right thing to do. Second, and more personally important, it let them run away before I could develop feelings. I hadn't always been so quick to tell my status, and I'd had my heart squished a time or two. That was a hard lesson to learn.

My hope was Tampa, a much larger city, would offer a wider variety of men, as well as a population of guys who had friends or exes who were also positive. I'd found those with even a little experience were less likely to run.

After a week of searching, my agent and I found a house I couldn't live without. The people of Seminole Heights had nicknamed it "The Castle on the Lake" because it was styled after a Spanish castle and sat at the top of a circle drive that wrapped around a small duck pond. A stonemason had built the house in 1923 for his wife, and his work was impeccable. I fell in love with the original hardwoods and tightly fitted marble the moment we walked through the door.

OVER THE NEXT COUPLE YEARS, I DID ALL THE THINGS A gay in his new town would do: discovered all the bars, explored eateries and hangout spots, joined the gay softball league, and created new profiles on every dating app imaginable.

The bars were filled with cute boys in tight jeans. For the first time in my life, I felt old staring at their unlined faces and pubescent bodies. Don't get me wrong—they were hot. I wouldn't throw any of them out of bed—and didn't—but the idea of dating someone so much younger made me pause. All they wanted was to party, to have fun, to shirk responsibility. I had a career now, a real job I loved, and a life I wanted to build. I'd been single for nearly nine years, but I still craved companionship.

Had I become…*an adult*?

The thought made me shudder.

Get over it, Peaches. We all age. The devil appeared in

a puff, bent over a walker with faux gray hair and spectacles. He was still shirtless with rippling abs and arms. *Well, we don't actually—we're eternal. But you lot do. Just slap some cream on it and go find a boy to slap. It'll make you feel younger in minutes—assuming you can last that long, given your advanced age and all.*

"I've found plenty of boys. I think I need something more now."

Oh shit. Emergency! Emergency! Angel, we need you, now!

The angel appeared with a toothbrush in his mouth and rollers in his freshly permed hair. He wore a white robe with pink frills at the collar and cuff.

Wha's wong? he asked before spitting out his toothpaste.

Our boy is trying to be responsible. I think he's—wait for it—growing up.

"Ha ha. You two are hilarious."

I still think you need to get laid. Let some muscle daddy fuck the second-guessing right out of you. It always worked before.

The angel sighed. *Oh, Michael, don't listen to him. He's like a rotten tooth, always wanting more sweets but ready to snap the next time you bite down hard—*

Hard, right. That's what I said. He needs to get hard, then take it hard.

"You two aren't helping, you know that, right?"

Fine. Figure it out on your own. I still think you need some dick, stat. Nothing puts you in a better mood than having some dude shove—

I believe he gets your point.

I'd rather he get some hot guy's point.

"Enough!" I waved my hand and the pair vanished. "I can't think with you two around."

My plan didn't involve thinking, the devil's distant voice rang in my head.

The freakin' angel laughed.

I hated those two sometimes.

16

SERENA V. GENERAL TSO

Part of giving up on dating involved deleting my Manhunt, Adam4Adam, and Grindr profiles.

Yes, I'd become a Grindr aficionado. It was basically the same guys that were on the other sites, only more convenient as an iPhone app featuring proximity and other pertinent details when an, um, immediate need arose.

That makes me sound like such a slut, doesn't it?

If the slipper fits, Dorothy, the angel's verbal whip cracked in my head.

Let's ignore him for the moment.

I deleted those profiles, and removed the apps from my phone. I also cleared out the history tab on my computer and removed them from the favorites bar at the top of Internet Explorer.

Sheesh. Everywhere I turned were little droppings… drippings…never mind.

You look good in glittery red shoes. Keep that pair.

I really needed a therapist.

Bottom line (and no, that was not a sexual reference, you deviant), I was freeing myself of my slutty ways. In fact, I was giving up on men altogether. None of my efforts were yielding more than one- or two-night stands, and I needed to devote more time to my fancy new job anyway. Guys were a distraction to my future success.

That brings us to a Sunday in early September, nearly seven years AR (After Ryan, please keep up here). I was stretched out watching TV, with Jesse sleeping peacefully on the other piece of sectional, when my phone lit up. If any of this sounds vaguely familiar, it's because it's almost an exact re-creation of my first date. You know, the one that started me on this insane, dark path?

This time, however, it wasn't a call from my roommate's friend. It was an alert from Facebook.

Huh. Facebook sent alerts. I hadn't known that.

I'd just signed up for Facebook a few days earlier, determined to replace my Slutisha ways with the more wholesome "share pics of your pups" social networking. I hadn't paid much attention to all the bells and whistles when installing the app on my phone, but there was, apparently, a setting that allowed Facebook to send alerts when friends posted pictures or changed information on their profiles.

I stared at the notice, debating turning that feature off, but something about it made me pause.

Your friend, Pedro Ramirez, just changed his status.

His status? What did that mean? And when did I friend Pedro? I hadn't seen or talked to him in nearly a year.

Curious, I clicked the alert. Pedro had changed his relationship status to "single."

Oh, that made more sense now.

Wait, Pedro had been dating someone?

I clicked again. He'd dated a guy named Heath for two months. Pedro hadn't posted any explanation for the breakup, nor had he trash-talked his ex. He simply posted a picture of himself and the greyhounds at the park. They spent more time at the park down the street from his house than they did in his house. It was kinda cute.

Now invested in this tale, I noticed Heath's name was a blue link, so I clicked it.

Holy shit. Heath was hot.

The first thing I noticed was his ridiculously white smile. The picture appeared to be a selfie taken outside a gas station or store, but the guy's smile was model-perfect.

Then there was his hair. I'm normally more of a chest and arms guy, but Heath's hair game was on point. I couldn't help but stare with envy. Dark, messy locks sprouted in every direction, giving the impression he didn't care that his hair was disheveled, while having placed every strand in exactly the right place.

Deep pools of rich brown smiled almost as brightly as his teeth.

I swooned a little, right there on my couch.

Jesse's head popped up as she glared accusingly.

"I know. You're right. I gave up on men. But I can still look, can't I?"

She gave me a low whimper, then laid her head back down.

I scrolled through Heath's profile. He had a ton of pictures—mostly impromptu shots—all with the same impeccable smile and infuriatingly sexy hair.

Despite his handsome appearance, there was something different about Heath. He seemed genuine, more down-to-earth and grounded than many of the guys I'd met lately. Yes, that was ridiculous to read from a picture or online profile, but it's what I saw.

On a whim, I clicked the Messenger button and sent:

Michael Reed: *Hey. Really nice smile.*

I locked my phone and dropped it on the floor before Jesse could judge me.

Seconds later, it chirped.

Heath Cox: *Cute smile yourself.*

That was fast. He liked my smile. I grinned into the phone.

Heath Cox: *How do you know Pedro?*

Holy crap. How had he connected the two of us?

Heath Cox: *I saw him on your friends list. He's our one friend in common.*

Oh.

Michael Reed: *We dated for a minute. The long-distance thing didn't work as well as I'd hoped.*

Heath Cox: *Yeah. I moved there, but that didn't make it work any better. He's a good guy, just a little scattered. Loved his dogs though.*

Michael Reed: *Did he take you to the park?*

Heath Cox: *LOL every night. You too?*

Michael Reed: 😊 *Yep.*

Heath Cox: *What are you doing right now?*

Well, that was fast. I thought Facebook was a safe zone. *What the hell?*

Michael Reed: *Nothing. Kinda bored.*

Heath Cox: *Want some company?*

Jesse sensed something in my mood and growled.

"Oh, hush. Daddy might get some dick today. We'll both be better for it."

She huffed and turned away.

Michael Reed: *Sure. I guess.*

Heath Cox: *One requirement. Do you have the Tennis Channel?*

Michael Reed: *Uh, maybe. I'm not sure.*

Heath Cox: *Serena's playing in the Open today. No Tennis Channel, no Heath.*

I fiddled with the remote, scrolling through the search function I'd never used. ESPN, ESPN2, ESPN3, Sports South, and a dozen other sports channels, but no Tennis Channel. I found the icon, but a message popped up informing me the Tennis Channel was a premium service that required an additional subscription. There was a button there to subscribe.

Did I *need* the Tennis Channel? Of course not. I didn't even like tennis. But there was a hottie willing to come over if I could flash him my Serena. I clicked "subscribe now."

I thought you were giving up men. The angel appeared, accompanied by a blinding flash of light I'd never seen before.

One thump later, he flashed again and vanished. His righteous indignation rang in my ear.

Michael Reed: *Oh, found it. Sorry, it was hidden among all the other sports channels.*

Damn, I sounded like a jock. What a stud.

Heath Cox: *Tennis is the only real sport. Send me your address. The match starts at two. I'll be there at 1:59.*

At precisely 1:59, the brass bell hanging by my door rang. The back door was propped open with only the interior gate shut to keep the dog inside. Jesse launched herself from the couch and skidded to a halt just beyond the metal bars. Her guttural growl echoed throughout the stone entranceway.

Jesse was a sweet baby, but the chow in her could

frighten the manliest of men. More importantly, she was a better judge of character than any animal—or human—I'd ever met. If she didn't like someone, they would never get to stand or sit next to me without her furry ass in between. Her eyes would *never* leave them, and she'd be ready to strike should the need arise. Daddy was well protected from suspicious characters.

If I'd only listened to her more, I would've avoided some really bad second and third dates along the way. A time or two I was sure she'd given me that "I told you so" look after a messy ending. She really was brilliant.

"Come on in. I'm just putting the match on," I yelled from the couch, grinning at the thought of my magical beast sizing up another meal—I mean, man.

The hinges squealed, and Jesse's growling silenced. I heard her breathing change from threatening to thrilled. When I peered over the couch, all I saw of my pup was her paws in the air. Heath was on his knees, bent over tickling the shit out of her. It sounded like they were both laughing hysterically.

I stood and gaped, unable to process the scene. "Jesse?"

They both looked up, both with a tongue lolling out the side of their mouth. If I hadn't been so shocked by her sudden change, I would've registered how insanely cute the image was.

"I think she likes me," Heath said.

Jesse's head snapped from me to him, then she pawed him to tickle or wrestle—or whatever you'd call what he was doing to my poor, easily manipulated dog.

Okay, maybe not easily manipulated, but it was impressive.

"I'd say so. She doesn't usually like anyone but me."

He beamed. "You just hadn't met *me* yet."

His teeth were just as perfect in real life, gleaming brilliantly like neatly pressed sailors in a row saluting up at me. My "I've given up on men" heart fluttered a bit. I swallowed down the feeling.

"Uh, I can leave you two alone if you need some time, but the match is about to start."

Heath leapt up faster than I thought his six-foot-one frame would allow.

"Sorry, pup, Serena's my girl." He mussed her head then strode through my dining room like he owned the house. "Hey. I'm Heath."

I wasn't sure whether to shake hands or hug or what. Did one do any of that before a tennis match? Was there etiquette for this situation?

Being a complete dork, I waved, as if he were standing in the house across the street rather than two feet away.

He grinned again, then pulled a hand out of his pocket and waved back.

Fuck. He'd out-dorked me—on purpose. By the shit-eating grin on his face, he knew it too.

Shit, his grin was cute.

Without another word, he bounded around me and fell onto the couch. Serena had just won the coin toss and was bouncing back to the baseline to begin her warm-up.

SERENA FOUGHT VALIANTLY AGAINST VICTORIA AZARENKA.

I wasn't into the tennis, but my guest was fascinating. He hung on every point. Actually, that's not accurate. He hung on every shot, every movement, every step Serena took. He went on about her "tiny step" as she approached the ball, her balance as she set up, and the easy power she got from her hip rotation and follow through. Every aspect of the game excited him.

I understood that she'd won, that's about it.

Don't get me wrong. I was athletic and played softball, and the basic mechanics of sport made sense to me, so I could follow most of what he said, but I'd never viewed tennis as being all that complex. Get the ball back. Wasn't that all there was to it?

Oh no. Tennis is freakin' hard. The more I listened to him, the more I realized tennis was a team sport wrapped in an individual effort. One person doing things ten should be doing—all at once. It wasn't only complex, it was incredibly difficult. The level of athleticism and coordination required to be decent was incredible. I couldn't even fathom the skill it took to be a professional.

And then there was Serena. There really wasn't anyone on her level. She played on a different planet from everyone else.

That's how Heath described it.

Between the first and second sets, when we realized the match would go much longer than expected, Heath asked if I'd had lunch.

"Uh, no, I hadn't even thought about it until now. I am kind of hungry."

He looked at me expectantly.

I ran a hand through my hair. "I, uh, haven't been to the grocery store in a minute. Mind if we order in?"

"No, that sounds great." He flashed me those damn teeth again. I tried to look away, but they were eye magnets, some form of demon magic pulling me into their deep brown eternity.

"Uh, okay, well, Chinese?" Fuck, I was stammering.

He grinned. "Sure. White meat only, please. General Tso's Chicken."

"Got it."

Thirty minutes later, we were at the "business end" of the second set. That's what Heath called it. Apparently, shit got real in a tennis match when the score reached 4–4. I didn't understand why, but sat forward on the couch, mirroring Heath, as though it was the most exciting thing ever.

You really don't know anything about this. You just want his cock, the devil snickered in my head.

"Shut it. I'm a little busy here," I whispered.

"What?" Heath said through a mouthful of spicy chicken goodness.

"Oh sorry, was somewhere else."

He cocked his head like a confused puppy, but turned back to the match.

Get this dumb game over so we can get him naked. The devil was persistent today.

"Yes!" Heath yelled at the television, masking my, "Fuck off," to the devil.

I caught myself watching him a little too openly a few times. He sat, leaned forward, literally on the edge of the couch, arms waving or clapping each time the chair umpire called the score. The tiny lines around his eyes curved upward when he smiled. A few rebellious curls kept falling into his face, forcing his hand up to brush them back. His fingers wove in the locks and slowly dragged them back.

Why was that simple act so sensual to me?

His eating *wasn't* sensual, by any definition of the word. In fact, he shoveled chicken and rice into his mouth so fast I wondered if he was bored with me and wanted to be done with our impromptu date. In a flash, his cartons were empty and cast aside, and his attention had returned to the match.

I beat my insecurities into submission and chalked his ravenous ways up to excitement over a great match.

I couldn't stop peeking as he roared at the screen.

Serena won in a thrilling third set. Heath was elated.

Then I looked down and realized Jesse had curled up on the couch at his side and fallen asleep, completely ignoring his outbursts and wild gesticulations. He'd been petting her throughout most of the match. She hadn't even sat between us—and she never let *anyone* touch her while she slept, rarely even me.

17

POST-MATCH RECOVERY

I picked up our plates and the leftover Chinese food containers while Heath rattled on about the match. It was cute to see him so excited. He hopped up from the couch and showed me a few moves, imitating Serena's forehand with surprising precision. When he tried to imitate her tiny steps, he made a *dat-dat-dat* sound with his mouth that cracked me up. He wasn't just into tennis, he was goofy-funny into it.

He compared the match we'd just watched to ones from the '70s, then explained how Steffi Graf was his all-time favorite player. There was something about her slice and movement. I think he said, "Her motto was, 'Hit it where they're not.' When they return it, hit it to the other side where they're not." That actually sounded like something I'd say as I tried to dumb down a very complicated sport.

Jesse had followed me dutifully into the kitchen, probably hoping Daddy would drop a few chunks of chicken. He did not. She then gave me the unmistakable signal that she needed to go potty.

"Hey, Heath. Want to take Jesse for a walk? Looks like she needs to do her business."

He dropped to the kitchen floor and she flopped into his lap, gobbling up every ounce of loving he offered.

I rolled my eyes. "You're such a slut!"

She looked up and grinned, understanding every word I'd said and claiming them.

Heath laughed as he wrestled her.

I shook my head. It was clear he'd won her over.

"Looks like I've won her over. What do I have to do about her dad?"

Holy shit. Was he in my head? And did he just say he wanted to win *me* over? A little tingle I'd thought long gone traveled up my spine.

"Uh, well, right now a walk would be good."

Why was I suddenly nervous?

We strolled around the pond. Turtles sunbathing on logs stretched their wrinkly necks as we passed. Ducks paddled toward us, likely hoping we'd brought an offering of bread. They were the fattest ducks on the planet thanks to the constant feeding by those of us who lived around the water. Heath drank it all in. Oddly, Jesse insisted on walking by *his* side. I finally handed him the leash so we'd stop having to change places each time she crossed our paths with her nylon tether.

That furry little traitor.

"So, what now?" Heath asked as I unclipped Jesse's leash in the doorway.

When I looked up, he was leaning against the wall in a way that pulled his shirt across his lean, muscular chest. A thick forest of black hair tried to escape out the top. His sleeves had rolled up slightly, straining against biceps that looked more like softballs than tennis balls. I blinked away the thought of what lay beneath.

"Well, um, I hadn't really thought that far ahead. This was all kind of last minute, you know?"

He gave me that damn smile again, and a lock of black silk fell across one brow. I nearly fell over trying to stand. His hand steadied my arm before I realized what was happening. When he pulled me up, we were inches apart.

English became my second language. Hell, I forgot English existed.

"Wow, uh, thanks. I'm not…I mean, I don't usually…fuck."

He laughed, low and sexy. God, that sound fanned the flame his touch had ignited. I tried to step back, to put space between us, but the damn wall was there. He stretched an arm out and placed a hand against the wall, leaning toward me.

I couldn't breathe. He smelled of musk and Irish Spring and General Tso.

Fuck you, General. Why did you have to be so damn spicy?

"You look tense. I have good hands, could give you a massage," he half whispered, half growled.

"Massage? Uh, what? Now? Really? I don't—"

Oh. My. God. Why had I turned into a thirteen-year-old girl about to get her first kiss? I'd fucked flight attendants into other time zones. Heath was just standing nearby and I was practically a puddle. *What the actual fuck?*

"Just a massage. Nobody's getting naked. We just met, after all."

I didn't trust my voice, so I nodded like the soon-to-be murder victim in a bad movie when the killer just asked him to go upstairs.

Heath smiled again. *Fuck.*

So, I did what any self-respecting idiot teen in a horror/thriller would do—I led him upstairs to my bedroom.

Jesse lay quietly at the foot of the bed, her fur tickling my toes, as Heath removed my shirt and pressed me gently down, face first.

"Close your eyes—and keep them closed. Just relax," he said.

Like that was going to happen. My heart was racing faster than a NASCAR driver on the final turn—or straight-away—or whatever NASCAR drivers did. What did I know?

The bed shifted as he stood and padded into the bath-room. I heard his footfalls accompanied by the squirty sound of a bottle shooting its goo into his hands. The bed shifted again, and I nearly leapt to the ceiling as cold lotion dripped between my shoulder blades. Heath barked out a low, rumbly laugh.

"Sorry, didn't realize it was that cold. I'll warm it up."

I bet you will, I thought as my heart tried to find its place in my chest once more.

And then his strong, steady hands began kneading my tight, chicken-shit-frightened shoulders and back. I forgot all about the cold sensation caused by the lavender lotion and let myself drift happily off into massage land. Damn, he knew how to use his hands.

He finished with my back and traveled up to my neck and shoulders where I carried most of my stress.

"Wow. Your neck is like a rock." His thumb dug into one side and I fought off a flinch.

"Yeah, welcome to my work."

"What do you do?"

"I'm an exec. for a financial company."

"Oh." Was that an eyebrow raise or snoozed reply? I couldn't tell. The meat of his palm pressed harder into my neck and I forgot to care.

When he finished rubbing my neck, I felt hot breath near my ear. "I need to warn you about something," he rasped.

"Huh?" was all I got out.

Two hundred pounds of muscle splayed against my back, pressing me into the bed. His cock twitched through his shorts, and my butt quivered.

"I make love like a wolf." His voice was thunder fucking lightning into submission.

Huh? My brain wouldn't function.

"I'm rough and powerful, and I growl when I like it— and I always like it." My dick was suddenly uncomfortable between our combined weight and the mattress.

"Oh." I was articulate as ever.

"But this is just a massage, so you don't need to worry."

"Uhh—"

Between his weight, his cock, and the idea of him fucking me like an angry wolf, words wouldn't form. Mental images of sex in the woods flashed through my head. I could hear his rumble, feel his breath, taste his—

He propped himself up, relieving my body of his weight. I wanted to reach back and pull him down again, but my arms wouldn't go that direction.

"Want to make out, just to see if there's a connection? I'd rather know up front if there's no chemistry."

I squirmed my way around to face him. His eyes strayed briefly down to my bare chest and abs, then back up. They brimmed with need.

"Yeah," I said. "Fuckin' kiss me."

Who the hell said that? Was that me or the devil?

All you, Massage Boy. Enjoy. The devil giggled.

Then the wolf pounced.

Lips locked. His tongue drove into my mouth and wrapped itself around my own. My breath was sucked out of me and I didn't care. Who the fuck needed to breathe when you could feel this good?

Holy shit, we fit together. His arms engulfed my whole body while his mouth devoured me. I tried to keep up, but he'd been honest. He was all wolf—all hunger and desire. It was passionate. No, it was primal.

Something in me began to panic, but he didn't stop. His weight pressed harder. He drove his cock down, and even through his shorts I felt its force against mine, and I wanted it.

My brain tossed the panic aside as I gave in to our lust. I gripped his arms, then his back, squeezing and clawing, pressing my fingers into the ridges of his deeply formed muscles.

God, his body was hard. There was no give when I pressed. It was like driving my thumbs into stone.

And that thought drove me crazier.

"Somebody's getting hard," he growled.

"God, yes."

His body trembled from a chuckle.

"Enough chemistry for you, Wolfy?"

He bit my neck, and I arched my back, pushing our dicks together and making him spasm.

"That's not fair," he protested.

"Fuck fair. Take your clothes off."

"Just a massage, remember?" he teased.

"Fucking take your clothes off and let the wolf off his leash. Now."

"So bossy." He pulled back, a wide, glimmering grin shining down. In one model-on-a-beach motion, he crossed his arms and whipped his shirt over his head, revealing chiseled pecs and rounded shoulders. A thick pelt of perfectly sculpted hair blanketed his chest, then thinned into the most luscious trail of sexual deviance ever to lead one to a pot of gold.

Fuck. Me.

I realized I'd been staring, exploring every curve and line with my eyes, while he loomed above, fucking grinning. "Everything meet with your approval? Need another minute to look?"

"Asshole."

He chuckled.

I reached a hand out and traced the line of his chest, one finger delicately running through his hair. His skin burned, and I was sure I felt him tremble at my touch.

"Keep doing that and this massage is going to need a happy ending."

"This stopped being a massage the minute you kissed me." I was in the red zone. There would be no turning back. "Pants. Now. And kiss me more."

Fucking grin.

Then our lips met again. He kissed me while we both fumbled awkwardly with our shorts. He didn't take his underwear off, just pressed his full weight against me again. Now only two thin layers of cotton separated our most important of parts—and his wasn't that of a normal wolf. Oh no, this was a genuine *Game of Thrones* dire wolf dick, all big and hard and—

He flipped me over before I could finish reliving parts of those books I didn't think good ol' George actually wrote in them. His cock was now rock-hard and pressed against the crease of my underwear. He didn't have to position anything. It knew where to go. His hips slowly ground up and down, teasing my butt without separating it. I was puckered so hard he couldn't have driven in a needle with a sledgehammer, but I fucking wanted him to try. The more he rubbed and finally pressed, the more I wanted him inside me.

While his dick teased my ass, he dragged his teeth across my neck, nipping and taunting. He pinned my arms above my head with his hands, and sweat dripped from his burning body onto my back. I wanted him to douse me, drown me in that salty, musky moisture. When he pressed his chest against me, the slickness of his sweat met the coarseness of his hair. Thousands of pinpricks of pleasure and pain tickled my skin. I could feel every hair, all of them together, as his ridiculously ripped chest and abs scrubbed away my last inhibitions.

And then he pressed his cock into my crack. It had somehow come free of the flap in his briefs and drove deep, only the cloth of my own undies stopping it from going further. My body screamed with need as he drove harder and harder, dragged his body over mine, bit my lobes and licked my neck.

"I need you in me now."

His mouth pressed against my ear. "Beg me."

"Please. Fucking please. Take me any way you want. Just take me."

He bit my lobe again, this time harder. I twitched at the pain, then leaned into it.

His hands released my arms and dove into the waistband of my underwear. Rather than rip them off like I expected, he gripped my hips and squeezed my buttocks, exploring my now exposed skin like it was new territory for his map. Then his fingers wriggled their way in front and a fingertip found my head. He gently teased a drop of slickness, then pulled his fingers away. Everything he did made me want more.

His hands vanished and I felt his weight lift as he pulled his own underwear off, flinging it across the room with his feet. Then one hand found my abs and lifted me up while the other slowly dragged my underwear to my ankles.

He stilled for a long moment. "Wow."

I turned my head to look.

"Don't move," he said. "I want to memorize everything like it is right now."

It was my turn to grin. Granted, it wasn't his model-perfect, pearly white gleam—no, it was a goofy high-school-band-nerd-getting-a-kiss-from-a-cheerleader grin—but it was a grin.

I lost track of how long his fingers gently traced every ridge of my legs, butt, back, and shoulders. The hungry wolf from moments earlier had retreated, replaced by a far more thoughtful, deliberate beast. I wanted so badly to ask what he was thinking, but his touch had the power to steal my voice. I couldn't speak or move—or think. All I wanted was to feel him—for him to never stop.

"Where's your lube?"

I could speak again. Just not English. "Uh, lube? Right.

It's…um…I have it…bathroom. No…drawer. Yeah…in the side table."

What the fuck? I was a blithering idiot.

He chuckled. "You talk good."

His lips pressed into my neck before I could respond, stealing my voice once more.

I heard the drawer slide open, then the pop of the bottle.

Reality returned to my brain. I was an adult. I had to be an adult.

I sat up. "Heath, I'm positive."

I tried to keep my eyes on his, but their will was greater and they fell to my hands.

His meaty palm cupped my cheek and lifted them back to his. "So am I. If you want to stop, we can. Or we can use—"

I shook my head. "No."

He cocked his puppy dog head again.

"No, don't stop," I said, with more force than I'd intended. "And no, I don't want to use a condom…unless you want to. In that case, I'm okay with it."

Michael Reed, what the hell are you doing? The angel's voice boomed in my head. His invocation of the house on the opposite side of his neighborhood caught my attention. *You might already have HIV, but there are other strains. For heaven's sake, there are other diseases you could catch. You don't know this guy. You just met. For all you know, he's a human petri dish. Think before you poke. Please.*

He's right, you know, the devil said. Fuck, they agreed. *The smart thing to do is use protection. Better yet, don't have sex with strangers. But when have we done the smart thing? Remember Fly Boy?*

Why was Fly Boy always his go-to? Sheesh.

Michael, this isn't a game. It's your life. It's his life too. Don't be stupid. The angel was practically begging.

Then Heath's freshly lubed palm found my cock and both sides of my conscience faded into the distance. In the back of my mind, I knew I was being irresponsible. Hell, in the front of my mind I knew it. In that moment, though, my mind was no longer in control. We'd passed that point. Right or wrong, I would deal with the consequences later.

Heath had watched my internal dialogue, knowing I was struggling with an answer. Only when my eyes met his with firm resolve did his hand grip my dick, saturating it with oily heat and tender passion. I reached down and gripped him, once more giddy at the girth of his godlike groin. It was already dripping and slick.

His other hand found my hole. I jumped, startled, then tried to relax as he teased and tested, leaving a layer of lube just outside—and inside. Then his weight was on me again. His knees spread my legs apart, and I lifted them over his shoulders. His cock slid against my hole, and my body lurched.

Holy fuck, he was big.

He pressed, and the tip slid inside me. I clinched involuntarily, and he slipped out with a *pop*.

He did that head-cock thing again.

"Sorry, it's been a while. And you're kinda—"

He snickered. "Yeah, I'm big. I know. Just trust me."

He leaned down and kissed me, softly, full of passion. His lips drank me in. As his tongue caressed mine, he entered me again. Slowly, tenderly, his tongue pressed deeper. Our lips parted for air and I realized he was fully inside me. He pulled back slowly, then dove in once more, again and again. His fingers gripped my hair and pulled my head back into the pillow as his lips and teeth found my neck again. He'd leave a mark, but I didn't care. I needed him inside me.

As moments passed, tenderness became urgency. His posture rose, gaining leverage. His thrusts grew more force-ful. Deliberate, methodical exploration devolved into desperate, driving passion. Grunts turned into growls, then groans. I freed my hands and gripped his butt, urging him deeper and harder. Faster. I wanted him so badly.

His breathing turned wild, and he leaned in. "If we keep doing this—"

"Shut up and fuck me."

He grabbed my wrists and slammed them against the pillows, then pulled my body toward him, thrusting him into me even deeper than before. Now fully on his knees, the wolf emerged to devour his prize. I heard myself growling and groaning in time to his thrusts and moans. Faster, harder, deeper. How could he go deeper? He gripped my hair again and howled at the ceiling. Drove himself with all his strength.

Our bodies shuddered together as he freed himself inside me. I'd not even touched myself, yet I painted his hairy stomach, whiteness smeared among the dark. He continued to thrust and shudder. My moans turned to whim-pers, then his died completely. He collapsed onto my body, still inside me, trembling atop me.

A moment later, he kissed my neck.

"That was some massage," I said. "Sure glad nobody took their clothes off."

He shoved his semi-hard cock. "Very funny. You weren't complaining."

"Oh, I'm still not. You felt…amazing."

He beamed. "Really?"

Wow. In that blinding moment, I realized he had no idea how incredible he was.

"Heath, damn, you were rock-star level. And those kisses…"

"Yeah. You're pretty good yourself."

He kissed me again and my heart flipped.

As he sat up and pulled away, I heard him snort a laugh.

"What's funny?"

"Um. Party foul."

"What?"

"You got shit on my dick."

"Eww," I gasped. "Sorry, I really wasn't expecting to get fucked today, certainly not have a freight train shoved up my ass."

He snorted again as he walked into the bathroom to clean up. "Freight train. 'Choo choo,' says the Choco Train."

I fell back onto the bed and tried to hide the brilliant rouge flooding my face. He was waving his dick like it was rolling down a track, making *chugga-chugga* sounds.

Thanks a lot, Serena.

18

BALLOON PARTY

H eath came over for dinner the next night. I made roasted pork stuffed with goat cheese, cherries and nuts, glazed with a port wine and cherry reduction.

Don't get all hot and bothered. It was a recipe I'd found in a book about grilling meats. It sounded complicated and foo-foo, but was actually super easy to prepare. The trick was to get the cook right on the pork. A little under and, well, one might kill one's guest with raw pork. That would be a clear party foul. A little over, and the pork became dry and tough, losing all its sumptuous flavor. No amount of glaze or goat cheese could help a lifeless, gray piece of pork.

Jesse lay dutifully by his feet, staring up as he took his first bite. I stared from my chair opposite his at the table. He closed his eyes as he chewed, and I knew from the wet-dream look on his face I'd nailed the cook.

"Oh, Jeeeeesus. You never said you could cook like this," he muttered as his chewing slowed to a reverential crawl.

I grinned and shrugged. "It's just pork. Nothing special."

You're such an ass. You know it's amazing, the angel whispered with a slight giggle.

Ass? Are you allowed to use big words like that? the devil snarked.

Fuck off. I can say a lot more than you might think. I just have to say it for the greater good.

I took a bite of pork and all the voices vanished. Holy shit, Heath was right. This might've been the most delicious thing I'd ever cooked.

"Told ya." My eyes popped open to catch him grinning. "First bite? It really is fantastic."

I nodded and chewed, then moaned.

"I remember that sound." His grin grew wider.

I gave him a look that said, *Really? At the table while eating pork?*

Then my brain processed what I'd just thought, and I laughed out loud. He'd *porked* to get that moan. The irony was as thick as—

After dinner, we skipped the planned viewing of whatever reality show had caught our attention and raced each other upstairs, giggling like four-year-olds all the way. There were no careful caresses or slow massages. We tore off each other's clothes and had wild, mindless rabbit sex— you know, the kind where you mean to go all night, but bunnies were made in zero-point-three seconds flat?

"Uh, that was…um…quick." He sounded embarrassed.

I chuckled. My head was nuzzled on the bed of fur just beneath his chin. "Quick can be fun too. I don't think my butt could've handled thirty minutes of the USS Heath firing its long guns after what you did yesterday."

"USS Heath? You going all navy on me now?" His voice was playful.

"Sorry, you fucked my brain cells dry."

My head bobbed as his chest heaved with laughter. God, that felt good.

My mind spun.

I will not *like this guy. Absolutely not. I've given up on men, on dating—and most definitely on relationships. My heart can't take another bad ending. Hell, it hasn't even had* a beginning *in years. Nope, definitely not liking Heath. No way.*

As I lay there, I heard his heart beating. His deep, slow breaths mirrored my own. When he wrapped one arm around me and pulled me tighter into him, I thought I might die right there. When he kissed the top of my head and his other hand stroked my hair, I stopped thinking altogether. All I could do was close my eyes and sigh—and smile.

Absolutely not. No, no, no. I refuse—

It had been years since I'd felt so warm and safe, so *wanted.* I drank it in, savored it, willed the moment's tranquility throughout my mind and soul. We didn't know each other, and I knew it was silly to feel this way on a second date, but my brain wasn't functioning—and for once, my Gemini twins of a conscience remained blessedly silent.

In the safety and comfort of Heath's arms, enveloped by his warmth and soothed by the rise and fall of his chest, I drifted into a peaceful, dreamless sleep.

A HOT, WET TONGUE ROUSED ME. I BLINKED BLEARILY TO find the sun rising and Jesse standing on the bed beside me, her nose centimeters from my own, her tongue lapping at my mouth.

"Yuck. Baby girl, do you mind *not* French kissing Daddy?"

A deep rumble to my right nearly startled me out of the bed. I looked over to find Heath propped up on one elbow staring at me. The annoyingly camera-ready fucker wore a shimmering smile, perfectly mussed hair with one curl begging for escape from its brethren, and nothing else. He lay on top of the covers in all his furry, naked glory. My eyes drifted down, and either he was happy to see me or mornings were a very good thing in his world. Hell, they were a good thing in mine now too.

"Morning, sleepy."

I smacked my disgusting morning-breath-laden lips and mumbled, "Morning."

He chuckled. A hand shot out and gently stroked my cheek. "You mumble when you sleep. I couldn't make out the words, but it sounded very serious."

My eyes widened. "Really?"

He nodded. "Yeah, it was cute. It took me a while to get sleepy, and I didn't want to move you. You were so peaceful laying there on my chest."

I didn't know what to say to that. Peaceful was *exactly* how it had felt.

"Uh, yeah, it was…nice, I guess."

He grunted. "You guess?"

"No, sorry, it *was* nice. I'm not a morning person. I need coffee."

I could feel his grin behind me as I rose and padded into the bathroom.

"Want to go get some?" he asked.

My head popped around the doorframe. "Huh? What?"

"Coffee. Want to go get some?" He shook his head and chuckled. "You really are out of it in the morning."

A weak smile and shrug later, I said, "Yeah. Always have been. And sure, let's go get something to eat and a caffeine IV, stat."

I showered and changed. Heath washed his face and threw on the clothes he'd worn the night before. They had that "recently used for fucking" look, but he didn't seem to care. I liked that.

Over coffee and the finest fare Denny's had to offer, Heath verbally daydreamed about the US Open. I could see him traveling to New York in his mind as he described the courts and players, the vendors and spectators. He was more passionate about tennis than anyone I'd ever known.

I took a bite of waffle and nodded like I understood. I was clueless.

"What's so special about the US Open?" I asked. "I mean, is it really that different from the French or the other majors?"

I may as well have slapped him.

"Seriously? Did you really just ask me that?"

I shrugged.

For the next twenty minutes, he described attending the last three Opens, the up-close view of the practice courts, seeing Roger Federer walk out on Center Court (or whatever it's named—he called it by some old player's name I recognized but couldn't place).

Then he compared it to the French and Australian Opens, and Wimbledon. The Australian was too hot, held in the dead of the Down Under summer. He loved the French because the red clay slowed the ball, creating long points where twenty or thirty shots were common. Apparently, that was a good thing. Wimbledon was the only tournament he allowed to be somewhat on par with the US Open, giving the Brits credit for their traditions and flair. After all, any tournament with a Royal Box had to be special, he reasoned.

"Royal Box," I chuckled. "Sounds like some bad gay porn."

He gave me a syrupy grin. "You liked my Royal Box last night."

"All thirty-six seconds of it, sure."

"Oh, you're gonna pay for that," he growled.

"Promises, promises."

The conversation trailed off as he turned to slam his Grand Slam. Mid-bite, he looked up, chewed hard and swallowed, then asked, "You free Friday night?"

"Uh, sure. I think so. Why?"

"My best friend is throwing a birthday party at their hotel. Should be fun. I'd love you to be my date."

Dammit. I'm not *dating. No, no, no.*

"Sure, sounds great."

Fuck.

HEATH STAYED OVER WEDNESDAY NIGHT. I WAS ACTUALLY sore and slightly bowlegged Thursday morning.

During the day, he trekked fifty minutes down to Sarasota where he coached gymnastics and all-star cheerleading. When I'd quizzed him about pom-poms, he swatted me and explained that all-star cheer was different from the poodle-skirted chant-callers I knew from basketball games. These were highly athletic, highly choreographed teams of girls and boys. They worked for endless hours perfecting their stunts and routines, then traveled, sometimes hundreds of miles, to compete against other teams. To Heath, all-star cheerleading was the perfect marriage of gymnastics, dance, and performance art.

I couldn't wipe the image of my muscular Heath and his pom-poms from my mind, but rolled with the explanation without protest. He promised to drag me to a competition sometime so I could experience the thrill of victory for myself. Something in the back of my mind warned against that course, but I couldn't help smiling at his enthusiasm. He was passionate about everything he did. It was endearing.

He stayed at the castle again Thursday night. We rationalized that since he didn't have to work in Sarasota on Friday, it would be easier to just go from my place to the party than to try to meet up sometime Friday afternoon—or to just meet at the party. Never mind that I had to work in the office on Friday. He could just hang out with Jesse for the day.

That's logical, right?

I was *not* dating. He was *not* living in my house, or moving in, or—damn it—*anything* that looked like a relationship. This was a good time where the guy happened to sleep over and let me lay my head on his chest while he held me and kissed my forehead.

That's *nothing* like dating. Absolutely nothing.

Fuck you and your snickering.

Friday evening, when Heath walked into the den wearing tight dark jeans and a tighter deep-burgundy shirt that hugged his arms and highlighted his eyes, I nearly stumbled as I strode out of the kitchen.

"This look okay?" he asked, glancing self-consciously down at his outfit.

"Oh, yeah, you look…really…I mean…great."

He beamed up. My knees wobbled when our eyes met.

"I'll take that."

Shit. Now all I could think about was one of us *taking* something the other had in abundance—and it wasn't smiles or good intentions.

"You almost ready?" he asked.

I looked down at my shorts and T-shirt and laughed awkwardly. "I need to get dressed. Give me ten minutes. Jesse can keep you company."

He sat on the couch and my traitorous pooch hopped up to snuggle beside him. She'd accepted him in the pack. That was almost as shocking as the first time I'd seen the anaconda beneath his undies.

Moments later, I descended the stairs in light blue jeans and a green collared shirt I'd found at a store in the mall marketing itself as the adult version of Abercrombie. It grated on me that I was too old for A&F, but life went on, I supposed.

A low whistle snapped my head up.

"You look like a present I need to unwrap." Heath rose to his feet and I could see through his jeans how much the rest of him was also rising. I giggled inwardly at the thought that *I* caused that. Pride warred with my PK awkwardness. Before I knew it, he was standing before me, cupping my cheek, kissing me deeply. I moaned at his tongue's touch.

"I missed you while you were upstairs. Please don't leave me like that again."

I am not fucking dating. Besides, that's a terrible line. Absolutely stupid—

"God, I missed—"

Who said that?

His mouth stopped whatever I was about to say. It stopped me from thinking too.

My eyes were closed when he pulled back. I felt his warm breath tickle my nose. He smelled of wintergreen mouthwash and sweet cologne. "We'd better get going. Teri's a ball of energy. Brace yourself."

His thumb brushed hair off my forehead. I still hadn't opened my eyes. His lips met mine for one last taste, tenderly this time.

I breathed out. "Okay. I'm good. I mean, we should go. Yeah, let's go."

Before turning away, he flicked the hair he'd just moved back onto my forehead. "Somebody needs to mess your hair up a little now and then. Leave that there."

I grinned. "Yes, sir."

HEATH HADN'T PREPARED ME FOR THE PARTY, OTHER THAN the one offhanded comment about Teri. We waltzed into Teri's family hotel, a historic building in the heart of Ybor City. Everything in the place was original; period pieces and art dating back a hundred years or more. A smattering of twenty and thirtysomethings dressed in their best night-on-the-town outfits stood in groups of twos and threes.

We'd made it halfway across the elegant lobby before—

"Heeeeeeeeathy-poo!" a woman's voice squealed.

Before I could register a snappy retort to my new favorite nickname that would haunt Heath as long as we knew each other, a tall, thin woman with dark hair that fell to her butt raced across the room and nearly knocked Heath to the ground with her hug. I took an involuntary step back and watched the collision—and Heath's ensuing discomfort —with sadistic pleasure.

"Hey, Teri-poo," Heath said as he nuzzled her neck with his nose and kissed her cheek. When he surfaced, they shared a wide smile, staring at each other a moment. Then he remembered he wasn't alone and pulled back.

"Teri, this is Michael."

She turned to me and, without a second of hesitation, barreled into me just as she had Heath. The only thing that saved me was her lack of space to gather speed. Two strides did not a runway make.

"Hi, Mikey," she said, calling me my least favorite variation of my name. I received the same peck on the cheek, but did not offer her the requisite neck nuzzle.

In a blur, she untangled our arms, pecked Heath again, and sped on to her next victims.

"That was a Teri drive-by. You may want to call your insurance," Heath said with a wide smile.

"I guess you warned me."

"Oh, that was calm Teri. Just wait."

"Awesome."

Heath reached over and dusted the makeup off my shoulder. He called the lipstick or makeup left in Teri's wake "Teri droppings." It seemed appropriate.

"Let's go downstairs. The others should be here by now. I want you to meet my friends."

Meeting friends is a dating thing, isn't it? Something I clearly am not supposed to be doing. Nor getting nose-nuzzled.

"Sounds great," I said as he took my hand, interlaced our fingers, and pulled me like a puppy on his first leash.

Nor interlacing fingers. What bedeviling fuckery is at play here?

We wound our way around an antique staircase you might see in an ancient library, the kind that winds in a circle so many times you're dizzy by the time your foot steps on the floor below. I thought the wrought iron was cool until the room started spinning. Heath never let go. He never unlocked…de-laced…unlaced…pulled our fingers apart. Whatever. I was screwed.

The first thing I realized as my feet touched down was the lighting in the party room was several lumens lower than in the lobby, giving the place a swanky vibe that fit perfectly with all the antique furniture and their velvety coverings. A trio played jazzy music in the corner as servers in red vests and black ties roamed throughout the small crowd with appetizers on silver trays.

"Heath!" virtually every voice in the room called as my non-date appeared. Guys strode over to clap him on the back or give him a sturdy hug. Women pecked his cheeks and squeezed his biceps appreciatively.

Something odd bubbled in my chest at that. Why did I suddenly dislike those women?

Weird.

"Come over here. Look, they're taking pictures."

In the corner was a wall of red balloons pinned to a shiny green backdrop. It looked like Christmas and Valentine's Day had mated and their baby was a photo booth. Heath pulled our still-interlaced hands and positioned us dead center.

"Can you take several? I want to pick the best one. Okay?" Heath seemed really excited about these pictures. I'd always hated having mine taken, was self-conscious of how the camera washed out my pasty skin. Being the awkward kid never fully left a person. On that night, I didn't have a choice. There was no running from that camera.

Flash. Flash, flash. Pop, flash, flash.

I blinked. The room was filled with dots.

"That's perfect. I love it," Heath said, examining the screen on the photographer's camera. "Can you email those to me?"

A moment later, the dots had cleared and Heath was showing me our pictures.

Our pictures. Our *first* pictures.

On the screen, Heath stood on the left. His teeth reflected the flash like a freakin' mirror. They were stills, but his hair somehow flowed. His skin practically glowed. How could anyone be that photogenic?

The washed-out guy next to him had a decent smile. One errant curl of reddish hair bobbed on his forehead.

"You look so cute there." Heath squeezed my shoulders and kissed my head.

"You look like you just stepped off a photo shoot. How do you do that?"

"What?" His smile was so wide it *had* to hurt.

"Always look good in pictures? Every pic you've ever taken on Facebook is model-perfect, even the candid ones and selfies—especially the candid ones. There should be a law against being that good in front of a camera."

He kissed me again. "It's a curse. Hope you're okay with it."

I snorted. "I guess. Any other tragic flaws I need to be aware of?"

"Plenty, but no cheating. You'll have to learn those on your own." His head snapped up and he called out, "Karl!"

Then he bounded across the room to be enveloped in the arms of a giant. I'd thought Heath tall at six foot two, but this dude had to stand six seven, maybe six eight, and he was thick and muscular, not skinny like some really tall guys. With Heath in the way, all I saw were massively thick arms and a losing battle over thinning hair. When Karl looked up, I realized the follicle fight didn't matter. His face was striking with or without a fancy 'do.

"Babe, come here." Heath motioned me over.

Aww. He just called you babe, the devil mocked.

I froze. *Shit.* He was right, he had called me babe. Was that allowed? You know, for guys who were definitely not dating?

You're so dating. Just admit it. You want more than just his dick, don't ya? The devil was relentless.

Hey, angel, a little help over here, I silently pleaded.

Not a chance. For better or worse, he's right. You let your ass do the talking, and this is what you get. Good luck.

"Come on. This is Karl." I'd been too lost in thought to see Heath approach and grab my hand again, pulling me over to stand before the Giant of Judgment. Shit, he was tall—and hot. I gaped up. My mouth wouldn't work.

"Nice to meet you, Michael. Heath's told us good things." The giant extended a hand. My own disappeared into his palm as he squeezed the life out of my knuckles. I don't even think he was trying to squeeze. His natural strength level was set to maximum, and he didn't know any lower. I gritted my teeth in a painful approximation of a smile while pretending not to be dying inside. My poor hand.

When I turned to Heath for help, he'd vanished.

"He's gone to check on Teri," Karl said. "He usually helps her get set for parties like this."

"Okay." I didn't know how to respond to that. Were parties a common thing? I thought this was her birthday—

or the giant's—I couldn't remember. And what was there to set up? I looked around the room and hotel workers had done all the setup I could see. I shrugged it off and made small talk with the big man.

Ten minutes later, Teri and Heath reappeared. She talked a thousand words a minute and bounced from one group of friends to the next. When she settled by my side, she practically melted into Karl's body. Their kiss was so intimate I felt like I was intruding by watching. That kiss offered the only breath in her otherwise unpunctuated, Charles Dickens-esque dialogue. She spoke so quickly I could barely keep up.

Then Heath spoke and he matched her energy. He babbled incessantly while she prattled on, neither bothered that the other spoke at the same time. I watched them carry on two separate conversations aimed at the other, and I swear they knew exactly what the other was saying. It was dizzying.

I looked up to find Karl grinning down at me. "They're a lot, especially together. Let's get you a drink."

We left the party around one o'clock in the morning. The hotel sat on the edge of Ybor, making it an easy walk to the party district of Tampa. Most of the guests were headed down the street to continue their celebrations. Heath said he usually went with them, especially if Teri and Karl were leading the charge, but that night he just wanted to take me home and do nasty things together.

He rubbed my leg all the way home. It wasn't the gentle fingertip stroking I'd come to know. It was the firm, hungry rubbing of a man who wanted to strip naked the moment the door slammed shut.

So we did.

That night, in two rounds of reckless, passionate,

animalistic sex, Heath fucked me so hard I thought my uterus might fall out—and I don't even have one of those puppies.

I didn't know what had gotten into him, but I liked it. Fuck, I loved it.

He threw me onto the bed and spread my legs apart like he owned them, like he owned every part of me. There was no foreplay, no lovey-touchy-kissy lead in. He grabbed the lube, doused us both, then dove into me. I'd never been driven so hard or fast—or hard. Did I say hard? *Fuck.*

As we neared the end of round two, Heath was up on his knees with my ankles tossed over his shoulders. I swear he had a leg up my ass all the way to his knee, and he was shoving with all his might. That's when we heard it.

A loud *crack.*

Heath froze mid-thrust. His eyes were wild and wide. Mine were bleary.

Another *crack*, this one louder.

Then the bed fell and Heath tumbled out of me and over the side.

I hopped up, now fully alert. "Heath! Are you okay? Holy crap. Talk to me."

It started as a low rumble, then grew to a roar. Before I knew it, Heath was laughing hysterically. He pointed. My eyes followed his finger. His laughter redoubled, then mine joined his. Tears were streaming down our cheeks as we lay on that floor howling.

The mattress lay askew. The wooden railing that held it was no longer visible; only shards.

We'd broken the bed.

19

DRAWERS

I didn't see Heath for a couple days. No, it wasn't because of the bed. He had to go see his mom in Alabama. Something was going on with his sister, and his mom needed help. It was odd. He hadn't held back with any other subject, but his family was a sore point. He seemed almost, I don't know…ashamed. It was weird. I didn't press, just told him to have a good trip and drive safely.

On the first day of his trip, I went to a local furniture store and picked a replacement for my utterly destroyed bed frame. I couldn't help the chuckle as I strolled through the showroom with a most helpful sales lady, who asked what was most important to me in my new bed.

"Durability," I said through laughter she couldn't understand. I think she expected an explanation, but there was no way I was giving her one. She'd just have to speculate.

In the end, I chose a very sturdy mahogany frame with six built-in drawers fitted neatly under the mattress. My house was historic, but its closet and drawer space were historically lacking. Plus, if Heath wanted to continue sleeping over, I thought it might be nice to have a place for his underwear and things.

You're so dating, the angel quipped.

Yep. Gotta agree with Glowy over there. You're whipped—and not just up the ass like—

"Thanks, guys. I got it. No mental image needed."

You broke a bed. Your mental image is very physical—and in pieces. The devil howled with laughter as he vanished.

The angel actually patted my cheek in pity. That was a new low.

On the second day of Heath's trip, I sat on my sectional on one end of the L while Jesse sprawled out on the other piece. She glared at me like I'd done something to scare her new bestie away.

"He's gone to see his mom. I promise I didn't disappear him like in the movies. He'll be back soon."

She looked away, unconvinced.

I stared at the television. And, for the first time, realized I missed him.

20

ALABAMA

Heath came straight from Alabama to my place. I'd rehearsed his return in my head. There would be no running from across the room into his arms. No, I would not do the fawning, "I missed you" thing. Never mind that I *had* missed him. I wasn't supposed to be dating, and a single guy didn't miss another single guy he wasn't interested in.

The moment the door handle wiggled, I was off the couch, running to the door, and buried myself in his chest and arms.

"Woah," he laughed as he set his bag down and raised his arms to hug me. "Can a guy get in the door before he's expected to perform? Sheesh."

I pulled back and punched his chest. "Dork."

He pulled me back into him and kissed me deeply. "I missed you too."

I fucking melted. *Dammit.*

He lifted his duffel over his shoulder, and I led him upstairs.

"So," I said over my shoulder as we ascended. "I have a surprise, but don't read too much into this. My rule stands."

"Rule? You have a rule?" He smacked my butt.

"Not about sex. You broke all those. No moving in before a year of dating. That's always been my rule."

Okay, yes, most observant reader, I shattered that with Ryan. Stop judging.

"Oh, I don't want to move into this shabby place," he teased. I knew he loved the castle. Then he stepped into the bedroom and whistled. "Now that's a bed. We'll have to work extra hard to break that puppy."

I barked a laugh. "I'm afraid I'll be in more pieces than the bed if you break this one. It's built like a tank."

He wiggled his bushy black brows. "Have you met the USS Heath? It's a battleship. Ships beat tanks."

I rolled my eyes and laughed, then pointed down below the mattress. "Those two are for you."

His eyes followed my finger, then those bushy brows slowly rose. "My own drawers? So I won't move in?"

"Shut up," I said in my most mature voice.

He tossed his duffel on the floor and grabbed me roughly. "I've never wanted to break a bed more than I do right now. Fuck the drawers."

We were naked before I had time to show him the headboard's mini-drawer and its new pump-action bottle of lube. The fucker found it without any help.

***

"How's your mom?" I asked while trailing my fingers through his sweaty, lube-slicked chest hair.

Yes, he had lube up there. Don't ask questions.

He grunted. "She's okay. She wants to move down here."

I waited for him to explain. When he didn't, I asked, "That's a good thing, isn't it? You'd be closer to each other."

He grunted again. "Yeah, we'd be closer."

This time I just waited. I thought he'd fallen asleep, but he finally spoke again, this time in a quiet, pensive voice. "I didn't have the same childhood as…well, anybody else. I don't even know my dad. I think I know who he is—which one he is, I mean. My mom was very…popular."

I didn't know what to say to that. My childhood could've been on an episode of *Leave It to Beaver* or *The Andy Griffith Show*. I knew other families weren't always like ours, but I had no idea some were so irrevocably broken.

"My mom was drunk a lot when I was younger. I'd find her in the hallway passed out, half naked, sometimes totally naked." He thought a moment. "I was six, maybe seven, the first time I found her naked and had to help her into bed. I remember eating Froot Loops at the table with some man the next morning. He hadn't been in her bed when I put her there, but he ate breakfast with me. He wore a uniform and had a gun. I think he was some kind of cop. I never got his name."

I sat up and leaned on my elbow and watched his eyes drift further into the past. My hand never left his chest.

"My brother was murdered when he was a teenager. He was a really bad guy, ran with a lot worse, but nobody deserves to be murdered. Cops thought some drug gang executed him." He shifted onto his side and looked up. His eyes pleaded. I wasn't sure for what. My heart ached for him. "My sister tried to kill my mom."

"What?" I was stunned.

He nodded slowly. "Stabbed her a dozen times through the covers while she lay in bed. Docs couldn't believe Mom even made it to the hospital alive, but she proved them all wrong and lived through it. My sister's been in jail ever since—but she's getting out. That's why I went home."

What could I even say to any of that? This poor man.

"My mom wants to move here so my sister doesn't know where she is. She's scared."

"I bet she is."

He looked up, tears brimming in his eyes. "But you don't know my mom. She's a sweet little old lady, but she's manipulative. If she comes here, she'll try—"

"She'll try what?"

He shook his head. "I'm sorry. You don't want to know all that. It's terrible enough I have to know it."

I cupped his cheek, turning his eyes back to mine. "Heath, listen to me. I'm here, and I'm not going anywhere. I wasn't planning on dating. Hell, I was trying to avoid it. But what I feel for you—"

He smiled for the first time in long moments. "I feel it too."

"You shattered my no dating rule. Then you broke my bed. Now you're moving shit into drawers. Heath Cox, you're going to be the end of me, aren't you?"

He gripped my head in both of his strong, meaty palms. "Only if I'm lucky."

I lost myself in the kiss that followed.

That's when I stopped fighting it—the idea of dating or relationships or whatever. I stopped fighting the idea that I could be happy again. Or hurt again. I stopped fighting

Heath and his ridiculous smile and maddening, knee-weakening eyes.

My heart had known long before my head caught up.

It had only been a few weeks since Serena beat Azarenka—and yes, every part of that sounds ridiculous when I say it out loud—but I knew we'd find a way.

21

DO YOU LIKE YOUR BALLS HARD
OR YELLOW?

The following Saturday marked the beginning of the fall softball season. Tampa, being a wonderfully tropical Florida enclave, enjoyed warm weather most months of the year, affording us the opportunity for outdoor sports leagues when other cities were huddled about fireplaces roasting weenies—or whatever miserable people up north did. I was thankful not to know the right answer to that question.

Heath surprised me by offering to come play with me. He'd never played softball on a team, but was extremely athletic and confident in his ability to master any sport he tried. I loved the idea of playing on teams together, as it would let us bond within a shared circle of friends while spending more time together.

We warmed up and our coach came over to watch and evaluate. Heath was a beast with a bat. His first few swings launched the ball twenty yards over the fence. I thought our coach was going to run out onto the field and hug him. He later told me the mechanics of batting felt a lot like the snap of a forehand in tennis. It just made sense to him.

Once he mastered the timing, balls flew. It was a thing of beauty.

Satisfied with his offensive skills, we switched to defense. He picked up the hand–eye coordination required to catch almost immediately. Coach had him field fly balls in the outfield, and he ran down everything they hit at him. When moved to the fast-paced infield, he did even better. Years of swatting at tennis balls had taught him to follow the line of the ball better than most guys on the team. The buzz about our new player was beginning to build.

And then he threw the ball.

Let's not be generous—his throwing was *beyond* terrible. He had a clinically diagnosable case of throwing dyslexia, perhaps the worst case ever seen. It was chronic. There was no treatment. He would not recover.

Old friends from Atlanta introduced me to that term, explaining it occurred when a softball player tried to throw the ball in one direction, but it consistently chose its own path. Poor Heath. I tried helping him. The coach tried. Half the team tried. It was useless. His tosses went sideways or backward or, worse, straight down into the dirt. Any time he caught a ball and had to throw to a baseman during a drill, the entire infield cringed; some ducked instinctively. No one knew where his toss would go, least of all him.

For a stud of state-championship athletic proportions, he was dreadful.

We were a C-level team, meaning most of the players knew which end of the bat to use, but we weren't highly skilled. Heath's hiccups with throwing fit in well with our Bad News Bears fielders and batters. In fact, his incredible skill in those two areas balanced out some of our weaknesses. Coach decided to play him at first base, where he would catch far more than throw. It just made sense. As we neared the end of our first practice together, the future was looking bright for our softball season…

Until coach put Heath back in the outfield for more fly ball practice and my dummy non-boyfriend dove for a foul ball. Who dives for a foul ball in practice? Let the ball drop. He didn't know that little unwritten rule of laziness in adult sport. He dove…and dislocated his shoulder.

I raced him to the hospital, where a spindly-looking doctor who mustered more strength than I thought he possessed snapped everything back into place. Heath's writhing ceased immediately.

In the car on the way back to the castle, he turned to me. "I really liked softball today. You know, until—"

I didn't mean to chuckle, but he was poking fun at himself. "You're supposed to let fouls drop during practice."

"Now he tells me."

I rolled my eyes.

"Maybe I should stick to tennis. Would you ever want to learn a new sport?"

That gave me pause. *Huh. Tennis.* I'd never played, other than smacking balls over the fence a few times. I was pretty sure that wasn't the goal, but it had felt good at the time, like a home run in every other sport that mattered.

On a whim, I said, "Sure. Sounds fun. Know anyone who can teach me?"

He grinned.

I knew that grin. I was so screwed.

<hr>

HEATH TOOK ME TO HIT A FEW DAYS LATER. HE SCOWLED at my racket. It was the same aluminum-framed beast I'd used when I tried out for my high school team. All the other kids had started playing when they were three, while I was walking onto the court for my first time thinking, "This will be easy."

It was *not* easy. I did not make the team.

We started near the net with something he called "mini-tennis." It felt weird standing only a few feet away, trying to keep the ball just over the net, but he swore it was one of the best drills to get a feel for the ball. We eventually stepped back to the baseline and tried to rally. Heath was amazing, and not just because his hair bounced as he moved. At nearly forty years old, he still played at a small college level. I was lucky just to track the ball, much less hit it. More of my strokes smacked the back fence than the court. After ten minutes of futile feeding, he motioned me up to the net.

"So, I think we may need to start with different lessons."

I hated being bad at anything. Damn it, I was athletic. This shouldn't be so hard.

"Don't beat yourself up. Tennis is one of the hardest sports. People don't think that, but it is, and everything is up to you. There's no team to help you or have your back. You did fine for your first time, but we need to spend more time doing footwork and basic drills before you're ready to rally—at least, until we get your level up to…well, just up."

I liked him wanting to help me get it up, then I realized he was talking about my tennis level. The boner that was starting to form deflated.

"Okay. Put me in, coach."

"Wrong sport, but I'll take it." He chuckled and shook his head. "We'll need a basket of balls and a hopper."

"Hopper?"

"It's a wire basket with a long handle to help pick up balls. You'll see."

He spent the next thirty minutes teaching me basic feeding and footwork drills, hitting patterns, and how to properly toss for a serve.

Yes, there is a proper way to toss a tennis ball.

These drills became part of our routine. I went to the office. Heath drove to Sarasota. We'd meet afterward on a tennis court and drill, followed by dinner at the castle—which I cooked because he was a terrible cook and I dreamed of becoming a chef. We ate on the couch while Jesse stared intently from the other end of the sectional. Her head would rise like a telescope when she'd hear Heath's fork land on his plate the final time. How she knew it was the final time was a mystery. She just knew.

Yes, we let her lick the plates. Neither of us could refuse my baby girl.

While Jesse hoovered the glazing off the porcelain, we'd flip through channels, usually landing on *American Idol*, *Survivor*, or some random match on the Tennis Channel. It didn't matter who was on, Heath clung to every stroke.

Of the tennis matches…*tennis* strokes. Stop being dirty!

Then we'd get naked and other strokes took over.

Now you can be dirty.

He never again slept in the bedroom he rented from an older married couple across town. Five months after Serena, we drove to the house and retrieved the last of his things.

He ended up using *all* the drawers in the new bed.

Most nights, I fell asleep on his chest, reveling in his steady breath and beautiful warmth.

Most mornings, I woke to his fingers tracing my back or shoulder, or his lips kissing my neck as Jesse tickled my toes with her devilish tongue. She would not be out-loved by some man—not even the man she'd fallen for the moment he'd walked through our door and fell to the ground to greet her before acknowledging my existence.

What can I say? My baby girl has good judgment.

22

FOIE GRAS

Heath introduced me to the joys of the GLTA—the Gay and Lesbian Tennis League, a world tour of local organizations and tournaments in more than seventy cities around the globe. Florida boasted four of these tournaments: the Citrus Classic in Tampa, the Orange Blossom in Orlando, the Art Deco in Miami, and the Clay Court Classic in Fort Lauderdale. There was even a tournament where each of these four key cities competed against each other team-tennis style, called the Florida Cup.

Heath was already a member of Advantage Tampa Bay, our local club. After a quick investment in a new racket, bringing my equipment out of the Dark Ages, we signed me up as a member of ATB so I could participate in local league play. Heath was determined I get as much match play as possible, arguing it was the only way to "learn to win."

Who was I to argue? He wasn't just a stud. He was a tennis stud.

Did I mention how watching him play made me weak at the knees? Fuck. How could a big guy like that move so well? While he got to almost every ball, Heath didn't look fast on the court. I nicknamed him Turtle, which he absolutely hated. Once I learned how much he hated it, I did the only thing a respectable boyfriend could do—I ordered a turtle vibration dampener for his racket.

Magically, that nickname became his favorite. I overheard him bragging about his turtle dampener on more than one occasion before a match. It made me giggle.

Nine months after we met, the baby came.

Stop that! Of course there was no actual baby. We're dudes—and my uterus fell out chapters ago. Keep up here.

Fourteen months post-Serena, we played in our first GLTA tournament together, the local Tampa Bay Citrus Classic, played on the Har-Tru green clay of the Harbor Island Athletic Club. Heath entered in the A division, the second highest, while I competed with the other rookies in D.

Heath won two rounds, but was defeated by an arch-nemesis from Fort Lauderdale in the third round.

I won my first trophy, besting the seven others in the Bad News Bears division.

Heath cried when they presented me the blown-glass orange with "Champion" emblazoned on the metal tag. I still remember the look in his eyes as I walked off that court. No man—not even Ryan—had looked at me with such pride.

I promptly tripped over the raised lip of the sideline and gasped as the sacred orange rolled across the clay to rest at his feet, thankfully unbroken. The queens around him roared with laughter, and we joined them as soon as he helped me up and dutifully dusted the clay off my knees and shorts. His hand lifting me from my fall sent tremors through my heart. There's nothing like knowing someone is there to pick you up when you fall to make butterflies dance. Why is that?

A few guys let out "Aww" at his display.

I didn't trust myself to speak after he kissed me in front of them.

I suppose the Citrus Classic was our first true coming out as a couple. Heath was well known in the gay tennis community, but they'd never seen him with a serious boyfriend. I lost track of the guys who whispered, "Good for you," or "Finally, someone got him."

We left Harbor Island exhausted, and I think there was clay lodged in places it didn't belong, but we held each other's hands as we walked to the car, only letting go long enough to hop in and buckle up. I was a reigning champion for the first time, and he was just the most beautiful man alive. There's a trophy for that, isn't there?

We played three more tournaments over the following six months. I didn't win anymore trophies. Neither did he. We did, however, receive the same "Awws" and "Good for yous" in every city we visited.

Those were better than any damn orange.

———

THE SECOND ANNIVERSARY OF SERENA ROLLED AROUND. We celebrated with a trip to the US Open in New York. Our girl was there, whipping every ass she encountered.

Not literally. On the court. Serena's a lady.

You behave.

When we arrived at LaGuardia Airport to return home, Heath grabbed my hand and pulled me away from the security line.

"What's up, babe? You okay?" I asked.

"So, I kind of did a thing."

My brows rose.

"You have the next week off from work."

"What?" I was dumbfounded. "How—"

"I talked to your work son, who talked to your boss, who talked to HR. You have the week off. They're not letting you back in the building."

I wasn't sure I liked him tinkering with work. That could go in all sorts of bad directions—and would impact us both—but I let him keep going. Something was seriously up if they'd agreed to his mysterious plan.

"We're not flying home from here," he said tentatively.

"Uh-huh."

"Look, I'm no good with words on the spot. You know that. Take this." I glanced down at the boarding pass in his hand. The airport code wasn't one I recognized upside down. I took it and held it up.

It was a flight from New York to Paris.

My eyes snapped up to his. He was positively beaming.

"You...we're...we're going to Paris?"

"Happy anniversary, babe."

"You're taking me to Paris?" It still wasn't registering. My body was numb. Heath didn't make a ton of money as a coach. This would've set him back months of salary, maybe half a year. My eyes traveled from his face to the ticket then back up. They were losing a battle with an approaching tsunami, and he knew it. That fucker.

"Heath Cox. What am I going to do with you?" I stood there, in the middle of the bustling airport, surrounded by hustling passengers, with tears rolling down my cheeks.

"Kiss him!" a woman in a small crowd I hadn't seen gather yelled out.

"Go on. Give him a wet one," another yelled.

We both laughed, then I threw my arms around him and kissed him as deeply as I ever had. With the exception of our applauding peanut gallery, the rest of the traveling public ignored us. They had flights to catch. Then I remembered the time printed on the boarding pass. So did we.

<hr>

PARIS WAS EVERYTHING I'D EVER DREAMED IT WOULD BE. Napoleon's design was stunning. The people were fashionable—and friendly, no matter what anyone says. The Parisians we met were warm and kind. They appreciated that I tried to remember French from college, but quickly switched to English before I could permanently mar their unparalleled tongue.

I suppose they were right to do that. My French was awful.

Oh, but Heath's was worse.

On our first day, he tried to order for himself at a breakfast restaurant. The server spoke perfect English, but Mr. Confident Turtle wanted to impress me. He gave his order. The server quirked a brow, then repeated it with a very large question mark. Heath nodded emphatically, pointing at the menu. The server, now befuddled, turned to me.

"Monsieur veut des escargots pour le petit déjeuner? Vraiment?"

I spit my coffee and doubled over. The waiter joined me.

Heath crossed his arms. "What's so funny?" he demanded.

"What did you order?" I asked. He had to tell me. Even the waiter hung on his next words.

"Well—" He no longer sounded so confident. "I

ordered eggs and ham on some kind of bun or bread, maybe a muffin. I couldn't get that word."

The waiter and I exchanged a look and cracked up again.

"What?" Now he sounded wounded.

"Babe, you ordered snails—for breakfast. You were looking at the dinner menu."

His face fell as he stared down at the menu.

The waiter and I wiped tears away, and I ordered for us both. From the kitchen, I could hear the waiter's excited voice replaying the scene. The roar of laughter told us the server would get miles out of the episode.

Our hotel sat diagonally across from the Louvre. We could walk to so much: shops, the Arc de Triomphe, restaurants, art galleries, you name it.

Notre Dame had yet to burn, and we marveled at the detailed splendor of its carvings. Neither of us was particularly religious—yes, I know, ironic for the PK—but there was no denying the majesty of France's most famous cathedral. For those who never saw the place before its tragic fire, you missed something special.

We visited everything from palaces to parade grounds. The Eiffel Tower had only recently begun lighting up at night, and we were both amazed when the glittering began. We were among the many couples holding hands and kissing in the lights beneath a full moon.

As beautiful as everything was, my eyes always found a way back to his. There was no sight in Paris to rival his chocolaty orbs. I could've skipped the tours and lost myself in his gaze forever.

What am I saying? We were in *Paris*. I needed to see everything. There would be plenty of time for eye-gazing after the day's activities.

Heath had it all planned out. He knew I loved to make the most of a trip and would want to see every sight we could cram in, but he also managed to schedule some downtime.

On our last night in Paris, we ate at an outdoor café. The air was crisp, and we were both bundled in our most fashionable coats and scarves. Like most cafés, the tables faced outward so diners could observe the streets. Heath and I sat side by side and people-watched as we ate. Our hands parted to take a bite or cut something, then found their way back together without word or command. We were alive in the most enchanting city either of us had ever visited, and we breathed in its magic as though life itself was at stake.

Heath stared out at the passing tourists. I couldn't stop watching him. His eyes positively glowed in the gas lamplight of the restaurant's façade. He wore a silly beanie he knew I hated, more to poke at me than to stay warm. His lips were parted in a slight smile that never quite left his lips.

Maybe that's what struck me most. His beautiful smile never faded—not when we were together.

As he gazed outward and I turned to avoid being caught staring, a man walked by. He was slim, but athletic. I could see that through his tight-fitting shirt, which was an oddity since it was chilly. He wasn't wearing a coat.

Now curious, I watched him more closely.

There was something familiar. The slight curl to his deep brown, almost black hair. His confident gait. I couldn't place what felt so recognizable—until he turned and glanced at our table.

It was his eyes. I could've sworn they belonged to—

No, that's ridiculous. Joseph would've been nearly fifty.

The guy walking by didn't look a day over…well, shit. It could've been him.

Joseph. My first.

The guy vanished into the night, leaving my mind drifting wistfully into the past. I watched my younger self walk into Joseph's antique-filled apartment. I could smell the leather of his high-backed throne, see his wall of movies.

A smile tugged at the corner of my mouth, and I barely suppressed a chuckle as the image of Stephen Baldwin sandwiched between a guy and a gal popped into my head.

I'd been such a dork. How could any human being have been that clueless? Seriously?

Despite supreme naivete, that night had opened so many doors, doors I never even knew existed. I'd been so innocent and wide-eyed, so afraid to consider who I might be, or might become.

That night taught me to question. I learned that sometimes answers affirm our beliefs. Others force us to challenge and discard them. *Discard* may be a poor choice of word. *Respectfully disagree* might be more appropriate. However it should be defined, one thing was certain. That night with my roommate's friend changed the course of my life. It changed what I knew, and what I *thought* I knew. It changed how I saw others, and what I sought in them.

I didn't know it at the time, but that night changed *everything*.

The memories were so vivid and present in my mind's eye, yet it felt like a lifetime ago.

"Babe, where'd you go?" Heath said, as he squeezed my hand and nudged my shoulder affectionately.

Startled out of the recollection, my head turned toward him. His gaze was strong and pure. There were only possibilities in his eyes, opportunities and chances he wanted to take with me, a *lifetime* of them. In that frozen moment, bundled against a chilly, clear Parisian night, my heart finally and fully opened to a beautiful, boundless life of laughter and love.

So many times I thought I'd known *forever*. So many times I'd been wrong.

That night, beyond reason or doubt, I knew Heath was my forever.

He was my last date.

EPILOGUE

Dearest reader,

We need to talk.

It's not usual for an author to address a reader directly. In fact, it's viewed by some in the literary community as a shattering of norms and rules that should guide all texts of quality. While I understand the style in which I wrote may seem unusual or awkward to some, the singular goal was to present a fun, honest story in a new and personal way.

Therefore, to those who cried foul at this attempt at innovation, I wish you well as you read other works. Every book isn't for every reader. I'm good with that. We're still friends. Sort of.

To everyone else—yes, I'm talking to *you*—thank you for sticking with me on this journey. Your emails, reviews, and DMs were filled with amazing comments and suggestions that never failed to lift my spirit. *You* are the reason I write, and hearing how much you love my characters or enjoy my stories makes my heart full.

Curiosity is a terrible beast when left unfed. So, before we wrap things up, I would like to address a few comments and answer questions raised throughout the writing of this series.

Is this really a true story? I get this one a lot. Yes, sir or ma'am, this series really is a true story. I changed names, locations, and altered some timelines, but the guts of the tale are indeed my real-life adventure. Yes, the foam party *really* happened—exactly as it was described. It was the single hottest sexual experience of my life (to date). One day, I'll recover. I doubt those who watched ever will.

Some authors advised me not to reveal the autobiographical nature of this series, but I thought you should know. I *wanted* you to know. I wanted to have an open, honest dialogue with readers by telling my own story in my own snarky voice.

Were you really that clueless? Surely not. No one is that clueless. Au contraire, mon frère, I was indeed that lost little lamb who'd been sheltered from the world and all its bountiful gayness. My childhood was in the '70s and '80s. It was a different time. And yes, my dad really was a part-time preacher for fifty-six years. *Sheltered* barely defines what I was.

IN THE FIRST BOOK, WHY WASN'T YOUR SATURN TOTALED WHEN you had that accident? Well, ask the insurance company that one. I'd had the car a month when I wrapped it around that tree. They saw fit to pay a ridiculous amount to have it repaired. I wasn't given a choice. Sad, but true.

WHERE WERE THE CONDOMS? I PROMISED YOU HONESTY, right? I said I wrote what I recalled, not a work of fiction.

Here's the truth: I was a complete and total moron, incapable of respecting HIV and its deadliness—or respecting myself enough to use protection. I knew better. Claiming ignorance was an excuse. The truth was that I didn't like condoms and made the moronic choice not to use them. You see how that turned out in this last book. Kids, don't be like Mike. Wrap that puppy. Pee-pee balloons are your friends.

WHY DIDN'T YOU KEEP THE SERIES LIGHT AND FUNNY? So many people have asked me this. I had a blast writing the first two books, laughing along with the characters as they said and did ridiculous things. But do you remember my promise to keep things real, to stick to what happened? Life wasn't always funny. Sometimes it hurt or sucked, or both —and I don't mean sucking in the fun, tingly way either. Breakups are hard. Lord knows I experienced enough of them. A piece of me died each time I lost someone I loved (Carter's kids in particular), but that was life. In order to keep the series consistent and take you through the real life of one main character, you had to experience it all. These were deliberate choices, and I don't apologize for them.

As with life, there will *always* be more humor and laughter. I promise—it gets better. Keep your chin up.

WAS HEATH REALLY YOUR LAST DATE, AS THE TITLE STATES? As of the writing of this book, Heath and I have been together for over eleven years. We've traveled the US playing tennis tournaments together, vacationed in Europe and the Mediterranean, and taken cruises throughout the Caribbean. We are truly blessed.

We were officially married at the end of November 2020. We live in Florida with our two Australian shepherds and old-man cattle dog, Cooper. Heath took me off the market for good.

TO ALL THOSE FRUSTRATED BY THE BREAKUPS AND repeated HFNs (Happy For Now, to the uninitiated) in the previous books, Heath is my real-life Happily Ever After.

I love him with all my heart.

You're welcome, and thanks for waiting for him, like I did. 😊

Casey